HANS HABE

Ilona

Translated from the German by
MICHAEL BULLOCK

THE BOOK CLUB
121 CHARING CROSS ROAD LONDON W.C.2

To My Wife
Licci Balla-Habe
with love and admiration

First published in Great Britain 1962
by GEORGE G. HARRAP & CO. LTD
182 High Holborn, London, W.C.1

German edition © Verlag Kurt Desch GmbH 1960
English translation © George G. Harrap & Co. Ltd
and Harcourt, Brace & World Inc. 1961

Printed and bound by
The Hollen Street Press Limited London W1

ILONA

THIS panoramic novel depicts the lives of three women —mother, daughter, and granddaughter. Ilona, the mother, is the dominant figure, as the woman of the turn of the century. The two subsequent generations are represented by Zita, the woman of the transition period, and Eva, the young woman of to-day.

In the changing guise of the changing periods the novel shows us three first experiences of love, three births, three radical changes in an individual's destiny. It becomes the story of an epoch.

We see Vienna and Budapest at the time of the Emperor Franz Joseph, the St Petersburg of Rasputin, the Italian front during the First World War, Germany under the Weimar Republic, France battling with inflation, Germany during the nights of bombing, America in the course of the Second World War, and, finally, liberated Europe.

"Ilona" is undoubtedly Hans Habe's most important novel yet.

Contents

BOOK ONE

The Mother

Part One: 1886 to 1913

December was heralding a white Christmas, this year of our Lord 1886.

The red-brick building of Kisnémet railway station and the Hungarian plain behind it lay beneath deep snow. For days on end nothing but the hungry cawing of the ravens broke the silence.

In the bedroom over the first- and second-class waiting-room the woman had been lying in labour for eight hours. Three children she had borne in pain; now the fourth was on the way. Each time she had been certain she was going to die. Now she was tired of wrestling with death. She was waiting for it.

The man sat at the window staring out.

He had held her hand; then she had sent him away. Down below the station was sleeping beneath the snow, with the railway-lines shovelled clear. The halt sign on the signal stood out against the grey sky like a tiny red moon. In an hour and fourteen minutes the red would change to green. Would the child be there before the express went by?

Now and then children's laughter echoed through the house. The stationmaster, Mihály Horváth, knew the voices of his children: the lilting laugther of four-year-old Teréz, the grunting laughter of three-year-old Lajos. As usual the two elder children had excluded Margit, who was not yet eighteen months old, from their game. Should he stop them from laughing?

The woman was groaning softly. He turned round to the high, dark-brown bed. His eye came to rest upon the oleograph of a bright-blue *Madonna* by Raphael hanging over the bed.

He wanted to pray, but the Lord God gave him no words with which to pray. Pray? The Lord God always decided things differently. ". . . not my will, but thine be done." Perhaps there was no other prayer.

The stationmaster was just twenty-seven, but he could remember many unheard prayers. When he was a child he had made the Lord God many promises, and just as often threatened Him. But the Lord God had always ignored both promises and threats.

The door creaked softly, apologetically. Erzsi néni, the midwife, came into the room. She marched across to the bed with steps of a dragoon and busied herself with the groaning woman, brushing the man aside, as midwives do. Then she came over to the window and said, louder than she had intended, "We must fetch the doctor."

The stationmaster knew what that meant. Erzsi néni had delivered Ilona three times without medical assistance. The responsibility for a new human life she could bear alone; the responsibility for death she wished to share.

The doctor came. It was the Jewish doctor, Dr Grünfeld, a tiny man with a red beard. He enjoyed a widespread reputation for great wisdom.

He did not send the stationmaster out of the room. Mihály stood at the foot of the bed and gazed into the woman's white face. Suffering had not disfigured it. Her face was like fine porcelain that had become slightly cracked.

He had married her six years ago, and he had never ceased to marvel at her beauty, as at something that was present and yet not of this world. He loved her with patient passion, with the tenacious hope of winning her back when he lost her, as he did over and over again. After every birth she rebelled against the restrictions of domestic life, and she grew gentle every time she was expecting again. The time when she was expecting was like the brief, happy period of their engagement, and the time afterwards was like their honeymoon—full of bitterness and disappointment. It had been so this time. He wanted to promise his Lord God that now things would be different, but he couldn't remember what he had done wrong, and he didn't know what he could have done differently.

He looked at his watch, an heirloom from his father that he carried on a heavy chain in a pear-shaped, yellowed case. He had to see whether the points had been shifted, whether the signal was at green; he had to stand in front of his lit-up office and salute.

The pointsman had shifted the points correctly, as always. Máté, the village idiot, whom Mihály employed on his own initiative as postman, porter, and domestic servant, was already standing outside the office saluting, because he imagined himself to be the stationmaster. He ran quickly into the over-heated office and brought Mihály his cap. The stationmaster did not put it on immediately. The snow was falling slowly, in big flakes. His thick black hair turned white.

"The doctor has come," whispered the village idiot, and grinned suggestively.

"I know," said Mihály patiently.

Now the signal changed from red to green. One of the steel manikin's arms dropped languidly; the other shot stiffly up. A noise like the rattling of chains ran through the frame. The stationmaster looked at his watch again. The express was two minutes late.

At last it sped past, even faster than usual, as though to say that it despised small stations. The stationmaster raised his hand to the badge on his cap. The village idiot, behind him, did the same.

"Máté, lock the door," said the stationmaster.

As he was mounting the stairs—he reproached himself for climbing too slowly—he heard the wailing of a child. He could tell that it was a new voice.

The doctor met him in the doorway.

"Don't go in," said Dr Grünfeld.

"A boy?" he asked.

"A healthy girl."

He wanted to push Dr Grünfeld aside, but he sought his strength in vain.

9

"You must be brave," said the doctor. "We couldn't help her."

He looked at the little man with the red beard without comprehending. He appeared dead and made of clay, like the dwarfs in the garden behind the station building.

"Think of the child," said the doctor. "The child is the most important thing."

Why did the dwarf try to console him? How dare he say that the child was the most important thing? He seized the doctor by the chest and thrust him aside.

In the room, the midwife picked up the child by its legs. She dipped it in a washbasin. The bed was full of blood. A white cloth lay over the woman's face.

2

His wife had been dead for ten days.

He was making his way to Christmas matins through the crunching snow along the narrow path. Behind him lay the sleeping station. In front of him lay the scattered farmsteads and the village. There were lighted Christmas-trees in the windows, but since the houses themselves were invisible, it looked as if God had lit up the trees in the wood.

The stationmaster loved his village; more than a village, already half a small town. Kisnémet lay on the main line from Budapest to Debreczen, but far from the capital, east of the Tisza, in the north-east of the country, a fortuitous patch of houses, narrow streets, gardens, chestnut-trees, and acacias planted in the endless expanse of the Hungarian plain. Kisnémet possessed a main square with a large Calvinist and a small Catholic church; a chemist's shop, and elementary school, and a mill. It even possessed a stationer's shop that was famous for the beauty of its proprietress and an inn with a coffee-house and a billiards room, the Hotel Rákoczi. The importance of its railway station was, however, due to the Aporfalvy estates. The possessions of the masters of Aporfalva, Kisnémet and Gulyakút comprised an area of a hundred thousand yokes; the castle was only five miles from the railway, and although Kisnémet was not an express station, the express nevertheless stopped there—whenever the landowner arrived or left. The twentieth century had not yet dawned. No one was surprised when great exceptions were made for great gentlemen.

Muffled figures came towards the stationmaster from the farms. He greeted them, but he passed by quickly. He didn't want pity, either false or genuine. False pity was hateful, and genuine hurt. Why should he disturb the festive gaiety?

He wanted to feel only pain, but a gentle sadness had overlaid his pain. Do we weep for the dead who have gone into eternity? We weep only for ourselves. Birth was a miracle, but death was no less of a miracle. He had known his wife for seven years, almost to the day. He could no longer remember the time before he knew her, but it must have existed. When they had seen one another the first time it was like a reunion. Then she had become living to him, and one day he would die for her.

10

He was drawing nearer the village, but the village seemed to be drawing nearer him, a cool hand approaching a fevered brow. The woman was lying under the snow, in the cemetery. She had always longed to get away from here. Now she belonged to the village. And he too now belonged to it, not because he had been born here, but because one truly belongs to the earth only after it has swallowed up the dead.

He wanted to stay here. He didn't want to become anything more than he now was. He who achieves much wants more. He who possesses much fears to lose it. He who hopes to-day will be disappointed to-morrow. Only the unknowing rebel. There is no sorrow in resignation.

The path entered the main street. More and more people joined him. The church received them.

3

He stayed at home. He became no more than he was already. The century in the middle of which he had been born came to an end.

People did not know what they were doing when, on New Year's Eve 1899, they celebrated the birth of the new century with jubilation. It was as though they were greeting the rain, not knowing that it was not going to cease until the rivers rose from their beds and turned the meadows into lakes and "the waters rose fifteen cubits above the mountains." They did not suspect that the waters would not fall upon a single day, but would rise gradually with the years. They did not suspect that the Lord God was tired in this twentieth century. They drank to the Flood.

The rain fell invisible to men. It was now 1903. The stationmaster of Kisnémet was forty-four.

He had been a handsome man, and he was still a man of imposing appearance—only of medium height to be sure, but slim; with glossy black hair and a glossy black moustache twirled up at the ends; brown, fiery eyes; healthy, sun-tanned skin. In his black uniform, especially his full-dress uniform, with which he wore a tall cap ornamented with silver braid and a silver button, he looked more like a high-ranking officer than a provincial stationmaster.

His quiet gaiety flowed like a wide, eternally calm river into the rough sea of other human lives. The marriageable daughters of officials and local notables, who later became owners of businesses or large farms, all regarded him as a desirable match. He disappointed them.

Yet there was nothing mournful about his young widower's house. People called it 'his' house, although the single-storey red-brick building thickly overgrown with vine beside the railway-track did not belong to him. It belonged to the Imperial and Royal Hungarian Railways. It was not the Imperial and Royal Railways, however, who had provided the geraniums that adorned the pointsman's windows; nor the winter garden that Mihály had planted by the station in which he grafted, tended, and paired; nor the cosiness of the home in which cooking went on by day and night as if in preparation for a wedding.

11

The smell of food that impregnated the wooden benches in the waiting-room, the smell of smoke that permeated the house, the fact that the three Horváth girls flitted in and out of the office—all this lent a touch of the personal and private to the official business of the station.

Mihály no longer believed that the Lord God was deaf to his prayers. When Ilona was born—for the last born had received her mother's name at baptism—Teréz was four, Lajos three, Margit not yet two. People wondered how a young man would manage with four small children. But they were like the grass, whose blades cannot be distinguished from one another and which grows by itself. Later flowers grew between the blades of grass, mysteriously different. By then the Lord had given counsel to His servant.

The most mysterious was Ilona. When the stationmaster was alone with his flowers he was often startled, as he looked at a flower of delicate and exceptional colour, by the feeling that he was holding his youngest daughter in his hands. His sense of justice strove against the bias of his emotions; for years he deceived himself into believing that he loved her no more than the other three. Then he gave in and admitted to a love that overshadowed all others. He often recalled that with her first breath the little being had killed his wife, but instead of being angry with Ilona he told himself that there was no room for two miracles: they could not live alongside each other; one had to take the other's place. Now he understood what Dr Grünfeld, the doctor with the red beard, had meant when he stammered that the most important thing was the child.

4

Two days after Ilona's seventeenth birthday, on December 16, 1903, Aunt Rosa arrived from Budapest. Although the express had not stopped at Kisnémet for her benefit—cursing, she had changed into the slow train at Püspökladány—her arrival resembled that of the fine ladies who from time to time visited the Aporfalvys. A multitude of trunks, two hatboxes, rugs held together by leather straps, umbrellas, and even a senseless yellow sunshade came tumbling down the steps of the first-class compartment, so that the stationmaster, his staff, and his three daughters were barely enough to transport Aunt Rosa's baggage into the station building.

Mihály Horváth had not seen his elder sister for six years. She had written regularly and had referred more than once to the prosperity and success of her fashion house, but those who lived in this little provincial town hadn't sufficient imagination to form a proper picture of Aunt Rosa's status.

Victory over the trials of life was written all over her face: it radiated from her whole personality. She did nothing to hide it. What good was success in the big world if it were not adequately esteemed in the little world of the family.

Aunt Rosa's visit was planned to last only four or five days; by Christmas she had to be back in the capital. So the Christmas festivities were advanced for her benefit. Day and night, clothes were tried on,

12

scrutinized, exchanged, and ironed: clothes of heavy red material with black embroidery, high collars, fringed epaulets, and fashionable narrow ending in a puff round the wrist; costumes with big buttons and wide lapels over *jabots* of gauzy fabric or with loose blouses of silk-muslin.

Yet Aunt Rosa bore no resemblance to Santa Claus, whom she portrayed. She must have been about fifty; the nose, mouth, and forehead of her freckled face were wide, as though bloated with alcohol, which she did not drink, or with worries, which she did not have. The new fashion, which commanded that everything women carried in front of them should be pulled out of sight, irrespective of where it was to go, had been invented for her special torment. When she last visited Kisnémet she had been blonde; now her hair was a horrible violet-red flame colour; the stationmaster could not deny that it was dyed.

It was no use denying anything. Nothing was sacred to this big-hearted woman who seemed, with the magic trunks, to have opened Pandora's box. She referred to love affairs at Court as though to harmless fairy-stories; she let fall the names of mistresses in her conversation as though they were hallowed by history; she retailed the scandalous affairs of her clients from inside knowledge and without disapproval. She spoke in such frivolous terms of the city in which she lived that her brother looked out at the railway-line in front of the station and shook his head, as though dumbfounded to think that this innocent pair of rails should end in Sodom and Gomorrah.

5

On the third day of her visit the stationmaster finally succeeded in so arranging things that at a late hour in the evening he was left alone with his sister. Teréz, Margit, and Ilona had gone to bed; Lajos was with the Army and was not expected home till Christmas.

The stationmaster, who had undone the top button of his uniform jacket over the tight celluloid collar, had remained sitting at the table. His hands lay on the brightly coloured woollen tulips embroidered on the velvet cloth. Rosa had made herself comfortable on the sofa with the high, tapestry-covered back and gleaming brass lions' heads. Her short, beringed fingers were picking dainty chocolate confections from an enormous box. For several minutes now the stationmaster had been playing in silence with the pink shell shaped like a paper bag and bearing the fading words "Greetings from Abbazia."

"I know what you're thinking." Rosa broke the tense silence. "You're wishing me to the devil."

"You're exaggerating as usual, my dear Rosa," her brother replied. "I'm merely thinking that you've put a lot of ideas into the girls' heads, and it's not going to be easy for me to drive them out again."

"You're speaking of Ilona."

"Why should I be speaking particularly of Ilona?"

"You're always speaking of Ilona." She ignored his gesture of dissent. "And I agree with you, for once. Nothing can happen to

13

Teréz. She is the born model pupil. She takes after you. One or two things have happened to you in your life. But never through your own fault. That doesn't count."

"Perhaps," said the stationmaster, "Perhaps. . . ."

"And Margit? That child is unlucky. She looks too much like Ilona. Only to-day I watched those two. They were sitting side by side. . . . " She tapped the plush seat of the sofa. "They looked like twins, and both of them so much like your poor wife."

Mihály puckered his forehead. Rosa hated his wife beyond the grave. He didn't want his sister to speak of her.

"But how different those two are!" Rosa went on. "Men can feel that clearly, believe me. 'Why her and not me?' Margit will ask all through her life. And, of course, you will never have the courage to tell her how little mirrors know."

The stationmaster had stopped playing with the shell. Men, he thought . . . as though men were so important.

"You sit here in your little out-of-the-way village and let the trains go past," Rosa continued. "You gaze after the expresses, and your mind is at ease because they run on rails. And because they will return to-morrow, on the same rails. The twentieth century has begun, Mihály! There are no more rails. The trains that have passed will not come back."

The stationmaster stood up. He pushed his index finger in between his collar and his neck.

"Trains can't run without rails," he said.

The stationmaster was now feeling cold. He walked across to the stove and put on more fuel. With his back to Rosa and looking into the ashes, he said, "You were going to say something about Ilona."

"Do you know what the child said to me to-day? 'For once,' she said, 'I should like to live in a house that didn't have the word Kisnémet written on it. The travellers,' she said, 'lean out of the carriage windows and ask where they are. How I should like not to know where I was for once,' she said."

The man had straightened up.

"Did she say she wanted to go away?" he asked.

Rosa poked about among the empty little paper sweet containers. The rustling noise got on the stationmaster's nerves.

"Does the child know what she wants?" said Rosa. "She must get away from here, Mihály. Away from this horrible plush furniture." She pulled at the brass ring dangling from the lion's mouth as though she wished to tear it away from the beast. Her eyes lighted upon the huge, old-fashioned German sideboard with the double tier of shelves and the fruit-bowls with earthenware fruit protruding from them. "It is not good to live among other people's memories."

The stationmaster walked up and down.

"And who will she get to know here?" commented Rosa. "A few farmers' sons, the young teacher, the son of the Hotel Rákoczi. She speaks of young Count Aporfalvy as though he were a fairy prince, because he is serving with the Ninth Hussars. The whole of Budapest is full of Ninth Hussars."

14

"We're not engaged in a husband hunt," interrupted her brother.

"Do you think you can keep her for ever? Like your flowers, till they fade. You're an egotist, Mihály! Keep Teréz and, as far as I'm concerned, Margit. Ilona is not made for this godforsaken hole. With me she can learn dressmaking. The highest society comes to my salon. She can choose her husband—yes, a husband, even if you do look at me as if I were talking about Old Nick in person. If I'm wrong I'll send her back to you. Then at least she can teach the ladies of Kisnémet not to have themselves dressed by the paperhanger."

He tried to imagine his life without Ilona. Seventeen years had passed since his wife's death. The Lord God erected a building, then He slowly removed all the bricks, and yet it did not fall down. People said time healed all wounds. A fine doctor who healed wounds and brought the patient daily closer to the grave! But Ilona wasn't dead just because she was going away from him. It took nine hours and fourteen minutes to travel from Kisnémet to Budapest, including the change at Püspökladány. Perhaps he ought to take a holiday and go with her.

For a moment the stationmaster felt quite light-hearted. Then he thought of his return to the empty house. A house without Ilona seemed an empty house to him.

"Did she really say she wanted to go away?" he reiterated.

6

Ilona leant out of the window and waved.

The station slipped slowly back into the afternoon mist. The white handkerchief's no longer showed up against the white background of the snow-covered landscape. Only the lamp in the window of a house still gleamed through the mist and smoke. If the last thing I see is Papa's cap everything will be all right, thought the girl. Up to the last moment she saw the stationmaster's cap.

It was bitterly cold outside. She pulled up the lowered window with the leather strap. She didn't move. She knew every stick and stone: the red school building, the two-storey mill with the large house belonging to the mill-owner, Korcsmáros, Dr Grünfeld's cottage. Then came the promenade of which Kisnémet was so proud. It ended in railway gates. The lads and girls used to stand there on summer evenings waiting for the express. The only thing waiting behind the gates at the moment was farmer Szentirmai's open carriage. The old coachman was sitting wrapped up on the box. He probably had no idea that Horváth's youngest daughter was leaving. The train limped round a bend. The cemetery came into view over the top of a low stone wall. The wheels turned faster. Kisnémet passed out of sight.

Ilona sat down. She was alone with Aunt Rosa. Cases, rugs, and hat-boxes were piled up on the luggage-rack and on the red-plush seats of the first-class compartment. Ilona's travelling basket, closed with an iron rod and a padlock and with a picnic basket containing a cold chicken, red wine, and a napkin standing on top of it, looked poor and shabby among the other luggage. Aunt Rosa had taken out a novel as soon as they started. Carefully, so as not to crumple her new hat, Ilona leant her head back against the white lace antimacassar behind her. Conversations with her father, visits, packing, and farewells to her friends had left her no time to think. Now the trains were no longer travelling past her; she herself was travelling in one of them. She crushed her wet handkerchief between her fingers. She didn't want to cry any more. She had always suspected that she was chosen. Now she knew. Life seemed to her like a children's jigsaw puzzle: once they were put together the meaningless little pieces produced a scene from Little Red Riding Hood or Snow White, produced something beautiful and intelligible.

She hadn't been a good pupil at school; she wasn't quick to learn like Teréz, but the teachers had never treated her roughly as they did the other children, and after the final exam naturally she was chosen to recite the poem of thanks to the headmaster. Two years ago there was a charity bazaar—she could still smell the dry leaves with which the tent was decorated—and when the takings were counted up she had naturally sold most lottery tickets. Last summer she had been allowed to go to her first ball; her sisters had prophesied that she would be a wallflower, but naturally young Aporfalvy, an ensign in the Nádasdy Hussars, had danced the first csárdas with her. Naturally all these things happened—because that was what Nature intended.

Naturally, too, Aunt Rosa had chosen her from among her sisters. She had spoken of a splendid match, a millionaire or a count. She couldn't help smiling when she thought of her sisters' sour faces. Not that she was in any hurry. First she wanted to get to know the city with its suspension bridges and horse-drawn trams and shop windows, the royal palace and the tunnel under the Gellérthegy, the cafés from which gipsy music echoed, and the theatres in front of which black carriages waited for beautiful ladies and elegant gentlemen. Then she would marry—a millionaire or a count. Some one she didn't know yet. She thought of Sándor Bihari, the hotel-owner's son, who had asked for her hand when they were both seven; of Feri Aporfalvy, the landowner's son, who had hung about the station-house for days after the St Anne's Day ball. She also thought of Zoltán Szomoru, who on August 28—she remembered the date—had tried to kiss her; the next day he had left for Budapest, where he was a student at the Academy of Music. Perhaps she would meet him in Budapest and he wouldn't recognize her; but it might be better if she didn't see him again. It was as though the people she had known were slipping back into the mist like Kisnémet station.

The carriage door was pushed to one side. The guard, a great bear of a man with a thick iron-grey moustache, came in. He opened the milky-white hemisphere of the ceiling light and put the wick of his little lamp to the mantle of the gas-lamp. There was a hissing sound in the carriage; then it was drenched in flickering light.

"Well, how are you, little missie?" asked the guard as he took the tickets from Aunt Rosa.

"Fine, Józsi bácsi," said Ilona, trying to smile.

She didn't find it easy. She had known Józsi bácsi ever since she was

16

born. For as long as she could remember he had been travelling in the passenger train between Debreczen and Püspökladány. Her father had jestingly entrusted her to Józsi bácsi when she left.

"When do we reach Püspökladány?" she asked.

"At six-forty-three."

She had to turn her face away. It suddenly dawned on her that she didn't know the guard on the Püspökladány-Budapest express. Papa didn't know him either. His hand reached as far as Püspökladány and no farther.

"Feeling homesick already?" joked the guard.

She couldn't answer. Reckless of her round travelling hat, whose brim was crushed against the window, she pressed her face to the glass. Her tears mingled with the moisture on the darkening windowpane. Outside, the lighted windows ran along the snow. Józsi bácsi didn't know how hard it was. He didn't know that he was the last link in the breaking chain between Ilona Horváth and the stationhouse at Kisnémet.

7

Aunt Rosa's apartment was in Buda, the old part of the city on the right bank of the Danube. Beside the chunky realism of the new Pest it seemed to be made up of dolls' houses. Buda hill was dominated by the Royal Castle. The houses round about looked like His Majesty's toys. The great porches were surmounted by armorial bearings carved in stone. The people belonged to the houses.

Ilona noticed a coat of arms over the porch of the dainty 'palace' in which Aunt Rosa lived; it was made up of a fish and a sword; the fish was swallowing the sword. The house lay in a narrow backstreet bearing the name of Fortuna, the goddess of luck. The ground floor was occupied by the owner of the house, Baron Rozsnyai, and his son, a bachelor. The two old gentlemen were as alike as twins. The only means of recognizing the elder was by the way he kept shaking his head as though continually saying no. But it was due to an illness.

Aunt Rosa had four small rooms on the first floor—two bedrooms, a drawing-room, and a dining-room. There were no old-fashioned German sideboards here, no plush furniture, no earthenware vases, no oleographs. Everything was new, or, rather, genuinely old: silk-upholstered Biedermeier chairs, glass cases containing porcelain as fine as lace, paraffin lamps of transparent coloured glass.

Budapest was getting ready for Christmas with a gay bustle of activity, as though the shops were giving away what they sold. Ladies and gentlemen who rarely showed themselves in public crowded the white streets of the *belváros*. The shop-windows seemed to be bursting with clothes, jewels, boxes of sweets, toys, and all manner of beautiful and superfluous objects. The Váci ucca was filled with the tinkle of sleigh-bells; closed carriages waited outside the Konditorei Kugler; liveried serving-men and maids in kerchiefs walked along behind their masters and mistresses carrying parcels. The lamplighters lit the gas-lamps early. The Gizellatér was like a white ballroom. The streets smelt as though acolytes had strewn them with incense.

17

Ilona noticed that her aunt took no part in this incessant waving, greeting, stopping, and chatting. She herself received admiring glances from the gentlemen. From time to time one of them would turn round with unashamed gallantry. It also struck her that Aunt Rosa didn't go into the house on which a small marble plate announced that the "Salon Rosa" was on the first floor. Aunt Rosa pacified her curiosity. "Don't be impatient. We shall celebrate Christmas Eve in the family circle."

8

Under her aunt's watchful eye Ilona began to dress.

The full white dress of diaphanous muslin had a high neck, but it allowed the still childishly pink skin above her little breasts to shimmer through. The coquettish little collar which showed up her long, already very feminine neck to the best advantage was held together by a narrow black-velvet ribbon. In her hair she wore a tortoiseshell comb, dark-blond like her hair, the most valuable item left by her mother, which the stationmaster had slipped into her hands at the last moment. The black-lace fan with the white-ivory handle, which she was swaying to and fro in her hand, had also belonged to her mother.

When Aunt Rosa, satisfied at last, had gone Ilona stood in front of the cheval-glass that tilted in its brown frame. She was pale, but her very pallor brought out the perfect symmetry of her features, as engravings look nobler when no colour is added to them. Her nose was straight and not too small; her mouth was all the more exciting because a narrow upper lip seemed, as it were, to seal the full lower lip; her eyes varied bewilderingly from grey to blue; her ears were tiny and flat against her head; the serene hand of the Creator had not trembled as He drew this face.

Ilona wrinkled her forehead, as she always did in front of a mirror, not out of displeasure, but because she hoped it would make her look older. She gradually lost the feeling of disquiet which she had experienced all day long. What could Aunt Rosa have meant by the "family circle"? She was probably referring to her companions at work, who after all would now be Ilona's too. She had longed for new faces: she had no reason to fear them.

She smiled. Mirrors had always been kind to her, almost as though they had an energy of their own which they generously expended when the girl stood in front of them. Mirrors talked with her. They said, "We are old, and we are grateful because you rejuvenate us." "I shall always try to cheer you up," replied the girl. She knew she was beautiful. The Lord God, who had been so kind to her regarding her face, couldn't fail to have a bright future in store for her as well.

9

As she entered the Salon Rosa uneasiness seized her again.

She had pictured a fashion house quite differently. Long wall-mirrors reaching down to the ground in gilded frames multiplied the light from the bronze chandeliers; the wallpaper glittered silver, like a mirror; statues of half-naked women in twisted postures held all sorts of costly articles; the pictures showed scenes of amorous shepherds; benches upholstered in green velvet ran right round the room, almost as in a ballroom. To the left of the door were three fitting-rooms, but their green-velvet curtains were drawn aside; laid tables and champagne buckets could be seen. Amid all this splendour the big Christmas-tree looked strange as if in a shop-window.

Suddenly Ilona was surrounded by a host of young ladies. They had slipped out of doors to right and left, out of an uncanny number of doors. They relieved Ilona of her winter coat and her parcels; they admired her dress; whirled her through the room to the accompaniment of jokes, like a 'new girl' in a boarding-school. They only gave their Christian names. They were of various ages; the youngest not much older than Ilona, the oldest undoubtedly over thirty. Although they were all in the same trade, they resembled each other neither in clothing nor behaviour: one noisy and blonde, another sickly and brunette, a third cool and bored.

Ilona thought of the stationmaster with fierce, painful homesickness mingled with a feeling of reproach. The girls' dresses, which left their necks and shoulders bare, would have horrified the stationmaster. In addition they were all made up, like Juliska, who had once been a servant with the Horváths and whom the stationmaster had turned out. Ilona wanted to hurry to her aunt, wanted to ask her what she had meant by "family"; but Aunt Rosa, like an innkeeper's wife expecting guests, was too busy giving instructions to the housekeeper, who had come with them, testing drinks and straightening tablecloths.

When a grave-looking girl of about twenty-five in a green evening-dress came up to her she welcomed her gladly. Aranka was from the country, from the region of Lake Balaton, but she must have been living away from home for many years. She asked Ilona about her previous life with a curious air of longing, like a convict inquiring of a new arrival in the prison about the freedom he himself had lost long ago. She said one could "get used to this life," could "make the best of it"; at the same time she looked at Ilona pityingly. Two girls near by were whispering; when they realized that Ilona was listening they stopped in embarrassment and hurried off to another group, still glancing at her.

Ilona wished she could faint. Her sister Margit always fainted when she could see no other way out. But she wasn't Margit; she wouldn't faint. She was wrong; she was sure she was wrong. A few months ago she had read Emile Zola's scandalous novel *Nana*, so secretly that not even Teréz knew. Now its characters were coming to life as though in a nightmare. As in the feverish dreams of her childhood, the figures moving about the glittering room grew bigger and bigger, more and more unreal: the severely dressed, dried-up Gizi, who looked like a ring-mistress in the circus, as if she were brandishing an invisible whip; Denise, the French girl with a face like a pretty skull; Paula, who was so tall and powerful and high-bosomed that her pin-head looked ridiculous.

19

The old housekeeper, welcomed by a burst of reassuring cheers, brought the Christmas punch in a white soup-tureen. The girls drank one another's health, giggled, and put the parcels under the tree to the accompaniment of a great deal of noise.

Silence fell. Aunt Rosa lit the candles. A pleasant warmth streamed out from the Christmas-tree. The girls formed a semicircle. The nightmare faded. Their faces were like those of the angels on the pink confectionery wrappers. "Silent night, holy night." The lights played on the coloured glass balls. The stars of light from the 'sparklers' hopped up and down on the parcels. Aranka took Ilona's hand. Others were also standing hand in hand. The thin little girl, who couldn't have been more than seventeen, clung to the big buxom girl with the pinhead. Tears trickled down the French girl's high cheekbones; the rouge ran into her red mouth. "Silent night, holy night."

The lamps were relit. Their monotonous humming filled the room. Aunt Rosa distributed the presents. There was a note of relief in the hubbub that broke out, as though the religious mood had been a threat that had now passed. Zsuzsi had embroidered a cushion for Aranka; the French girl received a lace corset; the full-bosomed Paula a prayer-book bound in white leather; the Salon Rosa presented Magda, the brunette, with a damask tablecloth and table-napkins for her trousseau. Ilona could almost have believed that the fashion house was really Aunt Rosa's family, when the Christmas melody was shattered by a strident discord.

Two Hussar lieutenants had entered the room, obviously the worse for drink. They embraced Aunt Rosa and kissed the girls on the cheek one after the other. Before Ilona knew what was happening they had both fleetingly embraced her too. Now the door never stayed still. A stream of guests poured into the room, a singular stream. They couldn't belong to the family: there was a tall bald-headed man, evidently a business magnate; a sarcastic, taciturn man in evening-dress with a high collar; a man in boots who dropped on to the green bench with a groan and immediately fell asleep and snored. It was true that the guests brought presents—an ugly mountain of tissue-paper piled up in the middle of the room—but they were shameless presents, and the recipients accepted them shamelessly. Paula held up a pair of transparent knickers in front of her red evening dress; Zsuzsi waved a black nightdress in the air like a banner of mourning. The guests called noisily for drinks. Aunt Rosa uncorked bottles of wine and champagne with a practised hand, admonishing one man to go easy, exhorting the other to drink to his heart's content.

Ilona was left alone by the Christmas-tree. Kisnémet lay nine hours and fourteen minutes from Budapest. In her thoughts she clung to the timetable. In the living-room at Kisnémet the Christmas-tree was standing between the stove and the grandfather clock. Teréz was bringing in the Christmas goose. They were bound to be talking about the youngest daughter.

Aranka approached Ilona. Ilona stretched out her hand to her, but immediately let it fall again. The girl had turned round and was hurrying towards a new guest. He was a crooked little man. When you looked more closely you noticed that he had a hump. He was dressed with painful smartness. He took Aranka round the hips. She didn't resist, but bent down to him and kissed him on the mouth. As they passed the bald-headed man, closely intertwined, the latter touched the hunchback's shoulders. "That brings luck," he laughed. The little man didn't protest, but laughed himself. Paula, the white prayer-book still in her hand, was sitting on the lap of a major who had his monocle wedged over his eye. He was studying her bosom through it. The French girl had sat down beside the snoring man and was playing with his frizzy hair, staring absent-mindedly into space, as though the sleeper's head were an inanimate object. Aranka and the hunchback disappeared into one of the fitting-rooms. The green curtain ran along the brass rod.

The room was spinning round Ilona, who felt like an uninvited guest. She had hardly drunk any punch. A hateful mixture of knowledge and bewilderment rose in her. She was drunk and sober. The lieutenant of Hussars was hanging by his boots from the ceiling; the naked bronze statues let the glass balls fall from their hands; Aunt Rosa's lips turned into red ribbons that floated through the room; the mirrors magnified everything to infinity. The Christmas-tree stood in the corner bare, as on Twelfth Night. The man on the bench was snoring through the laughter. Behind the curtain the hunchback was laughing.

Ilona drew a deep breath. She looked at the entrance door, but the door moved away into the distance; all at once it was as far away as the farthest point at which the railway-lines converge. At last she found the side-door. With an effort she pressed down the latch.

10

She found herself in an ill-lit room. It was a cutting-room containing two or three covered sewing-machines, a clothes-rack with loose garments hanging on it, blue patterns lying on an unplaned table, and a headless tailor's dummy with sensual curves. She clung to the stuffed doll, then let go because the doll, having only one wooden leg, began to wobble. She tore open the window.

Snowy air poured into the room. Sound had vanished from the streets. Lighted Christmas-trees stood in the windows. Homes that were normally far apart seemed to have been brought together. Church bells rang incessantly. Their booming was accentuated by the tinkle of high-pitched sleigh-bells. Snow lay on the leaded window sill. Ilona picked up a handful of snow and put it on her face.

"Am I disturbing you?"

The man's voice—a warm, pleasant-sounding voice—came from the door.

Ilona turned round, still holding some snow in her hand.

It was the slim gentleman in evening-dress who had caught her attention because he took no part in the activities in the Salon.

"It's all right," she said.

The snow was dripping from her hands on to the floor.

The stranger sat down on one of the small tailor's chairs. His face with its strongly marked cheek-bones was almost as white as his cravat. His big brown eyes had a mocking but not malicious expression, like the eyes of sick people who mildly despise a healthy world. He took a cigarette from his gold case and lit it, but hardly drew on it once: it hung down between his bony fingers and slowly turned to ash.

"What's your name?" he asked.

"Ilona Horváth."

She regretted giving her name, when the stranger apparently had no thought of introducing himself.

"So I was right," he said. "How old are you exactly?"

"I was seventeen in December."

Again her answer was too precise. She shut the window.

The man glanced at the patterns, the sewing-machines, the flat-irons. His eyes came to rest on the dummy. As though speaking to the dummy, he said, "I've been watching you, young lady. You and your gem of an aunt. When did you come up from the country?"

Ilona wrinkled her forehead. Her anger made her forget her fear and disgust.

"If I told you," continued the stranger, "that you are in a house of assignation you might not know what I meant. The lady without a head will wait for a dress in vain. The French call it a *maison de joie*, but it is also called a brothel. I prefer brothel; the word joy shouldn't be taken too lightly—it is too rare and too precious. A house of sadness would be more accurate on an evening like this, when only the saddest seek the company of *filles de joie*."

Now that she had heard from the mouth of a stranger what she hadn't dared to admit to herself she no longer felt afraid. Aunt Rosa had deceived her father. She could forgive her everything but that.

"It's a pity about you, my child," commented the man. "You are young, charming, and exceptionally beautiful. Yes, exceptionally. I suppose your aunt promised you a fine match. It's not impossible that she honestly meant it. Whores are very fashionable just now. Every age has its own romanticism—sugary water that it pours over its misery. Historians will one day say that it was very significant that the dawn of the twentieth century was marked by the romanticization of the whore." He let the unsmoked cigarette fall from his hand by simply opening two fingers. "But it would be one chance in a thousand. Get your hat and coat—I'll take you home."

"But I don't know you . . ." said Ilona.

"Beautiful, charming, young—and clever too. You don't trust me. You're quite right."

Ilona walked across to the connecting door. With her hand already on the brass handle, she stood still. The Christmas bells were pounding wildly. But they weren't pounding so wildly that they drowned the sounds from the Salon—the shrill laughter of the girls, the drunken laughter of the men. She thought of the man snoring on the bench, of the hunchback behind the curtain. She turned round and leant her head back against the door.

The man had risen.

"It is the privilege of youth to demand plain speaking," he said. "You guessed right. I have nothing against you losing your innocence, only I shouldn't like to share you with others. A mistress isn't a prostitute. Your aunt will understand that. She's an understanding lady. Please be my advocate with her. Mention my name. It impresses every one who thinks that everything can be bought."

The blood flowed back into Ilona's cheeks.

"I'll think your proposition over," she said, like the ladies in her novels.

She cast another glance at the stupid dummy that had no head and only one leg. Then she went to the door that led into the ante-chamber. No one noticed her leaving.

11

She sat in the corner of the black carriage beside the gentleman in the top hat and full evening-dress overcoat.

The streets had come to life. Men and women were sitting in open sleighs wearing heavy fur coats, wrapped in rugs and hugging one another. A group of men staggered along the pavement singing and blocking it to other walkers. On the Gizellatér, under the huge Christmas-tree, a few freezing beggars stood slapping their arms round themselves, like birds unable to fly away. The white lions on the Lánczhid bridgehead looked down sullenly.

Ilona was overcome by self-pity, the emotion that is ashamed of itself and, unlike pity for others, deepens the wound it would like to heal. She even envied the freezing beggars and the sulky lions. She would probably have borne the terrible insult that had been inflicted upon her more easily if she could have vented her whole rage upon her aunt. But the childish trust she had displayed towards her aunt justified the woman in taking advantage of it. The experience of the last few hours had not made her more mature; rather, it had made her aware of her own tottering immaturity. And yet perhaps she *was* chosen. Even the monstrous happens only to the chosen.

The man remained mute. Only once did his knee touch the girl's knee, but he quickly moved it away. As though ashamed, he averted his face.

Outside in the street of the goddess Fortuna he helped her out of the carriage. The snow had spread a thick carpet over the pavement. The lights of a poor bachelor's Christmas-tree winked through the curtains covering the windows of the apartment occupied by the Barons Rozsnyai. The man went to the door and rang for the porter. Only then did he press his card into her hand.

"Thank you," said Ilona.

The stranger raised his top hat. She ran up the stairs.

When she reached the top she was out of breath. She lit the gas-lamp with a trembling hand.

Her eyes fell on the card. In an elaborate script it bore the name "Prince Taszilo Kontowski." She went into her room and sat down on the edge of her bed, her hat still on her head

She had been sitting in the bath for half an hour already. She enjoyed the flattery of the hot water afresh each time she used it. There had been no bathroom in the station-house at Kisnémet.

She hadn't left, neither on Christmas Day nor later. Nor had she become the Prince's mistress. She had never again entered Aunt Rosa's 'house of sadness.' Now there was no snow on the roofs. March breezes were drifting through the city.

The old housekeeper was bustling about outside. The aroma of morning coffee came in through the cracks. The baker's boy had just brought the crisp crescent rolls. A new day was beginning.

Every morning in the bath she thought over what had happened and made new plans, scarcely aware that she would no more carry out the new ones than she had those of yesterday.

Aunt Rosa had denied everything; everything that mattered. To be sure, no dresses were cut in her Salon; it was a house of assignation, as the Prince had said. But did that mean that she meant to prostitute her own niece? Only ingratitude could impute such base plans to her. She wanted Ilona to enjoy a truly royal education. What did it matter to her niece where the money came from? And did Ilona imagine she could still be happy in the narrow atmosphere of her little provincial town? Even if she told her father the truth, how was she going to explain her return to her sisters and the scandal-loving village? When Aunt Rosa had finished it was clear to Ilona that she had her aunt in the palm of her hand. If the vicious woman feared nothing else she feared her brother. The stationmaster's hand reached far beyond Püspökladány.

To begin with, Ilona really believed that she was only staying in order to savour her triumph over her aunt. As a rule Aunt Rosa was still asleep when she went out for a walk. From the near-by Fisherman's Mount one could see the whole city. A sea of roofs, and under each roof heaven knows how many destinies. The great city was mysterious; it was full of riddles waiting to be solved. The broad Danube looked as though it were flowing between two separated railway-lines. But these rails didn't come from Debreczen, didn't lead to Püspökladány. They began in distant countries and ended in the sea. Ilona no longer got lost in the streets of Pest. Admiring stares followed her, happy mirrors that walked along with her. At lunch her aunt occasionally talked about her business, not lasciviously, but like an innkeeper's wife complaining about a maid's dishonesty or a guest's carelessness. As a rule Ilona listened to the madam's monologue in silence; occasionally she astonished her aunt with the acuteness of her ingenuous judgment. In the afternoons she wandered through churches, galleries, museums. When one of her aunt's girls kept her company the suspicion arose in Ilona that Aunt Rosa had not completely abandoned her artful plans for her education; but she enjoyed seeing how coquettish her chastity appeared when reflected in the mirror of sin. Once a week her aunt took her to the opera, a theatre, or a concert; she was forbidden by the madam's ludicrously strict morals ever to go out alone in the evening. When she stayed at home she read till late at night, as delighted by her freedom to read what she liked as by her freedom to live as she liked.

But the more she enjoyed her new life, the prettier the dresses Aunt Rosa ordered for her, the more lavish the pocket-money she received, the greater grew Ilona's feeling of discomfort. She had meant to punish Aunt Rosa; now she had become her accomplice.

There was a knock on the bathroom door.

"Miss Ilona, the coffee is ready."

Ilona pulled out the plug by hooking her outstretched toes in the loose chain. She slid down deeper, as though slipping under a protective blanket. Slowly she raised her flat stomach and her little breasts out of the water. She splashed her body with cold water. Not until the water was below her hips did she stand up.

Wet and with a towel tied round her head like a turban, she stood in front of the tall mirror on the wall. The warmth of the circular brown wood-burning stove warmed her back. Holding the towel diagonally across her back like a bent bow, she rubbed herself until her skin turned pink. Ever since that night in Madame Rosa's Salon her body had been seized by an inexplicable restlessness. The thought of a man's embrace filled her neither with longing nor with aversion, but only with restlessness. She had begun to be afraid of herself. In her Sleeping Beauty's sleep she had dreamt of a prince who would wake her. Now she had woken of her own accord.

13

At the end of March Aunt Rosa surprised her with the information that she had a tier-box for the première of *The Teacher*, a comedy by Sándor Bródy. Although it wasn't Wednesday, Aunt Rosa's day off, she intended to go with her niece to the Vigszinház.

It wasn't Ilona's first visit to a theatre, but she had never imagined the splendour of a Budapest first night. The Comedy Theatre had only recently been opened. The boxes soared above the red-plush stalls like little white-and-gold gondolas; a thousand lights scintillated from the cut-glass chandeliers; the white-bosomed marble women played on golden harps. And what a select public! The ladies in off-the-shoulder evening-dresses with long trains, their arms bare and with low-cut necklines; the gentlemen in full-dress uniform or evening-dress, ulsters or chesterfields, with stand-up collars, patent-leather boots, and white kid gloves. The scent of perfume and powder hung about the theatre and, when the curtain went up, mingled with the smell of dust from the stage.

The main interval was long, longer than was appropriate to the sentimental play; but most of the spectators had come for the sake of the interval, during which they could show off their dresses, make supper dates, and hatch intrigues. The ladies stayed in the boxes, cooling themselves with their fans and letting themselves be served with refreshments by the gentlemen, who for their part crowded sweating round the buffet. There was much bustling to and fro between the boxes. Bachelors from the pit paid decorous visits to young ladies waiting with their mothers in the boxes. And once again the girl in the box felt that she had come from her small village to a big one, where everybody knew one another and only she remained a stranger.

Not that she could complain of having insufficient attention paid her, not by any means. Sitting with blushing cheeks at the balustrade of the box, she held her head high in the crossfire of stares. The gentlemen put their heads so close together behind their opera-glasses that it was almost as though they had four eyes apiece; no doubt there were whispered inquiries in the boxes and among the stalls as to the identity of the unknown beauty. Meanwhile nobody addressed a greeting to the right-hand tier-box. What sense of shame had been left to her was submerged by contempt for these respectable gentlemen who exchanged scornful remarks, but in an hour's time would very likely be knocking at the door of the house in the Galamb ucca.

It had gone dark again. Programmes rustled, here and there some one gave a little cough, the curtain moved slightly. It hadn't gone up yet, as though it were waiting for the expectant hush to become complete. Then there was a low knock at the door of the box.

The two women looked round.

A ray of light fell into the box. At the same moment the curtain rose.

Ilona immediately recognized the man who entered. He was wearing the full-dress uniform of the Ninth Hussars—a dark-blue attila with narrow trousers and white olives and a white shako, which he held to his waist. Count Feri Aporfalvy, son of the landowner of Kisnémet, approached on tiptoe. He wore his dark-brown hair rather too stiffly and straightly parted; under his well-shaped but insignificant nose he had a small, square-cut moustache. His whole exterior was that of a model pupil.

Ilona gave only a fleeting response to his greeting. He waited till it was dark, she thought. She turned back to the stage.

"I beg the ladies' pardon," stammered the ensign. "I didn't see Miss Ilona till the lights were just going out. What a surprise!"

Since Ilona made no move to introduce him, he bowed briefly to Aunt Rosa.

"Take a seat, ensign," whispered the madam with professional amiability.

He sat down behind Ilona. She could feel his breath on the back of her neck. He was breathing irregularly, as if he had just dismounted from his horse after a long ride. She couldn't see him, but she knew he was sitting upright with his white-gloved hands on his knees, like a schoolboy on his best behaviour because he has come to class too late.

She had great difficulty in following what was happening on the stage. Since the young Count had sat down behind her it was as if the village had caught up with her on her flight. It wasn't an unpleasant feeling; it was rather like the warmth she had felt in her childhood

26

when they were playing hide-and-seek and her father found her and took her in his arms. She was no longer aware of the scent of perfume and powder. The smell of the Hungarian plain passed through the Royal Comedy Theatre, the smell of soil, plants, and bushes. She heard the croaking of the frogs and the chirruping of the crickets. The previous summer was there too, the St Anne's Day Ball at which she had danced with Feri Aporfalvy—the first csárdás and many dances after that. Then they had stayed alone together on the stone terrace. The scent of elder-bushes drifted in among the trees. The pollen on the leaves was like pearls. His hand on the cool balustrade had touched her hand.

The performance was over.

"May I take the ladies home?" asked the ensign, rising quickly.

"Would you really do that?" replied Aunt Rosa, without giving Ilona time to speak. "You come like a guardian angel. I have an urgent appointment elsewhere, and it's a long way to Buda. May I leave Ilona in your care?"

The Count slipped too quickly into the shadow at the back of the box, thought Ilona.

"I can take a droshky," she said.

The ensign protested.

"What are you thinking of, Ilona kisasszony? It will be a pleasure."

He helped her into her coat. She shrugged her shoulders. He didn't seem to notice the offensive gesture.

14

It was obvious to Ilona that her aunt had only pretended to have an urgent appointment in order to leave her alone with the Count. She walked beside him to the carriage in silence. He asked her the address and shouted it up to the coachman on the box; then he sat down beside her with a sigh of relief.

"Thank God she has left us alone together," he said. "In heaven's name, what are you doing with that awful woman?"

"That awful woman is my aunt."

"You don't mean that seriously?"

"I might ask you how you come to know my aunt."

"Every one in Budapest knows her. But your father—he can't have any idea. . . ."

Quickly she said, "No, he hasn't any idea!"

Up till then it had never occurred to her that anyone might suspect the stationmaster on account of her actions. She found the thought unbearable. With only half an ear she heard the Count say, "You must go home at once. I'll get you a ticket."

"I could go home on my own, Count. I don't want to go home."

He asked her not to address him as 'Count.' He took her hand, asked her to explain everything. "There's nothing to explain," she said. The more urgently he spoke the more certain she became that he thought she formed part of her aunt's Salon, like the Zsuzsis and

27

Arankas. She didn't admit this, but neither did she deny it, seized by the usual pleasure in punishing some one, although she didn't know why her sin should be a punishment to him in particular. The more shocked his questions became the more frivolous grew her answers. Hesitantly, then more and more pressingly, he asked her to go back with him to his apartment. It was in Buda, quite close by. To-morrow he had to return to his regiment at Sopron. "I can't leave without knowing what is happening to you here." She agreed, "for an hour at the most," because his entreaties moved her, because she didn't want to be deprived of his presence so soon, or because she still wasn't sure whether he really thought her a scarlet woman. He pressed the little rubber ball encased in silk mesh by his seat and told the coachman, through the speaking-tube, to go to his home.

The little baroque 'palace' was situated in the Dísz tér, only a few steps from Aunt Rosa's house.

It was not until they were mounting the stairs that Ilona's heart began to beat wildly like bells hammering out a fire-alarm. Her agitation did not decrease when Feri stopped in the dark passage and whispered, "Go quietly, please! My batman is from Kisnémet!"

He opened the door, tiptoed across the entrance-hall, lit a match, and entered the study, shielding the flame with his hand. Then he came back, took the girl waiting in the dark by the hand, and led her into the room.

Most of the space was taken up by a large desk and two black-leather armchairs. Besides the chaise-longue, which was covered with a white bearskin, stood a low Turkish smoking-table. Two or three Persian carpets hung on the walls, the remaining areas of which were decorated with weapons—ancient pistols, worm-eaten sporting-guns, and curved sabres. No one lived here; here people were merely put up for a time.

Ilona wondered whether to sit on the divan or in one of the black-leather armchairs. She decided in favour of the armchair. She sat there without moving, in her high-necked, girlish, but very fashionable mauve silk evening dress, which Aunt Rosa had had made for her only a few days ago.

Feri took two little coloured glasses and a cut-glass bottle from a cupboard. He offered her a glass of liqueur, emptied his own, and sat down. She sipped at her glass. Warmth rose into her face.

"Now tell me all about it," he said.

She couldn't lie any more. The village had come after her. You could lie anywhere in the world except at home. Just as she couldn't have concealed from her father when face to face with him that she had spent Christmas Eve in a 'house of sadness,' so her intention to act the part of Zsuzsi or Aranka melted away before Feri's eyes. She told him about Aunt Rosa's visit, about her first few days in Budapest and the sinister Christmas Eve. She mentioned everything save the pale man. "I simply ran away," she said with a forced laugh. "I haven't been near the place since." She talked eagerly about her studies, as though she owed him an explanation. At one point he interjected, "She's kind to you, as the witch was kind to Hänsel and Gretel: she fattening you up in order to slaughter you." She quickly replied, "I'm taking revenge on her, don't forget that; she has to give me everything and gets nothing in return."

He looked at her sadly.

"You don't sell yourself," he said, "but you live on venal love. Your aunt's girls sold themselves for the dress that you are wearing. Every guinea you spend has lain on a bedside table."

She was overcome with rage, as happens to people whose excuses fall on deaf ears. He had slipped into her box in the dark. He had wanted to buy her a ticket. She wasn't even sure that he believed her story.

She stood up. He immediately rose too, took her by both hands, and pressed her back into the chair. His hands were damp.

There was a feeling of security mixed with her anger. Perhaps she wasn't in a bachelor apartment in the strange city at all, but in a room in Aporfalvy Castle. She felt secure, and for that very reason a wave of even more intense misery swept over her. She hadn't been able to picture the village without her; now she couldn't picture it with her. Nor could she stay with Aunt Rosa.

She fought in vain against the twitching of her lips. She let her head fall back against the back of the chair, hid her face, and began to sob. At the same time she saw her own figure merging with that of the hapless girl in the picture.

Feri had sat down beside her. His hands touched her arms. Shaken by sobs as she was, she didn't catch everything he said. He was accusing himself. He was talking about the St Anne's Day ball at which they had danced, of the days that followed. No excuse to visit the station-house had been too silly, he said. He had told his father about her, and his sister. Didn't she understand, he went on, why he had come into her box to-day at the risk of compromising himself? Back in Kisnémet he had lacked courage. "I was a coward." He had been afraid of his father, his sister, the village. "It's all my fault, Ilona, all my fault."

It wasn't his fault, she knew that; but a wave of gratitude flowed over her. He relieved her of the agonizing burden of self-pity that had been weighing her down. She didn't ask herself if she loved him. The village wasn't pursuing her; it had come to her, it was taking her to itself. She opened her eyes and smiled through her tears. She let him draw her to him. She felt his moustache on her cheek, the buttons of his uniform pressing into her breast. She felt his mouth, without feeling his kiss. All at once she was wide awake, like a sick person. The man's agitated hands fondled her back, looking for the buttons of her dress. As though from a distance she heard his confused apologies as he blamed himself for not having declared his love at the proper time, and also for not being able to control it now, when it was too late. She wanted to love him, but she couldn't think of a single word to say. Later. She would love him later. She let herself be led to the divan, and only wondered why he didn't take her to his bedroom.

She felt no pain, like some one who can no longer be hurt. What was happening to her was happening to some one else. She saw the objects in the room quite clearly: the Turkish brass table, the pattern on the Persian carpets, the rusty weapons. Later, she thought, later. . . .

It was 1904. . . .

When Ilona woke next morning in her bed she was surprised that nothing in her room had changed. Everything was the same as the morning before: the white furniture, the little mirror, the books on the bedside table, the curtains. But she herself was no longer the same. She had given away something that she could not give away a second time.

She crossed her arms under her loose hair.

She touched her hair, but she was afraid to touch her body. Her body was no longer hers, and yet it was hers, like a lost possession that becomes doubly valuable when we find it again, because we feel it to be a gift. It was a new feeling, and she observed it watchfully, like a new pain. But it wasn't painful, it was blissful. Later, she had thought yesterday. Now was later. Her lover's face became transfigured. She closed her eyes and relived without pain what yesterday had hurt her. There had been passion and love in his eyes: only the love remained. Perhaps she hadn't loved him before he possessed her—but wasn't it enough to love him now, since she belonged to him? Must surrender follow love? Without a doubt love followed surrender. Something you only possessed once must be precious. To a person who considered herself precious the person to whom she gave herself must be precious.

She was certain that he thought just as she did, that the pain was greater than the pleasure, the cry greater than the happiness. What he had received was something rare. He must know that it was rare.

The thought that now she could marry no one else didn't frighten her. It was ordained that men, when they sacrificed their freedom, demanded that their young wives should give them the only thing that another, who sacrificed nothing, had not received. Feri would sacrifice his freedom. He would marry her.

She jumped out of bed. It was still early—seven or half-past. The March sky was young over the old roofs. The street was empty. There was only old Baron Rozsnyai coming back from his morning walk, shaking his head as though to say no. Every now and then he looked up at the gutters in which birds were preening themselves and bathing, because it had rained during the night.

She wondered why she felt no remorse. Hadn't she been a bad girl? She gave a laugh of relief. People talked about bad girls, but they meant stupid girls. Bad meant silly. A bad girl was a girl who gave what was irreplaceable and got nothing in return. Feri wasn't a thief. Since he wasn't bad, she couldn't be bad either.

When she leant far enough out of the window she could see the roofs of the Dísz tér. Was Feri already awake? If only she could have told him she loved him! The thought that she felt no love for him
30

hadn't shocked her during the night when he was bent over her. To-day, when she loved him, she was afraid that he might discover she hadn't loved him yesterday. She wanted to run to him and tell him a girl belonged to the man who had made her a woman. Nothing she had said, thought, or felt before was true, because she had been dead, and now she had come to life. Now that her body was no longer complete, she was complete.

She was no longer the same. She was happy.

It was 1904. . . .

16

Feri had to leave the same morning for his garrison at Sopron.

Every time the front-door bell rang Ilona ran out, certain it was a message from him. For two days she hovered between hope and despondency.

The perpetual fluctuation of her emotions couldn't remain hidden from Aunt Rosa. Ilona didn't want to hide anything from her.

Forty-eight hours later Feri's telegram arrived from Sopron. "Expecting you," it said. "Have taken a room for you in the Old Post Hotel."

She held the telegram in her hand, trembling all over her body. Not to obey his call was unthinkable, but she had no money, and she couldn't leave the house without telling Aunt Rosa everything. First, she thought, she had entrusted herself to her aunt's protection, then she had become her victim, finally she had taken a cheap revenge on her—now she had to make an ally of her.

They were sitting at the lunch table when Ilona announced that she had to go to Sopron. And before Aunt Rosa could ask any questions she added that young Aporfalvy was waiting for her there.

The madam eyed her niece from the side. She didn't feign surprise.

"And what do you expect to gain from this journey?" she asked.

"What should I expect to gain from it?"

"So you are merely obeying the voice of your heart?"

"We shall marry."

"Has he proposed to you?"

"There wasn't time for that."

"You think he'll find more time in Sopron?"

"We love each other."

"Of course, of course. And you seriously imagine that's enough. My dear Ilona, that's how it started with all my girls. The worst thing about whores' stories is that they're true. I don't say that because I object in any way, but only because I want to make sure you can't reproach me with not warning you. You may be able to go back to Kisnémet from me, but from Sopron you will only be able to come back to me. Have you thought of that?"

"You don't know Feri."

"Women judge men more accurately when they don't know them. When we get to know them we discover all sorts of differences, but they are in ourselves, not in them. Men are all the same when they

31

enter my house; then they appear to become different, but they all look the same again when they leave it." She put down her knife and fork. "And don't imagine that your father won't know about this trip."

"Will you tell him?"

"I shall find some excuse—that's the least difficult thing. But you forget that Lajos is serving in Sopron with the Fourth Honvéds. Sopron is a small town. . . ."

That was something Ilona had forgotten. Her brother, who was not yet twenty-one but full of strict principles like her father, was serving with an infantry regiment in the West Hungarian garrison town. What would she say to him? How could she explain her presence?

"Well, that's your worry," Aunt Rosa continued. "I've warned you." She made a deprecatory gesture with her hand. "Feri Aporfalvy is no worse than the rest. At least try to be sensible. Above all, don't be lazy! It is comfortable to consider every one decent. Your father considers every one decent because he's too lazy to bother about them. He lives with his flowers: they don't disappoint him; at the worst they wither." She reached for a box of sweets; she always ate a few sweets after lunch. "And one more thing. Men always have to be forced into marriage. It really is silly to support another man's daughter. In my youth they married a girl because otherwise they couldn't possess her. That was in the nineteenth century, but you're living in the twentieth. Now men marry to keep a girl who would otherwise slip through their net. No one will pay you for something you like doing. The more willing you are the lower your price. I've even forbidden my girls to call their guests 'love' or 'darling': it's bad enough having to act affectionately towards them; there's no need for the girls to give the impression they enjoy it as well. Feri possesses you now, there's no changing that. Don't give him the feeling he can easily hold you."

Ilona wouldn't listen to her aunt's offensive words. The only thing that mattered was that she didn't oppose her journey. She left for Sopron next morning.

17

She had stopped thinking: she thought neither of Aunt Rosa, her father, nor Lajos: she was completely filled by the bliss of anticipation.

She was still sitting by the window. Although she now possessed many clothes, her Aunt Rosa had given her only the old travelling-basket, saying, "I can send your other things on later." The picnic-basket, carefully packed, was also perched on the luggage-rack. Ilona didn't touch it.

Everything was new to her, even the landscape. She had never seen mountains before. Now, as the train headed straight into the setting sun, mountains and hills seemed to be crowding round the track. They rose up on the horizon on both sides as though they had wrenched away a piece of the earth and a piece of the sky. In Ilona's homeland Christmas-trees arrived on lorries; here they stood in thousands on the mountain-slopes, the huge, dark-green, fragrant warehouse of Santa Claus. The young green leaves of a few deciduous trees were already peeping out from beneath the gloomy firs and melancholy pines, and yet the landscape appeared to the girl at the window stranger even than the stone sea of the city she had left.

When the train reached Sopron gas lights were burning in the imposing station. Ilona, alone in her compartment, shook herself out of her rigidity, straightened her dress and hat, took a quick look at herself in her pocket mirror, and opened the window. Her face was glowing, her heart thumping in her throat.

The cold air of evening struck her. Her eyes sought Feri, but white vapour rose with a whistle from under the carriage, and the people on the platform were nothing but will-o'-the-wisps in the gaslight.

Fear had no time to take possession of her, however; no sooner had the train come to a stop than she heard some one calling her name. It was a man's voice that she didn't recognize, because she had been hoping to hear a different one. Then a pale-blue Hussar's tunic and a pale-blue Hussar's forage-cap appeared directly under her window.

The forage-cap was perched at an angle on the small black-haired head of Mátyás, the peasant lad from Kisnémet who was serving as Feri Aporfalvy's batman. He was the same batman against whom Feri had warned her when they entered his apartment. Now he seemed to have no secrets from him.

"His lordship sends his apologies," Mátyás shouted up to the window, paying no heed to the other travellers. "I have a letter for you, Madam. I'm coming straight up to fetch your luggage."

He was already in the compartment, already taking the travelling-bag and the picnic-basket down from the luggage rack.

"The Colonel called all the officers to a conference this evening," he told her, talking so fast that Ilona had no chance to ask questions. "His lordship was heartbroken. I am to take Madam to her hotel and see that Madam has supper. Madam is to have a good night's rest and not to leave the hotel to-morrow morning until his lordship comes to fetch her."

He put the luggage down on the platform with a sigh of relief, as though he had to get his breath back after carrying out his difficult mission. He drew an envelope from his breast pocket.

Ilona took the letter, but she didn't open it. She didn't want to read it in the batman's presence.

They drove through Sopron in the light of evening in Feri's yellow trap. Nothing preoccupied Ilona so much at this moment as the servant on the coach-box. What did he think of her; how had Feri explained her stay; had he sworn him to secrecy, or would the batman to-morrow tell his relations in Kisnémet about the visit of the station-master's daughter?

The Régi Pósta Szálló was an immensely old building in Beloiannis Square next door to the Keksketemplom. It was built on two storeys and had winding stairs, round-arched passages, white pillars, closed oriels, and heavy oak doors, and was so awkwardly designed that after passing the porter's lodge guests had to cross the coffee-house to reach the staircase. Ilona imagined that all eyes were turned on her as she hurried through the coffee-house, followed by Mátyás and a boots in a green-baize apron.

Mátyás insisted on ordering supper for her from a room-waiter in a greasy dinner-jacket; the boots unlocked her wickerwork case and drew the iron rod out of the plaited loop.

Not until the men had left did she notice the big bunch of red roses standing on the commode between the two high, dark-brown beds. The beds reminded her of the bedroom at Kisnémet.

When she had at last taken off her coat and hat she sat down at the big oval table on which a highly decorated paraffin lamp was burning.

Outside it was night. The bells of the Keksketemplom loudly struck eight o'clock. As she opened her lover's letter with trembling hands she became aware that for the first time in her life she was alone. She read the letter, which welcomed her and apologized in loving terms for the writer's absence. She folded the letter and put it down on the table in front of her, but she couldn't rise. She was waiting, though she didn't know what for.

Thus the time of waiting began for Ilona Horváth.

18

A fortnight after her arrival Feri rented an apartment for her. It was on the first floor of a venerable house in the main square, and consisted of a large drawing-room, a pretty little bedroom, and a small dining-room, all furnished in the Biedermeier style. The windows faced the municipal tower, from whose round, roofed loggia the watchman had once announced the approach of friend or foe with merry or furious horn-calls. Ilona would sit for hours at the drawing-room window reading or doing some handwork and looking out at the tower; at the Trinity column, whose stone clouds seemed to be floating away; at the fronts of the burgher's houses, forbidden by ancient law to be wider than the tiny shops on the ground floor.

She was not yet eighteen, and completely satisfied by the simple fact of being independent. She had a maid, Marcsa, a sixteen-year-old peasant girl who sang melancholy soldiers' songs all day long, and for whom she was always having to buy things. She never knew when Feri would come, and, as at home in the old days, boiling and baking went on all day long so they should be ready to receive him at any time of the day or evening. She bought a fat cookery-book and devoted herself to this art she had neglected, ruining much and proud of every success.

She was alone a great deal without feeling lonely. She wasn't conscious of her emotions, but she instinctively realized that loneliness springs from the presumptuous demand to be pampered, courted, and entertained by one's environment, and, moreover, without giving it anything—for the generous are never lonely—so that in the last analysis loneliness is nothing but the inescapable aloneness of the egoist. Because she didn't imagine that the world owed her anything she was saved from boredom—the sort of nervous irritation experienced by people who feel cheated when life fails to entertain them.

Feri never stayed overnight. Ilona often lay awake for hours. Horses' hoofs clattered on the cobbles. A ray of light passed over the ceiling. To begin with, she managed not to think about herself. She lived in a light-hearted lethargy. Her state was not unlike the half-sleep in which we already know that threatening light is coming in through the drawn curtains, but still have the tired strength to go on dreaming a sweet dream. When the shopkeepers asked about the "little lady's" parents she stammered a lie, and when they began to stop asking questions she looked around for other shops. To her father she wrote gay fairy-tales about the fashion house where she worked; she took the letter to the post with a sigh of relief, but a few days later she was already thinking with trepidation of the next letter, which she repeatedly postponed writing.

She never had to ask Feri for money: on the first of every month he left an envelope behind, and because she was thrifty by nature the money piled up in her commode. A friendly relationship had been established between the two of them—the money and the girl. Often when she stayed in bed late in the morning—for she had learnt to start a long day late—she would take the banknotes and the coins out of the drawer and set them out in rows on her blanket. To begin with, the copper, silver, and gold pieces marched in narrow rows: a copper drummer at the head, then the silver N.C.O.'s and the copper privates in twos, and finally a golden lieutenant to bring up the rear. Later the ranks became four deep and longer, and a few blue notes—mounted officers—joined the column. Even this vacillated between dream and reality. She didn't know yet against what dangers her army of gold and silver was to defend her, but her need for a defence was already awake and ready.

Every morning she awoke with the resolve to wheedle or force a declaration of his intentions out of Feri. When evening came she always found an excuse to delay the execution of her plan, which she had worked out down to the last detail of the imaginary conversation. On one day Feri brought guests with him; on another her resolution melted in the notes of a gipsy orchestra; on a third she dared not destroy the happiness of a quiet evening. Plans for flight passed through her head; she pictured to herself what Feri would do if he found the nest empty; then again it seemed to her of no importance that her man was not her husband.

It would have been simple if she could have believed the proverb that says a good conscience is a soft pillow. Which of us has only one conscience? The bed was full of pillows. On Feri's pillow she slept peacefully. When she thought of her father her conscience was as crumpled as a pillow after a sleepless night.

Weeks passed, then months. She could no longer keep thoughts of herself at bay. What excitement had hidden, routine brought to light. In the monotony voices grew loud and echoed through the silent bedroom.

She had tried to forget, and for a time had forgotten, that her brother was in Sopron.

Soldiers passed through the town almost every day. During the first few weeks Ilona used to stand at the window and look out through the gauzy curtains. When the Hussars rode by with their gleaming boots, red trousers, and sky-blue attilas her eyes sought Feri, and he too looked up at the closed windows; he would slightly dip his drawn sabre as a sign that he knew she was behind the curtains. When the Fourth Honvéds marched past, announcing their approach from a distance by the rolling brass of their military band, Ilona rarely went to the window, either because she left enthusiasm for the infantry to Marcsa or because she was afraid Lajos might be among them and discover her. But once May was over and June began to usher in a hot summer she found it impossible to stay in her room. The booming of the drums, the challenging notes of the military bells, the call of the trumpets, drew her into the open. She went out on to the little wrought-iron balcony to wave to the soldiers marching past, until they disappeared into the avenue of chestnuts, and only the whirling dust and echoing music recalled the colourful picture.

One morning early in June she caught sight of Lajos in the seventh or eighth rank of marching men and, as though her eyes had drawn his, was discovered by him. She stared at him, and the hand that had been waving a lace handkerchief went rigid. She acted as if she hadn't seen him, as children shut their eyes in order not to be seen.

After a week she began to hope that she had really succeeded in deceiving Lajos. One evening—it was about six and she was getting ready for Feri's visit—there was a knock at the front door. She ran into the hall. Lajos stood before her.

She hadn't seen him for a year, and was surprised how much he had changed. He was now twenty-one, but he looked and behaved as if he were a great deal older. He had come to look even more like his father. The little twirled moustache under the straight but rather too fleshy nose, the protruding cheek-bones that made the face look almost square, the long, thin hands that contrasted with the sturdy figure—it was as though a coarsened version of the stationmaster were standing in front of Ilona. Only the big, golden-brown, rather moist eyes differed from their father's: it was like looking into the red-hot glow of an overheated boiler restrained with difficulty from exploding.

He gave his sister a fleeting kiss on the cheek. She walked in front of him into the living-room.

Then they sat facing each other, she in her red dress with the wide sleeves and wine-red velvet collar, he stiff and uncomfortable in his dark-blue walking-out uniform. He looked at the oil-painting hanging on the wall behind her—an unknown woman in a lilac dress with a yellow rose in her hair. She looked over his shoulder at the picture of the Emperor in a white full-dress uniform and a green hat with feathers. A faint smell of perfume hung about the room. Outside, Marcsa was singing the song about the soldier's farewell.

"How are you?" asked Ilona at last.

"I've known for a long time that you were here. Father wrote that you were working in a fashion house."

"Why didn't you come?"

"I didn't want to write the truth to Papa. Nor did I want to lie. I pretended I was kept too busy to see you. What lie did you tell?"

She involuntarily thrust out her lower lip.

"The same," she said. "And now? . . ."

"Margit is getting married. No doubt Papa will write and tell you himself. He would like us both to go home for the wedding."

"Who is she marrying?"

"Young Bihari."

She wasn't surprised. It could only have been young Szomoru, or young Korcsmáros, or young Bihari. It was a good thing it wasn't Zoltán Szomoru, the music student who had tried to kiss her last summer. So it had to be Pali Korcsmáros or Sándor Bihari. They had both been wooing her since her childhood. Margit looked like her twin sister. It was perfectly all right for the innkeeper's son to take Margit because he couldn't get her. And yet she felt a pang at the thought that Margit would marry before her. She had been waiting, and meanwhile in Kisnémet life had gone on. The Emperor in his white uniform and green hat looked down at her pityingly.

"Will you go?" she asked.

Lajos shook his head.

"A soldier doesn't get leave just because his sister is getting married. What about you?"

"I don't know."

"Do you have to ask the Count's permission?"

She went red.

"I don't have to ask anyone's permission."

"Oh, yes you do," said her brother.

Marcsa had stopped singing. Only the grandfather clock was ticking in the silence.

"I'm not reproaching you," said Lajos. "I'm merely surprised."

"What about?" she asked irritably.

"I have to wear this uniform. The Emperor's coat, as they call it. If it were up to me the Emperor could keep his coat. Or it could be worn by monkeys, who enjoy giving and receiving orders. You know I never liked playing tin soldiers."

He broke off with a gesture, as though to say she wouldn't understand what he meant.

She had never heard anyone talking like this, and certainly didn't understand him. Every one was proud to wear the Emperor's coat. She didn't dare to look up at the Emperor's picture.

"I'm surprised at your stupidity," he said. "They forced this uniform on me, and if I take it off too soon they'll put me against the wall. I can't become an officer because I only went to the elementary school. I have to serve in the infantry because Papa is a stationmaster. I'm only a tin soldier."

She wanted to tell him that she would soon be married. But as he looked at her, long and thoughtfully like her father, she couldn't bring herself to lie. It was easy to lie in letters. Letters didn't blush.

"But you?" he went on. "Do you have to serve them? Do you think you're one of them because a count dresses you prettily? You weren't fetched by the police. They won't shoot you if you run away. Margit, our stupid Margit. . . ." He stopped. "Do you remember? We always used to laugh at her. We never let her play with us. . . ."

She remembered. The garden behind the station in summer. The dwarfs. The fence, the ditch, the acacia-trees. Anaemic carnations, dusty poppies. Police and robbers. She was allowed to play with the boys. Margit used to run crying to the stationmaster. In winter the living-room with the dark-red velvet tablecloth and the stove tiles glowing red. They used to play at horse-racing with dice. Margit didn't understand the game and sulkily pretended she didn't want to play.

"What are you really trying to say?" she asked. "I can have ten Sanyi Biharis on every finger."

"Yes, ten on every finger," he laughed. He stood up and smoothed out the creases in his tunic. "Margit is a thousand times cleverer than you. If you're not ashamed of yourself—I'm ashamed of you."

Only now did she notice that he hadn't even unbuckled his bayonet. She wanted to hold him back, but it was pointless. He was like her father, austere, just, and sometimes hot-tempered. If he had accused her, sworn at her, called her a whore! But to have compared her to himself, a serving soldier!

"Won't you come back?" she asked despondently.

"No, I don't want to meet your Count," he said.

The kitchen door was ajar as they went into the narrow, dark hall. Marcsa poked her round head out inquisitively. She opened her eyes wide when she caught sight of the young corporal. She smiled ecstatically, as though to say, "Your place is in the kitchen with me."

Then Ilona put her arms round his neck and kissed him on both cheeks.

Dumbfounded, Marcsa retired into the kitchen. Dumbfounded, the corporal left.

20

Ilona went back into the living-room. She felt stifled. She undid her high, tight velvet collar.

Wedding in Kisnémet. She could only think of the brothel. She remembered the pale Prince Kontowski. For him too she felt a strange tenderness. "Will you become my mistress?" He had put his cards on the table. She had become a mistress. Every one knew that—Feri and the butcher, Lajos and the greengrocer woman, Aunt Rosa and Marcsa. She was the only one who didn't. Everybody was dressed and she was naked, as in a nightmare. The ridiculous person is the person who doesn't know he is ridiculous. The ice under your feet didn't grow any firmer because you walked with firm steps. It broke under your feet.

It mustn't break. Wasn't she still Ilona Horváth, whom destiny had chosen? Chosen—for what? To be special and different was nothing. Criminals and beggars, cripples and whores, were different and special. It wasn't enough that people turned their heads to look at you. You might be proud that they looked at you, while all the time it was because you had a hump. All at once a thought she had never thought before took shape in her mind. That person was truly chosen who saw himself. She hadn't seen herself since the station-house had slipped away into the December mist.

She rose and fastened the collar of her dress. She was standing like that, in the middle of the room, when Feri walked in.

He kissed her quickly on the mouth, and sat down in the armchair under the picture of the Emperor.

"Have you plenty of wine?" he asked. "I've invited a couple of friends round after supper. Gyuszi Herberstein and Béla Böszörményi. They may bring Mitzi with them."

She hadn't moved. She was standing with her back to him, staring at the lilac woman with the yellow rose.

"Do you mind?" he asked jokingly. "We've been alone every evening this week. . . ."

She went without a word to the door of the larder.

They may bring Mitzi with them. Mitzi was the girl-friend of First Lieutenant Böszörményi. She was a twenty-five-year-old Viennese. She had previously been old Prince Rátóthy's girl-friend. And before that some one else's. Mitzi was running to fat and looked like a blonde doll that had swallowed too much sawdust. She's an old doll, and I'm a new one, thought Ilona.

"We can eat,' she said.

There was no gaslight yet in the dining-room. The paraffin lamp hanging over the table in a transparent red-glass bowl was smoking. Ilona turned down the wick. She coughed.

Marcsa brought the soup in a flower-patterned tureen. Ilona put a plateful down in front of Feri. When Marcsa had gone out she said, "My brother was here."

"The corporal I met downstairs? I didn't recognize him. He looks good in uniform."

"My sister is getting married."

"Teréz?"

"No, Margit."

"Congratulations. Who is the happy man?"

"Sándor Bihari."

Feri took a spoonful of soup.

"Bihari? Isn't he the owner of the Hotel Rákoczi?"

"His son."

She left her soup untouched. How could Feri confuse Bihari the father and Bihari the son? Aporfalva Castle wasn't Kisnémet.

"I'm going to the wedding," she said.

"You're joking. . . ."

"Why should I be?"

"My little girl can't just go off and leave me like that."

39

"I'm not a soldier," she said. "I don't need a leave pass."

He looked up.

"What's the matter with you, Ilona?"

"Nothing, except that I've had enough. I'm not a Mitzi."

She threw her napkin down on the table and stood up. Her dress reached down to the ground. She drew it up and walked quickly across to the window. It was curious that she could act spontaneously and yet be conscious of every gesture.

"I don't understand," he said.

"The whole town is full of Mitzis," she said. "You meet them at the baker's and at the hairdresser's. One of them is Count Pataky's girl-friend, the other Major Jasinski's mistress." She lingered on the word 'mistress.' "The whole garrison is a house of assignation." She was glad she had picked up the expression from Kontowski. Feri's reply that he could tell Béla not to bring Mitzi only increased her anger. Did he really imagine it was as simple as that? He couldn't love her if he understood her so little.

'I can't go back to my father," she said. She played with her handkerchief, as great ladies do. "And anyhow, I don't want to. I can live in Budapest. I'm too good to be a garrison mistress."

Feri had risen. He walked across the room with long strides, bumping into things. His patent-leather boots squeaked. It sounded as if there were a kitten in the room.

"Now, listen to me," he said. "For months I have been firing one letter after another at the regimental command and the War Ministry in Budapest. Months ago I gave my father an ultimatum. You know very well that no officer is allowed to marry without the consent of the War Ministry. The War Ministry will have nothing to do with you; nor will my father. I can leave the Army. I can also renounce my inheritance. But I'm not going to do either thoughtlessly. The Ministry has no reason to reject you. Nor has my father. I shan't rest till they both give in."

Ilona crushed the handkerchief she was holding.

"Why didn't you tell me?"

"I didn't want to hurt you. . . ."

The paraffin lamp had long ago started smoking. The smoke was getting in Ilona's eyes. Tears were running down her cheeks. She made no move to lower the flame.

"Do you really want to marry me?" she asked.

Marriage: that was the word round which all her girlish dreams had revolved. Marriage: that meant to put yourself in the hands of a man whose destiny was to protect you; it meant to bear a name not as though it were yours by chance, but proudly, like a medal you had won; it meant to belong to a man who had the joyous right to gratitude and to whom you could give what you received from him. Marriage was passion that was not ashamed of itself; blessed pregnancy; open domesticity; to see yourself in the mirror without vanity; shared pain; a world within the world and eternity within the transient.

Now everything was quite simple. The Mitzis and Kláris wouldn't

40

nod in obscene complicity when she met them in the street. "My fiancé," she would say when she spoke of Feri. To-morrow she would go to the Honvéd barracks and look for Lajos. "I'm engaged," she would tell her father in Kisnémet.

She twined her arms round Feri's neck and put her head on his chest.

He stroked her hair.

They were standing like this in the smoke-filled room when Marcsa came in. The maid grinned and went out again, shrugging her shoulders.

The smell of the burnt roast came in through the door.

21

A fortnight later Ilona left Sopron. She wanted to spend two days in Budapest buying presents for Margit, and arrive just in time for the wedding.

After long hesitation she decided to stay with her aunt, because she couldn't have explained to her father why she was staying in an hotel. She insisted on paying for her board and lodging, and refused to take the clothes that had remained with Aunt Rosa until the madam angrily agreed to accept at least a small sum for them.

June was warm and wafted the scents of the countryside into the city. Spring dresses and straw hats sprouted from the asphalt of the Váci ucca. Summer had already entered the suburbs. Women, always disposed to welcome the victors with flowers, were equipping themselves to receive it.

Ilona was just hurrying home in her new summer costume with a lace collar and cuffs, carrying several parcels, when her eye was caught by a poster.

She stopped in amazement. The poster bore the name Zoltán Szomoru in enormous letters. It was an unusual name; there could be no mistake. "Europe's youngest conductor," who was making his debut with the Budapest Symphony Orchestra, was her childhood companion, the son of the farmer's widow, Agnes Szomoru. A glance informed Ilona that the concert was taking place in the Vigadó. Without stopping to think, she hurried past the Hotel Vadászkürt to the Danube embankment, where she bought a ticket at the concert-hall box-office.

She invented an excuse for not spending the evening with her aunt. She didn't want to be seen in public with the brothel-keeper, and also she regarded what was to be seen on every hoarding as her personal secret. She therefore pretended to have been invited by friends from Sopron, so that she could enter the redoubt on her own.

"Europe's youngest conductor" had attracted only a modest number of music-lovers. The gallery was sold out, but the wealthier public were waiting for the verdict of the critics: spectators were scattered sparsely in the stalls, and the rows of boxes gaped like a toothless mouth. In the first row there were two seats vacant on Ilona's left and three on her right; since, in addition to occupying this isolated position, she was indecorously unescorted, she attracted inquisitive stares; so she quickly moved to the side of a well-to-do married couple.

Instruments were taken out, violins tuned, brass notes tested—the typical cacophony of the concert-hall that precedes the anticipated harmonies. Preparations went on for a long time before the conductor appeared, then strode rapidly to the rostrum, halted in front of the music-stand, and gave a brief, almost unwilling nod. Either through the magical contrast between his youth and all the staid grey-haired or bald-headed men surrounding him, or because personality invariably creates a charmed circle, the young conductor immediately took possession of the suspicious public. If painters, in response to some secret prejudice, had not always depicted angels as fair-haired the youthful conductor could have been compared to an angel, one of those grave and masculine angels that come down to earth bearing not a palm-branch, but a sword. The big dark-blue eyes set wide apart, as in paintings by the Italian masters, were topped by a high, snow-white forehead, and this again by jet-black, silky, wavy hair. This archangel with the slightly aquiline nose, regular mouth, and cleanly curved eyebrows, holding a baton like a sword, looked out into the auditorium confidently, challengingly, without a trace of shyness.

Ilona wasn't exactly unmusical, but the classical harmonies were strange to her: she took in the music more with her eyes than with her ears. The rostrum was a general's hillock and the conductor a general. It is power that casts a spell upon women, especially the power of a man over other men; but what was enacted before Ilona's eyes was the drama of the power of one individual over many. When the slender baton rose in the white hand notes rose from the orchestra; they seemed to cower, to bow down humbly, when the imperious baton was lowered; a short stroke through the air, and the instruments that had been lamenting so loudly fell silent; then they cried out to heaven again because the man up there had opened out his arms to heaven. The conductor was a prophet and a magician—a prophet because he foresaw what was coming, a magician because he brought it to pass. Bass notes approached obediently when he enticed them; the violins grew wings when he spread out his arms as though to fly; the ear confirmed what the eye conjured up. An unfamiliar bliss filled the girl's heart—such a violent, almost painful pride that she would have liked to stand up and announce that the man up there sowing the storm and reducing it to nothing belonged to her, was bound to her by birth and descent and a half-kissed kiss.

When the interval came Zoltán Szomoru bowed to an enthusiastic public that was applauding itself for its own discovery, Ilona finally knew that the conductor had noticed her.

He thanked the audience pleasantly, but not without a certain arrogance, like a man who hears the confirmation of something that he himself has known for a long time. But when he looked down at the pink-cheeked girl clapping he smiled faintly, with his eyes alone and without screwing up his mouth. In spite of the modest nature of this greeting, Ilona abandoned herself during the second half of the programme to the happy fantasy that Zoltán was conducting for her, the orchestra was playing for her, the composer had written the symphony specially for her. The composer had doubtless translated quite a different song into musical notes, but Ilona only heard the song of her homeland. She saw the railway-lines by which she had stood with Zoltán on hot summer evenings; saw his mother's single-storey farmstead in the heat-haze of a summer's noon; saw him stripped to the waist walking through the waving fields. It was as though even in those days music had accompanied every one of his movements, and only she had not heard it at the time. The feeling of being chosen swept through her more strongly than ever, for she alone in the reverently listening hall knew the sky out of which the black-haired angel had descended.

The concert was at an end. The conductor had to bow over and over again, and now he did so with a triumphant gaiety and also with a jaunty modesty, as he pointed to the orchestra and compelled his musicians to stand up with a lifting gesture, as though they were hanging from his fingers. Ilona was assailed by trepidation, less because she was unable to catch the conductor's eye again than because she was aware that his triumph had carried him into alien regions foreign to her, had suddenly taken him away from her. She wished she had realized who he was earlier and alone, so that he did not have to share the discovery with others; she almost wished he had suffered a defeat, so that she could have hurried to him and spoken to him consolingly of the victory that still awaited him.

She resisted the temptation to visit him in his dressing-room. She told herself that he would think of her more if her presence in the front row at the Budapest Vigadó remained mysterious. She was capable of that much cool thought, although she left the concert-hall stirred to the depths of her soul and blind to her surroundings.

Back in the apartment in Buda, the cold supper was left untouched. Glad that Aunt Rosa was out, she retired to her bedroom.

As some one waking from a deep narcosis slowly recognizes people and objects, so the last few months of her life took shape before her eyes. She didn't love Feri, had never loved him. She accused herself, acquitted herself, accused herself again. She wasn't guilty of deceiving Feri. She had deceived herself. Deceived herself because she had escaped Aunt Rosa's 'fashion house' and yet hadn't wanted to go back to Kisnémet? Because she had been guided by impatience at the parting of the ways, and impatience had always indicated the wrong path? Feri's face grew pale, like the face of a dead man. She was guilty of his death. But who could detect the false when she had not met the true? The sweet thrills that had run through her body in Feri's arms seemed to her an attack of the shivers compared with the sensations of this evening. She had never felt dirty, not even while hesitantly learning the lessons of love. The purity she was discovering now dirtied her. The thought of marriage made the sweat break out on her brow.

The clocks in Aunt Rosa's apartment talked together for a long time before sleep set Ilona free from the conversation with herself.

She woke feeling dizzy and sick and quickly got up. Her knees were so devoid of feeling that she looked down to see if they were moving. She remembered that she hadn't eaten anything since mid-day the previous day. The feeling of oppression didn't go until she had drunk a cup of coffee and eaten a roll.

Aunt Rosa took her niece to the station in a one-horse cab. Throughout the journey she kept repeating her instructions.

"Where did you meet Feri?"

"I know. At a charity ball in Sopron."

"Who took you to it?"

Numbly, she rattled off the answers she had learnt by heart. The one-horse carriage bumped over the cobbles. She felt sick again. Fortunately Aunt Rosa was in a hurry. She embraced Ilona in the carriage.

The discomfort she had felt at the prospect of going to Kisnémet vanished as soon as she saw Zoltán. He didn't seem to notice her. He was engaged in an animated discussion with four or five young men on the platform. Ilona hurried past him, followed by her porter. She chose an empty second-class compartment in the carriage next to Zoltán's. She dealt absent-mindedly with her luggage, then took a mirror out of her pocket and devoted herself attentively to her beauty.

No sooner had the train broken away from the outskirts of the city, with the washing hanging out to dry, the faded posters on the walls, and the dirty children—Ilona felt that every one who lived by a railway-line must be sad—than Zoltán entered the compartment.

He was wearing a fashionably cut travelling-suit in a large check pattern, a fancy flannel waistcoat, and a wide, carefully knotted cravat. He had his travelling-cap in his hand. His hair was slightly untidy. Under his arm he was carrying two or three folded newspapers.

"Didn't you want to see me, or didn't you see me, Ilona?" he asked, shutting the door behind him.

He sat down facing her by the window.

"I didn't want to interrupt your good-byes," she said.

"Why didn't you come to my dressing-room yesterday?" he began. "Didn't you like the concert?"

"It was wonderful. It was overwhelming."

He smiled, the same superior smile that had caught her attention the previous evening. Smiling, he said, "The criticisms in the mid-day papers aren't bad, not bad at all."

He handed her the newspapers. They were open at the music reviews.

He's waiting for me to read them, she thought with pleasure. As she read the fulsome praise, the matter-of-fact admiration, the well-meaning admonitions addressed to the great discovery of the musical world, she knew that Zoltán was scrutinizing her. She didn't forget that her long dark-blonde lashes were perhaps her loveliest feature, nor how lowered eyes suited her. She smiled, grew serious, smiled again, busy reading, but paying attention all the time to the charm of her changing expression.

"Magnificent, magnificent, Zoltán!" she cried when she had finished. "I'm so proud of you! And how pleased your mother will be!"

"That's why I'm going home. In the last resort one's home village is what matters most. And that's why I was so pleased when I spotted you in the front row yesterday evening."

"Was that the only reason? . . ."

"No, not the only one." In the most natural way, he took her hand. "But to have a witness of yesterday evening going to Kisnémet is better than all the reviews. After all, I owe everything to Kisnémet. My mother would never have found the money for my training, for my further training. Because, make no mistake, it has only just started."

"What has that to do with Kisnémet?"

"The Aporfalvys. They're paying my fees."

"What of it?" she retorted quickly. "They're rolling in money. They have to do something with it besides organizing banquets and horse-races. In the old days princes used to keep Court jesters; now they keep musicians. . . ."

For the moment she had toyed with the idea of saying to Zoltán, "I shall soon be a Countess Aporfalvy." But she dismissed the idea—the idea of telling Zoltán, and almost the idea of becoming the Countess Aporfalvy. She talked herself into a heat. She talked like Lajos. She didn't know why she was arraigning the Aporfalvys. She had been seized by the need to erect a wall—on one side the Aporfalvys, on the other side herself, alone with Zoltán.

The young man let go of her hand. He was leaning back in his seat. His black hair stood out against the lace antimacassar. Framed in red velvet, he looked like the pampered princes in Spanish paintings. He stared at Ilona in astonishment, like a person who has discovered something new about a familiar object.

"What has happened to you?" he interrupted almost roughly. "You've changed more than I have. Where have you been since we last met?"

She reflected. How simple was the truth and how difficult a lie! Once one has begun to lie one has to tell each person a different lie. The fairy-tale of the little miss learning dressmaking in the big city was not for Zoltán's ears.

"I've been having a look round the world," she said mysteriously, with lowered eyes. She played with her gloves. "I'm just going home for Margit's wedding. Next week I'm coming back."

"To Budapest?"

She looked up. "Yes, to Budapest," she said, hoping he would say something about his own return. As he remained silent she continued casually, "But let's talk about you. How did you come to be conducting the Symphony Orchestra?"

He didn't need asking twice. Leaning forward, his elbows supported on his knees, he talked about the Conservatory, where he had begun by learning the violin, but had soon found his true vocation. He talked

45

about his colleagues, his teachers, and, when he realized that she was listening intently, no less animatedly about his views on music, composers, orchestras, and conductors.

She barely understood every third sentence, but the finest of woman's arts, the magic art of listening attentively, came to her easily.

"How wonderfully you listen!" he said. "I haven't spoken so much for years."

"I wish you would tell me some more."

He took her hand and kissed it. The courteous kiss went through her whole body: she felt it in her ears and in her knees. She remembered that he had tried to kiss her once; but this kiss meant more—it was a tribute to an adult woman.

At Püspökladány they changed trains. Zoltán called a porter, took Ilona gently by the elbow, paid the porter, made sure their trunks were safely on the train. Every now and then she closed her eyes for a moment. Mr and Mrs Szomoru on their honeymoon, she thought. She had to open her eyes because she felt giddy again.

The second class in the local train was packed. They put their gloves down on their seats and went out into the corridor.

They spoke little. Evening was weaving its net over the Hungarian plain. The sky was yellow, a great herdsman's tent. The white cattle were lying on the black earth. The herdsmen were leaning on their staves watching the train go by. A horse ran alongside the train, but was finally left behind. The evening sky swallowed up the outlines of the wells, with their long, almost vertical arms. Geese were waddling home. Little peasant boys drove the geese, and old peasant women drove the little boys. Pots containing geraniums stood in the windows. Flower-gardens encircled the signalman's boxes. The signalmen sat outside their boxes smoking long pipes.

"Well, well, the stationmaster will be pleased," Ilona suddenly heard a voice say beside her. It was Józsi bácsi, the elderly guard, broad, grey-haired, moustached. He was holding the candlestick in his hand. "I should hardly have recognized the little lady," he went on, turning to Zoltán. "So young Mr Zoltán is paying us another visit too? . . ."

Zoltán gave him both their tickets.

Józsi bácsi immediately turned back to Ilona.

"The stationmaster told me you were coming to the wedding, Miss Ilona. That's how it should be: first the elder sister, then the younger. It's going to be a fine wedding. A good lad, young Bihari." He looked at the clock. "Another thirty minutes. We're punctual, as usual."

"Punctual, as usual," repeated Ilona, smiling.

23

Ilona had been in Kisnémet for four days, and for four days she had known that she was pregnant.

Teréz was the only person to whom she could have confided the distressing news of her happy state. Teréz was twenty-two, four years older than her sister. She had completed a teacher's course at Debreczen, coming out top of her class. She could have found a job long ago, but the stationmaster couldn't spare her. So she stayed. She always did the right thing and never expected it of anyone else, as though she knew that goodness disappears as soon as it is made into a criterion. The village girls, and even older women, used to come to her for advice, because she judged calmly—that is to say, without condemning. She was like the priests, who understand lovers: her understanding was pure because it did not flow from the murky fountainhead of experience. At an early age she had learnt to distinguish between sicknesses, which are hateful, and the sick, who are merely pitiful.

Ilona didn't confide in her sister. Other unmarried girls might expect a child, but they loved the man by whom they were expecting a child. How was she to explain to Teréz that she was not suffering on account of her disgrace, but because the child's life had begun to germinate simultaneously with her own? Nor did she mention her engagement. She was waiting for a miracle.

On the eve of the wedding the young men of the village performed a serenade for Margit. They stood on the platform with their instruments, singing and playing to Margit's window. *"Csak egy kisleány van a vilagón"* ("There is only one girl in the world").

Ilona was sitting with Teréz and her father in the dining-room. No window but Margit's was allowed to be lit up. They were sitting in darkness. The June rain had cooled the air. A mild wind swayed the curtain over the open window.

The bride had shown herself at last. The orchestra moved off. There was the sound of footsteps on the gravel. Ilona thought she could recognize voices. The double bass scraped over the railway-lines. Then Teréz lit the lamp.

"I'm going across to Margit," she said.

"Yes, do," said the stationmaster.

He was sitting at the table. He was wearing his best uniform; he had been wearing it for days, perhaps to get used to it.

Ilona had moved her chair over to the window.

"I'ts getting cool," she said, and closed the window. She sat down. "I must talk to you, Papa."

"That sounds very serious." The stationmaster was smiling.

"I'm engaged."

"Engaged? Who to?"

"To Feri Aporfalvy."

"Is he here?"

"No, at Sopron. We met at a charity ball."

She churned out her lies. The stationmaster didn't interrupt.

"Don't you want to ask any questions?" Her voice sounded irritated.

"Does his father know?"

"He has written to tell him."

"Has the Count given his consent?"

"No, the Count hasn't given his consent. But what about you, Papa?"

The stationmaster stroked his moustache with the tip of his ring finger.

"The Count is right," he said.

"Aren't I good enough?"

"That's not the point."

He reflected. When two people marry, he explained, it is as though two boulders had broken loose from their mountains. They roll towards one another, but on the way they drag other stones along with them. By the time the boulders come to rest there is a large number of stones.

"Do you understand?" he asked.

"No."

"When your mother and I married we dragged a lot of stones with us. Her friends and mine. Her family and mine. Her father didn't come to the wedding. My mother never went to the Szapolczays because she didn't have a black-silk dress."

"And yet you were happy."

"No, we were never happy."

He looked at his daughter calmly. All her life he had lied to her, to her and to his other children. Now Ilona's happiness was at stake. He was ready to give up his life's lie.

"It isn't good for people to make sacrifices," he said. "They regret their good deeds as well as their evil ones."

"Who says Feri is making a sacrifice?"

"Both of you are making a sacrifice, both of you. His father will never give his consent. His sister will never speak to him again. Especially his sister. He will have to leave the Army. But Margit and Teréz and I would be out of place in the house of a Countess Aporfalvy."

"Aunt Rosa says we are living in the twentieth century."

"Aunt Rosa expects miracles of the calendar."

Ilona had risen. She had turned away from her father. Her forehead was hot on the windowpane. Didn't her father sense that she had no choice?

The stationmaster walked silently over to the window. He put his arm round his daughter's shoulders.

"Many parents think their children must discover every form of suffering for themselves," he said. "But what are parents there for?" He took her thin face in his hand so that she had to look at him. "Do you think I understand nothing about love, Ilona? I understand enough to know that you don't love him sufficiently."

"What makes you think that?"

"You don't love him sufficiently to put up with all that lies ahead," the stationmaster continued. "You kept it from me for four days. You couldn't have kept it from me for four minutes if you had been serious in your heart. You left the letter from Sopron unopened for an hour. And you asked after Zoltán Szomoru. Do these signs mean anything different in the twentieth century from what they used to mean in the nineteenth?" He smiled again. "My child would be good enough for His Majesty the Emperor. But she would have to love him enough."

She laid her head on his chest. He was trying to help her. But how could he help her, since he knew only half the truth? She loved an-

other man than the one to whom she was promised. And she was
expecting a child by the one whom she wished to renounce.

"There's something else I must tell you, Papa," she whispered.

"To-morrow," he said soothingly. "To-morrow is another day. Now
we must go to bed. You want to look your best for Margit's wedding,
don't you?"

He waited gallantly till she was at the door before pulling the little
brass chain of the gaslight and following her across the dark room into
the passage.

24

Margit was already asleep when she went into the bedroom and
undressed.

Beside her bed, which was only separated by a commode from the
bed of her quietly sleeping sister, her presents stood in a pile. She had
spent every gulden she possessed on wedding presents. There was an
evening-dress with ribbons, lace, and ruches, a ridiculous dress such as
no one in Kisnémet could wear without exciting hostility; there was a
no less provocative hat, a gold medallion, a tobacco-box ornamented
with semi-precious stones, a flower-vase, a table-clock.

Ilona was seized with panic at her own foolishness. How foolish to
have left her best dresses behind with Aunt Rosa when the presents
themselves would immediately betray to the little town that she was
living as some one's mistress! One didn't marry a stationmaster's
daughter. But still less did one marry a mistress.

The family had seen the parcels, but they had no idea what was in
them. She must find a hiding-place. She thought of all sorts of places;
none of them seemed to her safe.

There was not a sound to be heard in the room but the quiet
breathing of the bride.

She's dreaming of the day-to-day provincial life that lies ahead of
her, thought Ilona, without envy, but without arrogance either. The
burden of being 'chosen' weighed as heavy as a hundredweight sack.
And you never knew what the sack contained. To be different was a
harsh piece of good fortune.

The bell of the Catholic church tolled midnight, followed two or
three minutes later by the bell of the Calvinist church.

Ilona got out of bed.

She dressed hastily and felt for the parcels. She couldn't get rid of
the big boxes containing the evening-dress, or the vase. She didn't
touch the little box containing the medallion. She opened the hat-
box and stuffed the other parcels into it. The tissue-paper rustled.
Margit slept on.

She tiptoed through the house with the hat-box over her arm. The
key grated in the door.

She didn't notice how cool the June night was. She avoided the
gravel and was careful to walk on the sleepers as she crossed the railway-line. On the other side lay a half-dry stream. In summer the
croaking of the frogs could be heard in the house on the other side of

49

the station. Now it was silent. The sand of the plain glittered in the moonlight.

She wanted to throw her presents into the stream, but the water was too shallow. She ran along the slope. When she came to a stop she could see in the distance two sleeping farmhouses. Beyond them lay the fields belonging to Zoltán's mother. It was uncanny how far one could see. The moon was an eerie sun.

She knelt down at the foot of the sandy hillock skirted by a narrow path. Here she was protected from the night wind. Her knees were freezing cold. I should have brought a spade, she thought. She began to grub up the soil with her bare fingers.

She worked for a long time, perhaps half an hour. Gradually the parcels vanished into the earth. When she came to the parcel containing the tobacco-box she hesitated. She loved semi-precious stones. Then she went on digging. Her fingers hurt.

Now there was nothing left but the hat.

She straightened up. She was seized by an obstinate desire to put it on. It was a beautiful hat—big, with white, black, and green feathers. They curved down almost to her shoulders, like the branches of a weeping willow. She tidied her hair as though in front of a mirror. She stood there in the moonlight in her plain dress with the hat on her head. The wind caught the feathers. Ilona swayed like a weeping willow.

Suddenly she heard a voice. Was the wind carrying it from a distance? Some one was singing half-aloud behind her on the sandy hillock.

She tore the hat from her head and threw it into the pit. The feathers snapped at once. When she looked down it was as if a dead cock were lying at her feet.

25

The day had started well.

During breakfast Máté, the village idiot, who delivered the post, had brought her a letter.

"You do look smart, Máté!" she cried.

"There's a wedding to-day," he said with a wink, as though it were a secret.

In the stationmaster's worn-out suit, which was too short for his arms and legs, he looked like a decorated tree. A thin iron chain dangled round his neck, with an old railway trumpet suspended from it. Coloured ribbons, a celluloid doll's leg, and an alarm-clock with one hand hung from the highly polished silver buttons of the waistcoat. Round one arm he had tied a red, white, and green bow bearing the words "Dance Committee."

"Everything must be saved up," he whispered. "Nothing must be lost."

Ilona took the letter with a smile.

It was from Feri.

"In great haste to let you know that I have been promoted

50

Lieutenant and transferred to Budapest," he wrote. "I've already had your things taken to Budapest. I am waiting for you in *our* house." The word 'our' was underlined. "Yours longingly, Feri."

The anxiety of the last few days diminished. She no longer avoided thinking of Feri. Perhaps she had only wanted to betray him because she was afraid he would betray her.

She thrust the letter into the bodice of her dress.

The wedding was in the afternoon.

The bride walked down the nave of the church in her mother's lace dress. Ilona and Teréz, also in lace dresses, carried her train. The stationmaster walked in front of Ilona. She admired his dignified gait. He looked like a general.

She kept her eyes decorously lowered, but nothing escaped her.

The church was decorated with bright-coloured wild flowers. John the Baptist, bending down in front of the side-altar, seemed to be plucking Hungarian wild flowers from the waters of the Jordan. The main altar also looked gay rather than solemn. The crucifix was wreathed in flowers. The letters I.N.R.I. were scarcely visible for flowers. The sun came in through the coloured window-panes and fell on the pews of light carved wood.

Máté, in his fool's costume, was standing pressed up against the wall under a picture of the Calvary. He was grinning. The notes of the organ seemed to be bursting the walls of the little church.

Ilona's eyes sought Zoltán. His mother, a skinny little peasant woman with a black head-scarf was standing next to the mayor. Had Zoltán left without a word?

The bridal procession had reached the altar. The stationmaster stepped back; the bridegroom moved to the side of the bride. He was wearing a suit that was too tight and in his buttonhole a white flower that was too big. He was rather shorter than Margit; during most of the ceremony he stood on tiptoe. His young face was bright red. Why do I have to see everything that is ridiculous? thought Ilona. Margit was playing her part with a smile and perfect naturalness.

The two families were now standing in the front row to the left of the altar.

On Sundays the first row on both sides was reserved for the Aporfalvy family. Ilona looked down at the little brass plate fixed to the lectern in front of her. "Countess Mathilde Aporfalvy of Aporfalva and Gulyakut." Feri's dead mother. My child's grandmother: the thought filled Ilona with bitter merriment. She looked across at the Aporfalvys. To the right of the altar, alone in the first row, stood father and daughter. Countess Consuela had married an Italian prince a few years before, but six months later she was back with her father. With his slightly bent back, iron-grey head, and aquiline nose, Count Endre Aporfalvy looked like one of the greyhounds he bred. The Princess, with her black hair lying close to her head, stood beside him —the picture of a woman devoid of charity.

Ilona looked at the bride from the side. Yes, she and Margit looked alike. Beauty no longer seemed to Ilona sufficient protection. Couldn't she too one day be satisfied with a small-town splendour, the tasteless presents of household utensils, the envy of the village girls, the condescending congratulations of the Aporfalvys? She saw in front of her the dead cock in the pit she had dug. The long plumes seemed to be struggling, as though the cock were trying to fly again. She was ashamed of having retreated before the celebrating village; she was even ashamed of her prayer. It was no punishment to be different. A count's mistress? Why not? She felt Feri's letter in her bodice.

Outside the church the young couple received congratulations. Ilona stood behind her father. The Count came up to him, then the Princess. The Count avoided Ilona's eyes, which met only those of the Princess. Who would lower her eyes first? The Princess lowered hers, as though ending an unworthy duel. The stationmaster placed himself in front of his youngest daughter as if to protect her. People took off their hats. The Count and the Princess strode past them nodding. The liveried servant opened the door of the landau. The black-clad coachman with the little beribboned hat set the horses in motion. The carriage disappeared in a cloud of dust. Freed from constraint, voices now grew loud.

The bridegroom's parents had decorated the Hotel Rákoczi in gala fashion. In the gilded dining-room places were laid for over a hundred people. The long tables stood round the walls under the huge gilt-framed equestrian portrait of His Majesty Emperor Francis Joseph I and the slightly smaller gilt-framed portrait of Her Majesty Empress Elisabeth. The gilt-framed mirrors had brown freckles. The dining-room looked twice as large in them, but also restless, like the reflection of a landscape in water. Red, white, and green cockades had been stuck in their frames. Next door, in the coffee-house, the gipsies were striking up a dance. The plates rattled to the vibration of the csárdás. There was a smell of dry leaves, as at rifle-club parties, of beer and sauerkraut. Pigs had been killed. There were black-puddings, tasty liver sausages, warm hams, legs of pork, bacon, smoked pork. The earthenware wine-jugs passed from hand to hand.

Then Zoltán came towards Ilona from the other end of the room, from the open folding-doors leading into the coffee-house. The clouds of smoke were like the pigs' bladders that hung in the butcher's windows. Zoltán seemed to be pushing them aside. He was wearing a grey, urban, almost foppish suit, as though to say, "I don't belong here; I don't give a damn for you." Count Aporfalvy himself would not have looked more out of place than this farmer's son, Zoltán Szomoru.

She hurried towards him, not caring whether anyone noticed. She forgot the letter in her bosom, forgot the proud plans she had made when she saw the Count's family. The faces of the drinkers came close to her and moved away again, at one moment enormous, at the next tiny.

He didn't greet her; he merely said, "Shall we dance?"

She followed him into the coffee-house, swaying slightly as she walked through the smoke, as if banging her head against the pigs' bladders.

In the doorway he stopped. "Or shall we sit down instead?" he asked.

They sat down on two chairs with thin curved backs beside the billiard-table, which had been pushed into one corner.

"Weren't you at the church?" asked Ilona.

"I was standing at the door. I watched you."

Ilona looked at him; the dance-floor had begun to spin round; it was as though she were dancing herself.

"I'm going back to-morrow," he said.

"So am I," she lied.

For a while he said nothing, simply scrutinizing her, amused and slightly pitying.

Then he said, "Too bad about the beautiful hat."

"So it was you? . . ."

"You were quite right. It would have looked ridiculous here. . . ."

"Why didn't you say something?"

"I enjoyed spying on you."

"It wasn't chivalrous."

"I don't give a damn for chivalry. You were beautiful with the plumed hat in the moonlight. Anger suits you. Never stop being angry."

She looked round. The billiard-table covered with an oil-cloth sheet reminded her of a wooden box in which she had once seen a corpse carried away, old Tabányi's corpse. The couples were dancing with red faces. The men's hands rested on the girls' hips; the girls' hands rested on the men's shoulders. Two steps to the right, two steps to the left. They were a little drunk and very contented. The bride and bridegroom had already slipped away.

Through the smoke came Zoltán's voice.

"Four days ago I too still thought the village was heaven knows how important. Now it's behind me. It will never see me again. After Budapest come Vienna, Paris, Rome, London. We imagine people ought to love us because we herded pigs with them. But they don't say, 'Here comes the great conductor who used to herd pigs with us.' They say, 'Here comes the swineherd.' They hate me because they're afraid I might despise them. They're right. I do despise them. When you have flown high enough everything down below becomes tiny. To the eagle Aporfalvy Castle is no bigger than a pigsty."

He noticed that he was only talking about himself, and he became silent.

"You're not a swineherd to me," she said. "Isn't that more important?"

Yes, that was more important, he said. But he didn't hate the village any the less for it. There was something he knew which she didn't know yet: they had both outgrown the village.

What he said was flattering, but it sounded almost menacing because he didn't explain it. His art had raised him above Kisnémet and Aporfalva. What distinguished her from the dancing peasant girls? He, the conductor; she, the Count's mistress—wasn't that what he meant by greatness?

53

She was trying to dispel the thought when he said, "It's no coincidence that we're leaving to-morrow. We could miss our connexion at Püspökladány. We could spend the night at Püspökladány.

The blood rose into her head. She had felt admiration for him, first love. But he despised her as he despised the villagers. He had no time. To-morrow Paris and Rome. To-day the Püspökladány junction. What had she expected? The fact that she was no longer a virgin was written all over her face. There was no need for a hat with feathers to betray that.

"I'm engaged," she said.

He laughed softly. "They're talking about it in the village. But you won't marry him."

Was it her destiny to be insulted? Her love changed into hate.

He said, "I didn't mean to offend you. I felt attracted to you as soon as I saw you at the concert." He went on: "You're too good for him. He's a simpleton. He belongs here. You didn't go away in order to come back again."

The red had disappeared from her face.

"Perhaps *you're* a simpleton," she said. "You're certainly a simpleton if you imagine I'm going to spend a night with you at Püspökladány."

"Don't pretend to be so indignant."

"I'm not indignant. You're a silly boy whose head has been turned by success. Didn't you say you owed everything to the Aporfalvys?"

"I shall pay them back." Now he had become unsure of himself.

"That isn't necessary," she said immediately. "We shall continue to show you our favour. I respect this village, Zoltán, because it bore me. I respect the Aporfalvys because I shall be one of them. You will prowl around castles for years, and one day, if you're lucky, they will let you in. But by then I shall have been living in castles for a long time."

She broke off, as though exhausted by the words, which she only thought of as they came tumbling out of her.

Zoltán laughed. "How could I have so much overestimated you?" he said.

She put her hand on his in an almost motherly way.

"I know where you're going," she said. "But we're going by different routes—and mine is shorter and better." She rose. "My eagle's flight doesn't start from a provincial hotel in Püspökladány."

She lifted the train of her dress.

She hurried across to a high window in the dining-room. The window was open. Darkness had fallen. She drew a deep breath. Never stop being angry, he had said. He could rely on her. She wouldn't stop being angry.

26

She didn't see Zoltán again; she didn't confide in either Teréz or her sister; a week later she left for Budapest.

She lived in Feri's little 'palace" in the quiet Dísz tér in Buda, where even the houses came of a good family. Feri was out all day long, and his batman was also away most of the time. She was frightened of the cook, a gaunt woman who accepted her only grumblingly. Feri had forbidden her to see Aunt Rosa.

She rarely thought of Kisnémet. It wasn't easy to imagine that she was the same person who had lived in the station-house over the nameboard. The girl who had gazed after the soldiers who marched past in Sopron was a stranger to her. She was maturing fast because she pondered over herself a great deal, or did she ponder over herself a great deal because she was growing mature?

All this passed through Ilona's mind as she strove for clarity and became more and more confused. Maturity is the attempt to live with ourselves, complete maturity peace with ourselves. Ilona was still at the beginning of the road, rarely capable of living with herself, never of being happy with herself.

She often thought of Zoltán, and her heart beat faster when she read his name in the papers. Because she imagined she had been insulted, because she thought Fate avenged the insulted, she dreamt of satisfaction. She saw him as a suppliant at the gates of the Aporfalvys' castle; she saw herself with Feri in the box of the concert-hall in which the conductor was whistled off the stage; even saw him as a violin-playing beggar in a café which she visited with her husband. But what followed? If she consoled him she wouldn't be obtaining satisfaction; if she didn't console him he wouldn't be aware of her triumph.

She tried to console herself by drawing close to Feri. Only through a man, she thought, could she win a victory over another man. She had no idea that her feelings for Feri had jumped years; they had matured prematurely; they had cheated time. If they had been married ten or twenty years people would have said, "What a happy couple!" But even happiness is subject to time; time has prescribed a definite sequence for happiness; as in music, cacophony is produced when the correct sequence is not followed, so Ilona had cheated herself of the early notes of happiness. When they came late they sounded out of tune.

27

She had confided in Feri the very first day of her return. Her pregnancy had dismayed him, but he finally accepted it with masculine resignation. She was a little hurt by the fact that he never spoke of the child, as though an unmarried man had no right to do so. He spoke all the more about their marriage. His optimism angered her. He interpreted a letter from his father, which contained not one word about Ilona, as silent consent; he hailed a birthday present from his sister as a happy omen; he read acceptance into an evasive reply from the War Ministry.

Three months passed in this self-deception. Then came the final refusal from the Imperial and Royal War Ministry, and, a day later, the no less final letter from Count Aporfalvy.

Was Feri to break with his family and leave the Army? His

optimism was not to be so easily discouraged. It was 1904. Fathers and Ministries were not governed only by inexorable destiny, but also by His Apostolic Majesty Francis Joseph I, by the Grace of God Emperor of Austria and King of Hungary. The Emperor had given time the time to weave its legends. He was now seventy-four, and had been ruling for fifty-six years. There seemed to be almost no family in the realm that had not had a share in the Emperor's clemency. As a young man he had had thirteen rebellious generals executed on the spot, but since then he had suffered much. His son had died, and so had his wife. Merciless fate had made him merciful. Twice a week he held audience at Schönbrunn or Hofburg, and legend had it that he had more than once interposed his authority when a young face touched his old heart. Ilona was immediately ablaze with enthusiasm when Feri suggested that she should go to Vienna and see the Emperor in person.

Of course, it wasn't as simple as the reading-books used in the monarchy's schools made it appear. Weeks passed in nerve-racking preparation. Feri dared not turn for help to Prince Montenuovo, because of the Lord High Chamberlain's close relations with the house of Aporfalvy. The commanding officer of his regiment, Field-Marshal Count Franz Leopold Nádasdy zu Fogaras, politely but firmly refused to intervene on his behalf. Finally a friend of Feri's, Count Khuen-Héderváry, found an unusual but, as it turned out, promising solution. A Hungarian artist named István Borsonyai was painting the Emperor's portrait, and as a result of the Emperor's once accidentally addressing him as 'Baron' had been raised to the ranks of the hereditary nobility. This Herr von Borsonyai, as he had thus become, a friend of Count Khuen-Héderváry's, approached the Count chancery, who, in the erroneous belief that the Emperor had promised the Court painter to grant her an audience, fixed the reception of Ilona Horváth from Kisnémet for Friday, July 8.

Ilona's excitement grew from day to day. Now she was actually to see the capital city, the magical world in which every stone spoke of the greatness of the empire and its ruler. There would be an end to her impatience. At last she could take her destiny in her own hands. The girls who were described in the reading-books, and sometimes even portrayed in coloured pictures—the gentle, intelligent creatures whom the Emperor received and whose afflictions of the heart he immediately understood—resembled her to a hair, so that they seemed to be accurate pictures of herself already on her knees before the Emperor. Her mission was bound to succeed. The Emperor and she would understand each other.

Her preparations were interrupted by a visit from Lajos.

Her brother came unexpectedly, unannounced, on a rainy summer afternoon. The storm that had descended upon the city had brought no drop in the temperature. The warm rain seemed to be washing away the little baroque 'palace' in the Dísz tér. The equestrian statue of

General András Hadik was so thickly wrapped in mist that it looked as if it were still waiting to be unveiled.

Feri was at the barracks; his batman had gone to town. The door was opened by the cook.

Lajos had no overcoat on, and his uniform was dripping wet. For a long time he sat in silence in the black-leather armchair in the study, the same one in which Ilona had sat during her first visit. The water ran down from his hair into his face and from his boots on to the Persian carpet. He looked wretched.

Ilona could see that something bad had happened, but what she actually heard was far worse than her expectations.

Once he started he spoke fast and without pausing, staring down all the time at the steadily growing pool round his feet.

He had run away from his regiment at Sopron, he told his sister, deserted, ten days ago. "They're on my heels," he said. "If it hadn't been for Aunt Rosa they'd have caught me already." The good woman had taken him in at the risk of her own safety—not in her own house, to which he was bound to be trailed, but in the brothel, which, as Ilona knew, lay in the heart of the city.

"Why in heaven's name did you desert?" Ilona asked when she finally managed to break in on his confused confession.

"I called a lieutenant a cur," replied Lajos, "and he is a cur, who bullies his men. I don't regret it." In any case he had passed the remark in the canteen, he went on; no officer had overheard it; only an officious sergeant-major had reported it to his superiors. Although he had denied it, because "things will have to change before anyone can speak the truth in our glorious Army," he had been condemned to four weeks' solitary confinement on bread and water. "On the second day I broke out, not because I was afraid of prison, nor because I didn't like the bread and water, but because I've had enough, absolutely enough, of this dog's life, enough of the officers and enough of my comrades, who drum and trumpet or move their arms like Aunt Sallys that make music when you shoot them in the stomach," he said continuing to stare down at the puddle on the Persian carpet.

Ilona tried in vain to persuade him to return to his regiment.

"The punishment for desertion in time of peace is twenty years," he said. "For escaping from the military prison it's life."

When Ilona asked what she could do he didn't answer. He talked of flight, of crossing the Italian frontier, over which many deserters had escaped. He wove fantasies about America, the strand of the stranded, the asylum of liberty, the great, brave republic over the ocean. He suddenly stood up, strode across to Ilona, took her by the shoulders, and stammered incoherently. He couldn't take back all he had said in Sopron, because what she was doing was wrong, and he hadn't wanted to see her again, let alone come to her for help. He talked himself into a passion, and she had to interrupt him. He surely hadn't come here to give her a lecture; he had deserted, and they would have to see what they could do to put matters right.

At last he spoke of money. "Only for Italy; I shall manage to get across to America on my own, as a stoker or a cabin-boy; people do that every day. Anyone who flees from despotism is welcome over there."

It annoyed her to hear him declaim, as though he had deserted from despotism, instead of from the barracks. But he was her brother. She was humiliated to see him humiliate himself.

"I'll send you back the money from America," he said. "Don't imagine I want to keep the wages of shame you receive from Aporfalvy."

He became insulting, as though only abuse could protect him from humiliation. Exhausted by abuse and humiliation, he dropped into the leather armchair.

Ilona remained unperturbed by his anger. She was no longer the little officer's mistress he had bawled out at Sopron. The same words no longer had the same meaning. She looked at her brother, looked through him. Behind him stood the stationmaster. She thought about herself, quite impersonally, about Ilona Horváth from the Horváth family. She couldn't remain a mistress, couldn't bring an illegitimate child into the world. Nor could she be the sister of a deserter.

"Can you stay with Aunt Rosa for a few more days?" she asked, and when Lajos replied that he could she went on: "You must give me a few days. Don't ask now; I shall come and see you in a few days. You must promise to do nothing in the meantime. Nothing, do you understand? I'll find a way."

He thanked her in a low voice, reluctantly. Then he left.

She watched him through the window. It was still raining. The water was gushing down through the drain-pipes into the street, as though the only purpose of the gutters on the roofs was to flood the streets. A chambermaid from one of the big houses ran laughing across the square, holding up her skirt, pursued by a baker's boy dressed in white, but spattered with mud. The soldier staggered through the puddles like a drunken man; he didn't look round; he took no notice of the rain. The Emperor's coat was getting dirty.

Ilona went through the half-dark apartment to her bedroom.

She had promised Lajos she would find a way, so she had to find a way. To 'desert the flag' was a terrible thing. Her brother wouldn't 'desert the flag.' It was all nonsense about Italy and despotism and America. In school readers you saw the flag on every page—the red, white, and green flag, or the black and yellow one. In school readers heroes died under the flag. The flag must be right; on no account could anyone desert it. She would never desert the flag. The school readers reminded her of the Emperor and that she would soon be standing in front of him.

She called the cook. The old woman came, with her pointed white nose, offended, ready to object to any order she was given.

"Pack," said Ilona gruffly. "It's getting late."

She wasn't even afraid of the cook any more.

Ilona was met at the landing-stage by the painter Borsonyai. She had sailed up the Danube for half a day and a night. It was the 8th of July.

The painter Borsonyai looked like a thin man who had slipped into a large barrel. Skinny legs supported an enormous body topped by a gaunt head. He carried his accidental barony around with the same difficulty as his heavy body: he looked round in surprise every time some one addressed him as 'Baron.' The straggling wig wreathing his pale bird's face caused him discomfort. Drops of sweat fell on to the barrel.

It was a hot morning. The sun blazed down on the open fiacre. There was a lot of traffic, but because of the heat it moved lethargically. The horses at the cab-ranks stood with lowered heads; they thrust their muzzles into their nose-bags, but they didn't eat. The women wore white blouses with stiff white collars and big hats with feathers or tiny saucer hats of yellow straw. Even the nurse-maids in the dresses of the various provinces of the monarchy, pushed the prams along slowly. Only the soulless tram-cars hurried. Not a breath stirred the dusty chestnut-trees.

Borsonyai told Ilona the names of the streets as proudly as if he owned them. Like all Hungarians, he was proud of Vienna.

"Every one has gone out of town," he said apologetically. "There's not a single well-to-do person left in Vienna. I'd have gone long ago, if I wasn't just painting His Majesty's portrait." He realized his tactlessness and blushed. "Of course, His Majesty is at Schönbrunn. Schönbrunn isn't Vienna. Schönbrunn is Schönbrunn."

"Tell me, Baron," asked Ilona, "how do you talk to the Emperor? I mean, we didn't learn much German at school."

"I'll let you into a secret, my dear young lady. I have never spoken a word to His Majesty. He has occasionally deigned to speak to me, but he has never asked me a question. Rothbichl has been massaging him for forty years, and he has never addressed a word to Rothbichl."

"But I must speak to His Majesty."

"The Emperor speaks the languages of all his peoples."

Borsonyai ordered the coachman to make a detour. He explained everything there was to be seen from his own standpoint—the artistic. The Imperial Museums, built by Semper and Hasenauer. Between them the statue of the Empress Maria Theresa by Zumbusch. And, finally, St Stephen's Cathedral, a miracle, eternally unfinished.

She felt afraid. It was the fault of the Empress Maria Theresa's statue, with the enthroned monarch and the four stone horses. Maria Theresa, 1717 to 1789—she remembered the dates from her history lessons. A hundred and fifty years ago she had still been alive. She was an ancestress of the Emperor Francis Joseph I, the man before whom, in exactly five hours, she, Ilona Horváth from Kisnémet, would be standing. The most powerful man she had ever known was Count Endre Aporfalvy. On his account trains stopped at Kisnémet. But no Aporfalvy sat on a stone armchair with stone riders at his feet. Perhaps she ought to turn back, beg her father's forgiveness, and give birth to an illegitimate child.

The one-horse carriage stopped in a narrow street behind St Stephen's Cathedral.

A hunchbacked boots carried Ilona's case into the hotel The porter appeared in the doorway, a round hat in his hand. The painter suddenly began to behave with stiff dignity. He addressed Ilona as "my child," as though afraid his position might be misconstrued.

"I shall fetch you on the dot of two, my child," he said. "Your audience is fixed for three-twenty. On no account leave your room."

Ilona was very fully occupied. She had to rid herself of the dust of travel, prepare her clothes, and get dressed. Worldly-wise, she set the little hotel in motion. The hunchback brought jug after jug of warm water, while a second boots saw to Ilona's shoes.

She had chosen for the audience a simple dress of dark-grey silk with long sleeves ending at the wrist in a narrow band of lace. She was worried by the fact that the dress left her throat bare, but she had brought a beautiful scarf with her, also of silk and shimmering opal in colour. She decided to put this round her neck and tuck it into her heart-shaped décolleté. While the hotel chambermaid, prattling incessantly, ironed her dress she desperately tried to remember the pictures in the readers; but the girls in the pictures wore Biedermeier dresses; they were old pictures, because the Emperor was old and had been reigning for a long time. Perhaps he was no longer so benevolent as in the paintings..

The room waiter brought her a light meal. She ate only a few mouthfuls. The room was low and sultry. She went to the window. Beyond the roofs she could see the slender tower of St Stephen's Cathedral. She turned to the boots.

"How far is St Stephen's Cathedral from here?"

"Two minutes, miss; three at the most."

She threw a scarf round her shoulders and went out.

It was shady in the cathedral, exactly as in Kisnémet church on summer afternoons.

She stopped beside a huge pillar and looked aloft. The vaulting above the pillars ran together like fingers touching in prayer. They were mighty and gentle, the fingers of God. This vast palace had been created as His house, but He had many houses and dwelt in heaven.

Ilona was glad that she hadn't obeyed the painter's admonition. Apart from the evening prayers and the Lord's prayer, she knew only the twenty-ninth psalm about the power of God over floods. She had learnt it by heart because she was afraid of floods. She was carrying a child under her heart, and an Emperor was to decide whether or not it was to bear its father's name. It was a long way from her to the Emperor, but it must be even farther from the Emperor to God. "The voice of the Lord is powerful; the voice of the Lord is full of majesty." The monument to the Empress Maria Theresa was now quite small.

She knelt down before a side-altar. She repeated the Lord's Prayer. She was praying for her child. She remembered Lajos. The thought of

60

him was painful, more painful than the thought of her child. She had promised to do something for him. Now she could only pray for him.

30

It was exactly two. A fiacre with two horses turned the corner. The Baron got out and helped her into the carriage.

The sun was blazing down, as if trying to burn a hole in the veiled sky. Vienna was plunged in its midday slumber. The streets were almost empty. Ilona opened her sunshade. She was prone to freckles. They made her look younger; she didn't want to appear before the Emperor looking like a freckled child.

The painter gave her instructions as to how to behave.

"You must only speak when you are asked a question," he explained, "and on no account must you address a question to His Majesty. Don't be afraid; the Emperor likes people to have confidence in him. The Emperor isn't an aristocrat. Before the French Revolution, you must know, there were several different estates, but there was never a royal estate. That's the point. The aristocracy is class-conscious, and class-consciousness is arrogance. The Emperor is so high above the classes that he can't distinguish one class from another. By the way, you had better end every sentence with the words 'your Majesty.' "

She nodded absent-mindedly. Did the Emperor hold audience in this heat? She silently hoped they would find the castle gates barred.

The gates were not barred. Borsonyai, who had been eyeing her coquettish sunshade with distaste throughout the ride, took it from Ilona with relief. He promised to wait for her, however long the audience might last.

She crossed the rectangular courtyard, and was suddenly standing at the foot of a flight of steps bearing a notice that read "Lord High Chamberlain's Office, Audiences." She followed an arrow, and immediately found herself in a plain-looking office seething with people —soldiers and women, black-clad civil servants, gentlemen, even children. Behind an ink-spattered desk sat a manikin with a bureaucratic nose which he stuck into a large book as the petitioners for an audience filed past him. On the one hand he scrutinized the petition, on the other those who had presented themselves for an audience. Every now and then he came out from behind his desk, straightened some one's tie or flew into a passion because a pair of patent-leather shoes did not shine sufficiently. When he had "tried the hearts and reins" of a petitioner and reduced him to a suitable state of dejection he signed to a lackey, who led the petitioner away. Ilona was dealt with quicker than the others—either because the Court official was impressed by the name of Baron Borsonyai, or because he didn't understand Hungarian.

In the large waiting-room into which she was taken there were three men and a woman, besides two lackeys, who kept watch in front of a high white door. They were almost like the stone riders on the statue of the Empress Maria Theresa. An elderly gentleman, a district

c

61

governor, was standing by the high window; he wore a dress-coat with a sword and an impressive-looking hat, and looked as though he were accustomed to grant audiences himself. Under a gigantic landscape painting representing a Court excursion in the open air a grey-haired general was talking with a fair-haired, girlish-looking lieutenant. A woman of the shopkeeper class was sitting by the white stove. Ilona sat down beside her.

The woman immediately began a conversation. She was one of those people who in some inexplicable way manage to find out every one else's business. In order to lure Ilona's secret from her she took her into her confidence. The tobacco-shop she ran in the Lerchenfelder Gürtel threatened to fall under the pickaxe; the owner of the house had decided to build a cinema on his property. An old customer of the shop, a privy councillor in the Ministry of Education, indignant at this infraction of a long-established right, had arranged an audience for her with His Majesty. The old gentleman over there in the dress-coat, the district governor, she went on, had come to thank the Emperor for the bestowal of a high order. The lieutenant had been called to an audience in order to receive the imperial thanks: he had courageously thrown himself in front of a carriage that threatened to run over a young archduchess. Finally, the general—the cigar-seller's voice was now almost inaudible—had a hard mission. His son, a lieutenant in the Uhlans, had 'forgotten' to pay his card debts: if the Emperor's grace didn't save him he could expect to be dismissed from the Army with ignominy. But what brought the little lady to His Majesty?

Ilona had to disappoint her talkative neighbour. Her school German barely enabled her to understand half the latter's story, let alone tell her own. Moreover, the stiff lackeys with the white side-whiskers were looking at them disapprovingly.

She fell silent. She looked at the old general with compassion. He was talking in a dignified but kindly way to the lieutenant. Without a doubt, he wished the heroic lieutenant were his son. And yet he had come to intercede for his son. But she? She had come to ask His Majesty's permission for a marriage which her heart did not desire and which she would long since have renounced if she had not been pregnant. Lajos was hiding in Aunt Rosa's brothel. Ilona started with horror. In the next room the Emperor was receiving his subjects, and she was thinking of a brothel! She was only thinking of her brother. The stationmaster. He wasn't likely to lose his job if his daughter gave birth to an illegitimate child. But could the father of a deserter remain an imperial and royal stationmaster? Which would the stationmaster be least able to bear—his daughter's disgrace or his son's?

The governor had vanished through the door of the audience chamber, reappeared, and hurried out with a nod to the general. One of the two lackeys called the lieutenant. The afternoon sun fell perpendicularly into the room. The air stood still. After a few minutes the lieutenant came out; the shopkeeper from the Lerchenfelder Gürtel pushed past the servants and through the white-and-gilt door. The lieutenant, bright-red in the face and looking now like a baby in uniform, clicked the heels of his patent-leather shoes before the general.

Ilona was alone with the general. He seemed not to see her. His dignity fell away from him. He walked nervously to and fro between painting and stove, stove and painting. All at once he looked like a retired stationmaster. Only when the lackey addressed him did he grow back into his uniform. He marched towards the door as though into enemy fire. Ilona pressed her fingers together: she meant to stay like this until he came out again. She scarcely listened to the shopkeeper as the latter told her triumphantly that the house-owner would not carry out his devilish plan: the Emperor understood that the shop in the Lerchenfelder Gürtel must remain. Ilona was thinking about the lieutenant who hadn't paid his debts. He took on Lajos's features.

She had no watch; time became endless. She counted the minutes. If you counted to sixty a minute grew into time. If you did nothing but count seconds, one to sixty, one to sixty, you could prolong your life to eternity. It was a good sign that the Emperor listened to the general for so long. When at last he came out he looked rejuvenated; he was young, almost like a lieutenant. The lackey had to call Ilona's name twice before she went towards the door.

As the door closed behind her she didn't see the Emperor at once. Carrying out her instructions, she remained in a deep curtsey. Somewhere at the other end of the room she saw something white and motionless; something golden also glittered from down there; perhaps it was the collar of the white uniform; perhaps it was the gilt frames of the pictures on the brown-lacquered wall. The curtains had been lowered; it was cool and almost dark in the little audience-chamber. There was the same cosiness in the stationmaster's office on warm July days. And the fact that there was nothing to be heard but the singing of the birds outside the windows also reminded her of the stationmaster's office.

The white, motionless figure moved at last.

"Come closer, Fräulein Horváth!"

She rose.

His Apostolic Majesty, Emperor Francis Joseph I, by the Grace of God Emperor of Austria, King of Jerusalem, Hungary, Bohemia, Dalmatia, Croatia, Slovenia, Galicia and Lodomeria, and so forth and so on—the Emperor was standing in front of a high, brown-lacquered desk, not behind it, but on the same side as his visitor. Now she recognized him, but she couldn't believe it was really he. He was standing upright, like old men bent by gout, or rather like old men who hold themselves doubly straight to prove that they are not bent. He was supporting himself with one hand on the desk. He looked like the pictures in the station, in the Hotel Rákoczi, in bedrooms and offices. Only he was far older. Ilona thought she had never seen such an old man.

"Do you speak German, Fräulein Horváth?" asked His Apostolic Majesty.

"Very badly, your Majesty," she said. She wasn't sure whether he could hear her voice.

"Then we'll speak Hungarian. Where do you come from?"

"From Kisnémet, your Majesty."

The Emperor's eyes rested on Ilona. It was as though he were trying to see from her face, as from a map, where Kisnémet lay. Hundreds of cities, thousands of towns, tens of thousands of villages, belonged to the Emperor. He couldn't remember all of them.

He cast a glance at the desk. There, painted in ink, stood the name of the petitioner for the Emperor's grace; there, too, in one or two words, stood the reason for her visit. A pair of round, unframed spectacles lay on the desk. The Emperor reached for them, but seemed to change his mind.

"What is your wish, Fräulein Horváth?"

She lowered her eyes. She had many wishes, but she couldn't state them all. She had made a long journey; in a few minutes she would be outside again like the others. She thought of the general.

"My brother is a deserter, your Majesty," she said. She had almost forgotten the words 'your Majesty.'

"A deserter? What do you mean?"

"He is serving with the Fourth Infantry Regiment at Sopron. He left the barracks without permission, and hasn't been back for two weeks." Now she had said it; now she wanted to tell the Emperor everything. "He was accused of insulting an officer, but it was all a mistake. He really didn't do it. He was locked up, and he ran away. He's in Budapest . . . your Majesty." She knew she ought to have waited for a question from the Emperor, but she didn't wait. She saw the pictures in the readers clearly before her. The Emperor hadn't changed. She fell to her knees. "My father would never survive it, your Majesty."

"Stand up," said the Emperor. "Your father . . . what is your father?"

"He's the stationmaster at Kisnémet, your Majesty."

The Emperor looked at her for a long time, a very long time, it seemed to her. It was as though he were trying to picture the station at Kisnémet and the stationmaster. There were many stationmasters in the Monarchy.

"Did your father request the audience for you?"

"No, he knows nothing about it, your Majesty."

"How old are you?"

"Just seventeen."

"And your brother?"

"Twenty-one, your Majesty."

"Any other brothers and sisters?"

"Two sisters."

"Are you the youngest?"

"Yes, your Majesty."

The Emperor nodded, as though he had known this all along, but also as though he found it hard to believe that anyone was seventeen years old. Again he reached for his glasses; again he left them untouched.

If he puts on his glasses I'm done for, thought Ilona. Obtaining an audience under false pretences. Was it punishable by imprisonment, or possibly death? Why had she talked about Lajos? She wanted to say something, wanted to rectify herself; but she remembered Borsonyai's instructions and waited.

"And now you want me to quash the court martial, Fräulein . . ." said the Emperor. He had suddenly forgotten her name. "You're asking a great deal, a very great deal. Discipline is the foundation of the Army. You think the Emperor is all-powerful. But even the Emperor obeys discipline. Do you understand, Fräulein Horváth?" Now he had remembered her name again.

The Emperor let his eyes run over the shiny walls, as though the answer he couldn't find was there on the brown lacquer. Ilona began to feel sorry for the Emperor. That a soldier had deserted affected him personally. The stationmaster wore just the same sorrowful expression when a train was late. Old people were all the same; they looked very sad when the order of things was upset. She had to reassure the Emperor.

"All he wants is to be a soldier again, your Majesty," she said.

The Emperor's voice sounded broken as he replied.

"That's what they all want. First they get into debt playing cards, then they send their fathers here. The uniform means nothing to them any more, nothing. But they whine when they have to take it off." He coughed and went red. "Why should I pardon him?" It wasn't clear whether he was speaking of the card-player or Lajos. "Why him and not another?" The Emperor was speaking as though to himself.

Ilona had sacrificed her child's name. Now she had nothing to lose.

"You should pardon him because of my father, your Majesty," she said. "He has been stationmaster at Kisnémet for twenty-one years. Make inquiries about him, your Majesty. There isn't another station like ours in the whole of Hungary. He has never taken a holiday. He was always so proud of Lajos."

"Your brother's name is Lajos?"

"Yes, your Majesty."

"Where is he serving?"

"With the Fourth Infantry Regiment at Sopron."

Now the Emperor put on his glasses. He was smiling. This could be seen clearly, because his moustache was moving.

"Fourth Infantry Regiment at Sopron," he said. "Colonel Von Jerzabek." One could see he was glad to have remembered the name. "Colonel Jerzabek," he repeated as he picked up his pen. Was Jerzabek still commanding the Fourth Infantry at Sopron? Or was Jerzabek dead? Whenever he inquired after a regimental commander he turned out to have been dead for twenty years.

Ilona saw nothing but the glasses on the fleshy nose in the emaciated face. The Emperor looked at the white foolscap sheet lying in front of him. He put the pen back in the shallow groove of the desk. He looked at Ilona.

"It says here 'marriage permit for an officer.' It says nothing about desertion. How do you explain that, Fräulein? . . ." He looked at the paper. Fräulein Horváth?"

Ilona went scarlet.

"It only happened yesterday, your Majesty."

"It happened yesterday? I thought he ran off a fortnight ago—your brother." All at once every detail was clear to him.

"That's to say, I only heard about it yesterday—about my brother, your Majesty. It was too late. I really didn't plan it. I had already been commanded to appear in audience. . . ."

The Emperor moved his head slowly up and down. Ilona didn't know what it meant. For a moment she wondered whether to speak of Feri. But the Emperor had already picked up the pen. To speak now would spoil everything. She waited for a question.

"And for your brother's sake you are prepared to renounce your marriage?" asked the Emperor.

"Yes, your Majesty."

The Emperor turned away. He rested both arms on the sloping top of the desk and dipped the pen in the ink. There was no sound in the room but the scratching of the pen. "Marriage permit for an officer." The Emperor drew a line through it and made a note.

"Tell your brother to report back to his regiment immediately. I shall send word to Jerzabek to pardon him. A few weeks' confinement to barracks will do him no harm." He repeated the words "confinement to barracks" as though they reinforced the shaky discipline of the monarchy. He looked at Ilona. "Self-pitying youth. They get harder and harder and more and more sorry for themselves." He recollected himself. It was growing late. The strokes of the church bells came in through the lowered blinds, muted, as though muffled by the curtains. How many fathers and sisters were still waiting? How many card-players and deserters? The Emperor nodded. "And tell your father he should bring up his sons as he has brought up his daughter." He had forgotten that the stationmaster at Kisnémet had only one son and that all the rest of his children were daughters. "You may go, my child."

Ilona retired, keeping her back to the door all the time as she had been instructed. She bent her head low. The white, motionless figure moved into the distance. The narrow red carpet under her feet grew longer and longer, as if it were being unrolled in front of her.

When the servant left her at the flight of steps she broke into a run. She ran across the rectangular courtyard, past the black-and-yellow sentry-box, ran through the wrought-iron lattice gate.

Now she knew why Borsonyai had said the Emperor wasn't an aristocrat. The Aporfalvys, who imagined a jewel would fall out of their crown if one of them married a stationmaster's daughter, didn't possess a crown. She turned round once more. There, at the top of the flight of steps, was the Emperor's room. He could prevent the building of a cinema and hang orders on an old man's chest and give a father back his son. It was good that she hadn't asked of him anything so trivial as permission to marry an officer. Perhaps he was gazing after her through the curtains. She would give the stationmaster the Emperor's greetings.

31

She went straight from the landing-stage to the Salon Rosa, which she hadn't re-entered since that Christmas Eve. It was morning. An old woman was dusting the half-naked women. The more dust she wiped off, the dustier the Salon appeared. The windows were open. A smell of beer rose from the street. Lajos was sitting on the green bench outside one of the fitting-cubicles. He had been glancing through the fashion magazines.

She didn't go home till she was sure Lajos would take the next train to Sopron. There was an iron ring round her heart. Good deeds were easily done, but it was hard not to regret them. She was alone with her magnanimity.

She kept nothing from Feri. He didn't reproach her. He became silent and sad. Even before her trip he had been sparing with plans: now he lived from day to day.

July passed; August was maturing. In the little garden behind the house the trees were bending beneath the weight of plenty.

She was now in the third month. The attacks of nausea had stopped. She ate with a fierce and capricious appetite. Her face grew even younger. Every morning she stood naked in front of the mirror looking at her curving hips and swelling breasts. She could understand that she was pregnant, but she couldn't understand that she was expecting a child. The changing body belonged to an alien life.

She never once wondered whether it would be a boy or a girl, fair or dark, like her or like him. It never occurred to her to prepare for the child's arrival, to knit stockings, jumpers, jackets, and mittens. One day her body would become slim again. Feri told her to see a doctor; she didn't go. She thought of the birth even less than of the child.

She wasn't ashamed of her pregnancy. In this she was like all women, who suddenly boast of their condition after long keeping it a secret. She didn't even deceive the domestic staff. She seemed more inclined to deceive Feri, to whom she always showed herself in voluminous dresses or tightly laced up, as though she didn't want to share her hope with him, or as though it would be unworthy of her to remind him of his duty.

She read a great deal and learnt a great deal. Because she bore a miracle within her she was close to everything miraculous. The fruit in the bowls was not miraculous, but it was miraculous so long as it gleamed on the bough. The children playing in the Dísz tér were miraculous because they were still growing. The little clouds that went up behind the Gellérthegy, sped towards the other clouds, and united with them into a storm were a miracle. Existence was full of magnificent mysteries. The embassy secretary Von Berthold once let fall a remark, quickly, and embarrassed as soon as he had spoken. His little son had scarlet fever; his wife was with him. She didn't fall ill. Children didn't infect their mothers. A night-time storm snapped a telegraph-post, but it didn't snap a single flower in the garden. Didn't storms know what they were doing? Not everything mysterious was threatening.

Feri spoke more and more frequently these days of a trip to Kisnémet. He had made up his mind to confront his father with Ilona. With her, or with her pregnancy? She thought of the station-master, whom Feri didn't mention. Earlier than most people she had chosen her tribunal. Her court of law was the stationmaster. Feri thought she feared the Count's anger, but all she feared was her father's pain.

She persuaded him to go alone. He was to leave on a Monday.

32

On Sunday—it was August 22—a gymkhana was held at Alag, near Budapest, in which officers from the most select cavalry regiments competed.

Feri had to be at Alag in the morning. Count Nádasdy's Ninth Hussars spent the whole afternoon practising daring jumps over stone walls, artificial ditches, and white gates. The Colonel had warned them not to underestimate the First Hussars and the Prussian Uhlans. It would be a nice mess if the Uhlans carried off the trophy from the Soproners, and that in the most gracious presence of Her Imperial Highness the Archduchess Auguszta.

Ilona set out for Alag after lunch.

The special train was filled to overflowing. A general who looked as if he were retired was the only man in her compartment. The gentlemen had given their seats to the ladies. They stood in the corridor discussing the gymkhana. The blue, yellow, and red tunics and gleaming sabres contrasted with the soot-blackened railway carriage.

Outside the little station of Alag the carriages, landaus, dog-carts, and phaetons were waiting. Mátyás was there too. He helped Ilona up on to the backward-facing seat of the yellow trap. He knew about her pregnancy, which was not visible in the lace dress corsetted round the hips. Much to her annoyance, he treated her with the anxious care with which valets dust their master's porcelain.

"The Count has been riding magnificently," he reported. "He has done two clear rounds. He is riding seventh, directly after First Lieutenant Török and before Captain Von Lilienfels." He seemed to twist his tongue on the German name.

The carriages trotted towards the course in a serried line. The horses' hoofs sank deep into the sand; the dust swirled high in the air. Ilona opened her sunshade. On the horizon to the west, where Budapest lay, heavy clouds were piling up, still hesitantly. They were moving into position like howitzers before a battle. The rays of the sun were sharp, like cavalry sabres.

"There's going to be a storm," said Mátyás. With peasant certainty he added, "But not until the races are over."

The show-jumping had started. The first rider, a lieutenant in the Prussian Uhlans, put his bay over ditches, gates, brick walls.

Ilona looked round. The boxes were packed. Only she was alone. The box on her right was occupied by a grey-haired colonel and his three chattering daughters. The colonel looked at Ilona through his

68

monocle, complaisantly and provocatively, as men eye beautiful, home-less women; but at the same time as though apologizing for his three marriageable daughters. She turned her head towards the box on her left, in which three gentlemen—a high-ranking officer and two civilians in pearl-grey jackets—were dancing attendance on a lady with parch-ment-yellow skin. Here every one knew every one, knew about the others' inheritances, jealousies, affairs of honour, and successes; only Ilona knew nobody and nothing, and yet was one of them, because there had to be women among them whom nobody knew.

Mátyás had been mistaken. The clouds overran the sun. Ilona closed her sunshade. She switched her eyes from the strangers to the well-kept grass that was slightly yellow from the long summer. First Lieutenant Török completed his run to desultory applause. His horse had refused the last ditch. He had to give it the spurs twice before it jumped the water.

It was Feri's turn. He was riding Csárdás, his best horse, a grey, with a noble gait, a broad neck, and a tail trimmed to a point. The lieutenant looked handsome on the grey, with his red breeches, dark-blue attila, white olives, and white shako. He rode past Ilona's box, turned his head slightly to the side, and smiled. A little farther on, in front of the box occupied by the Archduchess, a fat lady behind a multitude of veils, he reined in his grey and saluted. The Archduchess waved graciously. He galloped back to the start. The storm was now quite close.

Feri headed his mount towards the course. Effortlessly the grey jumped a white fence. With reins tight Feri approached the brick wall. He gave the horse its head and leaned forward over its neck, his slim torso pressed against the horse's broad neck. The hoofs flew over the red wall, almost touching it. The rider looked round, as though to make sure the wall was still standing. He urged the grey along the course, took the first ditch, a second gate, a third. Applause thundered through the approaching thunder. A few people had already risen; the ladies were already drawing up their skirts. Large drops were falling from the sky.

The rider was approaching the last ditch between the Archduchess's box and Ilona's. He gave Csárdás the spurs. The horse jumped. Then it seemed to lose its balance in mid-flight. It landed on the other side of the ditch, but it didn't land on its hoofs. It reminded one of a circus horse going gracefully down on its knees to acknowledge applause. It fell on the knees of its forelegs. The slender knee-joints gave way. The head and neck shot forward; the back and the broad croup followed; finally the hind legs went straight up into the air. The horse remained lying on its back. Feri lay under its full weight. His head was out of sight; only the bright-red trousers and blue attila projected from be-neath the body of the grey.

The spectators were frozen to the spot, as they sat, as they walked, as they ran. Then everything was in motion, double motion. Men ran towards the track—officers, soldiers, grooms, batmen, and a few gentlemen with flying coat-tails and grey top-hats. Others, men and women, fled the scene; fled bent double, their hands over their faces or over their heads; fled from the sight or from the rain that was coming down in torrents. The storm had broken over the course.

Ilona ran along behind abandoned boxes, down three or four steps and over the black gravel. She ducked under the fence, her sunshade in her hand.

Rain and excitement wiped away what she saw; what she thought became all the clearer. He would have married her if she had not had to beg the Emperor's pardon for Lajos. To-morrow he had been going to Kisnémet. To-morrow might have been to-day. What difference did it make to things when they didn't happen in the right order? She was carrying his child under her heart.

She forced her way through a wall of men.

Feri's body had been freed from the weight of the animal. Horse and rider lay side by side. The grey animal was red with blood. Feri lay on his back, his head on one side, as he had often slept beside Ilona, always on his back with his face turned towards her. The gesture had been voluntary, even in sleep. Feri no longer did anything voluntarily; everything happened to him. His head was freed from the natural limits of movement. It seemed no longer to belong to his neck.

"His neck is broken. He's dead," said an officer who was bending over Feri. He wore the velvet collar of an Army surgeon.

Ilona pushed him aside. She knelt down. Dirt splashed up over her. She wanted to take Feri's face is her hands, but her hands remained hanging in mid-air: his head, she felt, would come away from his neck. Her throat was tight, as though she were trying to block the path of her tears. She laid her head on the man's chest, tenderly, as she had always done. His chest was warm.

Some one raised her up.

She immediately straightened. She stood straight in the rain.

"He must be taken to Budapest," she said. She felt the man's questioning look. "I am Countess Aporfalvy," she said.

Now she was no longer a tiresome woman, but an object of sympathy. She took no notice of the sympathy, knowing that it was directed towards a name that did not belong to her. Calmly she made arrangements in a voice that hardly trembled. The regimental surgeon stood beside her, passing on her instructions and issuing his own. She turned away. It was a good thing she didn't have to look at anyone. It was impossible to look up in the rain. People scurried to safety, as though the rain were more terrible than death.

Through a veil she caught sight of Mátyás. He was standing to attention in front of the regimental surgeon, mechanically repeating his orders. Tears were running over his furrowed peasant's face, mingling with the raindrops. When she saw him tears came into Ilona's eyes. Shared, the pain was doubled. She was grateful to Mátyás for not giving her away.

"May I take you home, Countess?" she heard a voice beside her ask. "Baron Felsenburg. I'm in Feri's regiment."

He was a very young ensign, little more than a child. She felt old beside him.

70

"Not home, thank you," she said, shaking her head. "Just take me to the station."

She found a corner seat in a compartment occupied by a single family. It was a colonel with his wife and two young boys, twins. She made sure no one recognized her as the woman of the racecourse. The family had left the gymkhana early. They didn't know that Feri was dead. They talked about nothing but the accident till the train left. Then they talked only about the weather that had spoilt the fun. The door to the corridor was open. Outside they were discussing the mishap. "He would have won without a doubt," said a Nádasdy Hussar. "A devil of a fall; I can't imagine that he'll pull through," grated a Prussian voice. "Do you know who the girl in white was?" asked a third voice. Ilona drew back deeper into her corner.

In Budapest she took a one-horse carriage. The storm had passed over. The water splashed up out of the puddles on to the pavement. A patch of blue sky, still dull after the rain, peeped out above the Imperial Palace. The thunder was fleeing behind the Gellérthegy.

Not until she entered the house did Ilona realize what had happened. When they look back people can never understand how they could have failed to foresee what was coming. Ilona had never seen a dead man before; no one close to her had died. Twice a year she used to go to her mother's grave in the cemetery. But the dead in the cemetery had always been dead. She wanted to weep, but she couldn't. She felt no panic, only an impotent rage. The dead were evil. They didn't finish what they had begun; didn't fulfil what they had promised; didn't make good what they had spoiled; didn't allow the living to propitiate them. They stole away—supercilious, offended, malicious.

She came to a stop in front of the wall mirror in the bedroom. She was still wearing the white dress splashed with mud and the tall hat, like a top-hat, with a pink veil. She took no steps to rid herself of the soaking-wet dress. She put her hand on her belly. The dead were irresponsible. Now she understood what to be pregnant meant. It meant to become a mother. A boy or a girl, fair or dark, healthy or sick—a child. She saw it in front of her—playing with other children, a satchel on its back, on her knees, in the garden. Its father had deserted, and no Emperor could pardon his desertion. But she was there with her child—a proud whole. She stopped thinking about the dead. She wasn't ashamed of the hot feeling of happiness in which her anger vanished, as her sorrow had vanished in her rage. She felt her twofold life and acted according to the commandment of the living.

There was no one at home but the cook, her lurking enemy. She didn't care what the woman thought of her. In a few minutes she had changed her clothes. She began to pack. She hurriedly stuffed everything she possessed into her trunks. There wasn't enough room in her trunks; she ordered the dumbfounded woman to fetch Feri's trunks. They stood around everywhere, in the bedroom, in the drawing-room, in the study, open, closed, wholly or half packed.

The money she had saved was in the commode. She pushed it into her bodice. She sent the cook out of the room. Feri kept some money, a few gold thalers, and one or two pieces of jewellery in a wooden casket lined with velvet on the study mantelpiece. She knew where the key was, but she couldn't remember. She took the whole casket and hid it between dresses, underclothing, and scarves. It never occurred to her that she was stealing. She was taking what was due to her, to her and to her child. People would soon be arriving with the dead man. Strangers asking questions. Who she was and what she was doing there. She couldn't lie a second time. Feri's father would come, and his sister. Who was she, since she was nothing but the mother of his child? Flight was good. She thought of her room in Sopron, of the bed on which she had set the coins marching in ranks. Before her eyes the coins rose into a golden wall. She was determined to raise a wall of gold round her child. It wasn't going to be so easy for death to outwit him who was still unborn.

The cook came back with a suitcase. Ilona didn't care whether she noticed that the casket was gone.

"Fetch a cab," she ordered.

The trunks were locked. She sat down. She sat in the black-leather armchair in which she had sat during her first visit. At last she was able to weep. She made her peace with the dead man; now she recalled that she had loved him.

The coachman fetched the luggage. It was difficult to get so many trunks into a two-horse carriage. Ilona helped him. The cook stood by, her hands folded in front of her: she was parading her disapproval before the coachman.

"The keys . . . ," said Ilona. She handed the woman the keys, which were hanging on a flat, shapeless metal band.

As she put her foot on the step it struck her that she had given no thought to the goal of her flight. Aunt Rosa! A shudder ran down her spine. Was she not Ilona Horváth? Was she not chosen? Her aunt's prophecy should not be fulfilled. She was fleeing, but she was not surrendering.

"Where to, miss?" asked the coachman.

"To the Hotel Hungaria," said Ilona.

33

The Hotel Hungaria was the capital's smartest hotel. Landowners who had come to Budapest to enjoy themselves stayed there, so did aristocrats from the crown lands, and also high-ranking officers and courtiers who accompanied the Emperor on his rare visits to Budapest.

The hotel faced the Danube. On the other side of the river rose the Imperial Palace. Old Buda lay at the Emperor's feet. Between twelve and one elegant Budapest strolled on the Danube promenade under the windows of the hotel. The ladies took dogs and clothes for a walk. People sat in the sunshine on little iron chairs. A military band played in the pavilion outside the Hangli. In the evenings a gipsy orchestra fiddled in the restaurant as softly as if they were rehearsing chamber music. When Ilona's windows were open she heard the gipsies.

She sat by her window all through the night. The yellow mantles flickered in the gas-lamps. Couples sat on the benches. Every now and then women's laughing voices rang out from the restaurant.

She had been to supper in the Hotel Hungaria two or three times with Feri: that was why the name had occurred to her. She had never looked at the bills, and now she hadn't the courage to ask the price of the room. There were no single rooms. She had a spacious bedroom with a small drawing-room. Her savings were not inconsiderable, but she didn't know what could be regarded as considerable here. Only the contents of the casket reassured her. There were golden Maria Theresa thalers in it, and jewellery to the value of almost three thousand gulden. She had had it valued by a jeweller in the Váczi ucca.

She had been living in the Hungaria for two weeks, and no bill had been presented as yet. She didn't dare speak to the black-clad gentlemen at the reception desk. She ate in small inns and smuggled bread and cold roast meat into her room. She smuggled the stale bread out of the hotel again and gave it to the pigeons in front of the Petöfi Memorial.

She didn't regret having put up here. She was a woman, and therefore born to be helped by men. They didn't help those who helped themselves. She thought more and more often of Zoltán. Posters announced that he was going to give a concert in Budapest. She walked furtively past the Vigadó, but she didn't go in. She silently hoped that she would meet him in the street, but once when she thought she saw him in the distance she lowered her head and hurried away. She hadn't become Countess Aporfalvy. But at least she was staying at the Hungaria.

She woke with a single thought and fell asleep with the same thought. She must find a father for her child. The thought wouldn't let go of her. Men could deny their children, because they lost them in begetting them. Women received, and what they had received they had to keep. A child that bore its mother's name had no name. Its certificate of baptism didn't say "Father dead," but "Father unknown." The baptism certificate lied. She studied the men in the street, wondering whether one of them would marry a pregnant woman. Once, when the room waiter brought her breakfast, she very nearly asked him if he would marry her. The men in the entrance-hall of the hotel stared after her because she was wearing a black dress. She had no right to a widow's weeds, only to mourning. She hurried past the men and yet hoped one of them would speak to her. These were men who looked as though one could confide in them, as though they would take pity on an unmarried mother. Out on the promenade she looked into the padded prams and entered into conversations with the nursemaids. The children in the prams overflowing with silk eiderdowns were legitimate.

At night, as she looked out of the window, her gaze was lost in the water. The light from the gas-lanterns was reflected in the Danube. At times an illuminated steamer passed up river, towards Vienna. On quiet nights she could hear the singing of the passengers. Unmarried mothers jumped into the water. The water didn't lure her. Servant girls jumped into the water. So long as you were living in the Hotel Hungaria you belonged to the world that didn't jump into the water.

Beside the three electric bells on the door were three little enamel figures—a waiter in tails, a chambermaid with a feather duster, a boots carrying a case. You could ring for whichever you wanted. Perhaps you could also ring for a man to marry you. Miracles happened, but they didn't happen everywhere. They didn't happen in Kisnémet, and they didn't happen in the brothel. There might be a miracle hidden in the Hotel Hungaria, with its thick carpets, black-clad managers, gold-braided porters, lissom foreigners, fine ladies, and night-time gipsy music. It merely had to be found.

On the fifteenth day of her stay, after a sleepless night, she resolved to ask for her bill.

Even before the waiter brought her breakfast she hurried down into the hotel entrance-hall. It was empty. Green light filtered down through the coloured glass dome. The gilt stucco decorations on the walls looked like forgotten garlands left over from festivities the previous night.

The man in the black jacket sprang to his feet as she approached the reception desk.

"I should like to have my bill," she said. She had been practising the sentence all night long. "Room one hundred and one."

The chief reception clerk knew at once.

"His Highness has already paid the bill, madame."

He spoke with such ready discretion that it didn't sound confidential, hardly even discreet.

"Oh, I see, His Highness . . .," she said.

She went out into the street. It was cool. A few beggars were breakfasting on the benches. There was no one sitting on the yellow iron chairs by the Danube, because there you had to pay. The paying public were still asleep. The 'chairwoman' was going for a walk in her chair kingdom, a black cash-bag round her neck. Then the old woman sat down and blinked into the September sun. Ilona sat down beside her.

"Do you want a ticket?" asked the chairwoman.

"Yes, of course. . . ."

As she gave the old woman a kreuzer and received a long pink ticket in exchange she suddenly saw a tailor's dummy in front of her, high-bosomed and headless. The man had stared unceasingly at the dummy. He was wearing a dress-coat with a high collar. He was pale, and the unsmoked cigarette burned away in his long, bony fingers. It was Christmas. The church bells were ringing outside. She still had his visiting-card somewhere. His name was Prince Kontowski.

The following morning her supposition was confirmed. The visiting-card lay in a bouquet of red roses.

Four days later, on a Sunday morning, the Prince called upon her.

34

She recognized him at once, although he looked to her younger than on the last occasion. He was wearing a high-buttoned dark-blue suit and a wide silver-grey cravat with a large pearl sticking in it. He

74

carefully put down his gloves and walking-stick and sat uncomfortably in the low armchair, which was too short for his slender legs.

"Thank you for the lovely flowers," said Ilona. "They're still quite fresh." She didn't mention the hotel bill.

"I heard of your misfortune. I'm sorry. . . ."

"So you know? . . ."

"Since our first meeting I have never lost sight of you. I lay my admiration at your feet." In his mocking eyes there was no mockery.

"Admiration?" she said. "I don't know. . . ."

"I waited to see what path you would follow after Aporfalvy's death. I shouldn't have fetched you from the Maison Rosa."

Was he 'fetching' her from the Hotel Hungaria? She looked at him in surprise. At the same time she wondered why he found it necessary to mention her aunt's house.

"I hate lack of dignity," the Prince continued, "as I hate the new fashion for women to go without corsets. Women's bodies will fall to pieces if they are not laced together. We are too weak, my dear young lady, to manage without stays. What arrogance this uncorsetted youth displays! The soul needs a corset as much as the body. Bearing is a question of habit. That's true of most vices and virtues, by the way. People become what they get used to. You did well to move into the Hotel Hungaria. Fate doesn't like people to appear before it *en négligé*."

"And you have been playing Fate, Prince Kontowski?" She smiled.

He asked permission to light a cigarette.

"I should like to play Fate for you in the future as well," he said.

"Are you repeating the proposal you made to the girl in her aunt's 'house of sadness'?"

His smile betrayed his pleasure at her good memory.

"If you wish," he said.

"I must disappoint you. . . ."

"Have I come too late?"

"Too late or too early, I don't know. Have you really not noticed anything?"

He looked at her questioningly. She found his bewilderment touching.

"It's the corset," she said. "I'm in the fifth month."

She folded her hands over her abdomen. The joined hands clearly stressed its curve.

An unaccustomed red tinged Kontowski's face.

"I'm grateful to you for your honesty," he said. "You could have deceived me."

"You have been kind to me. Why should I deceive you?"

She was sure he would now get up and withdraw to the accompaniment of awkward apologies.

He remained in his chair.

"What do you plan to do?" he asked.

"I must marry. Feri would have married me. My child must have a name."

"I'm sorry that I . . ."

75

"I never asked you to," she interrupted him.

"You misunderstand me. It isn't because it's another man's child."

Now he looked as he had looked on Christmas Eve. Ilona began to feel that the miracle had something sinister about it. A man didn't go to the Maison Rosa on Christmas Eve by chance.

"Nor am I narrow-minded like the Aporfalvys," the Prince continued. "I don't despise commoners. My contempt for the whole of humanity preserves me from arrogance towards a particular category. I have nothing against commoners except that they are also human beings." He broke off. "You might be an archduchess and a virgin—it would make no difference. I haven't married because I consider marriage a reckless gamble. It is very unlikely that two total strangers will be able to spend their lives together in harmony. They come from two different planets, and don't become more alike because their paths happen to cross. And yet there is no other love than that rooted in similarity, since apart from ourselves we can at most love our reflections. To change love into a community of interest is savagely to maltreat it. The marriage with the best chance of happiness would be one between brother and sister, but, as you know, that is forbidden in our civilization."

His words did not cause her pain. There was something anguished in his scorn.

"I'm in my mid-forties. You're eighteen," he said. "A young mistress makes a man younger; a young wife makes him older."

"My dear Prince Kontowski," she reiterated, almost as though she were forty and he eighteen, "I really didn't make you a proposal of marriage."

"I know, I know," he replied quickly. "All the time I'm talking I'm thinking—though not about what I'm saying. We must find you a husband." He put the tips of his fingers together and stroked the sharp bridge of his rather overlong nose with them. "He must satisfy a number of requirements. An honourable name. He must be poor, otherwise my money would be no inducement. Preferably of an age where he has no further prospect of a wealthy match. Furthermore, there must be no risk of his falling in love with you." He struck his forehead. "I've got it! Baron Rattowitz! A distant relation of my mother's. I haven't seen him for years, but I occasionally give him money because he has a knack of writing the most absurd begging letters. He is one of those shameless beggars who retain their dignity. A few weeks ago he wrote and told me I absolutely must send him money because he had discovered an infallible system for breaking the bank at Monte Carlo. Fortunately I haven't answered his letter yet. I'll send him a telegram. He shall come and marry you. Then he can go to Monte Carlo and gamble away my money."

She had listened to the monologue in silence. Now she took her hands from her abdomen and laid them gracefully on the arms of the chair.

Naturally she would marry Baron Rattowitz. She wouldn't jump into the water like a servant-girl; she wouldn't return to the village with her shame; she wouldn't stay in a provincial hotel with Zoltán. She would

76

tell her father the truth at last. It was all natural. It was the way nature wanted it. She looked at the Prince gratefully, almost lovingly. Naturally she would become his mistress. A woman did not bear the burden of her own strength a day longer than it took her to find a man who would relieve her of it. You didn't fight the waves that carried you.

"Thank you," she said. "But . . ."

"But? . . ."

"I'm not as helpless as you suppose. Nor am I so bold. I could have paid my hotel bill. I'm not poor. Why should you pay Baron Rattowitz to marry me?"

"Because I don't know what to do with my money. Compared with me the Aporfalvys are paupers. One is only rich when money means nothing to one any more. I shall give you a life in which you will forget the value of money."

Why did he talk about money? They weren't in the Maison Rosa now. He wasn't young, but many would have considered him good-looking. He was a Kontowski. He had no need to boast.

He was already saying, "We won't deceive one another, Ilona. You don't love me—why should you? I shall be grateful if you don't detest me. So long as you are with me you will not dissipate my loneliness, but you will understand it. I shall not marry you, but I shall protect you from the contempt of the married women who would have liked to become my mistresses. I shan't hide you; I shall show off with you. And I hope you won't leave me until you have learnt all I can teach you."

He stood up.

She was too deeply sunk in thought to follow him immediately. Perhaps he underestimated himself. Zoltán was her first love, Feri her first lover; but he was the first man whom she wanted to get to know. She wouldn't leave Kontowski for a long while. At the same time she wondered what this man had been looking for in Aunt Rosa's 'house of sadness.' The Prince could have all the women he desired, and yet he went and enjoyed himself with whores. He was richer than the Aporfalvys, yet he spent Christmas Eve in a brothel.

Rising, she said, "May I ask you something, Prince Kontowski?"

He puckered his forehead. She noticed, and immediately gave her curiosity a different turn.

"Why me? Of all women, why me?"

He smiled with relief.

"I am no longer young, Ilona. Not that that's so terrible: people only become bearable after forty. Youth attracts me, but not the youth of to-day. It sometimes seems to me that the devil, attacking the weakest points like any good strategist, is in the process of depriving women of their reason. They are fighting for their rights— that is to say, for the right to toil like men, to share the burden of responsibility with them, to live unprotected, and to die alone. They are giving up their natural virtues in return for unnatural desires. I am buying you a husband, Ilona, because you have convinced me of your intelligence. You still respect prejudices. Anyone who no longer respects them is stupid. And anyone who is stupid is also immoral. I can make nothing of the youth of to-day. You are young and beautiful, very beautiful and very young, but you are a stranger in this paltry new century. I don't know any other young woman who still belongs to my century, the last one in which nature ruled. Is that enough for you?"

He took his top-hat, his gloves, his stick. He bent over her hand.

"I shall send a telegram to Rattowitz to-day. The sooner it takes place the better. May I hope meanwhile to spend an hour with you from time to time?"

"You know you are always welcome, Prince Kontowski."

When he had gone she walked across to the open window. The urge to mix with the gay throng became irresistible. She went to the cupboard containing her dresses and hats, opened it, and looked at them with satisfaction. She chose a matt green dress and a tall green hat.

She slowly peeled off her mourning dress.

35

In December 1904, a few days before Ilona's birthday, the stationmaster arrived in Budapest.

She had moved out of the Hotel Hungaria long before. The Prince had set up an apartment for her—three rooms in a little Late Gothic house in the Szentháromság ucca above the Pâtisserie Ruszwurm, an establishment left over from the Biedermeier period which now served as a rendezvous for romantic lovers. Besides herself, only the proprietors of the pâtisserie, an old Biedermeier couple, lived in the single-storey house. Walls, stairs, and passages were impregnated with the odour of hot chocolate. Along with the scent of chocolate something of the old-world quality of the pâtisserie had risen into the house, which, with its silk-upholstered furniture, lady's work-tables, knick-knacks, and niches, had preserved its cosiness against the new century.

Ilona was now in the eighth month of her pregnancy.

Only a few days before she had written and told the stationmaster everything—or almost everything, for she had not initiated him into the secret of the Salon Rosa and her change of mind during the audience at Schönbrunn. Once she had sealed and posted the letter she no longer felt afraid. It was strange about lies. You covered something ugly with a cloth, and under the cloth it became even uglier. Gradually you came to fear the cloth more than what it hid.

The stationmaster had expressly forbidden Ilona to meet him at the station. He had refused her invitation to stay with her. He had taken a room in a little inn only a few doors away from the pâtisserie.

Father and daughter were alone.

She had never seen him in civilian clothes before. He wore a black suit and a wide cravat with white spots, a wretched suit that nevertheless didn't look provincial—as though a village tailor could not detract from the dignity of this slim gentleman. The stationmaster felt ill at ease in civilian dress, like officers in whose wardrobes frock-coats are waiting for their owner's retirement. Ilona felt uncomfortable because she believed her father had dressed up like this only in order to leave the stationmaster at home.

Conversation began hesitantly. Ilona asked after Margit. "She's well," said the stationmaster. "She will be confined in March," he added, looking at the roses on the Biedermeier wallpaper. "And Teréz?" "The teacher is ill; she is helping at the school," he said. "She sends her love."

The maid brought coffee and cakes. Ilona sent her out and served her father herself. She did everything laboriously, not because of the weight of her body, but like some one anxious to gain time.

"The cakes are from the pâtisserie," she said. "It's the best in the whole of Buda." Her father nodded. There was silence. Coffee-vapour rose from the flower-patterned china pot.

"Would you be able to manage without Teréz?" asked Ilona.

"Teréz?"

"I should like to have her with me when the child is born. And afterwards. I shall be alone a great deal."

"Perhaps," said the stationmaster. "I'll tell her." Teréz was his last daughter. He too would be alone.

"I'm glad you came, Papa," she said. "There won't be anyone else at the wedding."

"I had to come. They wouldn't have understood in the village. . . ."

"What do they know in the village?"

"That you're marrying a rich baron. People envy me."

She looked at him over the coffee-table. His lips were no longer as full as they used to be. They were flanked by two parentheses, as though he wanted to enclose them. A few grey hairs gleamed in his moustache.

"Did you know nothing until you got my letter?" she asked.

"Four weeks ago I learnt everything. Zoltán Szomoru came to see me. He told me everything. About Rosa too."

She clutched at her abdomen. She always did when something affected her strongly, as though her heart had suddenly begun to beat far down in her womb, together with the child's heart.

"Zoltán? How did he know? . . ."

"He said he had always loved you. He had made inquiries about you here. He would have married you, he said. He stayed with me far into the night."

She laughed.

"He thought of it a bit late," she said.

"The rest I heard from Lajos."

"You aren't very lucky with us, Papa."

"Who says so?"

She lowered her eyes.

"It isn't difficult to understand your children when they are like yourself," he commented. "I should never have left Kisnémet. But neither could I have saved Lajos. I can't be proud of you and at the same time condemn you."

He stood up. With his hands folded behind his back he strode up and down in the room. This was the way he used to walk along the railway-line to make sure everything was in order. Everything always was in order.

"Why don't you stay here with me, Papa?" she asked.

"Because it is Prince Kontowski's apartment. I'm not giving him anything, and I won't accept anything from him. But that concerns me alone and nobody else." He came to a stop. "I don't know why you hid it from me. It must be my fault. Was I so strict with you?"

"You were never strict."

He shook his head. "Too strict. I didn't explain anything to you. I imagined you must understand. I was too strict and too thoughtless. I should have made inquiries about Aunt Rosa."

"Now you're blaming yourself for everything. I should have gone away even without Aunt Rosa. I don't belong in Kisnémet."

"Nor with your aunt. That's clear enough to me. You mustn't imagine you're bad. You didn't write to me because you thought of my life. It's easy for me. I live according to the timetable. That changes only once a year, in spring. Every one has always stayed good in Kisnémet. That's nothing to boast about in Kisnémet. Now let's drop the subject." He sat down relieved. "Just one thing, Ilona. Your room is just as it used to be. You don't belong in Kisnémet. But you belong to me. It's bad when parents are the wards of their children; but the reverse is quite natural. There will always be room for you and your child with me." He crossed his legs. The rays of the December sun fell on his face. He once more looked as young as she remembered him. He smiled. "Tell me about the Emperor!" he said.

She couldn't tell him about the Emperor yet. She stood up. Although her body was heavy, she moved easily. But she nearly knocked the coffee-table over as she walked round to her father. She twined her arms round his neck and kissed him on both cheeks. Only what he approved was good. She sat down at his feet and laid her head on his knee. She was able to draw up her legs. She was no longer afraid of the birth.

He stroked her hair.

"You mustn't excite yourself," he said.

"I'm happy," she said.

"Have you thought of a name yet?"

"A boy will have to be called Mihály, of course." It only occurred to her as she said it.

"And a girl?"

"Zita. What do you think of Zita?" She had only thought of a girl.

"Very pretty. Zita. . . ." He let the word melt in his mouth.

"I've bought all sorts of things already. And knitted some myself. Would you like to see them?"

She took him by the hand and led him into her bedroom. The chest-of-drawers was full to the top with pale-blue and pink jackets, blankets, hoods, and bootees. She spread them all out in front of the station-master. Then she stopped, so suddenly that the stationmaster looked at her in surprise.

"I don't know my husband yet," she said. "He's coming from

Vienna early to-morrow. Immediately after the wedding he's going to Monte Carlo. Kontowski wanted it like that."

The stationmaster was playing awkwardly with a hood.

"Teréz should have come with me straight away," he said.

"What about the schoolchildren?"

"What do I care about other people's children!"

They went back into the drawing-room.

Now Ilona told him about the Emperor. Her father wanted to know everything. What uniform the Emperor wore and whether he spoke fluent Hungarian; whether it was true that he never sat down during the audience, and whether he didn't look his great age. She conveyed his greetings to the stationmaster.

From Schönbrunn the conversation moved to Kisnémet. The stationmaster spoke without embarrassment of Margit's pregnancy. She wanted a boy. The Hotel Rákoczi was to have another storey added next year. Dr Grünfeld fell ill more and more frequently, but, stubborn as he was, he refused to put himself in the hands of any other doctor. Pista bácsi, the pointsman, had been given a wage increase: he had been forty years with the railways. And, of course, Máté sent Ilona his hearty good wishes: he went about the village talking all the time of "our Baroness." The stationmaster had to promise him a new trumpet.

The hours passed like minutes. Her father had taken her home.

36

The following morning Baron Rattowitz arrived. Ilona feared the meeting between the two men. She need not have done so.

The Baron was nearer fifty than forty. He looked older than the stationmaster. His soft, almost entirely grey hair fell over his forehead; his grey-blond side-whiskers made his red face look as narrow as it must have been before heavy drinking made it swell. He was exceptionally tall and walked slightly bent, in an obliging sort of way: he obliged the person he was speaking to by bending down to him. Even his weak-kneed legs, which he pushed rather than lifted when he walked, seemed to be trying to reduce his size to the scale of his fellowmen. If, as he emphasized on every possible occasion, he was a worthless fellow, a rascal, and a madcap it was in a superior kind of way, as though an amused observer were walking beside his ego.

Ilona observed the excellent understanding between the two men with relief. For the first time she became aware of the secret of the generations, the complicity between people who need have nothing in common beyond the closeness of their birth-dates.

If the Baron had pretended not to notice Ilona's advanced state of pregnancy, if he had fussed over his future wife, if he had tried to take himself or his rôle seriously—there would have been no end to Ilona's embarrassment. Baron Ferdinand Maria Leopold von Rattowitz was not like that.

"Yes, I'm leaving again to-day, my child, immediately after the wedding," he told Ilona, whose presence he had till then noted only casually. He had devoted himself exclusively to the stationmaster; with the *savoir-faire* of a man of the world he had concentrated on the things that interested the latter, as though he had been waiting for a long time to know more about railways, timetables, and life in a provincial station. "I'm leaving again to-day," he said, "because the Bank of Monte Carlo owes me a small fortune, which I now intend to recover. You will soon be relieved of my presence, but I beg you not to forget me entirely. Alcohol has attacked my liver, and my heart doesn't seem to approve of my way of life either. It's a pleasure to make you my wife; it would be a greater pleasure to make you my widow. Therefore I should like to entrust you with my papers, which your father"—he turned back to the stationmaster—"will be good enough to take care of, so as to spare you the formalities connected with the death certificate. I can assure you that my estate will cause you no trouble, since on the one hand I possess no earthly goods, while on the other—because people long ago stopped lending me money—I shall leave no debts."

On the stroke of eleven her father and her bridegroom made their way to the church in Kontowski's coach.

Kontowski had thought of everything. As the two-horse carriage drew up under the bare chestnut-trees in the sleepy Batthányi tér, two grave figures emerged from the shadows cast by the sunny morning. With their shiny top-hats, fur-edged winter overcoats, and side-whiskers reaching almost down to their mouths, they might have been cab-drivers; but, as it soon transpired, they came of a respectable family. They were brothers, Barons Károly and Géza von Dobay, and as like as two weasels.

Ilona wore a white wedding-dress without a myrtle wreath. The best dressmaker in the capital had cut it with such skill that veil and lace, tulle and taffeta-muslin, almost completely concealed the bride's curves.

She wasn't worried about her curves, but her footsteps were heavy. She dragged herself down the aisle to the altar on the right of the bought bridegroom. All at once it became clear to her that little more than the deed divided good people from bad. Every one had evil intentions, but the good didn't carry them out. In thought she had been through everything. She had strode down the church, light of foot, at the side of a stranger, her child under her heart, promised as a mistress to a rich man. She had been proud of the name her child would bear. The deed was different. In her fantasy she had had no accomplices, or they had no faces. Now she had accomplices, and they had faces—the bridegroom with his frozen smile, the funereal-looking witnesses, her father, whose thoughts seemed to be elsewhere. Her fantasy had been soundless. Now the organ was droning the wedding march, the same one the organ in the village church had played at Margit's wedding. Her fantasy had been devoid of smells. The smell of the incense was laden with childhood memories and made her feel sick.

The emptiness of the church increased her discomfort. It was empty, like a house which burglars break into after making sure it is un-occupied. The statues of the saints seemed to be keeping a look-out.

Ilona hadn't been afraid of the church. You deceived God everywhere or nowhere. It was difficult to deceive Him here.

The priest came. He was a fair young man with short hair and watery eyes. He looked at Ilona and the Baron without surprise, indifferently, not even politely. In his white surplice he appeared to be in fancy dress. Perhaps he wasn't a priest at all; perhaps he too was only an accomplice? The priest did what his office prescribed. It still wasn't too late. She could still prevent the hands from dispensing blessing. If she now chose confession, instead of the wedding, plan, intention, and fantasy would remain what they were—sinful thoughts, not sins. "Thou shalt not covet thy neighbour's property." Thou shalt not take it if thou covetest it. "Amen," said the priest. In Ilona's womb the child twisted round, as if turning a somersault. "Amen," she repeated. The Baron turned to her. "The rings," said the priest. She breathed a scarcely audible "Yes." Perhaps no one had heard it. The priest heard it so did the bridegroom. Nobody helped you avoid falsehood. She thought of Kontowski, the absent accomplice who was helping her to perform a falsehood. The Baron took the rings from his pocket. The church door clicked shut. Some one had entered the church, not knowing a wedding was going on. He knelt down, alone, in the last row. Ilona thought of the packed church at Kisnémet. She thought of Zoltán. He would have married her. Why hadn't he done so? Every one had good intentions, but only the good carried them out.

She knelt down; she stood up. She was wearing the ring on her finger. She was Baroness Ilona Rattowitz. Her child had a name.

37

They drove to the Buda Town Hall, where they signed the papers, shook hands, and distributed tips. The two witnesses tagged along behind until the party was outside the restaurant. Here they declined the Baron's invitation with thanks.

The lunch had obviously been Rattowitz's own idea, because the stage-management now went off the rails. Places were laid for five. Two had to be removed. The table was too large for three, and they found themselves sitting far apart.

It was late—past two. There wasn't a single customer left in the small, smart Buda restaurant. The only sound that entered the panelled private room was the rattle of plates and cutlery from the kitchen.

The bridegroom was in a munificent and generous mood. To accompany an excellent lunch—*bouillon* with egg, *pâté de foie gras*, grilled *fogas*, roast chicken with trimmings, chocolate cake with whipped cream—he ordered a Badacsonyer 1894 and a bottle of Pomméry 1889. Like most drinkers, he could stand scarcely a drop of alcohol. His cheeks quickly grew flushed, his eyes glittered, and his tongue obeyed him only reluctantly.

Ilona was nevertheless grateful to him for keeping the party going. Tales of a rich and miserly aunt who was for ever getting caught in the net of her own cupidity alternated with anecdotes from the casinos of Monte Carlo, and these again with stories of life on Polish estates, where the Baron had spent his youth. He mentioned Kontowski only once—"half Poland belongs to him"—then he reverted to his infallible roulette system.

"It's entirely a matter of calculating probabilities," he said, and since his listeners knew games of chance only from hearsay, he ordered the waiter to bring a pencil and paper and sketched out an accurate diagram of a gaming-table. "If seventeen hasn't come up," he said, people stake on sixteen and eighteen; but twenty-five and thirty-four are next to seventeen on the roulette-wheel." He pushed his plate, knife, fork, and spoon aside, spread out his long arms over the wedding-table, and immediately launched out into a welter of technical expressions like *cheval, colonne, carré, pair,* and *passe.* Now and again he took one of the flowers that lay scattered over the wedding-table and placed it on *rouge, noir,* or a number. "Then I double my stake," he said, pulling a carnation to pieces and placing eight pink blossoms on a transversal. Finally, realizing that he had been playing *croupier* long enough, he leant across the table with glazed eyes and said, "You will soon get to know all that for yourself, *me chère*—drawing-rooms and gaming-rooms, intrigues and gossip, hunting and fishing, Paris and Vienna, Warsaw and St Petersburg. I'll bet my last jetton that you do honour to my battered name." He brushed the flower-jettons away; they fluttered slowly down to the floor. "Enjoy what you experience and beware of boredom. Most of our follies are committed in the attempt to keep ourselves amused. But if you do encounter boredom get on a train at once and go to my friend, your father"—he laid his mottled hand on the stationmaster's shoulder—"for things are always most amusing in a station through which, if I understand right, the trains pass at full speed. Take good care of my papers." He now turned entirely to the stationmaster. "I herewith make you my executor. Your health!"

The stationmaster suggested it was time to leave. The Baron's train to the south left Budapest at five-twenty-three; the express the stationmaster had to catch, if he was not to miss the connexion at Püspökladány and was to be in Kisnémet in time for his official duties next morning, left half an hour later.

The Baron paid the bill, distributing tips left and right to the waiters on duty, who received them with ill-concealed astonishment. He gave Ilona his arm. On the table lay the crumpled diagram of a gaming-table and several mutilated flowers.

Rattowitz said good-bye to his wife and his new friend outside the Pâtisserie Ruszwurm. They gazed after him till Kontowski's carriage turned the corner. Then Ilona gathered up the train of her bridal dress that was peeping out from under her winter overcoat. The stationmaster touched her arm.

They sat in the drawing-room for a few minutes—the daughter in her white dress, the father in his Sunday best. It was slowly growing dark.

"Next week I'll send you Teréz," said the stationmaster.

"Thank you, Papa."

"You must come and see us soon, with the child."

"As soon as it is no longer possible to tell how old it is. I don't want to disgrace you."

"You won't disgrace me."

He stood up and kissed his daughter on the brow.

"Give my greetings to every one," she said. "You haven't forgotten Máté's trumpet have you?"

"No, I bought it early this morning."

He walked quickly into the antechamber. He put his coat over his arm, as though anxious not to prolong the farewell.

"It's cold, Papa," said Ilona.

"You should think about yourself," said the stationmaster.

As she opened the door for him the smell of chocolate met her in warm waves. It was four-thirty. Down below in the pâtisserie the first couples were meeting.

38

Good weeks began for Ilona. Her lies had been like fellow-prisoners in a cell. When she opened her eyes they were already there. When she closed her eyes they stared at the sleeper. Now they had gone.

Teréz arrived in Budapest only a few days after the wedding.

She was now twenty-two, only four years older than Ilona, but she looked twenty-six or -seven. Like Lajos, she resembled the stationmaster. The dark hair, which reached down to her knees when it was loose, and which she wore in close plaits above her smooth forehead, framed a face of such proud purity that the school-children obeyed her blindly, unknown shopkeepers gave her credit, and young men turned to other girls. There was a peasant hardness about the cheekbones in the small, slightly too flat face which it was hard but rewarding to get to know: if you studied it long enough it revealed deep-set eyes, a fine nose, a thin but expressive mouth.

She was the only one of the stationmaster's children who sometimes went to church on weekdays too, but she didn't go in search of consolation or hope or security; nor did she go to ask for things. Probably she only went to thank God for having made everything so well. She was sure no one needed her advice, for He who advised mankind knew better than she. To many people she appeared cold, although she loved them: she esteemed God too highly to heed her own powers. She wasn't indulgent, because only a person living on high could be condescending. Anyone who tried to guide the strayers on to the right path must imagine he knew which the right path was. She was kind to the poor, the old, and the frail, but she didn't doubt God's dispositions. She was free from envy because she didn't compare herself with others. Teréz felt no desire to experience herself what she saw and heard. She resembled her father more than merely outwardly, but since she belonged to a younger generation she was harder and more lucid.

Her relationship to Ilona also resembled her father's. The love she felt for her younger sister wasn't kind; it was almost selfish. Since she was able to give Ilona a great deal, she received a great deal. In

85

the proximity of Ilona her austere gravity diminished; she bore her own and other people's burdens more easily. From time to time she even allowed her sister to catch her in front of a mirror. She didn't quite understand Ilona, but she admired what surprised her and watched over what was strange to her. She was devoid of prudery: she didn't worry her head over her own virginity—it didn't even give her headaches.

Kontowski, who visited Ilona almost every day, took to Teréz at once. The village schoolmistress's attitude towards him was free from constraint, but by no means confidential, as though she had only come to help her sister through her pregnancy, not to give advice. "She has such a proud humility," the Prince once remarked to Ilona. On another occasion he had employed exactly the same words to describe true aristocrats.

During the last few weeks before her confinement Ilona ceased to go out. Twice a week she was visited by Herr Holzapfel, her German teacher, a shy young man who blushed easily; twice a week by Monsieur Poulain, an elderly Frenchman who looked like a frisky Mephistopheles, used the most modern teaching methods, and regaled the ladies with all sorts of Parisian anecdotes. The sisters competed in learning foreign languages, Ilona being the more skilled in imitating the correct intonation and Teréz the more thorough in grasping grammatical rules. Along with serious books, the Prince brought Hungarian, French, and German novels, as well as a mass of newspapers, periodicals, Society and fashion magazines, which the sisters often read pink-cheeked till late at night.

They frequently talked about Kisnémet. To begin with Ilona used to bring the conversation round to Zoltán Szomoru, till she noticed that her sister reacted to the subject with suspicion and aversion. Most often they talked of the future. Kontowski spent the greater part of the year travelling. He inspected his estates in Galicia; visited friends in the capitals of Europe; stayed in Vienna, where he pursued certain aims as yet incomprehensible to Ilona. When she listened to her future lover's plans, which now also related to her unborn child, Ilona was at first offended, then angry, and for a long time reluctant. He would take Ilona on his travels, he said, and no one could be more suitable than Teréz to look after the child in her absence. Only when Ilona discovered that Teréz accepted Kontowski's arrangements without surprise did she reconcile herself to the idea of long separations from her child. Just as she had come home from her wedding on her father's arm, so she shared her motherhood with her sister. Again the word 'naturally'—Ilona's favourite word—cropped up. Naturally Teréz had come when she needed her; naturally she was ready to sacrifice her own future for Ilona; naturally she paid the chosen one the tribute of her time.

39

The labour-pains began at four in the afternoon on January 31, 1905. It was a Sunday.

The few shops with telephones were shut. A neighbouring lawyer had one. Teréz hurried to him in order to ring Dr Sasvári, the obstetrician.

Ilona lay on linen sheets spread over rubber ones. The wide Biedermeier bed had been shifted into the middle of the room. On all sides large buckets were waiting for boiling water. Beside the dressing-table, which had been cleared of its scent-bottles, powder-boxes, and jars, stood a wooden peasant cradle, low, bright-blue, with a gay Hungarian tulip pattern. It had been Ilona's cradle; the stationmaster had sent it from Kisnémet. Ilona had never seen it before: her father must have kept it up in the loft. Folded and freshly ironed towels lay on tables, chairs, and commodes. There was a smell of sun-dried washing. The late-January sun filtered in through the drawn silk curtains on to the bed. The silence was broken only by an occasional groan from the woman.

Her mother had died when she was born, she thought. Her picture in a silver frame stood on the bedside table that had been pushed away. She couldn't see it. People said she was like her mother, but her mother looked old, like every one in old pictures, although she had been less than eighteen when the daguerreotype was made. In the meantime Professor Semmelweis had discovered that it was un-necessary for women to die in childbed. His white memorial in the Kossuth Lajos ucca was surrounded by grateful mothers in stone. She knew she wouldn't die, even without the Professor's science. The child had no father. It must have a mother. She wouldn't feel sorry for herself and die.

She had lived with a child for nine months, yet she didn't know whether it was a boy or a girl. She could pray for it to be a girl, but it was probably too late. Too late? God knew long ago that to-day she would pray for a girl. Why did people pray, when God gave them the words they prayed with? The more you thought about it the less you understood. God didn't want people to understand. That was why he made women carry an unknown burden for nine months. The mysteries were past understanding, especially those you carried within yourself.

The labour-pains grew more and more violent. No sooner had they appeared than they seemed to have been there all the time. What was it like to be without pains? The pains raged inside her, ebbed, and as soon as they vanished became unimaginable. She waited for the pain and waited for it to go.

Why wasn't Teréz there? Cold sweat broke out on her forehead. She began to discover the special nature of labour-pains. They came and went. They swept over her body like an evil cloud that emptied itself out over her and floated away, driven off by fresh pains.

The intervals between pains grew shorter. Fear came with them. She counted the seconds. There had been three hundred and sixty-six seconds without pain before; now there were only three hundred. There were hands in her abdomen, rough, bloody butcher's hands. They were trying brutally to push the little body out of her.

The pain dragged her body up into a sitting position. Her eyes fell on her mother's picture. It came closer, grew huge. She did look like her mother. She would die. She had killed her mother; now her child was killing her. Her life had begun wickedly. Everything wicked rose from her abdomen into her head. She had never loved Feri. She had robbed the dead. She had loved another, still loved him. She had lied to her father. And without loving she had enjoyed pleasure. The enjoyment seemed to her monstrous, the contact repulsive.

At last the door opened. Teréz was back. Soon the doctor would be there too.

Teréz dried the sweat from her sister's brow. Ilona sank back into the pillows. Her convulsive tension relaxed.

"What time is it?" she asked.

"Six."

Had the labour-pains really started only two hours ago? Nothing had happened in seventeen years, and everything in one. Nothing in a year, and everything in two hours. The clock and the calendar were frauds. It was a fraud that the hour contained sixty minutes, the minute sixty seconds, the day twenty-four hours, and the year three hundred and sixty-five days. Many days had three hundred and sixty-five hours, and many years were a second. The slow short hand of the clock showed pain, the hurrying long one happiness. Time mocked its instruments.

She seized Teréz's hand.

"I'm going to die," she said.

"Nonsense!"

"I can't stand it."

"You only imagine you can't."

"Why doesn't he come?"

"He'll be here in a minute."

Then the doctor arrived, and with him the midwife.

Dr Sasvári was a man of enormous girth. A sparse wreath of dark hair encircled a shiny bald patch; his round chin fell on to his chest in three folds, completely hiding his throat; his chest itself spread out in the shape of a cone, ending at the bottom in a ring of fat. Although the midwife was a good two heads taller, the dried-up, mousy-grey woman was totally obscured by the imposing personality of the doctor. He paid no attention to the rest of those present, but bent down over Ilona, feeling her body with practised hands, while a golden fish hanging on his watch-chain jumped up and down on the woman's naked stomach. Then he announced that "as usual" he had been called too soon, and that he would go and wait in the Pâtisserie Ruszwurm, from where Miss Puskás, the midwife, could call him when the time came. His too short legs carried him quickly through the narrow door.

Ilona hated him for going.

"He's leaving me to die," she repeated through clenched teeth to Teréz.

"He delivers a dozen women every day."

"But he's leaving me to die."

Teréz was holding her left hand; Miss Puskás took told of her right. Her nails bored into the woman's palms.

"Bear down! Go on, bear down!" ordered the midwife.

88

As Ilona did nothing she let go of her hand and pressed on her abdomen. She had hands of steel. The midwife's hands outside, the butcher's hands inside—they'll crush the child, thought Ilona. She opened her eyes. Why was the midwife wearing a black dress? It was a mourning dress. The black hurt her. She couldn't see a dress any more. There wasn't a midwife there either. A great ugly bird was hovering over her. The bird alighted on her.

"You must call the doctor," she said to Teréz. "He'll have to help me."

The pains had floated away again. She began to count aloud. One, two, three, four . . . twenty . . . a hundred. There was nothing in the room but the woman's groaning counting. One, two, three, four . . . twenty . . . forty . . . a hundred. A carriage bumped over the cobbles. People were talking outside the pâtisserie. They laughed. Their laughter was like pinpricks. A hundred and twenty . . . a hundred and thirty . . . a hundred and fifty. This time the pains did not float over her: they fell upon her. Knives that plunged into her flesh and twisted in it, screws with sharpened threads, sharpened forks with a thousand prongs.

"Yell if you want to," she heard Teréz say.

She tried to yell. She could only groan.

"Push, push harder," said the midwife. Her weight bore down upon Ilona.

Teréz's hand was too weak. Ilona let go of it. She clung to the bedpost, tried to raise herself up on the cold wood. The bedposts! If only she could sink her teeth into their timber!

Pictures flitted across the ceiling. She saw Dr Grünfeld's red beard. The doctor who had brought her into the world was dying. She too would die. She saw the Salon Rosa, and the Salon was spinning round as it had on that Christmas Eve. Aunt Rosa's red, freckled face bent down over her. Had Aunt Rosa returned? In her ears she heard music, drums and trumpets; the military band marched past; she was in Sopron on her balcony. A red carpet hung from the ceiling; it grew longer and longer, like the carpet under her feet in the Emperor's audience chamber. The Emperor had a red beard and looked like Dr Grünfeld. The horse stumbled and buried the rider under its weight. Was she still in Feri's house? The black armchair towered up in front of her; it looked like a coffin standing on end.

"I'm dying!" she murmured. "I'm dying!"

Again a face bent down over her. Was it a delirium-face, or was it real? It was a round, fat face; she didn't recognize the man; he had froth round his mouth like a mad dog.

It wasn't froth; it was whipped cream. Then she remembered that the doctor had gone down to the pâtisserie. He had been called just as he was eating a cream-puff.

From a distance came the doctor's orders. Towels, scissors, water. She only saw the froth round the thick lips. Not a mad dog. A cream-puff eater. Alfréd Sasvári, M.D., obstetrician and cream-puff eater.

She started laughing. The laughter shook her body, threw it up in

89

the air and down on to the bed again, pressed on her abdomen, tore at her shoulders.

The laughter was stronger than the pain; it overcame the pain. She felt nothing more. There was silence.

"Scissors!"

She heard the doctor's voice quite clearly.

Then the child's voice was the only sound in the room.

The midwife lifted up the child.

"It's a girl," she said.

40

Soon after Zita's birth Ilona moved with Teréz and her child to Vienna. The Prince took an apartment for her in the Bellaria, not far from the monument to the Empress Maria Theresa which she had once admired. It was very sumptuous, very cold, very princely, and comprised six rooms divided by a spacious hall, so that Teréz and the child could retire to their own rooms when Kontowski was there.

Three months after Zita's birth Ilona went with the Prince to his castle in Galicia.

Spring was as far away from Galicia as the gay capital from the endless wilderness. Winter ruled without fear of dethronement. The snow lay high between the firs of the forest, dirty snow that could neither renew itself nor melt. The north wind groped its way through the branches, a blind man searching. Hunger had driven the wolves down from the Carpathians into the valley. The valley was as bleak as the mountains. Wind and wolves howled in competition.

They arrived late in the afternoon and ate their meal at a small table by the fire in the hunting-room. To move even a few paces from the table was like going out into the night. It was amazing that there was no snow on the stags' antlers hanging on the walls.

Kontowski drank a great deal—wine and plum brandy and champagne; yet at this moment he remained sober, as though intoxication were resisting him, as love withholds itself from him who seeks it. It was as though he were drinking merely to make the hours pass. Every now and then he went over to the window, out into the cold of the room, away from the light of the candles. He seemed to be waiting for morning. Morning did not come.

It was late when they went upstairs to bed. An old servant carried the silver candlestick in front of him with a stony face. Ilona thought of Mátyás. Women like herself always came up against the servants of their joint masters. The candles flickered. Cold rose from the stone stairs. Every step was a dark block of ice. The wind whispered mocking songs through the crevices of the tall windows.

The struggle began at two in the morning and lasted until a pallid light that was not sunshine seeped in through the curtains. Then Ilona knew why the Prince had spent Christmas Eve 1903 in Aunt Rosa's 'house of sadness.'

The man was not struggling with the woman; he was struggling with himself. At times he seemed to have forgotten the naked woman beside him, as though she were not the cause, but only the renewal, of his

90

torment. He seemed continually aware of his body, a shapely, sinewy male body with a youthful skin, almost as he might have been aware of a servant who was ostentatiously present and at the same time disregarded his master's commands. He sought with words and gestures to arouse Ilona's resistance, and when it failed to appear he tried to fire himself on his own anger; but his wooing and his demands betrayed not longing, but weakness. He sought ecstasy in vain, for while he was trying to forget himself the thought of ceasing to think was ceaselessly hammering behind his veined forehead. The experience was as terrifyingly familiar to the man as it was terrifyingly unfamiliar to Ilona; he spoke and behaved like an actor in the midst of a nightmare in which he had to make a hundred appearances before rows of empty seats.

Previously he had scarcely spoken of himself; now he talked about nothing else. He blamed his parents, boasted of his youthful dissipations, enumerated his mistresses. He interpreted Ilona's patience as pity. Pity, the arch-enemy of love, took away his last vestige of restraint. If she repulsed him he tried to buy her. The buyer humiliated himself and the bought, but his offers did not offend her, although that was exactly what he had hoped to do; he felt that she had seen through him and began to rage. He talked and talked, as though he believed he could grasp and hold the passing hour. Just as he had feared the night, he now feared the morning. With infinite tenderness he settled Ilona on her pillows, but he shook her roughly awake when she closed her eyes as if to sleep, as though accusing her of sleeping away his last hope. He begged her to forgive him for having taken her for his mistress, although he knew very well she could never become his mistress in fact; no sooner had she pacified him than, punishing himself for lying, he covered her body with kisses again.

He refused to resign himself. Begging, imploring, and arguing, he had sought with half the whores of the Monarchy to wrest from his body an answer to the question of why it did not obey his desires. The white candles didn't burn; he had imagined that the black candles of pitch would burn. He was known in the filthy brothels of Rumania, under the gold coin of Parisian *maisons closes,* in Macedonian taverns, where black girls from North Africa offered their naked bodies for sale, in Viennese houses of assignation where experienced madams instructed their girls in the tricks of the trade—a rich unknown who travelled in search of defeats. Now he was seeking in purity what he had failed to find in filth, but he did so with a helpless subtlety, as though his body was a stranger whom he could trick. He dragged purity down into the dirt, transferred the speech and behaviour of Polish brothels to the bedchamber of his castle, and despaired because he was defeated in the latter as in the former. Then he accused himself. A drunken port drab in Hamburg, a strange creature who demanded satisfaction as well as payment, had once yelled mockery at him, called her ponce, torn his clothes off his back, and hounded him out naked into the street. Now he repeated the abuse that had been shouted after him, directed it against himself. Words of love followed the obscenities, obscenities in turn the words of love. At the pinnacle of his rage and in the depths of his humiliation he sought pleasure, but his body understood whispers no better than curses.

The idea that she might be to blame for the man's torment never occurred to Ilona. She was inexperienced, but experienced enough not to blame herself for an illness that had nothing to do with her. Curiously enough, it was the man's behaviour that calmed her tense nerves from the outset. That she could not miraculously cure the patient in a single night might be her fault, but his every approach to her, his every gesture, his every word, betrayed the age of his illness. Her inability to help him filled her with pride rather than shame: no lover, only a bought woman, could heal such a malady. Her blood was not whipped up, therefore she was not angry that it remained unassuaged. She felt nothing but compassion for the man who raved, humiliated himself, accused himself and her; it was not compassion with the man as such, however, but with the human being who imagined he would lose her because he couldn't possess her. How unspeakably deep he must have sunk and how unspeakably low the women he had met must have been that he should believe she would forget his fine, lovable, and estimable qualities because he did not possess the one thing that is a ponce's sole wealth!

Although she had long since pretended to be asleep, she was still awake when, wounded in the battle with himself, he at last fell asleep on her arm. She was not afraid of the future. She wasn't even sure that the unexpected, terrifying, perhaps terrible experience she had had was not a merciful dispensation, because she had never desired this man by her side, but might, who knows, love the sufferer. No man understood that a woman could rise from her bed unloved and yet undefeated. Men decided everything between man and woman; only the most important thing, happiness and unhappiness, was in the hands of women. She laid her hand gently on the man's damp face.

When the sun rose, a sun as pale and watery as the moon that had set, man and woman were sleeping side by side. Their faces were calm.

41

They returned to Vienna; Ilona adapted herself to her new life.

She was young and prodigal with time. Age looks at the clock; youth doesn't even look at the calendar. She didn't yet know that the only thing lost for good is lost time. She didn't understand when people talked about growing old. Youth has no inkling that we start to grow old the day we are born, that on the day we are born we start to die. She took her youth too much for granted to be proud of it. She was surrounded by people older than herself; the effort to understand them preserved her from the cowardly and coquettish pose of being misunderstood herself. Her desire for experience was so great that she feared no disappointments. He who defends himself against disappointments hides from life. She knew that you cannot mature without growing old, and because she wanted to mature she ungrudgingly paid the price in years.

During the first year in which she was Kontowski's mistress grea storms put an end to the great calm. In the eyes of the world Baroness Rattowitz, the young beauty from Hungary, was the Prince's mistress. Kontowski made her an accomplice of appearances. When he sat opposite Ilona at the breakfast-table after a white night he would take her hand and kiss it, as though in thanks for hours of joy. Then again the mute comedy would collapse. The man sought fresh defeats and reported them in monologues of weakness. He raged not only against himself, but also against Ilona, always ending by imploring the assurance that she wouldn't leave him.

At first she considered leaving him. She didn't long for any other man, but she despised herself for staying with this one. But before she even had time to tell herself that she was staying with him out of vanity, self-interest, indolence, and faint-heartedness, it was no longer true. Whether because she wished to punish herself for her moral lapse and her year of sin, or because she had to grow up alongside her growing daughter, or because she was convinced that the woman must be satisfied with what the man gave her—she came to terms with the unnatural situation and eventually came to consider it natural.

She hated Kontowski's monologues more than the nights at his side. Once she had realized that she couldn't cure him it became a question of softening his revolt against the unalterable. She didn't act without thinking of herself. The greater became her liking for the Prince the more easily he was able to excite her young body, but the more empty she was left in the loneliness of her half-satisfaction. Kontowski felt this, and because he felt it the half-love he was able to give was followed by tormenting self-accusation. With unspeakable effort, by the application of all her womanly tact and inborn shrewdness, she lengthened the intervals between the vain struggles and solitary joys. The rarer the despairing endeavours and the ensuing monologues became, the greater became Ilona's admiration for Kontowski; the greater the admiration, however, the less her pity, which finally she had no further need to conceal because it had entirely evaporated. Kontowski was ill. She didn't blame him for his illness. She helped him to hide it from the world. She had grown up in an atmosphere in which kindness prevailed. She recognized its importance.

The Prince read her every wish in her eyes. Nothing binds a man so fast to a woman as his bad conscience, unless it is gratitude because she doesn't take advantage of his bad conscience. Ilona asked for nothing and received everything. She became independent of him and nevertheless stayed with him: now he was certain that he was loved for his own sake. Yet she imagined that she gave him nothing but the time which she possessed in such copious measure.

42

She measured time only by her daughter, Zita.

The idea that children often resemble their grandparents seemed to be borne out by Zita. Her violet eyes, white skin, and delicate bone-structure came from Ilona's mother; her jet-black hair, full mouth, and confident movements from the stationmaster. As though nature wished to erase what was illegitimate, only her straight, rather too short nose recalled Feri, and she showed no other trace of the Aporfalvy family. During the early years Count Aporfalvy made clumsy attempts to see his only grandchild, but in Kisnémet Ilona avoided the vicinity of the castle, and when the Count tried to visit her in Vienna she sent word that his visit was unwelcome.

When Ilona was not travelling she devoted herself entirely to her daughter. She kept strictly to certain dates: she spent four weeks every summer, from July 15 to the middle of August, with her child. These weeks were closed to Kontowski. Only a few miles from Kisnémet station lay a house and garden that had belonged to an early-widowed Herr Von Keresztény. After his wife's death Herr Von Keresztény had moved to Budapest, where in the course of the years he had, so to speak, drunk away his estate a yoke at a time, till nothing was left but a large garden round the house; the house itself would undoubtedly have sunk brick by brick in alcohol if Ilona had not persuaded the Prince to buy it from him before it was too late. Although she laid no claim to any of the many other houses he owned, she asked him to register this one, which he was forbidden to enter, as her property at the Kisnémet land-registry office. It was not only homesickness that drove her home to the village, with its golden-yellow cornfields, roads deep in dust, dried-up streams, and sultry nights, to whose chirruping and croaking music the glow-worms danced—she wanted to give her daughter a home, and she knew no other.

It made her happy to see that Zita was happiest at Kisnémet. The child spent little time at Berény, as the shrunken estate was called, for a few minutes in the carriage took her to the station where her grandfather ruled. Aunt Rosa hadn't been a good prophet when she depicted the new century to the stationmaster as a threatening monster. There was no sign of the new century at Kisnémet. To be sure, Pista bácsi, the pointsman, was dead, and a younger employee who could operate the telephone and the telegraph had taken his place, but Máté was still collecting dolls' legs, chicken-bones, goose-feathers, and frying-pans with holes in them, still imagined that he was the stationmaster, and entertained the little Baroness with fantastic tales. The stationmaster joyfully indulged Zita's belief that the station was nothing but an outsized toy station and he himself nothing but the tin model of a stationmaster belonging to the toy railway. For four weeks bells were rung in the station, light-signals changed, trumpets blown, and, when there was no danger, even points switched, just as the little lady pleased. When Zita ate her spinach like a good girl or obediently slept for two hours after lunch she was occasionally allowed to spend the night with Teréz in the station-house. Everything had remained untouched in the girls' room. The child slept in the bed in which her mother had once dreamt of a house that didn't have the word Kisnémet on it.

The happy illusion of the summer months didn't deceive Ilona. She saw her child with clear eyes. Zita's streak of obstinacy grew stronger and stronger, her often senseless dislikes more and more marked, the tendency to contradict for the sole purpose of opposing more and more frequent. True, children try out their wills as young birds of prey try out their claws, thought Ilona, but the child's stubborn spirit was sometimes impossible to control. Ilona's moods were transferred to the child, but in the child's soul they grew to unnatural proportions, as though seen under a magnifying-glass. Her sobs frightened Ilona, so did her laughter. When Zita danced it was as if she were dancing on a frozen lake beneath whose ice the water threatened. Her lovely child's face was at times as ancient as stone. She reminded Ilona of the children in Breughel's paintings, who are as old as the adults, only much smaller. Ilona was disquieted most of all by the sometimes spiteful, sometimes cold, and sometimes sly aversion with which her daughter repulsed Kontowski's advances. Zita, who could run to an old park-keeper when he picked her a flower, who entranced Ilona's curmudgeonly coachman so that he slipped her lumps of sugar to give to the horses, who quickly got to know people and came back from every walk with new friends, remained impervious to the Prince's costly gifts. Once, having asked Teréz to explain the hierarchy of aristocratic ranks to her, she burst into bitter tears because she was a mere baroness, while Kontowski was a prince; she was only consoled when Teréz assured her that emperors and kings also ruled over princes. Later, when she went to school, Zita was the best in her class, but Ilona's pride was mixed with distress, because the child soon became aware of her superiority. She treated her schoolfellows with condescending, even contemptuous benevolence. Zita was gnawed by ambition, an ambition tending to resignation. Though she possessed many talents she lacked others; but she refused, sulky and offended, to learn what did not come easily to her by nature.

With every fault Ilona discovered in her daughter her love for the child increased. She didn't spoil her, but she had difficulty in not spoiling her. She sought the roots of her child's faults in herself. She already had an inkling of what seed she had sown in the furrow of time. Who could claim a clear conscience when he brought children into the world? A woman's life revolved around man and child. She had a man and a child, but in her life they were not one. She alone bore the responsibility for both of them.

43

She often thought of Zoltán. She had met him two or three times at balls or at the flower parade in the Prater—always in large gatherings. Her girlhood dream of seeing him humiliated was over and done with. The conductor's fame flew over the cities. He gave concerts in Vienna and Paris, at the Court of the King of England and at that of the King of the Belgians. He was so famous that people spoke of him simply as Szomoru—there was no further need to qualify the surname. Ilona also came across his name in the section of the paper devoted to local news. He cancelled concerts; threw out a trusted orchestra leader; lost his score and conducted without it. Women were crazy about him, and girls collected postcards with his picture. The more he despised the public the more they loved him. His popularity remained unscathed when it was rumoured that the daughter of a wealthy industrialist had thrown herself into the river on his account. A slight shiver ran down Ilona's spine when she heard his name. She knew she would come into contact with him again one day, but it must not be at a ball or a flower parade. It could only happen when she was more than Prince Kontowski's mistress.

During the early years she hoped that Kontowski would marry her. She heard regularly from Rattowitz—on her birthday, their wedding anniversary, and at Christmas. He never appeared in person. She could tell from his presents whether he was having good luck or bad. From Paris he sent her the first gramophone she had possessed, because he had guessed the winner at Auteuil; only a bunch of white lilac came for Christmas: Kontowski had to pay his debts at Monte Carlo. When Zita asked about her father Ilona, feeling her way along the truth, told her he was travelling, leaving open the question of whether he would ever come back. In the child's imagination the Baron became a fairy-tale figure with whom no Sleeping Beauty's prince could compete. She loved him more than the princes of fairy-tales, and had just as little wish to make his acquaintance: the slayer of dragons, conqueror of giants, and owner of seven-league boots would have been out of place in the Bellaria apartment or the Berény farmhouse.

Society, which she had feared, accepted her. But how strange Society was! She often thought of the old baron she had got to know during her first year in Vienna. His father had been chief of police, the same one who had planted himself outside the burning Ringtheatre in 1881 and shouted into the inferno: "No one is to go in! No one is to come out! Everything is under control!" Thereafter four hundred and forty-seven corpses were recovered from the ruins. "The cabbies raise their hats particularly respectfully when I walk past them in the Graben," the Baron had said. "They only remember that my father was already a big noise at the time of the Ringtheatre fire; that he was a big fraud, God rest his soul, has long since been forgotten. Here, my dear Baroness, you see an image of the aristocracy. You only have to be or do something long enough, never mind what, and people raise their hats. Not only cabbies, by the way. Everything that lasts a long time is respectable. The most decent thing that is new looks shabby besides the most indecent thing that has been going on for a long time. There is a deep significance in this. We fear nothing so much as time, and anyone who has stood up to time gains our respect. It really isn't easy to outlive life."

Ilona too needed time. Many drawing-rooms remained closed to her at first. She heard whispering behind her back when she entered the Konditorei Demel. When she appeared in her box at the première of *Elektra* opera-glasses probed her as a stethoscope probes the body of a sick man. But because the Prince refused invitations without her, because some of his friends broke through the cordon of prejudice, because the aged Princess Pauline Metternich, originator of the flower parade and patron of the fine arts, ordered the Baroness Rattowitz to be presented to her during the Freudenau races, a siege of the house in the Bellariastrasse began and did not cease.

Ilona had her hands full.

There was Kontowski, a man with a tendency to depression, cynical in all he said, sentimental in all he felt, who suffered over the times he lived in. She often contradicted him; learnt to distinguish between his wisdom and his bitterness, although they resembled one another like a pair of twins; erected embankments of optimism against the tidal wave of his gloomy fancies. She became as indispensable to him as he was to her. Boredom and loneliness were strangers to her, not so much because she was rarely alone as because every thought that came to her was immediately paired off with another thought and began to circle around it: what made Kontowski happy or dejected preoccupied her to such an extent that her solitude became populated by him, his friends, and his enemies. She didn't understand what certain women, who were to be met more and more frequently now, meant by the seductive phrase "a life of one's own." The people who remained true to themselves did best.

The day was filled even if Ilona had only to care for a single child. Provisions had to be bought; guests came and went and were not parsimonious with their admiration; a hospital bed had to be found for a pregnant maid; the vases thirsted for fresh flowers and the flowerpots for fresh water; the visitor had burnt a hole in the table-cloth, the child wouldn't say her bedtime prayers by herself; now it was evening and Ilona had to make herself beautiful for the man who came to praise her beauty. She had found a cold, sumptuous apartment when she arrived; nothing was left to recall this save the walls. It never occurred to her that she was only embellishing her apartment for her child, for Teréz, for Kontowski or his friends. She was doing it for herself. She often thought about growing old. Perhaps nobody would any longer praise her beauty. But guests would still congratulate her on her food; nobody would stop her from embroidering and knitting, playing new and old songs on the piano, advising old friends and watching new ones grow up. Women aged, but what they did remained young. It was good to grow older; it was good to be a woman.

People talked more and more about women's rights. From her balcony Ilona saw women parading the streets with placards and making speeches in public places. It struck her that most of them were ugly. They couldn't find men who would care for them and for whom they could care. They accused men of coercive domination, but it seemed to Ilona that they were merely trying to entice beautiful and attractive women into becoming as unattractive as themselves. They called themselves 'feminists,' but they looked, behaved, and talked like men. Perhaps they only cut off their hair because it wouldn't grow? And what were the rights they demanded? Ilona knew of no right that she didn't possess. She possessed power. The Prince, a powerful man, did nothing without consulting her. The men she received as guests asked her advice. Who would want to be a puppet when he could be the puppet-master?

She forgot the demonstrating women. She learnt more than languages, customs, and etiquette. She began to see behind men's flattery, behind their crudities and their tears, their smiles and their indifference. Sometimes a paradise was revealed, sometimes an abyss, sometimes a void. She no longer believed that men were good, but they were nevertheless a little better than their reputation.

"Maturity," Kontowski used to say, "is acquaintance with oneself; at best, friendship with oneself, but in any case coming to terms with oneself. Our feelings are planted in us like roots in the soil, but soil and roots are not the same thing. The soil is ourself. The roots grow into us, churn us up, fructify and poison us, thrust out from us, and thrust into us again. Growth is unrest. We have to live with it as the earth lives with its endless roots. The earth is mature when it learns to live with its roots."

She was barely twenty when Kontowski spoke to her like this. When she was twenty-six time was complete. She had begun to understand it.

44

The expresses that passed Kisnémet station came back; summer and winter timetables followed one another like the seasons; the geraniums flowered in the windows. In Kisnémet people didn't know that Aunt Rosa had been right. The new century had begun.

In the same year, in the same month, as Zita was born the empire of Japan and the tsardom of Russia signed a peace treaty at Portsmouth, on the soil of the American republic. The trench was invented. Men burrowed in among worms and larvae. Killing had become easier. The earth took revenge. The San Francisco earthquake lasted for two days.

An earthquake passed through the tsardom. The people revolted against their Little Father. Vladimir Ilyich Ulyanov, called Lenin, became the leader of the Bolsheviks.

At his seventh attempt Admiral Robert E. Peary reached the North Pole. Among his companions was the Negro Matthew Henson.

Great progress was made. Seventeen Negroes were lynched in the southern United States.

That year, 1909, Louis Blériot flew the Channel. Soldiers had sought protection in the earth; they knew nothing of the enemy in the skies.

Crises began to be numbered. The first Moroccan crisis ended with the defeat of Kaiser Wilhelm II.

Progress changed pleasures. Announcers no longer accompanied the wildly audacious happenings on the cinema screen with plaintive voices. The human voice fell silent; the sub-title had triumphed. Max Linder appeared in the "masterpiece of laughter" *Mariage Américain*. A little man with a little moustache tripped over his little stick. His name was Charles Chaplin.

The thunder of guns roared through the blue Mediterranean night. In the war against Turkey, Italy took Libya.

The ladies had freed themselves from the corset. *Art nouveau* showed people's fear of growing old. The train and the 'cartwheel' hat were soon dropped, too. In Paris Monsieur Poiret created the chemise dress: he undressed women by dressing them.

The body was naked; now the soul demanded its *décolleté*. In his consulting-room in the Berggasse, Vienna, Dr Sigmund Freud was working out the theories of psychoanalysis.

Near Newfoundland the *Titanic* ran into an iceberg. It was the 14th of April. Fifteen hundred lives were lost.

Serbia, Bulgaria, Montenegro, and Greece defeated Turkey. This was the first Balkan war. Wars began to be numbered.

The fireworks never came to an end. In honour of his jubilee the Emperor expanded his empire by the forcible annexation of Bosnia and Herzegovina. In a whitewashed single-storey house in the town of Sarajevo a boy with burning eyes spoke of the Emperor's "dirty laurels." His name was Gabriel Princip.

The Emperor's brother, Archduke Ludwig Victor, had his ears boxed in a public bathing establishment. He was wearing nothing but bathing trunks. His Majesty banished him for life to Schloss Klesheim.

Bulgaria had offered Johann Salvator, Archduke of Austria, the Tsar's crown. On May 6, 1911, the missing "Johann Orth, skipper on a long voyage," was declared dead.

During the flower parade in the Prater hundreds of fiacres trotted past on rubber wheels under the pink candles of the chestnut-trees. Burgomaster Karl Lueger waved from his carriage.

People wore Girardi hats, carried Girardi sticks, and smoked cigarettes in Girardi holders.

In Galician garrisons young officers were talking about the desire of the national states for independence and about revolution.

The new Hofburg was nearing completion.

In the Café Griensteidl young literati were gathering round Arthur Schnitzler and Hermann Bahr.

"If the mob comes out into the streets we shall have to open fire," proclaimed the police-chief of the Bohemian capital, Prague.

The Emperor, aged eighty, opened exhibitions. "It was very nice; I liked it very much." In his villa at Bad Ischl he received the ambassador of his "dear cousin" the German Kaiser. It wasn't nice; he didn't like it. "The future looks very black to me." The old man's eyes were dim. What he thought was the future was the present.

45

First splashing, then hissing and frothing, and finally lashing waves, the present surged against Ilona's drawing-room in the Bellaria.

More and more frequently the Prince received a small circle of friends in his mistress's drawing-room. He didn't wish to see them in his house nor to meet them in public places, not even the red-plush *chambres séparées* of the Hotel Sacher. What sort of people could these be? Ilona heard their names with relief. There was a Polish landowner, Kontowski's neighbour in Galicia; a Hungarian count whose father had been Prime Minister; a member of the Reichstag from the Bohemian crown lands; a very young general whose family name was familiar to Ilona from the history-books; an archduke of barely thirty whose name came only a little way after His Majesty's in the Court

Circular. Why these secret meetings? Why did the Prince bring his personal servant, who soundlessly served the drinks?

What Ilona heard made her heart stand still.

It was inconceivable. The Monarchy was in danger. Wasn't his Apostolic Majesty Francis Joseph I, Emperor of Austria, King of Jerusalem, Hungary, Bohemia, Dalmatia, Croatia, Slovenia, Galicia, and Lodomeria, still reigning? And wasn't he reigning by the Grace of God? In her mind's eye Ilona saw the Emperor as she had seen him long ago in the audience chamber. The Emperor was old. The many countries hung on him like the medals on the caved-in, old-men's chests of the veteran soldiers who were sometimes to be seen on the benches in the Volksgarten. They were proud of their medals, but they carried them with difficulty. The jingling gold seemed no longer quite to belong to them. They had to polish it every day, and could no longer remember when and for what they got it. The Emperor was content with his park at Ischl. But now Bosnia-Herzegovina had been "incorporated" into his world empire, as chancellery parlance phrased it. It was a new medal on the narrow, old-man's chest. "The Emperor has forgotten to die, that's the whole trouble," wisecracked the young general one day in Ilona's drawing-room. He wore the coat of the same Emperor whom he was urging to die. Ilona often thought of Lajos. The Archduke made more outrageous speeches than the deserter had ever made. From his balcony the Emperor saw Vienna illuminated. But his eyes were tired. Galicia was far away, and so was Bosnia-Herzegovina. The Emperor could no longer see that far.

"I'm no revolutionary," Kontowski said to Ilona one night after the others had left. She was lying on the ottoman; he was walking up and down with long strides, almost as though he saw no walls. "None of us is a revolutionary." He stopped by the window. "We love the Emperor as we love that memorial out there on which his great ancestress is enthroned. The Empress is almost alive again, like all those who have been dead long enough. She has left her throne up there in the Hofburg to her heirs. The Emperor is dead, but he still sits on his throne. He rules from a memorial and is surrounded by memorial figures. They sit high up on horseback. Their horses proudly raise their hoofs and prance—but they can no longer touch the ground. They're made of stone. Do you understand what I mean?" Again he paced up and down the room. "Perhaps it is too late to breathe life into the stone. Perhaps the memorials of the Monarchy are only alive in our visions. But if belief in the soul of our statues is lost nothing is left. Nothing." He came to a stop in front of Ilona. "What do we want? It would be better to ask me what we don't want. We don't want war. And we should be certain to lose it—with a stone Emperor, memorial figures, and petrified horses." He lowered his voice. "The Heir Apparent is with us. We have our men at Court, in the Reichsrat, in the Army. Sztankay's influence on the General Staff is increasing. Vitzthum is beginning to win a hearing in the Ballhausplatz. Francis Ferdinand will exert his personal influence to have me appointed ambassador to St Petersburg. A Prince Kontowski in St Petersburg would convince the Slavs of our upright intentions." He sat down beside her. The feverish glitter in his eyes disappeared; tired veils sank down over them again. "You must picture history as a closed circle," he went on. "There is no progress and no regress, for with progress we move back and with regress we draw nearer to the beginning. The end of one slavery is the start of another; with the end of freedom it begins all over again. Peace moves towards war, war towards peace. In hope there is fear and in fear hope. Happy is he who lives in unhappy times, and woe to him who imagines himself happy! The Flood itself, the end of sin, was the beginning of sin. Noah cursed Canaan, and his children's children built the Tower of Babel." He fell silent. "I shall neither impel history forward nor retard it. All my friends and I want is not to be statues when it takes place."

It was on a March night in 1911 that Kontowski spoke thus to Ilona. She tried to understand what he meant. She assumed the colour of the man, as the chameleon assumes the colour of its environment. She read the gazettes and observed what was going on around her with new eyes; she heard speeches, proclamations, conversations, and gossip with new ears.

The leaves of the calendar were still falling slowly, like leaves of trees on a windless autumn day. The year 1911 drew to a close; the year 1912 rose and sank. At the end of November the newspapers reported that His Majesty had been graciously pleased to appoint His Highness Prince Taszilo Kontowski Imperial and Royal Austrian Ambassador to the Court of the Tsar. The Imperial Russian Government had approved the appointment. Early in December Kontowski left for St Petersburg.

Six weeks later Ilona followed him.

It was January, January 1913.

Part Two: 1913 to 1918

ILONA LOOKED OUT OF THE DRAWING-ROOM WINDOW OF HER VILLA into the night. The full moon seemed to be frozen to the sky. It gave the impression of eternally illuminating an eternal light. The snow was blue, like a frozen lake.

She had been in St Petersburg for more than six weeks. The villa—fourteen spacious rooms with towers, nooks, and side-passages, a kind of temple in which no god would have felt at home—stood on the Krestovsky Island, one of the countless islands connected to the city by narrow bridges. At the bottom of the garden flowed the Neva. It made a dark band through the snow, as though invisible hands were rolling a black carpet across the white landscape. Gigantic blocks of ice were floating downstream. The church bells echoed plaintively through the rumble of cracking ice as if announcing some disaster.

Kontowski had been invited, with other ambassadors, to call on the Tsar in the Winter Palace. He lived in the embassy, but he spent almost every evening with Ilona. This was only her second evening alone.

She went across to the little Empire writing-desk and sat down. A letter from her father, written on a long sheet of foolscap in a neat chancery hand, lay upon it. Next to it lay an envelope bearing Teréz's upright and strangely restless handwriting. A coloured drawing peeped out of it, Zita's drawing. It depicted the Ringstrasse covered in snow. The Parliament building looked like the witch's gingerbread house, the trees like white dumplings on skewers.

Teréz's letter had taken several weeks to get there. Ilona thought of her own journey through Bohemia and Poland and endless Russia. "Russia is unconquerable because it is so vast," the British ambassador had said to her the previous day. It was vast and remote—remote from everywhere. She sometimes had the feeling that the endless field of snow through which her train had ploughed lay between her and her past. And yet the roads that lead back are a hundred times longer than the roads that lead forward.

To-morrow a diplomatic courier would leave for Vienna. The censor was difficult, so the courier provided a good opportunity to write to Teréz.

She dipped her pen in the ink, but could find no words. What she had to describe was unreal; Teréz wouldn't understand it. She remembered the supper Prince Gabriel Constantinovich had given in the ambassador's honour soon after her arrival. It was an "intimate gathering," with eighteen guests. Behind each guest stood two liveried footmen. At table Ilona sat facing a painting showing a banquet famed in Russian history. The picture was teeming with gold-braided red-white-and-blue uniforms, footmen in silk breeches, and ladies with crowns of feathers and brilliants; gold cutlery and cut-glass vessels glittered on the table. Suddenly Ilona realized that she was sitting in the same room, at the same table, which was laid with the same gold. Even the footmen seemed to be the same, although the painting must have been at least a hundred years old. She looked round to see if she was enclosed in a gilt frame. She couldn't be sure whether the picture had come to life or she had turned into a picture. Had the dead awakened, or was she dead?

She had always been afraid of dreams—of her own, and even of those related by others. What could be more uncanny than to see oneself and have no power over oneself? Even beautiful dreams were nightmares. St Petersburg was a nightmare, terrifying even in its beauty.

Once more she dipped her pen in the ink in vain.

During her first week she had been to the Marinsky Theatre, where Glinka's *A Life for the Tsar* was on, an opera as patriotic as the school performances on the Austrian Emperor's birthday. The gentlemen wore evening-dress embellished with decorations; the ladies ermine and chinchilla coats. There was a sparkling in the darkened auditorium. No one seemed to be listening. Nothing linked the stage with the auditorium. The actors were as much alone as during a rehearsal. The ladies and gentlemen were as alone in the boxes as in the shop-windows.

Ilona put down her pen. The strange furniture looked at her, not hostilely, but indifferently, as strange people look. Who had lived here before her? And who before them? Had they moved out, or had they

102

died? She became a stranger to herself as she looked round. She had wanted to rise high, and she had merely travelled far. She tried to feel proud of what she had achieved, but she couldn't manage it. People could feel proud when they had achieved what they set out to do. Had she wanted to become the mistress of the Imperial and Royal Ambassador to the Court of the Tsar? Had she wanted to spin political webs in princely drawing-rooms? Had she wanted to go so far from her father, her sisters, her child? The pinnacles still called to her. But she wanted to stand on them with earth under her feet. She didn't want to float above them as in dreams that were nightmares.

2

At length she wrote:

My Dearest Sister,

I was delighted to receive your letter, and hasten to answer your questions—those you have asked and those you have left unasked.

I should like to reassure you: my position here is not as difficult as you seem to suppose. It is true that Taszilo says scornfully that society is even more hypocritical than at home—"they imagine they are being perpetually watched not only by the Tsar, but also by God Himself"—but for that very reason their laws don't apply to les étrangers. They treat foreigners with great respect, though it may only be because they look upon them as beings from another world. Thus they see nothing amiss in a Hungarian baroness spending the 'season' in St Petersburg and enjoying the special patronage of the embassy. I am beginning to understand how much arrogance may lie in the tolerant exemption of foreigners from one's own austere principles. I am accepted here, but I shall never be at home here. (Was I at home in Budapest or Vienna? One is probably never at home anywhere except where one has asked a passing pedestrian the time in the playground.)

I am invited out almost every evening, to parties, the ballet, or clubs. The ballet at the Imperial Theatre—we saw Tschaikovsky's Swan Lake there—is the best in the world, and I am not surprised that Karsavina is revered as though she were the Tsarina. Such pomp prevails in the houses to which we are so hospitably invited that I haven't been able to return any of these invitations yet, although I have six servants besides the coachman. At every banquet conversation revolves around the next one.

I don't think it was only for personal reasons that Taszilo sent for me so soon. High politics are carried on in drawing-rooms to a far greater extent than with us. Every afternoon we take tea at the houses of four or five aristocratic women. When people aren't talking about parties they are discussing politics, and because the women have nothing else to do they have a great deal to say. (The men are very polite and pay one the most charming compliments, but they're in a hurry to proceed from politeness to politics.) There is far more talk here than in Vienna about a coming war. Taszilo considers that his task is to convince St Petersburg of our peaceful intentions. I am supposed to help him in this. Are you laughing about your little sister who is making history? I, on the contrary, tremble. Ever since Mr Páloczi tried to teach us history at school (I think I forgot to send him my condolences when his sister died) I have always imagined world history to be full of wise men, heroes, and royal women, who hold the key to great mysteries and speak with tongues that we don't understand. Things are quite different, Teréz, and terrifyingly simple. As we were on our way to tea with the Grand-duchess Maria Petrovna last Friday Taszilo told me our hostess was bound to ask me what people in Vienna thought about the prospects of war. "The Emperor is eighty-three, Imperial Highness," I was to reply, "and he does not wish to hear the thunder of cannon on his death-bed." We hadn't even gathered round the boiling samovar when the Grand-duchess took me aside and questioned me about feeling in Vienna regarding a war. How great was my surprise, however, when five days later Grand-duke Nikolai Nikolaievich, commander of the Imperial Guard, came up to me with a fatherly smile during an interval at the Marinsky Theatre and remarked, "You put that very neatly, Baroness, about the death-bed and the thunder of cannon. May God grant you are right!" My sally had made the rounds. He had heard about it at the Tsar's luncheon-table.

I've heard the most amazing things since I have been here. The Empress, Alexandra Feodorovna, is said to be completely in the hands of the "Staretz," a bearded peasant named Rasputin, in whom she sees "Boshy Tschelloviek," the Man of God, and whose miraculous powers she hopes may cure the Tsarevich, the heir to the throne. One part of the aristocracy hates the "Old Man" —that is what "Staretz" means, although Rasputin is little over forty—another woos his favour. They are called the "Rasputinitzky." To many people the Empress is a saint; others whisper that she is having an affair with the moujik. People speak of the Tsar as of a god, yet he is not held in nearly so much honour as our Emperor. The British ambassador, whom I like best of all my new acquaintances, said to me yesterday when we were taking tea with the wife of the Lord High Chamberlain, Mrs Narishkin, "You must distinguish between the mystical Christian religious beliefs of the people and the pagan Hellenistic beliefs of society. To the nobility the Tsar's Court is an Olympus, with the love affairs, jealousies, vanities, feuds, and gossip of the Greek abode of the gods."

But my letter is rambling on and on, and I am supposed to be telling you about myself. There has been little change since my last letter. I knew I was journeying into a foreign country, but I had no idea how foreign to myself I was going to become. When the Princess Maria Nikolaievna (she is the most beautiful woman in St Petersburg) keeps talking about the warlike deeds of her ancestors I think of Papa. Then I want to talk about Kisnémet station, and I'm ashamed of myself for not doing so. When I repeat the sentences Taszilo has taught me I feel a fraud. You may say that the height of arrogance is to want to stay true to oneself. Perhaps so. Anyhow, I know of nothing which I should consider it worth while to gain at the expense of losing myself.

Need I tell you how great is my longing for Vienna, for you, for my child? Taszilo, who is touchingly considerate, knows of my homesickness. He has promised that I can return home not later than the beginning of July, and for not less than six weeks. Let us hope we can all be at Berény again on July 15.

God bless you! My heart contracts when I think of Zita. I know that she has you and that she thinks of me less than I think of her. (Parents love their children more than they are loved by them. And with every generation children love their parents less. Will there be any love left in the end?)

I was reassured by what you wrote about the child. Did she get the Finnish doll for her collection? The courier is bringing a Russian one with him. The fur collar must be on the way. Is it true that she has completely recovered from her cold? I'd rather you rang Dr Schlichter too often than too seldom! Why doesn't Lajos write? But you couldn't know that; it's only to me that Vienna and Kisnémet seem so close together: all places seem close together and only St Petersburg far from everywhere.

Take Zita in your arms. I kiss you, my beloved sister.

Your

ILONA

P.S. Zoltán Szomoru is giving a concert here next week.

She sealed the letter with her signet. The red tears dropped slowly on to the envelope. She blew out the candle.

3

Not until twenty-four hours before the concert did she tell the Prince that Zoltán Szomoru, born in her own village, was conducting in St Petersburg.

It was afternoon. They were sitting in her boudoir, a small room next to the bedroom furnished in the rococo style, which appeared to Ilona the cosiest of all her rooms.

"Is Szomoru really from Kisnémet?" smiled Kontowski. "You've never mentioned it before. Kisnémet—birthplace of the famous!" He continued absent-mindedly: "Could you manage without my company? I'm expecting the courier from Vienna."

She agreed; indeed, she asked herself whether she would have gone to the Narodny Dom with the Prince. She had been alone when Zoltán first conducted in Budapest. Now she was driven by curiosity, like some one who has buried a treasure in the garden of his childhood and, long since grown-up, grubs in the soil to see whether the childhood treasure is still there. She wasn't sure whether she wanted to find the buried feeling; she was only sure that she must find out whether it was still there. This was her own soil, foreign to the Prince.

Kontowski lit a cigarette, inhaled deeply a few times, then held it between his fingers as though forgotten.

"The courier will bring no good news," he said. "The Turks have finally lost the Balkan War. By May at the latest they will have to give up the area west of the Enos-Midia line."

"At least there won't be any fighting," she commented absent-mindedly.

"It wasn't a war; it was a dress rehearsal. The victors are already fighting over the spoils. The Russians are egging on the Serbs, we the Bulgarians."

"Then is it true that we want war?"

"That's not the point. The statesmen of all nations wear Gessler hats. They are called prestige. For a time the hats are saluted by others. That is called greatness. Then they are no longer saluted. Prestige and greatness turn into war. It is fought in the name of an honour that doesn't exist."

"No honour? . . ."

He shook his head. "The concepts of honour for the individual have stood firm for centuries. To remain honourable it is enough to stick to them. There is no changing, no growing honour in private life: a man dies with the same honour with which he was born. But the honour of nations rises and falls like stocks and shares. It is negotiated on the stock exchange of power. The nations decide what is compatible or incompatible with their honour according to their power."

She was listening with only half an ear. Was it a matter of indifference to Kontowski that she was going to the concert alone? During the first few years she had suffered from his jealousy. She had more admirers now than ever, but Kontowski didn't notice. He seemed certain that she couldn't dispense with the wisdom he poured into her young soul, the excitement of his thoughts in which he allowed her to share. Out of pity or aversion, convenience or fear, she had tried to make him forget that she had a body. Perhaps she had succeeded.

She noticed that he was waiting for her to raise an objection. He was used to her interrupting him as a sign that she had understood.

"What you say sounds cynical," she said, rather too late.

He laughed. "I once looked the word up in a dictionary. 'Cynical' was defined as 'mean, shameless, impudent,' whereas a 'cynic' was defined as 'a man without illusions.' So a man without illusions is supposed to be mean, shameless, impudent. What nonsense! The man without illusions is humble because he respects reality, frank because he does not shrink from speaking the truth, and shameless only in the sense that he scorns universally protected tabus."

"Perhaps people are prepared to put up with misunderstandings," she said, "because frankness is unbearable."

He stroked the bridge of his nose.

"The conflicts between us are not insoluble," he said, "but the tabus forbid us to give them independence, while our morality forbids us to suppress them, although one of these two paths must be followed if war is to be avoided. I am alone with my cynicism, surrounded by honourable tabus. I can do no more."

106

She said nothing, she asked nothing, she maintained a stubborn silence. She was thinking of the dress she would wear to-morrow. The white one was too low-cut, the blue too discreetly high-necked; another white one too pompous, the black one too simple. She didn't care whether Machiavelli was right. The Prince reminded her of a peacock spreading out his feathers in a farmyard and hissing because the other animals take no notice of him. They are looking for grains, laying eggs, and mating. In vain the peacock shows them that he is more beautiful than they.

Kontowski noticed nothing. "In Vienna they think they can isolate the Russians," he said. "I can't convince the Ballhausplatz that the French and British are in deadly earnest."

An hour later he left. She was glad when he left. She wanted to get used to loneliness.

4

As though seeking to postpone the hour of sleeplessness, she wandered about the house. She feared the night.

At night she had often met Zoltán. She hadn't always seen his face. Sometimes he wore a mask, another man's features. But she knew that it was he. She feared the sweet nightmares, and yet, when she awoke from them, she wanted to go on dreaming. She often lay for a long time in a twilight state, her hot body feeling as though torn apart because she stretched out one hand towards the dream and the other towards reality to frighten it away. As soon as reality prevailed she began to be tormented by the question of why she received all the delight she had renounced more violently, more fiercely, more orgiastically, from the dream figure of Zoltán than she ever had in Feri's arms, why she had to remain faithful to him who had never possessed her. After such nights she felt she ought to confess what she had dreamed as if it had really happened.

That night she slept without dreaming, and the following day the only evidence of her excitement was the way she busied herself with all sorts of things she had postponed for ages or which were quite superfluous, as if she dared not think of anything joyful in case the joy might be exhaustion in anticipation.

Not till the afternoon did the embassy succeed in obtaining a seat in the second row of the orchestra stalls. The concert by the Budapest Philharmonic Orchestra was sold out. The fame of this conductor of only thirty-one had reached the capital of the Tsar, and it spoke for his audacity that among other pieces he had elected to play Tschaikovsky's Sixth Symphony.

Ilona studied herself in the mirror in five or six dresses. She still wrinkled her forehead in front of the mirror—no longer in order to look older, but out of habit or anger with the mirror for not slavishly answering "Yes" to all her questions. Finally she chose a rust-brown evening-dress made for her by Mademoiselle Lorrain from Paris. The patterned brocade clung closely round her knees, while the upper part fell like a gauzy curtain from the bust over the hips. A stiff lace collar framed bosom, throat, and shoulders; its white fused with the white of the skin, emphasizing the nakedness it concealed.

While the hairdresser was doing her hair for what seemed to be the hundredth time—she wore it on top of her head, in a style of her own, with a thick plait wreathing the rising waves—she made up her mind not to visit Zoltán, not to speak to him; on the previous occasion, in Budapest, she hadn't spoken to him either. A fleeting glance from the stage should be enough to convince him of her prosperity, her beauty, and her happiness.

She did not know that unhappy love always flaunts the happiness it has found without being loved in return.

5

March had come, but only the dirty snow lying like a discarded coal-sack on the Nevsky Prospekt bespoke the end of winter. The cold forced its way into the closed coach and reddened Ilona's cheeks. Her ears were numb. Music came from the churches and coffee-houses—organ notes and gipsy violins. She glanced at the clock on the slender tower of the Duma. She didn't want to be late, but she didn't want to be too early either. She was going to a rendezvous with some one who was quite unaware that they had one.

When she entered the concert-hall she was no longer alone. The girl who had once entered the Vigadó was walking beside her. Like a mother taking out her half-grown daughter, she looked at her shadow. How provincial was her invisible daughter's dress, how *gauche* her movements! And how radiant she herself by comparison! She regretted that the rostrum was still empty and the conductor could not watch the admiration inspired on all sides by the lady in the clinging sable.

Zoltán Szomoru looked older than she remembered him, older than his years. Two lines joined the wings of his nose and the corners of his mouth. The waves that had passed over his forehead had left undulations behind them. Wrinkles of experience, not of age, still superficial, still capable of being wiped away. Ilona compared herself with him. What had she experienced? She felt a greater likeness to her shadow, about which she had just been smiling.

For the first part of his programme the conductor had chosen Brahms's Fourth Symphony in E Minor, not by chance, but because he could rely on the Russian public's appreciation of such ecclesiastical music influenced by Bach.

The pious hush in the half-darkened hall and the pious melodies weaving this way and that within it were in exciting contrast to the personality of the conductor. It seemed to Ilona as though the gilded splendour of the hall were giving place to a cloistered twilight; as though the white shirt-fronts were turning into penitential shirts; as though the rounded arches of the boxes were changing into church windows, the red stalls into wooden pews. A devil, it seemed, was conducting in a church. Among willing witches, the devil is a dull fellow. But here he had crept into a convent, the only male creature among nuns. The nuns revered his sex. The conductor did no violence to Brahms's music. The seducer scorned force. The virgins threw off their clothes. Thirstily they offered themselves. Satan did not take them. Driven to ecstasy by his baton, the naked choir danced around him.

Or did all this exist only in the fevered imagination of the women in the auditorium? She turned away from the rostrum, as though to make the other women as naked as she. Her imagination undressed them.

Then the symphony drew near to its end. This was the part of the work that had led the conductor to choose this particular one of Brahms's symphonies. The liturgical music now became, indeed, a round-dance, almost a slow waltz in three-four time, the old Italian *passacaglia* against the background of an obstinate double-bass, so that the virgins seemed to be waltzing in a storm: a menace hung over the ecstasy, and the round-dance was being performed at the foot of the judgment seat.

The lights slowly returned. The applause was as orgiastic as the concert. The conductor, who had hurried away, had to show himself again. His way of expressing thanks was strange. He walked on to the stage with uncertain steps, his head lowered as though still enveloped by his music; once on the stage he came to an abrupt stop and, instead of bowing, raised his head stiffly to the gallery—a sleepwalker startled out of his dream, filled not with self-confidence, but with sudden consciousness of himself.

Because he seemed to see no one Ilona was sure he hadn't seen her either. She could still feel his hand on her body, as on nights when she had woken from wild nightmares. She had to follow it, search for it, find it. Her legs carried her, but they were soft like the carpets under her feet. Blindly she made a path for herself through the festal throng. She scarcely saw the attendant from whom she asked the way to the dressing-room. A steel door clicked shut behind her. In the semi-darkness she stumbled along between double-basses, violin-cases, harps, and music-stands. The dressing-room door was open.

Zoltán was surrounded by admirers. He was leaning against a bust accepting bouquets, which he passed on to a man standing behind him. He didn't notice Ilona.

She stood still and watched him, content to be able to spy upon the unsuspecting man as in her dreams, where he was helpless at the mercy of her imagination. She had difficulty in recognizing him. Was it possible that a moonstruck man shouted to on the roof-ridge could suddenly be so sure-footed? The face, changing swiftly from alert attentiveness, serious reflection, and jesting charm, was more like a mime's that a musician's. The deep-blue eyes were not gazing into invisible regions, but into the eyes of beautiful women and reverent men. Perhaps this wizard conjured music from violins, flutes, and trumpets as a fairground magician conjured paper flowers and rabbits out of his hat, to the amazement and delight of the crowd, but conscious of every one of his tricks and unmoved by his own hocus-pocus. He was a conjurer, not a devil. Ilona's strength returned.

"Ilona!"

The ladies and gentlemen round the conductor parted. Zoltán came towards Ilona with outstretched arms. He took her by the hand with an almost fatherly gesture. He led her into a corner, to the bust of Mussorgsky. His shirt was soaking wet, his collar crumpled. The damp had made his thick hair wavy. There were a few white hairs on his temples. It was good to see him exhausted.

"I haven't had time to change yet," he apologized, indicating the crowd. "How glad I am that you have come to see me! I've turned the whole of St Petersburg upside down looking for you."

"Did you know I was here?"

"How could I not have known?" He didn't explain further. "I'm having supper with some friends in my hotel. Will you come?"

"I don't know. . . ."

"You must! Suite three hundred and one in the Hôtel de Paris."

"You've taken me by surprise. I only wanted to congratulate you. . . ."

"In heaven's name! The concert isn't over. I've still got to deal the Russians Tschaikovsky." 'Deal' was the word he used. He took her by the wrist and held her out in front of him like a work of art. "How beautiful my little girl has grown, how bewitchingly beautiful!"

She blushed.

"Your little girl is married and the mother of a big daughter."

"I know. I know everything." He raised his eyebrows. The waves on his forehead continued into the waves of his hair. "Are you accompanied?"

"No, I'm alone." She regretted that the Prince was waiting for the courier.

"So much the better! An ambassador would have been out of place in our humble company." He beckoned to the man in evening-dress who had been standing behind him by the bust of Beethoven. "Mr Hajdu—the Baroness Von Rattowitz. The Baroness is going to give us the pleasure of her company after the concert. Will you accompany her. . . ."

"Thank you, I have my coach," interjected Ilona.

"I want to make sure you come. Hajdu, see that the Baroness doesn't give you the slip!"

"With pleasure, Maestro." Mr Hajdu bowed. "May I remind you . . ."

"Yes, I must go and change. See you soon, Ilona."

He kissed her hand. The dressing-room had emptied.

In the doorway Ilona looked round again.

Zoltán was standing alone in the middle of the room. He no longer saw her. His figure stood out black against the white background made up of the marble busts of Beethoven, Mussorgsky, Mozart. He was undoing his tie. He looked as he had looked on the rostrum. Yet music could not have transformed him now. He was gazing into the void, as though practising a lost look. He was moving away with swaying steps. The moonstruck man was wandering through the moonless night.

She didn't recognize Mr Hajdu immediately. It wasn't until she was sitting beside him in the coach that she lost sight of Zoltán. She thought of Kontowski. What would he say if he found out that she was on her way to supper at the Hôtel de Paris? She had no need to frighten away the thought, but she did try to get rid of the unaccountable feeling of satisfaction that came with it.

Mr Hajdu talked unceasingly. He was Zoltán's secretary, an unpaid secretary, because he came of a wealthy family and had no need to earn his living; he had been following the conductor for years across half the world. He resembled one of those rubber dogs that are given to puppies to try out their teeth on. The short-sighted eyes behind thick lenses lit up when he spoke of the "Maestro," and he never referred to him by any other name, like lackeys who measure their own rank by their master's. When he heard that Ilona had known the Maestro from birth he treated her too like a higher being.

Zoltán's drawing-room in the Hôtel de Paris was a large, oval room between two bedrooms, one of which was occupied by Mr Hajdu. The bedroom doors were closed. Flowers, anonymous flowers such as men receive, stood in vases, ice-buckets, and champagne bottles. Beside them the hotel palms in their blue earthenware pots decorated in the *art nouveau* style looked like paper plants. Two huge oil-paintings in thick frames depicted Napoleon's snow-covered retreat from Moscow and a gay sleigh-ride through St Petersburg. Between them hung a portrait of Tsar Nicholas II in a simple grey uniform. Ilona thought of the Austro-Hungarian Emperor. Compared with him the Tsar was a paltry tram-conductor. The city lights flickered through the half-drawn velvet curtains. There was a musty smell, like that in the entrance-hall of a mortuary.

Ilona found it not unpleasant to be the only woman among five men. The master of the house hadn't appeared yet. He was going to rest for half an hour, for he needed the relaxation, or, as Mr Hajdu put it, an "unmusical caesura." Three of the gentlemen were Hungarian, and since the legendary politeness of Hungarians comes to an end at the point where they have to speak a foreign language, the conversation was carried on in Hungarian. The two others, a Frenchman and a man of Slav appearance, seemed to have accepted this; in any event the conversation would have revolved around no other subject than the concert and no other person than the Maestro. The Frenchman, a Baron de Colignac, had joined the rest of the group years ago, while the Pole, a Mr Kollontai, had joined them months ago. With the exception of the grey-haired first solo violinist, they were all young men between twenty and thirty, wealthy idlers who basked in the rays of their self-chosen sun.

Two waiters were serving champagne. The gentlemen grouped themselves round the guest. They were visibly delighted by Ilona's presence, but she soon realized that their interest related solely to the woman who was able to chat so freely about the Maestro's childhood and youth. Mr Hajdu, who kept squinting anxiously at the bedroom door;

the old first violinist, whose approving smile seemed to apply once and for all to the whole evening; little Mr Weiss, a Budapest Jew, who replied to each of Ilona's tales with anecdotes about Zoltán and looked worried because his stories fell flat—they were figures on a monument and rather ludicrous, because the figure they adoringly surrounded hadn't yet mounted the pedestal.

At last one of the two bedroom doors opened. Incense filled the room. Zoltán was still wearing his black evening-dress trousers, patent-leather shoes, fresh white shirt, and white tie, but instead of the dress-coat he had put on a short wine-red jacket with silk lapels and a white chrysanthemum in the buttonhole. Halting for a moment in the doorway, he took a long cigarette-holder out of his mouth, and now Ilona noticed that he was smoking a special kind of cigarette that gave off incense instead of the usual tobacco-smoke.

The Maestro received the homage of his disciples. He seemed to do so without vanity, without false modesty, with a touch of irony that was directed towards no one but himself. As he came up to Ilona he stubbed out his cigarette and, bending down to her ear, said, "I have to bathe myself in incense so as not to feel the incense my ministrants scatter around me."

After he had sat down at the head of the table, with Ilona on his right, he finally brushed away the compliments like tiresome flies. He spoke only to Ilona, transferring the adulation of the company to her, so to speak, as if the place on the pedestal belonged to her and he himself were lying at her feet. If he drew the dumbfounded men into the conversation it was only to tell them stories of his youth in which Ilona played the main part. The distant village became the centre of the globe, the figure of the stationmaster huge, and the station-house a palace.

The food was copious and colourful in the Russian manner. The caviare-bowl was passed round. There were compotes of numerous fruits accompanying roast meat and fowl, salads and gherkins, and all kinds of delicacies. They drank *subrovna,* spirits smelling of perfume, from tubby little bottles. Afterwards the waiters poured out champagne. When the Turkish coffee had been distributed they left the table and gathered in small groups.

Zoltán and Ilona sat in plush armchairs under a potted palm, separated by a small round table on whose red-velvet top they had placed their glasses. The babble of voices seemed to come to them from far away.

"Is your daughter in Vienna?" asked Zoltán. He spoke in an intimate tone.

"Yes, with Teréz. How do you know?"

"Is there anything I don't know about you?"

He smiled. From a gold cigarette-case he drew a long Russian cigarette, not one of his incense cigarettes. Only a faint hint of incense still hung about the room.

"I knew I should find you," he said. "That's why I had plenty of time. When a man and a woman find each other they say they have

112

never lived before. The later they find each other the younger they stay."

"You have lived a great deal, Zoltán."

"People say so. They say it because they envy me. Not for my talent. Not for my fame. Others too have talent and fame. They envy me because I have the courage to live as I please. They will forgive you talent, success, and wealth. Only happiness they won't forgive. Undeserved happiness. They consider all happiness undeserved. It's really not you they're angry with, but Fate. Why should Fate have made you a present? They're unhappy because they daren't do what they would like to do. They call your courage happiness, their own cowardice unhappiness."

"Have you been happy?" she interrupted him.

"I could return your question. You and I have the courage to seek happiness. That is the adventure from which the others run away—into their miserable security. What you did was courageous. That's why you are my sister."

She thought of Kontowski. The happiest couple would be brother and sister, he used to say—if they weren't brother and sister.

He touched her hand. She looked up. The guests had left. Only Mr Hajdu and the Frenchman were standing by one of the high arched windows talking in low voices.

He leaned back. With half-closed eyes he said, "It's a fairy-story that love passes. It floats in space like the astral bodies of the dead. We still love all those we have ever loved. Why did I know that I had been waiting for you the moment I caught sight of you over the heads of my fans? Because the air is heavy with all the unkissed kisses. The wind carries them like pollen."

These were light words. She knew this, and yet she picked them up as if they were heavy. He spoke as though to himself, no doubt as a precaution against the banality of the words hurting her. She felt the caution and the banality, but she wasn't hurt by either of them. His face was no longer the face of the peasant-boy who had walked through the sunshine-yellow fields naked to the waist. It wasn't the face of the seeker after applause, nor the face of the mocker. But neither was it genuine, any more than his light words were genuine. She longed with a hungry curiosity to see the genuine face. She wouldn't put the light out as he bent down over her. She wouldn't close her eyes before his mouth.

He was talking about himself again, this time, too, without vanity. It was a breathless narration, as though he had to catch up on years in a matter of minutes, so that a stranger should not embrace a stranger.

"You and I together will be invincible," he said.

"Do you think I didn't know all about you?" she said.

She had long ago noticed that the secretary and the Frenchman had slipped away. Probably they always did that when the Maestro invited a woman to their parties.

The bells of St Catherine's Church struck the first hour of the morning. The other bells joined in. The bells didn't threaten, as in the lonely house on the Krestovsky Island.

She stood up.

He misunderstood her gesture, imagined she was going to leave. There was something like horror in his eyes as he rose to bar her path.

"I'm not going," she said.

She disarmed the seducer. Happiness was courage. He could take her because she gave herself to him.

The bedroom windows were open. She drew deep breaths of the cold night air. So he hadn't been expecting her. She felt happy because the windows were open.

She stood still in the doorway as he closed the windows. The curtain fell as though over a theatrical backcloth in which the lights of the city were only tiny dots.

He came up to her. She closed he eyes.

With closed eyes she felt for the golden cord of the bedside lamp. She didn't see the face that bent over her.

7

He sent her yellow roses. They turned the house on the island in the Neva into a rose-garden. He sent her a letter. "I have found you, and I shall never leave you again."

The same day he had to leave for Paris.

Again she wandered about the house all day long without doing anything. People only acted in order not to think. Why act when you were happy?

Instead of banishing the memory of the night, she called it up. She saw what the darkness had hidden. She filled every word Zoltán had spoken with a new meaning. He could break away from her, but he remained behind within her. Perhaps it is love for a man that first distinguishes a woman from a man. For him love was the extinction of her past; for her the conjuring up of his yesterdays. For him love was confirmation; for her transformation.

She called her conscience, but it didn't reply. Eight years ago, when she met Kontowski, she had slipped out of her body as one slips out of a dress. But then she was eighteen, and the dress she had taken off was new. Now she was twenty-six, and it was still new. Her conscience couldn't speak, because it was housed in her body and her body ordered it to keep silent.

For the first time she had not changed for supper when the Prince was announced.

8

Kontowski was even paler than usual. He didn't inquire about the concert. He didn't seem to notice the roses.

The little table was laid in the corner of the dining-room. The candles flickered in the heavy candlesticks. Beyond them the flames of the logs in the fireplace rose and fell. In the silver of the candelabra Ilona saw her own face, reduced in size and distorted. The Prince's face looked as if the yellow wax of the candles had flowed over his features. The early-spring storm was tearing at the window-panes. It was hot in the room.

"I must talk to you," said Kontowski.

She turned pale. In the nervous lights she couldn't see his eyes.

He spoke, but she knew he wanted to say something different from what he was saying.

"The news from Vienna," he said, " has exceeded my worst fears."

"What do you mean?" She had forgotten the conversation in her boudoir.

"War is only a question of time."

War! she thought. If war came she would have to go back to Vienna. Zoltán wouldn't be able to travel any more. The separation from Zita would be at an end. She didn't hesitate to translate the runes of the times into her own language.

"Shall we win the war?" she asked.

"We shall lose it. Not because we are in the wrong, but because we are the weaker."

"In that case the weaker would always have to give in."

"He has to at the end of the war anyhow. Madness pronounces a military defeat honourable, a peaceful one dishonourable." He picked at his fish, but didn't eat. "It will be the most terrible war of all time. Our world will perish in it."

Your world! she thought. Taken aback, she put down her knife and fork. She hadn't known before that his world was different from hers. The twenty or twenty-one years that separated them suddenly seemed to her as endless as the endless Russian steppes. But it wasn't the endlessness that mattered. Somewhere in the steppe rose boundary-posts. On this side of the turnpikes was the world in which they had lived together. But there was also a world beyond the turnpikes. This world was closed to Kontowski. What his tired eyes couldn't see mustn't exist. She didn't want to stop at his frontiers.

"The world won't perish, Taszilo," she said.

"It's beyond your comprehension."

"Because I'm too young?" she said irritably.

He talked about the war as though it had already broken out, as though it were already over.

"People standing on the edge of an abyss," he said, "don't ask themselves how they got there. They stare down into the abyss. It draws them. Do you know how they got there?"

"No," she replied, as though she didn't want to know.

He smiled. "They got there along a path. That is the one certainty. They must have got there along a path," he reiterated. "Instead of leaping into the abyss, all they have to do is turn round. But that's just what they don't do. They prefer to die rather than be untrue to the vain goal that is called 'Forward.' "

"If they are standing on the edge of an abyss," she interrupted him, "they must have taken the wrong path."

"Yes, but it wasn't wrong from the beginning. They must have gone wrong somewhere, at the crossroads."

"Where?"

"I don't know. We must go back to the crossroads. We must find the other path, which doesn't lead to the abyss. It exists. But it isn't

115

given to man to grope his way backward. He strides on, even if it is to destruction. He sees the past as a single road, although it is not a road, but an endless countryside, with countless roads, the trodden and the untrodden."

He spoke as though under a compulsion. He is spinning a web of words around me, she thought, and the words to which she had hitherto clung became for her horrible traps. She no longer fought shy of comparing him with Zoltán. He was like a shadow, deep, penetrating, frightening. His voice seemed to come from a shadow in front of which no body stood. Zoltán stood in the midday sun, shadowless.

A rumbling sound interrupted the Prince's speech. The March wind was sweeping the snow off the roof. It sounded as though big, heavy men were clattering about on the roof.

"Can we take coffee in the drawing-room?" asked Kontowski. He repeated: "I must talk to you."

Between the door of the dining-room and the armchairs that had been moved in front of the fireplace of the little drawing-room stood a high, round gas-lamp on a showy base. As he passed Kontowski put out the light. Then it was the turn of the little lamp on one of the small tables. He acted deliberately, like a householder at night-fall. Only one table-lamp was still burning. He didn't notice the yellow roses in the vases.

"I went to the concert yesterday," she said provocatively.

"Tschaikovsky?"

"Yes, Tschaikovsky."

He sat down by the fireplace facing Ilona. He shifted the armchair a little to one side, as though to avoid the gleam of the burning logs.

"The audience went wild," she said.

She glanced at the roses.

"The embassy should have held a reception for Szomoru," he remarked.

Coffee was served. Ilona poured out.

"He has already left for Paris," she said, after dismissing the maid. He lit a cigarette.

I could tell him I was with him in the Hôtel de Paris—he wouldn't ask any questions, she thought. He would talk about the end of the world, drowning his fear in his voice. He's not afraid of losing me. Perhaps he is waiting for the end of the world, so that he doesn't have to see that he has lost me.

"You will be defenceless in St Petersburg when war breaks out," he said.

Now her heart beat more violently. Now she listened.

"Who knows," he went on, "what war will mean to us? Perhaps the worst thing about times of war is that our virtues and vices, our weaknesses and our will, no longer count. Fortune and misfortune are fashioned by the times."

He is saying good-bye to me, she felt. She blessed the times that became a will.

"I understand," she said quickly.

"You don't understand," he retorted. His voice sounded irritable.

"Don't worry about me."

"I can't prevent world history, but I can arm myself against it." He threw the unsmoked cigarette into the fire. "I have written to Rattowitz. The Vatican must annul your marriage. I want to marry you." He leaned his head back. Only his knees in the tight black trousers were in the light. "As my wife you will have nothing to fear," he said. "You will enjoy diplomatic privileges and be under the protection of Vienna."

His hands were lying on his knees; the fire seemed to be burning them.

The clock on the mantelpiece struck eleven times. They heard it through the sound of falling ice.

She felt no satisfaction, no triumph. She felt anger. For eight years she had suppressed the feeling of humiliation. He hadn't asked her if she would marry him; he had graciously permitted her to act as if she would have said no. Now that he asked her and anticipated her reply, he humiliated her. Her anger faded. She felt pity for his arrogance. Eight years, and he had nothing to offer her but diplomatic privileges and the protection of Vienna.

"Taszilo. . . ," she began, without knowing what she was going to say.

"I shall ask nothing of you except that you should stay with me," he said. "From the day I met you I have trembled at the thought that I should lose you. That would have been natural. But I can't tolerate our being parted by outside forces, senselessly and prematurely."

"If war breaks out," she said, "you will have to return to Vienna. I'll wait for you there."

His head moved in the darkness. "I don't deceive myself," he said. "You only stayed with me because I was able to prove to you afresh every day that I was indispensable to you. In Vienna you would wake from the sleep into which I have lulled you." He rose and stood in front of the fireplace.

Again he had uttered what she was thinking. It wasn't cleverness, not cleverness alone. How he must love her to have grasped the metamorphosis that had taken place in her! Eight years were not wiped out in a single night.

"I'm incurable," he said. "I've been to all the great doctors in the world. To the doctors and the quacks. I shan't torment you any more."

"You don't torment me," she said weakly.

"Mankind fears the great uncertainties." As often before, he spoke of mankind to avoid speaking of himself. As often before, he was talking for the sake of talking. "I fear the terrible certainties. Is there any uncertainty so terrible as the certainty of growing old? Or that one will stand at the graves of friends? Or that miracles are growing rarer every day? Every leaf of the calendar is torn off by the hand of death." He stopped. "You are young. Very young and very healthy. I know you will deceive me. You would deceive me if I were healthy. My illness protects me from pain." He was speaking fast. "War is incalculable. You must be able to dispose of my property if anything happens to me. A Princess Kontowski will be welcome everywhere.

117

And you must always be able to come back to me—must always have to come back to me."

She sat where she was. He spoke of infidelity as though it were inevitable, like growing old and dying. Every one knew he would grow old and die, but nobody believed it. She couldn't obtain a charter for a future that lay behind her.

"I can't marry you," she said. "I have already deceived you."

She thought he staggered. He stepped out of the light.

"I knew it," he said.

What a frightful misunderstanding! she thought. He was talking about adventures she had never had. He knew nothing about the night that was separated from this night by only one day.

He sat down and buried his head in his hands.

It was so quiet that the drops could be heard falling from the roof on to the ground, as though a clock were ticking outside the window. Each drop was a second.

"It isn't you who have deceived me," he said. "I have deceived you. To be ill is a terrible offence."

Why did I say it? she thought. The truth is senseless and painful. He isn't arrogant. He is proud. And he is great because he is capable of overcoming his pride. She felt no more pity, only admiration. He hadn't talked his love to pieces, only hidden his suffering behind words.

She heard his voice:

"I am asking you nothing. I shall never ask you anything. Have pity on me. Don't leave me alone."

At last she had the strength to rise to her feet.

The path to the other side of the fireplace seemed endless. It was as if she were walking through fields of snow. She could no longer see the boundary-posts. Who was she, to feel arrogance before this bowed pride? Where would she have ended up without him, who had no body and yet was stronger than anyone else? She had never felt so small as now that he was lowering himself to her. She had never been so grateful as now that she had learnt how much he needed her. He was right. A storm was blowing up. You could not go against the wind. You had to turn round: only with your eyes could you go forward. And if some one stretched out his hand to you you had to grasp it.

She laid her hand cautiously on his head. He looked up. The tears had trickled into the furrows of his face.

The tears flowed over her cheeks. She wanted to say, "I love you," but the truth was harder for her now than the lie had been before.

"I shall be your wife," she said.

She bent down and took his head in her hands.

9

Although Rattowitz did everything to comply with his powerful cousin's wish—the Baron lay in a Rome hospital tormented by an insidious attack of gout—Kontowski's connexions proved insufficiently powerful to bring about an annulment of the marriage. Twice the

118

Papal Rota dealt with the case of Ilona and Ferdinand Rattowitz, but on both occasions Prince Orsini, Kontowski's influential friend at the Vatican, had to report to St Petersburg that the cardinals regarded the existence of a legitimate child as incontrovertible evidence against dissolution of the marriage on the grounds of non-consummation.

The Prince didn't give up hope. Their Eminences couldn't bring themselves to pervert the laws of the Holy Roman Church, but they did accord the petition favoured treatment: instead of being rejected out of hand, it was merely postponed. The Holy Roman Church, which had seen greater changes of heart than this, waited for a change of heart on the part of the petitioner.

Ilona was glad. When she promised to marry Kontowski she hadn't thought of Zita. Then she had realized the consequences for the child and herself. Her position was false as well as grotesque. Her child bore the name of a man who was not her father. Whose name would she bear after the dissolution of the marriage? Her first marriage had been "unconsummated," as it was called in the parlance of the Papal *votanti* and *referendarii;* now she was to enter into a second in the certainty that this could not be consummated either.

Her conscience had awakened: it did not fall asleep again. Winter passed without any fresh meeting with Zoltán. In May he went to America, to New York, Boston, and San Francisco, hurrying from one triumph to another; he wasn't due back till September. He wrote Ilona ardent love-letters, sent cards, telegrams, newspaper criticisms, photographs. She waited for the post, and her answers were no less passionate than his. If this was infidelity she could excuse it so long as it was limited to words, so long as she did not become Kontowski's wife while perpetually ready to obey Zoltán's call. In her dreams Zoltán no longer wore the face of a stranger. The gentle disembodiment she had felt during the past eight years was gone. She didn't return men's glances, but she felt them. She could silence her blood, but she had to bear her body. She blessed the Church that spared her from hurting Kontowski.

In the summer she went to Kisnémet for four weeks. She stayed eight, till the beginning of September.

10

Zita was eight and a half—at the age when half-years are still counted. She was tall and lanky; healthy, but pale under her black hair; with huge blue eyes that stood out from her delicate face; possessing the beauty of those teasing and malicious, charming and crafty elves who remain children for a thousand years, or act as if they were children. Ilona was happy when she watched the child playing, but she didn't trust her play, because the playing child seemed to be playing the part of a child.

Ilona treated her daughter warily, and was at the same time ashamed of her wariness. She was disappointed because Zita had greeted her without jubilation, indeed, almost indifferently; but she was also depressed by the fact that as the weeks passed the child attached her-

119

self to her with overflowing love. She was glad the child looked upon Teréz as her second mother, but she was not free from jealousy of her sister. She felt that she ought to correct certain tendencies in Zita's nature, but she feared to begin an undertaking that would remain unfinished. She was tormented by the restraint she had to exercise in order that the parting should not be unbearable. She knew that many things were not really good for Zita, but only good because she was growing up without her mother.

One event that probably would not have happened if she had been present disconcerted Ilona.

Teréz had been at Berény with the child since June. One day, on their way to Kisnémet, they had met Count Aporfalvy's coach. The Count stopped his coach, climbed out, and spoke to Zita. Next day he sent her a pony—brown with a white mane; then a riding-master turned up. Before Teréz had time to decide the proper course to follow the Count appeared at the station-house as though by chance when the child was there, and since Zita couldn't remain indifferent to such a generous gentleman, she henceforth divided her affections between the stationmaster and the Count. True, the Count avoided Berény, but he was seen in the vicinity of the station-house almost as frequently as his son had been while he was wooing the sixteen-year-old Ilona Horváth. Ilona met the Count in her father's office; they greeted one another briefly and awkwardly.

Then she learnt of the curious friendship that united the two men. They would often sit until late in the evening under the green lamp in the station office, and the younger man grew older and older till finally there was no further difference between the fifty-year-old and the seventy-year old. They were brothers who had lost each other and belatedly found each other again. They remained silent a great deal; sometimes they talked in low voices. They talked about the past century as about a good man now dead, whose inheritance was being squandered by a reckless son. "If the father only knew . . ." they said. The stationmaster had ceased to be surprised that the Count had become his brother. At times anger rose in them and they considered marching out against the wild windmills of the twentieth century, Don Quixotes both. Then they looked at Zita and smiled. You could rely on grandchildren. Only children were hopeless.

11

That summer Ilona talked a great deal to Lajos. He still caused her worry, yet she felt a greater affinity with him than with Margit, who devoted herself entirely to the hotel, her husband, and her two children; a greater affinity even than with Teréz, who was totally absorbed by her love for Zita. Lajos hated the world in which Ilona lived, but he seemed to know what he hated. He lived as a poorly paid day-labourer with a large farmer named Hegedüs only a few miles from Berény. Ilona used to visit him. The elegant lady in her riding-habit stood in the tiny room separated only by a wooden partition from the stable. The room was low, dark, and built on mud.

Harness hung on the walls. It smelt of manure and cheap soap. But the room was full of books; even the foot of the open bed with the red peasant pillow was piled high with them. There were a great many pink paperbacks among the books, including a cheap edition of the works of Marx and Engels published by *Népszava,* the Socialist newspaper. There were, too, German and English text-books, Molière's plays, a dog-eared *Faust,* Baudelaire's poems. "Those are my weapons," said Lajos. He was now twenty-nine, and looked very masculine, like a man who stands with both feet on the ground he owns. He was often in conflict with the police, but he befuddled them with highfalutin speeches, till in the end they shrugged their shoulders and gave him a fool's freedom.

Ilona didn't consider him a fool. His fantastic prophecies resembled to a hair those she had heard in Kontowski's circles, only he seemed to desire what Kontowski feared. He never mentioned Ilona's visit to the Emperor. She often thought of the young soldier who had flown from the Sopron barracks to her. He had managed to remain unchanged and yet grow up.

The stationmaster did not judge his son; nor did he consider him a fool; but he admitted that he did not understand him.

Kisnémet station was no longer an island. Mihály Horváth knew this. He read newspapers in which war and revolution were discussed. A conspiracy had been discovered in the barracks at Csenger, on the Rumanian border, not far from Debreczen. A whole railway train full of arrested workers, as well as a few peasants and soldiers, stopped at Kisnémet. It was night. The prisoners asked for water. Máté and the stationmaster brought it. The prisoners sang songs about some one called Pista, whom they wished on the gallows. Pista was the satirical nickname of Count István Tisza, the Royal Hungarian Prime Minister. Their song went on ringing in the air, mingled with the croaking of the frogs, long after the train had steamed away. Its ribald words echoed in the stationmaster's ears long after the singers had gone. In his dreams he saw Lajos among the prisoners, and he also heard the song in his sleep, although the station was sleeping as peacefully as ever. All at once Máté, the village idiot, felt he had to justify his hoarding mania. "It's in case of war," he said, as he fished a discarded frying-pan out of the rubbish-dump.

No, the stationmaster wasn't mistaken. His youngest daughter was living in St Petersburg with a prince to whom she wasn't married. She visited her own daughter almost like a stranger. Since his daughter couldn't be bad, it must be the world. Often the stationmaster would push the newspaper aside, put down the glasses he now needed for reading, and stare at the timetable hanging on the wall. It was odd that the trains still left and arrived on time. Kisnémet station wasn't an island. But if it wasn't an island it should be a fortress. The stationmaster asked himself how he could defend it.

It was a rainy September afternoon when Ilona left Vienna, where she had spent a week, for St Petersburg.

Teréz and Zita accompanied her to the station. The cab-horses were standing with lowered heads in the rain outside the East Station. The wet rugs stuck to their backs. The station was damp; rainy mist mingled with the steam from the locomotives. The rain was falling on the curved roof, monotonously, patiently, as though it knew it would go on falling for a long time.

Ilona had heared the parting, but it didn't seem to worry Zita. She compared the big city station with Kisnémet, and looked round for the stationmaster. She liked the porters with their red caps; she wished Máté could have one. She told the time from the big clock let into one of the glass arches of the station. When Ilona said they would see each other again soon Zita merely nodded, because 'soon' might be a day or a year. She could tell the time by the clock, yet time itself was still a mystery to her. Ilona bought her a raspberry-juice from a barrow on wheels; it was still possible to submerge the great distress in small joys. Not until the doors had been slammed and the guards had raised the green indicators and blown their whistles did Zita twine her arms round her mother's neck and start sobbing bitterly. She wouldn't let go of Ilona. She was still sure she could prevent the inevitable, suddenly, planlessly, with her child's arms.

The train moved off. For a time fluttering handkerchiefs followed it, like seagulls behind a ship. Ilona lowered the window, disregarding the protests of an old lady. She saw Teráz motionless in the crowd, in one hand her handkerchief, in the other Zita—a tiny blue dot in her blue mackintosh with the touchingly large hood. The adults were still visible, but the child was no longer to be seen. Now they were going out into the rain, thought Ilona, the woman in black and the blue mackintosh. For the last two months she had trembled over the child's every movement; her own worries appeared to her frivolous and spurious, since she was now leaving her child to the mercy of the elements, chance, and the eyes of a stranger. Only Teréz was still in sight, a black, nun-like figure, a stranger; then she too disappeared.

"At least you could close the window now," complained the old lady.

She shut the window, but she stayed where she was. The railway-lines ran after her, as though to persuade her with outstretched arms to turn back. Then they grew tired. The coach carrying Zita and Teréz was perhaps already bumping over the Vienna asphalt. Was Zita still crying? Children were soon consoled; but what sort of consolation was that, when it was you who had caused their tears? Her marriage to Kontowski, her love for Zoltán, the city towards which she was travelling, even war and peace—how unimportant it all was by comparison with her own guilt!

The rain beat impatiently against the window-panes. It seemed to be raining inside the compartment as well.

During the first months of 1914 Ilona felt with a sense of oppression how right Kontowski had been when he asserted that in the new century men would be ruled by powers which had interposed themselves between them and their Creator, and which will, character, and bearing could not influence.

The Prince had more reason than ever to send Ilona home. The spring was full of smouldering unrest. Ilona would sit all night long in the embassy while Kontowski waited for dispatches from Vienna to be decoded. He hardly slept. "It's as though I were afraid the disaster might surprise me in my sleep; as though it can't happen so long as I'm awake," he said. Nevertheless, he no longer talked about Ilona's return home. There was no one he could confide in. Since learning that he couldn't marry her he had surrounded her with more affection than ever before. He was waiting for outside forces to compel him to do what he hesitated to do on his own initiative.

Ilona didn't press him. Since Zoltán's return from America his letters had become less and less frequent. They came once a month, twice at the most. He scarcely spoke of his love any more. She blamed herself for not having followed his call, but she was too proud to speak of her love. She lived from day to day, she, too, dimly sensing the approach of an event that would change everything.

Summer had descended upon St Petersburg. It had been unbearably hot all day long. The air stood still, unrenewed, as though under a glass cover. In the house on the Krestovsky Island all the jalousies were down, but the dry heat seeped in through the shutters. Flies sat on the window-panes, vases, and lamps, too lazy to fly away.

Ilona was lying on the sofa in the drawing-room. It was shadiest there. The clocks ticked wearily. She hadn't dressed all day. Only a thin dressing-gown covered her body. She was waiting for evening.

That morning a letter from Zoltán had arrived from Vienna. It was a short letter, only two pages, in his large, self-satisfied, upright hand. There was not a word of love in it, and yet the letter had thrown her into a turmoil. He wrote that in July he was going to Kisnémet. His mother had died while he was in America. He had inherited the farm; he must finally see about the inheritance. She read secrets into all his letters; the more so the rarer and shorter they were. This time it was easy to read between the lines. Why had he put off till the summer this trip which he should have made long ago? He knew that she would be in Kisnémet by mid-July at the latest. She pictured their meeting. One morning she would go into the farm-house the Szomorus had occupied for centuries. Or he would come to Berény. She smelt the smell of the house; it was a special smell that seemed to be made up of peeled bark and rotting apples. They would go to the St Anne's Day Ball, the annual summer ball in honour of the strange saint who protected mothers and beggars. They would come to a stop by the railway-gate, like the time when he tried to kiss her. It wasn't true that youth passed. You merely moved away from it. You had only to go back to it.

There was a knock at the door.

She quickly drew her dressing-gown together and sat up.

It was one of her chambermaids.

"His Excellency's coachman has brought this letter," she said. "Madam is to go at once to the embassy. The coachman is waiting."

The girl withdrew. Ilona opened the sealed envelope. She read:

> *Dearest! The Crown Prince has to-day been assassinated at Sarajevo by a Serbian conspirator. The Archduchess is also dead. This means war. I cannot leave the embassy. Come to me at once.*
> *T.*

She dropped the letter on to the little table on which Zoltán's letter lay. Summer in Kisnémet was all at once as far away as if it lay not in the future, but in the distant past. The Crown Prince assassinated! This was the power that was more powerful than any individual. This was good-bye to to-morrow.

14

It was a sultry, sunless day when Ilona left the house on the Krestovsky Island. Many shops had been shut. The Imperial flag, the heraldic beast surmounted by a shot-down eagle, hung from the roof of the Duma. The church doors were closed; the singing penetrated to the Nevsky Prospekt only faintly.

Ilona stopped the coach outside the embassy.

Kontowski couldn't accompany her to the station. The Austro-Hungarian ultimatum to Serbia was expected. The embassy had taken half a first-class compartment for Ilona; there was no chance of any better accommodation. A sealed letter from the Imperial Russian Foreign Ministry had been pinned into her passport, instructing the frontier authorities to let the Hungarian citizen Ilona, Baroness Von Rattowitz, pass free and unhindered, and to render her every possible assistance. The Austrian authorities had been informed of her arrival by telegram. An embassy attaché and Kontowski's valet were waiting at the station to see to her luggage—two wardrobe trunks, nineteen ordinary trunks, and four hat-boxes.

"It is all too little," said Kontowski as she entered his study, "but everything humanly possible has been done. Send me a telegram the moment you have crossed the frontier. And, of course, from Vienna. I'm afraid we shall see one another soon." He smiled apologetically. "I shall undoubtedly get my passport in a few days." He came to a stop in front of her. "Now I ought to be at your side, and now of all times I can't be. The period of man's helplessness before Destiny is already beginning."

"Don't worry about me," she said. "I'm not afraid."

His eyes were tired, his cheeks hollow. War was coming, and he had forgotten nothing of importance to her well-being.

"If a miracle happens you will come back," he said, "as soon as summer is over."

It sounded like a question, and she replied, "Yes, I shall come back."

She felt a fierce tenderness such as she had rarely experienced before

124

—perhaps only for Zita. She would come back if he called her. But he wouldn't call her, she knew that. They might never see one another again. When she shut the door behind her ten years would be shut off—her youth. How often had she toyed with the idea of leaving Kontowski! In the end it had taken a war to separate them. She wasn't afraid for herself: she was too afraid for him. They would both be left alone, he lonelier than she. Perhaps you only loved those who needed you. Perhaps that was the only reason people loved children. She wanted to say something to him, wanted to thank him for his patience, his wisdom, his love; for the sure hand with which he had guided her; for the knowledge he had given and the knowledge he had withheld; for the questions he had answered and the questions he had not asked; for the sickness he had endured for her sake.

It was dusky in the embassy room, almost dark. Through the lowered blinds they could hear the tapping of blackbirds. The black-and-yellow and the red-white-and-green flags crossed under the picture of Emperor Francis Joseph I looked like tired military trophies in a war museum.

"Don't let's make it too hard for ourselves," said Kontowski. "We shall see one another again soon." He turned away. "I have had a few presents for Zita taken to the station. They are closed with the embassy's seal. Take care of yourself. God protect you!"

He took her head in his hands. He made to kiss her on the forehead. She threw her arms round his neck and kissed him on the mouth.

Half an hour later, when she entered the station, she was already far from St Petersburg. Stations stood in the midst of cities, but they belonged to the foreign country to which you were travelling. If the city had been dead, if it had dozed off sleepily in the July noon, the station seemed to be moving, to be travelling.

With some difficulty the young embassy attaché forced a passage for Ilona through the crowd of peasants, workers, middle-class women, officers, and soldiers. Soldiers were in the majority. Dressed in green uniforms or white tunics resembling those worn by the moujiks, and wearing short boots, they were pushing their way towards the dirty trains, the cattle-trucks standing on the lines. They lay sleeping on the benches in the waiting-rooms and on the platform, with their rifles beside them, and between the rifles bundles of provisions smelling of garlic. The reek of spirits came from the canteens and hung motionless in the hot air. A few elegant ladies were saying good-bye to officers, shedding tears, as though the men were already going to war. Peasant women taking their desperately clucking fowls to St Petersburg in wicker baskets thrust the ladies aside. A military train steamed out of the station. The soldiers were waving their flat caps and singing.

"Here are your luggage tickets, Baroness," said the attaché. "Is there anything else I can do for you?"

"No thank you, I have everything." When she was already on the steps she turned and smiled. "Look after His Excellency."

She was entrusting Kontowski to an attaché she had met for the first time an hour before.

15

They had now been travelling for two days and two nights.

The other half of the compartment was occupied by a gentleman who had introduced himself the moment the train drew out of the station. Now she knew his whole life story.

Dr Samuel Ginsburg, as he told her, was in his early fifties. Ilona had taken him for sixty. He was tall and slim; but the cautiousness of his movements, the stiffly conservative elegance of his clothes, and the dignity of his speech made him seem older. Ilona had to study him at some length before she knew why she had immediately trusted him. It was as though the rays of the setting sun lay upon the narrow face with the big, rather fleshy nose. It wasn't only the gold of the round, iridescent spectacles which created the impression that he was surrounded by gleaming gold. Little gold spots, tiny sun-coins, sparkled in his grey eyes. The thick hair above his high forehead was grey, but a pale reddish-blond shone through with a noonday warmth. As far as Ilona could remember, she had known only one Jew, Dr Grünfeld, the doctor at Kisnémet. The stationmaster had continued to put himself in Dr Grünfeld's hands even after two Christian doctors had settled in the village. Although Dr Grünfeld had been small and bearded and untidy-looking, exactly as one imagined a Jew, her travelling companion reminded her of the old doctor.

Dr Ginsburg was an antique-dealer, and had one of the most flourishing shops in St Petersburg, situated in the Nevsky Prospekt. Ilona had often admired it. Now the shop was shut. But that was Samuel Ginsburg's story.

His father had come to Russia from Vienna in 1860, before he was born. His father had travelled "in the opposite direction," as Dr Ginsburg put it. The Jews were fleeing from the pogroms, from Russia, Poland, and the East. Old Ginsburg went towards the East, because His Majesty Tsar Alexander II, called "the Liberator," had sought out the Jewish connoisseur and invited him to his Court. Samuel Ginsburg the Elder found the Tsar pleasant, St Petersburg a fine city, and business very much to his liking. He settled in Russia; sent for his wife, and opened his shop, which was patronized by the high aristocracy; but he wasn't willing to entrust himself completely to the country in which Jews were second-class human beings. Hadn't an Austrian Emperor, Joseph II, given the Jews special privileges, almost the right to feel themselves human beings? One couldn't be disloyal to Austria. Every time his wife, Charlotte, expected a child—and old Samuel's marriage was blessed with nine children—Ginsburg the Elder made a pilgrimage to the Austro-Hungarian consulate, where he formally obtained a certificate testifying that the newborn child held Austrian citizenship and therefore enjoyed the protection of a Most Gracious Habsburg.

Samuel Ginsburg the Younger felt no loyalty towards the Habsburg or Austria. True, he spoke German and had studied at the academies of art in Vienna, Berlin, and Paris, but Russian was his mother tongue and St Petersburg his native city. His parents were long since dead. They lay in the Jewish cemetery in St Petersburg. His wife was also buried there. His three sons had married Russian women; he showed Ilona photographs of them; only his daughter, by name Natasha, was the wife of a German doctor. Why had he himself not become a Russian citizen? The Russian bureaucracy was slow-moving—especially where Jews were concerned. "But I can't blame them," commented Dr Ginsburg. "After all, they remember my father, who rejected the gracious offer of Tsar Alexander. A great Austrian patriot, my father!" He said it without bitterness. Nor was he angry with the Russian authorities, who had suggested a fortnight ago, unofficially, of course, and "in his own interests," that he should close his shop in the Nevsky Prospekt "for the time being" and, if possible, leave the country. "I told you, Baroness, my father travelled in the opposite direction. We Jews almost always travel in the opposite direction. That's probably because Destiny travels with us; we're simply unaware of the fact."

Now Samuel Ginsburg the Younger was going to Berlin, to his daughter. "I shan't be a burden to my children, I hope," he said. He showed Ilona photographs of his daughter, Natasha, his son-in-law, his two blond grandchildren. She didn't like the look of the son-in-law, but she didn't tell him so. You carried a photograph round in your pocket and perhaps knew less about its subject than a stranger seeing it for the first time. That was why people travelled in the opposite direction, not only Jews. "I shan't be a burden to them," reiterated Dr Ginsburg. "Some of my most valuable paintings are in Berlin, among them a Rembrandt. Also part of my collection of clocks. And I flatter myself that I know my job. Fortunately antiques always remain new." As he spoke he stared out of the window, probably in order to hide how heavy his heart was. He was too young to live with his children and too old to find a new home.

The landscape was bleak. The railway-lines ran dead straight. There were no obstacles here for the train to avoid. Why did it run just here, not a hundred miles to the east or west? The lines seemed to have fallen from the sky, uncanny coincidences in the desert. It was impossible to believe that they led anywhere and didn't come to a sudden end in the everlasting sand. Since the track never curved, the travellers never saw the train in which they were sitting; perhaps there wasn't any engine in front; perhaps the carriage had been given a push in St Petersburg and would now go on rolling till it stopped.

As though he knew what Ilona was thinking, Dr Ginsburg drew her attention to every village they passed, every cluster of cottages on the horizon. They were wretched villages, wretched cottages. "Aren't these people completely cut off from the world?" asked Ilona. "What is the world, Baroness?" asked Dr Ginsburg.

16

The train had been travelling for three days and three nights.

When darkness fell Dr Ginsburg left the compartment and stayed away a long time, until Ilona had made herself more or less comfortable and put out the light. Then he slipped in again, without wishing her good-night, doing his best to make his presence forgotten.

Although she woke very early, he was no longer in the compartment in the morning; but no sooner had she finished washing in the barely clean toilet then he appeared with steaming tea that he had brought from the dining-car. Since the weather was very hot, she several times invited him to take off his jacket, but he merely thanked her politely and didn't even unbutton his waistcoat. When she didn't feel like talking he remained silent and read a Russian book. After two days and nights he looked exactly the same as when they set out—a gentleman in a travelling-suit with a gold watch-chain over his waistcoat and a wide tie faultlessly tied, sitting in a position that made him look as if he were not travelling, but merely having himself photographed in a travelling-suit.

Although the stations offered a welcome diversion, the stops seemed to last for ever. They stopped at the Government boundaries, at Saklinye, Karsovka, Dvinsk, Grodno. The officials entered Ilona's compartment, examined her papers suspiciously, asked questions she didn't understand. Dr Ginsburg interpreted. The officials left sullenly with a silent threat, as though the case were not settled, but merely postponed. Ilona thanked Destiny for having given her the antique-dealer for a travelling companion. The word that had been her favourite during her early youth occurred to her: 'naturally' a kind fate had entrusted her to Samuel Ginsburg. Once she witnessed a violent argument. A civilian official had turned Dr Ginsburg's luggage upside down and left it in a state of chaos. Dr Ginsburg went white. His straight back bent for a moment, as though a load had been placed upon it. But when Ilona asked him the reason for the quarrel he straightened up again. "He called me a pig of a Jew," he said. In consternation Ilona said, "They're making it easy for you to leave Russia, Dr Ginsburg." He replied, "One doesn't love a country because of its people, Baroness, but in spite of them." The little sun-coins were sparkling in his eyes.

The nearer they came to the frontier the more numerous were the villages, towns, cities; the more traffic there was too; and the more intense grew Ilona's disquiet.

The war was travelling with them; the war was coming to meet them. In Bialystok the train stood still half the night. She asked in a low voice, "Are you asleep, Dr Ginsburg?" "No, I'm awake," he replied. "What's happening?" she asked. "They're attaching cattle-trucks full of soldiers."

The following day several military trains passed them. The soldiers were standing in open cattle-trucks; some were sitting with their legs dangling outside. They waved to the passengers in the passing train as though they had to say good-bye to some one, no matter who. Officers, looking polished and neat, sat at the windows of the first- and second-class carriages; they were smiling, as though death was travelling only in the cattle-trucks. When the train stopped they saw soldiers waiting on the platform; they had stacked their rifles in the shape of a tent. Ilona thought about Kisnémet. Were steel tents that offered no shelter there too? Once their train stopped for four or five hours on the open track till a goods train passed them carrying cannon. The cannon

128

were held fast by chains; they were still harmless—chained dogs. When
Dr Ginsburg asked the guard how late they were running he shrugged
his shoulders. "In wartime delays are reckoned in days," said Dr
Ginsburg. "When men make war men don't matter. They let cannon
through first." Ilona nodded. "You're a brave woman," said Dr Ginsburg.

Was she a brave woman? She grew calm and serene at the thought.
In two or three days she would hold Zita in her arms. No power on
earth would keep them apart any longer. Courage didn't mean, as
Soltán had said, to do and leave undone what you wanted. Perhaps it
meant just the opposite, in fact. In any case courage was certainly not
the absence of fear. The most courageous person was the one who
feared nobody so much as himself. The perpetual fear of being unable
to stand one's own test; the tormenting impossibility of living with
oneself if one did wrong; fear of the accusations of one's conscience
coupled with the readiness to examine them; perpetual entreaty for the
inner tranquillity that could only be gained in perpetual war with oneself—that was courage. People were afraid of fear and had no inkling
that it was like the fever that drives out the poisons whose presence it
announces. Were criminals brave? They were cowardly, because they
fled from recognition of the fact that judgment is bound to follow
crime. The brave man was afraid of having to beg for mercy, therefore
he did not sin. You could defy the law, but not judgment. He who was
brave bowed down humbly before the law, so that he was not brought
to judgment for his arrogance. But Kontowski too was wrong. Man
was powerful, even the coward. The world could not touch the man
who feared himself more than the world. No storm, not even war, could
bend the man who was prepared to bend courageously. Perhaps they
were travelling into uncertainty. But what else was uncertainty than
the fear of tests one was afraid of not being able to stand? The
certainty of her youth had been a false certainty. Now she felt sure of
herself because she believed she could stand up to uncertainty.

17

It was ten in the evening when the train reached Mylovitz, the
frontier station between the Empire of the Tsars and the Empire of the
Habsburgs. Nobody had gone to bed. Most of the passengers had
already got out; the trucks carrying the soldiers had been uncoupled
long ago. The guard went through the train asking his guests to alight.

Evening had brought no cooling of the temperature. The starry,
moonless night was sultry. On the other side of the station lay Austria.
It smelt as at home in Kisnémet.

Mylovitz station wasn't much larger than Kisnémet. It was dirty,
wretched, dilapidated. The light from the paraffin lamps fell on the clay
floor. A few soldiers were sleeping on the earth. They could be heard
snoring. Four or five Jews in caftans, with long beards, were sitting on
their bundles, motionless, like people used to long waiting. Frontier
guards with fixed bayonets marched past them, to and fro, to and fro.
Every now and then the Jews looked up at the stars. They didn't look
up at the guards.

Six or seven passengers were taken into a waiting-room. A single narrow bench ran round the room. On the walls hung yellow time tables in Cyrillic script. The corners of the timetables hung down sadly because no train ran according to them any more. Between the time tables hung pictures of the Tsar and Tsarina. They had been put up the wrong way round: the Tsar and Tsarina had their heads turned away from each other, as though they were both ashamed of the dirty frontier station with the faded timetables.

For three full hours Ilona and Dr Ginsburg sat side by side on the wooden bench while a soldier with a gun stood motionless at the door leading to a second room. From time to time the sullen blue eyes of the soldier met the golden eyes of the old Jew. Then Dr Ginsburg's back became even straighter. The soldier looked tired and worn-out by comparison with him.

Ilona, in her tight-fitting, fashionable travelling-costume with a hat and veil, began to shiver. "What time is it?" she asked Dr Ginsburg. He took the gold watch out of his waistcoat pocket. "Twelve minutes past one," he said.

At last she was called. Dr Ginsburg at once rose too. The soldier at the door refused to let him pass. Dr Ginsburg protested. They argued in Russian—excitedly but patiently, as though they had the whole night to argue. "I can't leave you alone with that lot," Dr Ginsburg said to Ilona. She smiled gratefully. It was good to be weak. If you were weak and a woman you always found a man to protect you—even at a Russian frontier station; even if it was only an old Jew. In the end Dr Ginsburg slipped the soldier a gold coin. He took it in his hand and looked at it, hatefully and lovingly, as if it were the temptation we love and hate. He let them go in together.

A young officer, two N.C.O.s, and two civilian officials were sitting at a long table. One of the N.C.O.s shouted at Dr Ginsburg. The officer motioned him to keep quiet. He took Ilona's papers and held them under the paraffin lamp, but he didn't look at them. He scrutinized Ilona and stroked his short blond moustache with his little finger, on which he had a ring with a red stone. The stone was like a drop of blood in the paraffin light.

Meanwhile the others studied the papers. They turned each one round ten times. They whispered. They pushed the papers in front of the officer and whispered something in his ear. He looked at Ilona without so much as glancing at the papers.

"What were you doing in St Petersburg?" he asked.

Samuel Ginsburg translated.

"I went to see operas and ballets," she said.

Samuel Ginsburg translated.

"Tell her to hand over the maps," said one of the officials.

"Have you any maps?" translated Ginsburg.

"I have no maps," she said.

The officer stared at her.

Ginsburg began to speak. From his gestures Ilona deduced that he was pointing out the letter from the Imperial Foreign Ministry in her passport.

130

The officer glanced at the paper heavy with seals.

"Mobilization has been ordered," he said. "The document is no longer valid. You're a spy."

Samuel Ginsburg translated.

Ilona laughed. "Tell the gentlemen they will have the Austrian Foreign Ministry to deal with if they keep me here any longer."

The officer laughed. He suddenly understood German.

"Austria has the whole of Russia to deal with," he said.

The document passed from hand to hand.

There was a knock at the door. A soldier came in.

"He says there is nothing suspicious in your luggage," Ginsburg whispered to Ilona. "They have opened your luggage."

She was about to protest, but Ginsburg signed to her. She kept quiet.

Meanwhile the officers were studying the antique-dealer's papers. The officer pushed them away as though it disgusted him to touch them. He smiled.

"You can go," he said to Ilona.

She looked at Ginsburg and didn't move.

"You can go," repeated the officer.

"Tell them I shan't go until they let you go too," Ilona said to Ginsburg.

Ginsburg hesitated.

In broken German the officer said to Ilona. "Has he got your maps hidden on him?"

"You're talking rubbish," she said.

The officer turned to the soldier sitting beside him, a big man with a stupid face.

"Search him!" he said.

The man with the stupid face walked round the table to Ginsburg.

"Undress!" he yelled at him.

Ginsburg stepped back.

"Do you want to be present while we strip the Jew naked?" the officer asked Ilona.

"Yes," she said.

She turned round and went over to the little window.

On the platform the Jews in caftans were still sitting on their bundles, motionless, as though they were used to waiting. The soldiers marched to and fro, to and fro. Every now and then the Jews looked up at the stars. They didn't look up at the guards.

Behind Ilona the officer was giving his orders in two languages; Russian for his subordinates; German so that Ilona should understand.

"Coat! Trousers! Shirt! Pants! Shoes! Socks!"

Then there was silence.

"You can go," said the officer.

Ilona and Dr Ginsburg walked side by side to the train. They didn't look at each other, like people who are ashamed because they are human beings like the others who ought to be ashamed. When they were back in the compartment Ilona said, "Thank you, Dr Ginsburg." He said, "Thank you, Baroness." It was dark in the compartment. The Russians had put the light out; the Austrians hadn't lit it yet. A

131

shimmer of light came into the compartment from the station. Samuel Ginsburg sat by the window, erect, correct, rather stiff. It was as if the light were coming from him, a golden light. The train didn't move. At one point Ginsburg said, "Men don't know that they humiliate themselves when they humiliate others." Ilona said, "You'll be happier over there, Dr Ginsburg." He said, "What is happiness, Baroness?"

The mud huts, low cottages, and church of Mylovitz slowly emerged from the darkness. When the engine started up the luggage fell in a jumble. The Jews were still sitting on their bundles, motionless, as though they were used to waiting. The soldiers were marching to and fro, to and fro. The sky was pale and tired-looking. There were no stars left.

A few minutes later the Austrian frontier station loomed up. The black-and-yellow flag waved from a mast in the morning breeze. The train stopped outside a red-brick building. The building looked like every station in the Monarchy. There were geraniums in the windows.

Then it was hidden. There was a goods train waiting between Ilona's train and the station-house. Austrian soldiers were standing in the open doors of the cattle-trucks. Some were sitting on the steps dangling their legs outside. They had flowers on their field-grey caps. It was four in the morning.

18

It was Sunday, the first Sunday since Ilona's return from St Petersburg.

She had been in Vienna for barely a week, but the journey seemed to lie far behind her; it had become unreal.

She had found everything just as she had left it. The apartment in the Bellaria was shady and cool. It had been a happy reunion, with the ivory-tinted Augarten china on the breakfast-table; with the monograms on the towels; with the wide Biedermeier bed, her own; with the gleaming brass door-handles; with the blue writing-paper in the rack on the desk. It was good to talk with Teréz, whose image had become distorted by distance; who was less austere and nun-like than Ilona remembered her; who had an endless store of tales about Zita, and whose important preoccupation with a thousand little things almost convinced Ilona of the unimportance of the great things.

It was good to be with Zita. At a distance all the difficulties relating to the child had grown immeasurably; the child herself had changed with them, as though she were no longer a child, but a dwarf, small but old. Now Zita returned into her own body, became a child again—a child who cried when she bumped herself, was wildly delighted by small presents and only moderately by big ones, asked precocious questions and talked to dolls, took Ilona's presence for granted because she enjoyed it.

Ilona could scarcely imagine how she could have lived for so long without her child. Men too you loved with your heart, but it was a mistake to suppose that the love of the brain or of the sex, or both, enhanced the love of the heart; all other love than that of the heart robbed the heart of some of its love. Ilona had only to look at her child to realize that the 'pure love' people talked about was no moralistic phrase: pure in this context meant simply undisturbed, meant merely the undisturbed heart. Now she understood why the stationmaster hadn't married again; now that she was beginning to become a mother she understood her father.

She loved Sundays in the cities. They turned into villages, big, friendly villages. The people walked slowly, as though they were all coming from church. They looked up at the houses like strangers, because on weekdays they didn't see the city. They wore their dresses and suits carefully, like fragile china. The tram-bells sounded superfluous, like the childish bells of the ice-cream vendors. You could even hear the birds singing.

To-day was Sunday, but you couldn't tell. Two days ago the proclamation had been put up.

> *To my peoples! It was my most ardent desire to devote the years left to me by the grace of God to the works of peace, and to preserve my peoples from the heavy sacrifices and burdens of war. Providence has decreed otherwise. . . . I must therefore proceed to obtain by force of arms the indispensable guarantees that will ensure my state's tranquillity within and lasting peace without. . . . I have weighed and pondered everything.*

From her balcony Ilona could see people still standing in front of the proclamations. Each of them must know every line by heart. It was impossible to tell whether they kept standing in front of the proclamations in order to fan their enthusiasm with them; or because they couldn't understand how Providence could have decreed differently from the old gentleman who ruled by the grace of Providence; or because they wanted to make sure that the old gentleman really had weighed and pondered everything. On the opposite side of the road, on the advertisement pillars of the Volkstheater, the proclamation was framed by theatre posters. "Performance commences 8 P.M. Ends approximately 11 P.M." This performance had begun on July 29, 1914, but the people in front of the proclamation didn't know even approximately when it would end.

When the soldiers marched past with bands playing and wild flowers in their caps Ilona called her daughter on to the balcony. Zita ran out from her nursery, handkerchief in hand. Waving was one of the inexplicable pleasures of childhood. She stood beside Ilona pink-cheeked.

Since yesterday the nursery had changed into a railway station. The stationmaster had arrived from Kisnémet: several hundred stationmasters from the Monarchy had been called to the Austrian capital. In the nursery railway-lines ran round the carpet; the carriages of the toy railway were shunted to and fro. It was Zita's favourite game, preferred to any doll's house. To-day she was in heaven because on the floor, among carriages, locomotives, points, station-houses, and tunnels, sat a real stationmaster. It was splendid that Grandpapa was wearing his uniform. The Lilliputian railway looked completely genuine because it was commanded by a giant toy.

133

19

The following day two telegrams arrived—in the morning one from the Prince informing Ilona that Kontowski had been called to Stockholm for discussions and would have to remain there for at least a week; in the evening a second, from Zoltán. "I am at Baden with my regiment," it said. "You must come and see me on Sunday without fail."

For two days she hestitated. She talked it over with her sister, in whom she had confided the previous summer.

They were sitting on a bench in the Burggarten, opposite the Empress Maria Theresa memorial. Ilona had put up her sunshade; she was still afraid of freckles. Zita was playing with the other children. It was a warm afternoon. The birds were twittering in the maples, the tulips glowing in the flower-beds.

"I'm sure he wants to say good-bye to me," said Ilona. "Perhaps he is going up to the front next week already."

"Why ask me?" commented Teréz. "You will go anyhow."

"Don't you think I have to?"

"You have to because you want to."

"I want to see him again. That's all."

"The war is an excuse for everything. Perhaps that's why it is being waged."

"I have also made sacrifices these last few years."

"I know."

"Perhaps he will never come back."

"Not every one gets killed."

That's Teréz, thought Ilona. Lucid, honest, and a trifle hard. It was her fault that Teréz didn't understand her. Suddenly she became aware of the fact that Teréz was thirty-two. Ilona felt as though she herself had set the years between herself and her sister, like a bricklayer building a wall over which he himself can no longer see. Nothing was harder to understand and nothing easier to forget than that others had a life that was as close to them as one's own life was to oneself. There was no greater fault than forgetfulness. She had forgotten Teréz.

"Haven't you ever loved anyone?" she asked, as though a single question could make good the forgetfulness of years.

"No, I don't think so."

"You have sacrificed yourself to me."

Teréz gazed after Zita, who was bowling a hoop, dressed in her blue sailor suit and wearing a straw hat with fluttering ribbons.

"You have given me Zita," she said. "A husband could have given me no more."

"Haven't you ever thought of marrying?"

"I'm content."

It sounded so impatient, almost hostile, that Ilona asked her sister no more questions. They talked about the stationmaster, Margit, Zita, and the war.

Mothers were still sitting on the benches knitting .They watched their little boys and were glad they were no older. A soldier and a nursemaid passed; a boyish young ensign with his basket-hilt on his arm; and a retired colonel leaning on his wife.

Ilona talked, but she was thinking of Zoltán, of Zoltán and Teréz. She saw herself with Teréz's eyes. Teréz had no idea how little she herself knew of love. It hurt her to think that Teréz's eyes were false mirrors, but you couldn't argue with mirrors, neither with false nor with accurate ones. In her early youth she had tried to be as people saw her, to adapt herself to the mirrors. Vain metamorphoses lay behind her. She wouldn't become fickle, amorous, licentious, in order to resemble the picture Teréz had of her. At the same time she became aware of the hopelessness of trying to change this picture. That she had never loved Feri and would nevertheless have remained true to him for the rest of her life; that she had deceived Kontowski although she loved him; that Zoltán attracted her to the same extent as he repelled her—this was all inexplicable to another person. When she tried to explain it truth became simple and hence untrue, as if one were to open up one's heart, which, once visible, became an ugly, bloody piece of flesh, like all other hearts and yet like no heart. That's how it was with her heart and Teréz's heart. Perhaps her sister was right to give nothing away, to stand cold and stubborn on the boundary that separated understanding from non-understanding. Teréz was a mother, but she didn't seem to long for a child of her own; she envied Ilona and her supposed amours, yet she stayed a virgin and let her youth slip by; she spoke contemptuously of the 'feminists' who demanded masculine rights, yet she lived like them; she bowed humbly to the teachings of the Church, yet she was arrogant in her sacrifice; she seemed to forgive everything, yet she made no attempt to understand; she spoke of her contentment while unhappiness was carving premature furrows in her face—she was inscrutable, a human being.

"I don't need a war in order to find peace," said Teréz.

"I envy you," said Ilona.

One statement was as untrue as the other. She rose to her feet.

Zita ran towards them from far away, bowling the hoop along in front of her with a stick. The wheel hopped over the gravel, rolled towards the low iron railing round the flower-bed. Zita tried to grab it and fell over. She jumped up at once. Her knee was bleeding from a multitude of tiny grazes. She screwed up her mouth, but she didn't cry.

The two women hurried over to her.

"Have you hurt yourself, darling?" asked Ilona.

"It's nothing," said Teréz, as though it was more a question of pacifying the mother than the child.

"It'll be all right in a minute, Teréz," said Zita.

She clung to Teréz's skirt.

20

It had been raining all night. Drifting mist still hung over the fields as the Baden tram freed itself from the narrows formed by the tenements. The outlines of the Gumpoldskirchen vineyards were hazy. Although the weather was warm, the melancholy of approaching autumn was in the air, a quaking premonition. His Majesty's proclamations were still hanging on the wooden palings round a sports ground, great words tattered and lashed by the wind. The tram was almost empty, as though it wasn't Sunday.

Zoltán's telegram had said the Hotel Bristol in the Josephsplatz, right by the terminus.

The square was full of people—officers and men, men and officers. It was hard to imagine that so many uniforms had been waiting for their owners and then had suddenly crawled out of all the cupboards, all the boxes, all the warehouses, all the attics. They were field-grey, like mice; they ate up the colours. The women were senseless patches of brightness. A smell of sulphur came from the Josephsbad, with its fake Greek columns.

She asked the hotel porter for Zoltán, for Lieutenant Zoltán Szomoru. The porter handed her a letter. The lieutenant was no longer staying at the hotel. "Barrack-service," said the porter, as though it were a military secret. The letter asked her to wait in the hotel coffee-house; he would come as soon as his duties allowed him.

She sat down at a small marble table. The scent of coffee hung about the room, as though people had been drinking coffee here uninterruptedly since the Turkish siege. The Café Bristol looked like coffee-houses throughout the Monarchy; it looked like the coffee-house in the Hotel Rákoczi and the café belonging to the hotel at Sopron. Pictures of the Emperor and Empress hung on the brown panelled walls—the Emperor's picture under glass, the Empress's merely framed. The glass had been broken and not replaced. The Empress had been dead for a long time.

It wasn't yet midday, but the coffee-house was full of officers. They weren't drinking coffee: they were drinking wine and spirits. Old waiters were serving. Perhaps the old waiters had been taken out of the cupboards because the young ones had taken their uniforms out of the cupboards. The tail-coats of the young waiters were now lying in the cupboards like dead swallows. A few old gentlemen were sitting at their regular tables, spectacles or pince-nez on their noses, tubular newspaper-holders in their hands. Germany had declared war on Belgium; the Germans were in Liége. Japan had declared war on Germany, Austria on the Japanese, Germany on the French, Germany on the Russians. The old gentlemen read about the declarations of war and dipped their crescent rolls in their coffee. They shook their heads. It was impossible to tell for sure whether they were deprecating the war or the noisy gaiety of the officers. An officer's batman came in and halted with a salute at a table occupied by the noisiest group. The officers rose, called the head waiter, buckled on their sabres, and picked up their caps. Ilona watched them as they went through the glass door. In the vestibule stood a bride on the arm of a first lieutenant. The first lieutenant's cheeks were red. His bride stared fixedly in front of her, like a figure on a white iced cake. She was visibly pregnant. Bride and bridegroom hurried out of the vestibule; the wedding guests hurried after them. All over the Monarchy lieutenants were marrying pregnant girls. They quickly gave their names away before their names were put on wooden crosses.

136

At last Zoltán came in through the swinging glass door. He stopped at two tables occupied by higher-ranking officers, clicked his heels, and saluted. The officers returned his salute. A major waved his hand, as though telling the lieutenant to hurry. Even majors realized that young lieutenants were in a hurry.

"Forgive me for keeping you waiting so long, alone in this café," said Zoltán. "I couldn't think of anywhere else to meet."

He kissed her hand, sat down, but didn't unbuckle his sabre.

The uniform suited him. It wasn't a disguise like the tail-coat or the dressing-gown. You could see that he had once been a peasant lad, broad-shouldered, broad-chested, with slim hips. His sun-burnt neck in the high collar was slim. His dark hair was cut short, a youthful hair-style.

"I told the cab to wait," he said. "We can drive out into the Helenental. It isn't going to rain." He seemed to have made a pact with the sky.

"Did you know I would come?" she asked.

"I hoped so."

They drove out to the Helenental. Two white horses were harnessed to the 'rubber-wheeler.'

"We're off to the front to-morrow morning," he said.

She had told Teréz so; she had known it. And yet her heart grew heavy; it was seized by the panic that had seized millions of women throughout the Monarchy, married and engaged, lonely and pregnant, girls and mothers.

Why hadn't he got exemption from front-line service, she wanted to know. It was no secret that it wasn't impossible for anyone with connexions or achievements. He thanked her with a look, as though to say, "Loving women don't demand heroism of their men." He was no hero, he went on, and had no wish to be one. He was acting out of self-interest. All the young men in the Symphony Orchestra had been called up, and some fathers of families as well; the orchestra would never forgive him if he stayed behind as the result of 'patronage,' and still less would the stupid, heroism-loving public. "After all, I'm an officer in the reserve," he said. "I have to take the risk for the sake of the future. If I get killed it will be all the same, but if I come back crowned with glory . . ." He jested about death and glory.

They ate lunch at a restaurant in the Helenental. The robber knights' castles of Rauhenstein and Rauhenegg looked sadly down upon them, wise ruins. The Schwechat swirled round the old stones. A mild wind carried the scent of cyclamen from the Vienna woods. It rained once, but only for five minutes. The air was heavy and damp. The restaurant filled with officers and women. The hectic, unnatural gaiety threatened at any moment to turn into tears, as on a railway station. The women looked at one another. The men didn't dare look at one another. Each one knew what the other was thinking. They were quite naked in their common destiny.

They fled from the restaurant, as though from the common destiny. They spoke faster than they meant to, hurrying from one subject to another for fear of not having time to say what they wanted. Zoltán talked about his travels, about America, about successes and awkward incidents, about his mother's death, about his return to Kisnémet, about Mr Hajdu, his secretary. She talked about St Petersburg, about the ball during which the false news of Rasputin's murder had spread, about the house on Krestovsky Island, about the stationmaster and Zita and Teréz. She clung to their common memories and the people they both knew. She didn't mention Kontowski. He didn't refer to women, as though the earth were populated solely by men. Yet she couldn't help often thinking of Kontowski and what he had said about the helplessness of the individual in the face of Destiny. They couldn't talk about the future, the happy land of lovers, because an Archduke had been murdered in a Serbian village and the Germans were in Brussels.

Zoltán had hired the fiacre for the whole day. The driver had raised the black oil-cloth roof. Every time the lady and the lieutenant got in he buckled a black oil-cloth over their knees. Only the upper parts of their bodies were visible. Under the black sheet their knees touched. Their hands touched and did not let go of one another again. It was as if their hands and knees were in joint coffins. The horses trotted out into the Helenental. The passengers heard nothing but the tapping of their hoofs and, every now and then, the rain dripping from the wet trees.

Several times they stopped and got out—at the road-house with the odd name Jammerpeppi, at the Cholerakapelle, at the Krainerhütte. Time passed. It was not amenable to any entreaty, any reason, any cunning, any prayer. When they were alone in the cab they longed for people; then they fled from people into their black oil-cloth coffin. They scarcely spoke any more. They kissed, under the shelter of the rain-roof, with hurried passion. The childish occurrence by which they were surrounded, the war, had turned them into children, but they didn't feel ashamed in front of each other, because the menace looming over them had freed them from the burden of responsibility. When Ilona opened her eyes between two kisses she saw the passing tree-tops. It was as though they were travelling between tree-tops. The horses trotted on. The raindrops fell from the trees, the notes of a melancholy song.

Evening came early after the sunless day. "It's not as late as that yet," they said, but it was already later. The last tram from Baden to Vienna, the 'blue,' as it was called, on account of its blue rear light, went at ten. They had gone on and on, out of fear of the way back. It was too late to catch the tram.

They had supper in the Chapter-house Cellar at Heiligenkreuz. There was an infantry regiment at Heiligenkreuz. The customers were almost all men. The low stone arches of the cellar echoed with their singing. They sang old soldiers' songs; there were no new ones yet. A major came over to their table. Zoltán jumped up and clicked his heels. Ilona thought of the evening in St Petersburg, of the applauding crowd, of Zoltán's disciples in the reception-room of the Hôtel de Paris. Wouldn't the lieutenant and the "lovely lady" come and sit at the officers' table? "I'm afraid we have to leave in a minute, sir," said Zoltán. "Very good, lieutenant," said the major. Then they had to leave.

In the Chapter-house yard they stood still. Darkness had fallen. A yellow light shone from the cellar windows on the courtyard. The tenor was still singing. The tram hasn't gone yet, thought Ilona, although it was far too late to catch it. An old monk crossed the courtyard with short steps, carrying a bucket.

They climbed into the fiacre, which swayed from side to side. "To Baden," Zoltán told the cabby. The cab turned out of the yard past the plane-trees. "I have to be in barracks by six," he said. "We march off at seven." Up to now he hadn't named the hours.

Silently they counted the hours—nine till six. Silently they thought, Where shall we go? Zoltán no longer had a hotel room. The couldn't stay at an unknown hotel—the lady and the lieutenant who had to be in the barracks by six. The cab with the black rain-roof was their shelter. They kissed.

"Stop at the Krainerhütte," ordered Zoltán. A stage on the way back. The way back grew longer if you thought of stages.

The Krainerhütte was an old summertime restaurant, a popular spot for excursions. It was late: the Sunday visitors had gone home. Only two or three rooms still had lights on; they were visible from the street, through the garden.

Zoltán climbed out. She followed him with her eyes till he disappeared in the darkness. No doubt he was inquiring about a room. She would follow him. She had become a great lady; she had lived in castles; she had a daughter, a house, clothes, jewellery, servants. She had forgotten that she was twenty-eight. Perhaps it wasn't only the old whom the war made young.

The cabby had come down from the box. He lit one of the two candles in the square lantern. The candle had gone out. The cabby knew everything. Cabbies in garrison towns knew all about common destinies.

Zoltán came back. He stood by the cab in the light from the candles. He looked tired.

"We can still get a cognac," he said. "But it's cold inside."

The coachmen handed him the blankets—big, rough blankets. He took them under his arm. They walked through the garden, in which a few wet deck-chairs had been forgotten.

There were tables and benches on the terrace of mouldering timber. Zoltán put down the blankets on one of the tables.

They didn't speak a word as they stood by the bar. The grumpy innkeeper's wife poured them out a cognac each. Since Zoltán had put down the blankets outside they had no more secrets from each other. They were conspirators, shameless. Time had driven them through the afternoon, through the evening. They could trick time if they turned an afternoon, an evening, into weeks, months, years. Time afforded them no shelter, but they had only to overcome their shame in order to find shelter.

They left the bar-room and walked past the tables. Zoltán put the blankets under his arm.

They didn't cross the garden; they walked round the house, across a

139

meadow. Ilona's shoes got wet; the dew crept up to her ankles. The moon hung poised above the porous clouds, invisible, giving out a dim light, like the candles in the cab. Then the forest began. They waded through dry leaves that had outlived winter, spring, and summer and were waiting for another autumn, for new old leaves that would come to join them, even if now they still hung so green and proud on the branches. They stopped. Zoltán spread out the blankets over the leaves. The smell of horses mingled with the smell of rotting vegetation, damp, and cyclamens. They still hesitated. Then their last shame fell away from them—the pious lie of lovers that the one didn't know what the other desired, didn't want what the other longed for. They longed for the same thing, urgently, breathlessly, in a common struggle against time. They were not aware of the cold that rose from the earth, the smell of the horse-blankets, the lack of shelter. They scorned houses and roofs, praised the sky that was arched over them, a divine shelter. The lie that everything was meant to be like that and therefore was good came easily to them. They praised the war that had brought them together again and made them young and shameless. They rejoiced over the deception they were inflicting on time. Their love scorned fatigue, was renewed as though fresh strength kept flowing into it from the hours that were flowing away. If they spoke, between kisses, embraces, caresses, they spoke of the future which they could now talk about again. Had they ever been downhearted? Who said they wouldn't meet again, to-morrow, perhaps, or the day after? They felt as naked as the sky was naked above them, even if it was covered by clouds. The woman's cry was like the cry of a bird. Nature listened lovingly, protectively, without curiosity. Finally the rain made them retreat, leaving their kisses for another time, even though it fell gentle and warm on the trees as on a roof.

They talked with loosened tongues as the cab took them to Baden. It stopped in the Josephsplatz. The clock on the Josephsbad showed three-thirty. The restaurants had closed long ago. They looked searchingly through the dark windows of the Café Bristol. Inside, the chairs stood on the tables; the billiard-table was covered with a cloth. Once again they had nowhere to shelter. They had to part.

"You must take the cab to Vienna," said Zoltán. "Or spend the night here."

"No, no, I'll take a cab."

He looked at her and understood. Shame had returned. She didn't want to go to Vienna with the cabby who had waited for them outside the Krainerhütte.

He paid off the cab. They walked to the cab-rank, the terminus. There was one single fiacre. The driver was asleep. Water was dripping from his overcoat on to the street. Zoltán woke him; asked him if he would be willing to drive to Vienna and how long it would take. "Two hours, maybe two and a half," said the cabby. Zoltán paid him.

Then he kissed her once more, quickly, without a word The cabby was standing beside them holding the oil-cloth.

He buttoned the cloth over Ilona's knees. Only the upper part of her body was visible. Now she was alone under the black cloth. She didn't look round.

The beating of the horses' hoofs echoed through the night-time streets. Soon, when they came to the unpaved country road, they ceased to echo. The rain was falling more heavily. It slapped on the roof of the cab. The candles in square lanterns grew pale. The sun was rising.

21

Kontowski didn't return to Vienna. He was offered the post of Austro-Hungarian ambassador in Stockholm and accepted it. As soon as he was settled there he asked Ilona to join him.

She didn't go. A common destiny was a torrent in which you drowned, but it was also a wave that carried you. War, uncertainty, the growing transport difficulties, made her threadbare excuses easier.

She couldn't come to terms with the loss of the lost years. She was twenty-eight, but lost years count double. To snatch what lies behind means to run recklessly forward. The desire to recapture what was lost became an obsession.

She was aware that she had never loved anyone but Zoltán. This love suppressed every other thought: within it common sense became contemptible, consideration of others betrayal. She had always prided herself on being level-headed. She had acted level-headedly after the Christmas Eve at the Maison Rosa, after Feri's death, when she married Rattowitz, when she stayed the night at the Hôtel de Paris in St Petersburg. Now she discarded all the laws she had lived by, her own and other people's. Love became her only law. She had been thrifty with her existence only to squander it now. The things of which she had been proud now appeared despicable. She couldn't return to Kontowski because she didn't want to return to herself.

Although she didn't want to admit it, she was still herself: therefore she had to justify what she was doing. Whenever she looked around for justification the times were ready to help. The times were her best accomplice. Accomplices pacify conscience, facilitate the deed, stand guard—and run away. So long as the ground was firm under her feet, she told herself, she could stumble with impunity. Now the ground was shaking; she had to walk with firm steps. She thought of the prices at the market that were ceaselessly changing; they fell or rose while you were going from one stall to the next. In the best shops, however, new notices appeared. "Fixed prices," they said. The self-evident was no longer self-evident. She had to determine the 'fixed prices' herself and stick to them, like the honest shopkeepers, who had the two words scratched in glass as admonitions to themselves. Since what she had done after the night in the St Petersburg hotel seemed to her cheating, she had to act differently through and through. Love was the fixed price. Love couldn't be cheating. The thought that the fixed price might be too high, might be cheating, never occurred to her.

She accepted the offer of the times, made use of their penury. She couldn't live anywhere out of reach of the Army postal service; in any place where she would have to conceal her happiness and her fears and

141

perhaps her mourning. She discovered in herself a macabre readiness
to become for the second time the widow of a man who wasn't her
husband.

22

Should she first write to the Prince and then change her life, or
should she first change her life and then write to him? He might have
interpreted a premature letter of farewell as indecision. Her decision
must be irrevocable. She set about changing her life.

She possessed Berény, jewellery, quite a fortune in cash. She could
have kept the apartment in the Bellaria, but now that she was paying
the rent and servants herself the expense went against the grain of her
thrifty nature. Moreover, the apartment was that of a mistress, not
unlike hotel rooms, designed for the visits of a stranger. The little villa
she found in Döbling, a quiet and elegant suburb, the 'Cottage,' as
the district was called, met her wishes and also, with its pretty garden,
Zita's needs. It consisted of five rooms, which were not small, but in
the friendliest way compact. She had electric-light and a telephone
installed. Then she gave her lady's maid notice, retaining only the cook
who had been eight years in her service. Old Josephine—"Peppi," as
Zita called her—a moody little woman with the strength of a bear,
timid but fearless, felt herself part of the family. Her promotion to
'housekeeper' meant more to her than the increase in wages, and since,
moreover, she had already made life unbearable for a countless succes-
sion of chambermaids, she welcomed the changes in high spirits.

When the move had been made, with the approval of Zita, who, like
most children, took more cramped living conditions for better ones,
Ilona set about putting her financial affairs in order. She placed herself
in the hands of an old banker, Maximilian von Hämmerle, and spent
hours in his confidence-inspiring, dusty counting-house behind the
Bauernmarkt poring over lists of stocks and shares and market rates
till she was conversant with expressions like dividend distribution and
admitted and unadmitted stocks. The banker advised her to buy gilt-
edged securities and to invest heavily in War Loan. She deposited her
jewellery, which she didn't intend to wear during the war, in a safe in
Hämmerle's Bank. When she was sure that she could keep the house
and grounds of Berény free from a mortgage she was satisfied with her
financial operations.

Meanwhile autumn had come.

She heard from Zoltán at least once a week, and sometimes twice.
Field-post letters came from the region of Brody, in Galicia, where
heavy fighting was in progress. Pink field cards arrived; picture postcards with no less rosy scenes of women saying farewell and soldiers
waving; and also postcards intended for children, bearing humorous
drawings of children wearing paper shakos, dragging wooden cannon
behind them, and playing at destruction. Zita began to collect these.

Every morning Ilona opened the door to the postman herself. If she
went out in the afternoon she felt impelled to be home in time for the
second post. She carried Zoltán's letters in her handbag and read them

over and over again. She had no further need to read between the lines, as she had done in St Petersburg: Zoltán's longing was clear from every word. It was no less than hers—perhaps even stronger, because it was coupled with a longing for home. Not all love was proud, but when pride was added to it love became complete.

The letters were censored, of course, arbitrarily, ruthlessly. Eight or ten lines were left out of a four-page letter; the rest was crossed out with opaque black ink. The lines that were spared, meaningless half-sentences, were like notices of bereavement framed in black. Ilona's exhortation to Zoltán to remember the censorship never reached him. The censors considered the exhortation dangerous to the state. The thick black railway-lines continued to run through Zoltán's letters.

The whole Monarchy was groaning under the censorship. Postmen went through the towns and villages like horsemen of the Apocalypse. They were angels and devils in black uniforms, heralds of happiness, messengers of death. People believed the almost unintelligible letters, although every one knew that the 'good news' that was conveyed from landing to landing, balcony to balcony, cottage to cottage, door to door, meant nothing, since the writer might have been dead before ever the letter was sent off. The censors allowed some letters through quicker than others. Letters from soldiers were sometimes held back and overtaken by condolences from the regimental commander or announcements of death from the War Ministry; as a result, letters from dead men arrived weeks after the news of their death.

Ilona was oppressed above all by the thought that since she was not Zoltán's wife, and not related to him either by blood or marriage, she would not be informed if he were wounded or dead. Alongside fear of disaster marched the oddest of human fears—the fear of not hearing about the disaster.

23

By late October, when she finally made up her mind to write to Kontowski, her last doubts had disappeared. And yet she found the letter hard to write, and not merely on account of the pain it was bound to cause Kontowski. She ought to have written: "I love a man; I am happy." It was as simple as that. But she didn't write this—either because she wanted to spare Kontowski's feelings or because the times, her accomplice and accessory, offered her conscience a refuge in which it could hide.

"You spoke of the great helplessness that would descend upon us," she wrote.

It has already come over me. It is a cruel helplessness, because I experience it with open eyes. I hear and see, speak, think, and act, but I do it all helplessly. Do you remember telling me during those last weeks in St Petersburg that you couldn't sleep because you were afraid disaster might fall upon you in your sleep? The more I feel threatened by my helplessness the more I cling to my wakefulness. I feel that I must stay awake or sleep in my armour like a warrior. In our good years I didn't miss my own will. It was superfluous for me to want anything. You took all decisions from me. I am grateful to you. But now that the times are taking our decisions for us, I must preserve what little is left of my will.

She opened Kontowski's reply with trembling hands.

He scarcely spoke of himself. "We live in a time of parting," he wrote.

Wives part from their husbands, mothers from their sons, we all part from the past. But what is parting? Is it not a sad contempt for the future? If wives knew their husbands would come back, if we could hope that the times we were parting from would return, we should not call it parting. We should call it a temporary separation. But we don't believe that we shall see each other again, we don't believe that at some future date we shall have an opportunity of saying good-bye in our own time. You are leaving me as a precaution, in order to avoid one day having to leave me without saying good-bye. I cling to the hope that what you foresee will never happen. I am not cautious. . . . I had intended to retire from the diplomatic service. Now I shall stay on; I am too much of a coward to throw every hope overboard at the same time. Write to me! I shall always know where to find you.

24

As though it hadn't been hard enough for Ilona to arrange her life without the aid of a man, to be independent contrary to nature, Zita now perpetually talked about her father.

The children in the state school she attended had fathers, and because their fathers went off to the front, became heroes, figured on lists of missing, or fell on the field of battle, they became important. One day the headmistress asked to see Teréz when she came to fetch Zita. The child had told them her father had been posted missing at the front and had probably been killed: the headmistress requested Teréz to convey her sympathy to the Baroness.

Ilona and Teréz decided not to mention the child's grim boast in her presence. But how much the mystery of her father must be on Zita's mind to cause her to make a hero of him, and even to kill him off! You couldn't rely on a child's forgetfulness.

What was Ilona to do? The fairy-story of the world traveller couldn't be repeated; Zita wouldn't have understood a divorce, and anyhow it wasn't true. Ilona didn't know where Ferdinand Rattowitz was, and on no account could she introduce the dissipated old man to Zita as her father. Should she really fall back on the common destiny send Rattowitz to the front, and make him die? She rejected the idea of such a humiliating comedy.

One evening she was sitting on Zita's bed: she read aloud to her every evening. When Zita asked about her father again she told her that he had disappeared on one of his adventurous expeditions while Zita was still a little girl. Ilona invented all kinds of details regarding the fruitless search for the missing Baron, who had never been heard of again. "Was there a war then?" asked Zita. "No, why?" Zita wrinkled her forehead. "Can people be missing when there isn't a war?" She was

144

less concerned about the possibility of her unknown father having been swallowed up by the jungle or devoured by wild beasts than by the impossibility of mourning him as a fallen hero.

Ilona didn't return to the drawing-room where Teréz was waiting for her till an hour later.

"I piled lie upon lie," she said. "Nothing has been gained except time. . . ."

25

Ilona's twenty-eighth birthday passed, so did Christmas: the war was still not at an end.

The newspapers came out late, with big white patches. Like the black lines in field-post letters, they represented the forbidden truth. The lists of killed and missing grew longer and longer. Death had become prolific. People stared at white patches and black borders. They gave up their seats in the overcrowded trams to women in widows' weeds. They bought stamps for "widows and orphans" and put them on Army postal-service letters addressed to those destined to leave widows and orphans. War-wounded flooded the city—men with one arm, one leg, blind. They didn't take off their uniforms; they groped their way through the city on sticks and crutches, conscience in field-grey. People deplored them and avoided them.

'Society,' that curious construction that determines its own limits; 'Society,' that knows no other laws but its own, laws which, with fluctuating stringency, serve no other purpose than self-preservation; that has for centuries introduced changes, but always disclaims responsibility for them, and since it has torpedoed the ship itself knows in advance exactly where the lifeboat is to be found; 'Society,' which possesses an inimitable capacity for deploring events without finding out their cause, so that ignorance becomes a condition of acceptance into its circles; 'Society,' that resembles those magnificent Venetian *palazzi* beneath which flow the filthiest canals—'Society' began to show stirrings of conscience, or, rather, of the astute desire to buy itself free from the great disaster by small acts of charity.

Since Ilona had ceased to be the Prince's mistress, since the years had smothered the source of her wealth, she belonged more than ever to this Society that prefers to see the symbols of money rather than its sources. To begin with, she thought she had no friends, since she knew only Kontowski's friends. She avoided the circles in which she had formerly moved, but word of her presence in Vienna soon got round, and the doors of the reception-rooms were immediately opened to her. 'Society's' life-urge compelled it to rejuvenate itself from time to time: for fear of being outpaced by strangers it took in the frontier-dwellers who urbanely crossed its frontiers, even if they did so on forged papers.

The ladies vied with one another in charitable works. Warm socks for "our boys" were knitted every Thursday in the house of Princess Ilani; Countess Laube zu Laubenstein ceaselessly organized balls, the "net proceeds" from which went to widows and orphans; Countess Ina von Alberthausen, the wife of a distinguished general and corps

commander on the eastern front, was actually requested by th
Emperor to recruit volunteer nurses from among the ladies of Society

When the Countess first encouraged Ilona to come "to us"
sounded like an invitation to a hen-party. Countess Gina repeated th
invitation at every opportunity—she never missed either the knittin
afternoons or the balls or the ladies' gatherings—and one day she eve
came to see Ilona in her Döbling villa. Finally Ilona agreed. Thre
times a week, from three to six, she attended the nurses' course con
ducted under the supervision of Surgeon-Major Wilhelm von Berg i
the Rudolfinerhaus.

By spring 1915 she had passed the intensive course with honour.
It was around this time that an idea which she had long harboured i
silence began to take solid shape in her mind.

26

The medical examination of girls and women who had complete
the nursing course and volunteered for duty at the front took place i
Simmering. The poor suburb did not run gently out among green field
but ended in the streets of tombstones sculptors and the forest
monuments of the central cemetery. The barracks fitted into thes
deathly surroundings.

Thin partitions had been erected in the barrack gymnasium. The
formed seven or eight dressing-rooms and a number of crooke
labyrinths, like the halls of mirrors in the 'Wurstelprater' intended fo
the amusement of children. Young girls in nurses' uniforms with th
stern mien of the newly qualified were issuing orders.

Ilona was shown into a cubicle in which two naked women wit
towels round their waists were already sitting on a narrow bench.
nurse thrust towels into Ilona's hand, pushed a pair of felt slippers
front of her, and told her to undress.

One of the two naked women rose with a brief, military nod, almo
as though she were simultaneously clicking her heels together, but didn
shake hands with Ilona. She was exceptionally tall, a 'hop-pole,' as the
said in Vienna, about forty, bony, with slack breasts that hid betwee
her bones and seemed to be mocking her erect bearing. Her short ha
that only half covered her ears betrayed that she was a suffragette, fo
whom short hair was as good as a uniform.

Fräulein Von Segelmann, as she introduced herself, had obvious
dragged her companion, Fräulein Wagemut, to the barracks with he
for the small, fair-haired girl sat huddled in her corner, clinging to th
older woman as though in frightened trust. Whereas nakedness seeme
quite natural to the ugly woman, the pretty one kept hiding her fu
rather too large breasts behind her arms; she also kept shifting t
skimpy towel round her loins, thereby revealing the very thing she w
trying to keep hidden.

Fräulein Von Segelmann looked with utter disgust at the dain
underclothes which Ilona began to peel off.

"Do you really want to go to the front?" she asked, as though n
body who came to the medical examinations in such gauzy pant
could possibly be credited with patriotic intentions.

146

"Yes," replied Ilona curtly.

"Which course did you attend?"

"The one at the Rudolfinerhaus."

"I thought so."

"Why?"

"The Rudolfinerhaus supplies very few volunteers. The ladies Countess Alberthausen recruits prefer to stay in Vienna." Gesticulating with her long hands, Fräulein Von Segelmann began to grow angry. "Most of them only force their way into hospitals in order to find a husband. They don't even know how to empty a bed-pan properly; they flounce through the wards as if they were on a dance-floor, doing more harm than good. No sooner have they tricked some poor, unfortunate casualty into saying 'Yes' than they drag him off to the altar, and no sooner have they celebrated a 'war wedding than they throw off their nurse's uniform and become nice little women again." She sat down, crossed her thin legs, and examined her toes. "None of these wretched women understands that the war is our great opportunity. Now or never we can shake off the yoke. The longer the war lasts the more positions we shall capture. To-day I saw the first tram-conductress. But that's only the beginning. . . ."

"The women will be glad when they can stay at home again," said Ilona.

The little blonde looked at her out of stupid eyes, admiring and shocked, as though Ilona had put into words what she herself dared not say.

"Why do you take up a profession if you think like that?" objected Fräulein Von Segelmann like an examining magistrate

"I shall become a nurse for the duration of the war. Like the tram conductresses."

Ilona had slowly undressed. As she did so she caught herself shamelessly displaying her nakedness to Fräulein Von Segelmann, as though there could be no better answer to the challenge of the flat-chested girl. She hung her panties over her lace-trimmed petticoat like the pink banner of femininity. But because such cruel coquettishness was alien to her, she begun to scrutinize the reasons for her irritation.

She didn't want to "take up" a profession, as Fräulein Von Segelmann had expressed it, as though a profession were a club or a gun. People spoke of 'professional women' as if they were something new, but in reality women could only change their profession, since they already had one. They were wives. They were mothers. Working women? Were there any others? The women who boasted of being 'working women' merely wanted to change their place of work. They wanted to get out of the house; they fled from a vocation to a profession. To whom did they intend to leave the housework, the cooking, the bringing up of children, the care of the family's happiness that was in their hands? To nobody. They wanted to keep what they had and capture what they were not entitled to. They sought adventure, conflict, excitement. Wasn't it exciting enough for them to be the protectress of a second life, the more important one? Did they, who had hitherto held mankind's happiness in strong hands, really want to become the weaker sex?

Ilona took off her stockings. All at once she had the feeling that there had been a terrible misunderstanding. Was she 'taking up' a profession as soldiers 'take up' the weapons that are thrust into their hands without a by-your-leave? All she wanted was to get to Zoltán. There was no other way to the man she loved. He had been torn away from her at the moment when they had become one. Now she was a half. The Hungarian word for woman was *feleség*, halfness. There was no more beautiful word. One half strove irresistibly to reach the other. It had nothing to do with profession, conflict, or captured positions.

The little blonde had been called. She left the cubicle, without having addressed a word to Ilona, and tripped along with her loin-cloth, her arms crossed over her breasts, pink and terrified, a piglet going to the slaughter.

"My neighbour's daughter," commented Fräulein Von Segelmann contemptuously. "I don't know why I brought her here. She'll run away at the first cannon-shot. . . ."

"Who can be sure he won't run away at the first cannon-shot?"

"Ridiculous! Men don't run away, even though they're cowards."

"Do you hate men, Fräulein Von Segelmann?"

"I despise them. Don't imagine I'm going to the front for sentimental reasons. I'm thinking of the future. If we leave the war to men they'll go one boasting of their deeds until they feel like starting another. Only if a sufficient number of women go to war on both sides shall we be able to call their bluff." She was talking like an election candidate. "We mustn't leave the men alone together. They only make war in order to be on their own, as they are during their beer-parties and skittle evenings."

"And you want to nurse men? You'd rather strangle them."

Fräulein Von Segelmann gulped. Her throat moved up and down as though she had an Adam's apple like a man.

"It's my patriotic duty," she said evasively.

Ilona was considering what to reply to the election candidate when the curtain of the cubicle was thrust aside.

"There you are, my dear," cried Countess Alberthausen, spreading out her arms. "I've been searching for you frantically. The idiots have kept you waiting. Take your towels and come with me."

Ilona tied the large towel tighter round her waist and put the other round her shoulders. Then she followed Countess Gina through the maze of the gymnasium.

There was a smell as of too many women. They looked at one another with hostility, as only naked women can look at each other— with the eyes of the absent men. It was as though none of them wanted to be here and yet denied the others the right to be here. They wore their bare skin like a prison uniform.

Countess Gina, grey-haired, powerfully built, in a pastel-blue spring costume with an enormous feather hat and a large enamel brooch bearing the Red Cross on the whalebone-stiffened collar of her white blouse, ruthlessly forced a path for them through the mass of naked bodies with her blue umbrella or sunshade—it was impossible to tell which it was.

Ilona felt ridiculous, an adult locked up in a nursery. She could have been friendly with Countess Alberthausen for years without ever appearing before her naked. She stumbled along behind her, past the sweating women, stripped and wearing huge mens' slippers that disgusted her. She understood what Kontowski meant by the new helplessness. It was not the powerlessness that goes with the loss of consciousness, a paralysis without actions or thoughts. He who was attacked by this new and as yet nameless disease thought and acted, but he didn't act as he thought; he was not paralysed—indeed, he moved with the hectic eagerness of a twitching marionette—but like a marionette he had no will of his own and was powerless in the face of a dominant will; a part of events and yet not a participant in them. She hadn't wanted to learn nursing; but she had become a nurse because others had become nurses, although they didn't want to either. She didn't want to go to the front, of which she had only the vaguest notion and where she saw no one but Zoltán; but she had to go to the front, because the compulsion that dominated him begot further compulsion. She didn't want to leave Zita; but the compulsion that dominated her was transmitted to the life of the child. She didn't want to parade naked before Army surgeons, dependent upon their 'fit' or 'unfit'; but in a minute she would be standing in front of them, powerlessly subservient to their will.

Countess Gina opened the door of the examination-room without knocking. She left Ilona standing in the doorway, strode up to a long table with four or five doctors sitting behind it, whispered something into the ear of one of them, a surgeon-major, and beckoned Ilona with her umbrella. A woman with petty-bourgeois skin, who wore her towel like an apron, was quickly dealt with. The doctors turned to Ilona, while the Countess sat down on a stool, as though to say that her presence alone could afford a sure guarantee against the word 'unfit.'

Ilona found the politeness with which she was treated by the gentlemen in white gowns over uniforms embarrassing, because it revealed the absence of that impersonality which alone makes a medical examination bearable. All the doctors were elderly, yet the naked woman's beauty seemed to confuse them. They applied their instruments, cold wooden stethoscopes, to her cautiously and awkwardly, as though testing the heart-beat of a marble statue. A sigh of relief ran round the table when the chairman of the examining board, an old gentleman who leafed importantly through his papers during the examination, finally requested Ilona to go and have her ears and eyes tested.

"I'll see you in your dressing-room," the Countess called after her.

Ilona was glad to escape with her nakedness into the anonymity of the adjoining room. At least half a dozen naked women were standing about in here. The fact that they were not given time to dress before the test letter-cards were set up in front of them and all sorts of words were whispered into their ears increased Ilona's discomfort.

She was left alone, and stood by the window, waiting.

Her name was called out.

She read the large and small X, B, R, S, T, F. She repeated the words whispered by the Army surgeon from the other end of the room. She shuffled back to her cubicle in her man's slippers.

The Countess was waiting for her.

27

During the night she stood bending over Zita's bed watching the sleeping child.

Zita was sleeping on her side. Her hands under her cheek were like two tiny pillows on the pillow. A ray of light shone through the crack of the door on to her hair. The goblin restlessness that emanated from her by day and vanished from her face. Tiny beads of sweat glistened under her slightly tip-tilted nose. Everything about her seemed perfect, not because it was perfectly beautiful, but because, in this unsuspecting tranquillity, it betrayed the hand of God that creates man tranquil and unsuspecting. From time to time her lips moved softly. She was evidently dreaming.

There was nothing more peaceful than a sleeping child and nothing more helpless. The peacefulness and the helplessness were one and the same. Adults slept just as peacefully when they believed that God was watching over them. Only the person who was sure of help was so helpless. Few adults believed in God. All children believed in their mothers. God didn't slip away. Mothers shouldn't slip away.

Ilona felt like a traitress. On the journey from St Petersburg she had sworn to herself never again to leave Zita. That was less than a year ago. Now she was waiting for the order to desert her child.

She thought of the medical examination. She had become a child without a will of her own, a humiliated animal. Why hadn't they branded her as they branded the horses which the soldiers drove away from the pastures? In her youth she had thought herself chosen. Now her flesh seemed to become one with the flesh of other women, a shapeless lump with hundreds of breasts, navels, thighs, a seething mass grave. Men had to die in order to fill the mass graves, on both sides of the line, like the brass scales of a weighing-machine: equilibrium demanded it. Women died voluntarily.

She wasn't an animal, a child, or a man. She could go and cancel it all.

Zita moved. In her sleep her hand felt for the blanket. Ilona covered her up. The child murmured something. It sounded like thanks and made Ilona feel ashamed.

How great must her love for Zoltán be, since it made her shameless! She searched far back in the past. Feri had died a cowardly, shameless death. Then came Kontowski, came the loveless years of her youth. Finally Zoltán, already in flight. She had a right to catch up with him. That was her right to happiness. "What is happiness?" Dr Ginsburg had said. Wasn't happiness lying in front of her, in the little bed, helpless?

She didn't find what she was looking for in the past. She had thought only of herself: that was why she didn't find it. She must think of Zoltán. Her child was not in danger. Nothing would change in Zita's life. She might have lived with Kontowski in Stockholm. Then she wouldn't have looked for an excuse, and yet it would have been a betrayal. It wasn't a betrayal if she went to the front. She wasn't only a mother—she was a woman. Love for Zoltán couldn't cancel out love for Zita. Zoltán had written to her about a comrade in the regiment who had been wounded and met his wife by chance in the field hospital. Such coincidences, such miracles, did happen. Her heart beat so violently that she was afraid Zita might hear it. She had a right to the miracle. She would meet Zoltán. She would put her arms protectively around him and lead him out of the fire. If he was unhurt she must preserve him from wounds. His hands belonged to the world. If he was wounded she must tend his wounds. Nobody knew who he was. She alone could raise him up out of the mass. If he was dead, then she must find him among the dead. Nobody could find him but she.

The creaking of the door betrayed that Teréz was standing there waiting.

Ilona tiptoed past her. It seemed to her that her sister was looking at her reproachfully. Probably Teréz only meant that she had stayed too long in the nursery. She pitied and envied the quiet, arid girl who would never leave Zita's nursery.

28

Ilona was still in Vienna.

She was working in a hospital, or, rather, a school that had been converted into a hospital. Hospitals were full to overflowing. Wounded soldiers were brought to Vienna, but that didn't mean that fewer inconsiderate civilians fell ill. The desks and blackboards still stood pushed together in the corridors of the suburban school. There had been no time to get rid of them. Duty-lists of doctors and nurses were now pinned to the blackboards on which teachers had formerly written the ABC. A few stuffed owls and stiff hares stood in the corner collecting dust. The maps in the schools had become meaningless by comparison with the maps in the coffee-houses. The groaning of the sick came from classroom IIa or IIIb.

Ilona worked from eight to six five days a week, and often on Sunday and in the night. She got used to the groaning of the wounded, scarcely heard the monotonous anguish. She eyed the ladies who distributed books and cakes angrily, as she herself had formerly been eyed. The volunteer sisters who had reported for front-line duty had to be hardened. To be hardened meant to become hard. An old territorial's leg had been amputated. He complained for days about pains in the leg that had long ago been thrown away like an unwanted bandage. It fell to Ilona to tell him the truth. He began to cry; the tears trickled into his long black beard. A young infantryman from a small village near Linz asked Ilona to write and tell his fiancée to come, because he was going to die. He died, but his fiancée didn't come. The medical superintendent called Ilona in to help with operations. "You're a brave woman," he said. Dr Ginsburg had said the same thing.

At the beginning of July she received a field postcard from Zoltán. She had been without news for four weeks. He wrote that he had been transferred to the Second Tirolese Imperial Rifles in Italy. The unit had been sent south hurriedly and secretly. He was well. He said nothing about leave. Perhaps the censor had crossed out leave.

A few days later she received her own posting—to Galicia.

She drove straight from the hospital to Countess Alberthausen. She asked for help in getting her posting changed. Nurses were needed on the Isonzo front too. "This is war, my dear," said the Countess. "Our brave boys can't choose where they want to go either." She always called the soldiers "our brave boys," as though they were children. Under pressure, Ilona admitted the reason for her request. "This is war, my dear," reiterated the Countess. Ilona had only a bare week left. The greater the difficulties the more certain she became that Zoltán expected her. She no longer felt Kontowski's "great helplessness"; she opposed her will to it. She moved heaven and earth. The banker Hämmerle had connexions. She knew General Von Schneider-Wolin at the War Ministry. On Sunday she drove out to Rodaun to see Princess Ellani. Everywhere the same wry looks. Had Baroness Rattowitz not acted from patriotism? Had it perhaps been from love? Everywhere the same shrug of the shoulders. "How do you hope to find him on the Isonzo front?" asked old Hämmerle. Everywhere the same answer. "This is war, my dear."

Two days before she was due to leave for Galicia she carried out a decision she had put off again and again.

Kontowski was in Vienna. He had retired from the diplomatic service and returned from Stockholm. He had telephoned Ilona immediately after his arrival. Now she telephoned him. He invited her to supper the following week. No, she said, she must talk to him to-day. "At five o'clock," he said.

The medical superintendent didn't let her go till four-thirty. He shook his head. She left the room before he could say that this was war.

29

She remembered the afternoon when she had driven to Schönbrunn beside the painter Borsonyai, to the Emperor. Suddenly he was standing before her in his white uniform, groping for his glasses. He was now eighty-five. He had been ruling for sixty-seven years. She had to call the figures to mind in order to be sure that he was really still alive. The tobacconist in the Lerchenfelder Gürtel must have died a long time ago; a cinema had long stood on the site of her shop. Perhaps it hadn't been a good thing that the general's son was allowed to stay in the Army. Perhaps his name was on the list of missing. Time was stronger than the Emperor. It pulled down houses; gave the lie to his promises; turned his grace into disaster. When you were tired you stretched out your hand to the past. "Permission for an officer to marry," had been written on the foolscap sheet. She had asked pardon for Lajos. Now

152

she was going to Kontowski to ask his help in getting to the front, to her beloved. Suppose she changed her mind this time too? Suppose she stifled the voice of her blood, the longing that knew no consideration for others, no 'helplessness,' no shame? Suppose she asked Kontowski to set her free from the uniform into which nothing had forced her but shameless love? Then she had been carrying Zita under her heart. Now Zita was ten. Must she betray her child a second time?

The Prince was once again living in his palace in the Prinz-Eugen-Strasse.

It was an enormous house, not built for a bachelor, and scarcely for a living family. It was a museum of dead Kontowskis. Hundreds of years ago there might have been a family that needed such spaciousness, a family that included a fat princess, a dozen *infantes*, aunts, uncles, major-domos, footmen, cooks, and permanent guests. It seemed as though one could still hear the rustle of silk and velvet in the ancestral portrait-gallery, the shuffling of dancers under the painted ceilings and the footsteps of the servants on the marble stairs. They were all dead. The footman walked ahead of Ilona, a mute guide. She wondered why the house wasn't heated, although there was no possible reason for heating it, since the July sun was blazing outside. Why hadn't the footman greeted her more cordially? His name was Julius; she knew him. Old servants weren't so considerate as their masters; they didn't forgive women the pain they caused their masters.

Julius opened the library-door and let Ilona in.

Kontowski was standing at one of the bookshelves with his back to the door. He had a book in his hand. He turned round, put down the book, and came towards her.

He was wearing a pearl-grey summer suit with a wide, dark-red tie. Although he possessed countless suits, she had known them all. She didn't know this one. Small things like this revealed what strangers they had become to each other.

He kissed her hand and led her to a laid tea-table by the window.

"How glad I am to see you!" he said. "You haven't altered."

"Forgive the way I'm dressed," she said. "I didn't have time to change."

"The nurse's uniform suits you, as everything does."

"You haven't altered either, Taszilo," she said, although it wasn't what she thought.

He looked tired. His skin was yellow. The grey hair had spread, hesitantly, like autumn snow.

He poured her a cup of tea. He asked after Zita, Teréz, the station-master. The more he spoke and the more she told him, the greater strangers they became to each other. There were still bridges linking them together. But beyond the bridges lay two alien worlds, hers and his. "Have you still got Berény?" he asked. "Yes, of course." How could he ask? "Are you going to take a new post?" she asked. "No, I've retired." How could she ask?

"You wanted to speak to me urgently?" said the Prince. "Are you going to the front?"

"How do you know?"

153

She was no longer certain that she could carry out her plan. As once before—at her wedding—she felt the gulf between intention and act. She had intended to spare his feelings, not to tell him why she was in a hurry to get to the Isonzo front. Half the truth was not enough. The whole truth seemed to her mean. She herself appeared mean in her own eyes. Would she, in peacetime, ever have thought of getting her past lover to smooth the path to the bed of her present lover? Was it because her lover had no bed that she felt able to do so? Did the trenches excuse everything? She suspected herself of having kept her nurse's uniform on intentionally. The uniform merely meant that she was young enough to nurse young men. The world was splitting up into the fit and the unfit. The insolent robustness of youth was everywhere giving itself airs. Whoever was too old to die was unfit for life. The young were proud of their crass ability to die. Wisdom no longer counted, nor did nobility of soul or the fruits of experience; nothing counted now but the body that could be transformed into dust. Her nurse's uniform was ostentation. The whole truth was sensuality and death.

Ilona looked round. The afternoon sun was shining in through the tall pointed arches of the windows on to the old leather volumes. The books were old, weather-beaten faces. They seemed to be smiling with tired wisdom, like old men sitting in the afternoon sunshine. The books wouldn't crumble to dust. The teaset with the Kontowski arms bore the pale reflection of the setting sun. She had deserted this world for the noisy, youthful, arrogantly dying street. Now she had come back as a petitioner.

"Yes," she said. "I have to go to the front."

"Do you want to be exempted from service at the front?"

The Emperor hadn't made it so easy for her when she saw him at Schönbrunn.

"No," she said. "I want to go to the front."

He lit a long Russian cigarette and, as always, allowed it to smoulder away between his fingers.

"Not from patriotism or a sense of duty," she said quickly. "I want to be near a man."

"I know. Zoltán Szomoru."

"He's on the Isonzo. I'm supposed to go to Galicia the day after to-morrow."

"I understand. Do you know which regiment he is with?"

"The Tirolese Imperial Rifles."

"Which regiment?"

"The Second."

"How does he come to be with the Austrians?"

"I don't know."

"Which hospital have you been assigned to?"

"The Forty-first Field Hospital."

The Prince rose. He walked to the door. With his hand on the brocade bell-pull, he stood still.

"Shall I have him recalled to Vienna?" he asked.

"No, no, that's impossible. He doesn't want to. . . ."

154

Kontowski still didn't ring.

"Have you thought it over thoroughly?" he asked.

"Of course."

"It's not of course. I hope you don't believe the lies the Government spreads through the bulletins. A hero's death is no kinder than any other death." He smiled slightly ironically. "Your face won't be seen at the front. Nurses have to wear gas-masks, like every one else."

"I know," she said. She had known, but she had never thought about it.

The Prince tugged the bell-pull.

"Get the War Ministry on the telephone for me," he ordered as Julius entered. "I want to speak to General Von Plötzeneder."

Julius went out. Ilona said,

"I shouldn't have come to you if I could have found any other way."

"The others wouldn't have understood." His hand was still on the bell-pull. "Love is the only thing that makes sense in these senseless times."

The footman came back. Kontowski followed him.

I'm humiliating myself more and more, thought Ilona. She felt as naked as in the labyrinth of the medical examination-rooms at Simmering barracks.

Kontowski re-entered the room and sat down.

"It's settled," he said. "You must be patient for ten days, till the next troop train leaves for Italy. You have been assigned to the Schönpass casualty-clearing station. It's not too far from the Col di Lana, where the Imperial Rifles are stationed, but not too close to the lines either. One mustn't carry heroism too far, otherwise it becomes ridiculous. Report to-morrow to First Lieutenant Stanitzky at the War Ministry."

"Thank you," she said. Tears forced their way into her throat.

"Stop that," he said, "otherwise I shall start feeling noble. I had no alternative but to fulfil your wish. Heroes are beyond rivalry. We have created these heroes; now, for better or worse, we must live with them."

"Are you happy?" he asked.

She was sitting stiffly in the armchair in her light-blue nurse's uniform. She nodded.

"Did it start in St Petersburg?"

"Yes."

"And you would have married me in spite of it?"

"If I had married you I shouldn't have seen him again."

"Does a scrap of paper mean so much to you?"

"I didn't marry you. Isn't that enough?"

"Will he marry you?"

"You know the Vatican won't annul my marriage."

"The war doesn't halt even at the gates of the Vatican. Do you hear from Rattowitz?"

"No."

"He isn't well. I had him taken to a sanatorium near Budapest. I don't think he will survive the war. He will die with the Monarchy. In his own way he is a hero."

"I'm sorry . . ." she stammered.

"You needn't feel sorry for him."

It sounded arrogant, as though to say, "I lent you Rattowitz, but now I'm taking him back. It's none of your business what happens to Rattowitz. We shall both die with the Monarchy."

The sun was setting in the trees of the Lichtenstein Park, a red ball thrown up into the air by children at play. The library was like the turret of a fortress. It was impossible to imagine that the house lay in the middle of Vienna, in the boiling-hot summer city with its workers, men, on leave, war-wounded, profiteers, women, soldiers, widows, and orphans.

"Will he marry you?" reiterated Kontowski.

"Why don't you ask me whether I would marry him?"

"Women attach importance to scraps of paper."

She wanted to leave. With every minute Kontowski became less of a stranger, and with every minute she hated him more. He hadn't asked her any questions until he had been able to show his power. Perhaps for fear that if he questioned her she might not ask any favour of him. Or perhaps because his nobility, his arrogant nobility, called upon him to act like this. Now he was demanding the price.

"I want you to be happy," he said.

"I am happy—I've already told you so."

"How long has he been at the front?"

"From the beginning."

"Hasn't he had any leave?"

"No."

"That's unfair." He threw his cigarette into the ash-tray, still burning. "Then you haven't seen one another often?"

"No."

The smoke rose into her face. She stubbed out his cigarette.

"Sorry," he said mockingly. "He is to be envied. Our women are not as faithful as our heroes deserve. Did you know him while you were still Aporfalvy's fiancée?"

"I've always known him."

"Do you really know what awaits you out there?" he asked, as though at last willing to drop the subject.

"Yes."

"Nurses get killed too."

"I know."

"I can't promise that you will remain in the casualty-clearing station."

"I didn't ask for that, Taszilo."

"Fresh wounds are different from scarred ones."

"I've seen a great deal here in the hospital."

"And you could stand it?"

"Yes."

He looked at her hands, as though he thought they would betray to him what she did not betray.

She drew back her hands.

"You must love him very much," he said.

It had been an illusion: he hadn't changed the subject. His questions

156

rained down on her. Had she really discovered her love so late? Had Feri Aporfalvy known about Zoltán? Had it happened that evening in St Petersburg when she went to the concert alone? Why hadn't the conductor obtained exemption from front-line service? Did he love her enough? Was she more to him than an adventure? How long had he stayed in Petersburg? Did she go with him to the base, and why not? How often had they been together? Did she imagine that she would meet him on the Isonzo, that they could be alone together? Was he really so young? Had she a photo of him in uniform? Did he return to Petersburg that time? Over and over again Petersburg. . . .

She answered Yes and No, No and Yes. Her finger-nails tore the leather of the armchair. These were the morbid questions he had asked during their first years together. These were the questions that had detached themselves from the monologues, from the accusations against her and against himself. In those days she was able to tolerate his illness. In those days she had been compassionate. In those days they had been alone; no healthy third party stood between them. One didn't love the illness of people one loved, but one tolerated it. Illnesses became repulsive when one ceased to love the sufferer. She now considered him capable of any baseness—even a secret telephone-call to the War Ministry. His power began to seem to her almost as nauseating as his illness.

"I must go," she said. "Thank you, Taszilo." There was no longer any emotion in her voice.

He accompanied her. It was almost dark in the gallery. He didn't put the light on. He took her hand. His hand was damp.

They went down the marble stairs.

"I'm leaving for the country soon," he said. "Julius will always know where you can find me."

"Thank you," she said again.

The warm summer evening absorbed her. The jasmine on the walls of the Lichtenstein Gardens gave off an overpowering scent. A lorry-load of soldiers rattled past. The soldiers were not singing.

Ilona felt like singing. She hastened towards the boiling-hot summer city with its workers, men on leave, war-wounded, profiteers, women, soldiers, widows, and orphans, as though towards a lover.

30

She stayed only one night in Schönpass. When she arrived, after travelling for days, she heard that an offensive had been launched on the Isonzo. No one seemed to know whether by the Italians or the Austrians.

"We have had instructions to send all nurses who come from the interior straight on to Sant'Andrea," explained the chief surgeon at the casualty-clearing station. He looked at the nurses. "Field Hospital Number Four," he said. "A cart will be placed at your disposal."

At supper a young doctor sat down beside Ilona.

"It's a crime to send you to the front so unprepared," he said in a low voice. "But our nurses are exhausted. They can't be sent forward."

During the night the nurses who had come from the 'interior' were issued with their field kit. There was only a paraffin-lamp burning in the stores. The sergeant-major who issued the equipment was smoking a cigar; in the smoke from the cigar and the paraffin-lamp he was almost invisible. Rucksack, water-bottle, gas-mask. The rubber of the gas-mask was soft and wet in Ilona's hand. She remembered what Kontowski had said.

Next morning a cart stood waiting for them. Although it was early, the sky was deep blue. The wings of the birds furrowed the sky. An Italian summer day was breaking.

Four nurses and five soldiers returning to their units climbed into the cart. None of the soldiers belonged to the Tirolese Imperial Rifles. Yes, they had heard that the Imperial Rifles were not far from Gorizia. Gorizia wasn't far from Sant'Andrea. The Col di Lana? Yes, that was a mountain. There were a lot of mountains. The wagon bumped over churned-up roads and trackless fields. Flies sat on the sweating backs of the horses. When the way led uphill the nurses and soldiers had to get out and walk. The sun blazed down on the stony karst soil. The sun was as hard as the rock.

Ilona's feet hurt. She tried not to show it. She marched on, smiled, joked with the soldiers, clambered up into the cart and down again. She felt at times as though she were pulling the cart herself. Less than ever could she picture what 'the front' meant. As seen from Vienna she had reached the front long ago. But the people at Schönpass talked about the front as though they themselves were in Vienna. The front was somewhere out ahead. But where?

She walked alongside the horses as though she were a stranger alongside herself. Was she really Baroness Rattowitz, who lived in a Döbling villa and had a child, smart friends, soft shoes, and countless dresses? Only what she had left behind seemed to her real.

They ate their lunch rations in a devastated farmhouse. Its occupants had left it in haste. Soldiers had looted it. There was a grandfather clock in the best room. Every now and then it struck. Soldiers looted provisions, slaughtered chickens, slashed linen, but clocks they wound up. The driver watered the horses at the spring from which silvery-clear water flowed, as though it had to go on flowing till the farm-people returned, something flowing yet permanent amid what was static yet transient. A cow had been left behind. It was running round and round in a circle in the field behind the house. Its udder was full. Its bellowing filled the air. One of the soldiers ran after it. The others watched the performance—the bellowing cow that grew wilder and wilder with pain, and the sweating soldier grew more and more furious because the animal didn't know that he wanted to relieve it of its suffering.

Shortly afterwards they began to feel the proximity of the front. There were isolated farms, and still a few peasants to be seen trudging heavily across the fields from whose soil stones projected as though stones were all that it bore. They didn't look up. Not until the cart had bumped past did they turn round and stare after it malevolently, as though the occupants were enemies. Soldiers were enemies, their own

158

side as well as the others. The nearness of the front couldn't be seen or heard, but it could be smelt. There was a sweet smell of decay. Dead horses. Perhaps the whole front smelt like a putrefying horse.

The cart travelled westward, towards the setting sun. Now there were no more surly peasants. Slender church-towers or rough stone announced the presence of dead villages. Only the churches didn't look deserted. He who dwelt in them had not fled.

In two or three of the villages soldiers were quartered. They were standing around the black "goulash cannon," the mobile field kitchen, with mess-tins in their hands. Some were sitting outside deserted houses. One of these houses had been struck by a shell. There was a hole in the wall, a round window. As they passed they could see a grandfather clock in the room. When the cart stopped it was surrounded by soldiers. They eyed the nurses longingly, but their glances weren't so impudent as in the city barracks. The soldiers were children; the farther they went from the towns the more they longed for their mothers. There were no Imperial Rifles among them either. To them too the Col di Lana was only a mountain.

The road ran uphill and narrowed. Walls of rock crowded in upon it from both sides as though trying to block it. They passed a military cemetery. The wooden crosses stood in rows, like soldiers on parade. The crosses bore the name, the date of birth, and the date of death. Some of the names were burnt in, others only hurriedly scribbled in chalk. Born 1892, 1875, 1893, 1881. The dates of birth varied. Died 1915. It was a good year for death.

Ilona didn't believe the driver when he said they were near their destination. The cart had come from nowhere; it was going nowhere. Fatigue laid itself over Ilona's ears like a pair of hands: she no longer heard the tapping of the hoofs, nor did she hear when one of the nurses spoke to her. At the same time voices were raised in her which she had not previously heard, as though they had been in a prison yard guarded by the wakeful senses; now the guards were asleep and the voices had broken out. Love of Zoltán didn't justify what she was doing. True, she had written to tell him she was coming, but she didn't know whether he had received her letter. She was no longer sure that he wanted her to do what she was doing. She was not obeying the loved one, but only love, blind to all dangers, deaf to all voices; apparently so strong that it tore down every obstacle, but in reality so weak that it had to keep on going forward, forward. Fear sat beside her. The rocks would close behind her and block the road back.

The track grew steeper and narrower. They didn't go downhill, as though it were no longer worthwhile to spare the horses, the dead, floating horses. Cats screamed, love-mad and hungry. Through the clear, starry night came the rumble of distant thunder. A church-tower loomed out of the darkness. The moon rose behind it. The church-tower was like a stone saint encircled by a luminous halo.

"That's Sant'Andrea," said the driver.

That was her destination.

31

The distant thunder had been the rumble of guns.

The cart stopped outside a single-storey house built of heavy blocks of stone. All the houses were built of stone, as though they had been hewn out of the rocks, so that in spite of their solidity they looked unfinished. The house stood in a narrow street. To reach it the cart had crossed a square and passed a church standing all by itself in the centre—a toy church which the playing child had not yet put with the toy houses. The narrow street led out of this square, but it ended neither in another square nor in another street; nor did it run out into a field or meadow; it seemed simply to get lost, as though the earth curved over and came to an end.

Nobody took any notice of the new arrivals. The driver unharnessed the horses and brought them to safety, like a ship's captain, who, once in port, has no thought for anything but his ship and leaves the passengers to their own devices. The soldiers went off in various directions.

As the nurses stood there at a loss Ilona realized why the street seemed to end in the void. Searchlights were patrolling the sky. They were looking for a target, but they merely got tangled up with one another, swords of light duelling in the sky. Like drunken duellers plunging their swords into the body of their judge, they transfixed the moon. The duelling lights revealed that the road ended in a declivity. Down below lay the valley that stretched to the foot of Sant'Andrea. A few paces from the house were enough to bring into sight the Austrian artillery on the steep slopes, camouflaged with leafy branches from which the flames shot out like blossoms. Here and there tiny human figures dodged the light like crazy, light-shy moths, and gun-barrels flashed in the beams of the searchlights. On the horizon the sky lay in a night-time fever. Now they could not only smell the front, they could see and hear it. The mountains into which they had travelled multiplied the angry sound, as though the mighty, enraged at their powerlessness to quieten the din of battle, were whipping passions still higher. But because Sant'Andrea lay beyond and also above the front, everything they saw and heard became doubly terrifying: they looked down upon events as though from a box at the theatre. On the stage there was violent firing, men were buried by rocks, the actors fell down and died.

Finally an old man with a grey, stubbly beard, who looked like a ghost because he was the only one not in uniform, showed the new arrivals the way to the house through a small, stony garden.

The other nurses vanished; they went out into the street in search of their billets. On the way here Ilona had already been filled with envy of these women's independence. They felt at home everywhere, even at the front. While she herself stood there helplessly, waiting for a fresh outburst of anger from the older nurse, the old man who had directed them before reappeared. He took charge of Ilona, leading her across the street to a house in which the hospital kitchen had been set up. She didn't know which was east and which was west, confused right and left. "One shouldn't get to know a village during the night,' said the old man in German that sounded like Italian. The moon got caught up in a white flag and turned even whiter.

Meal-time was long past, but the bearded man, who darted to and fro with a candle in his hand like a goblin, found sardines and biscuits. "That's the best I can do for you, nurse," he said in a friendly tone. "To-morrow morning they'll look after you."

To-morrow morning. . . .

Then she stopped thinking. She had no other wish than to sleep. She saw a bed in front of her, enormously large, as soft as the sky. Her eyes closed.

When she woke her head was lying on her arm on the window-sill. The wrist-watch protected by a grille, which she had been given in Vienna, had stopped. She didn't know whether she had slept for a few minutes or several hours. In her sleep she had travelled on and on and on. The guns had thundered in her sleep, but she hadn't heard them.

It was quite quiet. The searchlights were no longer circling. Candles and a few paraffin-lamps were burning in some of the other houses. The village looked almost friendly through the glass-less windows.

All her fatigue had left her. She stood up quickly, and quickly straightened out her crumpled uniform.

Outside the door she came to a stop. The scene that met her eyes told her what the time was. An hour must have passed, perhaps a bit more. The nurse across the way had reckoned with casualties in one or two hours. Those who were to die or become wounded didn't know it at the time, but the nurse did.

A stream of casualties blocked Ilona's path.

They were being carried past on stretchers, hastily bandaged. Blood stained the bandages black, for in the moonlight there was only black and white. The light from the pocket torches danced over their faces like big, ugly glow-worms. A young face was turned to Ilona. Blood was trickling down over the soldier's forehead from under the head-bandage, running over his nose and into his mouth. He moistened his lips with his tongue, as though drinking his own blood.

Then for a time no stretchers passed. Soldiers trudged past with one arm in a sling. One hobbled on one leg, like a child playing. Blood dripped on to the cobbles from the foot he was holding up in the air. He hopped and screamed. Ilona couldn't understand what he said.

A man wounded in the thigh leaned on one whose hands were bandaged. He had put both hands on the shoulders of the man in front, like one gymnast about to leapfrog over another. The soldier with the bandaged hands shook him off and began to run. The other fell down. He couldn't stand up again. Then another lot of bearers came by with stretchers. They went past him. He extended both arms to them like a beggar vainly holding out his hands for charity.

Two bearers put down their stretcher. One of them bent down over the wounded man they had been carrying. "He's dead," he said. Then they lifted the stretcher again and walked on, corpse-bearers.

Human sounds filled the summer night. One wounded man was screaming. Each time the stretcher-bearers trod on a fresh cobble-stone he bellowed, as though the stone were piercing his body. There

161

were whines and whimpers, moans and groans. "I'm dying!" one man cried in German. They were screaming in Croat and Hungarian. They screamed like animals; that's why they were understood. "I'm dying!" they screamed, and imagined that others were moved by their deaths. The old screamed and the young, the good and the evil, the cowards and also the heroes. Not all of them died.

But Ilona didn't know that. She stood in the doorway, paralysed, aware that she was in hell, where men rise from the dead only to die again and again. What prevented her from screaming that she herself was going to die was not shame, but merely the feeling that she was already dead. But it was shame that prevented her from laughing at the thought that she had come to hell voluntarily—a woman and a volunteer.

The beggar was still lying on the ground.

Ilona shook off her paralysis. She ran to him and raised him up, as she had been taught, supporting him with her arms under his. No doubt she was hurting him. She almost had to laugh again at the thought of the Vienna hospital. Wounds that were not fresh were not wounds at all. Old blood flowed away easily. The dying she had seen had got used to dying.

"*Köszönöm*," said the man in Hungarian. "Thank you."

"*Csak jöjjön velem*," she said. "Come with me."

He looked at her as though he had seen an angel. He thought angels spoke Hungarian. He couldn't have been more than twenty. He reminded her of Lajos.

She had told him to come with her, but she didn't know where to go. In the main square in front of the church, which stood there crooked and forgotten, the stretcher-bearers split up into various groups. "One shouldn't get to know a village during the night," the old man had said.

"Well, what are you standing there for, nurse?" she heard a voice say beside her.

She found herself looking into the face of a regimental medical officer. He was wearing a white coat over his uniform. The coat was covered with blood. The moon was reflected on the doctor's bald head.

"Come with me!" he said.

He walked ahead to the nearest hospital building.

It was the only house in Sant'Andrea with two floors. It must have been the school or the town hall. In a niche in the wall over the door stood a statue of St Andrew. He was carrying a diagonal cross as though leaning it against the wind. The white flag with the red cross hung from the roof. A slight breeze swayed it to and fro in front of St Andrew's nose.

"For God's sake get a move on, woman," said the doctor.

32

Inside the hospital it was suffocatingly hot. Ilona fought hard not to faint.

A medical orderly took charge of the wounded man. She followed the M.O.

To her left and right soldiers lay on plank beds or straw spread on the floor. The place reeked of blood and pus and filth. The stench was viscous. The dark wooden ceiling was low. It hung over the wounded like a great coffin. When Ilona passed the groaning men they sat up, stretched out their arms, called for water, for help, or simply cried out that they were dying. They cried out in German, Hungarian, Czech, Croat. A helpless angel, she couldn't help them. Her feet waded through straw. The hospital was a byre. To right and left lay the dying cattle.

The doctor pushed open a door.

There were four or five paraffin-lamps in the small room. It was light and almost silent. An operating-table stood in the middle of the room. The arms of the soldier lying on it dangled lifelessly. His uniform was ripped to shreds. He was bleeding from the stomach. The blood was the only live thing about him.

A young doctor, fair-haired and offensively pink-cheeked, and two nurses hurried towards the regimental medical officer. They whispered. The M.O. issued his instructions with reassuring gruffness. He was a gigantic man, like one of those over-life-size statues created by an heroic age. When he moved about he did so at surprising speed, as though people were standing behind him pushing him along like a monument in a sculptor's studio. It seemed as though his almost square head was only bald because no hair could possibly grow on an object of stone. He went over to a wash-basin. One of the nurses poured water over his hands. His hands were like his face, angular, rugged, reassuringly hard.

Then he remembered Ilona again. He turned to one of the nurses. "A newcomer. Tell her where to go."

The second nurse had freed the man on the operating-table from the remnants of his uniform. The Emperor's coat lay on the floor. She picked up the pay-book, turned the pages, and said to the young doctor, "Corporal Paul Höfer. Number seventy-eight ninety. Tirolese Imperial Rifles, Second Regiment."

Ilona clung to the door. The desire to laugh took possession of her with such force that she had to press her lips together. So this was the goal. The Imperial Rifles were near by—the gallant Imperial Rifles. Filthy, bloody lumps of flesh. Perhaps Zoltán was much closer than she imagined. Had she heard the name right? Was the M.O. bending over Corporal Paul Höfer?

"Kindly don't faint," the pink-cheeked young doctor told her imperiously. "Haven't you ever seen an abdominal wound before?"

"Send her off to sleep," said the M.O.

One of the two sisters explained to her where she was to go. She nodded. As she shut the door she heard the young doctor's voice behind her: "They're really sending us the last dregs."

She went back through the room with the straw, the room with the dying cattle.

Outside the house she stood still. The moon had gone down. A cool wind heralded morning. From the woods the smell of pines streamed into the village. It was as though the pines were marching on Sant'Andrea, a mighty army of liberation that would carry the wounded and the dead away on its branches, away from the stench of blood and pus and filth.

33

Ilona got used to the front. She began to feel at home in the strange village. The houses were bleak and sombre, but not unfriendly. In the dark they had been like trees at night which look as though men are hanging from their branches. In the morning they are only trees. The wounded strolling through the streets nodded to the nurse; some of them turned round to stare and clicked their tongues. She was glad they desired her. The silvery bells of the ambulances rang through the afternoon. When the front was quiet they moved far away into the distance. Peace triumphed over war because it possessed scents and warmth, sounds and habits, all sorts of healing herbs. The mountains stood round the village protectively; snow lay on some of the peaks. The blackbirds warbled as in the Vienna Volksgarten.

For the first time since her childhood she didn't want to be chosen, and yet felt that she was. The war was not a matter for men, as some asserted, because it was not a matter for human beings at all. But still less was it a matter for women. If you remained a woman you were treated as a woman by the men. Naturally—here, too, everything was quite natural. Naturally Dr Jankovics, the pink-cheeked assistant surgeon who sneered at all the nurses and chased them all, soon stopped sneering at her and chasing her. Naturally she made friends with the bearded civilian who had brought her biscuits and made tea for her the first night. His name was Giuseppe, he spoke Italian better than German, but he was a patriotic Austrian who had refused to leave his house. He slept on the floor of the hospital kitchen, in the house that had once belonged to him. Naturally she had to prevent Giuseppe from stealing titbits from the kitchen for her. She cleaned fouled camp-beds; washed suppurating wounds; carried out a bucket containing a human foot, black with blood and putrefied. But naturally she always found a medical orderly to help her; sometimes the wounded even helped her themselves.

She no longer smelt the stench of blood and pus. When the sky on the horizon began to grow fevered she knew that soon the stretcher-bearers would be there with the wounded and the dead. The military cemetery behind Sant'Andrea grew larger. It had been placed on an eminence away from the village; but it crept ever closer to the village, as though trying to smother houses and hospitals with is crosses. Sometimes a dead man's name was written on a cross before Ilona had even had time to write the letter to his next-of-kin.

There was a militia regiment stationed near Sant'Andrea. This brought a good many elderly men into hospital. Ilona pitied them more than the young ones. The longer you lived the more natural death became, but it had to be a natural death. The old men asked for Nurse Ilona. They talked to her about their wives and children. Almost all of them promised her something: a carpenter wanted to make his finest table for her when peace came; a shoemaker to fit her with an elegant pair of shoes, a head waiter actually said he would give

164

her extra-special service. A young ensign held her arm fast half one night; in his delirium he was going to the altar with her. By morning his arm hooked in hers was cold and stiff.

At times she was surprised that she didn't make more effort to see Zoltán or free herself from the trap. But she thought little about Zoltán, and little even about Zita. She read Teréz's and Zita's letters wearily. Zoltán and Zita were far away; everything was far away that lay ahead or behind. Perhaps there was nothing in the whole world but Sant'Andrea, a dark mountain village in the Tirolese mountains that had slipped out of God's hand, fallen on the earth, and been swallowed up by the Flood. What was far away could not be painful. The stationmaster wrote that Lajos was on the eastern front. That was a different war, even farther away than peace. Máté was ill, wrote the stationmaster. Was Máté still alive, that he could be ill? The stationmaster was very proud of his youngest daughter, but his letter didn't ring true, as though he were no longer very proud of the war. Sándor Bihari had been killed, wrote the stationmaster—Margit's husband who had become engaged to Ilona when they were both seven. She saw him in her mind's eye, in Kisnémet village church. He had been shorter than Margit; during the whole wedding he stood on tiptoe. No doubt the black flag was now waving outside the Hotel Rákoczi. The village would be lying in the golden light of the September afternoon; the lads and lassies standing by the railway barrier; it would be striking six from the Catholic church, and immediately afterwards from the Calvinist church. Sanyi had been killed in Italy, perhaps quite close by. The crosses were creeping nearer to the village of Sant'Andrea. Between Ilona and despair stood weariness, a soft wall. You didn't beat your head bloody if you ran at it. Your head merely became dull. Weariness was a merciful enemy.

She hadn't got used to the front. She was merely tired.

34

The only person who treated her no differently from his other subordinates was Dr Franz Sales, the regimental medical officer whom she had met on the first night. Now she was assigned to him.

Although the M.O. didn't show any interest in her, she clung to him as the only being from her own world. At the front one was a stone among stones washed up on the bank. She didn't despise the nurses with whom she shared the dormitory; nor the doctors and nurses with whom she ate in one of the cottages; not even Surgeon-Major Bauer, who was already drunk in the morning and strutted through Sant'Andrea in top-boots which he struck with his riding-crop as though to spur his lethargic legs into a run. She despised herself, because she had conjured up the fortuitous circumstances that had led to this communal existence. In Dr Sales's presence she felt no humiliating fortuity.

Dr Sales, a man under forty, was completely out of place in an Austrian field hospital. He came from Cologne, and had belonged to a Prussian unit. When it was relieved Dr Sales himself was in hospital, wounded. He stayed on with the Austrians.

Perhaps because he was a foreigner, he was much talked about—in whispers. It was rumoured that he had been a priest in his Rhineland home, but had cast off the cassock. The malicious said the Church had cast him out. The malicious were not numerous, because the wickedness of men, like fire, needs fanning in order to spread. But for the fact that the M.O. stayed away from all religious services the fire would soon have gone out altogether.

Why should a priest be unfaithful to the Church? wondered Ilona. Because the word enticed him, because he loved a woman, because he had been guilty of a moral lapse, because he had quarrelled with God?

None of these seemed likely in the M.O.'s case. Love affairs between nurses and doctors began in the thunder of guns and while searchlights were prying into the night; the greater the danger to the flesh the greater its longing. The gigantic man who could stand in front of the old stone walls as though he was part of them seemed not to notice that the women were of flesh and blood. When bandages were late arriving or he received an order he didn't like he could bellow and curse obscenely, as if he felt an urge to take the name of his Lord in vain; but he ate almost nothing, never touched wine, and seemed not to need any sleep. The patients loved him as they loved nobody else, although he never addressed a friendly word to them, as though, since his job was to save a gangrenous leg or sew up a face, he wasn't prepared to waste any time on the soul.

Ilona became daily more subservient to him. She didn't understand it herself. He seemed to distrust her; gave her the dirtiest jobs; once even grumbled that the "Baroness" had no claim to special privileges, although she hadn't requested any. He had her woken in the middle of the night and didn't thank her when she came. If he was on duty on Sunday, so was she. She had to make coffee for him till late at night—he drank excessive quantities of coffee and smoked immoderately—but as soon as they were alone he found some pretext to be rid of her.

Her curiosity became so great that one day she spied on him through the window. He was sitting at a table reading the Bible that was always close by him. His features were transfigured. His eyes, which were shadowed by thick blond brows, as though they wanted to hide under them, were suddenly uncannily soft—uncannily because they no longer matched his face. Then he sprang to his feet, flung the Bible furiously on to his camp-bed, and paced up and down his small room like a caged beast. When he sent for Ilona an hour later he showed no sign of all this. He operated for five hours at a stretch, in silence, only opening his mouth to demand the instruments or occasionally to call the pink-cheeked assistant surgeon a "God-damned cretin."

Being unable to explain the attraction which the M.O. exercised on her, Ilona finally contented herself with the hypothesis that she admired him. She had admired men all her life—her father's kindness, Kontowski's wisdom, Zoltán's genius, even Feri's helpless honesty. When you admired a man you remembered you were a woman.

35

One evening at the beginning of September, instead of sending her out of his room, he looked at her and said, "Nurse Ilona, I hear you have a relative in the Imperial Rifles."

"Not a relative . . ." She blushed.

"Why didn't you tell me?"

"I didn't think it would interest you, sir."

He stared into his coffee-cup. "Now at least I know why you're here. I took you for one of those pampered ladies who have been bragging in their drawing-rooms until some unfortunate chance swept them to the front. These women torture the wounded, and for my part I torture them until they pull all the strings they can to get out of here."

"I'm not much better, sir. At least, my motives are no more patriotic."

"I don't give a damn for patriotic motives. You do your job, that's enough."

He stirred his coffee, although he drank it without saccharine.

"We rarely get wounded Imperial Riflemen. Field Hospital Sixty-one deals with them. I'll try to get you exchanged for a nurse from Sixty-one."

From the distance came the thunder of guns. The instruments rattled together in the glass case on the wall.

"Thank you, sir," she said. Her heart was pounding.

"What's his name?" asked Dr Sales.

"First Lieutenant Zoltán Szomoru."

"The conductor?"

"Do you know him?"

"I heard him in Berlin once. It was quite a long time ago."

The thunder came closer.

"We shall have work to do," said the M.O.

His features relaxed. Was he waiting for the casualties as for a deliverance?

"What are you staring at me for?" he asked. "Haven't you anything to do?"

36

It was Sunday. The front had been quiet for several days. Ilona was on duty, and she left her billets at seven in the morning.

The main square had been turned into a military encampment. Several companies, perhaps a regiment, were resting between the church and the hospital on their way to the front. The soldiers had been marching all night. Now they were sleeping on the stony ground, tin soldiers that had been knocked down. The morning sun was shining in the soldier's faces. From the hill where the heroes' cemetery lay came down the heroes' successors. Here and there a whistle rang out, a word of command. The sleeping men didn't hear them. A few wounded soldiers from the hospital, with bandaged heads and arms in slings, were going for their morning walk. They stepped carefully over the sleepers. Better wounded to-day than dead to-morrow, they seemed to be saying. When one of the sleepers opened his eyes he saw a bandaged head, an arm in a sling.

Ilona reported to Dr Sales in his office.

He slept in his office next to the operating theatre. It was a small room at the rear of the house. There was a crack in one wall, narrow and winding like a river on a map. Ilona had never seen the room untidy. The brown Army blanket was stretched tightly over the camp-bed. There were books lying on it. The two small windows looked out on to a meadow that rose gently to the woods. The M.O. was standing by the open window looking up at the woods. His bald head seemed almost to fill the whole window-frame.

"Good morning, sir."

He turned round and smiled. When he smiled a crack split his face. The folds on his face ran from above downward, from his eyes to his chin, from the wings of his nose to the corners of his mouth. His smile made a line cross them out.

"Have you seen the soldiers?" he asked. "I think there's going to be an offensive."

"Ours?"

"We shall call it ours in any case."

In the meadow soldiers were setting up the field altar. A few casualties were already sitting on the grass waiting for the service.

"You can look after the patients," said the M.O. "I've given Pásztor his injection. He was in pain. Don't let Fuchs get up. He's impatient, but it comes from the fever. Go easy on the bismuth: the swine have held up supplies in Schönpass again. We must send Lovász and Lieutenant Kozeluh back to their regiment, but they can wait till to-morrow. After all, it's Sunday."

He knew all their names by heart—a difficult and superfluous feat. It should have been her job to give Pásztor his injection. When had Dr Sales got up? Had he been to bed at all?

He turned his eyes away from her, the eyes that punished themselves. From the table, over which a cracked sheet of oil-cloth was spread, he took a telegram. He handed it to her and walked slowly back to the window.

"You have been transferred to the Sixty-first," he said. "I have written to the M.O., Dr Pollack. Perhaps he'll be able to get First Lieutenant Szomoru back for a few hours."

She supported herself on the table.

"How can I thank you?"

He didn't answer.

"Are you getting a replacement?" she asked.

"Don't be so sanctimonious! Only the people who make war imagine that people are replaceable. Yes, I'm getting a 'replacement'! Another nurse will hand me the same scissors. I don't confuse the gestures with the people who make them."

He was standing with his back to her, his eyes on the meadow.

Soldiers had put a crucifix on the altar, genuflected, and left. The cross glittered in the sun.

"Why don't you go?" he said gruffly.

She could have repeated her thanks and left. Once again she had put her trust in a man, and once again a man had helped her. In a few days she would be near Zoltán.

She stayed. Her curiosity grew more and more intense and more and more baffled. Probably she would never see the M.O. again. Most people whom the war seemed to be binding for ever parted for ever. She couldn't leave Dr Sales without finding out who he was and why he had helped her. Human characteristics were said to become as distinct at the front as artillery positions in the sudden beam of the seachlights. When the light fell on Dr Sales it revealed a statue on which stood a single word—duty. The statue stood there in wind and rain, in summer's heat and winter's ice. Human beings weren't statues; they couldn't possess only one single quality. But did she stay simply out of curiosity? As danger moved away from her the desire to conjure it up grew. Men and women at the front were bound by a painful sensitivity. Close to death men became more men, women more women.

"Why do you want to send me away, Dr Sales?" she asked almost provocatively. "Are you angry because I am grateful to you?"

He turned round. His eyes crawled out from their cover like soldiers from a trench. His jaw-bones moved; it was obvious that he was clenching his teeth.

"Go to the devil," he said. "And don't come back. I don't need you. You can go to the service."

She walked to the door. She felt his eyes on the back of her neck, at the point where the little blonde hairs peeped out from under the cap.

"There goes Eve, the everlasting seductress," he shouted after her. "But your seductive wiles bounce off me.'

"Doctor! . . ." She turned to him.

"Doctor, doctor. . . ." He imitated her. "Are you making fun of me? You know quite well you owe me no thanks. I want to get rid of you, that's all."

"I thought . . ."

"Don't think! Your presence is intolerable to me. I should have sent you away at once, the moment I picked you up outside the church. You didn't promise me anything? Why should you? One loves temptation for its own sake. Do you think I'm blind? People portray witches as ugly, because they are so stupid as to see the world as beautiful. The devil loves contrasts. In hell the witches look like angels."

She stood frozen to the spot, horrified by the harvest her curiosity had reaped.

"You want me to put it into words," he said. "I'll make you a present of that too. Go to your lover with the lascivious feeling that you are leaving a madman behind. Be reassured: I noticed your beauty. Don't worry: I desire you as I have never desired a woman before. You succeeded: I tore myself to pieces. Are you satisfied?"

He went to his camp-bed, ripped off the blanket, hunted under the pillow. She didn't know what he was going to do until he came towards her carrying a photograph. Invisible hands were rolling a boulder towards her.

169

"That's my wife," he said. "Those are my children. My wife isn't beautiful. I don't love her." He struck the photograph with a hard finger, like a usurer tapping his receipt. "I shall stay faithful to her. Faithful, do you understand? I didn't lay aside the priest's robe in order to exchange celibacy for a life of sin. I didn't renounce lies in order to lie, do you understand?"

Ilona's eyes ran quickly over the photograph. All the men at the front showed photographs of their families. What a beautiful wife, one said, what sweet children! I mustn't lie now, she thought, not now. Why hadn't she left before? Shame swept over her, the ridiculous traveller who always arrived too late. She turned her eyes to the window. She remembered an oil-painting that used to hang in the station-house—a Franciscan monk holding up a cross before the devil. She clung superstitiously to the sight of the cross on the altar outside.

All at once the M.O. became calm. Only his hands trembled as he put the family photograph down on the table.

"Get an indulgence from the parson out there," he said.

She had firm ground under her feet again. She couldn't leave now; it was too late. But she could try to make him forget what he had just said. So long as he didn't talk about her again. . .

"So it's true . . . ," she said.

He nodded. He dropped into an armchair. A bee buzzed in the room. It settled on the wall where the crack described a river.

"I've never regretted it," he said. "Otherwise I might now be standing in front of that altar. But I should take the twenty-sixth chapter of St Matthew as the text for my Sunday sermon. 'For all they that take the sword shall perish by the sword.' Every Sunday the Army chaplain blesses the weapons. And at the same time, on this day of the Lord, the same Church blesses the weapons on the other side. Brokers who don't want to lose any clients."

Ilona's knees were trembling. She had to sit down. She thanked God that Dr Sales was no longer raging against her. God would forgive him for slandering Him.

"You imagine I'm an atheist," he said. "If I were an atheist the idolatry out there wouldn't worry me."

"Have you become a Protestant?"

He laughed. "It's obvious you were brought up a Catholic. If I'm not an atheist I must be a Protestant. . . . Why should I have become a Protestant? New churches are nothing but an attempt to save the old ones." He was sitting with his back to the window. "Do you know why I became a doctor? Because the doctor has to help. If he is woken at two in the morning, if he is lying in the arms of his beloved, if he is bowed over his books, he has to get up and go to the aid of the patient. He must, do you understand? He has no choice. No one asks whether he loves the patient. He loves him inasmuch as he helps him. That is the law."

She was used to listening. She didn't mind missing the service. What he said didn't upset her. But the excitement she had sowed and reaped was still quivering in the air. She wanted to leave.

"Stay!" he commanded. "Or can't you bear to listen to me any more?"

She stayed in her seat.

"That man out there in front of the altar," he went on, as though he had won a victory, "is breaking the Law. He is insinuating into human souls the lie that it is easier to kill with weapons that have been blessed. He has thought about the Law and discovered how it can be broken. God didn't forbid Adam and Eve to eat of the tree of evil. Not of evil, do you understand? There was no tree of evil in Paradise. They ate of the tree of *knowledge*: they became evil of their own accord. Knowledge is nothing but an attempt to explain our evil deeds. Explain means justify. Man is born with a conscience. He acquires knowledge in order to pacify it."

"Man will never cease to strive after knowledge, Dr Sales," she said.

"You may call that the curse of Adam and Eve."

"And why did the Saviour come? Because God had pity on men. He renewed the Law. Whether men are believers or not, there is one thing they know: Paradise lies behind them. But they go forward. Who is leading them? The devil. The Garden of Eden has only one gate. But the devil shows men a thousand gates. Through all of them, he says, they can enter Paradise. If a gate shuts behind them two more open. Then four and eight and a hundred and a thousand. Every thought a gate. Every piece of knowledge a new gate. Big doors, little doors, cellar doors, heavenly doors, back doors. Every garden a Garden of Eden. In every garden a new tree of knowledge. The 'tree pleasant to the eye' the Bible calls it. Divine sarcasm!"

She was sitting facing the window. She saw the wounded making towards the altar from all sides. The hobbled along leaning on one another. A nurse was leading a young man; he had put his arm round her like a sweetheart. Giuseppe was busy at the altar. There were soldiers whom she didn't know among the worshippers. Perhaps they had woken from sleep.

"Reason also comes from God, you will say," he went on. "Yes—divine reason. The Law from Mount Sinai and from the Sermon on the Mount. But on its way to men the devil changed reason into folly. Doctrine turns into philosophy, the word into babble, and order into chaos."

She listened. She no longer felt fear of the man who sat bending over the table as though he wanted to crush it under his arms. His eyes were directed towards her, but he seemed not to see her. He could be an angel, but also the devil. Only the devil was so sure of being right. Earlier on, when he held his wife's photograph in his hand, had he not sought to prove that he alone knew the right path?

She said, "And what is the Law, Dr Sales?"

"Blessed renunciation." He spoke in a low voice. "You must picture humanity as a vast chaos in which every smallest molecule is gravitating away from the centre and at the same time from every other molecule. The molecule is man. The centre from which he is moving is God. Do you know what centrifugal force is? The movement, for example, of a stone tied to a string and swung round and round in a circle, which

171

exercises a continuous outward pull on the hand. Man is the stone. The greater the mass or its velocity the greater its centrifugal force. You can't explain anything to a stone. All you can do is to prevent it by force from flying away. That is the Law. The Law that prevents the doctor from going on sleeping, whoring, or thinking, when he is called upon to help."

"You want to replace knowledge by the penal code."

"The doctor doesn't think about the penal code any more than he thinks about the noble motives for his actions. The Law contradicts human nature, but miraculously it becomes nature, because it comes from God. Faith comes from prayer, because we pray for the favour of believing. So the action comes before the thought. Motive is the idol of our self-pitying age! If our motives were weighed on Judgment Day, God would be left so alone that he would seek warmth in hell."

He stood up. She rose at the same time. Involuntarily, she took a step towards the window.

The soldiers stood tightly packed round the altar, leaning on one another, on crutches and rifles. The Army chaplain had mounted the step to the altar. He was wearing the vestments over his uniform. The sun caught the gold of his robe. He raised the cross. Most of the soldiers kneeled down. A few remained standing because they couldn't kneel.

Dr Sales approached Ilona. She turned away. She felt his breath on the back of her neck.

"I had to stop you from thanking me," he said. "You have no idea how wretched I was. Once you were standing facing me by the operating table. Do you remember? Lieutenant Kereszthury. Shot in the lung. I looked up. You were holding the ether-mask. My hand trembled. Ought I to have forbidden my heart to desire you? I commanded my hand not to tremble. Mankind can never find the devil because they do not know his masks. He slips into people and slips out of them again. That priest out there blessing the weapons is the devil. In an hour, when he closes the eyes of a dying man, the devil will have gone out of him. When you stood facing me with the ether-mask in your hand you were the devil. One night I was writing a letter to my wife. You came in. You weren't wearing your cap. Your hair had been ruffled by the wind. I stared at my wife's photograph. I wanted to draw strength from it. But your hair fluttered over the picture. Then the devil had entered into the picture of my wife. I hadn't the strength to love my wife. But I told you to clear away the blood-soaked bandages from the operating-theatre. One evening you came into my room. You caught sight of my bed. Perhaps you were only thinking that the blanket was crooked. But our eyes met above the bed. The devil was in our eyes. Then I thought of the man on the Col di Lana. I tried to love him, but I hated him. That was the evening when I told you I would send you away. And now go with God!"

The wounded and the soldiers were standing erect round the altar. Some were supporting themselves on other men, some on crutches, some on rifles. One was supporting himself on a nurse, as though embracing her. The hymn rose into the cloudless morning sky. The

172

mountains echoed it back. It was as if the hymn came from the woods.

37

Auxiliary Hospital Sixty-one was only a dressing-station. It was not situated in a village, nor was there any village near by. The white tent formed a semicircle round an ancient, dilapidated farm. The camp was surrounded by high mountains, embedded in a hollow of the Buchenstein Valley somewhat resembling the crater of a volcano. The white Red Cross flag hung from a huge tree that had not blossomed for a century. When the wind moved the flag it was as though a hanged man in a white shirt was dangling from the branches. Even during the day the tents stood out gleaming against the stony ground, although they were no longer white. The shadows of the mountains spread a black cloth over the valley. Crows perched in the branches; they were part of the sombre trees, noticeable only when they cawed. The valley appeared all the more melancholy because the sky was blue. The sun was reflected in the snow of the peaks; in its arrogance it shone only on the *névés*.

The front ran along the heights of the Col di Lana. The mountain seemed close enough to touch, yet the front was not to be seen; it had its back towards the dressing-station.

The front was quiet, a lurking beast. Every now and then a shot rent the silence, spreading and echoing as though from a distant hunt. Every now and then the rattle of machine-gun fire rang out. In Sant'Andrea Ilona had only heard the boom of cannon. The quieter the sounds the closer the front. In the dressing-station they spoke of Sant'Andrea as contemptuously as in Sant'Andrea they spoke of Schönpass and in Schönpass of Klagenfurt and Vienna. The front despised the base, the base the interior, and the interior peace. If there were a gas attack, they said, no one would be left alive. Poison-gases hung stationary over valleys. They were proud of the closeness of death.

On the third day after Ilona's arrival regimental medical officer Dr Pollack informed her that in the afternoon or early evening Lieutenant Szomoru would ride down from his post on the Col di Lana "Night leave," said the doctor, without blinking.

Dr Pollack came from Vienna. His practice was in the Taborstrasse, in the former ghetto. He was a little man with a soft, mobile face reminiscent of the rubber animals thrown to puppies to play with. On his pliable nose sat a pair of regulation steel-framed spectacles. As a rule Dr Pollack put the spectacles in their case and, contrary to regulations, wore pince-nez, smiling as he did so, happily and slightly guiltily, as though he had played a trick on the war. At such times he looked like one of his patients from the ghetto, although he was very proud of his military record: he wore his medals even on his white coat, which was likewise contrary to regulations. He had received Dr Sales's letter, and welcomed Ilona like a prima donna starring at a provincial theatre. He never disclosed to her how he had conveyed the news of her presence to Lieutenant Szomoru, nor how he had arranged

173

for him to have night leave. But it was clear that he had done it willingly—indeed, with a childish pleasure, as though this too were a welcome opportunity of playing a trick on war.

She went into her tent, where a small white celluloid mirror hung on a string like a theatrical prop lowered from the rigging-loft. She tidied the little hairs peeping out from under her cap; powdered her nose; straightened her dress. The mirror rotated on the string, malevolently turning its back on her.

What she had done seemed more and more shameful to her. The front was no place at which to meet people you loved, at which to remain united with them for ever. The war passed on, wandered away from those who sought it, sought out those who were hiding from it. "Night leave," Dr Pollack had said. With how many nights had she paid, with how many more would she pay, for a single night? Every one in the 'Sixty-first' knew that she was expecting her lover: Dr Pollack, the card-playing soldiers, the assistant surgeon who was throwing stones at the crows, the nurse who was writing letters. Never had Ilona been so conscious of being a woman. Men didn't see what was wretched, drab and repugnant till they had proved their potency and poured out their passion; when their whipped-up blood had grown calm; when they possessed what they had desired. A woman didn't have to wait for exhaustion in order to become weak; didn't have to get dirty in order to long for cleanliness; didn't have to wait for passion to ebb before growing sober. Fever and reflection went hand in hand, dissimilar sisters.

The desperate urge to deride herself seized her in front of the swinging mirror in the hospital tent, because once more, for the hundredth time, she had tidied her hair, straightened her cap, smoothed her uniform, as though in preparation for a secret rendezvous, as though there were no war, no white tents, as though poison-gas—the drifting, stationary death—could not spread across the valley. She was worse than any whore, because whores, even if they made love to half a dozen soldiers a night, slept in their homes; they didn't leave families for the sake of a soldier's one night leave.

It was no longer enough, as in the past, for Ilona to wrinkle up her forehead in front of the mirror. As sometimes in her childhood, she had to make faces in the mirror, ugly faces.

Then even that wasn't enough for her. Her gas-mask lay on the camp-bed. She picked it up and forced it on, regardless of her starched cap, her tamed hair. She stood like this in front of the swinging mirror, white and slim, and yet, with the shapeless green gas-mask over her head, like the horrible figures in Shrovetide plays, the ugly heathen gods. She stared into the mirror from behind the huge skull's eyes of the mask, bending forward until she almost touched it with the round trunk.

"Ilona!"

She heard the voice muffled by the mask and recognized it at once. She tore the mask from her head. The cap got caught up inside it and flew away with it. Her hair was dishevelled.

174

38

They had been walking for almost two hours, uphill, downhill, farther and farther away from the front, from the tents of the dressing-station. The front was not something visible. It was an invisible presence in the landscape that seemed devastated, although it was not the war that had churned up the stones, but the earth that had spewed them forth in the course of the centuries. They had to be careful not to lose the way that led back into the proximity of death.

They talked, stood still, stole a glance at each other, talked again. Their first kisses were difficult, as if they had never kissed each other before. They were ashamed of their lust, like a couple kissing in front of thousands of lustful prisoners in a prison yard.

Zoltán was thin. His skin was burnt dark-brown; his white teeth and dark-blue eyes shone; for this reason one did not see immediately how emaciated and hollow his face was. The uniform was no longer pulled taut across his chest. It was dirty and roughly darned in several places; his puttees were ragged at the edges. His steel helmet was dangling from his belt. It banged against the metal buckle as he walked. The cropped hair had altered Zoltán's features: Ilona had to make an effort to remember what he used to look like. It had been easy as long as he was far away. Memory, a part of the past, makes the past present. It is not until two people meet again after much anticipation that they become strangers.

Their timid kisses brought them no closer. Words had to do so. They talked hurriedly, about important and unimportant things, interrupting each other, squandering the time they were trying to hold on to.

They wandered on, the soldier and the nurse. Although evening was coming down, it was still warm. The evening drew delicate veils over the mountains, as though Nature wanted to be alone for the night.

Zoltán asked few questions and spoke almost exclusively of himself.

"I must get out of here," he said. "As quickly as possible. In the next offensive the Italians will take the Col di Lana, even if they have to blow the colossus up. My guardian angel is obviously tired." He stopped. "Do you hear that?"

She listened. She had been hearing the noise for days, so continuously that she scarcely heard it any more. The song of birds, the splashing of water, the croaking of ravens, human voices, drowned the monotonous sound, but it was there all the time, like the buzzing of a bee.

"The borings," said Zoltán. "They're laying mines under the mountain. One night it will go up in the air. The Col di Lana is going to die."

"Don't the generals know?"

"On the General Staff maps the mountains are perfectly quiet."

They walked on, downhill, along a narrow path by the edge of the forest that seemed to have been for ages untrodden by any human foot. Men had laboriously laid it down between forest and rock, and now forest and rock had taken it back. The mountains were quiet, as on the General Staff maps.

"I don't want to die," said Zoltán. "Senselessly, like a dog, up there on the mountain." He stretched out his hand, as though when he stretched out his hand to the Col di Lana he could see unthinking death. "I don't want to lose my hand. When I saw you in Baden I had no idea what it was like. Christmas at home! People are beginning to forget me. Most conductors are already back home again. Or they were never so stupid as to play the hero at all. I'm no use here. All this nonsense means nothing to me." He flicked the unit cross on his chest into the air with his thumb and forefinger, like some one shooting away a fly. "The concerts in Vienna are sold out. The Opera is looking for a conductor. New, exciting experiments are being made in music. It's the same with heroism as with illness: people only talk about it while it's still new." He took her hands. "You must help me. You must get me out of here."

It was beginning to grow dark. The overgrown path had led them into the vicinity of a tiny mountain village. In the violet light of evening a church loomed up, with a rectangular tower. Five or six cottages lay scattered round this church, huts rather than cottages, as if the village had been left unfinished. A stupefying scent came from the pine-woods. In the west, where two mountains had taken a valley between them like two parents taking their child in the middle, there was still a streak of light on the horizon. Ilona felt as though she must defend herself against the beauty of nature, because it was deceitful amid all this humiliation and death.

Zoltán wanted her to "get him out." How wrong everything she had done had been! She remembered his letters. The censor had crossed out what he really thought. Instead of releasing him from the prison, she had entered this prison surrounded by the mountains like pitiless warders.

"How can I do that?" she asked. "I no longer have the power to decide my own life."

"Haven't you got influence in Vienna? Influence is everything."

"Of course, but . . ."

"You must go to Vienna," he said insistently. "You can only do it in person. Don't mention me straight away. Speak only of yourself. There's no shame in your not being able to stick it here. Didn't you tell me Kontowski had helped you? No one else could have done it. I'm sure you have only to write to him. . . ."

Lord, let me understand him, she thought. Jealousy falls silent when the mountain speaks. Love is drowned in the sound of the mountain. Lord, do not let me despise him! In the past courage had been alien to her; fear had been the woman's protective armour. No sooner had she put the armour aside than the rôles were reversed: the man was afraid. It was her fault. Reason was speaking through Zoltán; only she had sacrificed her reason along with her fear.

He hadn't let go of her hand. It was dark. They walked on. The steel helmet struck against the belt-buckle at every step.

"I could go on walking like this for days," he said. "The night ought to last for several nights. Then by morning we should be out of these loathsome hills."

Just as there are some doors in front of which one knows that they

176

are locked, even though they do not differ from other doors, so they knew that the cottages round the church were deserted.

They stood in front of the first cottage. The wind was whistling in the tree-tops like a herdsman playing his flute.

"Let's go in," said Zoltán. "You must be hungry. I've got bread and sausage in my pack. And a little wine in my water-bottle."

Bread and sausage and wine. The night in the Helenental. She had stayed behind in the cab. He had come back from the Krainerhütte and asked the cabby for blankets. Bread and sausage and wine and the horse-blankets. Lies one had to invent because of one's own shame. Would they never cease to look for shelter? Was any love great enough to endure in flight and shame?

He pushed the door open. It grated angrily, as though waking from a long sleep. Only now did he let go of her hand.

The light from the torch penetrated the room. There was nothing standing on the stone floor but a large peasant table, as though the occupants had been surprised by the war while eating and had taken everything with them—crockery and cutlery, chairs, table-cloth, and pictures—leaving behind only what was too heavy for them. He went to a door and shone the torch into a second room. It was empty. A crucifix hung on the wall. A dead dog lay on the floor, a stinking skeleton with a few filthy hairs. The fugitives had left the crucifix and the dog behind.

"I want to have a look round," said Zoltán. "Will you wait here? You're not afraid, are you?"

She remained alone in the dark room with the big table. Her feet were aching. She sat down on the table.

Then he went and 'looked round.' He was looking for a bed. A soldier with a torch, in a strange village, looking for a strange bed. She, Baroness Ilona von Rattowitz, née Horváth, daughter of the station-master at Kisnémet, mistress of the Imperial Austro-Hungarian Ambassador at the Court of the Tsar, owner of the Berény farm in Hungary, mother of a ten-year-old daughter, sat in a room in a Tirolese village waiting for a strange bed. Of course is wasn't true; it couldn't be true. She thought of Dr Sales. Do right, never mind why. Do not do wrong, never mind why not. What would he think of her, who was doing wrong without even wanting to? The "great helplessness," Kontowski had said. The "great helplessness" didn't excuse everything.

Fear began to grip her by the throat. All at once it seemed to her possible that Zoltán wouldn't come back. Perhaps, instead of walking away from the front, they had walked into the midst of it. What she had never seen in the light appeared to her doubly dark. If she were to stand up now and look for the door she would get one door mixed up with another. In the next room lay the dead dog.

She stood up.

The light from the torch shone in her face.

"I've found somewhere we can spend the night," said Zoltán.

His uniform was covered with straw.

He took her by the hand. She stumbled over the threshold. He put his arm round her waist. They walked past the church. The light from the torch crept up it. There was no bell in the tower; the church's tongue had been cut out. The church-bells no longer announced burials and fires.

The second cottage was next door to the church. The door was open. Zoltán led Ilona through an empty room.

In the next room stood a table, a broken chair, a bed. Mattresses and blankets had gone. Straw had been heaped up on the bedstead. It smelt damp and musty.

He took off his haversack and put his water-bottle on the table. His belt and pistol and steel helmet were already lying there; he had taken them off before leaving the cottage. He couldn't stand the torch on end, so he laid it flat on the table. The light shone on the cracked ceiling and formed a small yellow circle. Then he unscrewed the cup from his water-bottle. There was a gurgling sound.

He handed her the full cup.

"I'll drink out of the bottle," he said.

She put the cup to her lips. The red wine tasted acid.

"Have you another glassful?" she asked.

He refilled the cup.

"You must eat something."

"I'm not hungry."

He sat down on the edge of the bedstead. The bed sighed.

"We must get out of the war," he said. "I have longed for you as no man has ever longed for a woman. But it makes a difference whether the man comes to the woman or the woman to the man. It makes a difference where they meet. There are too many people dying here. I'm not one of those men who love better when they are about to die." He rested his elbow on his knee, he laughed. "Love can blossom even in a hovel. What a stupid lie! We are the people we are. We are not other people, you and I. We weren't born for cottages. We fled from cottages, from Kisnémet. Why should we be ashamed of loving what we have achieved? We have become great because we hate the small. Our love is not more superficial because it sails proudly over the surface, like a liner over the ocean. . . ."

He talked and talked with a loosened tongue.

His words were like cool raindrops after a sultry summer's day. The more he cursed the place where they had met, the ugliness that surrounded them, the times that gave them no time, the less hateful the times appeared to her, the less visible the ugliness, the pleasanter the place. So long as they felt the same it didn't matter what they felt.

"Don't talk," she said. She sat down beside him on the edge of the bed. "We shan't allow ourselves to be defeated, you and I."

She looked at him. She no longer wanted to see behind his face, as in St Petersburg. This was the face she loved. It was the face of the peasant lad walking across his mother's fields; the face of the angel on the Budapest concert platform; the face of the mocker at Margit's wedding; the face of the actor behind the doors of the Narodny Dom; the face that bent down to her in the St Petersburg hotel and in the wood outside Vienna. Peasant lad, angel, actor, devil, hero, seducer, genius, coward: even in her dreams, which had driven her here, into the village behind the front, she had seen a thousand faces and yet always the same one.

"Won't you kiss me?" she said.

The straw no longer smelt damp and musty. It smelt of fresh hay, like the hayricks on the Szomorus' farm at Kisnémet.

"Are you cold?" he asked.

"No," she said.

She wasn't cold as he undressed her, with hasty hands and yet slowly; as she lay naked on her nurse's clothes and his uniform, which he had spread over the straw, slowly, almost reverently, according to the shameless ritual of man and woman making a bed for themselves.

The light from the torch flickered once again, then it went out. The circle on the cracked ceiling vanished. It was impossible to see now where the bed stood. In the distance the humming speech of the mountain that was going to die could be heard again.

39

Ilona wrote to the Prince the same day on which Zoltán rode back to his battalion. She took refuge in that honesty which often goes hand in hand with shamelessness as its pleasanter twin. She didn't take Zoltán's advice to speak only of herself. When she had asked Kontowski to smooth her path to Zoltán she had cruelly shattered his hopes: it would have been crueller to revive them. She asked the Prince to put in a word for Zoltán as well as for herself.

The letter never reached the Prince; it never even left the cardboard box in which Dr Pollack kept the letters to be dispatched.

Four days after Zoltán's return to his dug-out a rider came into the camp from Sant'Andrea to deliver and collect post.

The rider had hardly reached the camp before the M.O. called Ilona to his tent. He was wearing his steel-rimmed spectacles for a change, and his small eyes, older than himself, moved excitedly this way and that behind them.

"My child," he began, "I'm afraid that I must send you back to Vienna. Please don't be worried, although it concerns your little daughter. Here, the telegram says she has scarlet fever; the Ministry of War has approved your transfer." He handed her the telegram. "I'm showing it to you so that you shan't be unnecessarily upset. If the child were seriously ill they would simply have given you home leave. Your daughter undoubtedly has scarlet fever. But you must have a powerful advocate who, quite understandably, has made use of the opportunity to get you transferred."

She held the telegram in her hand, incapable of deciphering the words. The M.O.'s remarks didn't deceive her. Zita was seriously ill, perhaps dead. Far more than she realized, Ilona held the childish belief that sin was followed by punishment; only she had ceased to believe that punishment followed so quickly upon sin—by telegraph, so to speak. Fear, which rejuvenates grown-ups till they became children, made her childish. As in her childhood, her first thought was to try to strike a bargain with God; but she couldn't even pray

179

fervently without thinking that she was only praying in order to calm her fears.

Dr Pollack had pushed a camp-stool over to Ilona.

"I've read about the scarlet-fever epidemic in the Vienna papers," he said. He was a doctor, and knew the reassuring effect of medical explanations. "It's a particularly mild form. There's hardly a single child who hasn't caught it. With our modern medicines we are fully able to cope with the disease. Really, the only important thing is to avoid after-effects. Nephritis, rheumatoid arthritis, and otitis media. But I'm sure your daughter is in good hands, and you'll be in Vienna yourself before the skin begins to peel."

"Do you know Dr Schlichter, our family doctor?" asked Ilona.

The thought of the old children's specialist was the only thing that could reassure her now.

"Dr Felix Schlichter? Of course. A first-rate man. You've nothing to worry about." He smiled, as though he himself were no longer worried. "Unfortunately you can't leave before the day after to-morrow. I can't spare our one and only ambulance, and we shan't be getting a second till to-morrow evening."

She stood up, ashamed of her weakness. Her fear gave way to self-accusation. Every child had scarlet fever at some time or other. Mothers didn't leave children who might catch scarlet fever to their sisters or the family doctor. They didn't run after their lovers; nurse unknown soldiers; lie to themselves about "great tasks." She must apologize to Teréz for having confused the fronts and deserted from her own. Would Zita be able to forgive her?

Dr Pollack warded off her thanks with embarrassment.

"You needn't send off that letter I gave you," she said.

Twinkling away over the top of his spectacles, Dr Pollack rummaged in the cardboard box. He was glad to be able to deal with something that had no connexion with the telegram.

Ilona tore up her letter to Kontowski. God, she thought, might take up her bargain after all.

40

When Ilona arrived in Vienna Zita was over her illness; only the skin of her little face was still peeling, as though after sunburn. On the other hand, however, otitis media had developed. The right ear had to be punctured. The specialist feared the left ear might also become involved.

Ilona had rightly surmised that she owed her recall to Kontowski. Teréz alarmed but resolute as always, had informed the Prince, who had immediately appeared at the Döbling Villa, called in the best specialist, and arranged Ilona's transfer to Vienna.

Ilona wanted to call on Kontowski, but the following day he came himself to pay a brief, very formal visit. He sat in the drawing-room, stiff and taciturn, his eyes turned almost continually upon Teréz, as though begging her not to leave him alone with Ilona. "I think," he said, "that we shall manage to win or lose the war without you. I couldn't prevent you from being posted back to the front. I shall

180

therefore arrange for your discharge from the services." He took his leave without waiting for Ilona's consent.

He was not mistaken in taking Ilona's agreement for granted. Her conscience was like a lazy schoolboy trying to catch up on his neglected homework with belated diligence. From the moment she arrived in Vienna after five days' journey, in passenger and troop trains, carts and lorries, dirty and tormented by anxiety, she had no other wish than to win back her child.

Ilona was soon sobered of the illusion that she had only to take Zita in her arms for the child to forgive her. Only adults have grown used to disappointments: to the child who hits the corner of the table on which he has bumped himself pain suffered and the desire for retribution are one. For every hour she had spent far from Vienna, Ilona had to pay with a night's vigil. If in Teréz's arms Zita had wept for her mother she now demonstated to the home-comer that she preferred Teréz to her. She clamoured for the most expensive toy, then ignored it and petted a broken doll given her by Teréz. Ilona, who at the outset shrank from no attempt at bribery, gradually realized that Fate deals with embezzled time as the Public Prosecutor deals with embezzled money: both are punished and can only be restored in kind. Not even love and tenderness replace time. He who borrows time must pay back time.

On this particular night, too, Ilona was sitting on her child's bed. Zita was in pain. Pus was trickling out of the punctured ear on to the pillow, which had to be changed again and again. The autumn wind rattled the window-panes. Every now and then an apple fell to the ground with a dull thud.

Ilona thought of Zoltán. Every day she ran through the lists of the dead and missing, and had even inquired after his name at the War Ministry. All over the Monarchy women breathed a sigh of relief after searching in vain for their man's name. Even in the second year of the war they knew nothing about the front. The men were devoid of responsibility, the women of imagination—and so the war went on. But Ilona could not escape from the scenes she had witnessed. The Italians occupied the collapsed caves on the Col di Lana. They didn't bother about the names of dead enemies. Many of the defeated were still wandering through the woods like hungry animals. Many found their way into the valley, but in the valley there were nothing but shattered houses and forgotten graves. Sant'Andrea had fallen. Lucky were the women for whom these words conjured up no picture. To Ilona the Sixty-first Field Hospital was little Dr Pollack with his pince-nez in their velvet case and gaunt Nurse Hermine with the white flag. Sant'Andrea was Dr Sales fighting with the demons around and within him. War was the bedstead in an empty cottage which she could never find again, because all she knew was that it lay behind the front. Behind, before— meaningless words.

Zita woke and complained of pains in her left ear. She cried. Her temperature rose to over a hundred and four. Ilona rang the doctor. "It's the crisis," said Dr Schlichter. He woke Professor Mellinger, the ear specialist. The house was seized by the wakeful unrest of houses in which some one is lying sick at night. They waited for the Professor as though everything would take a turn for the better as soon as he arrived. Zita screamed that she didn't want to see the Professor, anyone but him. Since he had punctured her ear she hated him. He was a quiet, kind man, but he had a hump, and Zita, like all children, was frightened of cripples.

Ilona and Dr Schlichter had to hold Zita while the tiny man examined her. The fever lent her abnormal strength. She tore herself free and scratched the Professor's face. Teréz and Josephine hurried to give their assistance. Zita sought refuge with them. The Professor pierced the eardrum. Morning, as superstitiously awaited as the Professor had been earlier, was trickling through the curtains as the Professor left.

It was twenty-four hours before Ilona went to bed. During this time she tortured herself with reproaches, was certain Zita would lose her hearing. Then the child's temperature fell as quickly as it had risen. "There is nothing more to worry about, Baroness; the danger is past," Dr Schlichter assured her. Zita sat up against her pillows and demanded the promised toy.

A week later Ilona learnt from Captain Reznicek, an acquaintance in the War Ministry, that First Lieutenant Zoltán Szomoru had been taken prisoner on the Italian front. The following day the newspapers carried a detailed account of the great conductor's heroic exploits in the battle for the Col di Lana. Ilona could still hear Zoltán's words: "You must get me out of here. . . ."

She went back into Zita's room, sat down on her bed, picked up the open book, and asked, "Where did we get to?" She heard her own voice as though from far away.

41

The year 1916 brought no decision either.

More than seven hundred thousand men fell at the battle of Verdun. The names of the strongholds of Thiaumont, Vaux, Douaumont, and Fleury became as familiar as the names of capitals. In Paris they fêted the president of a republic that didn't exist. The republic was called Czechoslovakia, its president Thomas Masaryk. The statesman sat bent over maps, cut them up, and put them together again. Europe was bleeding; it was already being divided up. Germans and British both hailed the battle of the Skagerrak as their victory. The heads of Hindenburg and Ludendorff appeared on the white-porcelain bowls of tobacco-pipes. A million soldiers perished on the Somme. People consoled themselves with the thought that there were only four hundred thousand German dead as against six hundred thousand British and French. The German submarine *Deutschland* paid a visit to the American port of Norfolk. All-out U-boat warfare was launched. The head of Emperor Francis Joseph I rarely appeared on pipe-bowls now. The successor to the throne, Archduke Karl, hurried to Vienna from his Galician garrison. Deserters hung from the trees along the dusty highways of Bukovina. "I shall not live to see victory," said the old gentleman in the Hofburg. All he could see was his own end.

Theatres, music-halls, restaurants, and night-clubs were full to over-flowing. The homeland enjoyed the life the front lost. The Chief of Police, who instructed his officers "to keep their eyes on such female persons as behave in public in the manner of prositutes so ostentatiously and provocatively as to offend the moral susceptibilities of their fellow-citizens," was a complete fool. Whose moral susceptibilities were going to be offended? The men were dying at the front; the women went on the streets. Night-birds returning home in the grey light of morning saw the women outside the lowered iron shutters of food-shops. Queueing became a national pastime. Ration-cards were issued. Bread turned black. The crown wobbled—on kings' heads, on foreign-exchange markets.

Ilona had heard from Zoltán only twice since he was taken prisoner. Printed cards—P.O.W. post sent through the Red Cross. Countess Alberthausen's ladies, who knitted socks for "our brave lads" and distributed biscuits among "our brave wounded" in the hospitals, seemed to have vanished from the face of the earth. General Alberthausen had been killed in Volhynia. Even generals got killed. At Kontowski's palace Ilona was informed that His Highness was away. She rarely went out nowadays. When she did go she hurried home early, arriving out of breath, as in her childhood, when she had fled from a dark room and torn open the door of the lighted living-room as though pursued by demons.

Again and again the stationmaster exhorted his daughter to come to Kisnémet with Teréz and the child. She hesitated, as though fearing that in her absence from the city the disaster would take place quicker. At length the stationmaster took a holiday and came to Vienna. Life was still tolerable in the village, he said. And, after all, the child was the main consideration.

In July 1916, when Ilona set out for Berény accompanied by the stationmaster, it was not, as normally, for a brief summer visit. In the Döbling house white sheets were put over the furniture. The Persian carpets lay rolled up on the parquet floor of the drawing-room. The chandeliers were covered up. They looked like women's heads in the motoring scarves that were now so fashionable. Josephine took all the keys with her, Zita her books and toys. "The Baroness is moving to the country," said the neighbours.

42

It was a hot summer. The green roller-blinds in the Berény house were down till late in the afternoon. There was a pleasant smell of wood and apples. In the spacious kitchen flies stuck in hundreds to the long, orange-coloured fly-papers. When Ilona looked out she saw the wheat-fields, which seemed to grow before her eyes, changing from green to yellow, absorbing the colour of the sunshine. Often she imagined that Zoltán was walking between the ears of what, stripped to the waist. In nature, where everything that ended immediately began all over again, there was no end.

She was not put out by the fact that the Army had commandeered her four horses and she had to go from Berény to Kisnémet on foot.

Even Zita didn't regret it. In the barn stood two carriages, the yellow-lacquered four-seater and the brake, the *szekér*. Zita sat on the box, holding invisible reins, and discovered that invisible horses went faster, were more manageable, and also less dangerous than visible ones. When Ilona walked to Kisnémet through the dust, which was as deep as sand, she felt as though her feet were resting from the asphalt of the city.

In the evenings she used to sit on the stone-flagged terrace behind her house. Everything was asleep. A single candle burnt in the hurricane-lamp. The crickets chirruped. The scent of the acacias was as sultry as the night. Ilona gazed into the candlelight, and immediately rejected the plan of having electric-light installed at Berény. The new conjured up no memories; he who lost memories became poor. There were more and more people who were afraid of being alone; they crowded together like cows in the rain. Perhaps they were alone because they had killed the only thing that would have stayed at their side till death—the child they had been. Ilona recalled that she would be thirty this year and that none of the three men she had loved was with her. To each of them she had given what she possessed, and yet she had lost nothing. In her language a sweetheart was *szeretö*, the loving one; therefore Hungarian was a good language. She had her child and she had Berény. Since she had been at home the scenes of the war no longer frightened her. She slept peacefully; no longer dreamt of the dark valley; no longer woke bathed in sweat, imagining she could hear the death-rattle of the mountain. Far from home you remembered home, but at home you remembered nothing. At the front she had often been tempted by pride; she had despised the people around her. She had outgrown the people of Kisnémet, but she didn't look down upon them. To be at home meant to be without pride.

43

The stationmaster was fifty-seven, but although his temples were grey, he looked no older than fifty. He had always lived according to his duty; now he considered it his duty to stay young.

It was not because he overestimated the importance of his post. The fire had gone out long ago. He had believed that the Monarchy would win the war so long as every stationmaster did his duty. At moments of honesty he admitted to himself that nobody could win it.

He did not draw his wisdom from the *Höfer*, the daily report from the front. There were other, more reliable signs.

The peasants had stopped bringing their chickens, eggs, fruit, and vegetables to market on Fridays. They called at houses where they could exchange the fruits of their toil for tobacco, spirits, and all kinds of articles—lamps, bed-linen, doormats, trousers, candles, even news-print and images of the saints. Often they stood in the doorway with their hats in their hands, still in the accustomed attitude of humility, but their eyes flitting over clothing and household goods, slyly valuing, as though examining things which to-morrow would belong to them. The schoolmaster had been killed on the Isonzo front; the children

184

were taught the ABC by a schoolmistress from Debreczen who was said to have an illegitimate child in the town. More strangers appeared in Kisnémet. In addition to Mr Ujlaki, who came round twice a year to talk to the peasant girls and domestic servants into buying mirrors, eau-de-Cologne, head-scarves, china dogs, and whatever else was absolutely essential to their trousseau, other travelling salesmen appeared, but they brought only tobacco and preferred to do business with the peasants.

Although the stationmaster never once exchanged spirits or tobacco for provisions and drove pedlars away with the words "you pack of thieves," the times soaked into his pores.

At the beginning of the war he had been sent a deputy, who was one day to take his place. The man embezzled the petty cash. The stationmaster tried to excuse his deputy, but he couldn't understand him, for the man didn't understand himself. Count Aporfalvy, who had become his friend, was dead. The castle was occupied by Princess Consuela. Unknown men came and went; the tumult of the festivities could be heard in the servants' quarters. The Count always spent the winter in the castle, although there was only a makeshift heating system; the Princess had central heating installed and fled to the city on the first cold day. In the winter the stationmaster received a letter from his sister; she sent him money, a great deal of money, and asked him to send her, "at any price," two crates of eggs. "Business is excellent," wrote Rosa. "You know how it is." He tore up the letter and sent the money back.

When war broke out Mihály Horváth made up his mind to stay young because he thought he could prevent anything from changing. Now that everything had changed, he had to stay young because he was one of the few who had been instructed to build Noah's ark.

44

After her father Ilona spent most of her time with Margit, whose three children—Sanyi, the same age as Zita, Kató, aged nine and Mihály, who was not quite two—were Zita's playmates.

It was not only the friendship between their children that bound Ilona to Margit.

The sisters no longer looked so much alike as in their childhood. Margit had grown rather fat, especially round the hips; although she was only thirty-one, she looked considerably older than her sister. She hadn't Teréz's balanced nature, but she adapted herself with serene composure to her destiny. When she came to Berény she could rummage for hours through Ilona's clothes and jewellery; she would listen with glowing cheeks while Ilona talked about the great world, but Ilona could detect no envy in her face. She, and even Teréz, were to Margit characters out of a novel which one enjoyed leafing through without wanting to live it. Since her husband's death in Russia Margit always wore a black dress, but she seldom spoke of him and burdened nobody with her mourning. She had inherited the hotel, and ran it with an iron hand: loved, but even more feared, by her employees; feared, but even more loved, by her children; respected and feared at one and the same time by shopkeepers, suppliers, and wine-growers; fully capable of turning out a group of drunkards with her own hands; always ready after closing-time, when her children were asleep, to sit for hours over bills, cash-slips, and account-books.

At times, especially when she came across one of her own wedding-presents in Margit's home, Ilona remembered the arrogant pity she had felt for the girl at the wedding altar. She was no longer certain which of them had been best treated by Destiny.

The more her esteem for Margit rose the more of a stranger Teréz became to her. She examined herself to see whether she was motivated by the wish to shake off the troublesome burden of gratitude; whether she resented the fact that Teréz knew too much about her chaotic life; whether Teréz's shadowy existence weighed on her conscience, or whether she was simply jealous of her elder sister because she still had to share Zita's love with her. She acquitted herself. The day with Teréz was not easy. Like all people who have long lived an unusual life, she considered herself unusual. Because she had never made a mistake she thought herself infallible. In her youth she had done right without condemning wrong; now she became impatiently patient. Every one who came into contact with her soon felt like a guilty schoolboy; first he would try to gain the favour of those stern eyes; then he became angry at his own servility and hypocrisy; and finally he avoided her company, as we avoid, so far as we can, our own consciences. Different as they were, Margit and Ilona had both loved, conceived, and borne children; they couldn't understand Teréz, who had renounced men and ceased to be a woman.

One Sunday, when the Horváths were once more gathered in the apartment over the office, the one missing member of the family, about whom they were talking, unexpectedly knocked at the door.

45

The following evening Ilona, Lajos, and the stationmaster were sitting on the stone-paved terrace behind the house at Berény. Zita had gone to sleep long ago; Teréz had retired with a headache. The meal had been cleared away: only a bottle of Badacsonyer and two glasses stood on the laid table.

It had been raining all the afternoon. A slight whiff of wet hay ran through the spicy smell of the earth, like a river flowing into the sea and still visible in the estuary. Gnats seeking death fluttered round the shaded candles. Ilona put out the candles, lit the paraffin-lamp in the dining-room, and opened the doors. They sat in the dark. Only a ray of light shone upon the terrace from the room.

Lajos had taken off the jacket of his uniform and was sitting in his shirt-sleeves. He had drunk the first bottle of golden-yellow Badacsonyer almost entirely on his own. He poured himself another glass and said, "I'm leaving to-morrow, Papa."

"I thought you had a week's leave," commented the stationmaster in astonishment.

186

"I don't want the police to pick me up here."

Ilona thought of the rainy day on which Lajos had suddenly appeared in Feri's apartment.

"Have you run away?" she asked.

"The penalty for desertion is death." He laughed. "I don't want to be executed. I haven't run away. You needn't go to the Emperor."

"Why should they pick you up?" asked the stationmaster.

"A few days before I went on leave they arrested two of us. They're going to be court-martialled."

"Who are 'you'?"

"Soldiers who want to end the war."

"They all want that."

"The others are waiting. We won't wait any longer."

"That's high treason," said the stationmaster.

Again Lajos laughed. "What are we betraying? The war? That's lost. The Monarchy? That's lost because the war is lost. Death merely prolongs the life of the rulers."

"Why must *you* risk your neck?" interrupted Ilona.

Lajos answered vehemently, "It's true you have made the acquaintance of the so-called historical class, but you know nothing about history. In nature ripe fruit falls from the tree. In history it's different. If the tree isn't shaken the rotten fruit hangs on the branches for decades."

"Are you one of the revolutionaries?" asked the stationmaster.

"You want to know whether I'm the devil."

"I want to know what you are doing."

Lajos emptied his glass. He stood up and walked across the terrace. His voice came from the darkness.

He spoke of the Monarchy, which deserved its fate. For centuries it had kept itself alive only by force. It had suppressed the minorities, the Czechs and Croats and Slovenes. "The nations are thirsting for freedom." The gentlemen in Vienna, he said in a voice quivering with emotion, had started the war in order to drown the nations' desire for freedom in a wave of false patriotism. "Do you know why millions have to die? Because the Aporfalvys are afraid they won't make enough money on their pigs."

The stationmaster replied, "That's what the Socialist papers say."

"Does that mean it isn't true?"

"It's too simple to be true."

The son spoke more and more heatedly. The gentlemen in Vienna care for nothing but their rotten domination. Revolution, 1848, the freeing of the serfs—a lot of rubbish. "If a day-labourer tries to leave one master and find work on another farm the police fetch him back. The peasant pays rent for decades; if he is turned out by the landowner he doesn't possess as much earth as he can take away on the soles of his shoes." All at once Lajos's voice sounded gentle. "It's probably all your fault, Papa," he said. "You're the decentest man I know. You taught me to hate injustice, but you forgot to hate it yourself."

Now the stationmaster poured himself out a glass. He said, "You have read more books than I, Lajos. I was busy with my timetables and my flowers. But I too have read a few. Revolutions always free people who don't want to be freed. You think you know what is good for me. Did I ever empower you to act in my name?"

Ilona drew a deep breath. She didn't know which of the two was right—her father or her brother. She merely felt that a threat hung over both of them.

Lajos spoke of the future, feverishly, passionately, and yet as graphically as if he were describing something already achieved. He was concerned with the peasants, he said. "The land must be divided up. We shall do away with large landed property. Those who do not cultivate the soil shall not own it. The Aporfalvys belong to the historical class because in the whole of their history none of them has worked." He came to a stop in front of the stationmaster. "Do you want those who are guilty of this disaster to remain unpunished?"

"I don't know who is guilty, and I doubt if you do," replied his father. "I only know that you imagine your revolution would make the world a better place. If that were true we should long ago have been living in Paradise. There have always been rulers and ruled, and the rulers have always been more or less unjust. If you have the power to distribute the estates you will distribute them unjustly. I don't say you mean to, but that's what will happen."

"No it won't!" cried Lajos. He emerged from the darkness, vanished into it again. How could there still be injustice when the people chose their own representatives? "Do you remember the last elections? Half the village was put in prison. Next day they let us out. It was a mis-understanding, they said. Meanwhile Dr Kasznár had been elected, the lick-spittle, Aporfalvy's candidate." There could never again be war, he said. "No nation wants war. Let the peoples fearlessly announce their will, and there will be no more war."

How did Lajos become a revolutionary? Ilona wondered. She remembered him as a little boy with big, dreamy eyes and curly black hair. He had always tried to make peace between his quarrelling sisters. All three always turned on him. She remembered him in the Sopron apartment. He had hated Feri. Would things perhaps have been different if she had not become the mistress of the young landowner?

"Are you sure you will live to see all that?" she asked. She was prompted solely by fear.

"They'll take care not to hang me," he said. "Of course they string up the poor devils at the front from the nearest tree. Our glorious army is accompanied by drumhead court martials. In the Galician villages the corpses dangle till they rot. I've cut down a few; I hadn't time to bury them. No isolated individual can escape the same fate. But they dare not execute us who stand together. Before their end the rulers always try to govern leniently. For centuries they knew no leniency. Then they restrain the executioner they have ordered themselves."

"And suppose things turn out differently?" asked the stationmaster. "Suppose we win the war? . . ."

Lajos came up to the table and filled his glass.

"Every revolution has its martyrs," he said. "Think of Father Martinovicz, think of Kossuth. And the Arad martyrs. A hundred years later monuments are erected to their memory."

Ilona pricked up her ears. She thought she heard a sound from the direction of the farm gate. "Some one's coming," she said.

The stationmaster rose and went to the balustrade at the side of the terrace. By day the gate leading into what was left of the Berény estate was visible from this point. The swaying light of an acetylene-lamp was moving towards the front door. It disappeared round the front of the house. "A cyclist," said the stationmaster.

Ilona had risen. All three were standing in the darkness. No one spoke. They could hear the frogs croaking.

Josephine came through the dining-room carrying a candle. Her thin plaits were hanging down on her shoulders. She had thrown a coat over her long nightdress.

"The Police Superintendent is here," she said. "He wants to speak to the Baroness."

"Bring him out, ordered Ilona. Her voice was hoarse. "And bring a couple of candles."

The Police Superintendent was a man in his mid-fifties, broad-shouldered, corpulent; he breathed heavily in his tight-fitting uniform. His thick black eyebrows looked like two little black fish moving their tails. Since his moustache was curled upward, moustache and eyebrows ran in a ridiculous parallel one above the other. On his head he wore a black policeman's billycock embellished with many dark cock's plumes, intended to give a martial touch to the civilian headgear.

He halted in the doorway and saluted, narrowing his eyes rather angrily, because they were unable to pierce the darkness, so that he didn't quite know before whom he had raised his hand to his hat-brim.

Josephine brought two candles, put them on the table, and left, bashfully holding her coat together. Not till she reached the dining-room did she look round and put her arms akimbo, thereby expressing her disapproval of the late visit.

"Please forgive me for disturbing you, Baroness," said the Superintendent stiffly. Without turning to Lajos he went on, "I have to arrest Sergeant-Major Horváth."

Lajos took his jacket from the chair-back without a word.

There must be a mistake, András," said the stationmaster. He had been at school with the Superintendent.

"Please don't make any difficulties, Mihály," said the Superintendent.

"Won't you take a glass of wine?" asked Ilona.

The man with the plumed hat looked round uncertainly. He had known Ilona ever since she was born.

He put his hat on an empty chair.

"Very kind of you, Baroness," he said. He wouldn't lose face, he thought, so long as he addressed her as "Baroness."

All four sat down round the table. The Superintendent sipped warily at his glass, as though he were keeping within the law so long as he didn't drain it. Ilona was smiling stiffly, the stationmaster biting his lips, and Lajos wrestling with the little hook on the collar of his uniform.

At last the Superintendent said, "Orders from Army H.Q. at Debreczen."

No one replied. The frogs in the pond were croaking in competition with one another.

The Superintendent stared into his glass.

"You don't see Badacsonyer very often nowadays," he said. "The peasants hang on to it."

"Do you know what it's all about?" asked the stationmaster.

"Army H.Q. doesn't tell us anything. We're just an executive body. Perhaps the Sergeant-Major has overstayed his leave."

There was silence.

"It's a case of high treason," said Lajos.

The Superintendent looked at him for the first time.

"Don't make silly jokes, Lajos," he said. He laughed. But because laughing made him hot he undid the button of his uniform.

Ilona filled up his glass without asking her guest's permission. She didn't know what she hoped to gain by it.

"We have to send the Sergeant-Major to Debreczen by the first train," said the Superintendent, turning to the stationmaster. He said "the Sergeant-Major" because he regretted having addressed Lajos by name. "You can have the door of a carriage opened on the other side of the station, Mihály. I should like to spare you the shame. That's why I came myself."

"Thank you, András," said the stationmaster.

The Superintendent slowly emptied his glass. A light wind was swaying the candles. The wine in the glasses gleamed golden. The only sound was the policeman's heavy breathing. He said, "Have you heard that old Widow Balogh is dead, Mihály?"

"I heard before I came away."

"There's going to be a nice row. Before she was even cold they were going at one another hammer and tongs."

They were talking about old Widow Balogh who had left her farm to her second son. It was illegal. Her eldest son was a drunkard. The second son was lame, and hence stayed at home. The two sons-in-law were no good. No young people were any good nowadays.

Ilona and Lajos looked at each other. Ilona's heart was pounding as though it were made up of a lot of little hammers. She realized for the first time how much she loved Lajos. When András bácsi had emptied his glass he would take him away. There was no certainty that they wouldn't hang him.

When she went to pour the Superintendent another glass she found the bottle was empty. She rose to fetch a fresh one, but he stood up.

"Will you stand security for him, Mihály?" he asked. "I ought to handcuff him."

"Of course," said the stationmaster.

The Superintendent buttoned up the collar of his uniform and picked up his hat.

"Have you a bicycle, Sergeant-Major Horváth?"

"I walked here."

"Then we'll have to push my bicycle," said the Superintendent.

The stationmaster shook his son's hand. Ilona threw her arms round his neck and kissed him on both cheeks.

The Superintendent turned away.

"You're a silly boy," he said to the Sergeant-Major.

The stationmaster looked at Ilona.

"I'll stay on for a bit," he said.

Lajos and the Superintendent went through the dining-room.

Immediately afterwards the bicycle-light moved slowly across the yard. The prisoner and his warder were pushing the bicycle through the summer night to Kisnémet.

The stationmaster took Ilona's hand.

"András is a good fellow," he said.

The light had disappeared. Ilona gave a sob.

46

In the autumn Sergeant-Major Lajos Horváth was condemned to twenty years' penal servitude, with the added punishment of one day without food, a plank bed, and one day's confinement in darkness each year. Twelve others were court-martialled along with him. The number was an administrative error, since it enabled the defending counsel to compare them to the thirteen martyrs of Arad. Three of the thirteen were condemned to death. None of them was executed.

The stationmaster requested his retirement. He showed his petition only to Ilona. It was written on a foolscap sheet in his careful hand-writing, with thick strokes and hair-strokes, the lines as straight as railway-lines, with flourishes that looked like the smoke from loco-motives. "The undersigned," it said, "had no knowledge of the treasonable activities of his son, Sergeant-Major Lajos Horváth. The undersigned believes that in his almost forty years of service he has always done his duty to the best of his knowledge and belief. Since, however, the dignity of his post as stationmaster of the Imperial and Royal Railways in incompatible with the disgrace that has come upon his name, the undersigned begs leave to request the earliest possible designation of his successor, while maintaining his right to a pension." Below this he set his signature: "Mihály Horváth, Imp. & Roy. Stationmaster."

While the Imp. & Roy. Stationmaster Mihály Horváth waited for the Minister of Railways' reply he frequently spoke of his father, a thing he had never done before. Horváth Senior had been an engine-driver; he had lost his sight in a railway accident, for which he had been held partially responsible. Four years later, when he was exonerated from blame, old Horváth had long since been travelling by the heavenly train. At this point Mihály, who had intended to become a teacher, changed his mind and became a railwayman. That was forty years ago. Now Mihály often thought of his father.

At the end of October—a raw autumn was heralding a cold winter —the stationmaster received a large envelope bearing the stamp of the

Ministry of Railways. On the excuse of all sorts of urgent business he left it unopened for half a day.

The refusal of his request was accompanied by a communication from the Secretary of State in the Imperial and Royal Ministry of Railways. "It cannot be our intention," wrote the Secretary of State, "to visit the sins of the sons upon their fathers. At the moment when our brave soldiers are shrinking from no sacrifice in their effort to achieve final victory we need on the home a spirit of unreserved self-sacrifice on the part of all Hungarian patriots. I therefore request you, also in the name of His Excellency, to maintain your tested loyalty and remain at your post. I have the honour, on behalf of the highest authority, to assure you of the complete confidence of His Majesty's Ministry."

The stationmaster walked to Berény to show his daughter the letter. Then he went back into his office. He was certain that Austro-Hungary would win the war after all.

47

Once a month a relative of the convicted soldier Lajos Horváth was allowed to visit the prisoner. The first time the stationmaster went to Debreczen himself. He travelled in civilian clothes, as he had to Ilona's wedding.

At the beginning of November it was Ilona's turn. She brought Lajos his favourite foods in a blue hamper with four compartments. He asked her to request permission to send him technical works on agriculture. She had never seen him in better spirits. The feverish glitter that had sometimes frightened her had gone from his eyes. Calm, confidence, and warmth emanated from them. They are no longer glittering, they are radiant, she thought. "For a long time I lived in fear," he said. "Now I live in hope." He didn't count the years of imprisonment that stood in front of him—he counted the months the war could last.

A fortnight after Ilona's visit, on November 21, bells started ringing in all the churches of the Monarchy. There weren't as many as there used to be, because many of them had been melted down. The bells still spoke in Kisnémet's two churches. Ever since Ilona could remember the Calvinist bell had always given precedence to the Catholic bell; now they both rang at the same time. The rain fell, slowly at first, then more and more heavily, an evil rain which seemed to know that in it "all flesh that moved upon the earth, both of fowl, and of cattle, and of beast, and of every creeping thing that creepeth upon the earth, and every man would perish." Black flags hung from every house and cottage, building and palace; the water dripped down from them; even the rain-water seemed to have turned black in this black Flood. People poured into the churches, but the bells that had called them did not cease to ring. When Ilona entered Kisnémet church with her father, her sisters, Zita, and Margit's children, it was already evening. All the candles were burning. She thought of the Sunday on which she had gone to Schönbrunn, sunshade in hand, to see the Emperor. In her memory she saw the Emperor much more clearly than she saw herself. No one was so dead as the child one had been oneself. Now the audience-chamber in which the general and the lieutenant and the presiding judge and the tobacconist had waited was empty. The Emperor's corpse was laid out in Schönbrunn Castle. The corpse of the Monarchy was laid out. The bells were pealing. The rain fell incessantly.

48

"The trains that have gone by will never return," Aunt Rosa had said one winter's evening shortly before Christmas 1903. The station-master hadn't believed her.

Now he remembered that brothel-keeper's prediction. It was the end of October 1918. The traffic on the line between Budapest and Debreczen was slackening off, like a clock that slows down before stopping altogether. Then the trains didn't come back at all. The stationmaster received a telegram giving him further instructions. Finally telegraph and telephone fell silent. He had a personal attitude towards the railway-lines: they seemed to him like abandoned women. The trains should have said good-bye.

And yet the rails were not quiet; they had mysteriously come to life. Soldiers popped up from all sides, as though invisible trains had spat them out on the track. They camped along the line, rested on the station benches, slept in the bushes on the embankment. Opposite the station stood an iron plaque bearing the words: "The public are forbidden to cross the track." Weatherbeaten, it rose up out of the past. The timetables on their wooden frames were weatherbeaten too. The soldiers didn't ask permission to settle in the waiting-rooms. They sat there waiting, without knowing what they were waiting for. When they asked how far it was to Püspökladány, Karcag, Kisujszállás, Szolnok, or Budapest they didn't mean how many hours by train. They wanted to know how much farther they would have to march, as though the rails were no more than sign-posts. The distances didn't frighten them. Their uniforms were dirty and ragged; one had no cap, another no belt, and a third actually had no trousers. Bare legs peeped out from under long greatcoats. Some wore red-and-green armbands. These were members of the Soldiers' Councils, the stationmaster was told. He didn't know what that meant. Just as, for almost forty years, he had gazed after the trains until the red light on the last carriage disappeared, so now he gazed after the columns of soldiers as they moved off between the rails. When the autumn mist had swallowed up the rearguard the stationmaster imagined the night train had gone by. He looked up at the signal that stood out like a small red moon against the sky. No train could possibly have gone by.

Now the columns advanced senselessly in both directions. The trains used to know where they were going; the soldiers didn't know. Once when the stationmaster sank into an exhausted sleep over his table he dreamt that the columns had collided outside the station-house like trains travelling in opposite directions on the same track. There were many dead. They lay on the tracks; the soldiers marched over them.

Every now and then a man would leave the column as though alighting from a train. They were peasants' sons, local lads. They laughed when the stationmaster asked if they were on leave. They stared at him and shook their heads. The stationmaster grew very old under their stares.

One night the soldiers lit a fire under his window. They warmed themselves, drank, sang bawdy songs. The stationmaster put on his uniform and went downstairs. They told him Prime Minister Count Tisza had been murdered. They were drinking to the murder. One of them spotted the little black-and-yellow rosette on the stationmaster's cap. He tore if off. The stationmaster seized the lad by the chest of his jacket. He had never struck anyone before, but he was sure he could finish the lad off with one blow. Suddenly he was surrounded by a threatening semi-circle of soldiers. Then one said, "Leave the old man alone!" The stationmaster bent down and picked up the little, round rosette. That night the soldiers hauled down the black-and-yellow flag from the flag-pole. They burnt it. The smell of the burning cloth rose up to the stationmaster's window.

For news from Kisnémet he was dependent upon people who came from the little town, exhausted, as though they had made a long journey. They told him the retired Colonel Lengyeltóthy, who had been playing chess with the notary in the Café Rakóczi for twenty years, had been beaten up in the open street. András bácsi, the Police Superintendent, had been arrested. Who could arrest the Police Superintendent? The messengers from the town shrugged their shoulders. They said Pali Falus, a miller's lad, had been elected chairman of the Revolutionary Council. No one knew who had elected him. During the night the dead Count's valet came to the station. János stood at the door muffled up and as pale as a ghost. Were there still no trains? he wanted to know. Princess Consuela had sent him. Soldiers were prowling round the castle threatening to set it on fire. The stationmaster went to the telephone. He turned the handle. The instrument made a clanking sound, and that was all. The stationmaster shrugged his shoulders.

On the morning of November 1, All Saints' Day, Lajos suddenly stood before the stationmaster. The civilian suit he was wearing didn't belong to him; it was far too small. He had a red-white-and-green armband round his sleeve. "Have you escaped from prison?" asked the stationmaster. "There isn't any prison any more," said Lajos. "I shall wait for a car to fetch me. They're sending me one from Budapest." The stationmaster thought of Margit, Ilona, and the children. It occurred to him that it was All Saints' Day. He asked if he could leave the station to Lajos for a bit. "Can you stay in the office for a few hours?" he asked. Lajos put his hands on his father's shoulders. He laughed. "I'll look after everything." The stationmaster took his coat. "I'm going to the cemetery," he said.

49

The sky knew nothing about All Saints on this November 1, 1918. The sky was not in mourning. It was blue and cloudless. The sun cast its golden seed into the black fields. It was as though the sky were smiling slightly at the sad visitors to the cemeteries who didn't know that the graves were empty, that both saints and sinners were living in clover up in heaven.

Ilona had intended to go to Kisnémet, but she dared not leave the house. Although Berény lay some distance from the railway, the track was visible beyond the leafless trees. The heads of soldiers popped up along it like ravens hopping up and down in the fields.

The newspapers were two days old. Ilona felt a shock of dismay every time she caught sight of them. They told of the humiliation suffered by Austria's truce emissary, Staff Captain Ruggera, at the Italian Headquarters; of the rapid advance of the Italians and British across the Piave; of Turkey's capitulation; of the unrest in Vienna and Budapest. While Ilona walked up and down in the house Teréz and Zita sat in the drawing-room playing draughts. Ilona couldn't understand why the stationmaster hadn't sent a messenger to Berény.

Soon after nine Teréz and Zita went to bed. Josephine sat down with Ilona at the dining-table. For days Ilona had put off checking the housekeeping accounts. It was reassuring to look into Josephine's leathery bird's face and listen to the old woman complaining about the prices. She banged the little blue housekeeping-accounts book on the table crossly a few times. Everyday life was the only thing you could cling to, like a balustrade on the edge of the abyss.,

Then both women pricked up their ears. "There was a knock at the door," said Ilona. They held their breath. Josephine rose. Ilona shook her head. She went to the front door herself.

There was silence outside.

"Who is that?" asked Ilona.

"Your father sent me," said a woman's voice.

Ilona opened the door.

The woman outside did not move. Josephine approached with a candle. Ilona recognized Princess Consuela. She was wearing a black dress and a black-silk scarf over her head and carrying a small suitcase.

"Come in, your Highness," said Ilona.

Josephine went in front of the two women carrying the candle. The paraffin-lamp was still burning in the living-room. The old woman left Ilona and the Princess alone.

"Forgive me for disturbing you in the middle of the night, Baroness," said the Princess. She waited, stiffly erect, until Ilona offered her a chair. "The revolutionaries have occupied the castle. I fled to your father. I shouldn't be safe in the station, he said. He said you would give me shelter for the night."

"Of course," nodded Ilona.

The Princess was still holding her suitcase Now she let go of it with a faint smile.

"My jewellery. Everything I could pick up in a hurry." She went on hastily: "I'm to tell you that everything is in order at the station. You are not to move till you hear from your father. Your brother has placed the station under the protection of the Revolutionary Council."

195

"Is Lajos there?"

The Princess lowered her eyes, as though she couldn't bear the gaze of the sister of a man who could put a station under the protection of the Revolutionary Council.

Ilona thought of Feri. She imagined she could hear the faint creaking of his boots. He was walking up and down in the drawing-room of the house in Buda. "I could overcome my father's opposition. But Consuela is inflexible." Ilona thought of Margit's wedding. She had been carrying Zita under her heart at the time. The Princess had looked her in the eyes; it had been a challenge to a duel. Now Zita was sleeping upstairs in her room, a beautiful young girl of thirteen. The Princess was sitting in front of her, begging a favour. The other's misery was the measure of her own triumph, a miserable triumph. Destiny took the duelling-sword out of one's hand and kept it till it was old and rusty. Living time killed everything, even hatred.

"You are very kind, Baroness," said the Princess.

"It's the least I could do," responded Ilona.

They scrutinized each other in silence. The Princess had still not taken off the black head-scarf. Her big dark eyes gave nothing away; they were like the heavy oak doors of Aporfalvy Castle, which barred the way to the uninvited. With her high arched eyebrows, too small mouth, too straight nose, and high forehead criss-crossed with little pale veins, she looked like Bellini's Madonnas, to whom we can imagine people praying, but whom we cannot imagine loving anyone.

"They will burn the place to the ground," said the Princess. "They will hang the aristocrats from the lamp-posts, as they did during the French Revolution. And the Revolution is led by one of our people, a Count Károlyi."

Ilona remembered having heard the name from Kontowski. What was going to happen to Taszilo? If Kontowski was in difficulties she must hurry to him. Kontowski had given her Berény—good, protective Berény. Lajos placed the station under the protection of the Revolutionary Council. A woman didn't know where she belonged.

"In a few days everything will have quietened down," she said. "You can stay here till it has, your Highness."

"Please don't call me your Highness, Baroness."

Ilona fell silent, because she didn't know what to call the Princess. The lamp was smoking. She rose and turned down the wick.

"I'm glad my father didn't live to see it," said the Princess.

Outside, the dog started barking. The Princess sat up yet more stiffly in her armchair, like some one steeling himself against blows that are about to fall.

"Bordi is on edge," commented Ilona. "As though he knew something was happening."

"My father loved his peasants," the Princess went on. "He was kind to them. I have always hated the rabble. When I went to church I used to pray to God for a humble heart. He didn't hear me. Now it makes no difference. They would have burnt the castle down just the same. The rabble cannot be won over by love. The rabble distrusts love, and they're right."

196

Ilona wished the Princess's words could make her angry. She knew what Lajos would have replied, but she wasn't Lajos, and she didn't reply at all. Perhaps the Princess was afraid Ilona Horváth might misconstrue the fact of an Aporfalvy accepting her hospitality.

"What do these people want?" asked Princess Consuela.

"I don't know."

"Everything great in the world has come into being through suppression. Everything that has endured, everything we admire, was produced by slave labour. People who think we are all equal falsify Creation. God didn't create men equal." She had folded her hands as though in prayer. "First revolutions tear down the masters' castles, then the masters' houses."

The paraffin-lamp was still smoking. Ilona rose and drew the curtain. There were hundreds and thousands of cold stars in the sky.

"I think we ought to go to bed," suggested Ilona.

The Princess didn't seem to hear.

"I have caused you much distress, Ilona," she said. "Feri would have married you. I'm sorry."

"That was a long time ago."

"I always wanted to ask your forgiveness. I could never bring myself to do so. Now it's easy for me. Don't misunderstand me; it has nothing to do with the Revolution." She made a dismissive gesture, as though thrusting the Revolution aside. "When he was asked what he did during the French Revolution Abbé Siéyès said, *'J'ai survécu*—I survived.' I wanted to ask your forgiveness. Ilona, because you survived the disgrace and gave Feri's child a name. There is only one way to become an aristocrat. You have to survive the danger of becoming a plebeian." She stretched out her hand to Ilona. "If we survive we shall be friends, shan't we?"

"Of course, Consuela," said Ilona, as though speaking to a sick person. "But you must allow me to show you your room."

The stairs creaked outside. Teréz entered. She was wearing a dressing-gown.

"Princess Consuela is going to spend the night with us," explained Ilona.

The dog barked again. Now Ilona and the Princess also heard what Teréz had already heard before—human footsteps, voices.

"Zita is awake," said Teréz.

A shot rang out. The howling of the dying dog came into the room. Fists hammered on the front door.

"Go upstairs, quick," whispered Ilona.

It was as though the Princess didn't understand. She stood in the middle of the room, as white as a sheet. She didn't move until Zita burst into the room, barefoot, in a nightdress, her long hair hanging down over her shoulders. For a moment she stood still in astonishment, then she hurried to Teréz for protection.

Ilona went to the front door.

"Open up!" came the shout from outside. "Open up!"

"Who's there? What do you want?"

"In the name of the Revolutionary Council, open the door! We

197

know the Aporfalvy woman is with you!"

Ilona waited till Princess Consuela had gone upstairs.

She couldn't immediately count how many men entered the house. They not only pushed Ilona aside; they also jostled one another. Some wore uniforms; others were in civilian clothes. Even they had rifles. Their faces were red, ugly with ardour and alcohol. They brought a sour reek of wine into the house. Ilona didn't know any of them. All the stranger, therefore, was the feeling she had that they were in disguise, that each of them was wearing some one else's clothes.

A lad seized Ilona's arm. His face was like curdled milk—fresh and mouldy.

"Where is the Aporfalvy woman?" he said.

"Let go of me! I don't know what you're talking about."

The others had forced their way into the drawing-room. Zita was weeping loudly. Teréz pressed the child's head to her, as though to prevent Zita from seeing the men.

"She fled out here, we know that," said one of the soldiers, evidently the leader, a giant of a man with a fair beard and blue eyes, wearing boots and an open-necked shirt.

Two or three of the intruders dropped into armchairs; one sank on to the sofa. Ilona thought she knew his face. He was too drunk to recognize anybody. In a thick voice he kept singing the first two lines of an old revolutionary song from 1848:

> *"Kossuth Lajos azt üzente*
> *Elfogyott a regimentje."*
> ("Lajos Kossuth told us to say
> His regiment is dead.")

He thought again for a moment, couldn't remember any more words, sang over again:

> *"Kossuth Lajos azt üzente*
> *Elfogyott a regimentje."*

"Search the house!" ordered the bearded man.

Some of the men crowded to the door. A shout from the leader stopped them in their tracks. He had discovered the Princess's little suitcase. The lock wouldn't yield. A man in civilian clothes thrust his fixed bayonet through the thin leather. The jewels poured out on to the floor. No one dared touch the diamonds and pearls, bracelets and necklaces.

Suddenly they shook off their paralysis, threw themselves on the floor, and snatched at the treasures, glittering reptiles that threatened to wriggle free. They tore tiaras, rings, and necklaces out of one another's hands. They dropped their guns and stumbled over them. When they straightened up each of them had a piece of jewellery in his hand. Laughter filled the room, the unnatural laughter of people who cannot explain their hilarity. An older man with a dark moustache put a diamond tiara on his head. A second looked at his fingers, on which he had slipped several rings; his fingers were too thick; the rings rested on the tips, shimmering finger-nails. The boy with the milky face put a necklace round his neck, swayed his hips, made movements with his hands which he imagined to be feminine, and crowed in a thin voice. The soldier with the moustache finally found what he had been looking for—a wall-mirror. Five or six others immediately crowded round the mirror; looked at themselves in the glory of their jewellery; laughed at themselves and the others. Only the leader had looted nothing. He stood there at a loss what to do. The drunken man was bawling: "*Kossuth Lajos azt üzente. . . .*" He couldn't even remember the second line now. Nothing remained on the floor but the suitcase and a few worthless objects that had fallen out of it—a silk nightdress, a broken scent-bottle, a toothbrush. There was a smell of sweat and chypre.

Ilona had sat down and drawn Zita to her. The child was no longer crying; she merely sobbed every now and then. Ilona felt she must get Zita out of here, but couldn't think where to take her. The Princess could have slipped out through the empty hall, but she was probably afraid to leave the bedroom. Why didn't Teréz do anything? Ilona was surprised that she could feel angry with Teréz for being horrified at the mere sight of the men. She was surprised that she didn't think of herself. The thought that she wasn't afraid filled her with pride. Out of the pride grew fresh courage.

"When will they go? When will they go?" Zita kept asking over and over again.

"Don't worry, they're just going," said Ilona.

Eventually the leader shouted at his men to take off their fancy-dress. They threw the jewellery back into the ripped suitcase grudgingly, like soldiers laying down their arms.

"Search the house!" ordered the bearded man. "You stay here," he said to the boy with the milky face. "Guard the women, understand? He pressed a gun into the boy's hand.

Again they all stumbled over one another. Only the boy remained standing in the doorway with the gun resting on his arm. The singer was asleep on the sofa. He was snoring.

Ilona tried to pacify the child. She thought of Ilona Horváth at the age of thirteen. She had grown up in the security of Kisnémet railway station. When she moved to Berény two years ago she had hoped that the land of her childhood would protect her child.

A shriek cut across the drunkard's snoring and Zita's low weeping. Ilona had never heard anyone shriek like that, not even at the front. Pain, resistance, humiliation, indignation, a cry for help, despair—all the misery of the human creature was contained in a single sound.

The boy in the doorway grinned. The freckles in his face became jumbled together.

Ilona rose to her feet. Zita fled to Teréz. She was screaming too.

The boy with the gun blocked Ilona's path.

"Let me go up!" said Ilona.

The boy pushed her away with the butt of his rifle.

"Stay where you are, or the same thing will happen to you."

Zita, imagining that the soldier was going to strike her mother, tore herself free from Teréz and threw herself between Ilona and the boy. The boy laughed loudly.

"There's no need to get excited," he said to Ilona. "You see, she's stopped screaming. She's enjoying it. She's been whoring around with counts for long enough."

Ilona listened. There was silence. The only sound was the creaking of a bed.

The lecherous expression of an old man came into the boy's face.

"I shall have a go too," he said. "I hope they hurry up. She's having a real good time, the aristo whore."

Ilona covered Zita's ears with her hands. What would happen if the men tried to violate her? The revolver the stationmaster had given her a year ago lay in a drawer of the commode in the bedroom. She had to get to the bedroom.

The door opened. The boy turned round. A soldier Ilona hadn't noticed before was standing in the doorway.

"It's your turn now," he said. His face was red and patchy.

The sound of an engine made him prick up his ears. The light from a headlamp shone in through the curtains

Ilona hurried to the front door. Two men in uniforms were standing outside. They both wore red-white-and-green armbands.

"For heaven's sake, help!" said Ilona. She didn't know why she thought the two men would help her.

They took no notice of her. One—a tall, slim man with a hard but trustworthy face—went up to the two who had followed Ilona into the hall.

"Have you found her?" he asked.

"Yes, comrade," said the boy.

"Where is she?"

"Upstairs."

With a mute gesture the man ordered his companion to go up, and then came into the living-room. His eyes fell upon Teréz, still standing rigid with fright, the weeping child, the snoring man, and finally came to rest on the suitcase full of jewellery. An expression of disgust and disappointment came into his face. He turned to Ilona.

"I'm sorry," he said. He spoke a cultured Hungarian. "Why did you hide Consuela Aporfalvy?"

"Your men have been behaving like pigs."

"They didn't know you were Comrade Horváth's sister."

Ilona laughed. The tension of the last few hours was released in irresistible laughter. Ilona didn't stop laughing until Zita began to cry, frightened even more by her mother's unnatural laughter.

" 'Comrade Horváth'!" she said. "Are you sparing me because my brother is your comrade?"

The man did not reply. He walked across to the sofa and shook the sleeper. All his fury was poured out over the soldier.

"You'd do better to worry about the Princess," said Ilona. "Or do you intend to have your fun with her too?"

The man walked quickly past her, head bent, out into the hall. The door remained open behind him.

Through the door Ilona saw the Princess being brought downstairs between two men. Her black dress was torn, revealing her naked breasts. She made no attempt to cover them. Her arms were dangling, as though disconnected from her shoulders. A dark streak of blood ran across her face. Her stockings had slipped down and were rolled over her shoes. Her bare knees were bloody. At one point she tried to straighten up, as though waking from a deep sleep. Then she collapsed again. The men caught her as she fell.

The drunken man sat up on the sofa and rubbed his eyes. He rose and staggered over to the door. He was muttering something. It sounded like the words of the revolutionary song he had been singing earlier.

Two men entered the living-room, passed Zita and the two women, stuffed the jewellery and toilet articles into the suitcase. Only the fragments of the scent-bottle and the toothbrush were left on the floor.

The man with the hard, trustworthy face came back.

"I shall not be able to prevent proceedings from being taken against you," he said. "You will keep silent concerning everything that has happened here. In your own interest. I repeat that I am sorry." He avoided Ilona's eyes. "We cannot put right a thousand years of injustice in a single day. You can't make an omelette without breaking eggs." He halted in the doorway. "I'll leave one of my men here for your protection."

"Thank you," said Ilona. "I don't want to be protected by criminals." The man shrugged his shoulders.

Ilona hurried after him. Now her conscience awoke, the eternally oppressed slave of the great mistress, self-preservation. She had thought only of her child. She had tried to save Zita from hearing an ugly word, while a dozen men were violating her guest in her house. Never mind what she could have achieved, what she could have prevented; petty considerations of success enslaved the oppressed conscience. She must try to set the Princess free.

The men and the Princess had vanished. The stranger started the engine of his car.

Ilona looked out across the yard. The dead sheepdog lay at her feet. The cock was crowing. The horizon was silvery-grey. All Souls' Day was breaking.

50

At the end of November—the trains had long since begun to run again—Ilona arrived in Budapest.

She had stayed in Berény only a few days after All Souls' Day. Zita had gone down with a violent fever. The doctor came from Kisnémet, but could find no cause of illness. He talked about nervous fever, shaking his head, as though children were not entitled to suffer from nervous fever. A few days later the fever vanished, but Zita remained weak and silent; she wept frequently and moodily. At first shyly, then stubbornly, she refused to enter the living-room. Away from Berény! thought Ilona. Houses are like living beings: what has once happened in them lives on in them. There are said to be haunted houses in which the blood of the murdered is always fresh on the walls. Are there any other houses?

In the Döbling villa Zita quickly recovered. Nevertheless, the house seemed to Ilona like a friend one has left young and healthy, but finds old and sick. The walls looked woebegone. We often confuse houses with ourselves.

Her first visit was to a banker. The greater part of her fortune, which she had put into war loan was lost. Maximilian von Hämmerle tried to console her, but he was more in need of consolation than she. He reminded her of Ferencz bácsi, who had been postman in Kisnémet during her childhood. The day on which Ferencz bácsi had lost a valuable consignment of money—it is impossible to tell why one memory remains and another pales—had been one of the experiences of her childhood. Old Hämmerle seemed to have grown so small that he scarcely came level with the top of his high standing-desk. His face was like a crumpled cloth. Instead of blaming the times he blamed himself, like the postman who had lost the money entrusted to him. Ilona's stocks and shares were no longer quoted on the Stock Exchange; "for the time being," Hämmerle said without conviction. The banknotes were being changed. "Am I poor?" asked Ilona. "You have your jewellery, Baroness, and you have Berény," replied Hämmerle. "I shall have to economize," she commented. "We all have to do that," said Hämmerle. She couldn't help smiling, because he had said it like the chairman of a club accepting her into the circle of the old rich who were now the new poor.

She instructed an estate agent to find her a new apartment with three, or at most four, rooms. The thought of having to part with her jewellery didn't worry her. She had ceased to wear it at the outbreak of war. In Sopron she had been in the habit of arranging the silver and gold coins and the blue notes in military formation on her bedspread. Her attitude to her jewels was precisely that of a general to his soldiers: if the need arose they must be thrown into the attack.

On the other hand, to squander something of value ran counter to her innate thriftiness. Apart from her banker, she had never discussed money matters with anyone but Kontowski. She found the palace in the Prinz-Eugen-Strasse shut. She was told that "Herr Kontowski's" telephone had been cut off. She learnt from acquaintances that the Prince was in Budapest.

That was one of the reasons for her journey to Budapest. The other was Lajos.

On the day she left Berény the papers had published the list of members of the new Republican government of Hungary. The Ministry of Agriculture was in the hands of Lajos Horváth, peasant from Kisnémet. Only when she told Zita her uncle was a Cabinet Minister, and explained what it meant, did Ilona catch herself feeling proud of Lajos. From the moment he had visited her in her Sopron apartment, in revolt against uniform, authority, Emperor, and King, he had gone towards his goal, a sleepwalker, always on the edge of the abyss, confident of his own steps. Had he been impelled by ambition? Had he been washed up on the shore by waves of filth and blood? He was her brother. The Horváths were chosen. There were people whom success destroyed and others whom it mellowed. She wanted to find out if he had changed—and in what way. Furthermore, the stationmaster had asked her to put in a good word with Lajos for Princess Consuela, who had disappeared, probably into a prison in the capital. "Perhaps you can talk to him," the stationmaster had written. "You are both young. Lajos and I no longer speak the same language. . . ."

51

A footman opened the door for Ilona.

Lajos rose behind his desk and came towards her with outstretched arm. He was wearing black boots, his Sunday suit, and a white shirt without a tie. They sat down at a round table.

The lofty, dignified room was filled with dark-brown, gilded Empire-style furniture. Three folding-doors opened on to a balcony occupying the central section of the edifice. The Ministry of Agriculture was housed in the building of the former Royal Curia. Important-looking portraits of the old gentlemen who had one administered justice here hung on the walls in gilt frames. The recent removal of two pictures from the wall above the desk had left dark patches. Although it was early in the afternoon, the electric candles were burning in the gilded wooden chandeliers.

"Do I have to address you as 'Mr Minister' now?" asked Ilona.

"Don't be silly. How are Teréz and Zita?"

"Teréz is the same as ever; you know her. Zita is very proud of you."

"I'm glad some one in the family is. I wish I had Papa's letter here. I believe he would rather I was in prison. What about you? What are you going to do?"

"I don't know yet."

"Do you need money?"

"No," she replied in confusion. "I still have enough. . . ."

They looked at each other—the brother in his peasant's Sunday suit, the sister in her smart costume. He hasn't changed, she thought with relief.

She recalled the summer afternoon at Schönbrunn. The brother for whom she had begged the Imperial mercy now resided in a room that was almost as sumptuous as the Emperor's audience-chamber. Did he bestow audiences? Was he merciful? Men deserted, made wars, murdered their masters, became masters. The women implored mercy. She wished she could feel ashamed of Lajos like her father. To be certain one was right was a blind blessing. She had been born at the turn of the age. She wasn't certain what was right and what was wrong. Perhaps there was no right and wrong any more, but only portraits of old gentlemen who had administered justice and decided in their own day between right and wrong. Although Lajos was older than she, she had always looked upon him as her little brother. Only the very young and the very old never doubted. But he had asked her if she needed money, as her father had asked in her childhood when she wanted to go and buy acid-drops from the sweet-shop. Women who thought they were like men forgot that every man was a child and a father. How could women be like them, since they were their mothers and their children?

She brought the conversation round to Princess Consuela. "Justice is running its course," he interrupted her. "I'm not Minister of Justice." "Has she committed a crime?" she asked. She had treated her peasants like serfs, he told her. Did he know what his comrades had done to her? she replied. "I'm sorry," he said. "You can't make an omelette without breaking eggs." She laughed. He looked at her questioningly. "That's what the fellow said at the time," she explained. "Can't you think of any other excuse for injustice?"

His eyes were weary from lack of sleep. A fire burnt in them, but they gave off no light. She could have hated him for his arrogance, or admired him for his confidence; but she could already feel that he was neither arrogant nor full of confidence, that in his eyes there only burnt a candle, a flickering light.

He said, "Justice is a reflection of the past. The greater the injustice that has been done the more difficult it is to be just. But to-morrow the world we are creating will be able to look into a clean mirror."

He went to his desk. He stood in front of the wall with the dark patches; his head rose into them; he was surrounded by an invisible frame. Looking down at the big desk, whose legs were decorated with Greek deities, he began to speak of the redistribution of the Aporfalvy estates.

She hadn't expected him to justify himself. He did so. He hadn't wanted to reside in this sumptuous room, he said; the sooner he could leave it the better. He hadn't dreamt of a post as a Cabinet Minister—it had been thrust upon him by necessity: there were few people who knew the best way to divide up land. In Kisnémet station they knew nothing of the misery of the *nincstelenek*, the landless farm-labourers; nothing of the wretchedness of the day-labourers, who were called *cseléd*, servants. They were nothing but serfs. Did she know that every second child on the Aporfalvy estates was born in a pigsty? "To live in a cow-byre was a piece of luck: there you could stand upright." What better proof of the new masters' goodwill could there be than the fact that the Minister-President had begun with the distribution of his own estates—eighty thousand yokes, almost as much as the Aporfalvys possessed. To be sure, the mob was trying to jump on the bandwagon of the Revolution, but it would very soon be shaken off. "You hate the mob? We hate it more; it is dirtying the mirror in which future generations will look. For heaven's sake don't imagine it was the mob that carried the Revolution to victory. The Revolution was carried to victory by the workers and peasants and the home-coming soldiers. . . . You were at the front; you can't have remained blind." He described a circle with his hands, as though cleaning a mirror. "The future," he said. Again and again. "The future."

"You know the land better than you know people," she replied. "Do you seriously believe that the new peasants will be content? Won't the competent soon outstrip the incompetent, and will the incompetent ever admit to being incompetent? In one part of the land it will rain; in another there will be drought. Can you compel the weather to be just?"

"The weather has changed little for centuries. Therefore one soil is better than another. We bear that in mind when we parcel out the land."

"The weather hasn't changed, nor has the soil. What makes you think men will change?" She rose to her feet.

The rain was beating against the tall French windows as though grains of sand were being thrown at the panes. The curtains had been removed. Parliament Square, in which the Curia stood, lay bare before her eyes. She saw the Parliament building with its three-hundred-and-thirty-foot dome, the bronze lions on the steps, the countless Gothic towers, arcades, windows, lobbies. Behind the Parliament building, on the other side of the Danube, the medieval fortifications rose out of the November mist. A few hundred enthusiastic demonstrators who had marched to the Parliament building had taken refuge under the arcades; they stood there, wet and with lowered, wet banners.

When Ilona turned round, Lajos was sitting at his desk with his head in his hands.

"Mercy?" he said. "The Emperor could be merciful. When he looked in the mirror he saw nothing but himself. Half a century lay between the revolution that was crushed and your visit. In fifty years we shall be equally merciful. Or, better, there will be no need for mercy. Don't you understand? That is the whole point. We call people who give alms kind, and forget what a wretched world it is in which there are beggars."

She could feel that he wanted to be merciful as the Emperor had been merciful. She remembered what the Emperor had said about the Army, about punishment and discipline. What was it that forced people to set bloodhounds between themselves and their kindness, animals trained to hunt down kindness? Discipline and revolution, army and future—they were bloodhounds. On their own men meant well, but their kindness was like nakedness, of which they were unashamed only when they were alone.

Lajos began to talk of the difficulties confronting him and his friends. She was right, he said; few understood what they were planning. "The slave-owners know we are their enemies—if only the slaves realized that we are their friends." He spoke of the terrible habit of slavery. "We can forbid a count to use his title, but it is hard to forbid his servant to address him by it." He looked up. "Can you understand all that? The women could help us, but of all slaves they are the stubbornest. They love everything they possess, including their chains."

She didn't know whether she loved her chains. She had never felt them. Her thoughts no longer revolved round Princess Consuela. She saw only her brother. She had expected to find fulfilled ambition or measureless effort. But he was so alone that he opened his heart to her, who understood nothing. Should she tell him that the love she could give him was worth more than the understanding he demanded of her?

As he accompanied her to the door he said, "The proceedings against you have been dropped. On my account. I shall see what I can do for Consuela Aporfalvy."

He forgot to ask her how long she intended to stay in Budapest.

52

She took a one-horse carriage to Buda.

As the carriage was trotting across the suspension bridge, through the dreary afternoon, she realized that in a few minutes she would be seeing the house in which Zita was born. Kontowski's friends in Vienna had told her he was living in the apartment in the Szentháromság ucca in which he housed her at the end of 1904, after his visit to the Hotel Hungaria.

Then she remembered her last visit to him in the palace in the Prinz-Eugen-Strasse, and gradually her thoughts moved to Zoltán.

She had heard from him shortly before leaving Vienna. He was still a prisoner-of-war. The repatriation of Austro-Hungarian P.O.W.'s was a slow process. The vanquished had to release their prisoners quickly, but the railway-trucks returned empty. Victors were not merciful. "We shall be home by Christmas at the latest," wrote Zoltán. Christmas had always been the great hope. Now Christmas 1918 was approaching.

She was thirty-two, and she thought about growing old. She was still as beautiful as in her youth; still wore her dark-blond hair combed up and crowned with thick braids, the curious hair-style which Petersburg Society had described as the "Ilona hair-style." The skin on her body was taut and flawless, but at times the shadows over her grey-blue eyes seemed to lengthen, as though heralding evening. If growing old meant that experience clipped the wings of imagination till it became frightened like birds behind bars—then she had grown old. If growing old meant to rely more upon the poor, powerless ego than upon chance, fate and luck—then she had grown old. If growing old meant to be niggardly with the ceaselessly passing hours, as though the sun went by the slowly creeping hands of the clock—then she had grown old. If growing old meant knowing that other people also had a life for which one was also responsible as well as for one's own, so that one carried an ever-heavier burden on ever-weaker shoulders—then she had grown old.

There was no cause for tears. Why did women want to stay young at any price? They couldn't escape old age, since it stood in front of them wherever they went—the faster they ran the faster they ran into its arms. Did they fear no longer to be desired? Their vanity outlived their beauty—but had they not countless virtues that would outlive their vanity? They imagined old age was clutching them with hard, bony, icy arms, whereas in reality it took by force only what it could not obtain by love; towards the willing it was gentle, friendly, loving. Why did these women imagine that happiness did not grow old along with them? They looked back at their youth and thought it held happiness in its grip. In reality happiness had come along with them, it was walking beside them, they could take it by the hand; but they didn't recognize it. They were like Lot's wife, who looked back and was turned into a pillar of salt. He who looked back saw his dead happiness and wanted it to come to life; or he saw what he had missed.

A great gaiety came over Ilona. She was no longer thinking of Zoltán; she was thinking of Zita. Growing old didn't mean steering a course towards the end; it merely meant that one life passed over into another. There was also the second youth, of which women spoke longingly. What did it matter that it was not one's own?

Ilona almost felt that happiness was sitting beside her in the bumping cab, a different happiness from the one she had known, perhaps, more weary and gentle, more wrinkled and quiet, more intelligent and modest, but still clearly recognizable, like the brother of some one loved and now dead about whom the dead man had talked a great deal.

The gaunt horse back home from the Army—a brother of the horses at the Col di Lana, released early and rather surprised to be alive at all—climbed slowly up the winding street to the Fisherman's Hill.

The cab turned into the Szentháromság ucca and stopped outside the Late Gothic house in which Zita had been born.

Ilona had been afraid the Pâtisserie Rotwurm might have been closed or requisitioned. The Revolution had spared it. Through the draped lace curtains she could see the red-plush furniture, the Biedermeier cupboards with their empty bonbonnières, dolls, dolls' coaches, papier-mâché tarts. Loving couples were sitting in the windows. A tremulous yellow gaslight seeped out through the yellowed curtains into the street.

As Ilona entered the building she imagined she could see Dr Sasvári, the fat doctor who had eaten cream puffs up to the last moment before the delivery. The smell of drinking chocolate came to meet her in warm waves. She ran up the stairs. She was surprised that she hadn't a key to the apartment.

53

The Prince came to meet Ilona. He had received her letter. He embraced her cordially, almost rapturously, like survivors from a shipwreck unexpectedly meeting.

He was in his middle fifties, but since he had always looked older than he was he appeared unchanged. She knew the short velvet jacket he was wearing, and the wide, silver-grey tie with the big pearl.

Her eyes betrayed her astonishment. He said, "One mustn't let oneself go. Not now."

He explained why he had moved into the apartment in which he had once housed the young Ilona Horváth. When she had moved to Vienna he had kept it on, for sentimental reasons, as a *pied-à-terre*, or because he wasn't quite certain of her—he couldn't say. Anyhow, it was a good thing. The palace in the Prinz-Eugen-Strasse in Vienna was far too big for his financial means, he said; he was trying to sell it. "Perhaps one of the new rich will buy it, or a Ministry—it comes to the same thing." His estates in Poland, Galicia, and Bohemia were lost; his stocks and shares had become worthless; the capital he had invested in War Loan had melted away.

He talked about his losses indifferently, almost gaily. "Around the turn of the century the earth was threatened by a comet," he said. "People were less afraid of it than of a cold in the head. The magnitude of suffering is in inverse proportion to the number of sufferers." As her astonishment gave place to admiration, he commented, "It must be painful to suffer small loss. Great losses are easy to bear."

She tried to recognize the apartment. This was the living-room in which she had sat at the round table with Teréz and the old French teacher. Teréz's sewing-maching had stood over there in the corner. That was the bedroom. Only the walls were still the same. None of the furniture remained. The Prince had furnished the three rooms with pieces from his requisitioned house near Budapest. They made one think of outstanding men thrown by chance into the company of inferior individuals. It was not that the Maria Theresa tabernacle, the wine-red leather armchair, the Renaissance tables, were too big: the rooms were too small. Nevertheless, the furniture did not look uncomfortable.

In Kontowski's houses the gold snuff-boxes, bonbonnières decorated with semi-precious stones, Gothic Madonnas, and Russian icons had been submerged by the spaciousness; here they came into their own. "Gulliver among the Lilliputians," said Kontowski. "It's not the small rooms. . . ." He stressed the word 'rooms.'

Julius, the old footman, served tea. A small table stood by the window, as in the Vienna palace. The porcelain gleamed as it had always done; Ilona had always been surprised to find that there were certain houses in which the porcelain gleamed like silver. It was the old porcelain with the princely coronet. Kontowski smiled. "Börne writes that it is very dangerous for revolutionaries to inherit a tea-service," he said. "They immediately start being afraid it might get broken. You will understand that tea-services don't mean much to me."

He wanted to hear all that had happened to her since their last meeting. He seemed to have continued to be concerned about her, to have followed the course of her life. He knew almost everything; she simply had to fill in a gap here and there.

As always when Ilona sat opposite the Prince, she became an attentive schoolgirl. Nevertheless, she had experienced too much any longer to be able to absorb the teachings without examining the teacher. Was Kontowski so inwardly rich that he could renounce riches, power, and habit with a shrug of the shoulders? Or was he clinging to his own dignity in the midst of the Flood? She remembered the doctor in the Sant'Andrea field hospital who had said that the Law contradicted human nature, but miraculously became nature. Was Kontowski trying to subordinate his nature to the Law? Or did he ultimately owe his ability to remain himself in the midst of destruction to his illness, or, rather, to the hope of ceasing to feel his illness in the midst of universal impotence?

"What did you expect?" he asked, when he became aware of her astonishment. "Am I to weep for the past and whine for what is lost? We imagine that we venerate suffering. Suffering is not worthy of veneration; it only becomes 'great' at the moment we surmount it. It is the same with age. An old man is not 'venerable' because he is feeble and ailing, but only if he has risen above weakness and sickness."

She had intended to speak of her worries and ask his advice, but once again she listened to him spellbound, convinced she would gain more if she did not call him back to reality.

"I didn't expect that you would give me hope," she said. "You couldn't give me hope if you had none yourself."

"Hope?" he reiterated. "Perhaps. It's probably because I am not a conservative over whom the Revolution passes and moves on. The revolutionaries think that's what I am. They think I'm harmless; that's why they don't treat me too unmercifully. I'm not a conservative—I'm a reactionary. I believe in action; I even believe in progress; only I'm not at all sure that we serve its interests by going forward. Since mankind moves, not forward, but in a circle, it always returns to all the points it has passed through; the important thing is to take advantage of past experience, which includes the Revolution, in order to stop the wheel of history at the right moment and set it in motion again. A few times in every century the word 'restoration' is high treason. But restorations have taken place with the same regularity as revolutions, Revolution, restoration, reaction, renaissance—they all share the prefix 're.' Counter-movements are also repeated movements. Restorations very naturally spring from memory, and are no more than a longing for a present which, like memory, sees the past freed from its dross. No sensible man believes that the past will return unchanged, but no sensible man can deny that in an altered form it always returns. Revolution punishes the past; restoration purifies it. The hope of revolutionaries ceases with the revolution; the hope of reactionaries begins with it—so why should I despair?"

He rose and stood by the window, the long cigarette in his boneless hand. The rain had stopped. Voices could be heard from down below —the voices of loving couples, to which Ilona Horváth had often listened in this room.

"Have you heard from Rattowitz?" she asked.

"He wrote to me a few weeks ago. It was the first time he didn't ask me for money. He is on the way to Vienna. His aunt has died. I shouldn't be surprised if he has inherited a not inconsiderable fortune. He writes of it with melancholy grandeur. 'What do I care for wife and child? . . . My Emperor lies in duress vile!' Shall I still find life worth living when the Rattowitzes are no more?" He looked out of the window at the narrow street with the little houses. "When I see the old houses with their creaking stairs, musty rooms, and wretched lights I often think of the people who live in them," he interjected angrily. "We can pull down the wretched houses and build light and airy blocks of flats. The world will then become healthier—and uglier. Can ugliness be healthy? If there is a block of flats on this side of the street there can be neither cottages nor a palace on the other. The man in the block of flats will look out at a block of flats. He won't see the chestnut-trees above the roofs." He turned to Ilona again. "Progress, liberty, justice— doesn't anyone think of the price? Perhaps there won't be any idlers like Rattowitz. But think how much knowledge, wit, and understanding he gave freely while he was idling away his time! Perhaps no foolish king will squander the people's money, but nor will any fool bestow his patronage upon a Richard Wagner. Perhaps every one will possess the necessities of life, but he will pay for them with the loss of his longings."

She interrupted him. She had not yet told him of her visit to Lajos. He sat down at the table again and listened to her attentively.

"He is a romanticist," he said, "and would probably call me a romanticist. I at least know that the happiness of the few is bought with the suffering of the many. He doesn't know that the happiness of the many is exorbitantly expensive. But why do I tell you all this? I'm indulging in one of my monologues again. And yet you wrote that you need my advice."

Hesitantly, she began to outline her financial position. She was afraid he would think she had come to ask for his help, but he dispelled her misgivings with a gesture.

He listened to her patiently till she had finished, rose to his feet, and walked up and down lost in thought. On no account, he said, must she sell Berény. Houses and land would probably retain their value even in the general upheaval. If the Bolsheviks really did come into power their dominion would be only shortlived. "The victors cannot tolerate an outpost of Soviet Russia at the invasion-gate of the West." How much ready cash did she still possess? It was too little; he too had omitted to provide himself with funds to fall back on in a neutral country. Like Hämmerle, he blamed himself for not having advised her better. "Most pessimists act as if they were optimists—that's the whole trouble." What about her jewellery? Never had jewellery been less valuable according to the law of supply and demand: husbands were now selling what they had given their wives in years gone by. Admittedly, the new rich were buying jewellery, but the money they paid for it was bound to fall victim to inevitable devaluation. "The vanquished can bear the burdens placed upon them only by forging money: anyone who can save himself from starvation by forging money will do so." The best thing, therefore, would be to pawn a small quantity of her jewellery—the less the better, of course. He went to his desk and wrote down the name and address of a Vienna jeweller, "a trustworthy man," who lent money on valuables. "You and the child have got to live. When devaluation comes you will be able to redeem the pawned jewellery with a postage-stamp. You will only be doing what every one is doing. Running into debt is the fundamental ethic of the new era."

She stowed away the slip of paper in her handbag and looked at him gratefully, but quickly lowered her eyes when she noticed that her gratitude embarrassed him. He began to stride up and down again. How did Prince Taszilo Kontowski come to know the pawnbroker, the "trustworthy man"? He himself must have pawned what he had managed to save. She wondered whether to offer her assistance, to force upon him some piece of jewellery she had received from him. The conversation they had had, the room in which it had taken place, and finally the unbelievable idea that she might be better off than the Prince, brought the extent of the upheaval, in which she was a tiny, whirling molecule, more clearly home to her than Lajos's power, the night at Berény, the desolate Hofburg, the beflagged city. Before she had time to say anything Kontowski rang for his footman, choosing just this moment to order him to clear away the tea things.

Alone with Ilona again, he stood leaning against the bookcase and asked, "Isn't there anything else you want to discuss with me?"

"Yes; of course, a great deal." She tried to smile, but she was gripped by the fear that he would talk about Zoltán.

He wrinkled his brow, as though to say, "Don't worry; I'm not thinking of Zoltán Szomoru. That was 'before.' Everything that was 'before' appears to me flat, childish, unreal."

"What I chiefly have in mind is Zita," he said quickly. "You have never initiated me into your life together. That's not a reproach; it was perfectly understandable. Nevertheless, I think about her a great deal. Perhaps it's this house. . . . How old is she now?"

"She was thirteen in January."

"January," he repeated. "Thirteen. . . . If I were you I should definitely stay in Vienna with her. It's safer than Budapest."

"Why are you? . . ."

"Why am I here? If I have a home it is Vienna. I find it easier to forgive the Hungarians—I know them less well. But let us talk about you. Thirty isn't a good age. One cannot yet live on the past, and one is no longer young enough to live only in the future. This earthquake doesn't spare women—spares them even less than men. When the walls of houses are torn open the wind blows through homes." He ran his hand over his forehead. "So Zita is thirteen now. Thirteen. . . Tell me about her."

She did so with pleasure in doing so. She talked of Zita's imperious, self-willed nature; of her inexplicably precocious maturity, which seemed to be bursting all the confines of a careful upbringing; of her sometimes frighteningly sober questions; of the not unloving, but occasionally mocking, condescension with which she treated Teréz, almost as though it was she who was experienced and Teréz who was immature; of her naïve and yet disquieting interest in the opposite sex; of her childishness, which was all the more touching because it contradicted a nervous sensibility revealed, for example, in the flight from Berény; of her moods and irritating reticences· of her astounding intelligence, with which Ilona's own at the same age was scarcely to be compared; and also of her astuteness, which was most manifestly expressed in the fact that she accepted the fairy-story of her father's disappearance without a word, and yet did not seem to believe it for a moment.

"I don't know whether she loves me," she said at length; "I really don't know. Do you think it possible that I can't see through my own child, thirteen years old and a daughter? You used to rate my knowledge of human nature so high—but how badly it fails me now! Could it be that she doesn't forgive me for my life, which she doesn't even know—my absence during the war, St Petersburg, perhaps even the year before her birth? I love her with all my heart—she must feel that, must know that—and yet when I stretch out my hand to her it is often as though I were grasping at the void."

The Prince had listened to her. Now he interrupted her.

"The void between you and her is the time we live in. You mustn't blame yourself. Think of your own childhood. Your mother was dead, but the times were your mother. They were good to you, those despised, evil, unjust times, which people now want nothing to do with. You have survived chaos, and will continue to survive it, because your roots are firmly planted in order. You have often said that I saved you, but how easy it was to save a young woman, how little she needed to be saved when—thirteen years ago—she was looking for a father for her child, at any price, even the bitterest! . . . Only what ripens in the sun ripens naturally. What you call precocious maturity, what frightens you, is not ripeness but unnatural fermentation."

They talked for a long time. Ilona would never have imagined that she could speak so freely of her child, who had remained from the beginning her secret. How was it possible that this man who had no child, who couldn't beget a child, knew more about children than she herself, more than all the women she knew who had many children of their own? Because she was sitting in this room, which she had left one December morning in order, grotesquely, to become the wife of an unknown man, she remembered Baron Ferdinand von Rattowitz again. Then, thirteen years ago, seeing how easily her father and her husband understood each other, she had become aware for the first time of the great alliance that existed between people of the same generation. Now she understood Prince Taszilo Kontowski, and he understood her. The abyss had opened; beyond the abyss stood her child; and when she looked round she found herself on this side of the abyss, the same side as the ageing man.

Evening came. In the past the apartment had been lit by gas; now the Prince went to the switch and turned on the electric-light.

"What a beautiful lamp!" she said. "It's just like gaslight."

A soft yellow light shone on the thick Persian carpets. The Prince went to the window and drew the curtains.

"We mustn't stay apart for so long in future," he said. "I shall always let you know where you can find me."

She smiled, because this sentence too she had heard many times. And she had always known where to find him.

"I could order a taxi for you," he said as she turned to go.

She refused. As they passed the telephone she thought of the winter's day on which Teréz had run to a neighbouring lawyer in order to telephone the doctor.

Slowly they went down the stairs she had mounted at a run. She heard the tinkle of coffee-cups, the babble of conversation from the pâtisserie. She was thirty-two. She belonged to the same generation as the quinquagenarian who was gazing out after her from behind the curtains.

BOOK TWO

The Daughter

Part One: 1921 to 1931

Zita stood naked in front of the open wardrobe, on the right hung Teréz's few clothes, on the left her own. Teréz's clothes cringed like whipped dogs against the wall.

Zita pushed the clothes-hangers to and fro, like some one impatiently turning the pages of a book, unable to find the passage he is looking for. It was as if each movement were designed to whip up her own anger.

She hated her clothes. The old ones were too young, were irritating, like small children challenging older children to a childish game. The expensive ones were too old; they looked offended, proud; pride was all they had left. The new ones were cheap, as though ostentatiously demonstrating to the old ones the cost of vanity. The girl put out her tongue at the clothes, but they simply hung there without doing her the favour of replying.

She took a step back. Her eyes fell on Teréz's clothes. They were black, like mourning garments. She was seized with a superstitious dread. Teréz's clothes would infect her own. She herself would become like Teréz, arid, joyless, old-maidish.

She ran into her mother's bedroom, tugged at the lock, which resisted at first, and then opened the wardrobe. There hung Ilona's clothes, loose and fitted costumes, evening-dresses, afternoon frocks. They weren't new, but then Ilona wasn't young either. When you were seventeen you hadn't much to draw on. Zita wondered whether she should take one of Ilona's dresses.

The reflection in the mirror really brought her inadequacy home to her. She was a head shorter than her mother. Her black, almost blue, hair hung down over her bare shoulders, but it did not flatter her: it was coarse and recalcitrant. The lashes of her large, almond-shaped eyes were long and dark and fell over the eyes like shadows. Her nose and mouth were rather too small, but shapely; her neck long, rather too bony; her skin radiantly white. Her breasts were small but round, as though made to emphasize the boyishness of her figure—provided she had new clothes and was allowed to wear them.

Even to-day, when Zita was inclined to deride herself by making faces, she admitted that people thought her pretty in a way that defied exact description, but was very attractive. But what use were the compliments of friends when she had formed a quite definite idea of her own appearance, and blamed Creation for it, even if in truth it might have favoured her?

She couldn't wear her mother's clothes. To do so required bearing, dignity, arrogance, and vain self-confidence. Nevertheless, the naked girl looked at her mother's clothes. That was a dress from the Kon-

214

towski period. This billowing robe she had often worn when Zoltán Szomoru came to visit her. Who was she going out with when she bought the pastel-pink evening-dress embroidered with pearls? 'Benefactors,' 'childhood friends'—hypocritical words for the lovers of yesterday. Her mother grew into the clothes, voluptuous, domineering, irresistible. White shoulders gleamed from the wardrobe, full breasts, rounded hips. Her mother was in the habit of bolting the bathroom door; Zita mustn't see how desirable she still was at the age of thirty-five. Zita shut the wardrobe door as though throwing a cloth over her mother's portrait.

She wandered aimlessly through the empty rooms. She thought of ringing one of her friends—Hermine, Lotte, or Eleonora—and conferring with them about what to wear. She dismissed the idea. They were all after Georg, with the exception of Eleonora; but she didn't know him. They were all jealous of Zita. Why had she felt compelled to tell them that the producer was wooing her, cautiously, but unmistakably? She had to boast of her successes even before they were successes, rushing past and ahead of them, till finally she was unable to distinguish between boast and reality. She was ashamed of her indecision in small matters and great ones. She would find the right clothes even without the false friends.

It was still too early. She sat down at the dining-table. Breakfast hadn't been cleared away. Washing-up became more difficult when the rings of coffee began to set. Her mother and Teréz had gone out to work, the former in a fashion house, the latter in a restaurant. It was Zita's job to tidy the house. Every morning she thought of herself as Cinderella, although she had only been doing the housework since the schools closed down because of the coal shortage. Teréz was not the haughty sister; Teréz herself was Cinderella. But Zita didn't remember the story as clearly as all that. The feeling of injustice, oppression, rejection, wasn't bitter; she even derived a sweet feeling of rebellion from it.

The green velvet of the armchair fitted snugly against her bare thighs. She crossed her legs and picked up the newspaper. Disarmament conference in Washington, hunger riots in Moscow, impossible demands on the part of the victors, one gold mark equal to thirty-five paper marks. Carl Froelich was experimenting with sound pictures at the Triergon Studio, Friedrichstrasse, Berlin. First performance of the drama of manners, *Jama, the Sink of Iniquity*. Perhaps Georg would take her to see it.

Her mood changed, describing one of its daily *salti mortali*. She looked at the clock, lit a cigarette, sauntered into the bathroom. The bathroom mirror was friendlier: it mirrored her moods. She slipped the cigarette into the corner of her mouth. Pictures of the naked dancing-girls she had seen in the glass cases outside the night-clubs, in illustrated papers, in books surreptitiously passed from hand to hand, sprang to her mind. She could look just as vicious as these girls; she could be like Jama, the Sink of Iniquity. Why did she try to emulate her mother? She thrust out her belly, made it rotate as though it didn't belong to her body, crossed her hands over her breasts in feigned

215

bashfulness. Then she straightened up, went into the lavatory, and let the wet cigarette fall straight into the pan. The clothes in her mother's wardrobe were old clothes, nothing more; they dangled slack and shapeless on their hangers.

After this she went back into her own room, where the wardrobe still stood open. She cast a glance full of hatred at Teréz's clothes. It was as though a dark cloud were rising from the black clothes. She took hold of them and crushed their material between her fingers. The cloud was gone.

She decided in favour of a dark-grey costume. Georg had liked it; "practical" he had called it approvingly. It probably wasn't smart enough if they were going to a smart restaurant, but it would attract all the more attention on that account. She was tired of the everlasting, hopeless competition. She looked for a gauzy petticoat.

When she had finished dressing she went back to her mother's bedroom. A few lipsticks lay on the dressing-table. She tried them on the back of her hand and chose the darkest. It wasn't dark enough. She bent down closer to the mirror and made up her mouth to look wider than it was. White powder hid the girlish pink of her cheeks. She looked ailing, her mouth like dried blood.

A faint smell of scent hung about the room. Zita saw the room in the mirror. Silver boxes, silver bonbonnières bearing the baronial coronet, cut-glass vases. On the bed a mauve coverlet with wide lace borders. The little round silk-upholstered stool in front of the dressing-table. Old-maidish bric-à-brac, such as a stuffed dog, a dead darling with glass eyes. The thought that she had to live among these alien memories once more cast a grey blanket over Zita's mood. The flowers in the vases were still fresh, but they smelt mouldy. Dead darlings, thought the girl.

2

One this December afternoon, 1921, Zita had been alone in the three-roomed Berlin flat.

The block of flats stood in a row with other blocks of flats, looking like married couples grown old and shabby at the same time; they bore their age with decorum, their shabbiness shamefacedly; they were poor but honest. The people who lived in them wore their Sunday best even on weekdays.

On the other side of the street stood a factory producing opera-glasses. The workers had plenty of time on their hands, for opera-glasses were as superfluous as operas. During the midday break they would sometimes stand shoulder to shoulder at the windows, passing the opera-glasses from one to the other, laughing. They could see into Baroness Rattowitz's windows; perhaps they would catch a glimpse of the little Rattowitz stark naked. The workers were all Socialists, to be sure, but you didn't see a naked baroness every day. It wasn't every day that a baroness with countless trunks, even wardrobe trunks, and hat-boxes moved into the street. The workers had watched everything closely. Opera-glasses were not always superfluous.

Every now and then Zita noticed she was being watched. She angrily drew the curtains. In the Döbling villa there hadn't been any neighbours. Only when the leaves fell did the other villas appear from behind the trees, discreet guests who had waited for a long time and now politely aired their roofs. In spring they vanished as they had come.

After Ilona came back from the war they had stayed for a time in the Döbling villa. Then the stationmaster turned up; there was whispering in the drawing-room; they left for Berény. Even at Berény Josephine carried the keys of the Döbling villa on a key-ring, in perpetual readiness to leave. When Zita thought of Berény she shuddered. Only at Berény had she felt what possession meant, the feeling of finality, pleasant yet deceptive. The sheds with the two carriages on which she had sat driving invisible horses. The distant whistle of the railway engines greeting Kisnémet station, and the stationmaster who stood outside his office saluting. The smell of fresh timber and rotting apples. Berény had belonged to them on paper for another two years after they had abandoned it. Zita felt as though they had lost it on the night when Bödri's barking woke her from sleep. A strange man was standing at the door, young and fair-haired, with a gun on his arm. The bed creaked. Whenever she recalled the faces of her mother and Teréz a wave of fury swept over her. Those powerless faces betrayed nothing but concern for her, the thirteen-year-old girl. She would have liked to beat them for their paralysed concern. Her feelings might be unjust: the perpetrators were strong, the victims guilty. The hypocrisy that caused her mother and Teréz to remain silent even to this day about a mystery which she herself had long since deciphered made her blush, as an adult might blush on finding, long after her death, lascivious love-letters written by his adored mother to an unknown man.

They hadn't stayed long in the Döbling villa after coming back to it. The house took leave of its occupants, a waiting-room in which they were perpetually looking at the clock. They moved to Hietzing. Opposite them stood a church. Every half-hour they heard its bells ringing. They couldn't sleep, but at least church-windows had no eyes. The Hietzing house wasn't a home. The big doll had been left at Berény. Before they moved from Döbling the superfluous toys had been given away—as though there were such things as superfluous toys. In Hietzing Zita wouldn't play any more. She was too big, she said. She didn't want to fall in love with any toys. They were bound to be left behind. She also hated the new school, because she felt she would soon be saying good-bye to the teachers and her fellow-pupils as to dolls that had been given away.

Zita had been fifteen when her mother lost everything. Berény was sold. Josephine kept house for the man who bought it. Parting from Berény was easier than parting from Josephine. Zita already knew that there were pawnshops to which you took jewellery, and that they were 'forfeited' if you couldn't redeem them. Had Josephine too been pawned, had she been 'forfeited'? She still wrote from time to time. The Baroness would come back, she wrote. Silly old Pepi! Nothing came back. Everything provisional was final, but the final had no permanency. Nothing remained but cut-glass vases, snuff-boxes, hand-mirrors with the baronial coronet, dead darlings.

People packed. They were always packing. The trunks were like children's coffins. Zita feared them, still feared them.

The next house was in Dornbach, a strange district of villas in Vienna; strange because it bordered on the suburbs of Hernals, which was said to be the home of the *Pülcher*, crooks and gangsters. There were Hernals houses which boasted of being in Dornbach; Dornbach houses which suppressed the fact that they were in Hernals. The new house was in Hernals, but Dornbach was on the other side of the road; they looked out at old single-storey houses with flowers in the windows. Perhaps what mattered was not where you were, but what you looked out on.

From Hernals or Dornbach—whichever it was—Zita's mother moved to Budapest. Trunks were packed, Ilona's trunks. Her mother always left when she needed her most. When she was at St Petersburg she had come to see them only during the summer. When Zita had scarlet fever she had been in Italy. Now Zita had received and given her first kisses; her body was in turmoil. She had concealed this confused passion for a school-fellow's father from her mother. He was forty, an old man. If he had at least been a monster, but he was a monster only very prudently; full of consideration for her honour and his own; in conflict with the law, yet without infringing the penal code; touching with dirty fingers the glass that he preserved from falling. Zita kept silent, but she hoped that her mother would guess her distress. Her mother was away, as she had been when Zita had scarlet fever.

Ilona had gone to Budapest, to Prince Kontowski. He was back in his palace. Lajos had long since ceased to be a Cabinet Minister. The Bolsheviks had turned him out; an admiral on horseback turned out the Communists. The refugee lived in Vienna, sat about in cafés, and made speeches as he had once done in the inns round Kisnémet. He didn't notice how different the speeches sounded when they were about the past instead of the future. From time to time he visited his sisters and his niece. Although she knew he was only two years older than her mother, he appeared to Zita ancient. He talked about the breaking-up of the big estates. But Kontowski, though he had by no means re-covered them all, had at least regained his Hungarian possessions. He was rich enough to appear richer than he really was. If Ilona had to go away, why did it have to be to him of all people? Why Kontowski over and over again?

They must be grateful to him, Ilona had said when she returned from Budapest. He had found Ilona a job in Berlin, a job "in keeping with her gifts," as the manageress of a fashion house. The little coffins stood in the hall; men came to collect them. Why Berlin? "Somewhere nobody knows me," her mother had said. Somewhere people took the dead darlings for possessions, although they were only memories. Where they could be hypocritical without being found out. Ilona went to work at nine in the morning. Teréz had to earn her own living as a cashier. Why hadn't her mother stayed with the Prince? She couldn't ask her.

Statues didn't answer. They stood on marble plinths, turned to stone in the act of walking, with outstretched arms, in gala dress. Only when it rained or snowed or birds dirtied them did she feel a little sorry for them. Ilona seemed to be proof against rain and snow. One day it would turn out that she was not proof against dirt. Then Zita would feel sorry for her, not till then.

They had come to Berlin a year ago—eleven months to be exact. She remembered the last Christmas in Vienna; they didn't give one another presents, not because they were poor, but because they couldn't take everything with them anyway; trunks were packed; this or that was "put in store till later," that meant never to be seen again: dolls at Berény, the child's desk in Döbling, girl's frocks in Dornbach.

On the other side of the street stood the factory where they made opera-glasses.

3

The bus was full to overflowing. It was impossible to believe that it could take more passengers aboard—at the corner of the Tiergartenstrasse, by the Gedächtniskirche, at the Zoo railway station. They came from shops and factories and brought their smells with them, the smell of leather, of metal, of meat, of bales of cloth.

The bus drove along the Kurfürstendamm. If Zita had been able to turn round she would have seen the Femina fashion house on the other side of the street. She knew that an evening-dress was being made for her in the fashion house where her mother worked A surprise for Christmas—but Teréz had given the game away. I hope I get a short dress at last, thought the girl. Whenever she went out she pulled her skirts up above her knees, letting them down again when she came home. The dresses didn't sit properly. Why did her mother have to order a dress from the most expensive fashion house in Berlin? She could have bought two or three ready-made dresses for the same money, and they would have been just as pretty. The dress was a present from Ilona to herself, a tribute to her own pride. If only she would come home late to-day! She was always late nowadays, on account of the Christmas rush.

The street-lamps flared up, all at once. Men were carrying Christmas-trees home, stunted trees, step-children of the forest. Outside a hotel a limousine was being packed with trunks. A gentleman in a fur coat came out. Hotel porters stood round him with outstretched hands. No doubt he was going home for Christmas.

The bus stopped with a jerk. Zita was thrown forward. Her knee touched the knee of a man sitting in front of her. He looked up; she looked down. He was about forty, wearing a close-fitting double-breasted blue winter overcoat. A white handkerchief twinkled from his breast-pocket. With the thin black moustache under his long nose he looked like a South American. He smiled. His lips were strikingly red, not rouged, but like the red lips of a woman. Zita smiled too. She liked to be looked at. If no one looked at her for a long time she felt miserable. The moment she thought she was being watched she began

to act a part. A shopgirl out for adventure. Or a consumptive actress.
A young painter from the Romanisches Café. Or perhaps the daughter
of an American millionaire in Berlin incognito. Who could the man
be? A white-slaver from the Argentine, a Stock Exchange speculator,
a film producer? The man's eyes glided over her body. There were men
who undressed you with a look. You remained unmoved, and they
suffered.

Two more stops, thought Zita. In a few minutes she would be
entering the school, a silent, cold building. Holidays due to the coal
shortage. An electric stove had been installed in the gymnasium
because the rehearsals for the school New Year play were continuing.
She had the main part in a fusty old play by Blumenthal and Kadel-
burg, *City Air*. Georg Busse was producing.

Her heart beat faster. Yesterday Georg had asked her if she would
have dinner with him after the rehearsal. In a low voice, so the others
wouldn't hear. But also as though taking it for granted that she
couldn't possibly refuse. She would tell her mother over the phone
that the rehearsal was going on longer. In no case would she let the
opportunity slip. All the girls were crazy about Georg Busse. She
would get him, already had him. He was thirty, perhaps thirty-two. He
had been a soldier, a prisoner-of-war, a building worker, an actor, a
stage-hand, an actor again. Now he was producer at the Settee cabaret.
The school committee hadn't really wanted to engage him, but more
famous producers were too expensive. Besides, the Settee was a literary
cabaret. The poems of Ringelnatz and Tucholsy were recited there.
The school had got no further than Von Arnim and Brentano's
collection of *Lieder, Des Knaben Wunderhorn*. The blue flower of the
Romantic movement. Withered flowers, cemetery flowers. The blue
flower was not for Georg Busse. He wanted to go to bed with her.
That was nothing special. Some said so frankly; others were hypocritical. There were at most five virgins in her class—Lotte Wegerode,
Hilde Meyer, Annemarie von Bredow. Every one knew they were
virgins. It was no honour to be one of them.

"May I offer you my seat?" said the man with the blood-red
woman's lips.

"Thank you, but I'm getting out here," said Zita. She had forgotten
him.

4

That morning Ilona had had a long discussion with Fräulein Behrens,
the owner of the Femina fashion house.

Although it was only December, they were already working on the
spring models. There could be no doubt that in the coming year, 1922,
the women of Berlin would also bow to the dictates of Mlle Chanel of
Paris. Jersey, 'Coco's' favourite material, would be the dominant one.
Fräulein Behrens wanted to know whether Ilona had read the *Berliner
Illustrierte*. It had just awarded a prize to the quatrain best describing
the new fashion.

He is a tailor of consummate skill.
He'll make a lady's dress for nil.
The latest fashion he strictly heeds;
A handkerchief is all he needs.

Fräulein Behrens laughed a deep, masculine laugh that sounded as if
it came out of a barrel. Her voice, which didn't fit her, seemed to
shatter the slender figure. It was easy to laugh, said Fräulein Behrens.
It was easy for 'Coco' with her clientèle of slim Parisiennes. But let
Mlle Chanel try making Berlin women look boyish, let her spirit away
bust and backside and make them look as if they had a board at the
back and front, and all this with only a narrow belt instead of a corset.
What did Ilona think about taking a man tailor, Herr Piscacek from
Prague, who up to now had been working for Knize, the famous
gentlemen's tailor? They would soon be wearing a man's dinner-suit
for evening-dress, with a very narrow skirt, only to the knee, of course;
trousers were only a question of time.

To pacify Fräulein Behrens was more a psychological than a fashion
problem. On the one hand, the necessity of taking on Herr Piscacek
made a mockery of Fräulein Behren's brave declaration that a man
would enter the fashion house only "over her dead body." On the other,
it was pure chance that it was 'Coco' who had imposed the new
fashion: Fräulein Behrens had long been wearing men's suits with a
skirt, blouse, and tie, even in the evening, for which purpose she made
them of black silk. Fräulein Behren's friends—who filled the fashion
house from morning till night, sitting adoringly on pretty parchment
pouffes at their little queen's feet, with cigarettes in their mouths and
books in their hands, peeping curiously behind the curtains of the
dressing-rooms, and sometimes waited five or six hours for Fräulein
Behrens—hadn't waited for 'Coco.' On the other hand Fräulein
Behrens seemed to have no wish to dress her clients in her own
uniform, least of all with the aid of this Herr Piscacek, who had
hitherto been disreputably employed taking measurements for lounge-
suits.

Ilona ate her lunch in one of the automatic restaurants that were
now springing up like mushrooms in the Kurfürstendamm. When she
emerged into the Kurfürstendamm it had started snowing. The grey
above the roofs was not the sky, but a grey sieve between sky and
earth. The snow was falling through the sieve. By the time it had
settled on cars, people, and trams it had turned into dirty rain. She
thought of Kisnémet.

"Baroness!" She heard a voice behind her.

She turned round, scarcely surprised, because an instant earlier she
had recognized the man hurrying past her, though she had not trusted
her eyes on this day when she was haunted by the past. He too seemed
to have doubted whether it was really she.

"Dr Ginsburg," she smiled, "how nice to meet you!"

When she last saw him, over seven years ago, he had looked older
than he was. Like most people who outstrip their age, he appeared not
to have aged. He was wearing a black overcoat with a beaver collar

and a bowler-hat, which he held in his hand throughout the conversation, although Ilona several times invited him to put it on. There was still the curious golden gleam in his eyes behind the gold-rimmed spectacles; only the gold had grown somewhat paler, somewhat more precious, like the gold of old coins.

He inquired into the course taken by her life, not feigning any delight at what he heard, but not in the least shocked either, as though he were not listening to the story of years, but of a single day, which would be without importance in the story of years. He inquired after Teréz, Zita, the stationmaster—tentatively in the latter case, as one asks after old people who may no longer be alive; he remembered every name, even quickly calculated Zita's present age. Ilona replied briefly. She wanted to know how he was, and his daughter and son-in-law. He was fine, he reported, shamefaced and immediately adding reservations. He was selling watches, old watches, of course: "most of them no longer tell the time, but you can't blame them for that in such times as these." He undid his overcoat and hunted in his wallet; as he did so Ilona saw the gold watch-chain over his waistcoat which she remembered perfectly. Yes, he had very little contact with his daughter; it was the fault of his son-in-law, "or, rather, of politics," he added in excuse. At last he found the card. If he might make so bold, he would be delighted if the Baroness would pay him a visit; he had a few very special pieces, Viennese work too, one of the first watches with a second-hand, dating from 1756; he was sure she would enjoy an hour among such strange timepieces. She promised to come.

On the way home that evening in the packed underground train Ilona thought about her daughter. She was carrying a big cardboard box containing Zita's Christmas dress. Worry about Zita never left her; it was always there, and came to life at the slightest provocation. Was Zita angry with her over the lost estates, as the daughters of the new rich were angry with their mothers over the estates they had acquired? Zita's nature wasn't as simple as that. It was in perpetual conflict with itself; vacillated between melancholy and levity, was frivolous and tormented, superficial and brooding, unassailable and fragile. Was Maeterlinck's *Blue Bird*, the book every one was now reading, the fairy-tale of the children who ran after happiness, really the symbol of the age? The blue bird was flying ahead of Zita, visible only to her; it settled in the treetops and on the edge of abysses; Zita ran after it, stumbled, grazed herself, got up, ran on. The child was running after the bird and the mother after the child; gradually both the child and the bird were moving out of sight.

How was it that she had so quickly grown accustomed to this narcosis, this earthquake, this putrefaction? Her strength was deeply rooted in the soil of Kisnémet. "It all depends on the second line of defence," Kontowski used to say. You built it before the attack, hoped for victory, reckoned with defeat. Parents were no more and no less than a second line of defence. Grass grew on them when the children were victorious. When the children were defeated they fled to them.

When she opened the door it struck her that Zita wasn't at home. She put down the parcel. I shall wait for her, she thought.

5

The producer had announced a break and gone out.

In the gymnasium, with its parallel bars, vaulting-horses, ropes, and mattresses, chairs had been arranged in a semicircle as on a rehearsal stage. The gymnasium was in the basement of the old, dilapidated school. You could see the feet of the passers-by through the dirty windows. Every now and then somebody would bend down and stare into the gym. There was a warm smell of girls' bodies.

Zita was sitting in a corner with two friends. The electric stove was a long way from them, but they imagined they could feel its warmth.

Since Georg Busse had left the room he had become the sole topic of conversation. Zita wondered whether to confide in her two friends, Hermine Stutz and Lotte Wegerode.

Her attitude towards Hermine Stutz was a mixture of admiration and disapproval. She condemned Hermine's actions, but would have liked to follow her example. Hermine Stutz was eighteen; she had been kept back in the same form twice over. She wasn't stupid, not by any means, only she had other thoughts in her head than Hannibal's campaigns or Klopstock's hexameters. Her father had been killed in the war. More accurately, he had been reported killed, at Verdun. Her mother hadn't worn a widow's veil, hence she had no need to discard it. Her new husband wasn't at the front; he was in a reserved occupation—making boots for those who were not in reserved occupations, who marched into death. Hermine was fifteen when her father came back. "The second marriage is null and void," said the authorities. "The first marriage is null and void," said the wife. "Dead is dead," she said. What right had the dead to leave their graves? The two husbands, the living one and the dead one, sat in the dining-room. Then the dead one left. Perhaps he lay down in his grave again; anyhow, nothing more was heard of him. One night the living husband slipped into Hermine's bedroom. Six months later he left both mother and daughter. They both took new lovers. Frau Stutz still sent her daughter to school for the sake of appearances, because people talked if a young girl from a good home stayed at home. At school Hermine told them all about the lovers, her mother's and her own. "Unfortunately we're the same type," she said; "the same men fall for both of us." But she quickly stressed that nothing like the situation with her stepfather, the shoe manufacturer, had happened again. Her mother preferred younger men, she older ones. "You can learn something from all of them," she said. So long as it wasn't a question of Hannibal or hexameters, she was positively obsessed with the desire to learn.

For Lotte Wegerode, Zita felt both affection and contempt, as though she loved her because she found nothing to admire in the short-sighted, ailing, and yet pretty girl. Lotte Wegerode was one of the few virgins in the lower sixth. Her parents were millionaires—in dollars: it was necessary to state the currency because it was beginning to be easy to be a millionaire in marks. Lotte Wegerode hated her father's millions. She always wore the same dress, although she must have had a few dozen. With her pocket-money she had taken out a subscription to the

Red Flag, which she brought to school, to the horror of the teachers. She knew Ernst Toller's works by heart. Once she was arrested for sticking red propaganda posters on the walls of a bank. The police were surprised to find that it was her father's bank. Later Lotte Wegerode only stuck the posters on the walls of other people's banks, but she did so with less conviction. No less hungry for knowledge than Hermine, she attended Marxist lectures in Red Flag House. If she didn't apply herself to 'free love,' this was only because she hadn't time. At night the portraits of Lenin, Robespierre, and a bearded cavalry general called Budenny hung over her bed. Every morning before going to school she hid the pictures in the drawer of her dressing-table, between scent-bottles that she never touched. After locking her door in the evening she took the pictures out again. Lenin, Robespierre, and Budenny smelt like *cocottes.*

"He looks wonderful," said Hermine Stutz.

"He's magnificent," commented Lotte Wegerode. "If he gets a chance he could be another Max Reinhardt. But, of course, young people don't get a chance. Not in our country."

"Irene is completely stuck on him," whispered Hermine Stutz. That was her favourite expression.

"Irene is a child," replied Lotte Wegerode. She screwed up her dark-brown eyes and looked short-sightedly around for little Irene Hass, who was leaning coquettishly against the parallel bars.

"Hark who's talking!" retorted Hermine Stutz immediately. "You're a member of the club yourself."

"What club?"

"The Demi-Vierge Club, of course," laughed Hermine Stutz. "I think it's completely disgusting." She began to hum the hit of the season.

> Everything I have is yours,
> Except for one thing, there I falter.
> That's reserved for the man who one day
> Leads me to the altar.

Irene Hass and two other girls, attracted by the song, strolled over to the three.

One of them, a tiny brunette in a close-fitting knee-length dress, said, "Do you think he'll go on rehearsing for long? I've got a date. I told them at home we'd be rehearsing till ten."

"As far as I'm concerned we can go on till twelve," remarked Irene Hass.

"As far as you're concerned we could go on till to-morrow morning," said Hermine Stutz. "You're all in love with him."

"He's taking me out this evening," said Zita.

"Well, I'm damned!" commented Hermine Stutz appreciatively.

"Well, I'm damned!" echoed Lotte Wegerode.

Her friends' amazement delighted Zita.

"I knew straight away that he was stuck on you," said Lotte Wegerode, involuntarily adopting her more mature friend's vocabulary.

"You won't be able to lead *him* by the nose, you know." Hermine

Stutz was riding her hobby-horse again. "He's no kid. You'll have to lay your cards on the table for a change where he's concerned."

"Why not?" replied Zita, although she didn't like the way her friend put it.

"You're beginning to see sense," remarked Hermine Stutz.

"Is he taking you home straight away?" inquired Lotte Wegerode.

"He said nothing about a night-club," replied Zita. It wasn't true, but she had long wanted to see the inside of a night-club.

"I'm sure he hasn't any money," warned Lotte Wegerode.

"Workers of the world unite," mocked Hermine Stutz.

Lotte Wegerode took no notice of her. She seemed as excited as if she had a date with the producer herself.

"Do you love him?" she asked.

Zita didn't know what to answer. She would have answered Lotte Wegerode differently from Hermine Stutz, but she was sitting between the two of them.

"He excites me," she said, deciding in favour of the answer she would have given Hermine Stutz.

"He's a real man," nodded Hermine Stutz. "An almost extinct species."

Conversation in the gym ceased. Georg Busse had come in. He showed two rows of gleaming teeth and clapped his hands.

"We'll try the last scene again," he said.

6

Zita rang her mother from a public call-box and told her the rehearsal was dragging on. She had expected an angry answer from her mother. "Take care of yourself," said Ilona. "Leave the key outside," said Zita. "I shall still be up," said her mother.

When she stepped out into the street Busse took her arm. He was wearing a trench-coat with a belt, the collar turned up, and no hat. He was a good two heads taller than she, very blond, with blue eyes which, although they were handsome, were not pleasant; they were too big and rarely moved. They might have been glass.

They ate in a little restaurant near the school. The producer offered no word of explanation as to why he had asked her out. She hoped he would pay her a compliment, however superficial; would touch her hand, as though by accident. He spoke of nothing but his cabaret. The Settee was doing well; it was sold out every evening; the place was too small. "We live on the masochism of the middle class," he said.

She listened wide-eyed, not so much because she was interested in the Settee cabaret as because she already knew that when men woo women they talk about their jobs. He certainly didn't take her for a girl from a middle-class family. He certainly didn't know she was a baroness.

"We're going to a very high-class night-club now," he said. "It's the only one I can afford; you see, the proprietor is a fan of mine. He comes to see each of our programmes three times. We give him a free beer. In return I can get a bottle of champagne from him whenever I like." He noticed her hesitation. "If the racketeers don't like your costume they can leave the place." It hadn't occurred to him that her hesitation might spring from the lateness of the hour. He certainly didn't take her for a child.

They went by taxi to the Bamberger Strasse. He didn't kiss her, but merely put his arms round her shoulders without drawing her to him. Her worry increased. It was past ten. She no longer had any desire to see the inside of a night-club. She accepted the inevitable row with her mother, but it had to be worth while. She couldn't have said what she meant by that. A second life that bore her own as though it were as light as a feather. A point of brightness and support in the midst of everyday existence. The certainty of not becoming like Teréz, whom happiness had passed by, nor like her mother, who arrogantly flung it away. Something she didn't have to share with anyone, as she had to share Teréz's old-maid's bedroom and the wardrobe containing the black clothes. The banishment of anxiety, the banishment of the picture over the beds.

The Don Juan, as the night-club was called, paid homage to the lady-pursued lady-killer from whom it took its name. The walls were decorated with paintings portraying the hero's life: they showed him fighting a duel, enveloping thinly clad women in his black cloak, kneeling before beauties, adored by beauties. In between hung photographs of famous actors who had played the part of Don Juan—slim Italians, American film stars, fat opera-singers.

Although the club was full to overflowing, the proprietor led Zita and Busse to a small table that had just been pulled out on to the dance-floor. More and more tables were being pulled out on to the dance-floor. Their legs were creeping towards the legs of the dancers. "There's plenty of material for you to study here to-night, my dear Busse," said the proprietor, who wore a diamond ring on his little finger and a pearl in his tie. "Another general," said Busse when the fatherly man had gone. "Well, I should worry. Bring the free drinks! A dry Henkell, waiter!"

Zita was glad Busse didn't realize that this was her first visit to a night-club. Nor did her costume attract any attention. Several women were wearing tailored suits and a few men lounge-suits, as if they had dropped in to the Don Juan by chance. Interspersed among them were men in dinner-jackets, even one in tails, and women in low-cut evening-dresses, with necklines down to the navel.

> "The universe now stops and stares;
> The pulse of life is still;
> The world is trying out to see
> If chaos suits it well or ill,"

quoted Busse. "Shall we dance?" The skirt of her suit was too long. Only young girls wore long skirts nowadays. She said she would rather watch. "So would I," he commented appreciatively. "The passengers on the *Titanic* danced till they went under. And were proud of it too, the idiots."

"I must go," said Zita.

The band played a *tango milonga;* this called for red lighting. The dance-floor was now so small that the merging bodies could no longer be distinguished from one another. It was almost as though two heads grew from one neck, a woman's and a man's facing in opposite directions. A torch-singer stood beside the saxophonist; she wore a dress covered in glittering beads; they sparkled red; she moved her lips, her arms, but she couldn't be heard.

"I can sing like that too," said Zita. A idea suddenly struck her. "Couldn't I appear at the Settee?"

Busse leant back, as though seeing her for the first time.

"Why not?" he said. His eyes moved a little. "What would your mother say about it? Or haven't you got a mother?"

"Yes, I have. But she doesn't come into it."

"You're a baroness, they tell me."

"So what?"

"So nothing. We'll put it in the programme. Baroness Rattowitz singing Schmidlapp. That's our librettist. You'd do well as a seaport whore."

"I'm sure I should," she said.

"I'm sure you wouldn't. But that's just it. Sex-appeal consists of contrast."

He pointed to the dance-floor. The frog-wife was dancing with a young man in a dinner-jacket that had been pressed to death. Zita had noticed it earlier. After every dance the old man with the pince-nez took out his wallet and pressed a few more notes into the dancer's hand. The wallet was brown, fat, and large, left over like the pince-nez from a less happy time. When the frog-wife danced past the band— "the finest dance is the shimmy. It's danced by Lou and Jimmy"—the black drummer stopped and hummed: "When I'm dancing with my baby, I'm happy, and I don't mean maybe." But he hummed this in German. The 'baby' smiled. The frog-wife smiled. The frog-husband paid out the notes. Only the frog-daughter did nothing.

"When the gigolo dances with the kid," said Busse, "no one thinks anything of it. He doesn't smile; he gives his exhausted lips a rest. But one immediately imagines the old woman in bed with the dancing trouser-creases. A seaport whore as a lady. You as a seaport whore. It's the contrast, I tell you."

Zita wasn't listening. He would take her home, and she would have had no experience. She was the only one who had no experiences. No one who had no experiences could be happy. Why had she said she wanted to appear at the Settee? The producer was used to people wanting something from him. He would want nothing himself from a person who wanted nothing from him. The 'Baroness' had frightened him off. Her mother, the 'Baroness.' She wanted him to imagine that she was ready to sell herself for a part in his cabaret. She didn't really want to sell herself. She simply didn't want to go home. Nor to school. She found the night-club unpleasant because it made her feel like a confidence trickster. She had a desperate wish to be something, not to pretend to be something.

The hoarse voice of the *diseuse* made itself heard at last.

> "If the first wife is a flop,
> Take a second, don't stop."

The dance hostesses nodded to the older gentlemen, encouragingly, as an accompaniment to the words of the song. Then came the comedy vocalist, a portly little man; he disposed of his songs like a street-trader selling razor-blades.

> "Who put lanolin on Grandma's bread
> Instead of butter? That's what I said.
> Mamie took a great big bite,
> But Carol thinks it's quite all right."

"I must go," said Zita.

She knew it was a risk. Georg Busse would take her home. The bottle was empty. He said, "Of course you will have to 'interrupt your studies,' as people say when they don't want to go to school any more. Why should you? *Non scholae, sed vitae decimus*. What are you learning that will be useful to you in life? Dead Latin. Do you want to be a pharmacist? History? Read the papers! Geography? The frontiers are coming together and being pulled apart again like a concertina. Mathematics? Make one into a thousand. Study the stock-market quotations! Do you imagine this lot here know anything about mathematics? If they did they would never have become rich." He beckoned the waiter and pressed a note into his hand. "The tip isn't on the house, unfortunately," he told Zita. So he had heard her say she wanted to leave. "We'll go to my place," he said.

She walked ahead of him. People were dancing; she could disappear in the crowd; no one could see that her skirt was too long.

Her heart was beating loudly, louder than the jazz drums, she thought. It was past midnight. At home her mother was waiting. But she would stop waiting, because Zita wouldn't be home before two, and perhaps not till three or four. Georg would ask her if she loved him. She wouldn't know what to answer.

7

The house lay in a side-street off the Leipziger Strasse.

Busse struck a match and lit Zita up the stairs. He walked backwards with his face to Zita, three steps above her. He used three matches, one for each floor. Only his chin was visible in the light from the little flame. His chin went up and up, three steps above.

He hunted for his key.

"Prepare for a shock," he said. "I'm only a tenant. My landlord and his family are away."

She saw at once what it was he had been afraid would shock her. Georg was an artist, a great artist; ugliness wounded him. There was a long corridor lined the whole way along the right side with cupboards, brown cupboards crammed together as in a furniture warehouse. They had to squeeze past them. On top of the cupboards stood row upon

228

row of red apples. Then came a dining-room with a round table in the centre covered with a velvet cloth. The chairs were upholstered with imitation leather embellished with stamped relief decorations. They stood around the table at arm's length, as though afraid to touch it. There were rows of red apples on the sideboard. Busse put out the light in the dining-room and lit it in the bedroom. Both beds were covered with bedspreads. Over one hung a picture of the Divine Family—Mary, Joseph, the Child, and the Holy Ghost in the form of a dove. Over the other hung the landlord's family—father, mother, and the four children arranged like organ-pipes. The room smelt of apples.

"I haven't a private entrance of my own," said Busse. "But that's going to be changed."

He switched off the light in the bedroom, and switched on the light in his room.

Georg must have been living here for a long time, for the landlord-style had given way to his own, although not without a stout rear-guard action. The brown bed, high and wide, was the twin brother of the landlord-beds. The wardrobe with the inset oval of wood of the same colour also dated from the landlord period. But there were a couple of chairs which belonged to the new period, as did the desk, which was covered with books and papers. Finally, the wall was pure Georg Busse. Photographs were pinned all over it—photographs of actors and actresses, of scenes on the stage of the Settee and also a restaurant menu, a pink railway-ticket, a flat leather bottle, and even a pair of pale-blue lady's panties pierced by a nail.

"I hang up everything that reminds me of something nice," said Busse. He took a bottle of wine and two glasses from the wardrobe. "Warm but exquisite." He uncorked the bottle and poured out.

She sat down, but kept her coat on. The room was unheated.

He lowered himself on to the threadbare carpet at her feet, his glass in his hand. He looked up at her. All at once his eyes were quite mobile. He put his head in her lap. He still didn't tell her to take her coat off.

She touched his head, stroked his hair. There was silence. She wanted to ask him what his childhood had been like and whether his parents were still alive, but she asked none of these things. The noise of a toilet being flushed broke the silence.

"That happens three or four times every night," commented Georg.

Her fingers touched his temples. She plucked up courage and asked, "Why did you invite me out to-night?"

"I'm growing old," he said. "I'm already falling in love with school-girls."

"I don't want to work in the cabaret at all," she said.

He emptied his glass and rose to fill it. Then he sat down at her feet again; he put his head back in her lap.

"Are you still a virgin?" he asked.

"Why do you ask?"

"Yes, of course, you're still a virgin."

"What makes you think that?"

229

"Since you're not a whore, you must be a virgin. Otherwise you wouldn't have been so ready to come with me."

"Perhaps I've fallen in love with you," she said.

He nodded, almost imperceptibly. "You know," he said, "you remember the first man for the rest of your life. The first woman too, come to that. The first man can do a lot of harm. Very few repairs are possible in life. Remember that. You can't put things right; you can only start afresh. It's difficult with love; there you can neither repair nor start again." He turned his head to her, clasped her knees. "I haven't a guilty conscience," he said. "We two . . ."

He didn't finish the sentence, but she thought she knew what he meant. We two are lonely.

"I feel hot," she said.

He stood up and helped her off with her coat. She shivered. The coat fell to the floor. He didn't pick it up. He stood behind her and kissed her neck. She felt his breath on the little hairs on the nape of her neck, and in her ears.

I love him, she thought.

He kissed her mouth, hungrily, like a poor man at a rich table thinking himself unobserved.

From a neighbouring church-tower came the notes of the hour. Zita didn't count them.

8

The schoolkeeper had answered the telephone at last. The rehearsal ended soon after eight, he had said. Fräulein Von Rattowitz had gone off with Herr Busse, he remembered distinctly. "She'll come home all right, Frau Von Rattowitz."

Ilona had already changed into her dressing-gown and put the champagne on ice.

She kept on looking at the clock. She saw Zita in a traffic accident, under one of the speeding cars. She had to walk down dark alleys on her way home from the bus-stop. Zita had left the school with Herr Busse. She had mentioned him once or twice. Did the school governors know whom they were engaging when they took him on? All the horrible stories she had read in the *Berliner Zeitung am Mittag* and the *Nachtausgabe* rose before Ilona. She caught herself thinking that she was more afraid of the Herr Busse than of the speeding cars. She was ashamed of this thought. The twentieth century was twenty-one years old. I'm a hundred, thought Ilona.

On the stroke of midnight the front door opened; it was Teréz coming home. Ilona thought to herself that she hadn't waited for her sister so eagerly since Zita's birth.

Teréz who was generally very excitable, listened to her sister's story quite calmly. "If the police were to go chasing after every seventeen-year-old who stays out at night they would be kept very busy," she said. She urged Ilona to go to bed. "You have to get up early in the morning. I'll wait up. There's no cause for alarm."

They sat facing each other, Ilona in her silk dressing-gown, Teréz in her black dress with the little white collar. From time to time they heard lorries bumping over the cobbles down below. Otherwise there was quiet, the deceptive quiet of the suburbs. The light from the cut-glass standard lamps on either side of the Biedermeier sofa caressed the furniture. Teréz had picked up some knitting.

Was this calm really indifference? Was it anger that had grown tired? Or did Teréz seek revenge because Ilona had taken Zita's up-bringing away from her with just as little ceremony as she had originally handed it over to her? It occurred to Ilona that once again years had passed since she last bothered about Teréz. You didn't bother about your shadow. It stopped when you stopped and turned round when you turned round, the only friend who remained faithful till death. Next year Teréz would be forty. When they moved to Berlin she could have gone back to Kisnémet. Shadows didn't run away. Nor did they make a nuisance of themselves. At midday Teréz went back to the restaurant; at midnight she came home. At the end of the month she put her wages on the sewing-box, always on the same spot. Only the wages changed: they became continually greater in amount and smaller in value. She had withdrawn from Zita's upbringing. At first she appeared offended, as though saying, "I'll do it on my own or not at all." On Sunday morning she walked to church without complaining of the distance. On Sunday afternoon she walked to the cinema and came back with flushed cheeks. She never described what she had seen. On Sundays she was even capable of looking pretty, as in her youth—a shadow that had acquired colour. Once—it was several months ago—Ilona found one of her lipsticks was missing; she came across it by chance in Teréz's sewing-box. She smiled, but said nothing.

The longer Ilona observed the black figure the more uncanny she found her sister's calm. That's the way nurses in mental hospitals must sit, she thought, peacefully knitting until the patients begin to rave. What did Teréz know? She recalled that sometimes Teréz and Zita had stopped talking when she entered the room. Children trusted another shadow; they trusted anyone except their mothers.

"What do you know about Zita?" she asked gruffly.

"Nothing," replied Teréz, but a tinge of red that crept into her cheeks gave her away.

"Do you know where she might be?"

"No."

"Has she told you anything about Georg Busse?"

"No."

The clock on the commode struck one-thirty. Of all terrors waiting is the most terrible, thought Ilona. She wouldn't punish Zita if she came home now. She wouldn't ask any questions. But Teréz would question her at once.

"Do you think she could possibly be having an affair?" she asked. "She is honest with you."

Teréz laughed softly, as though she saw through her sister's belated compliment. She spoke as though to her own hands, as though to the knitting-needles.

"You know nothing about young people, Ilona."

"What do you know about young people?"

"More than you. We confuse the issue by comparing them with the young people of our day."

"I asked you a question," said Ilona impatiently.

"I don't know whether she is having an affair."

"You say that as though you would find it quite natural."

"I should find it quite natural. Destiny weighs too heavily on Zita."

"Do you mean that it's my fault?" asked Ilona.

"It's certainly not mine." The reply sounded vehement, accusing. "You gave her a name, but no father. You abandoned her on account of Kontowski, on account of Zoltán. 'But the last few years. . . ,' you will say. They don't count. She considers you old. People who mend their ways when they are old do so because they are forced to, and that doesn't count. You never gave up a man for her sake. Why should she give up a man for your sake?" For a moment the knitting-needles came to rest. "Papa renounced his own life for our benefit. You have renounced nothing." She went on knitting. She sat in the armchair stiffly, almost like a person paralysed in the body and legs who can only move his hands.

Ilona leaned forward in order to see Teréz better.

"Love, love . . . you talk about love," burst out Teréz. "You have no idea what it means. Papa wasn't afraid we should go off the rails. He prevented us from going off the rails. That is love. Nothing else." She didn't let her sister get a word in edgeways. "You have never let anyone share in your life. Do you think we didn't all know that from childhood on you looked upon yourself as chosen? Only the blind think themselves chosen. And they only do so because they can't see other people looking at them. You were happy alone. Now you are suffering alone."

"I'm not suffering," said Ilona. She was tired.

"Of course you're suffering. Your destiny has become commonplace. You can't bear that. Zita doesn't want to be as unhappy as you."

Happy, unhappy, happy, unhappy, thought Ilona. Couldn't Teréz talk about anything else? Did every one want to live as though the end were near? She pondered whether to answer her sister. Hadn't she already done the wrong thing when she said she wasn't suffering? Vain tolerators fed on other people's suffering. Fair-minded destiny had afforded them the pride of suffering. They extolled their misery as profundity; they confused the awkwardness of their own nature with sublimity; their envy with just contempt. Because they themselves were incapable of rebelling they regarded the anguished cries of the others as the shouting of market salesmen.

"It's strange that you should think of all that now, Teréz," said Ilona. "I almost believe that you have always hated me. We hate those who dare to do what we should like to do ourselves."

Teréz had laid aside her knitting.

"I have never hated you," she said. "But at last I have freed myself from you. I'm going to get married."

"Married? Who to?"

"It would upset you too much. Another time. . . ."

"I want to know."

"A head-waiter. From the restaurant. I've been having an affair with him."

"That's impossible!"

Teréz laughed.

The crystal drops of the little table-lamp clinked together. They were like the tinkling of sleigh-bells. Teréz sank back into the armchair. Her figure looked tiny, as though compressed by laughter.

"Why not?" she said. "He's a man. Only three years younger than I. A widower in a secure position, as they say in the marriage advertisements that I have devoured all my life, but never answered. He loves me. Can you still remember what that means? He isn't a count, nor is he famous. Do you know how utterly unimportant that is when one doesn't live by appearances?"

"A widower in a secure position," thought Ilona. A head-waiter, only three years younger. Why did it shock her? Her father had been the stationmaster at Kisnémet. The Maison Rosa had paid for her education. A lover had bought her the title of baroness. Ought she not to feel ashamed of her prejudices? She didn't feel ashamed. Things happened as they had to. What wretched kind of freedom was it that allowed itself to be dragged down by its own roots? What kind of ambition which, instead of leaping up to the heights, tried to turn the heights into valleys? What kind of pride that injured its own dignity? They said equality and meant complacency. Neither at Berény nor in St Petersburg nor in Vienna had she felt so clearly what she had become. Only here, in this Berlin suburb, did she begin to grasp what it meant to be chosen.

The clock struck two. Both women looked at the clock. Then they looked at each other.

"I'll tell you something, Ilona." Teréz spoke in a low voice, no longer laughing. "Zita knows about it. Zita considers it quite natural. We had a secret from you, but it was mine, not hers."

It seemed to Ilona as though the black figure in the armchair were taking on the colour of flesh. She hadn't seen Teréz naked since they were girls. Now she saw her in front of her naked, as she often used to sit on the bed in the bedroom over the waiting-rooms. What was this poor naked girl trying to do? To punish her by marrying? To prove to her that she was young? To show her where they both belonged?

"I'm glad you're getting married," said Ilona.

"Margit was happy too," said Teréz provocatively.

"I know."

She stood up. Naturally Teréz had told her at the right moment, naturally. Ilona was no longer frightened. Zita was having an affair. Perhaps with Georg Busse. Teréz must know who it was and whether he was kind to her. It was not enough to worry about children; you had also to prevent them from going off the rails.

"Let us go to bed," she said.

"I shall wait," said Teréz.

"There's no need for that," said Ilona. "Put the key outside the door, Teréz."

9

Georg had wanted to take her home, but she had asked him just to go with her to a taxi.

The taxi drove along Unter den Linden to the Brandenburger Tor. It was four o'clock. Lights were on in a few isolated shop-windows, illuminating the Christmas decorations, which looked lifeless, as though Christmas were over long ago. The Allee was completely empty. A group of people emerged noisily from the Hotel Adlon. A milk-van bumped across the Pariser Platz. The horses were pulling sleepily, the milk-churns rattling. The taxi turned right after the Brandenburger Tor and passed the Reichstag. The driver switched on the spotlight. It had stopped snowing long ago. A thin drizzle could be seen in the light from the headlamps; the wind drove the raindrops against the windows, as though they were coming to meet the car. Water was dripping off the trees on to the asphalt.

Everything turns out quite differently from what you imagine beforehand, thought Zita. She had been afraid of the pain and had felt no pain. Her friends had talked about the first night as of a stony path that led to paradise. She had entered Paradise without even knowing how she got there. "Haven't you always been my sweetheart?" Georg had said. She had to laugh when she thought of his face, his amazement because she quickly discovered that she had only to take the lobe of his ear between her teeth to send him frantic. She had imagined she would lie swooning in the arms of the first man to whom she gave herself completely, but she hadn't lost consciousness for an instant. She had stayed alert and used all her inherited weapons; but this in no way detracted from her happiness; she was like a mountaineer who takes in with open eyes and expanded lungs the beauties of the heights he has scaled. She was glad she hadn't given away her innocence while inexperienced, grateful to the men who had contented themselves with love-play and not demanded love. Only for a few minutes had the scales tipped in favour of the man that night. When Georg switched on the light equilibrium was re-established—the beautiful equality of lovers who gave nothing involuntarily and received what they were given with senses wide awake. She wanted to rise from the bed happy but not vanquished. She felt the pride of the artist whose imagination takes on form in the work of art. Georg had no need to fear that her first love might prove a disappointment. The thought that she would never see him again passed through her head—an impossible thought, but not frightening. She wouldn't forget his kisses, his kisses on the backs of her knees, in the curves of her elbows, "the loveliest places," as he said. Only hypocrites demanded that lovers should swoon. How were you to know if a man loved you if you lost consciousness in his arms, if you did not blissfully perceive that he felt the same joy at the same time? If you did not see with open eyes whether he was generous or selfish, grateful or conceited, full of love or merely full of sensuality?

She was certain now that she couldn't have resisted Georg even if she had not already intended to give herself to him as she climbed the stairs. Since she could not have resisted him, she must love him. She had resisted the others, and her resistance appeared to her dirty; or, rather, the dirtiness lay in having mastered her excitement, set limits to enjoyment. "Inhibitions are sensible, therefore they contradict love," Georg had said. She hadn't received more than she gave, hadn't given more than she received. She had regained her innocence that night.

Under one of the arc-lamps on the Spree bridge drunken men were trying to stop another drunk from jumping into the river. They were yelling so loud that Zita could hear them through the window of the taxi.

She wasn't thinking of her mother. Her friends, Hermine Stutz and Lotte Wegerode, occurred to her. In the Don Juan she had made up her mind to tell them about her experience. Now she thought to herself that girls who boasted about their adventures had never known love. Let them think what they liked, she would keep her secret!

The driver asked for the number of the house; she told him.

Her only wish was not to think of her mother; to-morrow, the day after to-morrow—that would be different! Perhaps she would really perform at the Settee, where she could always be near Georg. Her mother came home in the evening, Teréz at midnight. If she herself went out in the evening she wouldn't be home till every one was asleep. She would be asleep when the others went out. In this way life would be bearable. She would very soon move into a home of her own. Not into Georg's room. A clever woman remained a mystery even to her lover. She dismissed the thought that she might have other lovers, later, later; but equally she dismissed the thought that the first must be the last. A wave of gratitude flowed over her. She loved him because he had not caught but liberated her. She hadn't wanted to become his wife, but merely a woman. He had understood.

As she paid the driver she looked up at the windows. A dim light was burning in her mother's room. The rain was beating against the big window-panes of the optical factory.

Was she afraid after all? For a moment she considered going back to Georg and not coming home till after nine o'clock. Her mother would see at once what had happened. To deny her love seemed to her as impossible as to admit it.

The light in her mother's room went out. Her mother had heard the taxi. A feeling of tenderness, which she was unwilling to admit to consciousness, gripped Zita's heart.

In the darkness of the hall she remembered that she had drunk too much. Circles of light spun round before her eyes, expanding and contracting, together with spirals and streaks and serpents, pink, pale blue, opalescent. She thought of a kaleidoscope her grandfather had given her; you shook it, held it to your eye, and the bright-coloured pieces arranged themselves in pretty patterns. Where was the kaleidoscope?

She bent down. The key lay under the woven mat.

10

Christmas, New Year's Eve, Zita's seventeenth birthday, came and
went. Gone, too, were the holidays due to the coal shortage, but Zita
did not return to school. After her success in the school play she had
informed Ilona that she was going to appear at the Settee. The
question why she had not confronted her daughter after the night on
which Zita had come home at five o'clock, why, after an initial refusal,
she had agreed to Zita's plans, preoccupied Ilona incessantly.

Zita had produced forceful arguments. She couldn't and didn't want
to go to the university, so what use was a school certificate? She had
learnt languages, "the only thing that was any use," not without talent
and with astonishing diligence, encouraged by her successes in this field
since childhood. Now that she had discovered her talent for acting,
she could have attended a drama school, but this was a long and expensive route, and, after all, life itself was the best school. And didn't
every woman have to have a profession? Was she to become a
secretary, for which she lacked the training, or a shop assistant, in
which there was no future? It sounded almost honest when Zita said it
was high time she contributed to her own maintenance.

It wasn't true that all women worked, but most of them did. Ilona
recalled Fräulein Von Segelmann, the narrow-chested girl at the
medical examination, who had predicted the triumph of the working
woman. It was a magnificent victory Fräulein Von Segelmann had
won. After the mass suicide of the men a great many positions had
become free. Now there was unemployment, but the women refused to
give up the positions they had conquered. They no longer had to wait
for their husbands to come home every evening, but could come home
late themselves, dirty, tired, ill-humoured. They no longer had to worry
about their growing children, but could leave them to men and women,
to offices, factories, streets, and cabarets. They no longer had to put up
with the false chivalry of men; they could dress up as men, carry their
own parcels, open doors for themselves, fight for seats. They no longer
had to subordinate their own personalities to husband and family;
when their work left them time they could be just as selfish, ambitious,
and neurotic as men had always been. Only there was something suspicious, thought Ilona, about the readiness with which men had
accepted their defeat, the ease with which they had given up their
strongholds. Was the eternal war of the sexes really over for ever, or
was this a masculine stratagem, a tactical withdrawal? Marital
tragedies, divorces, infidelities, households with mistresses, were everyday occurrences. Were men taking their revenge for their defeat by
ceasing to love the conquerors? And had they left their agents behind
in the evacuated strongholds, their allies in the enemy camp—the
women who had remained women?

At the school play, the fusty atmosphere of which struck and surprised her, Ilona had met the man whom instinct immediately told her
was Zita's lover. She drew Busse into her house. He eluded her, neither
friend nor foe, but simply a stranger. She could hardly believe that he
was thirty-two, barely three years younger than herself. His immaturity

placed him on a par with Zita. The schism in Ilona's mind was increased by the fact that she would more easily have been able to forgive Zita for a passionate love, but at the same time perceived with relief that her child's first love was unlikely to leave any deep wounds behind.

She went with Zita to a performance at the Settee, a night-club near the Kurfürstendamm which she didn't particularly like, but which didn't perturb her too much either. It was a small, semi-circular room filled with futuristic decorations, full of smoke and patronized chiefly by intellectuals, who sat the whole evening over coffee and a bottle of wine. The two female members of the cast, to whom Zita was to be added to make a third, left the theatre immediately after the performance. They were unsuited to the function of barmaids—a profession of which Ilona had the most terrifying notions—by the fact that they would never have forgiven the men for seeing them as feminine beings. Admittedly, one or two smutty songs were sung, but not in a provocative spirit; on the contrary, *chansonniers* and *chansonnettes* sang of love as something that fortunately was as completely outmoded as the plush settee from which the cabaret took its name and which was suspended on ropes above the stage—a warning symbol. The Settee was a political cabaret in which the "good old days' were satirized, the exiled Kaiser re-exiled, the falling currency ridiculed, and the Government caricatured. It was true that Ilona had the feeling that the Settee was no less fusty than the school play, the latter because it glorified the past, the former because it buried what had already been buried long ago; but she had to admit that these were weak grounds on which to object to Zita's chosen career.

At first Ilona thought she had behaved correctly with Zita. At the Settee they were rehearsing the new programme. The rehearsals took place during the day; Zita rarely went out in the evening, and generally came home before midnight when she did. Ilona couldn't remember ever seeing her daughter more submissive, patient, and gay. Ilona didn't imagine that she had become franker, but she was reassured by the fact that Zita had retained a remnant of modesty, and did her best to conceal what obviously could not have remained a secret from her mother.

It was only when the cabaret closed its doors and night rehearsals were held that Ilona became aware of her disappointment. She seldom saw Zita now. When she came home in the evening the child was generally already out; in the morning they only saw each other for a few minutes at breakfast, or Zita had pinned a note on her door: "Please do not disturb!"

11

One day at the beginning of February Ilona left the fashion house rather earlier than usual to do a little shopping.

As she entered the empty flat she was seized by a feeling of malaise. Since, as sometimes happened, the feeling anticipated her thoughts, she could find no explanation for it.

On her way she had stopped outside a florist's shop on the corner of the street in which she lived, attracted by a rather large and enchantingly beautiful pot of cyclamen glowing purple amid the suburban drabness of the rest of the shop-window. She had bought the cyclamen, although the price seemed to her excessive, and asked for them to be delivered to the flat.

The flowers had now arrived, and she looked round for the best place to put them. When she found it—on a small Maria-Theresa secretaire—she paused in dismay, realizing that she had reached the age of thirty-five without ever having bought herself flowers. The house at Kisnémet had been full of flowers grown by the stationmaster. Feri had sent her the first flowers in Budapest, then in Sopron, then in Budapest again. She remembered the roses with which Prince Kontowski had announced himself at the Hotel Hungaria. In the apartment over the pâtisserie, in the house in the Bellaria, in the villa on Krestovsky Island, the Prince had always kept her supplied with flowers. One evening Zoltán's yellow roses had stood in the vases; Kontowski hadn't noticed them. Later too, in Vienna, there had been plenty of opportunities for admirers, adorers, and even passing acquaintances to flatter Ilona with flowers. Now, in Berlin, she occasionally asked Teréz or Zita to bring back potted plants or a few cut flowers; to-day, for the first time, she realized why. She didn't want to buy flowers for herself.

She let go of the flowerpot, took a step back, and studied the graceful shapes of the cyclamen. The petals resembled a woman's mouth waiting half open to receive a kiss. As though in response to unknown forces radiating from the calyxes, Ilona underwent a transformation.

She looked around and felt herself encircled by the spectres of lifelessness, renunciation, and loneliness. She, lonely? She had fallen into the trap of the times. Around her were lonely women who drew all other women into their loneliness. Women who made their own beds, telephoned men who didn't answer, spent whole nights sitting up in their lonely beds playing patience, travelled home unescorted. Women who bought their own flowers. Perhaps she had failed as a mother. But it would not help her daughter if she also failed as a woman. Maybe the first defeat had led to the second. She must free herself from her paralysis, must break out of her solitude.

No sooner had she recovered her senses than her swoon was forgotten. She went straight to the telephone. The wife of an eminent lawyer whom she had met at the fashion house, a Frau Markstein, had long ago invited her to pay her a visit. She rang up; the invitation was repeated.

In a few weeks Ilona's life changed completely. At Dr Markstein's Dahlem villa she met eminent criminal counsels who had their hands full defending business swindlers from the clutches of justice and juvenile murderers from the applause of the public. The newspaper reports, which she had formerly read in detail from a desire at least to live by proxy, lost their mysterious attraction. The beautiful Hungarian woman was passed from hand to hand, and people seemed amazed that she had previously remained hidden. The city which she had been seeing as though through a veil came to life. Ilona did not understand

Berlin's anguished gaiety, but she experienced it with her senses alert. She attended spiritual séances, which were all the rage: those who were tired of the terrestrial took refuge in the supernatural. She saw most of Percy Nolan, an Englishman of Irish extraction, an elderly, moody, but warm-hearted bachelor who held the post of deputy ambassador in Berlin, and remembered the Baroness from the time when he was embassy secretary in St Petersburg. Percy Nolan saw to her dealings with the authorities, difficult purchases, or anything else that was troublesome. He liked to saunter through Berlin's art-galleries, and when she was accompanying him on one such expedition she ran into Dr Sales, her superior officer at the Sant'Andrea field hospital. The meeting left an impression that lasted for days. He had asked her to telephone him, but she hesitated, just as she had still not visited Dr Ginsburg. The mirrors, for long her only advisers—before which, curiously enough, she now spent only minutes, not hours, as at the time of her lethargy—advised her to let the past rest.

When, in mid-March, Zita made her first appearance at the Settee, Ilona was not hurt by her daughter's request that she should stay away from the opening performance.

12

Ilona had guessed right when she supposed that Zita's love would not consume her.

Zita loved Georg, but she loved the life he opened up to her—Life with a capital L, as she thought it—more passionately still. She often felt as though Georg had found her on an island lost in the ocean, as though they had been two castaways who were all in all to each other. Now they had been taken aboard a ship, an ocean liner teeming with people who loved, danced, acted, and played. What wonder, then, that her island companion began to pale like a still living but already fading memory!

She made new acquaintances in the cabaret, people who were not her mother's friends. Apart from rehearsals, Georg had little to do. He took Zita to his favourite haunt, the Romanisches Café, where his friends gathered at their regular table. Here Zita met the lavender-scented Yugoslav Milan Seftic, who spent the night dancing with elderly ladies in the dance-hall of a hotel, but during the day wrote poems that neither rhymed nor had any meaning, and were certain of the universal applause of the group round the table. Another member of the party was a Hungarian film director, Tibor von Homonnay, who was about to direct his first film; he turned up each week with a different 'fiancée,' pretty girls for whom he predicted a magnificent career and to all of whom he promised the same part, so that for simplicity's sake they were all referred to as Constance, the heroine of the film that had not yet been made. Werner Effeweg, an ex-sailor from the Waterkante whose revolutionary poems appeared regularly in several left-wing periodicals, always wore a black shirt without a tie. The uncrowned queen of the table was Erika Wegener, the daughter of a world-famous physicist from Jena, and the author of a book entitled *Suicides in Literature*; although already thirty-one, she was an advocate of the idea that only a mass suicide of youth could shake the world out of its lethargy. In addition to the foregoing, acquaintances of the regular visitors gave occasional guest performances. Two of these aroused Zita's particular attention.

Sonia Herz, a woman of unbelievable elegance that was quite out of place in the smoky, noisy, uninhibited atmosphere of the café, had a certain claim to fame. This woman, as slim as a willow-wand, with enormous green eyes, smooth black hair parted in the centre, and long, slender legs, looked sickly with that intentional sickliness which seems to imply that only disgust with life renders life worth living. Her first marriage had been to young Count Fehrbrugg, who had died during the war. Rumour had it, however, that he had not been struck by an enemy bullet, but killed in a duel behind the lines. Her second husband, an industrialist named Herz, after all sorts of fraudulent manœuvres to which he was said to have been driven by his wife's extravagance, had disappeared, having probably made off to America. To crown it all, Sonia had been found one day unconscious, in the company of a well-known gynaecologist, who was also a professor and the father of a family, in the private room of a discreet restaurant. The rumours that their collapse was caused by cocaine poisoning had proved false; the accident was due to a faulty gas-fire. There was no certainty that the Count had been killed in a duel, that the industrialist had ruined himself on Sonia's account, or that the gynaecologist had taken cocaine; there was no certainty about anything connected with Sonia Herz. She walked with her thin legs along a thin wire. Nobody knew why Sonia Herz came to the Romanisches Café, unless—but even this wasn't certain—she had in fact had a brief love affair with Georg Busse. Sonia Herz quickly allayed Zita's jealousy. Whereas the regular circle took little notice of Zita, because here women only counted when, as the group phrased it, "they amounted to something in their own right," and were not merely "brought along"—so that a kind of class distinction that had nothing to do with their ages existed between Erika Wegener and Zita—whereas, that is to say, Zita was more or less ignored by the rest, Sonia Herz treated her as an equal, drew the group's attention to her, and even invited Zita to visit her in her Grunewald villa.

The other stranger could not have been more than twenty, a brash youngster, ostentatiously dressed, generally in a loud checked jacket, with red hair, a freckled face, and always smoking a fat cigar from which he never removed the gilt band, but kept pushing it up the cigar till finally it began to smoulder. This athletically built young man, Hermann Müller, used to amuse the gathering with all sorts of inventions: once it was a walking-stick in which twenty cigarettes could be slipped end to end, another time a latch-key with a ward that shone in the dark. Georg's circle, which, although politically liberal, was as exclusive as a London club, did not accept Hermann Müller on account of his conjuring-tricks, but because the young man was always willing to pay for the group's current drinks, and occasionally even to settle the debts they had run up with the head-waiter. It was said to be he who met the Settee's deficit out of his own pocket. The story went that Hermann Müller had received a few green dollar-bills every month from an uncle who had emigrated to America and was working as a mechanic in Detroit; that with this sum, not large in itself, but quite considerable when changed into marks, he had begun to speculate; and that he was now considered on the Stock Exchange an infant prodigy, although he was not allowed to enter the premises in person because he was still a minor. Hermann Müller, like Sonia Herz, doubtless sensed that, although tolerated, he was not welcome at the round, marble-topped table in the Romanisches Café; he also sensed that Baroness Von Rattowitz was likewise looked upon as a *parvenue*, and he therefore attached himself to Zita with a positively childlike dependence. Zita felt sorry for the wealthy upstart who confused Molière, Maupassant, Musset, and Murat, would have given all his bonds for the ability to write poetry without verses or paint Dadaistically, and probably suspected that they began to laugh uproariously about him before the checked jacket under the short fur coat was even out of sight.

13

Zita's appearance at the Settee made no difference to the minor part she played both in Georg's life and at the Romanisches Café.

She was originally supposed to sing three songs, and a fourth in the event of wild applause; but they dispensed with the fourth after the first rehearsal, since it seemed unlikely that they would have to reckon with applause. The three were reduced to two, and since no *diseuse* could appear before the curtain with only two songs, these two were also scratched. Georg put her in four scenes. The dream of the seaport whore was ended, but Zita was allowed to strut mutely up and down in high laced boots in front of a piece of scenery indicating a house-front, in the rôle of a streetwalker, while Illa Ill coughed out her whore's misery into the audience from a lighted window—the real reason why Zita had asked her mother to stay away from the première. In two further scenes she had speaking parts, but very thankless ones, consisting of only a few lines each. In a fourth she played the part of Snow White, lay in a glass coffin, and was carried off by an inflation prince to his newly acquired castle. Her name appeared four times in the programme of the new revue—including the silent part, "A Prostitute . . . Zita von Rattowitz"—so that she didn't dare bring home this first printed proof that she was a rising star.

She was angry, disappointed, but not unhappy. Georg was right: she displayed her talent on the stage of life. Hermine Stutz and Lotte Wegerode were still keeping a school-bench warm; but she was appearing in a Berlin cabaret; she had received friendly notices in two reviews, even if her name only appeared "among others"; and Hermann Müller, though the rest had laughed at him, had asked for her autograph. You didn't have to have talent in order to love the theatre. Every evening when she walked through the empty theatre her heart beat louder. She didn't mind dusting the plush settee over the stage, helping the other two dress, and occasionally pulling the curtain-cord. She was a member of a community of kindred spirits; acknowledged the applause, even if it was not directed primarily towards her; was incensed by the success of rival cabarets, and, in all modesty, could consider herself the colleague of the Rosa Valettis, Gussy Holls, and Trude Hesterbergs. When Teréz came home at midnight Zita pretended to be asleep, or if she came home later herself she crept through the bedroom on tiptoe. She heard her aunt's exhausted breathing, or her cough. She took the pity she felt for the old maid as confirmation of her own status. Then it was as if the dark room became peopled by a strange company. The passengers from the first-, second-, and third-class waiting-rooms were jumbled together. Over Teréz's bed floated the customers of the middle-class restaurant; the landlord and landlady and the cook; the head-waiter, whom Zita pictured as a comical cabaret figure, bowing and scraping, the table-napkin under his arm. "Very good, madam; very good, sir," "Waiter, bill, please!"

She was grateful to Georg. He had taken her into the school of life. A bare four months, and she was convinced that 'surplus value' would strangle capitalism; that history developed according to economic laws, and that God was only there to divert people from their true problems. She believed that, as Sigmund Freud taught, one must overcome one's inhibitions; that girls hated their mothers and boys their fathers, according to the law of the Oedipus complex; that most actions were motivated by the inferiority complex. She knew that the heart beat on the left, and the enemy was on the right; that the classics were as dry as dust and representational painting shallow; that only old men and reactionaries doubted the equality of women, and that the world would perish in the very near future if the intellectuals did not stave off the disaster in time.

In love, however, Georg was not her teacher, not her master. During rehearsals she submitted to his capricious dictatorship; when he spoke she hung on his lips; in the circle of his friends she contented herself with a rôle that was even smaller than that of the girl in the glass coffin in the parody of Snow White. Alone with him, she took revenge for the slights she had suffered. He still hadn't found new lodgings, and since his landlord and landlady had come back she could visit him only in the afternoons. At first she found these afternoon visits embarrassing. Love rebelled against the limitation of time and the silent agreement. Soon, however, she learnt that a bad conscience was the most powerful male aphrodisiac, a man's love all the greater the more he had to make good. Now she was the stage manager. She arranged the scenery and the lighting; punished violent passion with restrained reserve; showed the tired man how to behave passionately; gave the cue only when it suited her; bewildered her partner by arbitrary impromptus; reduced the star to the level of an extra, and succeeded in making him attribute both her surrender and her detachment to her free will. At the same time she neither deceived herself about her pleasure nor learnt to despise the man who was so docile. Her enjoyment was all the greater the more clearly she bore in mind that no sooner was the naked man clothed than he became her master; the

242

more clearly she perceived the uncontrollable impulses of the naked man behind the imperious gestures of the clothed man. At rehearsal she saw him in bed, in bed at rehearsal. She was satisfied.

<h2 style="text-align:center">14</h2>

On this sultry June day of 1922 there was no performance at the Settee.

In the morning the Reich Foreign Minister, Walter Rathenau, had been assassinated in the Königsallee by two officers belonging to the "Ehrhardt Brigade," Hermann Fischer and Erwin Kern, and a student, Ernst Techow. When Burg Saaleck, near Naumburg, was surrounded by police the assassin Kern appeared at the window and shouted, "We are dying for our ideals! Others will complete the task!"

They had gathered in Hermann Müller's new flat because it was situated at the corner of the Lützowstrasse and the Lützowplatz, in the heart of the city, enabling them to see clearly what was going on in the street.

Although no demonstrations were taking place in the Kurfürstendamm, they could feel the unrest creeping from the suburbs towards the city centre. Offended by the noise from the suburbs, the shops let down their sliding shutters. "I hope we shall be able to get home safely to-night," Georg had said.

When they entered Müller's flat the only people there, apart from Müller himself, were Erika Wegener, Milan Seftic, and a student named Karl Baader, a distant relation of Hermann. Erika Wegener, her hair cut short in a masculine style that left her ears uncovered, was sitting on a tweed-upholstered couch smoking. As soon as he saw Zita the student clicked his heels together and bowed so deep that she could see his red neck.

The flat smelt of paint. The very light and spacious lounge was furnished in the most modern style. The pieces of furniture were so far apart that they seemed to be vainly stretching out their arms to one another. In the far corner on the long wall hung a single painting. One had the impression that the collector had started to hang his pictures and then been disturbed. It was the work of a young Dadaist painter who had not succeeded in eliminating all perspective, but whose perspective shortened towards the front, instead of towards the back, as though the painter were leaning forward from behind the frame to push the figures and objects out of it. The picture, Hermann told them, was called *Post-War*, and—eschewing all reality, yet unable to escape from it entirely—represented a fat-paunched individual dressed half in uniform and half in tails and with a bishop's mitre on his head eating worms out of a skull, while disabled ex-servicemen, beggars, and widows peeped out of the skull-bowl awaiting their turn to be devoured. A standard lamp of glittering metal open at the top cast the right light on the picture; there was no ceiling light. The modernity of the room would scarcely have struck the visitors if they had not caught a glimpse, through an open door, of the bedroom, the sentimental character of which hit them in the eye. Either from filial loyalty or lack of money, Hermann Müller had transplanted his parents' Neukölln bedroom, lock stock and barrel, to the Lützowstrasse: besides the dark-brown bed, the room also contained a standard lamp topped by a shade of dark-red silk embellished with braiding and tassels, a one-legged sewing-table, two oleographs of Murillo's street urchins, an open bookcase devoid of books, and two armchairs whose Gobelin backs portrayed belling stags. Two framed photographs of the strip-dancer Anita Berber dressed as Eve constituted the only link between bedroom and lounge.

The evening was sultry. The houses were bathing in the heat, emerging from the bath sweating. The windows were open. From the balcony they could see the Landwehr Canal, the end of the Budapester Strasse, and the tops of a few trees in the Tiergarten. The smell of a city summer came in through the balcony door, a poor people's smell, since the rich are never there to inhale it in summer. A dull rumble mingled with the sound of the evening traffic, a false, alien note. Milan Seftic, the poet and gigolo, said it was the noise of street-fighting. Demonstrators were converging from all sides on the Brandenburger Tor.

The room filled up. Werner Effeweg, the sailor and poet, had just come from the Brandenburger Tor. His face, dominated by an almost square chin that jutted out as though hurrying ahead of the face, was flushed.

The next to arrive, immediately after him, was Johann Schmidlapp, the Settee's librettist. He was rarely seen in the cabaret, never in the Romanisches Café. He was a man in his late twenties, pale and gaunt, but with a face full of energy. Even his glasses made his features seem sharper—two round crystals in a crystal face. Both Effeweg and Schmidlapp had seen large detachments of police, but they didn't know whom they were directed against.

The group spoke of nothing but the murder in the Königsallee.

Effeweg said, "You're like children who put out their tongues at a policeman and then dodge quickly round the corner. You hope to kill with ridicule, but ridicule kills no one. It makes people popular. When a politician is dead, people say he was killed by ridicule. It's the other way round: he is ridiculed because he is dead. The others couldn't kill Rathenau with ridicule; that's why they murdered him. We kill nobody." He turned to the librettist. "That cabaret number of yours, Schmidlapp, about the dead who rise and parade before the generals. . . . The generals think it quite right that the dead should parade before them."

Schmidlapp said, "We don't write for the generals. We warn. Are we to become criminals because the others are? We warn with all the means at our disposal, including humour, satire, and irony. Can't we agree with one another, Effeweg? Our people are not the best in the world, as they imagine, but nor are they the worst. What they lack is imagination. They don't see the prison till all the windows are barred. They don't know that boots march of their own accord. They can only imagine death when they stand on the edge of the mass graves. If we can excite the people's imagination . . "

Effeweg interrupted him. "Tripe, Schmidlapp! The people are desperate, but they're not bitter. You're bitter, but not desperate. Don't you understand the difference? Desperation is a genuine feeling; bitterness is its sublimation into the sphere of the intellect. The people shake their fists, but they don't stick out their tongues. You mean well, I grant you. But we Germans have never understood humour. You're comic grave-diggers."

Erika Wegener said, "Grave-diggers only bury the dead. They don't kill." She lit another cigarette. "You're children. You know nothing about dying. Dying is a pleasure. At any rate, no dead person has ever asserted the contrary. Germany is itching to die."

Zita was sitting on the red couch between Georg and the student. Every time the word Germany was pronounced the student straightened up. His head projected into the death's head of the Dadaist glutton. He might have been eighteen, or twenty-eight. He looked like some one who blushed at the dancing-class and went to whores. It struck Zita that he acquired colour only when he blushed. He was tall and broad-shouldered, but everything about him was pallid—his fair hair, his skin, the lips he compressed until they disappeared.

Zita tried in vain to understand what the men were talking about. It was as if they were continuing a discussion of which she had missed the beginning. The noise had grown louder. She thought of her mother. Had she reached home safely? Would she herself be able to get home to-night? Perhaps she ought to telephone. She immediately felt ashamed of the thought. So she hadn't yet freed herself from her mother's tutelage, hadn't freed herself entirely from her childhood at Berény and in the Döbling villa. These men were talking as though the fate of Germany, perhaps of the world, rested on their shoulders. Who could say whether it wasn't true? And she, Baroness Zita von Rattowitz, seventeen, a few months ago a pupil in the lower sixth, now Snow White at the Settee, was permitted to take part in their discussions, in the destiny they were moulding. Ever since she could think she had wanted to be different from her mother, she didn't know exactly in what way, but different. Her mother, who wanted to fashion her after her own image, had called her frivolous, pleasure-seeking, superficial. To which of them did this apply now? To her mother, who had a prince for her lover; who left home because she was ashamed of work; who read sentimental novels and browsed through fashion magazines; who sought the society of people with high-sounding names? Or to herself, who was directly affected by the Foreign Minister's murder, appeared in a political cabaret, and belonged to this circle of earnest men and women? She wouldn't ring up her mother. She must listen; she must understand. The debate grew more and more heated. Only Hermann and the student took no part in it. Hermann was smoking his fat Brazilian cigar with the gold band.

"You aren't drinking anything," he said, quickly standing up. "Wine or cognac?"

"Cognac," said Seftic.

"Both," said Effeweg.

"Shall I show you something?" said Hermann. He walked over to a

245

built-in cupboard and pressed a knob. A little door sprang open and dropped to form a shelf. "Hocus-pocus," laughed Hermann. An illuminated bar lined with mirrors came into view. The bottles appeared twice as many as they really were.

"Whisky," said Erika Wegener. "Neat."

An elderly woman came in carrying a tray on which stood two bottles of wine and a plate of open sandwiches.

"There's no point in starving," said Hermann.

The woman put down the tray without a word. Then she stood in the doorway, as if asking whether anything else was wanted of her. She had a narrow head and sad eyes. Zita thought she looked like the old servants in Kisnémet who had worked for a lifetime for the same employers.

"I must ring the hotel," said Seftic.

Erika Wegener went out on to the balcony, whisky-glass in hand. It was now dark. Zita followed her. It was quiet in the street. Gramophone music echoed from open windows. A low wind wafted the scent of lime-blossoms and human voices up to the balcony.

"It's a proper night for love," said Erika Wegener.

Zita didn't answer, because she thought the remark sounded offensive, as though Erika meant, "What do you know about Rathenau's murder? You only know about nights of love."

The Yugoslav came back with another young man. He said, "I'm free. There won't be any dancing to-night."

"I'm surprised," said Georg.

The new arrival was Fritz Schlesinger, crime reporter on the *Morgenpost*, a narrow-chested boy who had made a name for himself some months ago by his disclosures concerning the price-rings. His shirt was open at the neck and torn.

"Things are pretty hot," he reported. "There have been violent clashes in the Pariser Platz between workers and 'Ehrhardt Brigaders' in mufti. When I went to the office the police had just opened fire."

"Would you like a new shirt?" asked Hermann.

"I'm going in a minute," answered the reporter. He sat down beside Zita, who had meanwhile returned to the red couch. "Schlesinger," he said. He had forgotten to introduce himself before. "People are afraid there will be serious trouble during the funeral. Rathenau was a symbol."

"You're too young to indulge in leading articles," commented Georg.

"Rathenau was a symbol of our weakness," growled Effeweg.

Baader, the student, was sitting beside Zita with clenched fists. His colourlessness had grown a shade more colourless. She couldn't remember his having said a single word. He had done nothing but drink. An empty bottle of wine stood in front of him.

"Rathenau was a symbol of Germany's desire for peace," said Schlesinger.

The student jumped up.

"Rathenau was the symbol of the politics of compliance," he shouted. "He and Ebert and Wirth have sold the German people to the Powers who dictated the Treaty of Versailles."

They were all on their feet. They advanced upon Baader from all sides, in a radial pattern, drawn by a magnetic central point. Effeweg blocked their path. He wasn't defending Baader; he was facing him and pushing the others back with his huge hands, as if to say "Leave this fellow to me."

There was silence. The silence had meaning, as though it put an end to meaningless sounds. There was no longer any noise from the street either.

Erika was the first to get a grip on herself. Turning to Hermann, who was standing on one side, she said, "Where did you dig up that idiot, Müller?"

Baader took a step back towards the wall.

"You're wonderful democrats," he stammered. "Why don't you let any one express a different opinion?"

Seftic was standing beside Zita. She was enveloped in a cloud of lavender.

"Would *you* let anyone express a different opinion?" he yelled.

Effeweg cast him a reproving side-glance.

"Take it easy!" he said. He still had both arms outstretched like a policeman holding back a crowd. "So you defend Rathenau's murderers, Herr Baader?"

"They are Germans who have acted for the whole of Germany," he retorted.

"Must you quarrel?" asked Hermann in an attempt to mediate. No one took any notice of him.

Zita's heart was beating violently. She seized Georg's arm. Every day she had heard of bloody brawls, but she hadn't seen any. Perhaps Hermann was right. What were they quarrelling about? What were wonderful democrats and politics of compliance and the Powers who dictated the Treaty of Versailles?

"The murderers are amongst us," yelled Schlesinger.

Baader went red in the face.

"Are you blind?" he said, as though speaking only to Effeweg. "The Jews have sold us. The Jewboy is defending the Jewish Cabinet Minister."

Schlesinger forced his way forward. He was so small that he only had to duck his head to dodge under Effeweg's arm.

With his left hand Effeweg pushed him back. With his right he struck Baader in the face.

The student staggered back. He fell against the bar. His head struck the mirror-shelf. He dragged a bottle down with him. The mirror broke in pieces. The bottle broke too. The green Chartreuse mingled with blood running from his nose and mouth. The light in the hocus-pocus bar had gone out.

Every one bent down over Baader. Only Effeweg walked away and sat down on the red couch. And Erika Wegener strolled out on to the balcony. The heat of the Berlin summer's night streamed in through the door, a slow-flowing river.

"We must bandage him," said Georg. He knelt down beside Baader. "Have you got anything we can use for a bandage, Hermann?"

Hermann hurried to the door. On the way he put down his cigar. His lips were twitching like those of a child about to cry. Zita felt sorry for him.

Baader sat half upright, holding a handkerchief over his mouth.

Even before Hermann got back the old woman who had appeared before was there again. She had entered soundlessly, carrying a battered wash-basin and a sponge.

Georg held the sponge to Baader's face. The sponge turned green and red with liqueur and blood.

"We ought to call a doctor," whispered Zita.

"He won't die," said Seftic.

When Hermann came back the old woman was kneeling down beside the student washing his face.

"Poor little fellow!" she said. And to the men: "Carry him to my bed."

Erika Wegener was still trying to cool herself on the balcony. Effeweg was sitting calmly on the couch.

Schmidlapp and Georg lifted up the student. The woman went in front of them. When she opened a door that had hitherto been shut they saw an empty room. It contained only a bed and a commode. A crucifix hung over the bed.

"Who is that woman?" asked Zita.

"My mother," said Hermann.

The sweat burst out on Zita's forehead. She went out on to the balcony.

"Have you a cigarette?" she asked Erika Wegener. Although she had tried hard, she had never enjoyed cigarettes up to now. She rarely smoked.

Erika Wegener had a half-smoked cigarette in her mouth.

"My last," she said, and handed it to Zita.

They stood side by side, leaning against the wall. The moon had risen. The roofs of the houses in the Lützoplatz glimmered blue and silver like a frozen lake. Only a few windows were still lit up.

"Don't get excited," said Erika Wegener. "There are bloody heads to-day in every second house."

Zita inhaled the smoke of the cigarette deeply.

"I must go back to the Pariser Platz," she heard Schlesinger's voice say behind her.

I'll ring Mummy, thought Zita.

15

Sonia Herz still appeared at the Romanisches Café from time to time. Her guest performances there resembled those of a famous opera star. She arrived in a snow-white limousine driven by a coal-black Negro chauffeur; waves of the fashionable perfume *N'aimez que moi* accompanied her everywhere. There was no need to open a fashion magazine; what Sonia Herz wore to-day would be in *Fashion* to-morrow. Not only were her clothes of the latest cut; she was one of those women who, although born long before the prevailing fashion,

knew how to adapt themselves physically, even physiognomically, to
the ideal of the moment. Her legs were so straight that they seemed
not to have grown out of the loins, but, as it were, to have sprung from
the ground and risen side by side to the loins. She could wear a dress
that was open all the way down to her flat stomach, but her breasts
didn't show; they clung to the inside of the dress without disturbing its
straight shapes. Looking into the pale, beautiful face that was a trifle
too narrow in the region of the chin, one saw only the supernaturally
large eyes, which, though made up and encircled with mascara, nevertheless remained Sonia's own eyes, and not creations of Mlle Chanel or
Mme Viennot.

Even in the Romanisches Café people were bound to be struck
by the fact that Sonia Herz joined the circle solely on Zita's account.
They would have suspected a Lesbian courtship had Sonia's amours
not been the talk of the town, had they not known that at this very
moment she was having an affair with the banker Alfred Bumke, the
man who paid for her villa in the Grunewald, her clothes, and the
white car, together with the Negro chauffeur.

To begin with Zita found something uncanny about the interest
shown in her by the divorced wife of the speculator. As a matter of
fact, nobody knew whether she really was divorced: mysteries enveloped Sonia Herz like the scent of *N'aimez que moi*. Although some
of the strange woman's effulgenge fell upon her, Zita became shy and
reserved in her presence, either because Sonia could be no younger
than her mother, or because she was used to fighting for recognition,
and thus received presents with distrust. But the farther she moved
away from her childhood friends, and hence her mother, the less she
felt understood by her mother, the readier she became to grasp the
outstretched hand.

16

Sonia's car picked Zita up after the performance.

October rain was falling on the Kurfürstendamm. The wind whipped
the rain along, and the rain whipped along the dirt. The Kurfüsten-
damm was dead. The restaurants, cafés, and bars that had displaced
old business establishments during the last year looked like illuminated
doss-houses.

The Königsallee was gloomy. The villas seemed to have ducked
under the trees to get out of the rain. Little window-eyes peeped out
between the trees as though looking to see whether the rain had
stopped. The rain continued to fall. The wind whirled the falling leaves
along in front of it; they settled on the windscreen of the car, yellow
and wet, like dead butterflies.

Zita could see herself in the pane of glass between her and the
driver's seat as if it were a cinema screen and she a film heroine—
raincoat; black tailored suit; small, round hat with black curls peeping
out from underneath it; negligent posture; a white car in the night; a
mute chauffeur looking like a jazz saxophonist. Anxiety mingled with
her pride: she wasn't sure how the film was going to end; she was a

star without a scenario. She wanted to ask the chauffeur if it was much farther, but she didn't dare. In the light of the sparse street-lamps she saw his black neck; he was sitting stiffly, as though trying to hold the steering-wheel away from him.

The car turned off to the right, down an unlit side-street, then down a second. Something glittered silver through the trees. The house stood beside a hidden lake.

A maidservant in a black dress with a white cap opened the door. The house was warm, overheated. Zita took off her hat and raincoat and tidied her hair in front of a small rococo mirror. Was she the only guest? The comfortable warmth did nothing to allay her anxiety.

Sonia Herz kissed her on both cheeks. She was wearing a dress of gold brocade, simple from the waist up, with an open Chinese collar, but below wide, sumptuous, reaching down to the ground. A large cross, inlaid with stones, African native work, hung round her neck. Zita felt she had to apologize for her suit. "I always dress crazily at home," Sonia reassured her.

They were not alone, and yet Zita was the only guest. She was astonished by Herr Bumke's appearance. The only bankers she had seen were those in Dadaist drawings. Herr Bumke, too, resembled a drawing, but not a Dadaist one. He was fifty or fifty-five; Zita couldn't tell the age of men over forty. As he stood beside Sonia with his dark hair grey at the temples and his small moustache almost imperceptibly curled up at the ends, he looked like a drawing that had left the pages of a men's magazine to pay its respects to a drawing out of *Fashion*.

They had kept the meal waiting for Zita. Like the hall and lounge, the dining-room was decorated in the rococo style. Here, too, old rose was the dominant colour. Zita had the feeling of tripping along from powder-box to powder-box. Two different white wines were served, then champagne. Sonia only sipped at her glasses; Herr Bumke didn't drink. Apart from whisky, he said, he was forbidden all alcohol, yet he was an "alcoholic *voyeur*." Zita vaguely remembered having come across the expression in Freud.

A feeling of wellbeing and uneasiness rose simultaneously in Zita. She felt at home in the strange house, as though she had once lived there, in her forgotten childhood. Sonia and Herr Bumke were old friends. She nodded to them in recognition. But they also nodded to each other, as though two friends had met a third who was not in the secret. Whatever Zita said, Sonia cast a glance at Herr Bumke; she was demanding his approval. Herr Bumke nodded approvingly. It was as though the two of them were spreading out their wings over Zita—one wing each—as they all flew along together.

A second bottle of champagne, cooled on ice, stood in the lounge. Zita had drunk too much. She heard her own voice. Only when the other two were speaking did she hear the rain beating against the window-panes.

Alfred put on a dance record—*Always*, the current hit from America. Sonia sang in a husky voice, a fashionable voice.

Herr Bumke filled Zita's glass and watched how she put it to her lips. This time he explained what a *voyeur* was. Only recently he had been to an establishment for *voyeurs* in Paris. You sat at a little hole and looked into a room in which a man and a woman were making love. Or two women, if you preferred. Did the man and the woman, or the two women, do it for money? Perhaps not. He had watched an unsuspecting American woman and her gigolo—wonderful. Herr Bumke described it quite coolly as he sat in the armchair in his well-pressed suit. Only his small brown eyes watched Zita, as they had watched when she drank.

Zita felt hot and cold, cold and hot. Was it a matter of indifference to Sonia that Herr Bumke had been to an establishment for *voyeurs*—recently? Sonia was smoking a cigarette in a long meerschaum holder. She laughed. There were places like that in Berlin too. They could all three of them go to one together. Her laughter no longer sounded husky, as though in her excitement Sonia had forgotten to use her fashionable voice. The three of us, thought Zita. She had expected to find a large gathering at Sonia Herz's. Or else to be alone with her new friend. Her vanity was no longer flattered by the fact that the two of them kept making her the centre of attention. As though Sonia were saying, "I told you so"; as though Herr Bumke nodded, "Yes, you told me so." The car drove down the Königsallee, thought Zita. Where did it turn off? In thought she was standing out in the rain. In thought she was trying to find her way.

When Zita sat down Herr Bumke came and perched on the arm of her chair. He put his arm round her shoulder. "A delightful evening," he said, as though speaking of an evening that was past. His hands felt along the small hairs on the back of her neck, he stroked the back of her head. Sonia was bound to have seen. "Let's dance," said Zita. Herr Bumke rose at once, as polite as a pupil at a dancing-school. As they danced he held her a little to one side, as though to feel her breast better. "No brassière." He laughed. His knees moved along her thighs. Now Sonia is bound to get up and turn me out, thought Zita. Sonia beat time with her hands, long, narrow hands that were older than she.

Zita remembered Georg. She had laughed once in bed, she couldn't remember why. He had looked at her out of his immobile eyes and told her that laughter and sex were deadly enemies. Now she resolved to call the deadly enemy to her aid. She had drunk a great deal; she had no difficulty in laughing. She laughed senselessly. The song reminded her of something funny. The two of them looked at her. She didn't care if they thought she was behaving like a teenager.

Her laughter was infectious. Sonia told a funny story. Herr Bumke told another, with eyes that did not join in his laughter. Now Sonia was also drinking, quickly and in large quantities, as though to catch up on what she had missed throughout the evening. "Would you like to see Anita Berber?" she said. She stood up and danced. She danced alone, imitating the strip-dancer. Then *Jama, The Sink of Iniquity*, the rage of Berlin. And when Zita and Herr Bumke applauded she imitated Anita Berber again. She twisted her body violently. She had undone a few more buttons of her brocade blouse. When she bent forward her breasts showed, small, girlish breasts, rather whiter than

251

girls' breasts. The cross with the bright-coloured stones joined in the dance. Herr Bumke was no longer applauding. He was sitting beside Zita, his hand resting on her knee, a restless hand.

There were beads of sweat on Zita's forehead. "Take off your jacket," said Sonia. She went on dancing. Herr Bumke politely wanted to help Zita off with her jacket, but she shook him off. Sonia dropped into an armchair, breathing heavily. "Shall we dance?" asked Herr Bumke. "I'm too hot," said Zita.

She suddenly imagined she knew why Sonia had invited her. Alfred Bumke was looking for a new mistress. He was tired of Sonia. Perhaps Sonia already had a new lover. Zita's mood turned one of its somersaults. She wasn't averse to Herr Bumke. She wasn't averse to a villa in the Grunewald. Only she would furnish it differently, in a modern style. Her mother spoke contemptuously of do-gooders, just like Sonia. I'm merely doing good to myself, she would tell her mother. She would wear clothes of gold brocade; they would no longer hang beside Teréz's black clothes. She laughed. Now she really had thought of something funny—Teréz in the arms of the head-waiter. These two here in the lounge were funny too. They were childish and took her for a child.

"Let's drink to our friendship," said Sonia. Why not? She picked up her champagne-glass; he picked up his whisky-glass. They drank with linked arms. She felt his small teeth on her lips. "Can you lend me a blouse?" she asked Sonia. In a minute she would tell Sonia what she thought of her childish game.

Sonia took her into the bedroom. Zita stood stock-still, dumbfounded. It wasn't a rococo bedroom. In the centre stood a wide, low bed. All the walls were panelled with mirrors reaching up to the ceiling. The ceiling also consisted of mirrors. Zita was standing in a glass cube, surprised that she wasn't walking on mirrors too. When she looked up she was standing on her head. The furniture hung from the ceiling. It was a drunken picture, perhaps only a picture of her own drunkenness. The mirrors multiplied the figure in gold brocade, the figure in the black tailor-made costume. Whichever way Zita turned she saw only herself, as though she were blocking her own path. She walked towards herself from all sides. She forgot what she had wanted to say to Sonia. She thought of running away. The door had closed. She was no longer sure where the door was. Doors, cupboard-doors, all mirrors.

The figure in gold opened a cupboard-door. Many figures opened many doors. Zita hurried to the cupboard. Here was a way out, as though a window had been opened. Sonia took a blouse out of the cupboard and threw it on the bed.

Zita took off her jacket. Under it she wore only a slip, without a brassière. She bent down over the bed. All over the room slim figures bent down over the bed.

When she straightened up Herr Bumke had entered the room. He came across to the bed. From all sides male figures moved towards the bed. Herr Bumke sat down on the bed in front of Zita. She held

252

the blouse in front of her breasts. Herr Bumke embraced her knees, drew her towards him.

She didn't defend herself immediately. Her curiosity was still greater than her fear. She expected a cry, a protest, help. Sonia stood motionless beside the bed. "Don't be a child," she said. The old hand undid the last buttons of the gold blouse. "I'm hot too." The man's hands clutched at Zita's skirt.

She lashed out. Her fist caught him in the face. He fell back on the bed, but he didn't let go of her, he pulled her down with him. Her knees jabbed into his stomach. Her long fingernails tore his cheeks. He cried out and let go of her.

She quickly put on her jacket. The door, she thought. Herr Bumke had jumped to his feet. He looked like the bankers in the Dadaist pictures.

Zita didn't realize at first that the obscenities that were bubbling out of his mouth like the macaroni out of the mouth of the Dadaist glutton were not directed towards her. Then she understood. "Couldn't you find me anything better, you filthy bitch!" screamed Herr Bumke. "Any whore would have got me something better." He was standing in front of Sonia; the filth was being poured out over her. His curses were multiplied, as though the mirrors echoed. Each of the men, twenty times visible, was yelling. Zita looked up and still saw the scene in front of her, so that reality and its reflection became jumbled together. The bed was hanging feet down over the man's head. His head touched his own head, a circus act executed by a single acrobat. But Sonia stood there motionless, her hand on the cross she had been about to take from her neck. Now her reflection was wavering, as though on water into which a stone had been thrown. The man's hand had struck her in the face. "Just remember that before you bring me another such piece of dirt," he screamed. The blood ran out of the woman's nose. It flowed into the white powder, became a pink mush. Sonia didn't defend herself, didn't speak. Under the man's blows she fell on to the bed. Her pointed shoulders were twitching. They were poor, poor shoulders.

Zita had to overcome the temptation to go to Sonia's aid. She had found the door. She ran down a long corridor full of porcelain lamps and rococo pictures, ran through the lounge, into the hall, seized her hat and raincoat.

The silver lake glittered through the trees. The rain was friendly, a familiar sound. At the corner of the Königsallee stood two taxis. The second taxi-driver woke the first. He didn't want to do him out of a fare.

17

Not until the taxi drew up outside Georg's house did it dawn upon Zita that she couldn't visit him at this time of night. She hurried to a telephone kiosk. The telephone rang for a long time. At last he answered. What on earth possessed her to ring him at three in the morning? She must talk to him at once. All right, he said reluctantly, he would be at the front door in a few minutes.

He had thrown a trench-coat over his pyjamas. It was cold. He drew her into the dark entrance-hall.

He knew that she had been with Sonia. She told him everything, from the sumptuous supper to the punch in the face in the hall of mirrors. When she mentioned Sonia's bedroom he laughed softly.

For a short space of time there was silence, as if he were waiting for her to come to the point of her story at last.

"Is that what you woke me up for?"

"Isn't it enough?"

"What the devil do you expect me to do? Challenge Bumke to a duel?"

She asked herself why she had come. Georg would understand her, she had thought. He would understand that she couldn't simply go home this evening, that she had to tell him of her experience. She hadn't thought of a duel. She had expected him to take her in his arms.

"I expect you to tell me what it all means," she said.

"It means nothing because nothing happened. Herr Bumke likes to sleep with two women at the same time. Other people need cocaine. Or little girls, like Jennecke. Or maybe goats. Herr Bumke is sociable. Sonia gets him company. You must have given the two of them a fine surprise. . . ."

"You wouldn't have cared if I had gone to bed with the two of them? . . ."

"I should have cared if you had gone to bed with Herr Bumke alone. Or with Sonia. But it would have been time enough to tell me to-morrow."

"I'm going."

She was shivering. Georg seemed to her out of reach, as though she had lost him in the darkness.

He lit a cigarette.

"You're out of place in this world, Snow White," he said. He had called her Snow White from time to time ever since her first appearance at the Settee.

"Why should I be? . . ."

"Don't take it to heart. It wasn't meant to be offensive. You join in everything bravely, but you'll never belong to this world."

Was that the tenderness she had expected? To whom should she belong? To him, to Sonia Herz? Did those two belong to each other?

"You're like the airmen," he said. "We had a few zooming over our heads in Russia. They thought themselves pretty dashing. A few crashed. But if they didn't crash they flew back behind the lines. Had hot showers and hopped into bed, mostly not alone. They only experienced the war from up above. They didn't come in contact with the earth until they were dead. That's how you seem to me, Snow White. You make excursions into war, but you can go back. We're the infantry; we can't go back. You probably don't understand what I mean." He was talking as though explaining a stage part to her. "This Bumke . . . He can't help it. And Sonia? Men don't give her pleasure any more, nor women. Now she takes refuge in her own reflection. Or she can only stand men in the mirror—unreal. You can join in all that,

254

Zita, but you don't need it. You can fly back. I bet you were thinking about your mother the whole evening."

Zita leant against the wall. The wall smelt damp, like a damp cellar. Sonia's bedroom had smelt of *N'aimez que moi*.

"You're reproaching me with being healthy," she said.

"I'm not reproaching you with anything. And anyhow, I don't know whether you are healthy. Who is healthy? Probably Herr Bumke, banker by trade, is perfectly healthy. Anyway, he takes the pills he needs. He who doesn't belong to the times in which he lives regards the times as sick, and that again is healthy, because otherwise he would have to regard himself as sick. You don't mean 'healthy,' Snow White; you mean pure. But purity is superficial—a daily bath, a little soap. You have no idea how many pure dead are lying underground, their well-washed bodies decaying."

The insult inflicted on her by Sonia seemed to Zita slight by comparison with Georg's indifference. She could no longer understand why she had come to him in the first place, after the school rehearsal ten months ago. They had passed through the entrance-hall, the same entrance-hall. He had struck one match after the other; she had only seen his chin. She had known that some sort of experience awaited her at Sonia Herz's, and then she had fled to him horror-struck because she had indeed had an experience. But if she didn't belong with Georg, with whom did she belong? With her mother? With Teréz? She shuddered.

"You can't go back. Then where are you going?" she asked provocatively.

"Nowhere."

"That's an empty phrase." She remembered what Sonia had said.

His cigarette glowed yellow in the darkness.

"Let's go to bed," he said.

She didn't move.

He put his arm round her shoulders. Not till his body was close to her did she feel how cold it was.

"It's a pity you can't come up," he said.

"That wouldn't help." She freed herself from his arm. "Do you still love me?" she asked.

He threw away his cigarette. It smouldered slowly away on the stone floor.

"Of course I still love you," he said. "Only I don't feel too comfortable about it. I can't help thinking of the war again. We had a lieutenant; his name was Karl Sahne. He had just got married before it started. One day his wife got permission to visit him at the base. The crazy woman brought their kid with her. She smuggled Sahne Junior into the base, so that her father could see her. A shell hit the inn. They were in bed. All three were killed—Sahne, his wife, the kid. The child was in the middle. I sometimes have the feeling that I'm taking a child into the combat zone. You haven't lost anything at the front; nor at the base."

She began to find the darkness unendurable. She felt as if she were going blind. The alcohol went to her head again.

"Why didn't you stay with Sonia?" she asked.

"I don't know."

"But you belong together?"

"At least we can neither of us go back.'

"I'm going," she reiterated.

"You're offended."

"I'm not offended."

"You're always offended," he said irritably. "That's why you're no good at the Settee either. I've made something of more untalented women before now. They weren't gifted, but they were convinced."

"What of?" She felt her way to the door.

He seized her hand.

"What of?" It sounded like scorn. "You want to know everything. Where are you going? Do you belong together? What is conviction? There's nothing to know. We used to know it all. Kaiser and Fatherland, family and morality. And religion, of course. Only it was all wrong. Order was chaos. You need order. A nice little conviction, served up like a jam tart. Cut yourself a slice, Baroness. Pass it to me on a plate, Herr Busse. Explain it to me, Herr Busse. What does it all mean? What is Frau Herz after? What is Herr Bumke after?" He let go of her hand. "How should I know? Only dilettanti know everything. They have to know exactly what's going on. One step off the prescribed path, and they're in the ditch. There must be light all round them. When darkness falls they crawl under the pillows. Anything rather than see the darkness! I'm through with Sonia. Herr Bumke makes me sick. But they're genuine. They aren't dilettanti. If they go to hell they will console themselves with the thought that down there dilettanti are forbidden to peep through the keyhole."

He opened the front door.

It had stopped raining. The rain was dripping on to the asphalt from the roof. They could hear every drop.

"I can't take you to a taxi," he said. "Have you enough money?"

She remembered that she had given all the money she had to the previous taxi-driver.

He rummaged in his coat-pocket.

"Wait a moment," he said.

Now he's going up the stairs, she thought. He is quietly opening the door. In the hall there is a smell of apples. He is creeping through the bedroom with the pictures of the Divine Family and the landlord's family. The light is on in his room. She would never see the room again. Don't get sentimental. Nobody gets sentimental.

He thrust a few banknotes into her hand.

"You'll have got over it by to-morrow," he said.

She ran from the house.

18

She didn't appear at the Settee again. Nobody noticed the fact. She told her mother there was no part for her in the new programme. Her mother's disbelief didn't worry her. Georg rang her a few times, then the telephone fell silent.

She stared at the telephone, an evil black cat. Even the hand-crank reminded her of a cat's crooked tail. The clocks in the flat seemed to have stopped. She asked herself whether she longed for Georg or whether he had merely wounded her pride by accepting her decision so readily. It wasn't Georg; it wasn't pride. It was self-deception: she couldn't bear to be alone. The previous year she had merely lodged here; now she lived here, in the flat with the dead darlings. Officers who had been demoted must feel like this. Loneliness was debasement, solitude disgrace. When the telephone rang it was for her mother. The Baroness is at the Femina fashion house, she said. She gave the number; perhaps her mother had concealed the fact that she worked there. For a few minutes she felt satisfied. Then she was mocked again by the silence of the lurking beast. Of course the people who phoned her mother were men. What had her mother got? Greater beauty? Maybe, but she was no longer young. Youth was nothing, experience everything. Had her mother got 'sex appeal,' the mysterious power of attraction that emanated from the body, but whose seat in the body was impossible to locate? Herr Bumke had appreciated her own sex appeal. Astute reserve, experience of life, fine clothes? It was useless to reflect on it. One of the men asked who was on the telephone. "Baroness Rattowitz's chambermaid," she said. In the evening the man came to take her mother to the theatre. While Ilona was dressing he sat with Zita in the living-room. "Why did you pretend to be the chambermaid?" he asked. "Some one has to pretend to be the chambermaid," she replied. The man laughed. Next day flowers were delivered for Ilona. Georg had never sent her flowers. On the same floor there lived a retired judge who owned an English bulldog. The judge was ill; Zita took the dog for walks. She brought him into the flat. His name was Karo. She taught him to bark and bite at the word "Pick." Karo attacked the postman. When Ilona came home one evening with new shoes and stockings Zita whispered to the dog, "Pick!" It sniffed at Ilona's shoes, wagging its tail. In Ilona's presence men became doglike and dogs human.

She didn't answer the telephone any more. The bell rang shrilly through the flat. Six, seven, eight, counted Zita. The ninth ring was faint, a despondent sound. Zita looked at the instrument with malicious joy. At times she took the receiver off. The anguished engaged sign filled the room for hours on end. "The telephone was engaged all the time; it must have been out of order," Ilona said in the evening. "It wasn't out of order," replied Zita. "I was talking to friends."

Almost every day she considered going to the Romanisches Café. Once she even put on her hat and coat, then took them off again. She wouldn't capitulate to her loneliness. Without doubt some one else was sitting in her place, like the Constances beside the Hungarian film director. Who was Georg now calling Snow White or Sleeping Beauty or some other figure of fun?

One afternoon at the end of November she opened the telephone directory at the letter H. Herwarth, Herweger, Hery, Herz. She phoned

Sonia Herz. The bell rang three or four times. "Frau Herz's flat." She let the maid say "Who is there?" angrily several times. Then she rang off.

From that moment on she was like some one who has escaped from a mortal danger and thereafter sees the hitherto unnoticed beauties of life; like a convalescent for whom the most everyday things become wonders. She put on her prettiest dress, pocketed her savings, left a brief note for Ilona, and took a taxi to the cinema in the Kurfürsten-damm. She didn't know what she hoped to gain by this visit to the cinema; she merely felt that she now had the strength to offer herself to life again. Life would welcome its prodigal daughter with open arms.

As though they had been raised by alcohol or a deceptive drug, her spirits fell the moment she found herself standing outside the illuminated cinema. She tried to tell herself that this attack of weakness made no difference to her recovery. She had merely been upset by the thought of Teréz, who for months on end had gone to the cinema alone every Sunday. There was nothing sadder than women who went to the cinema alone. The miracle would take place, but not in the darkened auditorium where usherettes flitted to and fro like ugly glow-worms, the air smelt of disinfectant, and loving couples sought a miserable refuge.

She started to walk away, pushed her way through the crowd in this direction and that, avoiding two street corners. If any acquaintances happened to be leaving the Romanisches Café they would find her humiliatingly alone. She also avoided the corner of the side-street in which the Settee stood. The performance was in progress, but one of the performers would sometimes leave the establishment for a snack of eggs boiled in salt water, cutlets in aspic, or sausages. The two points attracted and repelled Zita; she wandered irresolutely to and fro between them.

She came to a stop in front of the window of a department store. The wax dummies stared at her with round wax eyes. They stood in the window like exclamation-marks with the dot at the top, holding in paralysed hands that dangled from the wrist price-tags bearing deleted and revised prices. Fifty thousand, a hundred thousand, two hundred thousand. Zita was seized by the desire to smash the window and take up a position among the dummies. Even wax dummies were company. Why couldn't she bear to be alone—why, why? Because she was empty, her mother had said. What could she live on? Nothing; she had nothing to fall back on. Wherever she reached for support she clutched at the void.

She turned away from the shop-window towards the Romanisches Café. Johann Schmidlapp was standing in front of her.

"What are you doing here?" he asked.

"I've been to the cinema. With friends," she added quickly.

"What did you see?"

Under the paper bosom a neon sign spelt out the title of an American film. She read it out from the neon sign.

The Settee's librettist was already walking along beside her.

"How about a glass of whisky?" he said.

258

She nodded. Was this the miracle she had been looking for?

19

In the KuFü cellar bar music was provided by three Negroes, the Triplets. The trumpeter, who also played other instruments, seemed to be trying to trumpet away the clouds of smoke. When they became increasingly dense he redoubled his efforts. There was only room for four or five couples on the dance-floor. All the tables were occupied. Eventually Zita and Schmidlapp were able to perch themselves on two high stools at the "American Bar."

She wondered why it had been Schmidlapp she had met, but she had no doubt that everything which happened to her that day must have a purpose. Of all Georg's friends Schmidlapp was the one she had seen least often. He was out of place at the Settee, out of place at the Romanisches Café, and most out of place of all in this bar. His dark suit was dapper, his white shirt spotless, his rimless spectacles glittered. With his fair hair and almost invisible eyebrows he looked an eternal model pupil. But in his eyes there burnt a perpetual, calm, flameless fire.

He was sorry she no longer performed at the Settee, he said. Not because of her talent as an actress; he couldn't judge that. Because of Georg. They had been friends for almost two years—since they had founded the Settee together.

"Do you intend to stay in the theatre?" he asked.

"I don't know."

"Then don't. Second-rate actors are third-rate."

"I should like to leave Berlin altogether."

The idea first crossed her mind as she uttered it, but she was glad to have found a scapegoat in the shape of a city.

"You're wrong," said Schmidlapp. "It's a wonderful city. You probably imagine that by leaving Berlin you can step out of your own skin. That's the reason so many people are on the move. The whole of America wouldn't be large enough to contain all the people who would like to step out of their own skins."

"Why do you think I want to step out of my own skin?"

Zita had swivelled her stool around and was watching the dancers. She crossed one leg over the other. It was a pity the female impersonator had interrupted their conversation. She was among people, the jazz band was playing, she had a whisky-glass in her hand, a man was sitting beside her, but it wasn't enough: she wanted to talk about herself, to test out her ideas on a stranger.

"Berlin isn't so bad," he said, also turning round. "It's true that Berliners go for singers like that, but they also fill the best theatres in the world. That gentleman there, under whose table the waiter is smuggling an empty champagne-bottle, is undoubtedly illiterate, but, on the other hand, we have never had so many great poets, and they have never been able to afford champagne. You must see Elisabeth Bergner—a tired light that outshines the footlights," he interjected. "It's less than ten years since they thundered against Lovis Corinth;

to-day they daren't smash the pictures of George Grosz and Otto Dix." He looked at her. "Stay in Berlin! Try to learn something. You get everything free nowadays, even knowledge. In the past only criminals forged money. Just think what possibilities forged money opens up to honest people."

She felt that she meant something to Schmidlapp, but she also felt in his interest an unselfishness she had not encountered before. Suddenly she thought she knew why the evening with Sonia Herz had set her in such a turmoil. She had wanted to be desirable and had become nothing but desirable. Her sex had broken away from her and run off on its own, like a sister who goes out into the world and becomes rich. She had stayed behind, poor, sick, and lonely. She felt as though Schmidlapp had picked up her poor, sick, lonely ego out of the gutter.

"I left school," she said. "Nearly a year ago. I don't regret it, but I can't find a place for myself anywhere else." She talked about her mother, Berény, Ilona's friends, the Romanisches Café, even Teréz. Schmidlapp's attentiveness spurred her on. "Georg was right. I don't know where I belong."

"Who says you should belong anywhere?" replied Schmidlapp. "If you listen like a good girl I'll tell you my story. My father's name won't mean anything to you, but he is still a famous man. For unknown reasons, or because we Germans are born suicides, as Erika Wegener will conclusively prove to you, he is still at large. General Johann von Schmidlapp—we have the same Christian name; he had to inflict that on me too—was Judge-Advocate-General. No single executioner ever dispatched so many people into the next world. I'm not speaking of murderers; at least they're individualists. One evening he asked me what I wanted for my birthday: my twenty-first was the following day. I asked for pardon for a deserter. I got a pair of cuff-links; the deserter was hanged." The female impersonator had gone back behind the bar; Schmidlapp ordered another whisky. "So home was no place for me. Besides, I married the same year. I was exempted from military service because I'm short-sighted, which is a paradox, because short-sighted people are just what they need at the front. My wife's father had a small farm in the Allgäu. We've got three children." He polished his glasses. "You can see how well I fit into the Settee. What else? The French, the most intelligent people in the world, coined the phrase *frère et cochon*. The same nation that died for *fraternité* sees swinishness in intimacy. Just because I was the son of General Von Schmidlapp did I have either to become like him or else a Bolshevik? Did I have to become a village simpleton because I married a country girl? Or do I have to sponge on my father-in-law because I write songs for the cabaret? Incidentally, I'm working on a play now."

No one had ever spoken to her like this before. When he mentioned his wife and three children she felt her throat go tight, not because she was touched by the domestic idyll, but because she was now certain that Johann Schmidlapp had quite simply invited her to a glases of whisky without any ulterior motive.

"I think this is the best evening I've had," said Zita. "I hadn't been to the cinema at all. . . ."

"I know," said Schmidlapp.

"How do you know?"

"You seemed to be looking for something."

"I hadn't been among people for four weeks."

"Mix with people, but don't look for groups. 'Avoid gatherings of people,' they say when an epidemic breaks out. Why only when there's an epidemic? Wickedness is no less infectious than smallpox. Our virtues are private property, our shortcomings the common denominator. And for heaven's sake don't try to be the way people see you. If you need advice come to me. Sometimes I shall be able to advise you, sometimes not. My consulting hours are from three to six in the Café Kranzler. I can only write in the café. I have a beautiful home and work in a café. Make sense of that. Or, rather, don't make sense of it. Things don't always have to make sense." She looked at him so gratefully that he couldn't help laughing. It struck her that this was the first time she had seen him laugh. His crystal-clear eyes were warm. "Don't rack your brains as to why you have found a friend. 'The best things in life are free,' as the Americans say."

Schmidlapp had turned to the band again.

"I thought I recognized that voice," he said.

The female impersonator had stepped down; in his place stood Hermann Müller, conducting the orchestra and singing *Tiger Rag* at the top of his voice. Every one seemed to know him. The customers at the bar shouted encouragement to him; the Negroes pretended to be guided by his conducting.

Müller turned round and acknowledged the applause. He caught sight of Zita and Schmidlapp and came towards them with arms outstretched.

"You stay on," Schmidlapp said to Zita, putting a few banknotes down on the bar. "Müller is bound to ask you to dance. I've been talking all the evening. Unfortunately I can't dance."

20

At three in the afternoon Ilona began to decorate the Christmas-tree. She was alone in the flat. She had bought a fine, big tree. It had cost a lot, but she still measured Christmas-trees by those of her childhood. The Kisnémet trees had been big. They had stood beside the grandfather-clock. The stationmaster had always decorated them himself.

Six parcels had arrived from Kisnémet the previous day—from the stationmaster and Margit for her and Teréz and Zita. To-day a letter had come, written on a foolscap sheet in his neat, flourishy writing. "Perhaps this is my last Christmas at the station," he had written. "I shall probably retire next year." He had first written "have to retire," then crossed out the words "have to" with two lines as straight as if drawn with a ruler. It was a gay letter, growing gayer and gayer towards the end, as though he had cheered himself up as he wrote. He didn't mention Lajos, although Ilona knew how much he suffered because his son was still living as an *émigré* in Vienna. "Margit and the children are coming over here," he wrote. "We shall think of you."

She hung a silver ball among the branches, a gilded nut, a red apple. She stepped back and looked at the tree with satisfaction. Her cheeks were glowing. The branches were regular and dense, the trunk invisible; it was a perfect tree of the kind children draw before Christmas.

Ilona sat down. For whom was she decorating the child's tree? For Teréz? They scarcely ever talked to each other nowadays. Teréz planned to marry in the spring. When Christmas was discussed she said nothing. Teréz had believed in Father Christmas longer than any of them; perhaps that was why she had lost her belief so completely. For Zita? Her mother's joy in Christmas must seem childish to the child. She had long ago announced that she would be going out after the distribution of the presents, soon after nine at the latest. "Hermann will be calling for me," she had said. Yesterday Georg, to-day Hermann. A small tree would have been sufficient thought Ilona. A ready-made tree from the pâtisserie for three adult women living alone.

She listened, but she could hear no church-bells. The street was silent. Not all silence was solemn. The workers in the optical factory had gone home.

Her strength left her. She sat where she was. There were still three hours to go. She had asked Zita not to come home before six. How childish was her desire to give the others a surprise, since they had no wish to be surprised!

Her eyes fell on the parcels. They lay everywhere, on the Biedermeier sofa, the commode, the chairs; parcels that had come by post, parcels in Christmas tissue-paper, sober and festive parcels. The presents for Zita and Teréz, carefully chosen in a moment of recklessness normally alien to her, were lost among the countless presents she had received herself. She hadn't opened a single parcel yet. In Kisnémet no parcels were opened till the candles had been lit.

Ilona felt ill at ease. The feeling crawled out to her from the parcels. Was she a child, to get so many presents? Was her daughter grown-up, that she had to be content with so few? When had the powerlessness begun in which she had lost Zita? She didn't want to explore the past. Then she had been young herself; it was all too easy to excuse her failure by her own youth. Now she was no longer young. Why had she allowed Zita to appear at the cabaret? She had never believed in her daughter's talents as an actress. On the day Zita went to the first rehearsal it was already too late: she had let go of the reins. Zita had no inkling that she knew everything, that she could guess everything she didn't know. The disappointment after the first performance; the quarrel with her first man; the vain search for friends; the weeks of silent brooding; now the hectic lust for life that was obviously bound up with this Hermann Müller, the shimmy-boy in the check jacket. She had waited for a word or a glance from Zita that called out for help. Why hadn't she spoken the first word herself? She didn't want to be severe for fear of losing the child altogether, and couldn't be understanding for fear Zita would mistake understanding for approval. Had she really let go of the reins? They had slipped from her hands. Was it because, at the very moment when she should have been living solely for her daughter, she had been thinking about her own life? The stationmaster would not have been proud of her.

She stood up. The room was filled with the scent of fir-trees, filled with a sweet disorder. It seemed to Ilona that she was decorating the tree for herself alone. Absent-mindedly, she attached the candles to the ends of the branches. Then she picked a few parcels from the floor and looked at them. A small, longish parcel bearing the label of a Berlin jeweller. Sender: Prince Taszilo Kontowski. A Cellophane box containing orchids. On the card the handwriting of the theatre critic Gottfried Esch. A large, shallow box from a fashion house with a very English Christmas-card attached to it, undoubtedly from Percy Nolan.

She piled all the boxes on top of the largest, carried them into her bedroom, and put them in the wardrobe. How poor her daughter was! The richness of her own life filled her with shame.

She quickly locked the wardrobe. The doorbell rang. As she slammed the wardrobe-door she recalled the cool morning on which she had buried Margit's wedding-presents by the railway embankment. Always she had been rich, and always she had been ashamed of her riches.

It was the postman bringing a parcel.

"Merry Christmas!" he said.

"Merry Christmas!" she said, and gave him a tip.

Her heart began to pound. The parcel was from Paris. *Par exprès*: presumably the sender had remembered at the last minute.

She opened it. It contained an antique mirror, entirely of gold, the finest goldsmith's work. On the wrapping was written in Zoltán's large, upright, vain letters: "As always, I shall be thinking of you. A merry Christmas and a very, very happy New Year, Zoltán."

She went back into the room and fixed a glittering angel to the tree. Couldn't she give Zita any of her happiness? Must she hide her riches?

21

Mother and daughter were sitting facing each other. It was seven. They were waiting for Teréz. Ilona had put on a black-silk afternoon dress; Zita was wearing her black tailor-made costume. The room was filled with a warm odour of Christmas. A big bowl of oranges, apples, and nuts stood on the table. It was hot, as though the owner of the block, who had been saving coal all winter, now wanted to make his tenant's a present of warmth. Ilona had tidied up the flat before Zita got home. The room looked virginal, innocent, expectant. The parcels lay carefully arranged on a white cloth under the Christmas-tree; to right and left Ilona's and Teréz's; in the centre Zita's, the most numerous. The Christmas-tree looked joyful and shy, like a bride at the altar. Angel's-hair and lametta glittered like a silver bridal-dress.

"Wherever has Teréz got to?" said Ilona.

"She's finding it difficult to say good-bye to her fiancé," commented Zita.

"She's going to see him at nine, anyway."

"Are you going to be all on your own to-night, Mummy?" asked Zita. She sounded dismayed.

Ilona nodded. She was smiling. Zita didn't realize that she had given her a Christmas present. It had occurred to her that her mother would be left alone.

"Are you going to Hermann's home?" she asked.

"Yes. Everything is shut. Besides, I want him to stay with his mother."

"I didn't know he had a mother."

Zita laughed. "Even Hermann has a mother. But I have to remind him. She's a proper Neukölln working woman. He's slightly ashamed of her. And yet everything good about him is inherited from her. Well, I'll soon put him right."

Ilona's heart went out to her daughter. Everything was different from what she had thought. Naturally everything was different, naturally. All at once it seemed to her perfectly natural that Zita should want to spend Christmas Eve with a strange man's mother. She had never known Zita. As though out of a mist in which Ilona had mistaken trees for people, meadows for chasms, the moon for mysterious lights, the figure of Zita came towards her, friendly and sympathetic.

"I'm glad," said Ilona. "You know—we could really be friends."

"But we are friends, Mummy."

It sounded cool, but Ilona took no notice of that.

"No, no, we're not," she said quickly. "We haven't been up to now. I'm sure it's my fault. I even know where I made the mistake. Teréz told me recently. She said I hadn't let you have a part in my life. She was a little unjust, no doubt. She didn't mention the fact that I have always tried to understand you. It's clear to me now that that isn't enough. You're a woman, like me. We ought to trust one another."

Zita picked up the silver nutcrackers. An hour ago this would have upset Ilona: one didn't disarrange the fruit-bowl; one didn't start cracking nuts before the presents had been distributed. Children did a great deal that one didn't do. It no longer upset her.

What attacks of sentimentality Mummy suffers from! thought Zita. It probably has to do with Christmas. Georg had taught her that sentiment and sentimentality were two different things, mutually hostile doubles. But in two hours Hermann would be calling for her. Why should she spoil her mother's Christmas mood?

"We just haven't got time for one another," she said.

"That's what I thought, too. But it's an excuse. If you like—I shall always make time for you. I tell you, it's my fault. I saw how miserable you were over Georg. I think I know exactly what happened."

"You can't possibly know."

Zita's distrust was aroused. She wants me to have a part in her life, she thought. But instead of talking about herself she's going to give me a lecture.

She will understand me only if I talk about myself, thought Ilona. "I too had queer ideas about love," she said. "I'll tell you about it some time." Her eyes fell on the parcels under the Christmas-tree. She was seized by a feverish excitement, like some one trying to make up for a great deal of lost time in a single hour. It had been a complete mistake to hide her presents. I'm growing old, she should have said, but I'm never alone. Men still spoil me, because I never throw down the gauntlet to them. It's not the presents that count—it's the tribute. But how was she to help Zita without holding herself up as an example, without rousing the child's envy? . . .

She had a sudden idea, and rose quickly to her feet.

"I have so many old friends," she said.

Let's hope she doesn't start boasting about her lovers, thought Zita. Let's hope she doesn't start writing out prescriptions no chemist can make up any more. Ether-drops, valerian, centaury, old-world remedies.

"They're still all my friends," Ilona went on. "It's because I have never wanted to be anything but a woman. I entrusted myself to their protection." She laughed. "Some one once said to me, 'The drowning man needs the straw, but curiously enough the straw also needs the drowning man.' Men are straws." All at once she became aware of her didactic tone. She must talk to Zita in her own language. A confidential, youthful tone, as frivolous as possible. "Perhaps you don't go about it the right way," she said.

Zita wanted to say that she had no intention of "going about anything the right way." She wanted to be herself, and if men didn't like her the way she was that was just too bad.

Ilona gave her no chance to speak. She hurried to the bedroom-door and there came to a stop.

"Can you keep a secret?"

"Certainly, Mummy."

Ilona didn't notice the bored tone.

"This afternoon a present came," she said, "that I want to keep secret from Teréz." She looked at the clock. It was past eight. "You know what a prude she still is. I haven't opened the parcel, but I'm sure it contains something beautiful. And I'm sure it will be something I shan't know what to do with."

She went into the bedroom and came back with the small, longish parcel, the present from Kontowski. As she caught sight of the sender's name again she removed the wrapping-paper before Zita could see it. Then she walked across to her daughter with the case in her hand and sat down beside her on the arm of the chair.

It was one of those velvet cases that positively radiate distinction and the admiration of wealthy men for beautiful women, the soft custodians of the glittering decorations awarded for services in time of peace. She still possessed many such witnesses; she had sold the jewels and kept the cases. Carefully she opened the case. Like all such cases, it had a quiet catch, a velvet catch.

The pearls lay in a graceful oval on wine-red velvet; a necklace, not too large but exquisite, pale-pink in colour, regularly spaced, narrowing down to a small diamond clasp.

"They will suit you magnificently," said Ilona, putting the pearls round her daughter's neck. "You must always close the safety-chain."

Zita had gone red in the face.

"Are they genuine?" she asked.

"Of course."

The girl ran to the mirror. Pearls from Kontowski, she thought. From Kontowski, again and again from Kontowski. Should she tell her mother she didn't want the pearls? One day she would be given pearls, or, better still, she would buy them for herself. Not pearls from her mother's lover, not from Kontowski. But that was also sentimentality. You took what you got. You didn't ask questions. Her mother hadn't asked questions either.

She had gone quite red in the face with happiness, thought Ilona. I'm trying to buy Zita passed through her head, but she succeeded in dismissing the thought. Her first pearls—she is happy, that's all.

"Are you really going to give them to me?" asked Zita. Joyful excitement quivered in her voice.

"Of course we'll tell Teréz they're artificial," laughed Ilona.

Zita embraced her mother. Then she looked at herself in the mirror again.

"Wherever has Teréz got to?" said Ilona.

22

The two women's uneasiness grew. Zita, to be sure, was convinced that Teréz had stayed with her fiancé, but she couldn't think why her aunt hadn't telephoned. She was afraid that Ilona wouldn't light the candles on the tree and would spoil her evening with Hermann. Ilona saw headlines in her mind's eye. Tragedy on Christmas Eve. She saw Teréz as she had seen her on the evening when she was expecting Zita. Teréz's face appeared to her like the faces of the dead that announce the approaching catastrophe in retrospect. Hermann Müller would come, she thought; she would have to celebrate Christmas with a stranger. "I shall go to a restaurant," she said. "All the restaurants are shut," replied Zita. It was almost nine. "Shall we light the candles?" asked Ilona. "I can go to a restaurant with Hermann later on and ring you up," said Zita with relief.

Ilona switched off the light and lit the candles. Through the green boughs she studied her daughter's face—a beautiful face, filled with the good restlessness of youth. The pearls encircled the slender neck. Ilona's worry became submerged in her happiness.

The candlelight made Ilona's features appear softer. She is still beautiful, thought Zita. She thought it proudly, without envy.

Ilona put her arm round Zita's shoulders. Thus nestling against each other, they stood in front of the tree.

Ilona switched on the light. For a few moments she hesitated, glanced at the door, at the telephone. Hermann would be here in a minute. She decided to open the parcels.

Ilona had spent more on presents for Zita than she could really afford. The sense of the worthlessness of money had not left her unaffected. New shoes, a handbag, a blouse, handkerchiefs, a travelling-clock. Zita was delighted with them all. She had bought her mother an evening handbag and a gold lamé stole. Zita had been reckless too, thought Ilona. She didn't even feel pained that the presents were unlovingly packed.

Ilona folded the wrapping-paper. Only Teréz's presents remained lying under the tree. The wax from a candle was dripping on them. Should she put out the candles that were slowly burning down?

The doorbell rang. Both of them hurried into the hall.

Hermann stood at the door. He was wearing a short grey coat with an opossum collar, like a landowner. His cheeks were red; he looked younger than Zita. In his hands, on which he wore padded gloves, he held a flower-pot, or, rather, a tree, a rubber tree, which towered above his head. As he put the tree down in front of Ilona he hurried to announce that he hadn't brought Zita's presents with him. The tree, of course, was for the Baroness. He picked it up again and carried it into the room. He also had another little thing, he said, rummaged in his coat-pocket, and pulled out a dozen electric plugs. "Don't laugh, Baroness," he said; "these aren't ordinary plugs; they shine in the dark —you'll see." He walked over to the switch, turned out the light, and looked for an electric point. They couldn't judge it properly, he said, because of the light from the candles. He was financing this invention and expected to make a fortune from it. Then he admired the tree, saying he had never seen a finer one. He also enthused about Zita's presents. At the sight of the pearl necklace he whistled through his teeth, which were rather protruding and wide apart, like a squirrel's. Ilona asked if he would like a vermouth or a cognac. A cognac, of course. "Your mother is waiting," said Zita. Ilona had the feeling that Zita was afraid Hermann might say or do something *gauche*. Yet she no longer found Hermann unpleasant—in fact, she thought him quite touching. Zita embraced her; Hermann kissed her hand.

She was alone. After putting out the candles she went into the kitchen and looked vaguely at the dish of cold meats. It wasn't worth making a Christmas roast. The kitchen clock showed half-past nine.

When she went into the hall the front door had just opened.

Teréz's appearance froze her to the spot. Her sister was as white as the wall behind her. Her face had become one with the wall, scarcely standing out from it, like the reliefs of pale Madonnas in churches. Only her nose was red; Teréz looked miserable and ludicrous. As she caught sight of Ilona her features changed. Everything in her face seemed to go down, like a curtain torn away by a clumsy hand and lying in a thousand folds on the ground.

Ilona stretched out her hand to her sister.

"Come," she said, "it's time to light the tree."

Teréz shook her head, pulled her arm away, and went towards her room. Ilona held her back. "What has happened?" she asked.

Teréz didn't answer, but hurried to her room as though running away from Ilona. Ilona followed her. Teréz sat down on the edge of the bed. Ilona helped her off with her coat. He sister let her take the coat off as though not noticing what she was doing.

"He's married," she said.

Ilona sat down beside her. She understood. There was no sense in asking questions.

Teréz didn't wait for a question, but started to speak. She told her story coherently and chronologically, as though reading out a newspaper report. She didn't cry; her lips didn't even twitch. It was no newspaper report she read out, but a sentence, a merciless sentence on herself. She had noticed days ago, she said, that Oskar was very evasive whenever she spoke to him about Christmas. In the end he agreed to meet her after nine. That afternoon, when they were all wishing one another "Merry Christmas" and the chairs were already upside down on the tables, he suddenly started making excuses. His mother had just arrived from Leipzig. He had forgotten that he had told her his mother had died long ago; every now and then he went to Leipzig to visit her grave. She let him go, determined to find out the truth. Another waiter gave her his address. Didn't she know his address already? No; he had always told her he only had a furnished room. Now Ilona asked herself where they had met in the past. Teréz put the question herself and answered it. She was prosecutor and accused. They had met in one-hour hotels. Just as she had previously described the restaurant, "Merry Christmas," and the upturned chairs, so she now described the one-hour hotels, emphasizing every detail as in indictments and verdicts. Most of the women who went to these hotels were prostitutes. While she was in the room with Oskar the occupants of the neighbouring rooms had changed three or four times—they could distinguish the different voices. Teréz didn't stop talking about the hotels till Ilona pressed her to. So she went after him, to Friedrichshain. The Christmas-tree in the porter's flat was decorated; she stood by the glass door. If she had knocked she would have found out everything at once. But the devil had got into her; she went up to the flat on the fourth floor. It was past six; she had been walking up and down outside the building for a long time. The flat had only a tiny hall; the living-room door was open, and so was the kitchen door. There were two children in the kitchen; one of them had opened the door, a girl of thirteen or fourteen. Her brother was eight or nine. They were waiting in the kitchen to be called for the distribution of presents. She described the children; the girl, in particular, looked like her father. Oskar and his wife were busy at the Christmas-tree. The woman was in the act of lighting the candles; Oskar was sitting on the floor putting the pieces of a Märklin construction-set together. "Märklin," she said; she even remembered the name. The bridge he had built collapsed as he jumped up.

At this point Teréz broke off her monotonous recitation; for a moment she was unable to speak. The worst thing had been his presence of mind. He introduced her to his wife. The cashier from the restaurant. He had forgotten to tell his wife; he had invited her; she came from Hungary and was alone in Berlin. He was so certain that he could make an accomplice of the girl he had deceived. Perhaps he might really have succeeded; she wasn't sure. Perhaps she would have spent Christmas Eve with them, in the family circle. The woman saved her from that. This wasn't the first time it had happened. Teréz

268

gathered from the flood of curses that was poured out over her.

"So she was the one you spent your Sundays with; she's the one you do overtime with," yelled the woman. No, Teréz hadn't answered. The children had come in from the kitchen. They weren't waiting any more for the Christ Child who was supposed to fly through the room; they gaped at the strange woman. Then they flung themselves on the presents; the distribution of presents began early in the head-waiter's home. The woman screamed; Teréz couldn't remember what she had screamed. She had clutched at the Christmas-tree with one hand, as if to throw it at Teréz. A few glass balls fell down, a few candles. Oskar tried to pacify his wife—only his wife. The children were sitting on the floor with their legs crossed. Teréz left.

Since then she had been wandering about the streets. She hadn't wanted to come home.

Now her face suddenly broke into movement. It looked like a railway station with hundreds of lines; a madman had pressed all the buttons at the same time; everything started to move all at once—the carriages, the signals, the points, the tracks. She still wasn't crying. "Throw me out! Throw me out!" she screamed, without saying why Ilona should throw her out. She blamed herself for coming home, for being too much of a coward to end her own life. Nothing that had happened to her seemed as terrible as her own cowardice. She apologized to Ilona as though it had all happened because the shadow had broken away from the body, because it had tried to become a body.

Ilona helped her to undress. Teréz let her do it passively, like a patient being taken to hospital after an accident. She peeled off her clothes, her thin underclothes.

Is it my fault that every one around me is so poor? thought Ilona

"Now put on your dressing-gown," she said. "We'll go into the other room and open your presents. Then we'll talk."

Teréz laid her head on Ilona's shoulder.

23

One cold, wet Saturday afternoon in the middle of January Ilona made up her mind to call on Dr Ginsburg.

He lived on the ground-floor in a prematurely aged house on the corner of the Hohenzollerndamm and the Fehrbelliner Platz. Dr Ginsburg had no shop; his flat also served as a shop. He had done his best to tone down the architectural splendour, so that Ilona couldn't help thinking of those house or church doors that are concealed by heavy velvet curtains when there has been a death. Dr Ginsburg, who guessed Ilona's thoughts, smiled. "I have tried to convert the cold splendour into a warm one; I hope I have at least succeeded in that."

She confirmed that he had succeeded wonderfully. The flat radiated a warmth such as its builders had never dreamed of. That was due to his trade, chuckled Dr Ginsburg. Ilona soon realized what he meant. In every room they passed through there hung, stood, or lay a dozen or more watches and clocks; almost all of them were going—ticking, striking, swinging, reassuring and trustworthy and monotonous. "I wind them all up every day," said Dr Ginsburg, "but I haven't set any of them since I got them; the important thing is that the clocks should go; it doesn't matter what time they show."

In the middle of the dining-room stood a large round table laid for three people, with precious old silver and Meissen porcelain that gleamed as it had gleamed in Kontowski's house. The heavy damask, the quantity of cutlery, the cut-glass bowls, suggested a menu sufficient for a big dinner, not a mere afternoon coffee-party. The smell of fresh pastry, of vanilla, icing-sugar, and nuts, drifted through the room. "I thought you would find it boring to spend a whole afternoon with an old man," explained Dr Ginsburg. "I've invited a friend I think you ought to meet. An unusual man. Only in his mid-forties and already a clock-lover. The publisher Stefan Herrdegen; perhaps you have heard of his name."

They sat down in a drawing-room that differed little from the other rooms, as though Samuel Ginsburg lived in a series of drawing-rooms. On the marble mantelpiece stood a gilt Empire clock—alabaster and gold in the shape of an urn; over Dr Ginsburg's head hung a Spanish clock from the year 1755 on whose chased face the figures were replaced by allegorical constellations; facing Ilona's chair stood a Swiss pendulum-clock from the mid-seventeenth century, an exact copy of the first pendulum-clock invented a little before that date by Jost Bürgis, as Dr Ginsburg proudly explained; in a glass case on the table lay watches made by the Paris master Romilly, Biedermeier watches, a Turkish chronometer, and a heavy gold watch supposed—"Supposed," said Dr Ginsburg—to have been worn by the Emperor Napoleon in the historic hour of the Moscow disaster.

Ilona, who was used to taking an interest in other people's interests, took up a phrase of Dr Ginsburg's.

"Only in his mid-forties and already a clock-lover," she said. "Does one have to be old in order to love clocks?"

"Certainly, my dear Baroness, certainly. Many derogatory things have been said and written about clocks, not least by Shakespeare. 'The time is out of joint: O cursèd spite, that ever I was born to set it right!'" he quoted. "What injustice is done to the cheerful clocks! They are our true consolers, because as they turn for ever in a circle they grow ceaselessly younger. They know nothing of the day's transience, they do not even distinguish between day and night. Perhaps you will understand what I mean when I tell you of a vision that returns to me from time to time in my dreams."

Ilona couldn't help smiling at his talkativeness. In the train from St Petersburg he had never spoken except when she had encouraged him to. Now he was her host and trying to entertain her.

"The world is ruled by a mutually hostile brother and sister," Dr Ginsburg continued. "The brother is hard, heartless, and sceptical and despises mankind. The sister is beneficent and indulgent and full of compassion for mankind. Prince Calendar and Princess Clock. I believe there is a calendar and a clock in each person's soul. The calendar warns us of transience; the clock reminds us of eternity. The

270

leaves of the calendar become fewer and fewer; we tremble as we see them vanish; the further the wind blows them away the more breathlessly we run after them. 'In vain you pursue me,' whispers Prince Calendar; 'all loss is final.' But then the clock speaks. 'Nothing passes away' she says; 'Nothing is final.' She ticks on; after twelve comes one, again and again. When Plato constructed his night-clock he wrote something to this effect: 'The earth, our nourisher, that rotates about the axis which is drawn through the All, makes her the guardian and begetter of day and night.' Guardian and begetter, a perfect description of my princess."

"A beautiful parable, Dr Ginsburg," laughed Ilona. "But I'm afraid your princess is a little deceiver. She keeps running through the same figures over and over again in order to make us forget that they are no longer the same hours."

Dr Ginsburg had no time to reply, because the door opened and the old housekeeper, whose vast proportions had caught Ilona's attention earlier, ushered in the second guest. Ilona had indeed heard his name before, since many new publications bore initials S.H., or, rather, a large H entwined by the smaller S, as a snake entwines a tree.

Stefan Herrdegen greeted Dr Ginsburg with a cordiality that at once made Ilona well disposed towards him. He was a good head taller than the tall art-dealer. The first thing Ilona noticed about him was his hair. He wore it rather too long, especially round the ears, behind which it was combed back not exactly untidily, but carelessly. The two strands thus combed back were white, not flecked with grey, but actually as white as snow, so that they contrasted with the thick black hair. A superficial observer might have thought this the head of an artist but neither the thin lips nor the steel-grey eyes were those of a dreamer; on the contrary, the whole man seemed to radiate a self-confidence that was neither vain nor arrogant, but merely reassuring, as though Stefan Herrdegen had acquired this self-confidence in order to pass it on to others. He created the impression of a man to whom one would like to apply for a job and whom none of his employees ever left.

Dr Ginsburg scarcely had time to introduce the publisher to Ilona. The housekeeper called them to coffee with the hint of a threat in her voice, as though she wouldn't tolerate its being allowed to get cold.

Ilona felt that Herrdegen, who was sitting opposite her, was studying her, neither shyly nor impudently, but rather as though he were searching his memory to see if he had met before. And although she was sure she had never met him, she too had the feeling that he was no stranger. Now he spoke to her, with a smile which, as though shining out from behind them, made his features look surprisingly carefree and youthful.

When the housekeeper appeared admonishingly in the doorway Dr Ginsburg remembered his duties as the host and encouraged his guests to help themselves; he also asked Ilona to pour out the coffee.

As she filled Herrdegen's cup from the Dresden-china pot her eyes met his again, and she blushed, for the first time for several years. He immediately turned his head towards Dr Ginsburg, who had begun to refresh the memory of his first meeting with Ilona. He did so with such

271

enthusiasm, so many flattering details concerning her composure and courage, that the suspicion arose in Ilona that her travelling-companion had not arranged the meeting with the publisher by chance, but had made up his mind, tactfully and tacitly, to play Destiny. The fact that she felt no resentment at this, but on the contrary an increasing gratitude, made her blush again.

They rose and returned to the drawing-room, which was two rooms away from the dining-room. On the way Herrdegen stopped in front of a clock that had just begun to strike: it showed one o'clock, although it was past five and the darkness of a January afternoon was sinking over the street outside.

"What kind of clock is that?" said Herrdegen. "I have always wanted to ask you about it, Dr Ginsburg."

The old man nodded with pleasure.

"I thought it would catch your attention," he commented. "It's a Black Forest clock from Russia. Isn't is curious? The Black Forest clocks embarked on their campaign of world conquest at the end of the eighteenth century; they were exported to places as far afield as China, always with little concessions to the national character. You can see it here: this cuckoo is a thoroughly Russian bird. It's odd, isn't it? I picked up this clock from a junk-dealer in Nizhni Novgorod; now, by many detours, it has come home again."

They sat down in the drawing-room, round a low, circular table, in extremely comfortable red-plush armchairs. Ilona thought to herself that she hadn't felt so cheerful for a long time. She was hardly surprised when Herrdegen said, "I warn you, Baroness, if you come here often you won't be able to escape the old wizard's magic spell. How many clocks and watches have you, Dr Ginsburg?"

"I've never counted them. A hundred, perhaps two hundred."

Herrdegen addressed Ilona again. "You see? There are a hundred or two hundred clocks and watches ticking in these rooms, and yet here more than anywhere else I have the feeling that time is standing still."

"Time, time," said Dr Ginsburg. "What is time, my dear Herrdegen? We use the word in so many ways that its meaning has become confused. 'I have no time,' people complain, complain more often nowadays than ever, doubtless meaning that they are subservient to the time they don't 'have.' 'In my time,' people say, as though they had a time all their own that belonged to no one else, but were now living in some one else's time, as though there were various times with various owners. But this time of their own might easily coincide with the 'time' of Napoleon or Kaiser Wilhelm, so that it belonged to them, as it were, but also to some one else more powerful than they, who presumably just lent it to them for their temporary use. 'My time is running out,' people say—a sad presumption, since time neither begins with our birth nor ends with our death. 'My time has come at last,' people say—a happy presumption; if in the previous case time was confused with a person's own life-span, now it is being confused with his own success in life. People talk about 'passing' the time—an extremely foolish expression, since we can neither pass the time nor stop it from passing us. Others, again, warn against 'wasting' time—an absurd phrase, since time is not a currency and retains its value whether we bustle about like a factory-owner or sit around like a Chinese monk." He looked round, then nodded to his clocks. "Even here time does not stand still." He turned to his guests again. "Whether we 'have time' or 'have no time'; whether we are approaching the grave or new life is stirring within us; whether we endure humiliation or flatter ourselves with success; whether we call upon the happy hour to tarry or try to put the unhappy one to flight; whether we pass, waste, use, or enjoy time—twenty-four hours remain twenty-four hours, day approaches night, night approaches day; the clock reminds us of the higher order with its strict regularity, its justice without exceptions; large or small, pocket-watch or grandfather-clock, of gold or of base metal, the clock, though made by human hands, is a continual reminder of God, a tiny house of God; its hands, it often seems to me, are the hands of God."

Ilona had listened attentively. At the same time she remembered that night in the frontier station between the Tsardom and the Monarchy; it no longer struck her as strange that Samuel Ginsburg had outlived both of them.

Herrdegen was leaning back smoking a cigarette.

"I wish I could follow you, Dr Ginsburg," he said. "Because of some books I am publishing I have had to study the theory of relativity a bit; it's on every one's tongue at the moment. But doesn't it say that in a moving system time passes so much the slower the faster this system moves in relation to a system at rest? If we think this idea through to its logical conclusion it is possible that time will one day be withdrawn from circulation, and the clock become a useless toy."

Dr Ginsburg leant forward. He no longer looked old and was visibly excited; in fact, there was something of the belligerency of the fighting-cock about him.

"You're right," he said. "Einstein has challenged God. That is the beginning of the struggle between the scientific and the believing man."

Ilona was surprised to find that she understood every word. She thought of Kontowski. She had learnt to listen, had grown richer every day, and perhaps had been thereby armed against the time of which the two men were speaking. She had no need to say much; understanding was mirrored in her eyes. Herrdegen was still watching her.

Dr Ginsburg sat down again. The conversation turned to more practical subjects, above all to devaluation, which was continuing unceasingly. It was approaching seven when Ilona realized that the last three hours had passed like a minute.

"Forgive me if I say that you have succeeded in 'shortening' time, Dr Ginsburg." She smiled.

Herrdegen looked at his watch.

"You're absolutely right," he said. "With all these clocks about one loses one's sense of time."

Two clocks began to strike, two birds in twittering conversation.

Herrdegen had risen at the same time as Ilona.

"May I take you home, Baroness?" he asked.

"Take the Baroness safely home," said Dr Ginsburg.

The little gold coins were glittering in his eyes.

273

24

A few days after meeting him in the Kufü-Bar, Zita had become Hermann Müller's mistress. She hadn't regretted it, still didn't regret it. She didn't ask herself whether she loved him; the tenderness she felt for him was new and made her happy. At times she thought she played the same part in his life that Georg had played in hers. Hermann looked up to her. His admiration had many sides, like a monument on which the single principal figure is surrounded by all sorts of adoring secondary figures round the base. He was proud of her title, and never failed to introduce her as "the Baroness Von Rattowitz." The superficial education she had quickly acquired appeared to him of vertiginous profundity. He gave way completely to her taste, even sacrificing his check jacket. Since his sudden rise he had always been ashamed of his mother, but, kindly as he was by nature, he had been even more ashamed of the humiliation she suffered through him. Since Zita treated the old woman politely—indeed, with great consideration—he now did the same, and with an easy conscience.

For her part, Zita had long felt the need to try her wings. Unaware that almost every one experiences the wish to beat his teacher, she felt a definite urge to shake off Georg's tutelage. Those who have grown up like to try out their strength on people who didn't know them when they were still small. Now she no longer played a minor part; she played all the leading parts. Moreover, she had never before possessed another person. Now Hermann was her property. Although she could do what she liked with this property, she handled it with care, as though to prove that she acted differently from her mother, who had been reckless with her possessions. She was too proud to despise what belonged to her. In one sphere alone was Hermann superior to her, but in this sphere his superiority was astonishing. More than once she had seen some one warn Hermann against a particular speculation, which was nevertheless successful. When Hermann warned a friend and the latter disregarded the warning he was ruined.

And Hermann was only twenty-two. She had no need to feel ashamed when she wanted to go dancing, when she was enthusiastic about a film, when she didn't utter a sensible remark for a whole evening.

He didn't annotate love with intellectual glosses. Not until she got to know Hermann did it dawn on her that with Georg she had never laughed.

With Hermann she could laugh about everything. When the tireless dancer entered a night-club the band immediately struck up his favourite songs. Since he had bought a little sports car, the country-side round Berlin was opened up to her. But the best thing was that Hermann always had time. He had no office, no tools; he only had instinct. He never left her alone.

25

That evening they had stayed at home. There were five of them in

Hermann's flat. She had known Sigmund Braun and Hugo Steinmetz for some considerable time; to-day these two had been joined by Paul von Oppel.

The whole evening Zita kept hoping Hermann's friends would leave. What she had begun to fear soon after Christmas had become a certainty during the last few days. She could no longer hide her pregnancy from Hermann.

Conversation revolved around business. The value of the mark had fallen to thirty thousand to the dollar; it would continue to fall. They would reckon in millions, in milliards. Hermann said so; he ought to know. They spoke of 'hard currencies' as of hard metals. Other currencies, Oppel asserted, would soon come tumbling down after the mark—the Austrian krone, the French franc. The secret was to run up debts, declared Braun. All agreed. The thing to do was to acquire capital goods—houses, antiques, stamp-collections, machine-parts, mines, estates, sugar, castles—to leave the purchase price outstanding and pay later in devalued currency. There was nothing much left to be had in Germany, of course, said Steinmetz. The peasants didn't even bring their produce to market any more; they preferred to let it rot. They must turn their attention to Austria, or, better still, to France.

Although it was warm in the room, she shivered. She sat up and reached for a cushion. Oppel, who was sitting near her, got there first and handed it to her. She thanked him with a smile and laid the cushion on her abdomen. Only now did she become aware that she had found Oppel's presence irksome the whole evening.

He was in his late twenties. He had dropped the noble 'Von' long ago; when introducing himself he mumbled his name as unintelligibly as possible. The private banking house of J. Oppel and Co. had celebrated its centenary the very year of Paul's birth. J. Oppel had died long ago; his grandchild, Felix von Oppel, now governed the bank in the Unter den Linden. Paul, the founder's great-grandson, was considered the black sheep of the family. His daring—indeed, reckless—speculations were discussed and admired in Hermann's circle; in the J. Oppel and Co. bank he was looked upon as a renegade, a traitor, if not a criminal. The condemnation of his family and the bank didn't worry Paul Oppel in the least; it spurred him on.

Zita knew all this, and yet she felt a violent aversion towards the dark-blond, rather too pretty, smartly dressed Paul von Oppel. Didn't he speak like a man trying to talk the language of the lower classes with his servant? Didn't he try too zealously to belong to the turbulent younger generation? She felt as a deserter would feel who had hardly run away when a second deserter popped up beside him, sharing the same fate and the same aims, and for that very reason a danger to the first one.

Why was she so preoccupied with Paul Oppel? She turned to the other two guests.

Sigmund Braun, the oldest of the group, was a Viennese, but spent a few days in Berlin every month. Hermann occasionally called him his master. People said Braun was a millionaire, and not merely in kronen or marks. He was a modest, silent man with yellowish skin and slit eyes that made him look almost Japanese or Chinese. He seemed always to keep close to the wall when he moved about, and when he started to speak he raised his hand in a curious way, as though warding off a blow. Ever since Zita had known him he had always worn the same black suit and black-silk tie, like some one who has no confidence in his own taste, but is clever enough to avoid a gaffe. He was said to have acquired his fortune during the war, and in a manner as contemptible as it was astonishing. It had one day occurred to the head of the Supply Department that the Monarchy was incapable of coping with the flood of Russian prisoners-of-war, and could not house, let alone feed, them. Thereupon little Braun paid a visit to a general in the War Ministry and declared that he would relieve the Imperial-Royal Ministry of responsibility for the Russians if they would simply pay him so much per head and leave the rest to him. A few months later hundreds of thousands of Russian P.O.W.'s were in Braun's care, and not one lacked a roof over his head or went short of food. To be sure, a few thousand died, but then people do die—that's nature. Who could blame Sigmund Braun for not reporting the death of every single Russian immediately; for prolonging their lives a little; for letting the money for the dead Russians' keep continue to flow into his safe?

Hermann had sat down beside Zita and was holding her hand. She had always been touched by the brash lad's almost feminine intuition. He could feel her malaise, though he could not dispel it.

She was not afraid of the discussion with Hermann. The thought that he might "abandon her to her shame," as the melodramas put it, barely entered her head. He would suggest marrying her.

That was what had worried her the whole evening. She had no wish to leave Hermann; she was certain that he would never leave her; but even the prospect of a new loneliness was more bearable than that of finality. Hermann Müller's mistress, as long as it brought them both happiness—yes; his wife—never! She had seen to it that old Frau Müller no longer ate in the kitchen; had taken her to the cinema two or three times; even felt a certain affection for her; but the mother of a lover was a different matter from a woman whom one would eventually have to call 'Mama.' You could explain to a lover that it wasn't done to eat fish with a knife; it was amusing to take the knife out of his hand, but, of course, only so long as the waiter knew you were not Frau Müller. Hermann was a trapeze-artist, a rope-dancer; if he were one day to fall from the 'big top' of his shady business deals she would minister to him, but that didn't mean she wanted to don tights herself and perform the 'leap of death' hand in hand with him. The picture that came into her mind reminded her of her dream with the springboards. There were high and low, easy and dangerous springboards, but springboards were not intended for setting up house on. But suppose she didn't marry Hermann! An illegitimate child? That was unthinkable. It was ridiculous to condemn an unmarried mother; such narrow-minded prejudice was a thing of the past. Only in her case, just her case, it was impossible. An abortion? Day after day the newspapers discussed the repeal of Paragraph 218. Only it hadn't been repealed yet. The paragraph-sign curled up in front of Zita like an embryo crouching in its mother's womb. Midwives carried out abortions; perhaps doctors did too. Who knew them? Their names weren't among the small ads in the newspapers; they were in police records, under the heading "Prosecutions." Zita turned pale. She had to shut her eyes and breathe deeply to overcome her nausea.

Oppel was the only one who noticed. Although he had been taking part in the conversation, he had kept his eyes on Zita all the time, as though demanding her approbation. He had been staring at the cushion she was clutching to her abdomen.

"I think we had better go," he said. "The Baroness isn't feeling well." He always said "the Baroness."

Hermann immediately stood up and almost rudely urged his guests to leave.

"You'll stay, won't you, darling?" he said.

Steinmetz boyishly shook hands. Braun bowed slightly from a little distance. Oppel kissed her hand.

"Forgive me if I don't see you out," Zita said to all three.

26

Hermann had taken off his jacket and opened the collar of his shirt. He was striding up and down the room. Zita's heart softened. He was in the habit of marching about the room like this while waiting for one of his inspirations. She trusted him.

He sat down beside her on the couch and took her in his arms. His red, boyish face was burning.

"My poor darling," he said. And in the same breath: "Of course we'll get married."

So that was the great idea, the inspiration.

"We can't get married," she said.

"Why not?"

"We're too young." It was all she could think of.

"Don't talk nonsense, Bunny Rabbit. I'm of age. If I can do business in millions I can marry."

"But I'm too young," she said. "Bunny Rabbit," the pet name he used when they were alone, irritated her.

"Eighteen isn't too young."

She freed herself from his embrace and leaned back against the cushions.

A monotonous noise broke the silence in the room. They looked at each other and knew at once where it came from. Frau Müller was snoring in the next room. Hermann cast a glance full of hatred at the door of his mother's bedroom.

"That's why you won't marry me," he said.

"Why?"

"Because of my mother."

"You know perfectly well . . ."

"I know perfectly well," he interrupted, "that we aren't good enough for you."

He spoke in the plural, in the name of his whole family. "After all, my father only repaired water-pipes. And W.C.'s too, in case you didn't know."

"Please, Hermann, . . ." she said weakly.

"I'm not a Communist, you know that. But I don't know what you lot are so proud of." Now he was addressing her whole family. "It's true we haven't a five-pointed coronet, or eight-pointed, or I don't know what. We make money. Five-figure money, or eight-figure money, that I know exactly. If I want to I can buy you all the clothes in the Femina fashion house." He narrowed his eyes. He could look malignant, like a malignant child or an old man. "In a year I shall be able to buy the whole of the Femina, your mother included."

She straightened up. "Leave Mother out of it!" she said.

He rose to his feet, sobered. Again he strode up and down the room. He came to a stop outside his mother's bedroom door.

"I'll murder her if she doesn't stop," he said.

He's stupid, thought Zita. He was trying to talk her into marrying him. Instead of veiling his face, he was baring it. She despised his stupidity.

"What do you intend to do?" he asked, as though pacified by his own roughness. "Do you intend to bring an illegitimate child into the world?"

"No."

He walked past the bar, slammed the door shut. The light went out. The bottles clinked together.

"So you don't want a child?"

"No."

"You don't want a child by me."

"I don't want a child at all."

She was speaking the truth. She didn't want to marry anyone. She didn't want a child. The very thought made her shudder. A meaningless coincidence couldn't ruin all her plans, put shackles on her, drive her happiness into a corner. The life that was proliferating within her wasn't a child; it was a disease. She thought she was hearing her death-sentence. Zita von Rattowitz, you are condemned to death. In eight months you will be executed. Till then you will wear a penitential dress. A maternity dress. After your death you may push a pram. Along the Kurfürstendamm. Past the Romanisches Café. Past the Settee. A year after your death you may have a second child. A third and a fourth. She seemed to see half a dozen children grinning at her out of a single pram. They had evil children's faces, old men's faces. Hermann's face. They clung to her breasts, drinking her life with the mother's milk.

Hermann's voice brought her to herself with a shock.

"That's impossible," he said. "Every woman wants a child. You don't want my child."

"I tell you I don't want a child at all." She clenched her teeth. "I've no wish to end my life."

He refused to be pacified. Everything he had put up with during the last few months, without knowing that he was suffering, now broke out. Why had his childhood memories had to go to the junk-shop?

278

What was wrong with his suits? The gentlemen who wore quiet suits had ragged shirts. Of course she was ashamed of him because he ate fish with a knife. What utter tripe! The knife didn't hurt the fish. He confused Molière with Maupassant. So what? The great writers had starved to death; so had those who knew their works by heart. They wouldn't let him join the tennis-club. Quite right. He could only play football with tennis-balls. On the other hand, he didn't go bankrupt; he wouldn't jump out of the window like the old banker Seelig, a member of the tennis-club. Did she think he hadn't noticed the glances between her and Paul von Oppel? Herr Von Oppel was an idiot, and if he started speculating with francs the J. Oppel and Co. bank might as well shut up shop. But of course she wouldn't mind having a child by Herr Oppel; she would marry Herr Oppel. Just as he had previously poured out all his anger over his mother, so he now poured out all his misery over Paul von Oppel.

She wanted to go, but she lay back and crossed her arms behind her head. At all costs don't answer, she thought. He was the father of her child. She didn't want to make things too easy for him. She had thought him kind and affectionate. He had been a dancing-partner, a playmate, a bedmate. As long as there was no obstacle in their way people danced around each other, played with each other, lay in bed with each other. Confronted by an obstacle, they pulled up sharp, looked at each other, hated each other.

He dropped on to the couch and buried his head in his hands.

"You want to have an abortion," he said.

"Yes," she said, without moving.

"Suppose it goes wrong?"

"It mustn't go wrong. It must be done by a first-rate doctor."

"First-rate doctors aren't abortionists."

"There are doctors who make their living by abortions."

"Aren't you frightened?" He looked at her.

"Of course I'm frightened."

He moved closer. She could feel that his anger had evaporated. He was waiting for her to stretch out her hand to him.

"It's my fault," he said.

"It's my fault too."

There was silence. The snuffling noise from the next room had stopped. She didn't look at him; she looked upward. From the Dadaist painting the man with the bishop's mitre, half in tails, half in uniform, grinned down at her. The worms were dangling from his mouth.

She hid her head in the cushions. She forgot that she had meant to remain hard. She sobbed.

He raised her up, covered her face with kisses.

"Just leave it to me," he said. "Everything will be all right, Bunny Rabbit."

27

Zita left her mother a note. She wouldn't be home all day; she would come back in the evening, but Ilona was not to wait up for her.

The doctor whom Hermann had traced through friends—there were doctors who specialized exclusively in interruptions of pregnancy—was called Dr Fritz Friedhoff. In spite of the double 'f' the name sounded much too like *Friedhof*, cemetery—a horrifying name for a doctor. But he was a doctor. A gynaecologist. An obstetrician. Zita had visited him two days earlier.

Hermann had fetched her soon after Ilona left for the fashion house. She sat down beside him in his small, low sports car, which he had christened "Dolly." "Bunny Rabbit" was sitting in "Dolly." Hermann liked pet names.

It had been snowing for several days already. Unemployed were clearing away the snow. They were in no hurry. They stood by the roadside gazing up at the grey sky, as though waiting for fresh work to fall. Where should it come from, if not from heaven? Work went slowly in the empty streets as the workmen shovelled the snow into heaps. The morning mist hadn't lifted. The trees in the Charlottenburger Chaussee had trunks but no tops. The street was like a forest of felled trees. A few cars had switched on their lights.

They didn't talk. Zita pressed her forehead to the window-pane. She was sure she was going to die. She had often felt life to be senseless, but it was not as senseless as death. And yet it was not a matter of indifference what you died for. Soldiers died for their country. Bullfighters died for their own fame. Old men died because their hour had come. Suicides died in order that their will should be done. Why did she have to die? To kill the unborn child—a double suicide. She wanted to kill the unborn child, and it was killing her. If she could at least have clung to life! People said the will to live overcame death. She didn't know whether she wanted to live: only she didn't want to die. Life passed indifferently by the cemetery-walls. Life didn't even look round at the graves. The graves were forgotten; there was no point in dying. She thought of her childhood. Her grandfather sat in the nursery playing with the electric train. She stood on a railway platform; her mother was going to St Petersburg. Kontowski had given her a dolls' house; it was a real castle with a dozen rooms. She started. At the hour of death the dying person's life was said to pass before his eyes. The hour was near. Should she persuade Hermann to turn back? She could wait a week, or maybe two. What difference would it make? Her mother had already noticed the morning sickness. Teréz had watched her with malicious, envious eyes. Why did Teréz still hesitate to go back to Kisnémet? Perhaps she was waiting for Zita to need her again. After her death Teréz would go back to Kisnémet. Then her mother would no longer have to wait for the catastrophe. It was not too late yet. She could become Frau Müller. Her mother would give her consent. "You're just made for one another." She could hear her mother's voice. A wave of cold ran down her spine.

"Courage, Bunny Rabbit," said Hermann.

The car had turned down a side-street leading out of the Alexanderplatz.

He helped her out, taking her carefully by the arm. He's afraid I might slip and break my leg, she thought. Or fall down and lose the child. The thought seemed so ludicrous that she freed herself from Hermann's grasp.

The door was opened by the doctor's wife. She was wearing a white overall and a snow-white blouse. Zita had noticed her at her first visit. She was young, pretty, and blonde, not more than twenty-five. Perhaps she and her husband had been students together. "We can only marry if I do abortions," her fiancé had said. Now she helped him with the birth of the unborn.

In the little consulting-room opening out of the flat everything had been arranged to reassure the patient. The consulting-room was spotlessly clean. It wasn't reassuring. The clean room looked too unreal in the dirty house, as though a gentleman-crook pursued by the police were hiding in the entrance-door of a slum house. Dr Friedhoff was not reassuring either. He couldn't have been over thirty, and might have been younger. He was fair, with blue eyes and a mouth and nose that were too small. His surgeon's gown was snow-white, starched, ironed. He looked like a waiter in a summertime restaurant or the assistant in a high-class delicatessen. His practical amiability impelled the customers to haste. Two hundred grammes of ham, one Edam cheese, a kilo of oranges—yes, madam, we'll deliver it all for you. Roast chicken with trimmings. The table is reserved. The next customer; the next guest, please.

Zita went weak at the knees. She sat down. The doctor's wife started to chat with her. She talked about the weather, very optimistically. The snow was going to stop at last. Zita tried to read from her demeanour whether she was nervous, whether she was frightened. She wasn't frightened. Or she was drowning her fear in the weather report.

The doctor took almost no notice of Zita; he talked to Hermann, admonishing him once again to extreme discretion. Why so much discretion if there was nothing to fear? He was only performing the operation—operation, he said again and again, as though seeking reassurance in the surgical term—because the lady's health made it imperative. The lady. Zita didn't know she had been ill. Who was Dr Friedhoff deceiving? He cleared his throat a few times, sought for words, and finally said something about payment in advance. By to-morrow the money would no longer be worth anything, he added quickly, as though it was the money, not the patient, that was in danger. He was really only acting out of philanthropy, as the gentleman knew very well. The gentleman. Yes, he knew very well, said Hermann. He put the fee, which had evidently been discussed in advance, down on the desk in front of Dr Friedhoff. A pile of paper towering up in front of the doctor—some hundred thousand marks. The doctor called his wife. He indicated that she should remove the money with a gesture of the hand that seemed to be an injunction to wipe the dust off his desk as quickly as possible. The cashier took the money and stowed it away in a steel cash-box. Dr Friedhoff looked at his watch, an overlarge, very outdoor wrist-watch. He expected the gentleman to call for the lady at six o'clock sharp, not earlier and not later. As he said, he couldn't keep her any longer under any circumstances. Now his voice sounded harsh. Zita heard this with relief; he no longer reminded her of a waiter or the assistant in a delicatessen.

As Hermann went up to Zita to say good-bye the door opened. A fair child's head appeared in the opening. His father shouted at him. He knew he was not allowed to come in here. Emil had taken his cannon, the boy complained; he wouldn't give it back. His mouth was twisted into a tearful grimace. Frau Friedhoff took the boy by the hand and led him out of the room. Her scolding could be heard through the open door.

"I'll be here on the stroke of six, Bunny Rabbit," said Hermann. He bent down as though to kiss Zita on the forehead, but he left without kissing her.

Frau Friedhoff came back.

"Emil is really impossible," she said to her husband.

"Please undress," said the doctor to Zita.

He went into the next room. A draught came through the door.

While Zita began to undress, the woman stood leaning on the table.

"Emil is the son of a colleague of my husband's," she said. "His wife is dead; the little fellow spends the whole day with us. He's impossible."

Zita now had nothing on but her petticoat. Although it was hot, she was freezing. Her body seemed to her thin, like a child's body.

"You can keep that on," said the woman.

She opened the door. Zita's teeth penetrated the flesh of her lower lip. I can still turn back, she thought. In a few minutes it will be too late. I shall sleep. These strangers will do what they like with me.

She saw a high white table, a glass case, gleaming instruments. On a small iron stove stood steaming water. The doctor turned his back to her and bent over the stove.

"Through here," said the woman.

I'm going to die, thought Zita.

28

On the stroke of six Hermann was there. His loud voice wounded her. It sounded even more hearty than usual. She could hear it from the next room. His voice seemed to be slapping the doctor on the back, so to speak. He was undoubtedly glad to have got it over. She had got it over.

They drove through the February evening in Hermann's car. "Dolly" was built for young people, for the summer.

It was cold. She felt every stone, the slightest unevenness in the asphalt. Hermann talked incessantly, as though paying Destiny in the coinage of many words.

Outside her house they sat for a long time in the car. He would have liked to carry her up the stairs, but that was impossible because of the porter. She gathered her strength for the endless climb.

Fortunately there was no one at home. She undressed and went to bed. Hermann was in a hurry. He crept away like a thief.

Half an hour later Teréz arrived. She no longer worked in the restaurant and had been job-hunting. She didn't feel well, said Zita, probably flu. Was her mother staying at home this evening? she asked.

Yes, for a change, replied Teréz. Zita heard this with relief. Ilona arrived soon afterwards. She took Zita's temperature. It wasn't a fever —ninety-nine point five, just a little above normal. Teréz made her some tea. Zita left it untouched. The nausea she had felt during her pregnancy returned. For a second the idea passed through her head that the doctor had merely taken the money, had tricked her.

She fell asleep early. The anaesthetic was still at work.

Again and again she woke up. The fairy-tale dreams had given place to nightmares. She was on her way to Dr Friedhoff before the 'operation.' "Dolly" stopped outside a cemetery. In the middle of the cemetery stood the doctor. He was wearing a white tail-coat.

When the bleeding began, around twelve, she thought she was still dreaming. Suddenly she was wide awake. She tried to remember Frau Friedhoff's advice, but it had slipped her mind. She got out of bed and groped her way with an effort to the bathroom. The bathroom-light dazzled her. Perhaps everything had to be like this; perhaps it was quite normal. She couldn't still her fear. The sweat broke out on her forehead.

The bleeding stopped for only half an hour. She lay awake in bed. The blood ran warm down her thighs. Teréz was asleep in the next bed, breathing regularly. Did she still dream of her head-waiter? Should she wake Teréz? She tried to sit up, but immediately sank back into her pillow. This was death. It had given her a few hours' grace, but it wasn't really grace. Death hadn't wanted to surprise her while she was asleep; she was to experience her death in full consciousness. What was she to say to Teréz? She would have to tell her the truth, but she couldn't. Teréz would have to ring a doctor, but on no account Dr Friedhoff. He was now lying in bed. He had his wife in his arms, in the same bed in which she herself had been lying a few minutes ago. Bed of sickness, bed of love. I've had the child aborted, she would have to tell Teréz. What child? Why hadn't she gone to Hermann? She couldn't have stayed all night with Hermann. He wouldn't come either, if she rang. Suppose things go wrong? he had said. When things go wrong you're alone. She said "Teréz!" but she said it so softly that the sleeping woman couldn't hear her. She was merely testing out her voice to see if she could speak. Her hand slipped down over her abdomen. Her hand became wet. Another minute, and she wouldn't be able to call out. In the morning they would find her dead in bed. She sat up.

She called out: "Mummy!"

Teréz was awake at once.

"Did you call me?" she asked.

"Mummy," Zita said weakly. "Call Mummy!"

Teréz switched the light on.

"Are you feverish?" she asked.

"I'm bleeding to death," said Zita.

Teréz, who was standing by the bed, pulled off the bedclothes.

"What's happened, Zita?"

"Call Mummy," Zita reiterated.

Teréz went away. She's offended, thought Zita. When she was a child

283

she had always called for Teréz. Now she wasn't a child any more. Only a woman could help her. She closed her eyes.

When she opened them she was looking into the eyes of her mother. She didn't believe she still had the strength to put her arms round her mother's neck.

"Mummy, help me," she said, twining her arms round her mother's neck.

Ilona laid Zita back against the pillow. A few words from Teréz and the sight of Zita had been enough: she knew what had happened. I would have helped her, she thought. Why doesn't she trust me?

"You must call a doctor," said Zita. "I've had an abortion."

She was about to say something else, but broke off because Teréz had entered the room. She stood at the foot of the bed in her long white nightdress.

Ilona turned round, gave her instructions, sent her into the bathroom.

"You must keep calm," she said to Zita. "Excitement is the worst possible thing. And please tell me the truth. Was it a midwife?"

"No, a doctor."

"What's his name?"

"You can't ring him."

Teréz had come back. She handed Ilona the things she had asked for, without a word, like old operating-theatre nurses who think they know everything better than the surgeon.

Ilona acted calmly. Her hand didn't tremble.

"Stay here," she said to Teréz. "I'll call a doctor."

She went into the living-room. Now that she was alone she had to hold on to a chair. Zita had been to a quack. The quack might have killed her. At the same time, she was certain that the worst had been averted. Zita had called her. Ilona had to save her child.

As she went to the telephone her thoughts cleared. What was the number of the paragraph one read about in the paper every day?

Women came before the court, were sent to prison. It was not enough to save her child's life. Dr Löffelholz was a stiff old gentleman. He would report the case. Dr Theobald. He was a charlatan himself. Whom should she telephone? She thought of Stefan Herrdegen with a feeling of security. Herrdegen would give her the name of a doctor. But there was not time to be lost. She had met Professor Westrup at Dr Markstein's. He was an amiable man and a famous surgeon. Her fingers flew through the telephone-book. She asked for the number and waited on tenterhooks. The telephone rang for a long time. Patience; after all, it was past midnight. At last a woman's voice answered. She was sorry, said the woman; the Professor was at a medical congress in Cologne.

Cologne. The name of the city rang some sort of a bell. She thought hard. Why was she trying to think what Cologne meant to her? Then she knew. There was a doctor who came from Cologne. And he was a man she could trust.

She didn't look for the card Dr Sales had given her. He must be in the telephone-directory. Why was the directory so large? Why were

there so many telephones in Berlin? There was his name. Sales, Dr
Franz, general practitioner. Dr Sales was a surgeon—was it the same
one? She didn't know the street. Where was it? Was it a long way
away? Why was the city so big? She asked for the number. Dr Sales
wil be at home, she thought. My God, let him be at home.

"Dr Sales."

She recognized his voice at once.

Ilona Rattowitz, she said." You must come at once. My daughter has
a haemorrhage."

"Do you know the reason?"

"Yes, but I can't tell you on the phone."

"Where do you live?"

She told him the street and the number.

"I hope I shall be able to get a taxi straight away," he said. "I'll be
there in half an hour at the most. . . ."

Naturally he was at home, she thought, naturally. He wouldn't have
been Dr Sales if he had let her down. She saw him in her mind's eye,
in his white surgeon's gown, in the Sant'Andrea field hospital. She
hadn't been to Sant'Andrea in vain.

"The doctor is already on the way," she said as she came back into
the bedroom.

Teréz got up from the bed, on which she had been sitting. She made
way for Ilona, as though to say, "You're Zita's mother; she called for
you; there's no place for me here."

Ilona sat down and took Zita's damp hand in her hands.

"You know, it's a doctor I was with during the war. He's the most
magnificent man I've ever met. You can rest easy; nothing more can
happen to you."

And she began to talk about Sant'Andrea. Once upon a time. . . .
It sounded like a fairy-tale.

29

At two in the morning Ilona and Dr Sales were still sitting facing
each other. The doctor had staunched the bleeding and given Zita
tablets. She was sleeping. Teréz had withdrawn. Dr Sales wanted to
stay till he could be sure the haemorrhage wouldn't start again.

Ilona had only once caught a fleeting glimpse of the doctor in civilian
clothes—when they met in the museum. In his correct, but rather
threadbare suit he looked even more massive than she remembered him.
She thought of Rodin's gigantic figures.

She had asked him about his life. His wife had died soon after the
war, of Spanish flu, which swept across the defeated countries like a
lackey clearing away what death had forgotten. His son was studying
medicine at the University of Freiburg. His daughter was a novice in a
Rhineland convent. He had moved from Cologne to Berlin and taken
over a friend's practice in Neukölln as a G.P. under the health service,
giving up his career as a surgeon. He spoke of himself coolly and
objectively; only when he referred to his daughter did a shadow fall
upon his face.

K

285

They had also talked about Ilona, cautiously retracing their steps to Sant'Andrea. Sales avoided mentioning Zoltán.

The longer he stayed the more worried Ilona became. When she telephoned him she had acted instinctively, forgetting the fanaticism by which this man was driven. He alone knew what he understood by duty. Could she be certain that he would not report the abortion, as his position demanded?

"Now that Zita's life is no longer in danger," she said cautiously, "what hurts me most is that she didn't confide in me."

"Why should our children confide in us?"

"Your daughter entered a convent; mine went to a quack—what a difference in our destinies!" she commented thoughtfully.

"My daughter has as little trust in me as Zita has in you. One has hurled herself into life early; the other has renounced it early—and both out of revolt."

"What can we do?"

"Nothing."

"But it's our fault, isn't it?"

"I might agree with you, but to take all the responsibility upon oneself is just as much an easy way out as to disclaim all responsibility. The excuse of modern youth is that they want to forget. But what is it they want to forget? What we have experienced. They lick their paws like wounded bitches; but it is we who are wounded, not they."

She could feel that she was getting nowhere along this path. Weariness covered her face with its heavy hand. She felt every finger; weariness closed her eyes and locked her mouth. Even the lamps under the yellow shades seemed to be emitting a weary light. She couldn't let Dr Sales go until he had promised to keep silent.

She still didn't dare to ask him outright. She therefore asked him whether he thought the doctor who had performed the operation was a quack. He hadn't made any actual technical mistake, Dr Sales replied; the bleeding had come about as the result of emotional shock and because Zita hadn't been able to stay with him for twenty-four hours.

"He's a child-murderer," he said. "That's enough for me. If he ever comes before the court the search for attenuating motives will start at once. It will all have to be sought, found, and explained—whether the explanations are valid or not. They will say he helped poor women, out of a social conscience. Or else the war made such an impression on him that he didn't want to supply the Kaiser, or the Republic, as the case may be, with any more soldiers." He ran his hand over his forehead. "Tell me, Ilona, have you ever heard anyone speak of a good or bad person during the last few years? Such descriptions are outmoded, positively looked down upon. This or that man is not 'good,' people say; he is merely helpful in order to satisfy his own vanity. Or he isn't 'bad'; he is merely trying to prove that he isn't soft. As though any of that mattered a jot! Communal life is not based upon motives, but upon deeds; it seems that what interests us now is not relationships between people, but isolated pieces of knowledge."

She had scarcely been listening to Dr Sales. Only now, when the tension had relaxed, did she become aware of what had happened. Her

286

daughter was eighteen. She had had two lovers, perhaps more. She had become pregnant and gone to a quack. She might have died. And she herself had done nothing to protect her child. Even Dr Sales might constitute a new danger to Zita. Was he just, or merely impatient? Was he moral, or merely inhuman?

She spoke as though to herself as she said, "Why did that have to happen to me?"

He looked up at her from below, leaning forward.

"What do you mean by that?"

She repeated her question, surprised that Dr Sales had heard her at all.

"Why, why?" he went on. "Why do the good suffer? Why do the evil triumph? Why does an innocent child die in the cradle? Why does a murderer escape punishment? Why does a girl in a disreputable house remain pure? Why did your child have to go off the rails?"

She hadn't the strength to embark on an argument with Dr Sales.

"Yes, why?" she repeated.

"I can't answer your question because I challenge your right to ask it. The question 'Why?' is for God to ask, not us. He asks why a human being acts thus and not otherwise. He alone has the right to judge not merely deeds, but also their motives. But if we ask why God acts in such and such a way we are presuming to be God's God."

Was the ex-priest trying to preach a sermon to her? She was grateful to him for helping Zita. All she wanted from him now was a promise to keep her secret.

"Why didn't you remain a priest, Dr Sales?" she said irritably.

"You already asked me that at Sant'Andrea."

"I'm asking it again. But this time I shall answer the question myself. In the time of the Inquisition you probably would have remained a priest."

He smiled for the first time.

"I believe you're right, and I'm not even offended by what you say. I should have no objection to torturing the celebrated inventor of wireless on the rack, because I believe he has overstepped the dividing-line between physics and metaphysics. It is only a step from conveying human voices through the ether, from impertinent human penetration of the atmosphere, to the antenna aimed at picking up the thoughts of God. From now on the final mysteries are at stake. In a few years' time human sympathies will be regulated by traffic-lights and love operated like a steam-engine. The age of technology? Not at all. That's past. This is the age in which technology encroaches upon theology. What about the Church? The devil sits in the microphone through which the Pope delivers his New Year message; consequently, what the Holy Father has to say is of no importance. The Church, which moves with the times, is straying away from God; it is already stretching out its hand for the tip."

Ilona was following his movements, and her anxiety was growing every minute. It was long past three. There was not a sound to be heard in the whole house. Zita was asleep in the next room. Ilona made up her mind not to go to the fashion house next morning, but to sit at Zita's bedside. She felt the shame Zita would feel as though it were her own. But the doctor to whom she had turned in her need talked and talked. He was acting like a bad pastor who, at the very last moment, tries to entice a dying man away from another church. Her gratitude was swamped by her exhaustion. Had Dr Sales changed so much? Had the times, which he was attacking, so altered him?

"Zita seems to be asleep," she said, controlling herself with an effort. He came to a stop in front of her.

"Yes," he said, "I'm going."

She rose to her feet. Now they were standing facing each other. He looked into her eyes.

"I know," he said. "You're sorry you called me, Ilona, sorry you called the Inquisitor to the sick-bed. You're afraid I might report your daughter to the police. I ought to. Zita isn't the first this false doctor has set free from an unwanted child; nor is she the last. You can sleep peacefully; I shan't do so. Don't ask me why not. I don't know myself." He took his black bag, made sure he hadn't forgotten anything, closed it as slowly and carefully as if he were locking up his conscience in it along with the little bottles, tubes, and instruments. "She should stay in bed," he said. "I shall look in to-morrow."

He left so quickly that she only had a chance to say "Thank you" again as he went out through the door of the flat.

She went into Zita's bedroom on tiptoe. A ray of light shone into the room through the crack of the door. Zita's face was calm. Ilona bent down over the bed. For the first time that night Ilona remembered that she had carried this child under her heart.

30

During the next few months Zita lived a double life, perhaps a triple one.

A few days after the night of his visit Zita had to go and see Dr Sales in his surgery. She went several times without having to. Then informed Ilona that she was going to work as Dr Sales's receptionist, and would perhaps work for her school certificate and study medicine.

Zita knew misery only from revolutionary tales told round the table at the Romanisches Café; she had even taken the lower-middle-class milieu of her own district of Berlin for poverty. Sitting for the first time in Dr Sales's overfilled waiting-room, she was suddenly confronted with misery like an accused man being confronted by unexpected witnesses for the prosecution. The encounter was all the more startling because the witnesses were dumb, dumb and sick. The demonstrating proletarians whom she now met frequently in the inner city of Berlin bore their misery before them like a billowing banner. They demanded justice, not pity. The mute witnesses in Dr Sales's waiting-room aroused only pity. Hunger did not scream from their faces; it had laid itself to sleep on their features like a beggar in a doss-house.

This was the beginning of Zita's contact with poverty. She took advantage of her second and third visit to Dr Sales to ask if she could

288

help him. He agreed, although he certainly guessed that her pity for the poor scarcely sprang from that simple goodness which, he believed, was beyond analysis. Zita, surprised and delighted by his 'yes,' did not rack her brains as to the reason for her sudden interest in the sick and oppressed; didn't ask herself why she was especially moved by the fate of poor children. The punishment offered itself to her feeling of guilt.

Her relationship to the doctor, whom she assumed to have saved her not merely from death, but also from prison, was far more complicated. The presence of Franz Sales cast a spell over her just as it had once cast a spell over her mother. He worked day and night to relieve the sufferings of the poor; gave away the medicaments he received; neglected to present his accounts; but he seemed to feel no compassion for the people to whom he did good. "I cure the pneumonia of the poor, not their poverty," he once said to Zita. In continual contact with Dr Sales's poor she soon learnt that in the poor quarter of Neukölln he had the reputation of being a saint, and was encircled by the halo of Biblical legend; but he evidently knew nothing about his saintly repute, or considered it preposterous. Zita wondered whether he noticed that she beautified the waiting-room and surgery with potted plants, fresh flowers, and all sorts of little things; if he noticed he never showed it. Once only did she learn that he was satisfied with her, and then by a roundabout way. One evening Ilona told her that, being worried because Zita was late coming home from Neukölln, she had rung Dr Sales, who had said, "She is needed too much for anything to happen to her." Zita blushed.

Nevertheless she led a double life. When she came home, often not until eight or nine, after a difficult journey by tram and bus, she felt not merely the need but also the right to resume her previous life at the point where it had been interrupted by her visit to Dr Friedhoff. Hermann seemed to be even more slavishly subservient to her than before. His business affairs were flourishing. He read her every wish from her eyes, loaded her with attentions and presents.

Zita felt no contradiction between her two lives. When she met people she held forth as an expert on all social questions. She calculated for the benefit of young men about town how many useful things could have been done for the price of a night's drinking, irritated them into argument, and, once they had revealed their bad conscience, went home satisfied. She didn't ask herself what purpose was served by converting speculators, gigolos, stockbrokers, café geniuses, and night-club heroes, nor to what creed they were to be converted, nor what false creed they were to renounce; but she had no doubt about her missionary task. On the other hand, she was convinced that she was peculiarly well fitted to bring a little light into poverty-stricken homes: how could she have done so if she had become as grey as these houses? If ever she felt any doubt she was quickly confirmed in her beliefs by her own strength: she never became tired, either at work after a night spent dancing, or while dancing after a hard day's work.

Meanwhile Zita's second life was also divided. The weeks in which she had been ordered continence were long past, but she had not resumed her love relationship with Hermann. In vain he assured her that the accident couldn't happen again: fear of another pregnancy was stronger than his impetuous wooing. At times she admitted that it was not fear alone. Easy as she found the transition from the poor district of Neukölln to the West End night-clubs, she found it impossible to throw a bridge from Dr Sales's surgery to Hermann's bedroom. Where once her mother had bent over her bed, Dr Sales now stood between her and passion. Her body remembered what had happened to it longer than she did. Her heart spoke so loudly because her body was silent; her soul was so susceptible because her body was dulled; her whole being was so wide awake because her body was asleep. She had no idea what must inevitably happen when her body woke up, came to life, began to speak and, like a vanished brother suddenly reappearing, demanded its birthright, and threw the peace of her soul into turmoil.

31

At the end of May 1923, on a Sunday, Zita and her mother took Teréz to the station.

Teréz had looked for a job in vain, either because it was genuinely difficult for an unskilled worker to find work or because she didn't really want to find work. She hadn't got over her disappointment—got over it all the less because she had been so weak as to open her heart to Ilona on Christmas Eve. Up to that evening she had not been happy in the home of the three women, nor had she been unhappy, for at least she possessed a moral superiority over the other two that satisfied her vanity. Now that she felt she had lost this too she suffered unspeakably from the comparison with Ilona and Zita which she kept on making, as though under a compulsion. She reached the decision to run away from the tormenting and lost competition during the night in which Zita's cry for help woke her from sleep. To the feeling of being superfluous was added the aversion she felt for Ilona's behaviour. Instead of punishing Zita—though Teréz had no idea what form this punishment ought to have taken—Ilona sat on her daughter's bed for hours at a stretch, becoming, so it seemed to Teréz, her child's accomplice after the event. Teréz couldn't even guess what the two of them were hatching up, but it was enough for her that Zita's freedom remained uncurtailed; that she adopted a profession that was beyond all possibility of surveillance; finally, that the 'criminal,' as Teréz called him in her own mind, even appeared in the three women's home. In her indignation Teréz managed to conceal from herself the fact that in reality the unfolding friendship between mother and daughter had robbed her of her last hope of winning Zita back. The news that the stationmaster was planning to retire and move into new quarters provided a welcome opportunity. Throughout her whole youth Teréz had suffered from the stationmaster's love for Ilona; now he should see which of his daughters he could rely upon in his old age. Ilona and Zita would also find out, when she was far away, what they had possessed in her. The women of forty was filled with the sweet bitterness of a child picturing its parents weeping over its coffin.

The May afternoon was unusually hot. It was not the steam from the locomotives that increased the heat in the station: it seemed as though it were the heat that was making the locomotives steam. Many tourists were returning home from their Sunday outings, forcing their way with rucksacks on their backs through the ranks of the staider travellers. Arrival and departure rubbed together like opposite poles, producing sparks. The smells of leather, smoke, and sweat mingled. The heat increased Teréz's irritability. Again and again she hunted for her travel-pass and ticket; was certain she wouldn't find the porter; insisted they had left home far too late. In her black dress, with a small dark straw hat on her head, her overcoat over her arm, and a suitcase in her hand, she walked between the two women wearing light spring costumes. The almost twenty years she had been living in big cities seemed to have swirled by her without leaving a trace.

She's already in Kisnémet, thought Ilona. It was better for Teréz. At home she would soon grow calm. In time she would turn her one and only sin from a terrible memory into a bitter one, from a bitter memory into a sweet one. She would go on talking for a long time of the Sodom and Gomorrah into which she had been swept. The people in the village would believe her. She ought really to write to the stationmaster, thought Ilona, telling him to believe everything Teréz said, or to act as though he did. Teréz's homecoming must not prove a disappointment too. Ilona was overcome by a great feeling of tenderness towards her sister. Nineteen years ago she had called Teréz. Why must the people to whom one felt the most grateful irritate one the most? Why was compassion offensive? Why did railway stations, places of punctuality, insistently say that one was too late? Ilona remembered the rainy autumn day on which she had travelled back from Vienna to St Petersburg. In her mind's eye she saw a blue dot that grew smaller and smaller, as though it were not the train that was moving out of the station, but the station that was being drawn away from her along the tracks.

That time Teréz had gone away with Zita; she had gazed out of the window after them. Now the circle was complete. Teréz was going away; she was staying behind with her child. It was too late to hold Teréz back, just as then it had been too late to stay. Not till you saw the railway-tracks did you realize what distance meant: the tracks didn't lie still on the ground; they ran away. The station clock, the hurrying people, the shunting locomotives, the timetables, the countless notice-boards—everything seemed to be repeating the two little words "too late, too late, too late".

Zita's heart too had contracted. Teréz was leaving her. Now her wish would be fulfilled: she would have her room to herself. She had called out for her mother, but it had been Teréz in the next bed who had woken up. She didn't like to think about her childhood, but she didn't want to lose it. It seemed to her as though Teréz had shut up her own childhood in her trunks along with her countless old-maidish odds and ends, every one of which she had packed. Nothing about

291

Teréz had irritated her as much as her aunt's obstinate memory. Of course you came running to me when that happened. It was a good thing I was there. I bandaged your kness. I brought you home in good time. All that had been very annoying and very true. And all my thanks was to turn her clothes out of my cupboard, thought Zita. The clothes had lain as though in a coffin. The porter was carrying four coffins; Teréz had another in her hand.

The luggage wasn't lost. The window-seat in a first-class compartment, which Ilona had reserved for her sister, was still free, although Teréz had insisted up to the last moment that it would have been taken long ago, and that she would have to stand in the corridor all night.

Then Ilona and Zita were standing by the train under Teréz's window. The fat gentleman was leaning out, saying good-bye to another fat gentleman standing beside Ilona and Zita. They shook hands; their hands were like two sausages hanging side by side. "Tell Kunisch not to be silly and turn down Czech kronen," said the man up above. "Kunisch knows what he's doing," said the man down below. Teréz could barely squeeze her head through the window; she was standing half bent over her seat; her hat had slipped sideways.

The train moved off. Ilona stayed where she was. Zita took a few steps alongside the train. Teréz had taken out her handkerchief and was waving. The fat man was waving too. In the steam that was rising from the undercarriage of the coach his handkerchief looked like a little white flag hanging from a thick flagpole.

When Zita returned to Ilona she noticed at once that her mother was in a hurry to get out of the station. She could feel that Ilona's haste had nothing to do with the farewell to Teréz. She was hurrying like an adult trying to get a child away from the scene of a bloody accident. If she had not behaved in this odd way Zita might not have realized that her mother had seen something which she wanted to hide from her.

A dirty little local train, the disreputable brother of the express, had come in on a parallel track. Homecoming trippers were streaming towards the barrier, bringing a touch of the springtime in woods and meadows to the city. Wild-flowers were peeping out from their rucksacks in surprise at the throng, flowers which to-morrow would be withering away in the windows of suburban homes or on office desks.

Hermann walked past the two women, wearing a town suit that Zita herself had chosen for him. He hadn't arrived with the train; he had been waiting for it. He had his arm round a girl's waist. She was rather taller than he, very blonde, very slim, dressed in a white blouse and a brightly coloured skirt. When she turned her head towards him they could see her pink cheeks and white teeth.

Ilona put her arm round her daughter's waist with a protective gesture.

Zita stopped in her tracks and turned round towards the train that had just left.

"She may be a relative from the country," said Ilona.

32

It wasn't until months after her visit to Dr Ginsburg that Ilona became aware how much her life had changed. She still worked in the fashion house; helped women to hide their figures; translated Parisian *chic* into Berlin *Schmiss*; but she felt no more weariness, as though the day only began in the evening. She spent almost every evening with Stefan Herrdegen.

She compared him with other men in the way women, far more than men, do test their feelings by comparisons. Feri was still the father of her child, transfigured by time, but also unreal, like one's own youth, which, heaven knows, might be some one else's. The memory of the time she had spent with Kontowski was more alive than the man around whom the memory revolved. She loved Stefan Herrdegen when she ceased seeing herself with the eyes of Zoltán. She had always made herself beautiful for the absent man, as though he might suddenly appear. She had worn her hair in the style he liked, longer than fashion permitted. Now she had her hair cut short, even if not so short as most women wore it. Blue was Herrdegen's favourite colour: she ordered a blue costume and a blue dress from the Femina fashion house. Since Stefan had poked fun at the *garçonne* fashion popularized by Victor Margueritte's salacious novel of that name, she reached a feminine compromise with the boyish clothes of the day. When she gained applause for an intelligent or witty comment, when she discovered that short skirts showed her long legs to advantage, when people paid her compliments, she thought of Stefan. In her youth she had read a great deal, but her education was full of gaps. Herrdegen published chiefly *belles lettres*; his firm financed a literary periodical. Ilona threw herself into the reading of modern authors with the zeal of a schoolgirl before an exam. She imposed reserve on herself in the literary conversations conducted in Herrdegen's house, but became daily more familiar with the topics discussed. Her innate or acquired ability to listen enabled her in a few months to grasp the technical, and even the financial, aspects of publishing, so that her sparing expressions of opinion astounded Herrdegen more and more.

She was more concerned with Herrdegen himself than with his interests; her real study was the man.

He was the son of the founder of the firm, Stefan Herrdegen the Elder. "My father," he was in the habit of saying, "gave me his Christian name so that the firm's monogram shouldn't have to be changed." The founder, the son of a small Berlin chemist, had acquired the family's now considerable fortune; the firm owed its outstanding reputation to the son. The father had played safe by concentrating on school-books and specialist publications. At first he regarded his son's publishing plans with the distrust of a man whose son sets out to make a fortune at poker. "I'd rather make the poets a present," he commented. "It's cheaper than publishing their books." In reality old Herrdegen was not opposed to poets; he was merely opposed to losing money. When "S.H." began to do incomprehensibly well under the son he retired to the scientific department of the firm, which now barely paid its way. "An honourable publisher is bound to lose money on a certain percentage of his books," he commented with wry humour; in the past his son had run the "luxury department"; now he was doing it. This was in any case only a manner of speaking, since in actual fact Stefan Herrdegen the Elder could afford any luxury he liked. As a young man he had married Eleanora Levy, the only daughter of the wealthy Frankfurt banker Wilhelm Levy. Up to his death in the First World War old Herrdegen was under the thumb of the enchantingly beautiful Jewess, whose salon was the intellectual centre of pre-war Berlin. Even now, when she was closer to eighty than seventy, Eleanora was surrounded by an aura of beauty, wit, and elegance. Stefan, her only son, loved the Frankfurt banker's daughter with an exclusive, domineering love. She had opposed his marriage to Yvonne Rochemont, the daughter of a French publisher, with blind disregard for her son's feelings. When the marriage turned out successful none the less, the old woman was left with only the two-edged satisfaction that it produced no children. In 1916, when Stefan was at the front, the daughter-in-law had a serious accident, and for two years was confined to her bed, paralysed. Fate now enabled old Frau Herrdegen to ease her conscience by demonstrations of love, the immoderacy of which recalled her previous cruelty. After fifteen years of marriage Yvonne died in 1918, a day before Stefan came home. He was then forty-three. In the post-war period, with its shortage of men, he became one of the most sought-after bachelors in Berlin; not by chance, as Ilona soon realized, for he possessed that feminine power of intuitive understanding which turns effeminate men into homosexuals and virile men into the favourites of women. If he remained unmarried this was no longer under the influence of his mother, whom—in this respect foolish—he held responsible for his wife's death, and who now, however right she might be, was always in his eyes wrong. He felt for the dead woman a posthumous love that brooked no rival and coloured his whole relationship to women: since on the one hand he only forgave himself relations with whores, and on the other avoided whores, he regarded women who succumbed to him as whores. These women were not clever, as Ilona quickly discovered. Either they carried on a hopeless war against the dead woman, or they tried to imitate a woman they didn't know, or they allowed themselves to be frightened away by the memories that surrounded Stefan Herrdegen like a bodyguard.

Ilona too was unable at first to escape the impression of entering a house that was a museum to a single person. The publisher's spacious villa in the Grunewald was in any case reminiscent of a museum because of its richness, the prudent good taste of its furnishings, and the coldness which these elements produced in combination. The drawing-room took its tone from a famous painting by Velazquez; with its ebony bookcases and an eighteenth-century globe, the panelled library looked like a Faustian study; the dining-room had the austere grace of a baroque refectory. But it was impossible to escape from the presence of Yvonne Herrdegen. In the lounge there hung a portrait of the anaemic, already other-worldly-looking woman by a celebrated English painter; on the piano and desk stood silver-framed photographs of her;

it was impossible to touch a piece of cutlery, unfold a table-napkin, or open almost any book without coming upon the initials Y.R.H.

It was probably not so much Ilona's intelligence as her robust instinct that caused her to avoid battle with the dead woman. The dead were dead; ghosts neither terrifying nor touching—there weren't any. After a very short time the photographs of the dead woman meant no more and no less to Ilona than the portrait of the Infanta by the Spanish master or a still-life by "Flower" Bruegel. She hadn't known the dead woman. When Stefan talked about her she listened patiently, but without any exaggerated attentiveness. She neither forced her way to her altar, nor did she attempt to take her place. She did not try to prove to Stefan that she was like her or different from her. There was no room in a man's heart for two living women; but since one of them was dead, it was sufficient if the living woman did not bring the dead one back to life.

Alongside a robust instinct, Ilona possessed patience, a virtue she had learnt. She had seen Herrdegen for the first time in January. It was now the beginning of June. They met almost every day, but Herrdegen had never spoken of love. She had been to his house at least a dozen times, and had played the part of hostess at large and small parties, but he had never once invited her by herself. She waited for him to find the path to her through the tangled undergrowth of his feelings. It never occurred to her that she was spinning a web round him. Men know best about everything. About happiness they know nothing. Women who teach men to find happiness are only doing what is incumbent upon them.

33

The discussion between Zita and Hermann had been stormy, but, like a duel fought in masks, it left no scar behind.

Hermann had immediately admitted his relationship with the pretty typist he had met at the station—indeed, he almost boasted of it. He still loved Zita, loved her as much as on the very first day, but after all he was hardly more than twenty and not "made of wood," as he put it. It was true that there could be eroticism without love, but there could be no love without eroticism, he emphasized; the aphorism wasn't his, but he was none the less convinced of its wisdom. Zita inwardly agreed with him. When she had refused herself to him she had left him. Since she had left him, he couldn't be unfaithful to her.

Just as she had compared her second love with her first, so she compared her second disappointment with her first. She succeeded in despising Hermann because he was able to live without her; indeed, she felt slightly sorry for him.

When Paul Oppel rang her and invited her to the theatre, when she began to go out with him frequently, she couldn't help thinking of Georg's theory that you could "work out who the next man in a woman's life would be": he was generally marked by those characteristics which the woman had missed in the "man before." She was flattered to be seen out with Paul. The jazz musicians in the night-clubs

295

didn't know him, but he was treated all the more politely by the head-waiters in smart restaurants. He had a high black Buick that smelt of good leather. Not only were his own clothes discreetly aristocratic; he also knew about women's fashions. When he talked about money he did so like a politician or a strategist. Thus, when he said "France must be conquered," he meant the collapse of the French currency.

She revelled in Hermann's wretchedness, but she suffered herself. Paul had a past with which she felt she had to compete. He had lived for two years with Zdenka, a beautiful Yugoslav woman of about thirty who was said to sweep men off their feet. She had left Paul and married an elderly industrialist. That also spoke in her favour. Zita was convinced that Paul still wanted to arouse Zdenka's jealousy: why else did he continually frequent places where he was bound to run into her? Would Paul go back to Zdenka if she called him? It was inconceivable that she should not call him.

Zita competed with the unknown woman. How did a woman sweep men off their feet? When she woke during the night she pictured Paul and Zdenka in the most obscene embraces. She made up her mind that next time she would prove herself an expert in love. And although she then left herself to his guidance, all her thoughts revolved around sex. She often had to sit down in the middle of her work for Dr Sales because she was overcome by mental images of past or future nights. The word 'subservient' was now very fashionable in conversation; it was thought to rhyme with love as moon had once rhymed with June. Paul had been subservient to Zdenka; he must become subservient to her. By leaving nothing untried that might whip up his passion she drove her own so hard she could barely keep up with it. The question of whether she loved him would have seemed to her childish. Her body had long since answered all the questions she could ask.

34

Paul Oppel's week-end cottage stood on the very banks of the Wannsee.

The July night was hot. The water smelt of fading flowers. The moon drew silver railway-lines on the water; they disappeared into dark tunnels which the night arched over the lake.

Paul and Zita had put on their bathing-wraps and run a few hundred yards along the beach. They only let go of each other in order to throw off their bathing-wraps. Then they stood naked, facing one another at a little distance, as though afraid of losing sight of each other.

A woman can love a man just as passionately as she is loved, Zita knew. But before she became Paul's mistress she had believed that only a man could be in love with shapes and movements. When she now looked at the naked man she saw nothing absurd in comparing him to a bronze statue. She admired his beauty, and at the same time felt herself to be a sorceress who did not need to touch, but only to look at, the statue in order to breathe life into it. We are perfect, she thought.

We love each other because we are perfect. She felt no shame, because she was able to love with happy eyes.

He drew her to him. She pretended to resist—a game they had often played in tacit agreement. They wrestled and hurt each other, till Zita no longer knew whether it was the pain she gave or the pain she received that whipped up her pleasure.

After they had made love they ran hand in hand into the water. The cool water didn't calm Zita. She could still feel Paul's hands on her breast, her knees, her back.

In the week-end cottage Paul had put a bottle of wine on ice. While he was fetching the wine and glasses she put a record on the gramophone. *Always*, sang the American tenor. "Always." Whenever she asked Paul whether it was for always he replied, "Always—with three l's," a recurring phrase from the coda of their love. A phrase like that would never have occurred to Hermann. Georg would have thought it sloppy. Georg simply couldn't distinguish between slop and feeling. She sat down on the little wooden veranda in her bathing-wrap, lit two cigarettes at the same time, and put one of them in his mouth: she had seen this in a film. Only the person who is not in love is afraid of sentimentality.

He sat down opposite her at the little bamboo table and crossed one leg over the other.

"It's terrible having to take you home," he said.

"Later . . . ," she said.

They had come out to the Wannsee the previous afternoon. Now it was Sunday, almost midnight; the new week was beginning. To-morrow morning she would be back in Dr Sales's surgery. She could smell the odour of sweat, medicine, the mortar of suburban walls. During the months with Hermann Mondays had been easy. She had sought justification and found it with Dr Sales. Her love for Paul needed no justification.

"I have to go to Vienna on Thursday," he said. "Can't you come with me?"

"You know that's impossible."

"Because of Dr Sales?"

"Because of my mother."

She was seized with fright. It was the Sunday-midnight feeling. She would see Paul during the week, too, but they would never be alone. Could he go a week without a woman? She was thinking of Zdenka.

He filled her glass. She had drunk hurriedly, and emptied the new glass equally hurriedly. The open bathing-wrap lay loosely round her shoulders. His nakedness was all the more exciting because he himself seemed unaware of it.

She stood up, went indoors, and put on a record, a shimmy. They danced. She remembered the first time they had danced together. There had been hundreds of people around them, but she had felt his body just as she felt it to-day, when he was almost naked.

"These Sundays are unendurable," he said.

"I know."

"It's senseless, our having to separate."

297

"I should like never to go home again."

He stopped the gramophone. They sat down. Voices reached them from the distance. They seemed to be coming out of the water. Waves were splashing against the bank.

He laughed softly. "What would your mother say if I turned up with a bunch of flowers to-morrow and asked for your hand in marriage?"

Little beads of sweat broke out on her forehead. What he had just put into words was something she had scarcely dared to think. They would marry. She would stop working for Dr Sales. She had only served him out of gratitude. Her debt was paid off. She would no longer have to lie awake wondering whether Zdenka had called Paul. They would go home together every night and share the same bed. Marriage did not necessarily have to become habit. She was a match for all the Zdenkas in the world. There wouldn't be any more Mondays.

She tried to laugh. "And what about me? Aren't you going to ask me?"

"I herewith request your hand in marriage."

She looked at him across the table. If he asked her to marry him to-morrow there was no need for her to go home to-day.

"When did you think of that?" she asked.

"I think it was when I first saw you lying on Hermann's couch."

"Wasn't it only when Zdenka married?"

"Perhaps. But that makes no difference. We often find happiness by a roundabout route."

"Are you sure you no longer love her?"

"We didn't belong together any more than you and Hermann."

She thought of Schmidlapp. He insisted that people didn't have to belong together; it was enough if they loved each other. Schmidlapp was wrong. Paul hadn't married Zdenka.

"When I saw you at Hermann's," Paul continued, "I knew at once that we belonged together. We have both finished with the world from which we sprang. But, thank God, we also despise Hermann Müller and his sort."

She looked at the naked man and thought of her mother. Her mother's horror became almost a physical pleasure for her. She was sorry she couldn't tell her that Paul Oppel had asked her to marry him just at this moment. "We're not children, Mummy," she would have said. "We aren't tottering blindly into marriage as you did. We know one another. We have put one another to the test. We didn't leave our compatability to chance. We dare to put everything into words. We don't hypocritically pretend that what happens in the bedroom is of no importance. We have fought one another, torn one another to shreds, but what bliss to know that we have only to touch one another to forget everything! You've nothing to fear, Mummy."

He rose, took her head in his hands, and kissed her eyelids.

They went indoors.

He helped her out of her bathing-wrap. She felt the warmth of his body on her back.

The moon had long since set when they made their way back to Berlin.

35

Ilona and Herrdegen had dined at an open-air restaurant. It was about ten. He asked if she wouldn't like to drink a glass of wine at his house.

They were sitting in the garden behind the house. Light shone on the terrace through the arched door of the lounge, but Stefan had placed the basket-chairs on the lawn. It was dark, and there was a heavy scent of elderberry flowers. The bushes were invisible; the scent seemed to be rising from the ground. The sky was like a big black apron from which thousands of tiny diamonds would at any moment fall upon the earth. Of recent years Ilona had always grown melancholy in summer-time, as though spring and summer no longer belonged to her, as though only half the year belonged to her. Now she dared to look summer in the eye again.

She had told Stefan about her daughter's engagement. She had seen Paul Oppel only two or three times and knew very little about him. The great love? Perhaps. Until a few months ago, she said, Zita had told her nothing about herself. Until the night when she had had to call Dr Sales—but she said nothing about that to Herrdegen. Now they had come closer together; she almost believed that Zita trusted her. It wasn't the daughters' fault that their mothers didn't understand them. Until a little while ago Zita had wanted to study medicine. Before that she had appeared in a cabaret. Now she was interested in the stock exchange. "It's all terribly amateurish," said Ilona. "As though these young women were continually going about looking for themselves. They have lost their vocation and are frenziedly seeking a substitute." What vocation? Their vocation as women, of course. They learnt everything, and everything only half. They were experienced and ignorant, acute of hearing and blind. Zita had talked about her marriage like a mature woman talking about her third or fourth. She herself had felt inexperienced by comparison with Zita, and hence younger than her daughter. "What is the meaning of this fear of one's own youth? Is youth still filled with the fear of being asked to die?" The fear of death outlives death itself. Enjoyment is the only certainty, a certainty that comes to an end with the enjoyment. And why Paul Oppel? He undoubtedly had a good name, good manners, a good appearance. "But he radiates a hectic restlessness, like some one who can do nothing without regretting it. He is probably one of those much admired men of action who are proud of acting without thinking. What is the reason for such a choice? Is there any reason? I'm afraid he will hurt himself and her."

He knew Paul Oppel slightly, commented Stefan, but he had known his father, Felix von Oppel, for many years. He tried to recall his meeting with Paul, but he had paid no attention to the young man. "Perhaps they will invite us together some time," he said. "I should like to form an opinion."

Ilona thanked him. Then she fell silent. This was the first time she had been in Stefan's house alone. She shouldn't have talked about her daughter. She was thirty-seven and not only a mother. The summer night of Baden came into her mind. Summer 1914. The whole garrison had been seeking shelter. The two-horse cab had stopped outside the Krainerhütte. What madness she had been capable of, what self-forgetfulness! Now she was talking about her daughter's lovers, about Zita's engagement.

Stefan had moved his basket-chair closer to hers. His hand was on the back of her chair. She loved this hand, in which Stefan's whole nature seemed to be contained. From the wrist to the fingers it was broad, masculine, traversed by thick veins; but the fingers were long, thin, delicate; it was a protective hand, a hand in need of protection. Her hand was also lying on the back of the basket-chair. Her hand was an autonomous living creature; it longed for another living creature.

At last he broke the silence.

"We are rare people, Ilona," he said. "Rare because we are mature. Not old, I mean, only mature. To be mature without being old is the great blessing. Or so I thought till now. But there are moments in which maturity becomes more of a burden than you can guess. For months I have been trying to tell you how much I love you. Love seems to possess a language that one forgets with every day of added maturity. Youth has no need to translate its feelings: feelings and language are one to the young. I look for the dictionary and can't find it. An eighteen-year-old could not feel any different from the way I have been feeling since the day I met you in our friend Ginsburg's clock museum. But can I speak like an eighteen-year-old? And what will happen if I try to translate my feelings into a mature language? They will become unintelligible. The mature man seems to be faced with a choice between the ludicrous and the prosaic."

He laid his hand on her hand.

"The young people you were talking about just now," he said, "have become so destitute of fantasy in this fantastic world that they have to put love to the test. Their adventures cheat them of the true adventure. What kind of feelings must they have if they fear them like some repulsive disease?" He stopped. "I have decided in favour of prosiness and am about to make myself ridiculous. I want to ask you if you will become my wife."

She had to take a grip on herself in order not to cry out. Her thoughts went far back to the spring of 1904 at Sopron. Then she had talked about marriage with Feri. Marcsa was singing outside the room, his boots were creaking, the paraffin-lamp was smoking. Nothing had changed. Of course nothing had changed. She still believed that a woman's highest happiness was to bear the name of the man she loved; still believed that habit and repetition were the servants of love, not its enemies; still believed that the shared day reached completion in the shared night. Her heart was beating so violently because, as often happens at moments of happiness, she was overcome by an anxiety that she might lose what she had just gained. Only the person devoid of happiness was devoid of anxiety. Did he really not know that she loved him? Did he really not know how much passion there was in this passionless hour?

She turned to him.

"I'm happy, Stefan," she said.

"Does that mean that you are willing to marry me?"

She laughed. "Did you doubt it?"

"Yes," he said.

She stroked his hair, his face.

"I want to marry you, but I can't at present," she said.

"Because of Zita?"

"Also because of Zita. But that's not the real reason. You know too little about my life."

She began to speak of her life. He knew about Kontowski, about Zoltán. She had rarely mentioned Feri, and had avoided discussing Rattowitz altogether. He had heard that she was divorced and had not given the matter much thought. Now she told him everything—about Feri's death, about the Prince's visit, about her wedding to the ageing Baron.

"I haven't heard anything of him for the last eighteen months," she concluded. "Eighteen months ago he sent me flowers on my birthday. He was back in Monte Carlo at the time. Heaven knows whether he is still alive; heaven knows where he is."

She had hoped that her own narrative would calm her, but she had grown increasingly restless. Only now did she realize how hard her renunciation during the last few years had become for her. She had played many rôles, an amateur like her daughter. And now that she had found her own rôle again the past was lurking behind the bushes, an accomplice long since believed dead.

It was beginning to grow chilly. The wind was blowing little transparent clouds across the starry sky, as though chasing along the smoke from distant chimneys. Ilona remembered that the house was in the city.

Stefan took her by the hand and led her indoors. The manservant had put out the lights. The only lights in the lounge were a table-lamp and the little strip-lights over the paintings by Velazquez and the portrait of the dead woman.

They stood still in the middle of the room.

"We'll find him," he said.

"It makes no difference whether we find him or not," she said.

She put her arms round his neck.

36

About ten days later, on a hot August day, Ilona received a letter written on the notepaper of the Auersperg Sanatorium and post-marked Vienna. It read:

MY DEAR ILONA,

At the very moment when I was about to sit down and write to you—though this is only a façon de parler, *since I have long been confined to bed and am dictating this to a lovely nurse—at this very moment I have heard from our friend T.K. that you urgently* wish to speak to me. There is nothing I should like better than to see you, for good reasons of my own which I shall explain.

First, of course, I must ask your pardon for having, for the first time, omitted to remember your birthday; this was not due to negligence, however, but to the fact that just before Christmas I was at death's door, and hence more concerned with my own dying day than with your birthday. You will smile and say, "Weeds never die"—one of the many popular fallacies, since weeds die just as much as any other plants. It is merely that, in this world that so prides itself on being able to distinguish weeds from useful plants, weeds are less noticed. I therefore wish to inform you that I am once again at death's door, and this time, my doctors assure me, there will be no turning back. Hence I cannot hurry to you, as I should like, but must instead ask you to come and see me in the Auersperg Sanatorium, and as quickly as possible, since I have no intention of giving the afore-mentioned doctors the lie a second time.

But have no fear, my dear friend. You will admittedly find me moribund, but in no way pitiable. Believe me when I say that dying is easier to get used to than living: the latter takes a lifetime, the former only a little goodwill. The death of almost all my old friends—as well as my diligence in visiting old and new cemeteries, the only diligence I ever developed—has convinced me that I shall be far less lonely in the next world than in this one, where I have almost no one else than acquaintances whom I bore with my monologues because they themselves are prevented by coffin-walls from conversing with me. People like myself, who outlive their generation, are to be pitied, and most of all to be pitied are the immortals, since they are misunderstood not merely by their own generation, but by all later ones as well. Nor am I much worried by the fact that I have a pretty useless life behind me, since God, to whom, as you see, I have drawn closer in more than merely a spatial sense, never considered it necessary to initiate me into His plans for me, so that my apparent uselessness may very well have served a higher purpose.

And now to the end, in more than one sense. I have no idea why you wish to speak to me—and T.K. doesn't seem to know either, if he is telling me the truth—but it is all the more important that you should hurry to my death-bed. It is true that I am dying as I lived, but considerably richer, since my good aunt—the same one about whose niggardliness I told you many amusing tales at our wedding—left a respectable fortune which, being prevented by all sorts of physical complaints and old age, I was no longer in a position to squander in riotous living. To add the finishing touch of tragi-comedy, I must confess that I actually made a last trip to Monte Carlo, where I staked the money scraped together by my aunt's noble meanness alternately on my unyielding and for ever untrue favourite numbers eight, eighteen, and twenty-eight—the final eights—with the result that within a few days I had doubled my inheritance. Now finally convinced that Divine justice, so *manifestly absent from the earth, was only to be found in the other world, I left the sunny scene of my defeats as a victor destined to expiate his sins on the heavenly roulette-table, where a single system prevails—the croupier's. Not to ease my conscience—since this, being non-existent, is untroubled—but because I have no heirs and it goes against the grain to waste my money, or, as the case may be, my aunt's money, on charitable institutions which would then be shameless enough to bestow the name of a gambler and ne'er-do-well on all kinds of virtuous foundations—out of the simple wish to place my inheritance in the loveliest feminine hands, I have made you, my esteemed friend and spouse, my sole heir. Since, however, a man may neither be born nor die without an official certificate to that effect, your presence in person is required for the signature of certain documents—to me incomprehensible. Further-more, my capital is not in one of those currencies by comparison with which—it serves the currencies right—gambling-counters may be described as reliable symbols of value. Hence I must initiate you into my financial circumstances as I once, I hope to no avail, initiated you into the mysteries of the roulette-table.*

May I ask you—whether your own business with me is urgent or not—to hurry, so that you may find me, if not actually alive, at least not quite dead.

With a cordial embrace from your devoted servant,
FERDINAND MARIA LEOPOLD BARON VON RATTOWITZ

Ilona read the letter to the end with mingled smiles and tears. For eighteen years she had borne Baron Rattowitz's name, but she had rarely thought of him. She saw him in her mind's eye as he walked with bent back to the altar beside her and searching absent-mindedly for the ring which she still wore; as he pulled the carnations to pieces in the private room of the Buda restaurant and placed them on invisible numbers; as he disappeared into the mist of the December afternoon with a last wave in Kontowski's carriage. Now Baron Rattowitz had re-emerged from the mist, perhaps only to die. She wanted to tell him that he need not die for her sake. She had wanted to ask him for a divorce. Stefan was a Protestant; the Church's approval of a re-marriage was not indispensable. But it was not on that account that she had looked for the Baron and sought Kontowski's aid. Zita was still a minor; hence she needed the consent of a living father—"an official certificate," as Rattowitz put it. Zita who never spoke of her father, as though she knew everything, had mentioned the Baron several times in the last few days—tentatively, cautiously, but not without malice. Ilona had felt an urge to confess, to tell her half or the whole truth. She had perpetually postponed doing so. Now the idea of taking Zita to Vienna with her crossed her mind, but she immediately shrunk from the gruesome comedy. She knew at once that she couldn't conceal from Zita the purpose of her trip to Vienna. She was overcome by a great feeling of tenderness towards the old man who, dying, had risen from the dead to spare her the humiliation she had feared for half a lifetime. She sat down at her desk to compose the telegram informing the

Baron of her arrival in Vienna. She drafted it several times and tore it up again. Rattowitz had asked her to hurry, but she didn't want to shock him by unseemly haste. She finally decided to tell him all the facts, including Zita's marriage plans. No doubt the doctors were wrong again. Baron Rattowitz must now be sixty-six or seven. The man to whom she wrote was barely fifty, a gay gambler, the friend of light women, an elegant vagabond, a foolish philosopher. The carriage bearing Baron Rattowitz turned the corner once more and stopped outside the Pâtisserie Ruszwurm. The mist rolled away.

37

The following day was a Sunday. Zita was not at home. Ilona had made herself a simple lunch, and was now sitting in the living-room trying to read a book, but too happy to be able to read.

The windows were open. Two women were quarrelling outside. Gramophone music could be heard. An Italian tenor was singing Cavaradossi's aria. He sang it over and over again. At the passage "In her soft arms she clasped me . . ." a fault in the record compelled the tenor to repeat himself. "Clasped me . . . clasped me . . . clasped me . . ." Then the owner of the gramophone intervened, Cavaradossi jumped a line, and continued singing on the word "caresses."

Ilona looked up in surprise as the doorbell rang.

"My name is Felix von Oppel," said the man standing in the doorway.

He apologized. Ilona took him into the living-room. She was annoyed with him for coming unannounced. She would have forgiven his impoliteness, but she knew at once that it was intentional.

Felix von Oppel looked like the malicious drawings of German capitalists that appeared frequently in left-wing periodicals. He was in his early sixties, of medium height and sturdily built. His hair was cut short and formed a bristly cock's comb over his forehead. A deep scar ran from the roots of his hair to his left eyebrow, so that on one side he seemed to have two eyebrows, an upper and a lower one. Another memento of student duelling described a line from his nostril to his cheekbone, where it ended in a scar that had healed badly and formed a small hole. He wore a monocle, which caused the right side of his mouth to twist as though one half of his face had been paralysed by a stroke. His cheeks revealed the presence of a high blood-pressure—a weather-chart announcing a storm. He was wearing a dark suit which, although made of the finest cloth and strenuously pressed, looked dowdy because it was inappropriate to the hot season.

He apologized again, and asked leave to come straight to the point. His polite phraseology resembled the carefully composed terms of an after-dinner speech, and shared with the latter the circuitous length of the sentences; the predicates drifted about the room like lost souls.

To the point, then. His son, his only son, had informed him of his intention to marry the Baroness. He said, "informed me of his intention," as though it was undignified to express an idea in a single word when one was wealthy enough to afford four or five. To his "regret" he must oppose the intended marriage. Why had he called upon the Baroness? His son was of age, at least in a legal sense. But he hoped to be able to convince the Baroness that the marriage could only end in disaster, so that, for her part, she could restrain the Baroness from taking a fatal step.

"I am sorry," he concluded, "that in the event of my son"—he never once referred to Paul by name—"marrying your daughter I shall have not only to deprive him of his inheritance, but also of his position in the bank."

While he was speaking Ilona's only thought was whether to close the window. Just as she was about to strangle the tenor he croaked once more: "Clasped me . . . clasped me . . . clasped me . . ." Then the music stopped.

"It is, of course, entirely your affair, Herr Von Oppel," she said, "if you wish to disinherit your son; but I assume that you would like to tell me your reasons."

"I am not anxious to do so, Baroness," he replied. "You may take it that it is a matter of principle."

"I scarcely think that will convince my daughter."

"As you wish. I will begin with my son. He is a weakling, destitute of all moral fibre. For a long time past he has been speculating, with my money, of course, in a way calculated to besmirch the reputation of my firm. While we are striving"—he didn't say whom he meant by "we"—"to rebuild our Fatherland that has been ground down by the so-called peace-treaties and the enormous reparations, conscienceless speculators, foreigners, Jews, and other scum from heaven knows where are seeking to shake the foundations of an economy which . . ." The subordinate clause remained unfinished. "The circles in which my son moves must be described as criminal. You will ask, Baroness, what that has to do with your daughter. I cannot conceal from you that she also belongs to these circles—in fact, is positively a symbol of their moral standards. As was shown by the investigations which I was obliged to undertake, not merely as a father, but also as a responsible individual, your daughter performed in a cabaret run by Bolshevist traitors to the Fatherland, had relations with a profiteer named Müller, and at present works as assistant to a doctor who, for unexplained reasons, gave up—probably had to give up—a successful practice in Cologne. I beg you to believe, Baroness, that I have no wish to arrogate to myself the right to sit in judgment on your daughter; but you will understand that I had allowed myself to hope that a marriage in keeping with his social position might have served to rescue my son from the morass in which, through no act of mine . . ." He sought in vain to catch the escaping predicate. "To return to my son. I have no doubt that he has turned your daughter's head by means of all sorts of mendacious stories, and I am no doubt also acting in her own interest when I inform her through you that up to the present my son has never earned a single pfennig himself, and pays for his extravagant way of life entirely with means which my name and the reputation of our firm . . ."

Ilona straightened up.

"Herr Von Oppel," she said, "I must interrupt you. First, I must tell you that I scarcely know your son, and in so far as I do know him I do not like him. His financial circumstances are of no interest to me, and I fear that they will interest my daughter even less. Ever since I invested my fortune in War Loan and lost it my confidence in old-established fortunes, as you will readily appreciate, has been shattered. I understand little about finance, but I do know that yesterday I held the first five-hundred-million-mark note in my hand, and that a litre of milk costs ten thousand marks. Your son did not cause the chaos in which we are living; I must therefore conclude that it was your generation—or mine, if you wish—that caused it. Please don't answer me: I have no wish to discuss the political or economic situation with you. If, however, you imagine that my daughter is speculating on your fortune you would appear to me to be playing the part of the heavy father in an outmoded melodrama. Nowadays the fortune of a dollar profiteer may be more secure than that of Oppel's Bank. As to your name, I appreciate the fact that in 1909 Kaiser Wilhelm II graced the Oppel family with hereditary nobility, but if I attached much importance to the seven-hundred-year-old title of the Barons Von Rattowitz I should be forced to regard yours as a title of very recent date."

The banker had gone red in the face. He was sitting even more stiffly on the edge of the armchair, as though he didn't know whether to go or stay.

As she spoke she became aware that she was defending with growing eloquence a marriage which she desired as little as her visitor. She was not doing so merely because Felix von Oppel had from the first moment provoked her into opposition, so that she felt that anything of which he disapproved must merit her approval; she was not doing so merely because she alone had the right to judge her child; but also because the old man, in a different way from that which he had intended, had conjured up her own guilt. She had more in common with this father than she would have wished, with this father in particular. They were both parents and united by their 'helplessness.'

"We may not understand one another, Baroness," said Felix von Oppel. "I admit, however, that inspite of your asperity you do not correspond to the idea I had formed of you. May I, therefore, be permitted to ask you a personal question, assuring you in advance that I shall rest content with your answer, whatever it may be?"

"Please ask your question."

"My inquiries regarding your husband produced no result, or, rather, I received a great deal of contradictory information. I was told that you were divorced, and then again that you were . . ."

She interrupted him. "I have been living apart from my husband for many years. Since we are both Catholics, a divorce was impossible. My husband is now on his death-bed. I am going to Vienna, probably tomorrow, where he is awaiting a visit from me at the Auersperg Sanatorium. It may reassure you to know that Baron Rattowitz has left me his not inconsiderable fortune."

306

Felix von Oppel bowed with the gesture of one raising his glass to drink an awkward toast.

In the next flat the Italian tenor had started to sing again. Through the window the hot wind of the summer afternoon brought the hackneyed aria from *Tosca*: "When the stars were brightly shining, and faint perfumes the air pervaded. . . ."

You have not convinced me in every respect, Baroness," said Felix von Oppel, rising. "But you have at least convinced me that you desire your daughter's happiness. Do you think that the children can be happy together?"

"I do not think that we can prevent them from being unhappy, Herr Von Oppel," she said.

38

Ilona arived in Vienna early in the afternoon and took a room at the Hotel Sacher. A telephone-call to the Auersperg Sanatorium informed her that the Baron's condition had deteriorated. His doctors had nevertheless given him leave to see his wife for an hour.

As Ilona's taxi turned down the Bellaria she looked up at the house in which she had lived for years. From this balcony, which must have been built for eternity, she and Zita and Teréz had waved to the departing soldiers. Who now lived behind the shuttered windows? Other curtains, other furniture, other wallpaper, other people. For a moment she was seized by the desire that comes over all occupants of yesterday to go up the stairs, ring the bell, and say, "I should like to look at the apartment; I used to live here once." Why must she think of the past? Why must she feel older than she was? It was a good thing that Stefan didn't know the big cemeteries.

When she entered Rattowitz's room she observed that she wouldn't have to be alone with the sick man, or at least not at once. The spacious sanatorium room was full of people. An elderly nurse was standing at the foot of the bed; a young doctor was leaning against the window-sill. Two gentlemen were sitting at a small table pulled up to the bedside.

Ilona would not have recognized the Baron, yet he did not create the impression of a dying man. He was sitting almost upright, supported by his pillows, his bony hands covered in brown patches resting on the blanket. His hair had become thinner, but its grey was still interspersed with a reddish-blond, as though advancing age had halted before the last memories of youth.

Rattowitz stretched out both hands to Ilona with a smile. He spoke in a weak voice, but clearly and coherently. He rather ceremoniously introduced his lawyer and notary, after which he besought the two gentlemen to get straight down to the formalities. Ilona had to read documents whose contents she barely understood, and to sign others without knowing exactly what she was signing. The doctor and nurse signed as witnesses. Finally Rattowitz asked the notary, a slim gentleman with a little black beard who bore a resemblance to Napoleon III, to read out the will. The doctor and the notary protested against this unnecessary formality. Rattowitz's white face turned red with anger. He insisted on having the will read out.

After the will had been sealed the notary stowed it ceremoniously away in his brief-case. Rattowitz instructed the notary and the lawyer to give Ilona their cards. "So that the Baroness knows exactly who to get in touch with." Finally the two gentlemen said good-bye, followed by the doctor and the nurse. In the doorway the nurse whispered to Ilona not to stay longer than half an hour.

"The silly goose," said Rattowitz, whom the whispering had not escaped. "As if there were any advantage in having a good rest before dying! Pull the chair up closer, my dear. Unfortunately I can only speak in a low voice." After she had done as he asked he nodded towards the door again. "You think it is a vain satisfaction to be present at the opening of one's own will. I never could forgo such pleasures in all my life. And now I am like Shakespeare's Prince Henry, who says of himself:

> So, when this loose behaviour I throw off
> And pay the debt I never promisèd,
> By how much better than my work I am,
> By so much shall I falsify men's hopes."

He wrinkled his forehead. "I've forgotten the rest of the splendid monologue, although, astonishingly enough, my brain goes on ticking, like the watch in a dead man's waistcoat pocket. What a magnificent monologue this self-communion on the subject of improvement is!" Then he remembered a few more lines.

> "And, like bright metal on a sullen ground,
> My reformation, glittering o'er my fault,
> Shall show more goodly and attract more eyes . . .

No, I don't know any more. Could anything be more fun than to prove oneself unworthy of the world's mistrust? The sad thing is that people only believe in our improvement to the extent to which our bank-account grows. But that's all one. I have made peace with my Creator, and am now striding into death as gaily as young Prince Henry strode into life. If, as I hope, my instructions have been carried out the priest who is to give me a hand as I climb into the black chaise is already sitting outside."

Rattowitz had closed his eyes. She thought he had fallen asleep, and began quietly to rise to her feet. A slight gesture of his emaciated hand held her back. "I am exceedingly grateful to you," he murmured. Why he should be grateful he omitted to say; but when she started to speak of Zita he remarked that although fundamentally every one died alone, it was nevertheless a great consolation to have a family. As he said this he smiled without any trace of the irony which in the past had always sparkled behind his smile. Since he had closed his eyes, life had gone from his features. Ilona had the feeling that she was talking to a dead man. There was now a slight touch of pink round his eye-sockets, but instead of giving life to his face the transient colour made it seem even more lifeless than before. When the skies let out a peal of thunder and the sick man nevertheless did not wake up, Ilona was startled. A flash of lightning painted the white room still whiter. The rain rode over the leaden window-sill as though with a thousand tiny hooves. Rattowitz was asleep.

The nurse opened the door. Ilona rose and took her umbrella, surprised that just on this particular occasion she had not forgotten it. The scent of the roses, which she had sent the sick man, had become doubly strong since the rain had started.

When she telephoned the sanatorium next morning she was put through to the medical superintendent, who informed her that Baron Rattowitz had passed quietly away at four in the morning after receiving the sacraments of the Holy Roman Church.

39

The wedding took place at the end of November. Since Zita was a Catholic and Paul a Protestant, there was no religious ceremony. After the formalities at the registry office Felix von Oppel gave a reception in the Adlon Hotel, Unter den Linden.

On the day before the wedding Zita developed influenza. She told neither Paul nor Ilona. As she was changing her clothes in the flat Paul had rented she took her temperature and found it was a hundred and one.

She lived through the reception as though it were a nightmare.

The large hall. Glaring white walls, gilt stucco. Baskets of flowers, a multitude of flowers. Her mother, in a dark-grey dress with a dark-grey hat. Beautiful, the most beautiful woman in the room. By Ilona's side Herrdegen, the publisher. Probably her lover, certainly her lover. Will he marry her? In a corner, surrounded by friends, relations, men who all look like him, Felix von Oppel. They seem to be sitting on sacks of gold instead of chairs. They can't move from them; they've grown on to them. They wait for you to come to them. They stare into the hall and occasionally whisper. Something derogatory, of course. Why did Felix von Oppel give his consent? He hopes to win back his son. One day Paul will sit with the others. Turned to stone, on a sack of gold. More congratulations. A look into the mirror. Red cheeks. That comes from the fever. Short dark hair. Flawless skin. The nose slightly short. Large eyes make up for the faults. An enchanting dress. A present from her mother, from the Femina. Who is this Rattowitz? Her mother is suddenly rich. A whole lot of beautiful dresses, already packed. In an hour it will be over. A sleeping-car to the south, Venice, no more fever. A few steps, away from the mirror. Her movements remind her of her mother. She has always tried not to be like her mother, but her walk betrays her. Unknown people. Friendly words. You look charming. Thank you. Paul is standing in the midst of a group of young men. He insisted on inviting them. Steinmetz, Braun, Citron, Höllriegel, Bronner. Only Hermann is missing. They are standing in the farthest corner, as far as possible from the group round Felix von Oppel. They would really like to throw the flowerpots at one another. A battle of flowers at the wedding. Is it ordinary flu? It might be Spanish flu, pneumonia. Death on the honeymoon. Her mother goes up to Felix von Oppel. The Buddhas rise from their sacks of gold. Herrdegen is standing behind Ilona as though to protect her. The place is crackling with hostility. The Oppels, her mother, Paul's friends. The waiters are serving champagne, going to and fro between the hostile groups, diplomats in tail-coats, peace envoys. Telegrams on silver trays. Many still unopened. A telegram from the stationmaster, from Teréz, from Aunt Margit. Two girls are coming towards her. Is it really they? Hermine Stutz and Lotte Wegerode. Did she really share a school bench with them? "Are you happy?" asks Lotte Wegerode. The clink of glasses. It's hot. Can you hear the hum of the central heating? It isn't true that when you have a fever everything becomes blurred. You hear sounds twice as clearly. People with no fever live in a world without contours. The clock says six. Has it stopped? "Yes, very happy," she says. She doesn't know.

At last she was able to withdraw. She was glad not to have to say good-bye to anyone. She changed her clothes for the second time that day.

Two cars drew up. Paul, her mother, Herrdegen, and she got into the publisher's, a huge Mercédès with a grinning chauffeur. Steinmetz, Höllriegel, and Braun followed in a taxi.

Her mother took her hand. "Your hand is so hot," said her mother. "Have you got a temperature?"

"No," she said.

"It's the excitement," smiled her mother.

"Yes, it's the excitement," she said.

The air did her good. She breathed deeply. Perhaps it was really only the excitement; the fever would disappear.

The Italian express. Paul went up to the sleeping-car inspector, a little man with a flat cap dressed all in brown, as though he had fallen in chocolate sauce. He explained something to him. The passports were still in two different names. Oh, I see, a honeymoon; that's all right.

They climbed in. The beds had been made. There was a smell of locomotive-smoke and fresh linen.

They wouldn't use the upper bed; they would both sleep in the same one. A cold shudder ran down her back. The fever. When she was ill she felt a need to be alone, as sick dogs do. Paul would understand. In the new flat they would have separate bedrooms. Double bedrooms and double beds were bourgeois. How would it be? Would he come to her or she to him? Two bedrooms meant a blissful disquiet. There were only a few minutes till the train left. She hoped her mother wouldn't come into the train, wouldn't see the opened beds.

The train steamed out of the station. The evening air came in through the open window, cutting and cold, Paul put his arm round her. She waved. Her mother, Herrdegen, the three men, the whole station, were moving away from her, as though she herself were standing still, as though the ground were being pulled away from under her feet. Her youth grew smaller and smaller until it disappeared from sight.

40

For the first few days Zita saw Venice only from her hotel window. Her temperature rose; the doctor had to be sent for. Out of the high, narrow window she saw the stone spirals of the church of Santa Maria della Salute. They were like the coiled buns in the Döbling pâtisserie. The yellow of the ageing sun lay like a triumphal arch over the façade. The sun went into the church. Every now and then she heard ships' sirens and the warning cries of the gondoliers.

After a week she was allowed to go out. The weather was uninterruptedly fine. The golden roofs of the *palazzi* gilded the pale-blue sky as though the sun were coming out of them. There were almost no foreigners in Venice. The palaces stood as mutely by the narrow waterways as though their builders had fled centuries ago. The doves paraded across St Mark's Square like well-fed company directors with tiny brief-cases under their wings. Only a few gondolas drifted down the Grand Canal. The air was clear, every oar-stroke audible. The museum attendants bowed and scraped like lackeys; the gondoliers waited patiently on the steps of the hotels; the barman at the Danieli woke from a doze when Paul and Zita came into the bar. Even the shop-windows in the Merceria were lit up for them alone.

Nevertheless Zita's happiness was not complete. Paul often spoke of his father—too often, it seemed to her. His lips went white when he referred to him. He told her how bitterly his father had opposed his marriage. Why did he have to keep telling her that? In the past she had been afraid he only wanted to marry her because of Zdenka. Now she suspected that he had married her to spite his father.

When he talked about the future she was horrified. He planned to leave his father's bank and start a private bank with Braun. His enthusiasm failed to communicate itself to her because it seemed to her like a boy-scout's enthusiasm for the next jamboree. He was a good twelve years older than she, and she found his boyishness embarrassing. When opportunity knocked, you must answer the door, he said. If the French currency went the way of the krone and mark, one could "buy up half France" and pay off later with "a postage stamp." She thought she had heard all this before, in the same words, from Sigmund Braun. She was upset to hear him repeating Braun's words.

One morning at the end of the third week the hotel porter asked her if she would take the money that had arrived by cable. The sender was Felix von Oppel. There might be nothing strange in a father sending money to his son. But wasn't it merely pocket-money that the son received from his father? She felt as though they were both children spending their parents' money. She was married. She didn't want to be a child.

In his arms she forgot her fears. Time an again they left their plans for the day unfulfilled. Paul surprised her in the bath, and after that they never got dressed. They lay down for a siesta, and didn't get up till the sun had gone down behind the Campanile. At night they slept locked in each other's arms. When he drew the curtains in the morning the light streamed into the room laden with the smell of salt and lagoons. In the sunshine she rediscovered her body, as if she had lost it in the darkness.

Although Paul frequently talked about his plans, he seemed in no hurry to return to Berlin. She couldn't understand this mixture of ambition and indolence. She looked over his shoulder while he was drafting a telegram to his father. It was a request for money. She insisted that they should end their stay.

They left Santa Lucia shortly before Christmas.

41

They moved into their flat near the Königsallee—four rooms in a smart new block. An interior decorator had arranged everything to look light, expensive, and practical. Zita suspected that Felix von Oppel had paid for the furniture.

They were never alone; they always had guests or were invited out. They drank champagne and ate caviare. In the theatres premières followed one another thick and fast. One had to have seen the Haller revue On and Off, in which Trude Hesterberg dressed and undressed. Max Pallenberg was acting in Molnar's One, Two, Three. Every one was wild about a Swedish film star called Greta Garbo. She was playing Gösta Berling. People danced the shimmy to Negro orchestras in the Jägerstrasse night-clubs.

Soon after their return from Venice, Paul left his father's bank. Sigmund Braun founded his own bank—S. Braun and Company. In vain Paul assured Zita that he was an equal partner with Braun; the anonymity of the "and Company" angered her. The unbroken chain of nightly amusements began to worry her, because Paul frequently didn't get up until midday and didn't go to the bank till the afternoon. On the door of the flat stood a plate saying in silver letters: "Paul Oppel, Managing Director."

The bank was in the Kurfürstendamm, in a building vacated by a bankrupt shoe-shop. The executive offices were on the first floor, in rooms previously occupied by a solicitor. In order to obtain the rooms Braun had taken the solicitor on as head clerk. He sat reading the newspaper in the secretary's office. Paul's office was to the right of this. He sat behind an enormous semi-circular desk that was quite empty. Zita had the inexplicable feeling that the desk had been built for a toy electric railway. The telephones hung unseen below the top of the desk, like black grapes. Paul displayed them to her proudly. They never rang. An outsize clock on the wall showed the exact time in New York, San Francisco, and Tokyo. Everything depended on the differences in time Paul explained. The success of a transaction might turn upon whether people were just waking up in San Francisco or whether the stock exchange was already closing in Zürich. On the other side of the secretary's office was Sigmund Braun's domain. He never left his room; no one entered it. He ruled through the telephone. He arrived at the office at seven in the morning, and was generally still there at midnight. It was said that the dark-green curtains were always drawn, as

312

though Sigmund Braun feared the light of day. Paul told Zita that Braun had brought his secretary with him from Vienna, a one-legged ex-captain. During the war the captain had arranged for Braun not to be sent to the front. At night the ex-captain would often hobble down to the Kurfürstendamm and bring one of the whores up to the sleeping first-floor offices. Half an hour later she would leave again. "No woman has even seen Braun naked," said Paul.

On nights when Braun wasn't working or receiving visits from whores he would turn up at the flat in the Königsallee. Just as in Venice he had rung in the middle of the night, so now he appeared unannounced and late. "He can't eat," said Paul. It wasn't clear whether he was referring to Braun's table manners, the state of his stomach, or both. Zita frequently went to bed, feeling tired; Braun didn't take this as a hint to leave. He would sit small and hunched up in his black suit in a corner of the lounge. He always moved out of the light cast by the standard lamp, becoming a shadow in the shadow. He and Paul generally discussed the conquest of France. Paul hung on Braun's words. Sometimes he would forget that Zita had been present at their discussion, and next day would repeat what Braun had said as his own pearls of wisdom. At such times Zita felt as though she were living with a gramophone that played only one record—a recording of Sigmund Braun's voice.

42

Like every one who refuses to admit his own feelings, she tried to find external causes for her wretchedness.

During the first weeks in which Braun stood between her and Paul, as unassailable as the souls of the dead Russians he had sold during the war, Zita imagined that she was merely defending her husband's future. Like most women, she had taken her husband's professed intentions literally. He had wanted to dethrone his father and sit in his chair. She had no idea that men rarely take their own professed intentions literally, and don't like to be reminded of them.

After a time, when she and Paul started to quarrel over the most insignificant pretexts, she asked herself whether marriage was not an institution in which two people joined forces solely in order to rid each other of those characteristics which they had loved in each other before they were married. He had only to criticize the way she had done her hair, and she would reproach him with wanting to turn her into a copy of Zdenka. Since Paul didn't like visiting Ilona, Zita discovered her affection for her mother. Suddenly convinced that it was impossible not to love Ilona, she saw in Paul's reluctance an inability to keep his end up in Ilona's set.

She was no longer concerned about Paul's business affairs, and scarcely about Braun, although she could feel that Braun had taken Felix von Oppel's place in Paul's life, and that it was harder to cut out friends than fathers. She suffered agonies because her love no longer stood like a dazzling protective barrier between her own eyes and the picture of her husband. She suffered agonies because she now saw him, which meant that she had not seen him before. He possessed neither his father's cold hardness nor his friend's ruthless passion; he was neither cynical, like Georg, nor moral, like Schmidlapp; he had neither the intelligence of her friends at the Romanisches Café nor the primitive robustness of Hermann Müller. He assumed a hundred colours and had none of his own. He was neither a railway king nor a railway bandit, neither a banker in the traditional sense nor a profiteer in the new sense, neither male nor female. He drove his Buick at 75 m.p.h. along the motor-road outside Berlin, and answered like a schoolboy when his father rang him up. When he talked enthusiastically about what he wanted to build up she couldn't help thinking of the toy bricks with which little boys play on the floor; when he talked himself into a state of hatred she thought of a child tormenting a cat. The similarities between him and herself, which she discovered increasingly frequently, repelled her. Whatever else she had expected from her marriage, she had wanted to grow older. But she had grown younger. They were Hänsel and Gretel walking through the forest. He might hold out his hand to her, but she knew he could never lead her out of the forest.

Not a day passed without quarrels. They often began to argue while dressing to go out in the evening. One word led to another, all spoken in anger. "You only married me because of Zdenka." "Of course I only married you because of Zdenka. You only wanted to take revenge on Hermann." "Of course I only wanted to take revenge on Hermann." "Your mother despises me." "Of course she despises you. Your father thinks I'm an upstart foreigner." "Of course he does." Neither of them knew what they were quarrelling about; each was simply trying to wound the other. In the meantime it had become far too late to keep a date or get to a performance in time—a fresh pretext for mutual recriminations. The argument died away. The tree had been felled, but the roots remained. As their souls became worn out the desire grew to test out on each other the power of sex.

It wasn't a sovereign remedy. For one thing, because they had not put out the fire where it burned; for another, because Zita, who had previously been ashamed only of her husband's weakness, was now ashamed of her own. No sooner had she been happy in his arms than he seemed, so to speak, to fall to pieces before her eyes, like a crumbling statue. He was no longer one, a single, unified man, as he had been for a few moments. Now he was made up of a clothed dwarf and a naked giant. First she hadn't wanted to see the dwarf; now she wanted to see the dwarf even in the giant, so that she should never again make herself utterly subservient to him. She was like Lot, who slept with his daughter without knowing who was lying with him. "And he perceived not when she lay down, nor when she arose."

43

Zita and Paul had spent three days in Vienna and were now going on to Paris.

The Vienna West station was black with people, as though all the trains were leaving at the same time, as though all the people were leaving the city at the same time

Sleeping-car inspectors stood in front of the carriage-doors like a row of brown buoys in a rough sea, looking at their passenger-lists in professional despair. "It's impossible, sir, impossible, madam, we're sold out . . . we've already telephoned . . . it was the same yesterday evening . . . every one is going to Paris . . . if you hurry you might still get a seat." Dollars, pounds, Dutch gulden, were slipped into their hands. "I'm sorry, sir, I'm sorry, madam."

In compartment 3/4 the luggage had been stowed away and the beds already turned back, as on the trip to Venice. Paul lowered the window. He was looking out for Braun.

The clock showed seven-forty-five: the train was due to leave in half an hour. A thin man with a pince-nez on his nose hurried along the platform. A thin spinster, also with a pince-nez on her nose, hurried along behind him with a notebook and pencil in her hand. The thin man showed his sleeping-car ticket, turned to the elderly spinster, and said, "Tell Berger to buy five hundred Trifailer and two hundred Semperit." The spinster made a note. Through the open corridor Zita heard: "Tell Klieber to find out about Zivnostenska. And tell Egon we need an export permit for Hungarian coal immediately." Below the window a blonde girl was saying good-bye to a fat man in knee-breeches. They were smiling as lovers smile, ready to hide their smile away in a case the moment they were spotted. The man kissed her and said, "Don't forget to unload three hundred Alpine." Then he gave her the name of a Paris hotel. Majestic, Mirabeau, Meurice—the names of Paris hotels could be heard on all sides.

Perhaps Braun will be late, thought Zita. If he is too late everything will be all right. Her mother had talked about a second honeymoon. The Champs Elysées was the most beautiful street in the world. The chestnuts were in full bloom in the Bois de Boulogne. The murmuring of the river and the whispering of the lovers found their way into the dreams of the *clochards* sleeping under the bridges of the Seine. She and Paul would stroll along the boulevards as they had strolled across St Mark's Square in Venice. She forgot the station and the wartime stations of her childhood. Voices, whistled signals, the noise of locomotives, footsteps, the rattle of chains, and the thudding of luggage became one, like the sound of an avalanche falling somewhere far away.

Then she saw Braun, outside the lit-up buffet, where people were standing in a queue, pushing and shoving one another away, stretching out their hands to the sales-girls over other people's heads. He didn't use his elbows, nor did he take his place in the queue. He ducked down, reappeared again, and was standing right in front of the counter. Then he came towards the train with his hands full of parcels. He was small and delicate, with his right shoulder rather higher than the other. The parcels seemed to be dragging him down. The steam from a train enveloped him. Suddenly, like a wanderer emerging from the mist and reaching the mountain-peak, he was standing in front of them. Putting the paper bags, parcels, and bottles carefully down on the ground beside him, he took out his ticket and handed it to the inspector in the chocolate uniform.

In compartment 5/6 the beds were not made. "I gave instructions," said Braun, as Paul and Zita entered his compartment. "I've still got work to do." They sat down beside him. As always, he was wearing his black suit and black-silk tie. He sat there in the corner seat by the corridor, as though in a carriage going to a funeral. "There's a dining-car," remarked Paul, looking at Braun's supply of food. "I haven't time," said Braun.

The bottles clinked together as the train moved off. Zita looked out. There were only a few people waving. The secretaries of both sexes, the mistresses who were also secretaries, had already left. In the corridor some one said, "The franc is quoted at twenty and a quarter in Zürich." "Forty per cent. down," replied somebody else. Braun shut the door.

The two men talked, Zita listened with half an ear. "A swarm of locusts," said Paul. "We're part of it," said Braun. It sounded like a warning. The May night was warm. The suburban houses stood black alongside the railway-line, a few of them with their backs towards it, as though they had turned away in disgust. Electric lights were burning sparingly in a few isolated windows: the poor were economical with their electricity. "There's even a brothel madam on the train," said Paul. "She wants to buy French girls cheap." Zita wondered how he came to know a Viennese brothel-keeper; but the pain she felt at the thought quickly left her. "I'm worried about the number of petty fiddlers," said Braun. "The French will be more on their guard than they are already." "There's nothing they can do about it," replied Paul. "The rot has gone too deep. The war is won!" He laughed. Wartime memories returned to Zita. Was she in a military train? Was she going to the front? Was there a trench running across the Champs Elysées, the most beautiful street in the world? The sparks from the locomotive flew past the window, dying out as they passed, glow-worms vanishing into the night. It was getting cool.

They left Braun behind in his compartment. For a few minutes, as they made their way along half the train to the dining-car, Zita dreamed again that she was on her honeymoon. Between the separate carriages, on the iron plates that slithered to and fro—with black shock-absorbers like huge extended cameras on either side— Paul stopped and held out his hand to her. She thanked him with a smile. He smiled back. She regretted having opened her heart to her mother. In Paris she would forget everything.

44

They had been in Paris for three weeks, staying at Claridge's in the Champs Elysées.

It was spring. The shutters were opened out, like two arms stretched towards the sun. The flower-girls in the Madeleine were selling the whole of spring. The booksellers by the Seine hid the old Bibles and got out Balzac's *Contes drolatiques*. The balcony-doors had been flung open. There was a smell of lilac and mothballs. The *gendarmes* were sauntering about, swinging their rubber truncheons as if they were walking-sticks. When Zita looked out of her window the rear lights of the cars seemed like hundreds of rubies rolling across the street.

Her discovery of Paris had been spoiled for Zita. When she was with Paul she was walking beside a blind man. He seemed to see nothing: neither the pink triumphal arch in the Tuileries gardens nor the artists' cafés on the Montparnasse, neither the Impressionist paintings in the Louvre nor the shops under the arcades of the Rue de Rivoli.

For the most part she was alone. Paul couldn't drag himself away from Braun. The two talked incessantly about the sale of France. In the morning they had bought a farm, in the afternoon a Rembrandt, in the evening a stamp-collection. They never saw either the farm or the Rembrandt or the stamp-collection. France was to be pillaged, but how was it that the French watched their own downfall so cheerfully? The conquerors from Vienna and Budapest, Berlin and Prague, were to be met everywhere. The Parisians greeted them with smiles. Paul told her how he had met Madame Donnadieu, owner of a bank, queen of the stock exchange, defender of the franc, in a café opposite the Bourse. She had sat in the café with her baby at her breast, giving milk to her child and instructions to her brokers. Zita pictured Madame Donnadieu and trembled for Paul.

He looked ill. He left the best dishes untouched; his knife and fork trembled in his hand. In the night Zita heard his sighs, his restless breathing. He had secrets. Although there were two telephones in their suite, she caught him using the booth in the entrance-hall. He kept the drawer of the desk locked. When she besought him to talk to her openly he irritably suggested she should go home. If she was to avoid quarrels she had to avoid conversation.

Once, finding herself alone with him, she tackled Braun. Paul was simply on edge, said Braun; that was understandable. There was talk of America propping up the franc. The French claimed that J. P. Morgan, the world banker, was on his way to Paris with the loan that would save them. A red herring, of course, a desperate rearguard action. They were already getting thirty-nine francs for a dollar. A left-wing Cabinet was in sight; that meant the end of France. "The French carry their wallets on the right," said Braun.

Zita refused to be pacified. Whether she was standing in front of the Venus de Milo, eating in Maxim's, or trying on clothes, she kept thinking about her nightmare on the Paris train. It didn't fade like other dreams, good or bad. It was as though in the balmy spring air she could smell the odour of decay.

45

The previous evening she had received a telegram from her mother. Ilona had married Stefan Herrdegen.

In the morning she went to Versailles in a car Paul had hired for her. He seemed determined to get rid of her at any price. He hadn't returned to the hotel until midnight; then he had spent hours telephoning. At some time during the night he had gone to Braun's room. She heard his footsteps from the lounge. She had asked no questions. She didn't want to hear any fresh lies.

She listened absent-mindedly to the guide at Versailles; heard the dates of wars and the names of royal mistresses; walked down the austere avenues. The angular trees stood there like the guards of dead majesties. They seemed to be untouched by seasons, dressed in foliage as though in uniforms. Their shadows fell on the immaculate lawns.

Now, for the first time, she thought of her mother. She had no feelings about Herrdegen, neither hostile feelings, as towards Kontowski, nor feelings of jealous admiration, as for Zoltán, and yet she was deeply hurt. Her mother always did the right thing; she always did the wrong thing. Her mother acted freely, she under a mysterious compulsion. How many years had her mother waited for this man? How was it that her mother, who looked upon men as higher beings, was able to live without men, while she who despised men needed them? Sir Percy Nolan carried Ilona's parcels; Dr Markstein sat for hours over her papers; Baron Rattowitz had actually done her the favour of dying at the right moment. Zita thought of the dead man and asked herself, as so often in her childhood, whether he was really her father. Her mother attracted men like a cold magnet. To please her men died and left inheritances. She compared Paul with Herrdegen. One of them was a boy, the other a man. Youth was no happiness when it made a child of you. Was happiness a trait of character? Or did luck, like stage-coaches, crinolines, stomachers, and goose-quills, belong to a particular period? She didn't envy her mother because of Herrdegen. She envied her for having been born so many years before herself.

She had lunch in a little Versailles restaurant that reminded her of Madame Montespan's fragrant boudoir. The restaurant was full of men, but none of them spared her a glance. There was tension in their faces. They talked excitedly, left their food untouched, passed newspapers from hand to hand. Zita asked the waitress to bring her *Le Matin*.

She understood at once. John Pierpont Morgan had arrived in Paris the previous evening. He was staying at Claridge's, perhaps only a few rooms away from her own. His picture was in the paper. He looked like Father Christmas. He was made entirely of ice—hair, moustache, eyes. Immediately after his arrival he had received the Prime Minister. The latter looked like a boar's head, except that instead of a red tongue, he had a pipe hanging out of his mouth. The boar's head had just formed a government of national unity. "*Messieurs, il vaut la peine de me piller* [I'm worth pillaging]," he had said to the waiting reporters as he left the hotel. "I'm carrying a million dollars in my pocket. The franc is saved. *Au revoir, messieurs.*"

Zita paid her bill. Now the men stared after her. Some of them laughed.

She told the chauffeur she didn't want to go to Fontainebleu. The car drove down the avenues of chestnuts towards Paris.

46

Nothing had changed in the lounge, but the feeling of emptiness was so great that she wouldn't have been surprised if all the furniture had disappeared.

She ran into the bedroom, opened a wardrobe, realized it was her own, tore open the second one. There was nothing in it but three or four of Paul's suits, with gaps between them, as if burglars had been caught in the act. His dinner-jacket lay on the floor, a lowered banner of mourning. His shirts had gone from the chest-of-drawers. She hurried back into the lounge and opened the drawer of the desk. It wasn't locked; it was empty. No message, no farewell letter. She turned the carpet under the desk, looked under the pillow of her bed. She thought of ringing her mother. Was her mother still in the old flat? where was she? Away on a honeymoon? Her mother on a honeymoon! She began to laugh. She laughed loudly, like some one catching sight of his own soot-blackened face in the mirror.

Her laughter brought her to her senses. She asked for Sigmund Braun's room. Monsieur Braun had gone out. Gone out or left? No, only gone out. Would Monsieur Braun kindly come and see her the moment he got back?

She sat down, stood up, walked over to the window, sat down. Every solution to the riddle contradicted itself, crossed itself out. In spite of her despair she was able to weigh her anger against her pain. She only felt anger. Baron Rattowitz had died to please her mother. Paul had disappeared, fled, perhaps died, to spite her.

Darkness fell. When Zita went over to the balcony-door she saw the crowd milling about in the Champs Elysées. The news-vendors were shouting special editions. What did they contain? Reports that the war had been won? What did things look like now in the train from Paris to Vienna? A beaten army in retreat, a beaten army of profiteers, speculators, swindlers, brothel-keepers. On the opposite side of the street the neon sign on a cinema announced the première of the René Clair film *Entr'acte*. The letters of light danced joyfully over the wall. Was she mistaken, or was the milling crowd really so joyful?

She made up her mind to put a call through to her mother. There was a knock at the door.

Sigmund Braun looked unchanged. He walked over to her with the soundless footsteps of a Japanese, bowed politely, sat down.

"I'm sorry you came home early," he said. "We didn't reckon with that."

"Where's Paul?"

"I hope on the ship for Brazil. Listen to me quietly, Zita. Paul asks you to forgive him—if you can. I'm to tell you that he loves you. He'll do everything in his power to arrange for you to follow him—if you want to." He kept looking down at his knees. He seemed now to have discharged his most difficult task. He had spoken of Paul's love as though it were an illness. Like some one who finds solid ground under his feet again, he went on: "Paul speculated too heavily in francs. It's impossible to tell yet what his debts amount to, but they come to at least fifty thousand dollars. He reckoned with being able to repay them all in devalued currency. The dollar loan shattered his hopes. The franc is rising hourly. He tried to get out at the last moment, but, with the franc standing at twenty-three in Zürich, the banks stopped carrying out his instructions."

Zita compressed her lips. He, he, he—Sigmund Braun kept speaking in the third person. Did he really imagine that she confused the puppet with the wire-puller? Paul had been only a puppet. The wire had broken; the puppet had fallen head first from the stage.

"What about you?" asked Zita. "Have you feathered your own nest in good time? Or have all your accomplices fled to Brazil?"

Brazil, she thought. South America. Like Sonia Herz's husband, who was still talked about. The face of the beaten woman appeared before her.

Braun made a defensive gesture with his hand, as though he were used to warding off blows.

"You're doing me an injustice, Zita," he said. "I'm completely ruined."

"But you're a hero and have stayed to face the music!"

"I see I must tell you the whole truth. I'm ruined, but I haven't broken the law."

"And Paul?" Her heart stood still.

"Paul confessed to me last night that he had issued bills of exchange and post-dated cheques in his father's name. I had always assumed that he had considerable capital at his disposal. He swindled me too. Believe me, I shouldn't have taken him into my bank otherwise. He had little ability. The big banks were more careful. They only accepted bills that had been endorsed by Felix von Oppel. Unfortunately Felix von Oppel's signature was also Paul's handiwork. He hoped to make so much at one stroke that he could pay off the bills of exchange and cheques before they were even presented. I suspect that the big banks saw through his fraud, but didn't want to miss the chance of ruining my bank. What are fifty thousand dollars if you can smash one of the new rich? . . ."

She didn't know whether to believe the little man in the black confirmation suit. It was all the same to her. She bore Paul's name. Only forty-eight hours ago his body had lain on her body. She thought of the return to her Berlin home. Sooner or later she would have to go home. Sooner or later her mother would come home from her honeymoon.

"I knew it. I felt it," she said, burying her head in her hands.

"I should like you to understand me," said Braun in a low voice. "Perhaps you will then understand Paul too. I helped him get out of the country because I believed that otherwise he would have taken his life. He forged his father's signature, but he clung to the code of honour which he was infringing." Braun was speaking as though of a dead man. "He clung to everything for which I don't give a damn. I don't gamble, I don't drink, I never know what I'm eating. My father pushed a vegetable-barrow in the Taborstrasse. For years I used to sleep on the counter of the draper's shop where I worked. All my life

I have hated the rich. They didn't give me a chance, so I took one for myself. But I'm not a deserter. I don't feel sorry for myself. I shan't do away with myself. I shall start all over again from the bottom. Paul was a deserter even in the past. He forced his partnership on me. I knew that he despised me just as he despised his father. Paul rang his father last night. Felix von Oppel could have saved him with a stroke of the pen. He didn't do so. He attached more importance to smashing me. He is sitting in his office waiting for the news of his son's suicide. For that I respect him. It was to show Felix von Oppel that I am still alive, not to save his son, that I paid Paul's passage." He rose.

Zita had also risen and was standing by the window.

"Why didn't he write to me?" she asked.

"He was too much of a coward," said Sigmund Braun.

He walked silently over to the desk, took an envelope out of his pocket, and laid it on the desk.

"I'm sure you haven't any money," he said. "Go home as fast as you can."

47

She waited till just after eleven. There was no reply from her mother's number. Why should there be? Her mother had never replied when she needed her. It had always been the same, in her childhood and afterwards.

She felt more and more sorry for herself. Not daring to go into the bedroom, she finally summoned all her strength and went down to the entrance-hall to order her ticket.

She tried to read from the porter's manner whether he knew about her husband's flight. He seemed to know nothing, since he asked her if she needed two tickets. He would try to-morrow morning, he said, but he couldn't promise everything. The trains from Paris were packed.

She remembered that she hadn't eaten anything since lunch. On her way to the dining-room a familiar voice caught her ear. She stopped, sure her senses had deceived her.

Zoltán Szomoru was standing in a group of three or four men, all in evening-dress. They were chatting in loud voices, with the unrestraint of men who are entirely sure of themselves. A few people were looking at them, having recognized the conductor.

A feeling of happiness streamed over Zita. In her childhood it had sometimes happened that during a street riot or an accident she had spotted a familiar face. There was no greater good fortune than to catch sight of a familiar face during a disaster.

Nevertheless she hesitated. She hadn't seen Zoltán for three years. Then she had been sixteen, he almost forty. She wasn't sure whether he would recognize her.

The men walked towards the lift. If he now disappeared into the lift she would have disdained the finger of Fate.

He didn't recognize her immediately, but he stared with knit brow at the woman standing in his path. Then he burst out laughing and held out both hands to her.

321

"What are you doing here?" he asked, then he embraced her.

She didn't know what tone to adopt. He always treated her more or less as a child, and she had looked up to him. Although his hair was white, she imagined he had grown younger, while she had grown older.

"Could I talk to you?" she said. There were tears in her eyes, tears of gratitude. He took leave of his retinue. The men smiled, politely and unashamedly.

The lights were on in his suite, a sumptuous suite. Mr Morgan couldn't be staying in a more sumptuous one. In one corner stood a black piano. There was a smell of flowers, bath-oil, and incense.

He ordered champagne. She was no longer hungry. While they waited for the wine to be brought he spoke of nothing but himself. Next week he was conducting *Don Carlos* at the Paris Opéra. Had she read that he had been invited to direct the Metropolitan? "I turned it down. I'm staying a gipsy." Then he sat down beside her on the sofa, took her hand, and said, "Now you can talk. What has happened? You're not alone in Paris, are you?"

She poured out all her wretchedness. As she spoke it grew greater and greater, as though she were not pouring it out, but pouring it in. Fate was bearable so long as you were curious to know what blows it would deliver next. She was no longer curious. "I rang Mummy," she concluded. "Of course she wasn't at home. Do you know that she has married?"

He let go of her hand. "Who?" he asked.

While she talked about Herrdegen she watched him. He didn't look as young now as he had done. There was a line of pain round his mouth. She remembered an insignificant little incident in Dr Sales's consulting-room. A wasp had found its way in and stung Dr Sales, who let out a cry. She couldn't help thinking of her delight at Dr Sales's cry, which seemed inexplicable at the time, as she looked at Zoltán. It was good to see the strong become weak.

She felt more and more drawn to him. She was convinced that this feeling was not new. In the past he had often come to call for her mother. While the latter was beautifying herself in the next room Zoltán used to sit with her in the lounge and ask her offensive questions about school, the dancing-class, her first flirtations. Then they left. Zoltán abducted her mother, but it seemed to her now that Ilona had abducted Zoltán.

She forgot to talk about her misery, and had to call it back to mind, like a person with heart disease remembering his doctor's instructions in the middle of feeling deceptively well. She looked at Zoltán. His hair had turned completely white during the last three years. At the same time, it seemed also to have become softer and more wavy, and she felt a desire to stroke it.

He merely nodded and refilled her glass. He had not yet emptied his first glass.

"The question is, do you love him?" he commented, diverting the conversation from Ilona.

"I never want to see him again."

"Good. I don't think you should go to Berlin to-morrow. The newspapers will report your husband's flight. If I know people like Felix von Oppel—and I do know them—he will try to fasten the blame on you. Let's allow the scandal to die down. Be my guest. Come to the performance of *Don Carlos*. I'll show you Paris. Meanwhile we'll find your mother."

"I don't need my mother."

She had emptied the bottle almost by herself. It was still not too late. A woman's life was like a pearl necklace. If you were clever you started at the smallest pearls and passed through them down to the bottom, where the pearls became bigger and bigger, more and more beautiful. But if you were foolish you climbed up towards the clasp, where they became smaller and smaller, paler and paler.

He went into the bedroom to fetch cognac.

As always when she had drunk a great deal, her thoughts no longer followed one another in a logical sequence, but to make up for it their outlines were clearer, each thought an independent whole. She thought about her bedroom. Had the chambermaid put Paul's pyjamas on the bed? She wouldn't sleep beside those pyjamas. Anything rather than be left alone to-night! Anything rather than return home beaten to her mother!

He brought the travelling-flask and unscrewed two silver mugs from it. He had taken off his dinner-jacket and waistcoat and looked young again, young in an old-fashioned way. One could imagine him in a shirt with a ruffle, like the poets who used to sing at the feet of beautiful women.

He drank to her and said, "You make me feel very old, you know. I wonder if I have really aged so much. You must be nineteen now. . . ."

"Almost twenty."

"Twenty, then. When I look at you I feel as if I were a hundred."

"Don't women love you any more?"

He laughed. "One doesn't feel old because one is less loved, but because one loves less. The women who love me are just as ready as ever to waste my time. Only I'm no longer willing to waste it."

"Then I'm old. Since I last saw you I have wasted so much time that I have no more to waste. Men have stolen my time."

"What did your mother say about it?"

"Must you keep talking about Mummy all the time?" He irritated her. He was still sitting there talking to her as if he were inquiring about the boys she had met at the dancing-class. "In a minute you'll be asking me how she's looking. Fine, thanks. And she hasn't had any lovers since you left her, if that makes you feel better. She is well preserved—in a vacuum."

"I thought you didn't want to talk about her."

"I'm talking about myself. I would rather have tortured myself and you to death than have given you up."

He put his hand round her shoulders.

The blood rose to her head. She wondered how she could offer herself to him. Pleasure was like blood-letting. Everything heavy and poisonous was washed out of the body by the hotly racing blood.

Bitterness was drained away in pleasure. At the same time the bitterness intensified the pleasure.

He took the bottle out of her hand and said, "You don't have to get drunk in order to tell me that you want to stay with me. I would have told you long ago if I weren't afraid of you. It has nothing to do with you, still less with your mother. Since my youth I have given up loving young women: that has been my only defence against my white hair. No forty-year-old man who sleeps with a twenty-year-old woman admits to himself that he is doing so because he is forty and she is twenty. I'm telling you this because I don't want to deceive you. I don't feel sorry for you. It's lucky for you that the silly boy you married has run away. Nor do I find you more attractive than other beautiful woman who throw themselves at me because I'm Zoltán Szomoru. And, finally, you must get rid of the idea that I care whether your mother has married—and that's the last time I shall mention her. I'm simply giving in to the wish to kiss you just at this particular moment. It may be that to-morrow morning I shall send you away. If I do you need not blame yourself. It will simply mean that I'm not as old as I imagine."

She rose without a word and went into the bedroom. She staggered a little and felt slightly sick. She wasn't certain whether he had spoken to her just now, or three years ago. Had she really been to Versailles that morning? Did she once have a husband called Paul Oppel? Was little Herr Braun sleeping in the same hotel?

There was a box of sweets lying on the bedside table. She quickly thrust a handful into her mouth.

He had been following her, and laughed as he observed her little theft. He kissed her on the shoulders.

When he put the light out, and when, from the bed, she heard his shoes falling, she said, "Are you sure you're not my father? You could be. I've never believed. . . ."

"Quite sure," he said. "You need have no worries on that score. . . ."

48

Ilona examined herself. Had the news caused her pain? Zita had got through to her in Herrdegen's house, which was now her own. "I have run into Zoltán's arms," she had said. "I'm going to stay with him." Ilona had begged her to come home, had offered to come at once to Paris herself. "He saved my life," Zita had said. "I should have killed myself."

Ilona was worried about Zita, but the news caused her no pain. Disgust wasn't pain. And even the disgust which she felt, violently at first, then gradually fainter, was not disgust with her daughter. She understood Zita. She had been lying in the street. He who picked her up was her saviour. Perhaps she imagined she was taking revenge on her mother. But what kind of revenge was it which proved nothing but that she was living in the footsteps of the person she hated? Were people growing weaker with every generation? Had they no strength left?

It was only when she thought of Zoltán that she was overcome with repugnance. What was a fantasy to Zita was to him reality. He had held this child's mother in his arms. St Petersburg, Baden, the Col di Lana, Vienna. Was it the lascivious curiosity to compare mother and daughter? Were men prevented from tasting the love of their children only by blood relationship, mutual agreement, and the law? Or was Zoltán's vanity so great that he wanted to test out his masculinity on the daughters? So primitive that youth alone was not enough, that it had to be the youth of this particular girl?

In time even her repugnance to Zoltán vanished. Fear remained. This increased with every one of Zita's rare letters, the boastful tone of which betrayed her insecurity. Ilona now understood why parents warn their daughters against older men. Most prejudices are wise, the essence of judgment, only made up of elements that are no longer recognizable. Since people were growing weaker with every generation, no generation was capable of defending itself against the one before. Zoltán had almost destroyed her, but only almost. She possessed the same weapons. Zita's weapons were too weak. Since women had stopped wanting to be women their unused weapons had rusted.

Not for the first time, but more deeply than before, Ilona suffered because she saw the disaster that was threatening her daughter. Zita always seemed to act like a drowning woman, even when nobody else could see the rising water. As though driven by a demon, she challenged those stronger than herself to compete with her. Now she had challenged her mother. Ilona knew that her daughter would misunderstand every word, every piece of advice, every admonition, ascribing them to an injured woman. She could only keep silent.

49

The genie which man had called up came to life during these years 1924 to 1933. It ran busily down to the riverbank of the times; the bowl filled with water, the pool swelled. Mankind couldn't remember the magic spell that would stop him. He was bringing the water in which sin was to be submerged. It wasn't only sin that drowned. The water rose up the walls of royal castles and farmhouses, of palaces and cottages, parliaments and asylums, flats and exchange-offices. In vain men called out for the old sorcerer. He didn't utter the magic word.

True, the flood of money was dammed up; a billion paper marks became one Rentenmark. But the number of unemployed was still reckoned in millions.

On February 28, 1925, special editions reported: "At 10.15 this morning President Ebert died after a brief struggle with death." Robbed of its gold, Germany looked for a gold collar. On April 26 a gold collar became president. Theodor Lessing wrote: "One might say, 'Better a zero than a Nero.' Unfortunately history shows that behind a zero there is always a future Nero." Four months earlier Adolf Hitler had been released from the Landsberg fortress.

"Get rich quick" was the order of the day. Some people tried to get very rich quick. As a result scandals acquired proper names. They were called Sklarek, Castiglioni, Kutisker, Barmat, Kreuger. The water-carrier was no longer idle. The victors' banking-houses sank in the water. On October 29, 1929, sixteen million shares were thrown on the market in Wall Street. It was Black Friday. On St Valentine's Day, 1929, the Chicago gangsters fought a bloody street battle.

There were other street battles. The Vienna Palace of Justice blazed. A policeman, half-Nero, half-zero, became Chancellor of the Austrian Republic.

> Neither of general nor of priest take note,
> But for Thälmann cast your vote.

bawled the Communists in the Kurfürstendamm. "Rather dead than a slave," bawled the posters of the Brownshirts in the Sportpalast. The S.A. marched past. The Reichsbanner, Stahlhelm, and Red War Veterans' Union marched past. On September 14, 1930, the number of National Socialist seats in the Reichstag rose from twelve to one hundred and seven.

Japan overran Manchuria by force of arms. Four thousand were killed in General Escobar's Mexican revolution. Leon Trotsky arrived in Mexico. Lenin's empire was ruled by Joseph Vissarionovich Djugashvilli, alias Stalin. America was hunting the kidnapper of the Lindbergh baby. In Berlin young girls were called "cocaine baby." In Neukölln the schoolchildren went on strike. The Charleston was danced. Starving inmates destroyed a lunatic asylum in Italy. The police kept watch on political meetings. Sexual murderers prowled undetected through the streets of the big cities.

> Oh, you monster born of Hell!
> Must the whole house drown as well?

people wailed. It was too late. The times were rising. The innocent perished with the guilty. Fires burned in the water. On April 10, 1932, nineteen million Germans put their trust in the eighty-four-year-old victor of Tannenberg. On May 31, he handed it over to a gentlemen rider. On January 30, 1933, the gentleman rider rode Germany to disaster.

50

Whereas during the first few years of this epoch in which human liberty was foundering everywhere world events rippled past Zita—for she was living with an artist, and that meant living in a world within a world, in which the tramp of marching feet was drowned by applause, the rising flood concealed by a sea of flowers, the sense of imminent disaster deadened by certain sucess—whereas Zita searched the news-papers for the music reviews and turned off the radio when the news came on, the doors of Herrdegen's house stood open to the times.

There had been many changes in the house under the pines of the Grunewald, though they had been gradual, as Ilona wished. The first Frau Herrdegen's portrait still hung in the large, yet very warm drawing-room, but there was no one now who compared the living woman with the dead one. It was a portrait by an English artist, no more. When Ilona happened to see Stefan putting away the silver-framed photograph of the Frenchwoman in a chest she acted as though she had noticed nothing. On her thirty-ninth birthday, December 14, 1925, Stefan surprised her with a strikingly large quantity of bed-linen, tablecloths, towels, and table-napkins. The following Christmas it was silver, bearing her monogram. At first she used the new household articles only when they had guests; gradually the monogram Y.R.H. disappeared. In the spring the furniture in their double bedroom was moved into the big guest-room; their former bedroom became the guest-room. There was a much better view from the new bedroom, said Stefan; how was it he hadn't noticed it before? Outside the former guest-room there was a balcony which he said was just right for break-fast in summer, didn't she agree? Of course, she said, she had already been considering it.

Once a week, on Wednesday, Stefan came home from the publishing house around five o'clock. The literary afternoons, of which he pre-served loving memories from his youth, and for which his mother had been famous, were revived. The guests came unannounced, among them many authors published by S. Herrdegen. They were as varied as their books. Each of the literary visitors was convinced that the trend in writing which he represented was the only one that offered salvation; hence it required great diplomacy and tact to take each one seriously, but not too seriously. Stefan, a diplomat to his finger-tips, used to say laughingly to Ilona, "Fortunately they don't write what they believe to be true; they merely believe what they write to be true." Along with the poets, novelists, and dramatists there were publishers, critics, and journalists, and also mutual friends of Ilona and Stefan—the criminal counsel Dr Markstein, Dr Ginsburg, and occasionally even Dr Sales.

The day became too short for Ilona. Stefan brought new manu-scripts home; they read them, either together or singly, and discussed them till late at night. Until her death Stefan's mother—on whose death at the age of ninety in 1928 it was discovered that throughout her life she had pretended to be five years younger than she really was—always lunched with Ilona and Stefan on Sundays; she wanted to make good by her love for Ilona the offences she had committed against Stefan's first wife. Just as her guests felt at home in her house, so Ilona felt at home in Berlin. She was convinced that Berlin possessed the best fashion houses, theatres, and restaurants and the friendliest and wittiest inhabitants; when she had been away she came back as though to her homeland, and she once wrote to her father: "Berlin is more than irresistible—it is impossible to be untrue to it."

Meanwhile other topics besides literature were being discussed in the Herrdegens' house. From year to year, then from month to month, Ilona was reminded more and more frequently of the last years before the Great War, the years in the Bellaria. There were straws in the wind. Gerhard Leer suddenly stopped appearing on Wednesday. He had found another publisher, said Herrdegen. A friend disclosed to Ilona that Leer didn't want to be printed by a "Jewish Publisher" any more. Obricht, the newspaper proprietor, told them he had taken on his former colonel. The latter knew nothing about newspapers, but it "created a good impression" to have an ex-officer on the board of directors.

Then—it was towards the end of 1930—it seemed to Ilona as if she heard the rotten beams cracking in her own walls. She had been distrustful of Stefan's old manservant, Reinhart, from the beginning. This man, six foot six tall, with a pallid, horse's face, crept about the house like an insistent shadow. In the manner of the semi-educated, he expressed himself in clichés or quotations, which he misapplied. He could draw the curtains in the morning with the words, "What snow conceals the sun reveals," or reply, when asked how the cook was getting on with the new chambermaid, "Hand in hand, on the edge of the sand." Reinhart seemed to hold the whole world responsible for his lack of education, which compelled him to be a servant. But since he was hard-working and devoted to Stefan, and since, moreover, Ilona reproached herself with being unjust to him, as she had been to Kontowski's old Julius, she did not mention her antipathy to Stefan. One day Stefan rang her and asked her to look up the name in one of Karl May's books. They had often laughed together about the fact that Reinhart's private library consisted of the "Collected Works" of this writer for boys. Reinhart was out. When she went to his room she found on his bedside table the swastika party badge. "I can't take him to task for that," said Stefan, "but I'll ask him about it." Reinhart declared that he had found the badge under a seat in the cinema. "Reinhart is incapable of lying," commented Stefan. Reinhart stayed on.

Their guests talked less and less about literature and more and more about politics, it seemed to Ilona. Everybody's personal destiny was inextricably mixed up with politics; it was as though they had to influence political events for their own good, and yet were powerless to do so. The chief topic of conversation was not books, but the leading article in the morning paper. During a performance of *William Tell* fighting broke out in the theatre. "Where is the hollow way?" they shouted from the gallery, because the producer had represented the hollow way symbolically. Stefan rejected a book by a writer on the the the staff of the *Völkischer Beobachter*; during the night two of the publishing house's windows were smashed and the walls daubed with swastikas. Speaking to Ilona in confidence, people passed well-meaning but repulsive remarks. A friend advised her to get Herrdegen to take an ' Aryan' partner. Why didn't he tell him so himself? asked Ilona. Stefan was a "half-Jew" and therefore sensitive, replied the friend; he could speak openly to her because she was an "Aryan." Another was less nervous. "Half-Jews count as Aryans," he said reassuringly, "especially when they were combatant officers."

Stefan spent long evenings trying to convince Ilona that his friends overestimated the danger. They no longer read under the drawing-room lamp. They talked and talked. The faint-hearted didn't know Germany, declared Stefan. Anyone could see through the demagogue's slogans, catchwords, and promises. "If we can't rely on the German character, at least we can rely on German intelligence," he said. She must understand the Germans. he added apologetically. When he spoke of

328

Germany he to whom all pathos was normally repugnant could wallow in pathos. He talked about the nation of Goethe, Beethoven, and Matthias Grünewald. These were the only conversations in their eight years of marriage in which Ilona did not frankly speak her mind. She was Hungarian. She didn't want to offend the German. Perhaps she really knew nothing about the nation of Goethe, Beethoven, and Matthias Grünewald.

In these rich years of prosperity and esteem, of mutual independence and wonderful dependence—only rarely dimmed by worry about Zita, the loss of friends, passing illnesses, and the latent consciousness of powerlessness—in these almost perfect years, Ilona and Stefan occasionally asked each other how their love would stand up to a stern test. The question was half serious, half jesting, either because they couldn't imagine any test, or because they were sure they would stand up to the sternest.

The test came in the year when the world itself was put to the test.

51

Zita was not yet twenty when she became Zoltán's mistress.

He had not sent her away next morning. He showed her Paris. She sat in the front row when the public at the Opéra cheered him. Everything was easier than she had imagined. She heard nothing from her husband. She sent his suits to his father. Berlin newspapers reported the failure of the S. Braun and Company banking house. The partner's name was given only in small print. Bankruptcies were an everyday occurrence. For a while the premises of private banks stared out at the street with empty eyes. Then the shoe-shops and solicitors' offices moved in again. Young Oppel's flight was discussed in restaurants and on the stock exchange, but when people spoke to fathers about their sons who had gone wrong it sounded almost as though they were congratulating the fathers. Felix von Oppel, the father, had suffered a defeat, but the banker had won a victory. Perhaps that was worth fifty thousand dollars.

Zita, as Zoltán often said, was a good pupil. She had a natural understanding for music; her diligence and intelligence were amazing.

In her own eyes troublesome lectures and lessons were made up for by the evenings on which Zoltán conducted. She loved the applause, as if it were directed towards her. It wasn't modesty when she said she was a "typical member of the public." The enjoyment of the music, hardly separable from eroticism, became physical through the sight of the man; the charm of the contrast between the emotional exaltation and the practised physical gestures was irresistible. Zita immersed herself in the excitement released by the conductor. At times she felt as though she were loving her beloved in the sight of a sensual multitude, which seemed to her all the more sensual the more solemn it was. She watched her love and felt that it was being watched. The conductor's ecstacy was meant for her; his arms were embracing her; his fingers stroking her skin.

329

She wondered how her mother could have left Zoltán, but she also wondered whether her mother had been happy in his arms. He was the slave of his own urge to perfection, tormented by it and abjectly subservient to it; serving the work and tormented by the fear of sacrificing fame and outward success. He was a usurer with his hours of sleep, more concerned about his youth in the eyes of the crowd than in his mistress's bed, earnest and histrionic, an ascetic and a spendthrift. In his youth he had been able to pander to all his vanities, had not had to sacrifice one triumph to another; like most vain men, he had been a selfless lover. Now he exhausted himself for the public, serving it alone, his true love.

Zita learnt the art of false ecstacy; she satisfied what remained to Zoltán of private vanity. She thought she was making a sacrifice, but the sacrifice was easy for her so long as a reflection of the footlights fell upon her bed, so long as the applause echoed through her silent bedroom.

It was not her relations with Zoltán that were difficult, but her relations with his entourage. The "courtiers," as he called them contemptuously, travelled everywhere with him. His secretary, Andor Razsahegyi, was a former ballet-dancer from the Budapest opera. Zita detected at once that he was one of those homosexuals who never dare to indulge their inclinations; she also detected the fact that Zoltán exploited his secretary's inclinations without taking any notice of them. She had to get used to being the target of this humiliated and yet indispensable secretary's hate-filled glances even at the breakfast-table; to his walking through the bedroom as if she weren't there, into the bathroom, where Zoltán liked to listen to the letters of his feminine admirers in the bath. Nor could she get on with a young American millionaire called "Pinky" because of his red hair; nor with an amateur conductor, Mr Wilson, from London; nor with Zoltán's orchestra leader, Helmut Sorge; and least of all with Emil, the valet. Above all she hated the travelling, although between the spring of 1924 and the autumn of 1928 all the exciting variety of Europe was disclosed to her. It was part of the rôle of the unworldly maestro that, although he travelled in the company of a woman, he didn't like to travel alone with her. Zita's trunks stood among the luggage of the secretary, the orchestra leader, and the valet. Herr Rozsahegyi, who, like most homosexuals, was petty, occasionally managed to lose Zita's trunks. She didn't travel with Zoltán; she travelled in his wake.

Yet it was not the conspiracy of the courtiers that bound Zita to the conductor. She swallowed her bitterness in the hope of one day turning her enemies out into the street and arranging Zoltán's life as she thought fit. Zoltán had never spoken of marriage, and she wasn't sure whether she wanted to marry him. "I have remained a peasant," he would say with a smile when Zita, like the rest, had to account to him for even the slightest expenditure. A mediocre review would throw him into despair, the cause of which he revealed to no one, but which he would pour out over Zita. She was all the more convinced, however, that she alone held his happiness in her hands. She alone told him the truth. The idea of having to tell him the truth had become an obsession.

It didn't seem a selfish idea to her. Even if the courtiers turned to ice when she told him that his compositions—like all great conductors, he suffered from his lack of creative genius—were pale reflections of Brahms; she was resolved to preserve him from thus wasting his time. It was no use their protesting when he turned up at rehearsals, whispering that in her presence the maestro behaved as foolhardily as a trapezist practising without a net; she was convinced that she could spur him on by merciless criticism to greater achievements. The courtiers merely hoped that she would renounce her personality, because it was precisely her personality that bound Zoltán to her. She refused to give up her own personality to please anyone.

The hour for which she had been waiting never came; the hour for which Zoltán's court had been waiting came in the autumn of 1926, in Naples. As though in a badly produced Italian opera, Zoltán caught Zita in a young Italian's arms. It was her first and only infidelity. She had been seduced by the heat of her blood, without any thought of leaving Zoltán. But the compulsion that forced Zoltán to find the public even when he was fleeing it made discussion, let alone reconciliation, impossible. His vanity made him display his defeat in public, no doubt in the belief that if he himself announced it no one would regard it as a defeat. He accused her in front of the whole court. He ridiculed her ludicrous assumption of superiority; called he musical understanding the amateurism of a middle-class young lady; pilloried her mindless sensuality; laughed at her presumptuous efforts to change him; and finally boasted of love affairs which she knew existed only in his imagination. She had no alternative but to reply with equal vehemence; to describe him as a dummy trying to live up to the splendour of his reputation; to reproach him with the pettiness of his character, which was in insoluble conflict with his art; to answer the accusation of ingratitude by listing what she had done for him; to compare him with the greater Toscanini, because this wounded him most deeply of all—and finally to leave.

The Italian, who had merely been out for an adventure, and was far more impressed by the maestro's tragic resignation than by Zita's favours, withdrew.

Paul Oppel had meanwhile returned from his exile in Brazil. The divorce, in the course of which Zita contented herself with a modest alimony, took place in Vienna. She wrote to Ilona that she had been forced to leave Zoltán on account of the divorce.

Like many people who imagine they will find their lost ego in strange streets, among strange houses, in strange rooms, Zita went travelling. The picture-postcards she sent her mother were her identity-cards, as unreal as the cloudless skies, cool palms, and people dozing in the empty streets which they depicted. The lonelier the hotel rooms in which, like all homeless people, she quickly conjured up the finality of a home, the gayer sounded her cards to her mother. She suffered from the newspaper reports that spoke of Zoltán's successes, reading them with a lust for self-torture. On such days she paraded her happiness, as though Zoltán would see it. She thought up humiliating tricks for letting him know where she was, so that he could call her, determined not to follow his call. She wrote on the notepaper of a smart St Moritz hotel to ask Rozsahegyi whether he had found the earrings which she pretended to have lost. A fortnight later she rang from Geneva to inquire whether the hotel was forwarding her post properly. She waited feverishly for the promised letter, which said nothing except that the jewellery had not been found, and that "every one" hoped she was having a good time.

She finally settled in Rome, where she had made the acquaintance of a young and extremely wealthy American woman interior decorator. She attached herself to Pamela Stotsbury because the latter knew 'everybody.' Not as though Zita needed an introduction to 'everybody.' She herself knew men and women everywhere whom she called friend, *cher ami,* or *caro amico.* She was simply tired of working out a 'programme,' yet it was precisely the programme for the next week, the next day, or the coming evening to which she clung as a mountaineer clings to the next spur in the rock above the abyss. Life, she told herself, was endurable only when one had "something to look forward to"; yet, on the other hand, when you had laboriously to create something to look forward to all the delight went out of it, like a bed whose warmth you could not enjoy if you had to turn it back yourself. Pamela, whose wealth and acuteness of mind did not help to counteract her ugliness, was herself a refugee from her own ego. She doubtless assumed that she and the beautiful Hungarian would become fused into a single person, for she was a "programme artist" of unsurpassable ingenuity.

She encouraged Zita to study interior decorating. As in her childhood, Zita learnt with love and perseverance those things for which she was naturally gifted. Her unerring taste made her studies easy. She no longer hesitated to ask her mother for money. Her wanderings were at an end. She unpacked her trunks in a tasteful little two-room flat beside the Spanish Steps.

She had always longed to be popular: now she was popular, although she wasn't sure exactly what the word meant. Did being popular mean that the telephone was never still? Did it mean that on many afternoons she was invited to two of those cocktail-parties that were now so fashionable? That in the evening she could choose with whom and where she should go out? Did it mean that a murmur of admiration ran through the company when, particularly beautifully dressed, she entered a reception-room or appeared in a ballroom or in the Borghese Gardens when the races were on? All these things were so. Only when she came home at night did doubt rise in her. Had she not wanted to be popular in order to be happy? Being popular didn't mean being loved—or did it? Sometimes she came home late at night to find the bed still unmade, the room still in the state of disorder in which she had left it in the morning. Then she hadn't the energy to make her own bed. Instead she sat at the window for hours in her evening-dress, until the sky above the Obelisk began to grow light and the first flower-women pushed their barrows across the Piazza Trinità del Monti. The people she had met became fused into a grey dough out of which human heads poked like worms. There were times when she didn't go out of her room, but stayed in bed playing one game of patience after another, till she swept the cards off her blanket in a fury. Life was like a prison cell, in which you could settle down, but which you couldn't break out of. Had other people's lives any meaning? Why should life have a meaning? Once when she was ill and couldn't leave her room for two weeks at a stretch no one came except Pamela. She gave Pamela her mother's address because she was seized with the fear that she might die and the charwoman would have her buried without letting anyone know. These were fever fantasies. She had the telephone, the friend of the lonely. Whoever was at the other end had to answer, could be conjured up like a rabbit out of a hat. Every now and then she dialled the time announcer. It was only a voice on a gramophone record, but at least it was a voice. Was she lonely? It was only that one becomes addicted to people as one becomes addicted to morphia. But these were moods, the scars left by a childhood injury which one suddenly discovers on one's body without remembering how and when they were inflicted. When she woke the sun was high in the sky. Yesterday's parties, conversations, films, plays, suppers, and faces were still a grey mass. But she had a programme. To-day things would be different.

At the beginning of 1930 she returned to Berlin for the first time. The previous summer, at an Italian resort, she had met a friend of Pamela's, the German architect Werner Ase. He was in his mid-thirties, fair-haired, and reminiscent of those statues which the imitator of the emperors was now having erected in front of public buildings. The imitator had commissioned the German architect, from whom he expected Teutonic precision, to design a few Government offices. He wasn't disappointed, for Werner Ase built a post-office which was like a gladiatorial arena, and in which, as you could see immediately, no Italian postman could lose a single letter. Zita felt that this awkward, generous, and shy man carved out of coarse stone would be wax in her hand. True, he had a wife and two children, but he lived alone and wanted to marry Zita as soon as the authorities granted him his divorce.

She no longer threw herself headlong into an adventure, a love affair, a marriage. She twice visited Ase in Berlin to make sure he had been speaking the truth. She was afraid of packing her trunks. The flat by the Spanish Steps, in which the dust settled thicker and thicker, was security, a line of retreat. When she went to Berlin for the third time she finally had her luggage sent after her. Pamela disposed of the flat. Her friend remained behind, like one of the many things she had left in the various hotels during the last few years. They seldom wrote to each other. Zita had found her own programme—weeks, days, nights, that she could look forward to.

In the autumn of 1931, when Werner's divorce still hung fire, she settled down in a small flat in Berlin which even Ilona admired for its good taste.

She was twenty-six, only a little younger than Ilona, Baroness Von Rattowitz had been when she moved to St Petersburg.

Part Two : 1931 — 1945

Zita didn't marry Werner Ase.

He was wax in her hands, but no less so in the hands of his wife. Hedwig Ase was one of those women who, while they don't love everything they possess, are not prepared to relinquish any part of it. Ten years older than her husband, she hated Zita—who was almost ten years younger than he—with the fire of a burnt-out woman. Werner had left her long ago, not because of Zita, but because she bound him to the lower-middle-class background from which, not so much through character as through talent, he had freed himself. Like so many women at this period, she had been widowed by a career. Like Solveig, she was waiting for her Peer Gynt. She didn't believe, she scarcely hoped, that he would come back; being the very personification of reproach, she had no need to reproach him; she accepted loneliness and humiliation; insisted on retaining her marriage licence. Her tolerance was exasperating, not only for Werner, but also for Zita.

Zita had found a job with an interior decorator. She was independent, arranged other people's homes according to her own taste. During the day she wore a plain tailor-made costume, which suited her magnificently. The rôle of a working woman satisfied her. She looked down upon 'kept women,' among whom she included married women.

Werner Ase's mistake had been to promise marriage. Frau Ase now took the same place in Zita's life as Zoltán's courtiers had done. She wasn't sure whether she would marry Werner, but she was sure he must get a divorce. She regarded his children as weapons in his wife's hand. Although she didn't fear her pathetically tolerant rival, she reproached Werner bitterly when he visited his former home, spied on him, and was furious when he omitted to tell her about a visit that had really been only to his children. In vain Werner explained that he couldn't force his wife to agree to a legal separation. She asserted that he was hard towards her and soft towards his wife.

Their love was gradually ground to dust in the mill of their nerves. Schmidlapp, whom she still enjoyed meeting—he was now the editor of a weekly paper, and was the target of almost daily attacks by the Press of the rising régime—had once said to her, with his own peculiar philosophy, "A lover or a mistress is a ludicrous figure. Half world literature, and more than half the world's light fiction, pokes fun at the deceived husband, the cuckold. Bit it's not the cuckold who is ridiculous; it's the mistress or lover who is dependent upon the mood, a cold in the head, the postponement of a journey or capricious changes in the plans of the husband or the wife—that is to say, of a third party. While the cuckold is sleeping snugly in a warm bed the lover stands freezing under the window."

Zita had no wish to appear ludicrous. She had waited too long for Werner Ase.

2

On New Year's Eve 1931 a Rhineland industrialist, whose bachelor flat in Berlin she had decorated, invited Zita to supper at a restaurant in the Kurfürstendamm.

The evening had started tediously, and reached its nadir at midnight, when they drank to the New Year. Zita couldn't understand why she had come. She hadn't wanted to celebrate the New Year with her mother. The Herrdegen household was pervaded by the atmosphere of departure; she remembered it from her childhood. The trunks weren't packed, but they stood invisible among the furniture. It made no difference where she went. New Year's Eve was a painful festival. A headmaster seemed to be watching over it with raised forefinger: if the children weren't jolly they would have to remain in the same class for another year. She should have stayed at home, but she couldn't stay at home on New Year's Eve.

Midnight was past. They were under an obligation to rejoice in the coming year. An industrialist who manufactured flags was aiming balls of paper at the neck of Zita's dress, recklessly dipping the balls of paper in champagne first. The wet balls rolled down between her breasts. If she threw them back he would take it as an invitation to a jolly battle. Things were jolly enough already. She sat there without moving, like an automatic machine having coins dropped into it. The ladies were taking turns at wedging a colonel's monocle in their eye. Zita wondered whether to drop it. An elderly gentleman who was short-sighted was throwing paper streamers at a corpulent lady. She was sitting opposite him, so she was the closest target. The blue, red, and yellow streamers hung in her hair, round her ears, in the neck of her dress. The chef brought in a piglet. It looked as sad as if a melancholic cook had modelled it in marzipan, but it wasn't marzipan, and it squealed conscientiously. The guests looked at one another: every one seemed to distrust everybody else's gaiety. Zita counted the roses on the red-silk wallpaper. She should have stayed at home. You were afraid of missing something, and in the end you counted the roses on the wallpaper. To fix a given moment for the beginning of a New Year was a stupid arrangement.

Just before one, when everybody was trying to think of an excuse to say good-bye, but no one dared go, three friends of the host arrived. They were greeted like an army of liberation come to relieve the citadel besieged by boredom. One of the men sat down beside Zita, and never left her again, barely rising to his feet when fresh guests came in.

Konrad Severin hadn't come from a New Year's Eve party, or, at any rate, not from one at which people threw balls of paper, streamers, and confetti. The leaders of the Party had celebrated the New Year at the Kaiserhof, he told Zita. The leaders of which party? The National Socialist Party, of course. No, he wasn't one of the leaders, he denied modestly; he was only an ordinary member. An old Army pal had taken him along. They had drunk to the year of victory, the coming year, the coming victory.

At first she listened abstractedly. She found him restful to look at. He was fair, with blue eyes, a rather overlarge nose, and projecting cheekbones that gave his face the appearance of a solid scaffolding. The wrinkles in this face—for although he couldn't be more than thirty-five,

335

his face was furrowed—moved like workmen on scaffolding. Every fold seemed to have a job to do. An architectural face, thought Zita.

Her attention was captured. She remembered the political discussions at the Settee, with Georg, at the Romanisches Café, in Hermann's flat. In her mind's eye she saw the student. His name was Baader, or something like that. They had struck him, and his face had become covered in blood. What had he said? Erika Wegener stood out on the balcony blathering about the suicide of youth. It had been bewildering, as bewildering as everything since then. She couldn't help thinking of a house she had passed a few days ago in Dahlem. It had been burnt down a little while before. Women and men were grubbing in the ashes; everybody was looking for something; nobody knew for what. All the people she knew were like these blind seekers. It was not what the man beside her was saying that affected her; it was the way in which he said it. He was not seaching; he had found. He seemed to be bringing order into a neglected room. He pushed tables straight, picked up chairs that had been knocked down, washed up dirty dishes.

"You listen to me as if you were hearing all this for the first time."

"I am hearing it for the first time."

He laughed. She was surprised that he could laugh so heartily. People laughed sadly, nervously, maliciously, or guiltily. Could a good conscience also laugh?

"That's the trouble," he said. "There are still women, there are still people, who don't realize what it's all about."

He quoted the Party Leader's New Year speech. They might be empty phrases; she couldn't judge.

"Do you believe all that?" she asked.

He looked at her in amazement, as though seeing her for the first time.

"I do believe it," he said firmly.

A man who believed. A man beneath whose bright gaze the pointless took on point. A man who was different from all those she knew, and also different from herself. She hadn't pictured a dreamer like this.

"Don't imagine I'm an idealist," he said. "Or rather, we are idealists with both feet on the ground. I was told you were an architect. In that case you know that for every building you need a scaffolding of ladders. On the ladders you soar above the ground. But they are as safe as the ground itself."

He stopped talking about himself.

She followed his eyes. False noses and paper hats had been distributed. The men preferred the noses, the woman the hats. They marched past the table, the colonel with the monocle in front, past Zita, past Severin. One or two raised a toy trumpet to their mouths and trumpeted in their direction. But no one invited them to join the line. Severin laid his hand on her hand. His hand protected her from toy trumpets, clowns' noses, streamers, and balls of paper soaked in champagne.

He looked at his watch. "Suppose we were to slip away?" he said. "I've been invited to a place not far from here. It would be fun if you would come with me."

336

She went with him as a matter of course.

3

Zita's mother had told her the fairy-story of the blue bird that
children run after. The blue bird kept flying away. Her mother might
still believe in the fairy-tale of the fugitive happiness. She held the blue
bird in her hand.

She was with Konrad almost every day, every evening. He was a civil
engineer, thirty-six, unmarried, and, unlike most Berliners, did not
originally come from Berlin. His father, a Lüneberg farmer, was dead.
His mother, the daughter of a technician whom poverty had prevented
from ever becoming an engineer, lived in Munich, where she was born.
Konrad had fought in Russia, been wounded three times, and decorated
for outstanding gallantry. He was now a first lieutenant in the reserve.
He earned forty-eight marks a month after deduction of income-tax.
The building contractors for whom he worked thought very highly of
him. He had been seriously in love twice and once engaged. His
fiancée had married another man. He lived in a furnished flat—two
rooms and a bathroom. Over his bed hung photographs of his parents,
a comrade killed in the war, his sixth form at school, and Adolf Hitler.
He had joined the Party when it was first founded. He liked good
books, especially poetry. His favourite poets were Hölderlin, Novalis,
and Platen. He admired Wagner. Zita learnt all this in the course of
their first few meetings. His life was as simple as a warrant of arrest.

She had come to distrust her own feelings, and examined them as
soberly as she could. Was it his simplicity that attracted her? There
was no contradiction between his words and his deeds. His pre-
dictability was exciting, not dull. He was like the books of the
immortals, which one enjoys reading all the more the better one knows
them. In Konrad's nature, as in these books, there was no tension, or
only in the higher sense that one observes with satisfaction that what
must happen does happen. It couldn't be his simplicity alone. It was
purity. Georg, Paul, Werner, and Zoltán more than any, had constantly
talked about themselves. Konrad rarely spoke of himself, as a rule only
when he asked himself whether he was doing his duty. A man like him
should have been cold, but he was passionate, full of fire—only it
wasn't the fire of ambition. He condemned ideas, groups, parties, but
almost never individuals. He had countless friends; Zita had learnt to
value men who had friends. Friends, not colleagues or courtiers.
People's secrets had burned around her like hidden fires. Konrad had no
secrets. Were these virtues, she asked herself, or were they merely the
absence of vices? His great virtue was his attitude to her. Her soul
grew still in his presence; she drew breath. Out of the jumble of
thousands of coloured stones he composed a beautiful mosaic. Everything that had appeared to her senseless suddenly made sense—not only
the present, but also the past. She no longer blamed herself for having
sought with crazy arrogance to change Zoltán's life, to change Zoltán
himself: she had no wish to change Konrad, so the fault must have
lain with Zoltán, not with her.

The magnitude of her love could be measured by her own readiness to do what her mother had always advised her to do—to stop insisting on always being right. Although politics engrossed him more than his profession, she did not attempt to vie with him in this field. She did not feel obliged to convince herself that he was right: what she considered right must be right. She never felt towards Konrad that dangerous superiority which she had felt even towards Zoltán. In those spheres in which he did not feel at home he handed the reins over to her without a struggle; on his own ground he brooked no contradiction.

After only a fortnight he had asked her to marry him. They were now planning their life together, as clearly as an architect designs the ground-plan of a house. Did she want to go on with her profession? Why not, so long as they had no children? At the same time, however, disregarding Zita's indifference, he drew up a strict balance-sheet of their income and expenditure. She sat beside him as he wrote down his neat figures in a black notebook. How charming such pedantry could be! He clapped the notebook shut. That meant finality, security, peace. He would have nothing to do with a flat such as Zita had in mind. He considered her taste absurd, a monstrosity born of an outmoded decadence. She found every piece of furniture he chose frightful, but was all the prouder of the sacrifice she was making to his taste. She had to swear that she had not herself written any of the Bolshevistic songs sung at the Settee. She gave him her word with a laugh, delighted by the seriousness with which, looking at the future, he probed the past. Her mother had once told her, in a moment of bitterness, that she had many talents, but no talent for living. She no longer needed any talent for living. Her life was in the calm hands of Konrad Severin.

She also agreed, not without objection, but finally with a certain satisfaction, to his wish that Stefan Herrdegen should stay away from their wedding. "The man must always be right": wasn't that her mother's theme-song, repeated *ad nauseam*? That was what her mother had wanted her to accept. Could she complain now? That Herrdegen was a half-Jew was bad enough, said Konrad, but that wasn't the main reason. He considered Zita's stepfather the representative of a literature that was undermining the national consciousness of the German people, destroying the nation's will either through snivelling pacifist propaganda or through pornographic diversion; moreover, he financed a newspaper that had been guilty of the grossest insults to the Movement. Konrad's friends would not understand, and he would not allow, the presence of such a man at his wedding, particularly when the man was actually a 'relation.' Of course, he had nothing against the presence of Zita's mother; he would welcome it.

He called on Ilona one afternoon, when he was sure Herrdegen was at the publishing house.

The visit was short, punctuated by long silences. They sat in the drawing-room, Zita and Konrad on the settee under the picture of the first Frau Herrdegen, Ilona in an armchair. Zita felt as though it were a visit of condolence at which every one avoided referring to the deceased. She had put her hand on Konrad's hand, which was slightly damp with excitement. She hardly spoke, merely agreeing when Konrad

338

said something. Although she was wearing a very *chic,* very practical tailored suit, Zita pictured herself dressed in a bridal gown before the camera of an old-fashioned photographer. There was nothing grotesque about this vision. From her earliest youth her mother had preached womanliness. Why did she now look so horrified? Why did she conceal her amazement so clumsily? No, thank you, said Zita, she had given up smoking; Konrad didn't like her to smoke. Yes, she said, that was how they were going to do it, that was how Konrad wanted it. No, Konrad said they couldn't afford that. Her mother ought to have been happy. She revelled in her mother's wretchedness.

"We're going to get married in Munich because of my mother," said Konrad. Zita had insisted on that, not because of Konrad's mother, but because of her own. "Of course, we hope to see you at the wedding," said Konrad. Zita nodded agreement. She was extremely sorry she couldn't come, said Ilona. "I wish you every happiness." She embraced her daughter.

On May 8, 1932, they were married in Munich. The Party had sent a big bunch of white carnations with a swastika ribbon attached. Ilona sent a basket of red roses. Inside it was a jewel-case containing a necklace, a bracelet, and earrings—old Hungarian goldsmith's work. On the card was written: "We are with you in thought and send you our heartiest good wishes. Your mother, Stefan."

4

On February 27, 1933, the Reichstag burnt. Zita experienced these events as though through a veil. She was pregnant, in the ninth month.

Dr Termoelen, her doctor, said it was a difficult pregnancy. During the last fortnight she was not allowed to get up. The maid was ill in bed and in need of care herself. Ilona, who had seen little of Zita since her marriage, and then without Konrad and sometimes in secret, spent the better part of every day with her daughter. Konrad telephoned every hour, and came home as often as possible. He was busy, however, not only with the construction of a new railway-bridge in Berlin, but also with preparations for the new elections which had been announced immediately after the Reichstag fire. The Party couldn't spare anyone. Konrad made speeches, took part in meetings, visited hesitating comrades. It was often midnight before he released Ilona from her watch at Zita's bedside.

It was a good omen. Zita thought, that Konrad was there when the labour-pains started. It was seven o'clock on the morning of March 3.

After a talk with Dr Termoelen, Konrad sent for a taxi to take Zita to the Charité.

The taxi headed towards the Brandenburger Tor, taking the most direct route to the Luisenstrasse. It was cold, but spring was already in the air. The sun wasn't sure whether to shine or not—a shy, early-spring sun. Flags and placards flew past Zita. A child with outstretched arms. A worker's fist. Rats with human heads. A mother with a child in her arms. A child. A mother. Swastikas, swastikas. Like one chair piled on top of another chair. Rats with human heads. A worker's fist. A child. A mother. The black-red-and-white Nazi flags ran alongside the taxi. The houses were moving, as though moving with the flags in the morning. A child, the worker's fist, the rats, running chair-legs, swastikas.

"I'm glad you're seeing Berlin once more before the election," said Konrad. He squeezed Zita's hand. "Our child will be born into a happier world."

The pressure of his hand hurt her. Her whole body was hurting. She wasn't thinking of her child. She wasn't thinking of the world. She was sure she wouldn't get to the hospital in time.

She felt a wave of anger because Konrad still had eyes for the street. The wide maternity dress, which she had always disliked wearing, became tight round her abdomen. She wanted to undo the zip of the skirt, but couldn't. Konrad didn't notice. What did he notice? Did they have to have a child in the first year of their marriage? Her abdomen would fall apart. She wouldn't design any more interiors. Berlin before the election. What did it matter to her? Power, power, power: couldn't Konrad think of anything else? But that was why she loved him. Stop thinking! Thoughts hurt, like the cobblestones that seemed to be jabbing into her abdomen. The swastikas were running after one another, leaning slightly back, with nimble feet, children's drawings.

Her eyes fell on the little leather case standing at her feet. Her mother had packed it days ago. Her mother had always packed cases. She hated this case as much as all the other cases, perhaps more. Why couldn't she bring her child into the world at home, as she had come into the world, as her mother had? She saw her grandfather before her, the signal-flags of the railway. She wasn't travelling in a taxi; she was travelling in a train, with signal-flags to right and left. Why hadn't she thought of calling Teréz? Teréz was the only one who could help her.

"I'm in terrible pain," she said.

"Be patient; we're almost there," said Konrad.

Near the Reichstag police stopped the taxi. Traffic was being diverted. The building was ringed by curious crowds. The stone riders watched over the burnt-out dome. A group carrying flags marched past. There was a smell of burning.

5

She seemed to be travelling an endless road when, barely an hour later, she was wheeled on a trolley to the operating theatre.

The trolley stopped outside the operating theatre. There was a red light over the door.

"It will be your turn in a minute, Frau Severin," said the midwife, bending over Zita.

She looked up into a young face under a white cap, a clean, so to speak sterilized face.

"It will be your turn in a minute," she repeated to herself. Why had she been brought up too soon? They knew what they were doing. But the red light was on! Had something unforeseen happened in the operating theatre? Would she give birth to her child in this hospital corridor?

340

"A difficult pregnancy," Dr Termoelen had said. A difficult birth. Hidden thoughts, hidden images, rose into her mind, as though the pain had torn the protective cover away from them. She saw Dr Friedhoff's consulting-room. She had had the child taken away from her. There had been no technical mistakes, Dr Sales had said. She almost laughed out loud. No technical mistakes: she had come through alive. The mother is alive; the child is dead. The child is dead, so there was no technical mistake. Who could say what damage the quack might have done? She could bear children. Dead children. The sweat broke out on her forehead. For days the child in her womb hadn't moved. "I'm sorry," Dr Termoelen would say to Konrad. "We could only save the child." "Why, why?" Konrad would ask. "She has been to a quack at some time or other. She can only give birth to dead children."

"Nurse!" she whispered.

The sterilized face bent down over her. She winced. Wasn't it Frau Friedhoff's face? Frau Friedhoff had talked about the weather, about the snow.

"Yes, Frau Severin?"

"Is it normal for the child not to move during the last few days?"

"Don't worry, Frau Severin. Everything is all right."

An evasive answer. If the child didn't move, what was it that was causing her such pain? The corpse in the womb. A huge suppurating lump under her heart. That was why she wasn't having labour-pains like other women. Not sharp waves of pain, but one continuous ache. During her pregnancy she had frequently thought that she didn't want a child. Dear God, forgive me! I shall only live for the child. I shall only be a mother. I have always wanted a child. Not Hermann's child. Konrad's child.

She tried to sit up. The red light was still on over the door of the operating theatre. She sank back. Kisnémet, the station, the red light of the signal. Even in her childhood she had felt the red light to be menacing. It forbade trains to move. And suppose they moved nevertheless? The locomotives crashed into one another. Carriages rolled down the embankment. Dead people lay under the carriages.

The door opened, and a doctor came out. He whispered with the nurse. "Give her the injection," she heard. The doctor went back into the consulting-room.

"I can't stand it," said Zita.

The nurse had a syringe in her hand.

"It will only be a few minutes longer," she said. "We have a lot of births to-day, Frau Severin."

Where was Dr Termoelen? Why hadn't he come out himself? Perhaps he wasn't there at all. To-morrow or the day after or the day after that there were elections. Dr Termoelen was making election speeches. He had no time, like Konrad. Another doctor would bring the child into the world, the dead child. Or was Dr Termoelen behind the red light? "A lot of births, Frau Severin." What did she care about other births, other mothers, other children?

She didn't feel the prick of the hypodermic needle. The pain was submerged in her greater pain.

A gentle hand was laid on her brow. From her brow it slid down over her eyes. She wasn't grateful to the hand for setting her free from pain. She fought for lucidity, in vain.

"You see, it's better already," said the nurse.

A feeling of gentle bliss overcame her. There was also anger in the bliss, as though left over from non-blissful times. Why had Konrad let her suffer for so long? Was he proud of her suffering? Her mother had wanted to have her taken to a private nursing-home. There they wouldn't have let her suffer. There the doors had no red lights over them. There they didn't have "a lot of births"; you didn't have to wait your turn.

The trolley moved. The pains came back, pressed her down, strapped her as though with a leather belt to the bed on wheels. She could see nothing but the ceiling. An endless white steppe, a desolate snowy landscape, was stretched out above her. She was moving along under a steppe. That was how the dead saw the earth. Voices came to her from far away, from out of the steppe.

She turned her head to one side. White people, instrument tables, wash-basins, tiles, oxygen cylinders, people, bottles of alcohol, rubber gloves, sterilizer-drums, white people. She was being wheeled into a white factory.

The glaring light of the operating-lamp dazzled her. She didn't close her eyes. At all costs she mustn't fall asleep, as she had done at Dr Friedhoff's. In her sleep she would give everything away. Was the man bending over her Dr Termoelen, or was it Dr Friedhoff? In the dazzling light she saw the street through which she had been driven that morning, a few hours ago, perhaps yesterday, perhaps years ago. A child, a fist, a mother, swastikas, rats with human heads, a child.

She heard a child crying. She knew that it wasn't the voice of her child.

6

"She will be brought up in a moment," said the nurse. "Congratulations, Herr Severin, A healthy girl."

Ilona breathed a sigh of relief. She looked at the waiting-room clock. It was eleven. The March sun shone dully through the window-panes.

Konrad Severin had telephoned her an hour ago, carrying out Zita's wish, dispassionate, correct, just in time.

Now he was standing beside the nurse, gesticulating vigorously, asking questions, forgetful of himself. His face, which always made Ilona think of a death's head, although she couldn't deny that it was the good, clean face of a living man, was red.

He loves Zita, she thought. He was probably the first man who had loved her. Now he would love her still more. Her and his child.

A slight warmth rose in Ilona. She tried to fan the glow. He was good to Zita. What more could she ask? Why did she have to see him with her own eyes? Why couldn't she see him with Zita's? Perhaps he wasn't only good to her; perhaps he was also good for her. Zita's life, which had been broken into a thousand lives, into fragments that still consist of the original material and yet are worthless, had become one again. She herself hadn't been able to collect the broken pieces, to fit them together, to glue them fast. This man had been able to.

She listened to every word the nurse said, and scrutinized him at the same time. Her own sight thrust itself in front of Zita's eyes like a yellow filter. Why did Zita love him? He looked attractive, as attractive as a thousand others. Perhaps that was it, this reassuring common-placeness. Or was it power that Zita felt? Not the power of a personality, but power *per se*, such as thousands, hundreds of thousands of molecules of the times, bore within them. Zita was not armed against the times; she opened her heart to them unconditionally, trustingly, hungrily. She had loved Georg when the times were fleeing into cellars, Paul when zeros were rising. Now it was the flag-bearers who symbolized the times. Was she unjust? Ilona asked herself. Jealousy? She had been jealous of Teréz, not of this man. What was it? Was it only the times? Was it the flags, the placards, the fire? How could she explain to Zita that she was frightened for her? What she felt wasn't jealousy or aversion, but only fear, fear of what would happen to her child at the side of this confident, calm, powerful man.

Now everything is going to be all right, thought Ilona, as she listened to the nurse. In the happy warmth that enveloped her, and also included the strange man, she didn't ask herself why everything should be all right now.

She went up to Severin and shook hands with him.

"You have a marvellous daughter," he said with a smile.

"You have a marvellous wife," she rejoined with a smile.

"You can go into your wife's room," said the nurse.

They hurried along the corridors, not speaking. One door was open. Half a dozen babies were lying in tiny cots. Severin walked along close to the wall, always one step in front of Ilona. She was afraid he would push her away, refuse to let her see Zita.

He opened the door and entered in front of Ilona.

Zita lay in bed with the baby in her arms. Ilona had never seen her daughter looking so beautiful. Her loose hair was spread out on the pillow. Her skin was transparent ivory. A great tranquillity emanated from her, the untranquil one, from the restless one a restfulness that filled the whole room. Ilona couldn't help thinking of Feri, as he slept beside her released from all care.

Zita lifted up the child. She did it easily, in spite of her weariness, as though the child were weightless in her arms. It was a baby like any other, looking like a little old woman, as though beginning and end met, and yet different from all other children. It had brilliant blue eyes, the yes of the blind and of children; a thin nose; thick dark-blond hair.

"She looks just like you," said Zita.

She held out the child to her mother.

Severin had bent down over his wife and kissed her on the forehead. Nevertheless, Ilona felt that something terrible and irreparable had happened. Fear smothered her triumph.

Quickly, as though to make good for the fact that Zita had given

343

the baby to her first, she laid it in the arms of the man.

"I'm sure Zita wants to sleep," said Severin.

Ilona exchanged only a few more words with her daughter. Then she said good-bye, pretending not to notice that Severin stayed behind. In the doorway she turned round.

"I shall be at home. Please give me a ring."

"Of course," said Severin.

She hurried downstairs and out into the Luisenstrasse.

A band came round the corner. The men wore brown shirts. The drums were booming.

Ilona was glad when the door of the telephone-booth shut out the music. She asked for the number of the publishing house and was put through to Herrdegen.

"We have a granddaughter, Stefan," she said.

7

"Germans! Defend yourselves! Don't buy from Jews!" On April 1 the notices hung on the closed doors of the "Jewish shops," with the brownshirts standing guard outside. It was as though they were afraid their people, the German people, might regain their courage at the last moment. The men in brown had nothing to fear.

"German students march against the un-German spirit," said the placards on the lorries that raced through the streets on May 10. They were racing towards the square in front of the State Opera House. Books were piled up on the lorries. The spirit was going to the stake. The mob yelled with delight.

A week earlier S.A. men had forced their way into the S. Herrdegen publishing house and taken hundreds of books away. Everything had proceeded in an orderly manner. No violence. Receipts issued. Barbarians in spectacles. Barbarians with receipts, carrying out instructions. Stefan rescued a few manuscripts of books not yet printed. He brought them home and hid them under the mattress in the guest-room. When he looked up Ilona was standing in the doorway. He blushed and walked past her with his eyes on the floor. How clumsily he had done it, how touchingly clumsily! She wanted to take him in her arms like a child, to stroke his white hair.

She begged him to leave Germany. She often thought now of the night at Berény, of Consuela. He still refused to go. Any day, any hour, the German people would wake from their mass hypnosis. He talked as though to convince himself. Couldn't he see, she asked, that it was beginning with books and would end with human beings? He shook his head. His noble face, with the clear, grey eyes, thin mouth, and thick hair, had aged. He was in the middle fifties, but he looked as though he were in the middle sixties. Almost overnight, in the night when the books were burned, the white at his temples had spread over all his hair. She knew that he suffered more on account of the men who burnt the books than of the books that were burnt. People don't know that they humiliate themselves when they humiliate others, Dr Ginsberg had said. Did Stefan still believe what he said? Or did he simply not know which way to turn?

Only after nights of vigil, in which they dared not go to bed, as though they feared to be attacked in their sleep, in which they sat under the drawing-room lamp and the room became a raft of the shipwrecked, driven to and fro in the night, only after persuasion and argument, did Stefan finally allow Ilona to go to Vienna and Budapest and investigate the possibility of a move.

He took her to the station. At the last moment she wanted to turn back. She was afraid to leave him behind with his beloved city, his beloved people.

8

In Vienna she had discussions with publishers, writers, newspapermen, friends of Stefan's. Every day she talked to him on the telephone. She wanted to reassure him; he reassured her. "While you're in Budapest anyway," he said "take the opportunity and pay your father a visit." Why had he said that? Was he, without admitting it to himself, seeking security in the only place where he knew that her security lay? Or did he think that she would never see her father again? "You needn't hurry back," said Stefan. She anxiously read every edition of the newspapers.

She planned to remain only forty-eight hours in Budapest. She had telegraphed Kontowski from Vienna. Flowers and a short, affectionate letter were waiting for her at her hotel.

His castle lay outside the city, at Hüsvösvölgy. It was evening. The car he had sent for her drove through the spring mist that ran out of the forest on to the road like a herd of shy deer. The May rain had been falling warm and soft all day long. The landscape was melancholy, as though it no longer believed in its own awakening.

The wrought-iron gate of the park was opened by an old caretaker. The gate was large, the man small. He put his shoulder to it; it creaked on its hinges. Then he shut it behind her. Didn't he know that she would be leaving again almost at once? Why was the gate opened, why shut? It seemed to her as though the gate stood in open country merely to be opened and shut, as senseless as a castle drawbridge in the twentieth century. The park was neglected; the weeds had grown tall. A dog barked.

The castle lay deep in the park. The door was opened by a man-servant who Ilona didn't know. She wanted to ask whether Julius was dead, but she said nothing. She remembered that she was forty-seven, and that many of the people she had known now inhabited cemeteries.

In the cold and wintry hall stood coats of armour with closed vizors. These highly polished knights seemed also to be suffering from the cold. From a balustrade hung standards bearing all sorts or coats-of-arms. Beside the door, to which the servant now led her, she caught sight of a tabernacle which she recognized. It had stood in the apartment over the pâtisserie. There it had looked huge, a magnificent piece. Now it had come home. Like man himself, it counted for little at home.

She had feared the prospect of meeting the Prince. She hadn't seen him for fifteen years. A few weeks ago she had sent him a telegram: it had been his sixty-eighth birthday. Would her own age be reflected in his eyes, in a frank, merciless mirror? And would she be able to conceal her own feeling of shock?

As she entered the library she observed to her relief that he looked neither old nor ill. He was still just as slim, and merely walked a little bent. His face did not seem to be furrowed by any more wrinkles than before; they had simply grown deeper.

He came towards her smiling, with open arms. The room, though far larger, reminded her of the library in his Vienna house. Among a thousand rooms she would have recognised a room occupied by Kontowski.

"Well," he said, "let us dispense with all empty phrases. No, I don't look unchanged, as people are in the habit of saying. As if that were a compliment! Not unchanged, but a spry septuagenarian."

"You're sixty-eight," she interrupted him.

"Thank you." He took her arm and led her to a small table by the window. "You're not unchanged either. If I tell you that you've become even more beautiful you won't believe me. Yet it's true—and it's not due merely to my ageing eyes. I can boast of having known it when you were eighteen. I told you at the time that youth didn't suit you—or something to that effect. Please sit down." He pushed the arm-chair into position for her. "Age plays practical jokes. It makes the mature younger, the immature older. May I pour you a glass of port?"

The port gleamed deep red in the cut glass with the princely coronet. Ilona sipped at her glass and smiled. She really did feel young. He had kind eyes, perhaps dishonest eyes. She looked young in the plain black tailor-made costume with the white blouse and a charming little straw hat on her dark-blond hair. Berlin, with its flags, drums, transparencies, and blazing pyres, was thousands of miles away.

He lit one of his long cigarettes.

"I still smoke fifty a day," he said.

"You mean you light fifty," she said.

"Quite right." The cigarette dangled unsmoked between his long fingers. His hand had grown old. Gristle had formed round the wrists, thin branches with frozen buds. "And now," he said, "we will continue the interrupted sentence. Friendship is the ability to continue interrupted sentences fifteen years later."

She was astonished, as she had been astonished for thirty years, to find that he knew almost all about her. A nod as she spoke, a brief question, made her story easy to tell. After only a few minutes she came to her trip to Vienna and Budapest.

When she had finished he pointed to the heavy, dark desk, on which lay mountains of books, newspapers, and pamphlets. They were garish, impudent, out of place here.

"Before we talk any more about you," he said, "I should like to tell you where I stand. Every one 'stands' somewhere nowadays. If you haven't seen a friend for as long as a year you have to ask him where he 'stands.'"

346

"I should have thought it was sufficient to know who he is," objected Ilona.

"You make it easier for me to explain. What is happening in Germany now, and will probably happen elsewhere, is not something I wanted."

"You don't have to tell me that, Taszilo."

He shook his head. "People say that it is revolt of the Right. If you want to understand me you must get the futile terms 'right' and 'left' out of your head. You know that I used to be a reactionary. But that means that I know neither 'right' nor 'left', but only 'upper' and 'lower'. Upper is the aristocracy. Not necessarily by birth, but the aristocracy of an historical class which, when its turn comes, makes a new spiritual choice. Lower is the people. Since politics has rested on the assumption that popular feeling is right, or at least healthy, it has rested on a lie, and because it rests on a lie it is leading the world to its downfall."

"Did you say that you used to be a reactionary? Aren't you one any more?"

"In my own sense, yes; but not in the generally accepted sense. I don't wish to move in a society that makes use of the mob to gain its ends."

"But dictatorship," commented Ilona, doesn't bother about popular feeling."

"That's what democrats say, thereby involuntarily paying the finest tribute to dictatorship. In reality dictatorship is just as much an expression of popular feeling as democracy. It oppresses the people with the help of the people. That is what distinguishes it from aristocracy, which, though it does not oppress the people, does not ask them their wishes either. Dictatorship and democracy, disagreeing about other freedoms, are agreed in granting the people the freedom to commit suicide. When the Germans start the war which they must start, and when they have lost it, as they must lose it, they will put on tearful expressions and say the people were led astray. If that were true it would prove conclusively that peoples, who can always be led astray *en masse*, are unsuited to govern. But it isn't true. The people are not led astray; they lead astray those who are not strong enough to oppose their debased instincts." He took a pair of spectacles with thick horn rims out of his breast-pocket and toyed with them. "You say your husband trusts the German people. He is quite right in so far as he is comparing them with other peoples who will certainly do him the favour of being no better. The German people cannot disappoint me—because they are a people, not because they are German."

"You really are continuing an interrupted sentence," said Ilona. "But the day of aristocratic regimes is now over for good."

Ilona thought of the countless hours in which Kontowski had sat opposite her, apparently speaking to himself, in reality leading up to a goal which she could not yet see. Now she had asked his advice. Had asked him what Stefan was to do. Kontowski couldn't have forgotten that. He took a sip of port and went on.

"Upper and lower, I said. To me that is not a class distinction, or not primarily. You must picture human and political values—they are

347

the same thing—as a mountain composed of several strata. The lowest stratum consists of food. A second, somewhat higher, consists of everyday pleasures—for example, travel, visits to the cinema, various luxuries. The third stratum, higher still, is made up of social benefits—freedom of movement, old-age pensions, and similar advantages. The summit of the mountain of values consists in true freedom—that is to say, freedom of speech and opinion, justice, and all the other intellectual and emotional, in the highest sense personal, freedoms." He glanced at the desk. "If the people are left to choose their own path they will remain lazy wanderers on the first or second, or at best on the third, stage of the mountain. They will either sit down perfectly content among the food or in the cinema, so to speak, or they will lie down in a hospital bed. In other words, once their bellies are full a visit to the cinema seems to the people very desirable; if they can go to the cinema they may possibly think of a comfortable old-age home. The idea of scaling the highest peak leaves the people utterly cold. There is no people that will fight for intellectual and ethical freedoms, because they are not interested in them. It is different if we make the people start the journey from the top; we can confidently give a people the highest freedoms—or, rather, force these freedoms upon them: they won't rest content with them. Tireless and undaunted, they will follow the path downhill— that is to say, via the old-age home and the cinema to food."

Ilona interrupted him. "Have not thousands," she asked, "died for those highest freedoms of which you speak? Don't you believe that thousands will die for them now?"

"Of course," he replied at once. "Otherwise there would be neither revolution nor reaction, which are fundamentally the same thing. But do you seriously believe that revolutions are made by the people? No more than counter-revolutions." He stood up and, still toying with his spectacles, walked over to the desk. He came to a stop under a picture of a Kontowski from the fifteenth century—Ilona remembered that it had hung in the embassy in St Petersburg. "Up to the present the Austro-Hungarian Monarchy was the last European state form, apart from the British, that tried to hinder the people in their descent. In vain!" He cleared his throat. "And now you are thinking that I have been enjoying the sound of my own voice again and only talking about myself. On the contrary, I have been talking about you the whole time."

She couldn't hide her astonishment.

He looked at her and laughed.

"You asked my advice: I have given it to you. Of course you and your husband must leave Germany. You tell me he has Jewish ancestors. People have been racking their brains for centuries to discover the roots of anti-Semitism, although they are perfectly obvious. The Jews, not only because of the thousands of years of their history and of their isolation, but also because their intellectual and moral interests always take precedence over their social interests, are aristocrats; hence, as these offensive leaflets and pamphlets say, they are "alien to the people." So, get out of Germany! But it would be a mistake to emigrate to Austria or here to Hungary. I regard the forms of government prevailing in the rest of Europe with no less distrust

348

than the new German government—to say nothing of the people. There are only Britian and America left."

"America?" she said.

"Yes, America too. America is a constitutional democracy—that is to say, not a democracy in which freedom is permitted, but a democracy in which unfreedom is forbidden. Hence it is a kingdom without a king —one can come to terms with that. When the American lawgivers convened in 1787 they wrote an aristocratic law which at most five hundred of their fellow citizens understood. They did not accept any freedoms from the people; they bestowed freedoms upon the people— on certain conditions. That is the reason, the only reason—it has nothing to do with the national character, which is neither better nor worse than any other—why the mob has never again ruled in America for the last hundred and fifty years." He sat down behind the desk. "I don't know your husband's financial circumstances nor his connexions outside Germany. I need not tell you that my small means and my small influence are at his disposal. Should you be in urgent need of help in Berlin," he continued before she could interrupt him, "please apply to Count Fontenau at the French Embassy. In fact, I shall give you a letter to him straight away. Every aristocrat knows another aristocrat some-where—this too we have in common with the Jews."

He put on his glasses and began to write, using an old quill-pen. The scratching of the pen was the only sound in the room.

Was it really thirty years ago that a pale, slim man in evening-dress had followed her into the room with the headless doll? thought Ilona. Her heart grew so heavy that it felt like a burden under which her body was threatening to collapse. In St Petersburg, when she said good-bye to him in the embassy, she had believed that she would never see him again. How easy was parting when you were young! She felt as though the old man were writing her a letter of farewell. He wouldn't post it; he would put it in her hand, shamefacedly, as he had done all his good deeds. She would go away and never see him again. The gate would click shut, the drawbridge be raised. And behind it the old man would die, alone, as he had lived, even when he was with her, alone, sick, proud, and kind. But she would be far away in a world where the only security there could be did not exist—people you had known when you were young.

Outside the rain had become heavier; it was pattering on the window-panes. It seemed to Ilona as though the light that fell on the paper did not emanate from the yellow parchment lamp but from the old man.

When the Prince had sealed the letter and was coming towards her she said, "I have one more favour to ask of you, Taszilo. I hardly dare put it into words. . . ."

He smiled encouragingly.

"Without my husband's knowledge I have smuggled out of Germany the few pieces of jewellery I possess. Would you keep them for me?"

"Willingly," he said.

She took four or five jewel-cases out of her handbag, brown, velvet-black, wine-red cases. It occurred to her that Kontowski had given her the first jewels she ever had.

He put the cases down on the table.

"It may be that we shall not see each other again for a long time," he said, averting his face. "The jewels will be with Baron Verböczy." He scribbled a name and address on a piece of paper. "If anything happens to me. . . ."

"Nothing will happen to you, Taszilo," she said.

9

She changed at Püspökladány.

The train steamed through the May afternoon. She was alone in the compartment. She had lowered the window and put her head out, as though it was not enough to see the passing landscape, as though she had to hurry towards it. She remembered that on the first railway journeys of her life, to Debreczen and back, her father had warned her not to put her head out of the window because of the trains coming from the opposite direction and the soot from the engines. You remember such warnings all your life. The old locomotive still emitted thick clouds of smoke. The May wind blew them away.

Peasants, men and women, stood in the fields watching the train pass, as they had watched it a thousand times. The earth was black, a spinning gramophone record. The people seemed to be spinning with it. Even the little white clouds in the blue sky were spinning; they disappeared behind the train and reappeared again. A gooseherd was standing beside a pond; he couldn't have been more than ten years old. The ducks waddled after their ducklings and could never catch up with them. In the garden of a signalman's house the signalman's wife was bending down over her flowers. Ilona gazed after her for a long time; the colours of the flowers accompanied the train. The plain was boundless, the sky its only boundary. There was a warm smell, as though the snow that had lain over the fields had been only a warm, white blanket, a featherbed laid down by God. God watched over this countryside lovingly, as though over His own garden. Nothing had changed.

There was the cemetery. It was impossible to see over the top of the cemetery-wall. There, among the other dead, lay her mother. Ilona's heart pounded. The platform barriers, the promenade, the house in which Dr Grünfeld had lived. The mill. What had happened to fat Korcsmáros? She still knew every house.

She saw them from a distance standing by the track—the station-master, Teréz, Margit. The stationmaster was in mufti. It hurt Ilona a little to see that he was in mufti. Behind him she caught sight of a bright-red cap; it must be the new stationmaster's.

The stationmaster helped her down from the footboards. He looked younger than his seventy-four years gave reason to expect, much younger. His hair was grey, his face full of wrinkles, but his eyes shone and his moustache was still as full and jovial as ever, perhaps even more jovial. There was nothing of the strained effort of old men about his walk. He walked as though he could walk as far as the plain extended. You could see that he had neither fought against old age nor

350

welcomed it. He had entered into old age as he entered the warm station office on winter evenings.

Teréz was not wearing a black dress. She wore a blue spring frock done up a little too high at the neck, too much of a Sunday frock, and yet more youthful than the clothes she had worn in the city. Her face too seemed younger than it used to be, a face that still expected something. Margit had grown fat; the last trace of resemblance to Ilona was gone. But Margit too looked young; there wasn't a single wrinkle in her round, rosy face.

Ilona was deluged with questions, especially about Zita and the baby. She asked after Margit's children. She would see Sanyi in the evening, said Margit. He was at the hotel, which he helped his mother to run. Mihály, the youngest, was in Debreczen at the university. He intended to become a doctor. Kató, who had married a farmer, was expecting her third child. "We're both grandmothers," said Margit.

The new stationmaster introduced himself to Ilona. He was in his late thirties, very polite and very officious. It was obvious that he was trying to oblige the old stationmaster. "Laczi will take the luggage into the house on the trolley," he said. Ilona didn't know Laczi. She thought of Máté. She still had the clock he had bequeathed her. The old letters were still under the window; they had merely been repainted, a gleaming black.

"We can walk," said the stationmaster.

He took Ilona's arm and quickly walked on in front with her, as though he wanted to reach the house alone with her.

Ilona laughed. "I can't walk as fast as you, Papa," she said.

"I manage all right," he said. "I've never had a day's illness in my life."

He had built the house near the station, not too far from the village, but closer to the station. The snow-white walls and red roof gleamed from a distance. A merry plume of smoke curled up from the chimney towards the afternoon sky. A conservatory had been built on to the spacious house. The garden was bright with spring flowers.

"I have a little surprise for you," said the stationmaster. He looked round to see if Margit and Teréz were following, and walked faster still. He led Ilona through the garden, through the hall, and straight upstairs.

"It smells the same as ever," said Ilona. "I'm sure you've been cooking all day long."

She didn't want to say that it also smelt of smoke and soot, as on the station.

At the top of the stairs the stationmaster stopped to get his breath back. Now he had won the race, he was alone with Ilona. He opened a door.

"That's your room," he said.

"My room?"

"As long as I have a house you have a room," said the stationmaster. She tried to hide her tears, and walked over to the window. From the little window she could see the railway-tracks. The train was just leaving the station.

351

The stationmaster came up beside Ilona, put his arm round her shoulders, and gazed after the train.

10

It was now late. Margit and Sanyi had left, and Teréz had retired to her room, magnanimous rather than offended.

Ilona and the stationmaster were sitting in the dining-room. The furniture was the same—the tall sideboard, the grandfather-clock, the table that was too big even for the new room. Only the settee with the lions' heads had disappeared. In the corner stood a built-in couch upholstered with a plush material that was new and at the same time old, such as was to be seen in the windows of middle-class furniture-stores everywhere.

"Have you heard anything from Aunt Rosa?" asked Ilona.

"I didn't want to write and tell you. She died last year. She was run over by a car. I went to the funeral. All her girls were there. She left all her money to her girls."

Ilona felt a stab in her heart, a little sharp stab. Aunt Rosa had not meant well with her, and yet good had come of her actions. A higher power guided the hand of men. What they did had meaning; they simply didn't know what the meaning was. Aunt Rosa dead! One became more and more lonely. Perhaps among Aunt Rosa's girls there was one whom her money would save.

Then they talked about Lajos, who had been in Moscow for the past six years.

"I'll show you his last letter," said the stationmaster. "He writes twice a year. Doesn't he ever write to you?"

"He wrote once last year."

"Can you understand him? First he had to run away from the Bolsheviks. Now he's in Moscow."

"He was tired of talking about the past in Viennese coffee-houses. Do you know what he is doing?"

"He doesn't tell me anything about that. He always sends a whole lot of postage-stamps; Sanyi collects stamps."

Again and again the stationmaster came back to Zita. Ilona showed him photographs. At every second photograph the stationmaster said, "I know that one already. I've got it myself." There were photographs of Zita all over the house. He gazed at the pictures of Eva for a long time, smiling. "A beautiful name," he said. Everything about Zita's child seemed to him beautiful.

Ilona began cautiously to talk about Zita's husband.

"What kind of man is this Hitler?" asked the stationmaster.

Ilona told him what kind of man he was.

The stationmaster shook his head, as if he didn't understand.

"Do you think there will be another war?" he asked.

"People say so."

He played with a china ballerina that stood on the small table in front of the couch. She wore a short lace skirt that looked like Turkish delight.

"I don't want to go through another war," he said. "Although I don't fear it as I feared the last one. I don't know if you will understand what I mean. The Great War was still part of the peace. Since then there has been war." He glanced towards the window, as though war were standing outside, stubbornly waiting. After a while he said, "If there's a war you must all come home. The house is large enough."

All the time she wanted to tell him she couldn't come home, neither in peace nor in war. She kept putting it off. The stationmaster still knew nothing about the great helplessness, the common destiny.

She spoke of Teréz.

"At the beginning it was difficult," said the stationmaster. "Gradually she told me everything. I believe Bicskei would have married her. The teacher, you know. They went out together a few times. Then he stopped coming; I don't know why. Perhaps she thinks she has to stay with me." He laughed softly. "Since I have been sure she wouldn't marry I have acted as if I couldn't do without her." He ran his little finger over his moustache, as he had always done. "There's no hurry—but could you perhaps, very carefully ask Zita if she could invite Teréz to stay with her some time? She is constantly talking about Zita."

"Of course," said Ilona. She thought, he doesn't know what kind of a man Hitler is, but he knows more than the rest of us put together.

The grandfather-clock struck twelve.

"You must be tired," said the stationmaster.

Ilona wondered whether to wait till the morning. Could one telephone to Berlin from Kisnémet? Perhaps she would have to leave to-morrow.

"We're going away," she said.

"Where to?"

"We don't know yet."

She told the stationmaster why she had been in Vienna and Budapest. She tried to explain to him what it meant to be the publisher of books and periodicals that were publicly burned. She told him that Stefan had had a Jewish mother.

He listened in silence, without interrupting, leaning forward a little as he sat with folded hands. There was a slight twitching round his mouth as he said, "How far away are you going?"

"I don't know yet, Papa. Probably to England." She said nothing about America.

"Of course you could come to me," he said. "But that might not be the right thing for Stefan."

She put her hand on his hand. It was cold, the gradually cooling hand of an old man.

"Shall I ever see you again?" he said.

She stroked his hand. She felt guilty, as though with rough fingers she had drawn a line through the leaf of a calendar on which 1918 stood, and had written 1933 in its place. Old calendars had hung in the quiet house as they had once hung in Máté's room.

The stationmaster straightened up and made a circular movement with his head, as though the celluloid collar of his uniform were still bothering him. He looked now like an old general.

"All right," he said. "Don't misunderstand me, Ilona. It sounds like

353

one of the maxims hanging in the kitchen. Even in her day your mother couldn't stand them." He stopped. "Now you must think only of your husband. Zita has found her own happiness. It belongs to her; we know nothing about it. I was talking nonsense. I shall still be here when you come back. Korcsmáros is eighty-six, Sümegi already ninety. Teréz will be here too, and Margit. When two people love each other they must stick together. Then the times cannot harm them. Not even these times."

She twined her arms round his neck.

Later they stood in her room by the open window. There was a smell of sun-dried washing. The fields were fragrant. A bird sang, very briefly, with a single note, as though it were singing in its sleep, as men talk in their sleep. The signal of Kisnémet station stood out like a green moon against the sky.

11

Ilona and Stefan quietly made preparations for their move to London. They told no one of their intention to remain abroad. They had many friends, but they dared not confide in anyone. The British consulate-general supplied Herr and Frau Herrdegen with an entry visa to Britain. People spoke of a visa nowadays as of buried treasure. There were words that grew enormous, mysterious, and were uttered with reverence. Visa was one such word, consulate another, passport a third. Their passports were with Count Fontenau at the French Embassy.

Although the Government had closed down the S. Herrdegen publishing house and forbidden it to publish anything more, Stefan kept postponing their departure. New laws prohibited Germans from taking money and valuables out of the country under pain of death. Herrdegen had only insignificant sums of money abroad. In vain Ilona assured him that she could very well adapt herself to a modest life in freedom. He felt guilty, suffered under the responsibility with which he had burdened himself, seemed to be trying by every means to make up for his omissions. Had he secrets from her? Or was he waiting for a miracle?

Something had to happen that touched him more directly than anything yet, before he could make up his mind to leave.

They had given notice to the cook and chambermaid. One morning —it was by now mid-September—they woke without being woken by Reinhart. His bed was untouched. All his possessions were gone. Stefan's desk had been broken open and his papers ransacked. Many were missing. Ilona and Stefan went through the empty house. The spare room looked as though burglars had broken in; the mattresses lay on the floor. The manuscripts that Stefan had hidden had vanished.

When Stefan left the house an hour later he immediately came in again. He was deathly pale. Ilona followed him out in front of the house. In white paint on the wall stood the word 'Jew' with the swastika daubed beside it.

12

The train was due to leave in the evening.

Ilona left the house early in the morning. Everything was ready. The course of the day was not to differ from any other. Only she wanted to say good-bye to Dr Ginsburg and Dr Sales. Stefan had agreed with a weary smile. "Women have to say good-bye," he commented.

It was a bright September morning. The air seemed to be full of gay beads. The sun above the roofs was a big yellow apple; it hung in the sky as though on an invisible tree laden with autumn fruit. It was no longer a summer sun; you could look up at it as at the tops of the trees.

Ilona shivered. It wasn't due to the slight cold she had been fighting against for several days. The day before yesterday, yesterday, and finally this morning she had rung Dr Ginsburg. A crackling in the receiver had been the only response. She was frightened.

As she mounted the few steps leading through the vestibule of the ostentatious building on the corner of the Fehrbelliner Platz and passed the cold marble walls decorated with mosaics she remembered the afternoon on which she had come here for the first time. She thought of her first meeting with Stefan. Her heart melted. She was grateful. All that had happened was good, good and natural.

She rang the bell and waited for a long time. There was somebody at home; she could hear footsteps. She rang again.

Timidly the door was opened, and Lina, Dr Ginsburg's majestic housekeeper, big, fat Lina, stood in the doorway. When she saw Ilona her features relaxed, as though a weight were falling from her. She began to sob. She threw her arms round Ilona and pressed her huge body against her like a child trying to hide behind its mother's apron.

They went into the drawing-room and sat down at the table at which Ilona had sat with Herrdegen and Ginsburg. Clock-keys lay on the table, old rusty keys with ornamental iron wards, a small mountain of them. A blue duster lay beside them. Lina took it away, quickly stuffing it into the pocket of her apron.

She told Ilona what had happened, interrupting her story with sobs, over-elaborating minor details, and losing the thread in the way simple people do.

They had taken the Herr Doktor away a week ago. The men in brown had turned everything upside down. It had taken Lina days to get the flat into some sort of order again. So that Dr Ginsburg should find it tidy when he came back. "He will come back, won't he, Baroness?" The men in brown had accused him of trying to flee the country. They said he had money hidden away, foreign money. They hadn't found any foreign money, but they had taken all the money that was in the house. "He was quite calm," said Lina. "He kept trying to reassure me all the time." The tears ran down over her fat face, fat tears. The next day they had come back, she went on, and taken away pictures, gold objects, clocks. "Our pictures," she said, "our clocks."

Ilona looked round the room. The glass case with the watches was empty. There were dark patches on the wallpaper. A few clocks were still hanging on the walls, ticking regularly.

"I wind them up every day," said Lina, pointing to the keys. "I had difficulty in finding them all. The Herr Doktor always wound up the clocks himself."

Then she went to Dr Ginsburg's son-in-law, Lina continued. The Baroness knew that the Herr Doktor didn't get on with the Herr Doktor, his son-in-law, the dentist. But, he was married to Dr Ginsburg's daughter. They had children. "After all, he's human, I thought. And a big noise in the Party.

"As soon as I came to him I knew what had happened," said Lina. "There was one of our clocks hanging in the waiting-room. He had denounced the Herr Doktor. I don't know what has happened to his wife. Perhaps he had his own wife taken away; I wouldn't put it past him. The children were still there; I saw them through the door."

She began to cry again, pulled out the duster instead of her handkerchief, and wiped her wet eyes with it.

The Russian cuckoo-clock struck in the next room.

Ilona gritted her teeth. It wouldn't help if she started crying too. She saw Dr Ginsburg before her, between the men who had taken him away. He had sat opposite her for days and nights on end in the train travelling across the Russian plain. "We Jews always travel in the wrong direction," he had said. He had travelled in the wrong direction, upright, dignified, with his gold watch-chain over his waistcoat.

The old woman gripped Ilona's hand across the table.

"You come like an angel, Baroness," she said. "I should have got in touch with you long ago. I'm sure you'll help him. I'm sure you'll bring the Herr Doktor back."

Now Ilona did begin to cry. She covered her face with both hands. He had helped her on the endless journey. He had stood with his hat in his hand in the snowstorm in the Kurfürstendamm. Then he had played Destiny a little. The gold coins had glittered in his eyes. "I'm sure you'll help him." Her train left in the evening.

13

Ilona looked out of the taxi-window, but she scarcely saw the street. The tears hung in front of her eyes like a veil. The streets were full of people. Many of the women were still wearing summer frocks. There were fashion dummies standing in the shop-windows. Buses were hooting. Workmen, shopkeepers, a woman with a pram, girls, postmen, a baker's boy on a bicycle—none of them knew about Dr Ginsburg. Her powerlessness came home to Ilona, tightening her throat. Why couldn't she cry out to these people and tell them what had happened? None of them would have listened. None of them cared about Dr Ginsburg. Every one for himself, and not a human feeling among them. Wasn't Kontowski right? They were all going downhill. To right or left, but downhill.

The taxi drove slowly along by the pavement to make way for an ambulance. The ambulance passed with sirens wailing. Ilona saw the white figure of a doctor, a bandaged body. She felt something she had never felt before—a terrifying feeling. She envied the accident victim.

He had had an accident like a thousand others. Dr Ginsburg's accident was different—his own. No ambulance carried him away; no doctor came to his aid.

She ran up the steps of the house in Neukölln.

Dr Sales opened the door himself. He was wearing white trousers and was in shirtsleeves. He had just been changing to make his calls. He took Ilona into the consulting-room.

She forgot that she had come to say good-bye. She told him of her visit to Dr Ginsburg's flat. "I can do nothing. You must help him, Dr Sales."

He rose from behind his desk and began to pace up and down. It was as though he wanted to run his broad, bare skull against the wall. "I'll do what I can," he said. "Have you any idea where they have taken him?"

"Lina said something about the Alexanderplatz."

"The Alexanderplatz!" he repeated. It sounded as though he were saying "To hell!" He came to a stop in front of Ilona. "I'll do what I can," he reiterated. "To-day. I wonder what the fellows in the Alexanderplatz will tell me." He picked up a retractor-hook and seemed to be trying to bend it double in his fist. "But don't let me raise your hopes. I have no contacts with that gang of thugs."

She told him the real reason for her visit. "We're leaving to-day," she said.

He pushed a chair up beside her and sat down. He had grown very quiet. She thought she could hear his breathing. He rested his head in his hands, as he had often done at Sant'Andrea.

"Listen, Ilona," he said. He spoke in a low voice that did not seem to be his own. "I've been sick of all this rubbish for a long time." He waved his hand through the air, as though he wanted to sweep everything away—medicine cupboards, examination couch, basin-stand. "My people have cancer. I'm tired of treating intestinal catarrh. There must be a few men in this country who don't go weak at the knees at the sight of that gang. I shall look for them, I shall find them, you can rely on that." His voice sank ever lower. "The devil wears a thousand masks, and human beings are so stupid that they don't see behind them. Once in a while the Lord compels the devil to take off his mask. Then people think a great day has come for the devil. 'Look,' they say, 'he is so powerful that he no longer needs his masks.' People are stupid. A devil without a mask is no longer a devil. The power rests in the mask, as it rested in Samson's hair. I don't know whether I shall be here when you come back, Ilona. But that's not important. Not important," he repeated. "You will come back, be sure of that. I'm sorry I can't see Herrdegen again before you go. Let him know that we aren't all swine."

He put his arm round her shoulders and walked out into the hall with her.

"God be with you!" he said.

He kissed her on both cheeks.

14

Zita held the baby in her arms. Eva had been six months old a
fortnight ago. She had red cheeks and shining blue eyes, not doll's
eyes, like those of other babies, but eyes that were mutely understanding. Nor was her nose wide and flat, like other babies'; it was
fully formed, the tiny model of a real nose. Her honey-blond hair
peeped out from under her pink hood. Zita had dressed her entirely in
pink. Her little jacket was pink. Ilona had knitted it.

The taxi approached the house in the Grunewald.

Zita looked down at the baby. Everything she wore had been given
to her by Ilona. Zita hadn't noticed this until Eva was fully dressed.
Without knowing it she had wanted to give her mother pleasure. Had
she ever wanted to give her mother pleasure before? Her throat was
tight.

She couldn't believe that her mother was really going away, although
she had often gone away before. When Zita herself had been moving
from one hotel bedroom to another she hadn't seen her mother for
years on end. That wasn't the same. Was the change due to the baby
in her arms? A mysterious bond bound mothers together, good mothers
and bad. The baby became heavy in Zita's arms, as though she couldn't
carry it alone. Was the change due to her own sense of guilt? Her
mother had often left her alone. Now that didn't matter any more. She
was driving her mother out. "Herrdegen could go alone," Konrad had
said. She had looked at him uncomprehendingly, a cold shudder running down her spine. She experienced the moment in which a woman
fails to understand a man for the first time. From then onward misunderstandings followed one upon the other, relentlessy, like the
minutes of a self-winding clock. Or was that not the reason either? She
hadn't needed her mother. She had said so to others, and to herself.
But her mother had always been there. Where had she been? The dead
were also somewhere, but they were out of reach. She pressed the baby
to her protectively, at the same time seeking protection from her child.

The taxi stopped. The driver helped Zita out. He looked into the
baby's face and smiled. As Zita was paying him his eyes fell on the
wall of the house. "Jew" was daubed on it, and a swastika. The driver
looked away from the wall and glanced into the baby's face again,
quickly, pityingly.

Zita ran up the steps and frantically rang the bell. If the door wasn't
opened at once she would collapse.

Ilona opened the door.

Zita laid the baby in her mother's arms and burst out sobbing.

Ilona stood there helplessly, not knowing what to do—whether to
press her child to her heart or put the baby down somewhere.

Zita ran into the drawing-room, as though running away from her
mother and her baby.

Ilona followed her without a word and made a bed for Eva on the
settee.

Zita gritted her teeth.

"She never cries," she said. "Not even at night."

"Just like you," said Ilona. "You never cried either." She didn't look at Zita but gazed into the little red face. She has dressed her all in my things, she thought.

They sat down.

"I saw the wall," said Zita.

"It was Reinhart. He was with Stefan for twenty years."

They said nothing. The curtains were drawn. The afternoon sun was shining into the room through a crack between them. Grains of dust were dancing in the ray of sunlight, forming a wall of silvery grains of dust between mother and daughter.

"Are you really leaving, Mummy?" said Zita.

"Yes. This evening."

They looked at the baby. She was asleep. In her sleep she moved her finger. Fingers were the most wonderful, the most incredible, things about babies. Her fingers were still tiny and yet completely adult. They were the fully grown human being already present in the baby.

"I told Konrad, Mummy," said Zita. "You forbade me to, but I told him. He sends you his good wishes; sends you both his good wishes," she corrected herself. Shame came upon her, like a crowd of grinning carnival figures circling round her, refusing to let go of her. "All at once I hated Konrad," she said.

"You must be sensible," said Ilona. She managed to smile, although she was afraid that she would have to cry if she smiled. "We go where our husbands go. It's harder for you than for me. I know that Stefan is right; you mustn't ask whether Konrad is right."

"I'm not you," said Zita.

She wanted to provoke her mother, but she was no longer able to. She wanted to say, "I'm not you; I have to understand a man in order to love him." It didn't sound provocative. I don't hate Konrad, she thought. But why don't I hate him? Her love flowed out to her mother, fierce and hot and powerful.

What good would it do if she hated her husband? thought Ilona. What ought I to wish her? She had always known what she ought to wish Zita. What could have happened that a mother no longer knew what she should wish her child?

"The child is the most important thing, Zita," she said, quickly continuing, "There is just one thing I want to tell you. Remember that Grandfather is always there. And Teréz, of course. Papa is the same as ever. He has set aside a room for you in the new house."

She wanted to say, "You can have my room. I shan't need it." She was leaving behind everything she had loved. Her father, her child, her granddaughter. But she didn't feel sorry for herself; she simply felt that a link had broken out of a chain, and that she was this link. The strongest link had broken out; the chain was falling to pieces.

There was silence again. Both of them were thinking that it would have been better if they had not seen each other again. Both of them were trying to think of moments when they had hated each other. Neither of them could remember any.

"Did you see Peppi?" asked Zita.

"Peppi is dead. She died in March."

Zita bent over the back of the chair and hid her face in her hands. She knew that she wasn't weeping for Peppi. "Do you really have to go away, Mummy?" she said. She didn't expect an answer.

Ilona thought of the day on which Zita had twined her arms around her at the last moment on the Vienna East station. She had gone to St Petersburg. That time she hadn't had to go.

She stood up. It was getting late. She had to call Stefan. He had been sitting at his desk in the library the whole afternoon. She had left him alone. He had sat at this desk for years, long before she had known him.

At the settee she came to a stop and looked into the face of the sleeping baby. The night at Berény sprang to her mind. Upstairs a woman had cried out for help. She had held her hand over Zita's eyes. Children slept or were mute. Or pretended to be. They were witnesses, mute witnesses, mute accusers.

"Stefan wants to say good-bye to you," said Ilona

She went into the library. Stefan was sitting behind his empty desk. Only his hands were on top of the desk. He stood up and followed her, saying nothing, his head bent.

When they entered the drawing-room Zita was standing in the middle of the room dressed to leave, her baby in her arms.

Ilona stood aside while her husband and her daughter exchanged a few friendly, awkward words.

Then Zita and Ilona went out into the hall. Stefan stayed hesitantly behind in the drawing-room doorway, as though willing to help, but at the same time feeling superfluous.

Zita caught sight of the trunks standing by the wall. She hadn't noticed them when she arrived.

She was overcome by sobs. Her throat had been holding her tears in check; now it let them go free. She wept so violently that she couldn't hold the baby. Ilona wanted to take it from her, but Zita didn't give it to her. She went up to Stefan, forced the baby upon him, and twined her arms round her mother's neck.

"Mummy, Mummy!" she cried over and over again.

The two women stood bending over each other. The man stood in the doorway with the baby in his arms.

At last Zita tore herself away, took Eva, and rushed out.

Ilona covered her face.

She felt Stefan's arms round her shoulders.

"It's my fault," he said.

She kissed him on the cheek.

"We should have ordered a taxi for her," she said.

15

Ilona and Stefan stayed in London for three years.

They lived in a small flat in one of the two-storey brick-built houses in Kensington that never cease to look respectable however cheap they may be. "An Englishman's home is his castle," runs the saying. So the English have built thousands of little castles side by side with curved walls and black doors; castles occupied by shopkeepers and clerks, writers and doctors, a nation of aristocrats; not a people at all, Kontowski had said, so that this people should not give the lie to his contempt. The windows of the old house with the Victorian furniture looked out on to one of those tiny gardens that live like thousands of little hearts in the middle of London, as though the English forbade their city to encroach upon these hearts, being a cool people who know how to keep their hearts intact. A few steps led up to the door, as they had led up to the door of the villa in the Grunewald. To the right and left of the steps stood cast-iron lanterns that looked like merry sea-lions playing with glass balls. The garden was encircled by a high fence whose iron uprights resembled the spears of royal guards and turned the garden into a royal park.

London held its hand protectively over the two refugees from Berlin —a huge masculine hand. They grew calm. It was unseemly not to be calm, and because in this city people appeared to be unaware of the unseemly, they too gradually ceased to be aware of it. Stefan compared London with Berlin. One thing the two cities had in common: they were stronger than the people who inhabited them. They were like certain crack regiments that are not necessarily composed of crack individuals, but whose members behave as though they were crack individuals in order not to let down the regiment.

They had no need as yet to touch the money they possessed. They knew what they had, yet they didn't know whether it was a lot or a little. That depended upon the duration of their absence. Their absence from where? And would it ever end? Stefan had scraped together some money—the payment for books which he had sold abroad just before the end. The gilt-edged securities left to Ilona by Rattowitz were deposited with a bank, one of those curious British institutions which give the impression that the old clerks take the money home with them every evening and bring it back again in the morning, for safety's sake. Also deposited in the bank was her jewellery, which a friend of Kontowski's had brought from Budapest. One of Ilona's few pleasures since their flight was being able to talk to Stefan about money. This was the only sphere from which, in the past, he had excluded her, like the men of earlier generations, who regarded money as an indecent subject about which it was better not to speak in the presence of ladies. He gradually abandoned the amiable fiction that women must receive money like rain from heaven, which fell or did not fall, but was under all circumstances of supernatural origin. They had lived together; now they budgeted together.

A fortunate exception among his countrymen, Stefan had found a job soon after his arrival. It was badly paid, because he had no labour permit—a new expression in many people's vocabulary, like consulate, visa, and identity-card. "Adviser" was his title: he advised an English publisher he had known for a long time about German manuscripts— some written by refugees, others sent from Germany. He had no office and worked at home. Twice a week he went to the West End and picked up books and manuscripts from the publisher. He was often exhausted when he came home after a tiring journey by Underground.

Ilona admired the matter-of-fact way in which he adjusted himself to his new life. They often discussed their fate, and Ilona was certain that his contentment was not assumed. He looked as he had looked during the good years again. "Success is a great danger," he joked. "When you no longer have to lug books around you imagine you couldn't if you had to."

At first post from Berlin came regularly. "A letter from your daughter," said the postman when Ilona opened the door to him. He was an old man with a white moustache who reminded her of Józsi bácsi. Because he had been delivering letters for thirty years he knew what was in them. Zita's letters spoke of Eva. She sent photographs. She wrote about Eva's first steps and her first tooth and her first words. Ilona said to Stefan, "Zita has never written such cordial letters, and they were never so distant. It's as though she were telling us everything about one part of her life in order not to have to tell us anything about any of the other parts." Later the letters became rarer. Ilona wrote every week, generally on Saturday evening. She didn't answer anything, since there was nothing to answer, nor did she expect to receive an answer. The letters travelled to and fro and passed each other, like trains in the night.

After arriving in London they had let their house in the Grunewald, through a friend, to a lawyer, who paid the rent punctually into a deposit account. One day Stefan brought home a letter that had reached him care of the publisher for whom he worked. The house in the Grunewald had been seized by the Party. The new director of the S. Herrdegen publishing house had claimed it for himself. His name was Reinhart Stuck. It was the valet. He had moved into the publishing house with the purloined manuscripts. Ilona watched Stefan. He wasn't indignant, as she had expected, not even hurt, as she had feared. "The curious thing about these times," he said, "is that they have no discernment about metaphors. People talk about the 'publisher who is a lackey,' but, of course, they mean 'lackey' metaphorically. That is a mistake. He really is a lackey." Ilona had to talk him into going to see a lawyer to protest against the theft of the name S. Herrdegen. The German consulate-general in London passed on the protest, and passed back Berlin's rejection of it. The times lacked imagination. They could think up the idea of having a lackey as a publisher, but they couldn't think up a new name for the firm.

The number of German books published in London grew smaller and smaller. The majority of refugee writers were still in France or already in America. Many were in Vienna or Prague. When the German language beat against their ears they imagined they were at home. The great figures of the past were no longer translated, because abroad the language of Hitler was confused with the language of Goethe. The London publisher had very little need now of his German adviser. At the end of every month Stefan felt as if he were receiving charity. In the summer of 1936 a New York publisher offered to pay the Herrdegens' fare to the United States and to employ Stefan as a reader.

In October they left their home-in-exile.

16

December 14, 1936, was a Monday. It was Ilona's fiftieth birthday.

She was not allowed to get up until the birthday-table had been laid. It stood beside the breakfast-table. She inspected the black crocodile handbag, the white-kid gloves, her favourite perfume, Nuit de Noël, the delicate silk nightdress trimmed with Brussels lace. Long-stemmed yellow roses were gleaming in the vases.

Three times a week a coloured woman came to do the cleaning. Her name was Leilah, but Stefan called her "God's Blessing," because she had a habit of saying "God bless you" on every possible occasion. Leilah wasn't coming to-day, but the little flat was clean; there wasn't much to do. The flat was on the first floor of one of these old houses in Lexington Avenue that were built at a time when immigrants still thought they could take their old homeland with them on the soles of their shoes. In New York people didn't have homes, but only addresses. "Lexington and 77th" was a good address. If you lived there you had to do without a large flat: you paid with the number of rooms for the number of the street. Stefan and Ilona had only a bedroom and a large living-room, whose furniture Ilona had pushed this way and that until the room could be taken for a living-room, a dining-room, or a study, according to its use at the moment.

She sat down at her dressing-table. She had had the round stool upholstered with pink chintz; the dressing-table was covered in lace, which, along with so many superfluous things, she had brought with her from Germany; the cosmetic cartons, powder-puffs, and silver boxes made her think of a royal mistress's boudoir.

When she looked down at the bottles, phials, mirrors, and pots she couldn't help laughing. She couldn't part with a scent-bottle so long as it still contained a single drop. She was beginning to grow old and crotchety.

The mirror reassured her. She was wearing he hair longer again, combed up in a way that was reminiscent of the "Ilona hair-style" of her youth. Here and there a grey hair mingled with the dark-blond, a chance thread of silver. It had never occurred to her to pull them out. The fine tracks of the years lay round forehead and eyes, but nose, mouth, and chin had remained untouched. Her face, which she scrutinized daily, was still the same as ten or twenty years ago, her body unchanged.

She thought of her fortieth birthday. Four was an angular number between the round three and the round five. She had been married to Stefan for two years at that time. The day women fear had passed like a mild autumn day still full of summer sunshine.

The mirror wished her a happy birthday. There are said to be people who triumph over age. She couldn't remember having fought against age. Perhaps it was because she had the same attitude towards age as towards men. She had neither fought them nor been subjugated by them. Fighting ended with victory or defeat. Defeats are bitter; victories dearly bought. It is the same with age. People look embittered when they defeat it. It wasn't to spite age that she made herself beautiful, but *for* age, as though for a lover. Age likes to see a woman looking beautiful, just as men do. It becomes cruel if you fight it, as soft as wax if you meet it half-way, just as men do. It refuses to be robbed of anything, but enjoys giving, just as men do. Furthermore, it also lies as men do. It avers that there is a substitute for beauty. There is no substitute for beauty; but even that isn't sad. A woman is beautiful when she pleases; what other explanation can there be for the changing ideals of female beauty? A woman can always please, provided she doesn't imagine that it is sufficient to hide the signs of age under make-up. Is it so difficult to stroke a man's brow? He sees only the hand. Is it so difficult to make him a home in which the flowers do not wither? He confuses their freshness with the woman's freshness. Is it so difficult to make her blood, which previously listened only to its own melody, listen to the rhythm of another's blood? It is only difficult when she wishes to remain young and beautiful for her own benefit or for the benefit of other women. Women's eyes are malevolent mirrors. Men's eyes are friendly mirrors; but mirrors themselves are nothing but the eyes of the one who looks into them.

Fifty years, thought Ilona. She couldn't help laughing, because she still wrinkled her forehead in front of the mirror, although thin lines had long since begun to run across it; little folds lay round her eyes, and her skin woke up after she did and went to sleep before she did. What difference did it make? At parties men flew towards her; in the street they turned round and stared at her, even if they weren't the same men as in the past. Men paid her compliments, mirrors paid her compliments, age paid her compliments.

She thought of the nightdress Stefan had given her, a youthful, coquettish nightdress. Not to want to be younger than one was, but to accept the tribute of loving blindness gratefully—perhaps that was the secret.

She looked in the mirror again, and her heart beat for Stefan as it had beaten for him every day of these happy and terrible twelve years.

She had sat there for half an hour in front of the mirror admiring her own beauty. It was all quite different really. The truth was that she had been looking at herself with his eyes. The secret was to be fifty years old and loved.

17

The news became more and more frightening.

In October the Roman imitator had attacked defenceless Abyssinia; the world watched the attack without stirring. Japan attacked China. Spain was on fire. Criminals issued moral licences to one another. "Duce, I shall never forget what you have done," telegraphed the German misleader when the Roman imitator gave his approval to the rape of Austria. The free world held the ring for him when Hitler made his "last territorial demand" and occupied Sudetenland. It was 1938. Moloch was insatiable. His belly grew fatter and fatter, his appetite larger and larger. He swallowed countries and peoples.

Stefan's work, his modest but fortunate job, brought him into contact with Americans, but he found them hard to understand. Their absolutely infinite patience drove him, who was patient by nature, to impatience. Their friendliness seemed to him too general, and he distrusted it. The speed with which his colleagues in the publishing house changed, so that he barely had time to say good-bye to them, set his nerves on edge; the senselessness of an address and telephone-book containing only the names of nomads exasperated him. That an author, no matter how famous, was worth no more than the success of his latest book was incompatible with his feeling for value and achievement. He found it as difficult to get used to addressing the head of the firm as "Fred" as he did to being addressed himself as "Steve" by the humblest book-keeper. He was humiliated by having a woman under thirty as his immediate superior. Twenty times a day he shut the door of his office, which was left open twenty times. He was baffled by the practice of eating a stand-up lunch of sandwiches with salad and mayonnaise. He told himself in vain that the incomprehensible disorder in American working life was nevertheless better than the chaos in his homeland; the business methods which he condemned, gentle by comparison with the organized criminality of Germany; the vulgarity of everyday life noble by comparison with the brutality of the freed lackey. Day by day he became more "European."

Stefan jestingly called Ilona his "ambassadress to the United States." She tried to live up to the part. What good would it do Stefan if she gave way to his moods? For the first time in their marriage she had to fight against them. In any case, like most women, she had quickly made friends with America. If one of her European friends commented that the skyscrapers were "rocks with lavatory windows" she would only hear the word "rocks." Manhattan was indeed a rocky landscape, beautiful in its gigantic ugliness. She showed Stefan the city by night, when darkness covered up all the ugliness and made all the beauty shine out. The skyscrapers grew small, looking, if one only wished them to, like thousands of little biscuit houses one on top of the other. Could Stefan deny that Broadway resembled Berlin's best theatre district, that there was no musical event in the world to compare with the Sunday-afternoon concerts at Carnegie Hall, that the department stores could compete with the smartest shops in the Kurfürstendamm? The people's friendliness sprang from guilt-free hearts. The milkman who showed her photographs of his children, the delicatessen-keeper who talked Yiddish to her, thinking it was German, the postman who apologized when he brought no letter from Zita, the taxi-driver who tracked down her address to return a forgotten umbrella, not to speak of Leilah, "God's Blessing"—they were all new friends to Ilona.

She sometimes reproached Stefan with ingratitude. America had given him asylum. Stefan agreed with her, and remained as distant as before. In the evenings they often went to the cinema, for the sake of the news-reel, which Stefan followed with burning eyes, and in which, as she knew, he saw only the background, European landscapes, German cities. When they walked home at night through the silent streets she would put her arm through Stefan's, acting as though she were seeking his protection, though in reality she was lending him support. He walked along the walls, as though afraid the stone giants would crash down on him; he blinked at the lights like a blind man; a desert seemed to spread out around him. At night, when he embraced her, it sometimes seemed to her as if he were clinging to his homeland. She had to be more to him than she had been.

18

That Saturday Ilona spent the whole day altering her black-velvet dress which she had brought with her from London.

It was at the beginning of 1939. A few days earlier Ilona had stumbled on the name Zoltán Szomoru in the *New York Times*. He had landed in New York on the *Queen Mary*. The newspaper said that the world-famous conductor did not intent to return to Europe. "I hope," he had said, "that my decision will induce many other prominent artists to leave Germany as a protest against Hitlerian barbarity." The maestro had refused an invitation to conduct in Hitler's presence. "Next Saturday Szomoru is giving a concert in Carnegie Hall, the whole proceeds from which will go to the victims of Nazi persecution from Germany and Austria. He will conduct Beethoven's *Ninth Symphony*." A photograph showed him at the rail of the ship, his white hair fluttering in the wind. He wore no overcoat, but only a thick woollen scarf round his neck. He looked young.

Until yesterday Ilona had hesitated about accompanying Stefan to the concert. He knew of her youthful love; knew about the years Zita had lived with Zoltán. As a representative of the refugees, Stefan couldn't stay away. Like all men, he was jealous of his wife's past. Unlike women, men believe that the present and future cannot touch them, but they suffer all the more from their powerlessness with regard to the past—from their powerlessness or from their fear of comparison. Not without coquetry, Ilona enjoyed Stefan's touching jealousy. She did not disclose to him that she could now scarcely understand her youthful love. It was only when Stefan, half seriously, half in jest, taxed her with not daring to see Zoltán that she made up her mind to go to the concert, on condition that Stefan would go on alone to the reception that was to follow it. As the needle sped on over the old black dress she was convinced that she was attending the concert only to please Stefan.

They had aisle seats in the third row centre. The tickets were expensive, and only a few refugees were present. The audience who could afford the tickets was exceedingly smart. Ilona wondered whether her dress didn't look shabby. Stefan's compliments—was he paying her more compliments than usual to-day?—reassured her. The dress left her shoulders bare. Her décolletage, with the long neck, gently curving shoulders, high bosom, and full white skin, was as beautiful as in her youth. No one would notice that the dress was a little faded.

When the conductor appeared on the podium the audience rose to its feet. The demonstration was not directed exclusively towards the conductor. Nevertheless, Ilona remembered the evening at the Vigadó, when she had had to move next to a married couple because the rows of seats were empty. Then she had been young. To be young meant to hold the future in your hands, like a bird that you could shut up in a cage or allow to go free, just as you liked. Later you can only gaze after it.

Zoltán looked older than in the photographs. Everything noble in his face had been refined still more. The furrows on his forehead were like petrified waves. There was nothing about him now of the country boy who had walked through his mother's fields stripped to the waist.

The conductor seemed astonished by the applause that had greeted him. He ran his hand awkwardly over his white hair. This time, too, he didn't look at the audience, but stood there with head raised, as though the applause were ringing out from a celestial gallery. Was it a pose? Time is kind to vanities; it causes them to become second nature.

Ilona had heard Beethoven's *Ninth* many times, but she was sure that it had never before been performed with such power. From the very first beat the symphony seemed to be striving towards the finale, surging and majestic, mighty and controlled. The symphony was like an alpine chain: the listener stood in a valley and saw all the peaks at the same time at a single breathtaking glance.

Ilona tried hard only to listen to the music, but her thoughts kept wandering to the man in front of the conductor's stand.

She had known Zoltán ever since she was born. If she had been told that he was receiving favours and honours from the monster, she now admitted with shame that she would have believed it. And here he was conducting in Carnegie Hall; conducting without payment in order to ease the want of the victims of persecution; calling upon Europe's artists to revolt; sweeping the orchestra along into a furious protest in its own language, the language of Beethoven. What did one know of the person one imagined one knew best of all? When she thought of Zita she was overcome by revulsion against the man up there, but at the same time she felt that human beings were this as well as that, good and evil, petty and great, wonderful and terrifying in the multiplicity. She had seen the coward in the forests of South Tyrol, and now she found it hard not to glorify the hero. She saw before her the face of the actor in the St Petersburg dressing-room, and she saw his inspired humility as he brushed aside the applause as if it did not belong to him. It wasn't age. He was the same man he had always been—but who was he?

Her thoughts returned to herself. One day in a half-empty Budapest concert-hall she had felt with overwhelming force that she loved this man; she had come from the arms of another and was carrying her child in her womb. Then, one winter evening in Russia, her body had been in a turmoil, and she had betrayed the man to whom she owed everything. Now Zoltán's magic meant nothing more to her, and yet it comprised the meaning of her life—love for another, sacrifice, a common destiny, and, perhaps, belated victory. She heard Dr Sales's voice. There must be a higher being to whom all are subject and who causes all to act as if their acts were independent of their will, so that they serve each other by unwilled deeds, by deeds performed in despite of their will.

It seemed to Ilona as though the chorus were answering her thoughts. There are times when the glittering gilt falls from pathos and pathos itself becomes simple and quiet. Ilona's heart was constricted. If only her child could have heard the message! Would Zita have understood the message? And would the message not have thrust her yet deeper into misery? Had she forgotten human speech, had her mother taught her so badly? The song soared through space and time, the song of the suffering and victorious. Where there were victors there were defeated. What kind of triumph was it that the mother won over the daughter? And did the daughter's defeat have to be announced by the one man whom mother and daughter had loved?

She seized Stefan's hand. He was sitting bent forward, his jaw clenched, his jawbones projecting. She knew what he was thinking, and loved him more than before. He was draining to the last drop the chalice of language, of his beloved language, that had broken free and was echoing through the New York concert-hall. The language was already travelling; it was on its way home. Stefan did not let go of Ilona's hand again.

The conductor seemed to hold the orchestra down with both hands. His whole body was turned towards the chorus; he bent down, although the chorus was on a higher level than himself, like a miner digging precious stones out of the ground. Ilona who now looked up to him, saw that he was singing.

When the symphony was at an end there was silence for a moment. The conductor scarcely heard the applause; it was as though he were running away from it. Even the musicians gazed after the fleeing man in surprise.

The applause fell like hot rain. The audience stayed in the hall, applauding on their feet. The maestro didn't appear. The man and the woman in the third row looked at each other. Was it that the conductor wanted to withdraw behind Beethoven's work, behind his own achievement? Was it false modesty? Who could say what was false and what was genuine?

19

A dim light shone through the drawn curtain on to the man's face. Konrad had fallen asleep at last.

Zita lay on her back with her arms crossed behind her head. She could still feel the man's arms round her waist, his hair on her bosom, still felt his warmth in her loins.

She had put Eva to bed earlier than usual this evening. Konrad had read to her from a book of fairy-tales. Now she was sleeping in the next room, unsuspecting. When she awoke her father would be gone. His regiment was on the Polish frontier. It was war.

The happy weariness that follows love had not come. Zita could not get to sleep.

She thought back on the eight years she had lived with Konrad. She tried to imagine that they had been happy years. Before that her life had been meaningless—whether good or bad, meaningless. How often in those days had she asked herself why she lived! Konrad didn't understand the question, and had taught her not to ask it.

Everything had become simple and peaceful. When you are loved by a man you cease looking for love in the eyes, gestures, and words of strangers. When you have a home, a profession, minor and major worries, mutual joys, you do not compare your life with more exciting, greater, more turbulent lives. When you have a child who needs you and whom you almost painfully love you do not search for more mysterious tasks. When a man's touch is enough to set your blood boiling you do not ask why it is so. She had ceased searching and asking.

She sat up. What she had just thought seemed to her insincere—in fact, intolerably mendacious. During the years of her marriage, especially the first years, when she still thought a lot about the past, she often told herself that she had been a liar, of the worst sort, because she had lied to herself. Had she not been convinced of her love for Paul, for Zoltán, for the others? Had she not confused turmoil, passion, fascination, with happiness? After becoming Konrad's wife she had sworn never again to lie to herself, had looked down contemptuously and pityingly and incredulously upon the liar she had been.

The sweat broke out on her forehead. Was there anything more terrible than the realization that you had not changed? She had learnt to hate the woman she had been, and now felt that she was still the same woman.

She started, as though afraid her thoughts might wake the sleeping man. Could it be that only weariness had driven her to this man? That she had tottered forward because she was too tired to stand still? Could it be that the loneliness in her soul had become a dark room which she had fled, even if she had gone from it into a thousand darker rooms? Could it be that her love for her child was not as pure as she thought, that she was not a support to her child, but sought support from her child? Could it be that she had humbly put her brain in her husband's hands, not out of humility, but simply because he was willing to think for her? At all costs stop thinking, stop thinking tonight!

Her thoughts refused to be driven away. If she could have blamed Konrad! She blamed herself. He was drunken. With every victory he became more drunken. But she? She had felt no triumph as the German lands came home. She had been overwhelmed with shame as the books burnt, as the truckloads of Jews passed her in the streets, as friends left without daring to say good-bye. Only a few hours ago Konrad had spoken of the imminent victory over Poland. "We shall force them to their knees. We shall all be home by Christmas." Now he was calmly sleeping, tired by love, peacefully looking forward to war. Suddenly she hated this calm, this peace. It occurred to her— occurred to her now—that he had forbidden her to write to her mother. How often she had hoped that the postman would come late, when Konrad had already left the house! Her mother's letters lay under the linen. She hadn't thrown a single one away. Why did she collect what she feared? She had taken her own letters to the post herself, had put false sender's addresses on the envelope for fear the letters might come back. Her mother had never mentioned it. Even from a distance she had to humiliate herself before her mother. It wasn't Konrad's fault. Konrad was blind. But she wasn't blind, and yet she hadn't spoken . . . she, she, she.

How was it that everything had suddenly become so clear? Perhaps she was only lying to herself afresh. What was her distrust of others compared with her distrust of herself?

She lay back on the pillow; tried to ask herself why these thoughts had crawled out of their hidden holes to attack her now. The war! He had promised her peace and had led her into war. He had sailed with her over the smooth surface of the water, and many-armed octopuses, flashing stingrays, slippery eels, and horrible toadfish had been lurking below the surface. Was he ingenuous, or had he wanted what was happening? It made no difference. He was abandoning her.

Ought she to be proud of him, like the women who lovingly stroke the uniforms, the robes of their executioners? He had to go to war. What did that mean? Did there have to be war? She only knew that he was leaving her alone. She had fled to him from her loneliness, and he was thrusting her deeper into loneliness. The shared bedroom! He had insisted on it seven years ago. Separate bedrooms were unseemly —that was what it said in his book of law containing all the laws which she had made her own. She felt like laughing. Now they would have separate bedrooms after all. She here, in half a bed, and he somewhere in Poland. That wasn't unseemly; that wasn't against the law! . . .

She felt an irresistible urge to shake the peacefully sleeping man, to tell him what she had been thinking. When she sat up she saw his face, and a great weakness came over her, like the weakness she felt as she melted in his arms. She gently touched his hair, and hated herself for her tenderness.

Konrad opened his eyes. The first rays were coming in through the curtains.

20

Occasionally in January, when she picked up the *New York Times* along with the milk-bottles that stood outside the door every morning, Ilona was overcome by an inexplicable disquiet. Perhaps, she thought, it was only because Stefan had gone to the publishing house earlier than usual, so that she was alone with the newspaper, so to speak. Every morning they read the newspaper together. In the evening he brought three or four home with him. People were living on newspapers and radio reports.

She sat down at the breakfast-table again and leafed through the fat newspaper. There was nothing unusual in it. The news had shifted from Hitler's victory in Poland to its consequences. New regulations for the "solution of the Jewish question" had been promulgated in Occupied Poland. There was a photograph of Danzig celebrating. The first few pages were full of reports from the Russo-Finnish war.

Then the newspaper turned to ice in Ilona's hands. Or was it her hands that had been frozen to ice? She couldn't understand how she could hold the paper and read the lines. It was inconceivable that, faced with the inconceivable, one did the everyday thing, the habitual and ordinary.

Right at the back, under the heading "Obituaries"—after a long article on the death and career of an American banker and an illustrated account of the death and career of a once celebrated baseball star —stood the brief report:

> Prince Taszilo Kontowski.
> Budapest. Yesterday morning the former Austro-Hungarian Am-
> bassador to the Court of the Tsar, Prince Taszilo Kontowski, died
> of pneumonia in his castle near Budapest after a brief illness. He
> was seventy-five. The Prince, a scion of one of Poland's oldest
> noble families—his mother was the Hungarian Countess Maria von
> Szebenyei—withdrew from political life after the First World War.
> His efforts to avert the First World War were repeatedly ack-
> nowledged in Allied circles. The Prince's estates in Poland and
> Bohemia were confiscated after the First World War. Prince
> Taszilo Kontowski was unmarried.

Taszilo was dead. She couldn't take it in. She saw only the naked lines of the announcement. So that was all the world knew about Prince Taszilo Kontowski. That he had been an ambassador and that he had tried to preserve peace and that he had lost his estates. The world knew nothing of his wisdom, kindness, love, and suffering; nothing about his fight against illness; nothing about his revolt in renunciation; nothing about two tired but always wakeful eyes that had gazed after a woman all her life long. Ambassador to the Court of the Tsar. Unmarried.

Now he was laid out in the cold castle beyond the drawbridge. She knew what he looked like in death. He had had two faces, but in death every man had only one face. She had seen this face one day when he brought books to her in the apartment over the pâtisserie: "You must learn a great deal, Ilona"; when he had put the first pearls round her neck in the apartment in the Bellaria: "I must know that you are staying with me of your own free will"; when he had asked her to be his wife on Krestovsky Island: "A Princess Kontowski will be welcome everywhere"; when she embraced him for the last time in the St Peters-burg embassy: "I've put some toys for Zita in with the luggage"; when he gave her the name of a pawnbroker in the small apartment in which Zita had been born; when he gave her a letter so that she should find a job in Berlin; when he told her to turn in case of need to Count Fontenau. Now he was dead, and she hadn't even been able to say "Thank you" to him. Nor could she hurry to him to kiss his hand. The drawbridge had been raised. Behind the drawbridge were Zita, her granddaughter, her father, the dead man.

The door of the flat was opened, and Leilah, the coloured cleaning-woman, came in. She entered the room, saw the weeping woman at the

371

table, hurried over to her, put her arms round her.

"Have you had bad news, honey?" she said.

Ilona nodded.

21

On December 11, 1941, Germany and Italy declared war on the United States. A year later the German Sixth Army, sections of the Fourth Armoured Corps, and several Rumanian divisions were encircled by the Russians at Stalingrad. A year later Stalingrad, the Afrika Korps, and Italy had capitulated. The Red Army was standing on the Lower Dnieper. Bombs were falling on Dresden, Cologne, Nuremberg, Brunswick, Münster, Würzburg, and Frankfurt-am-Main. Bombs were falling on the German capital, Berlin.

On that November morning in 1943 the sky over Berlin was as clear as on a spring day. People looked apprehensively up at the sky that was arched over the city as transparent as a bell-glass. Since spring the sirens had at times been sounding during the day as well as at night. The sky belonged to the enemy. Good weather foretold a bad day.

Zita had come home an hour ago after taking Eva to school. Since the architect's office in which she had been working had closed down she had devoted herself entirely to her child. Three times a week she helped in a hospital. A few days ago she had received the order to "undertake war work" at a building project in Munich. She was to report on January 1.

She paced to and fro in the empty flat, coming to a stop in front of a photograph of Konrad. He had sent her a great many photographs. From Poland, after the victory. From France, after the victory. From Russia, in the midst of the victory. From his dug-out near Smolensk, from an officers' club near Minsk, from a field hospital near Minsk, from a second near Taganrog. He had been wounded twice, once slightly, once severely. At Taganrog he had won the Iron Cross. Eva was proud of him.

In August—it was a hot summer—he had been home on leave for two whole weeks.

She came to a stop in front of the photograph on the dressing-table. It had been taken during his last leave, and showed the three of them—herself, the Major, the child. All three were smiling.

They had talked little about the war in August. Heroes didn't talk about the war much. Only air heroes occasionally talked about the planes they had shot down, or how they had escaped death. As they talked they described the movements of soaring seagulls. In the sky they played with aeroplanes till they crashed and were dead. The earth was no nursery. On the earth people didn't play; they merely died.

Did Konrad still believe in victory? Once or twice, when she was lying in his arms, she had wanted to ask him. He wouldn't have told her the truth. Belief had to be voluntary. If there was nothing left but belief it wasn't belief at all. She herself now believed in victory. Why should he have told her the truth when she was deceiving herself? He had no longer slept peacefully. Once he shouted out so loudly that Eva began to cry in the next room. When he started to awake he woke her too, embraced her hungrily, wouldn't go to sleep again. This great hunger, this enjoyment of every hour, every minute, as though it were being spent with a prostitute who had to give value for money—this was the great love. Then his leave was over; they went down the steps of the hotel that let rooms by the hour. The hero said good-bye to wife and child.

On her wandering through the room Zita caught sight of herself in the mirrors. She ran away, but they ran after her. She had been thirty-four when the war broke out, four years ago. Now she appeared to herself to be a hundred. Her hair was untidy. She had merely run a comb through it before taking Eva to school. She had long ago stopped making up, and rarely used lipstick. In the evening, when she looked in the mirror, she tried to comfort herself with the thought that fatigue had distorted her features: next morning the wrinkles would be gone. Next morning they were still there. They weren't guests for the evening, but tenants who couldn't be turned out. Konrad had extolled her beauty. In the dark he had asked her if she had been faithful to him, anxiously, threateningly, piteously. Men feared the infidelity of their wives at home as they feared the enemy at the front. The heroes believed they had a right to fidelity, as though the women cared that it was to the war that they had deserted. She would have liked to deceive him. She had often come close to it. Once she had sat down late at night in front of the mirror and made herself up, till finally she looked as she had looked in her youth—four years ago. Then she had put on an evening-dress with a plunging neckline, a Paris dress. She had meant to go out on the streets like the whores; to sleep with the first man who came along; with a soldier on leave—after all one owed them something; or with a draft-dodger, who hadn't deserted to the front. But then she had caught sight of herself in the mirror again—a painted clown. She hadn't gone on the streets. Nor had she deceived him. She was too tired.

She went into the kitchen. Last night's dishes hadn't been washed up yet. They seldom were washed up in the morning; the flat generally hadn't been tidied by the afternoon. She opened the kitchen cupboard and took out a bottle of brandy. There were only a few drops left. She would have to get a new bottle. Although she needed drink more than she had ever needed anything, she had been too tired during the last few days to haggle for it, as she would have had to.

She poured the remains of the bottle into a tumbler and sat down on a kitchen chair.

22

She knew that the bombs were falling in the neighbourhood of the school. There was nothing to suggest it, nothing rational, nothing tangible. But she knew.

She raced down the stairs past the occupants of the other flats, who looked at her disparagingly: they thought she was in a hurry to be first into the air-raid shelter.

The street was almost empty. Only here and there pedestrians were scurrying to air-raid shelters. She didn't see them. The sirens were still wailing, and she ran after the sound, as though it came from a particular direction, and not from all sides.

It was possible to reach the school in fifteen minutes comfortably. That would be too late. She ran so fast that no one could stop her.

How could she have imagined that her life had no meaning? God would punish her because she had looked for the meaning which He had so clearly set before her. If there was a God He would punish her.

She pictured Eva in the burning school, under the rubble. It was her fault. She could have taken Eva to Kisnémet long ago. Her mother had thought of that as she said good-bye. Her mother had known. But she hadn't been able to part from Eva. Was there anything more despicable than a mother who, instead of taking her child by the hand, clung to her child's hand? The child to whom she clung in search of help appeared to her infinitely weak, infinitely delicate, infinitely in need of help. Eva was looking at her with reproachful eyes.

She stood still. Somewhere bombs were falling. Not near by. The sound was faint, as though far away stones were being dropped into water one after the other. The school was quite close, yet she imagined that the explosions were coming from the direction of the school.

She ran on, her overcoat unbuttoned in spite of the cold, her hair flying in the wind.

If you help me, God, I will take the child away from this hell. This very day. Never again shall I leave her alone for even a moment. I shall endure being alone if I must. Only she must be in safety. I was always in safety. My mother left me alone, but where she left me there was peace; war hadn't become War yet, my mother knew that.

The streets were becoming more and more empty. A policeman called out after her, tried to catch up with her, but was left behind. The white arrows pointing to the air-raid shelters ran after her like white ghosts. Houses blocked her path. Heat rose up from the icy streets like fever from a freezing body. The explosions were coming nearer. Far away above the rooftops the morning sky was stained red. The glass of the sky was melting in the fire.

She almost ran past the school. There it stood, untouched, grey, and indifferent as ever.

She didn't stop to think. She was already in the entrance-hall. In front of her towered the wide stairs, pillars, walls with black-framed timetables. When she looked up she saw butterflies behind glass, busts of German poets, a painting of Ancient Greece. Not a soul in the whole building. They were all dead—Hermine Stutz, Lotte Wegerode, her child, she herself.

On the right a flight of steps led down to the air-raid shelter. She ran down the steps and flung open a door.

The children were sitting in the shelter. They were sitting there quietly, facing each other, like the patients in Dr Sales's waiting-room. Hot steam came towards Zita. The pipes of the central-heating systems ran above the children's heads. The candles were burning in glass shades. There was a smell of damp walls. The children were playing together, behaving admirably. There was the sound of children's laughter.

Zita forced her way through between the legs, tripped over a shovel, a bucket, toys. The teachers stared after her, so did the children.

Eva was sitting at the far end of the line. She had a puzzle on her lap. The two girls beside her were pushing the pieces to and fro on her lap.

Eva looked up, cried "Mummy!" and stretched out her arms to Zita. She pressed the child to her.

Some one said, "Frau Severin, what are you doing here?"

The pieces of the puzzle rolled across the stone floor.

23

They changed trains at Püskpökladány.

It was mid-January. Zita had had great difficulty in obtaining a permit to travel to Hungary, particularly in Munich, where she knew nobody. But a few days ago she had received a telegram from Teréz saying that the stationmaster was seriously ill. Now she had the necessary papers.

Apart from Zita and Eva, there were two passengers in the compartment—a Hungarian lieutenant who had lost a leg and was on his way home to Debreczen, and a fat young woman, the wife of the mill-owner Korcsmáros from Kisnémet. The lieutenant was sitting in the corner hidden behind a newspaper, which he had finished reading long ago. The mill-owner's wife had recognized Zita, and asked after Ilona. She was surprised that "the little one" didn't understand a word of Hungarian. No doubt she was going to Kisnémet to see her great-grandfather again. Old Mr Horváth was very ill.

Eva couldn't understand the conversation between her mother and the fat woman. She sat by the window, or, rather, kept standing up to look out. She asked questions that Zita patiently answered. Eva was eleven; Zita was used to answering questions. Eva's questions often showed astonishing discernment; then, again, they were astonishingly silly. Both kinds delighted Zita equally.

Now Eva busied herself again with her doll, whose attention she drew to a sledge at the level-crossing. Mrs Korcsmáros had at last stopped talking about the war, and Zita could look at her child undisturbed.

Eva resembled her grandmother even more than before. This wasn't only due to the colour of her hair, her eyes, the shimmer of her skin; not even to the erect yet shy walk, into which Zita also frequently lapsed; it wasn't due merely to individual habits, such as wrinkling her forehead in front of the mirror. It sprang from the cool immaculacy which Zita had admired or envied in her mother.

Konrad had gone to the front four years ago. Eva had grown up without her father. Terms like purchasing-permit, ration-card, camouflage-net, poison-gas, sandbag, air-raid shelter, and incendiary-bomb were as familiar to her as Little Red Riding Hood or the Seven Dwarfs had been to Zita. Eva didn't think twice about getting up in the middle of the night and spending the winter's night wrapped up to the ears in a cellar. She had seen rubble, shattered walls, fires, a crashed plane, dead people. She had never suffered hunger, but she knew what it was. Her father was alive, but many children no longer had fathers. Air-raid warnings and all-clears had wailed through her nights. She knew that people killed in order to stay alive. She had seen her mother drunk. But she had remained untouched, as though dancing light-footed over the horrors. Her eyes were clear and happy. When Zita was unhappy she comforted her. She had so many friends that the flat was always echoing with children's voices. But she hadn't cried when they moved to Munich.

Mrs Korcsmáros began to talk about the war again, expressing herself very incautiously about the Germans, who had dragged Hungary into the war. The lieutenant put down the paper, lit a cigarette, and stared out into the corridor. Eva played with her doll. Zita remembered the old doctor in Vienna who had treated her when she was suffering from otitis media. He was a hunchback; therefore she didn't like him. She had no need to tell Eva not to stare at cripples. Eva paid no attention to the lieutenant. Perhaps my worry about Eva is unfounded, thought Zita. Perhaps children fall from God's hand ready-formed.

24

Zita and Teréz were sitting on the couch in the dining-room. It was three days since Zita and Eva had arrived in Kisnémet.

The sound of steps crunching through the snow could be heard outside the window. The doctor had just left. Only the table-lamp behind the couch was alight, because the door to the next room was ajar, and the stationmaster lay in there.

Before the doctor came they had been talking about Eva. Teréz picked up the thread again.

"You mustn't think of yourself," she said.

"I'm not thinking of myself."

"Then who are you thinking of? In six months Eva will speak Hungarian as well as you and I. I'll teach her myself."

"She won't want to be separated from me."

"You know very well that's nonsense," Teréz retorted sharply. "Children don't cling to their parents half so tenderly as parents would like them to."

What does Teréz know about children? thought Zita. What did she know about me when I was a child? She said, "I'll ask Eva."

"That's the last straw! What kind of modern nonsense is that? You are there to think for Eva—not the other way round."

She had raised her voice, and now quickly lowered it again. Both listened for any sound from the half-open door. They heard the stationmaster's heavy breathing.

"Bombs will fall on Munich just as much as on all the other cities," said Teréz. "They can do what they like with you. The war is lost."

"I know," said Zita.

"Then stop it!"

"We can't stop it."

It struck her as ludicrous that she should say 'we'. In Kisnémet it was very easy to 'stop it.' In Kisnémet everything was easy.

"So you want Eva to grow up under bombs?" demanded Teréz.

Teréz is right, thought Zita. How am I to tell her that I can't live without the child?

"Is it really impossible for you to come here?" asked Teréz.

"I've told you already; I have to stay."

"But you can visit Eva often."

"It's not as easy as you think."

Outside a wind had risen. It was driving the snow against the window-panes. Scraps of snow were racing past the window like sledges emerging from the mist.

"You're jealous," said Teréz in a low voice.

"Of you?"

"Yes, of me."

"Perhaps you're right," said Zita.

I shan't do her the favour of denying it, she thought. She robbed me of my mother; now she wants to rob me of my child. Who knows, perhaps my mother never wanted to go away at all. Teréz always sent her away, as she is now trying to send me away. Was she to tell the old woman sitting facing her, severe, helpful, and self-centred, that she couldn't replace a mother? She had never been able to replace a mother. Teréz had no idea how much she had needed her mother when she lay ill in the Döbling villa; after the first kiss from the first man; when Teréz slept in the next bed dreaming of her head-waiter. Teréz had no idea how much she hated her mother, even to-day, when she longed for her more than ever. She would see to it that Eva never hated her. She would rather they died together.

"You have never thought of anyone but yourself," said Teréz challengingly.

"What about you? Did you ever think of anyone but yourself? Did Mummy ever think of anyone but herself?"

"That was different."

"Why? Why was that different?"

She too had spoken too loud. She looked at the door in alarm.

"I once reproached your mother with imagining that she was chosen," said Teréz. "But I believe she really was. You can't live like your mother, because you're not your mother. If you had been your mother you would never have married that man."

I shan't reply, thought Zita. Am I to tell her she is wrong when I know she is right? Am I to say she is right and give her my child? She felt as weak as during the nights of air-raids, and even weaker. In thought she had tried to blame her mother, Teréz, and Konrad. All her life she had blamed others. Every time she made an accusation her conscience had been lightened. She felt a pang of terror because suddenly there was no one left to accuse.

She stood up.

"We shall wake Grandfather," she said.

25

She had taken a powerful sleeping-tablet, as she had every evening for the last year or two. Nevertheless, she was awake the moment Teréz called her.

Teréz was fully dressed. She hadn't gone to bed, but had watched at the stationmaster's bedside.

"Stay with Papa," she said. "I must fetch the doctor." Her voice broke. "And Margit."

She threw her coat over her shoulders and hurried out. Zita put on her dressing-gown and went into her grandfather's room.

There was only a small lamp burning in one corner, covered with a silk cloth. It was a yellow cloth: there was a dull-gold light in the room.

The old man lay on his back. He was wearing a white nightshirt trimmed with thin red braid. His hands lay folded on the blanket, still, as if he were asleep. His eyes were open. They too were still. He seemed to be looking at the picture hanging over the bed, an oleograph of a Madonna by Raphael. His breath came in gasps.

He noticed that Zita had come in, and beckoned to her with his eyes.

"Has Teréz gone to fetch the priest?" he asked.

"The doctor," said Zita.

The stationmaster laughed, as though he knew better.

She sat down on his bed.

Why did Teréz think he was dying? she wondered. The doctor had said the death-struggle might last for days more. The stationmaster had been struggling with death for weeks already. He was eighty-four, but his heart was good, as the doctor had said. Zita repeated the sentence inside herself, and all of a sudden understood it quite differently from the way in which the doctor had meant it. The stationmaster had a good heart. Perhaps there was no one else in the world who had a good heart. Zita thought of Eva, and how from the very beginning she had run to the old man. Like herself a hundred years earlier. The old man was a great magician. He turned the nursery into a railway station; he could hold up trains and switch points. He could also make a red light go on in front of death.

The stationmaster rattled in his throat. What would she tell Eva when he died? That he was in heaven? Nothing good had come to Eva from heaven, from the sky. It was no consolation that the dead were in heaven.

"I'm glad you've come," said the stationmaster in a faint voice.

"You mustn't talk, Grandfather," she said.

He pretended not to hear her.

"You should leave Eva here," he said. "In the station . . ." He didn't finish the sentence, as though remembering that he wasn't lying in the bedroom over the waiting-rooms.

For a while all was quiet. The wind gradually died down. Only in the stove was there still a whistling sound. The stationmaster seemed to prick up his ears.

Zita watched his eyes. They seemed to be looking for something. He tried to turn his head, but he was too weak.

Finally she understood. On the marble-topped commode stood a photograph of Ilona taken in St Petersburg. She was wearing a fur coat and a tall fur cap; in the background stood a church with a bulb-shaped cupola. One could almost feel the cold that had reigned on that day in St Petersburg.

Zita passed the photograph to the old man. He took it in his hands and thanked her with his eyes.

"I promised to wait for her," he said.

He ran his fingers over the photograph. He couldn't see it.

There was no sound but the ticking of a clock. The stationmaster coughed.

Zita gave him a spoonful of the medicine that was standing on the commode. She put her arm round his neck and raised him up a little. The back of his head was cold. A cold shudder ran down her spine.

A drop had run out of the spoon down the stationmaster's chin. He carefully wiped it away.

She heard voices outside and quickly stood up. The stationmaster seemed not to hear them.

Teréz was standing in the hallway with Margit and Margit's son. The door opened again. It wasn't only the doctor. The priest had come.

The doctor went into the room first. The others stood waiting in the hall. No one spoke. Nobody dared look at anyone else.

The doctor came out, leaving the door open for the priest, as though the earthly physician were handing over to the heavenly one.

Margit sobbed. Her son had put his arm round her shoulder. Teréz stood motionless in the doorway. She has never been able to weep, thought Zita.

Then the priest came out.

They went into the room and stood round the bed.

The stationmaster was still holding Ilona's photograph between his hands. He spoke in a low voice, murmuring; it was hard to understand what he was saying. He was talking about Máté. Máté was to do this that and the other. He was giving the village idiot orders. Then he raised his voice and demanded that Dr Grünfeld should be called. Then there was nothing to be heard but the rattling in his throat. "You can stay with me," he said.

He closed his eyes, slowly, like foils being lowered after a duel. He breathed deeply, but it was as though he were not breathing the air in, but only breathing it out, relieved, content.

Then the stationmaster died.

BOOK THREE

The Granddaughter

1944 to 1956

All that day Eva had felt restless. The feeling didn't leave her even after school was over and they had a snowball fight. Her hands were freezing cold, although ordinarily the snow seemed to her quite warm when they had snowball fights.

She walked home with Adél, her best friend, who was twelve, like her, and also lived on the road between Kisnémet and the station. Adél's father, a butcher, had been killed during the war. Aunt Teréz encouraged Eva's friendship with her, because a butcher's widow was a person to keep in with.

They walked through the village. It was very quiet. The sliding shutters were down. The emaciated acacia trees were shivering. They envied the old chestnut outside the Hotel Rákoczi, which had completely wrapped themselves up in their white cloaks. It had been snowing for days. No one had cleared the snow away. Narrow paths led to the houses. Each house seemed to be entirely isolated from the others. The roofs wore thick, white fur caps. The soldier on the memorial to the dead of the First World War also wore a thick fur cap, and he was waving a white flag. The bell of the Catholic church struck twelve, followed immediately afterwards by the Calvinist church.

A few boys threw snowballs at the girls. Adél giggled and hid behind Eva. You could rely on Eva; she was considered a champion shot. This time she didn't take up the challenge, but walked on faster. They had left the village and sauntered along past the piles of snow at the roadside, swinging their satchels.

Adél kept talking all the time. Eva didn't understand everything she said. She had been in Kisnémet for almost a year and had learnt Hungarian quickly. She had missed a year of school, but she had no trouble in following the lessons. It was only when Adél spoke too fast that she had a little difficulty in understanding her.

"Do you know why all the shops are shut?" said Adél.

"Because it's the middle of the day, of course."

"You're quite wrong. They're not going to open again at all."

Eva looked at her friend questioningly. She thought Adél a bit of a show-off.

"The Russians are already in Debreczen," said Adél. "They will soon be here."

Eva stopped in dismay. There had been a lot of talk about the Russians during recent weeks. She had no very clear idea of the Russians, but they must be terrible, since people were so frightened of them.

Adél bent over to Eva. Her dark, protruding eyes grew even larger as she whispered, "Mummy says there won't be any Christmas."

"What rubbish!" She immediately regretted saying it, because one didn't pass disrespectful remarks about the owner of the butcher's shop. "There's always Christmas," she added pacifically.

"If the Russians come there won't be any Christmas," declared Adél.

Eva pressed her satchel to her. She thought of last Christmas in Munich. That hadn't been a proper Christmas either. They had just moved from Berlin, and the little flat that had been supplied to them was still in disorder. They had had only a very small Christmas-tree, whose thin branches had bent under the red apples. But then it had been quite fun after all, because the woman they were billeted with had a son. He was two years older than Eva and his name was Peter. He had written to her twice since then and sent a photograph. It was inconceivable that there shouldn't be Christmas. Aunt Teréz had promised her that Mummy would come for Christmas.

They parted. Eva finished the journey alone. She ran, although the road was iced over; she stumbled over piles of snow. Her feet were cold.

At lunch the feeling of disquiet grew more distinct; it was the feeling she had at school when she hadn't done her homework and had a premonition that she was going to be questioned on it.

Auntie Teréz didn't say a word. She didn't even tell her to hold her knife properly and finish up her *rakott krumpli*, although Eva had no appetite and left a few potatoes.

"Is it true that the Russians are coming?" asked Eva. "Adél says so," she went on, as though quoting an authority.

"You needn't go back to school this afternoon," said Teréz. "I have to talk to you." But she said nothing more.

After lunch Eva wanted to help clear the table. They always cleared it together. Then Teréz washed the dishes and Eva dried them. Generally it was done in no time.

Teréz left the table just as it was. She sat down on the couch and signed to Eva. Eva stood in front of her. Teréz took her by the arm and pulled her to her.

"You're a big girl," she said. "I have something to tell you. . . ."

"I know: there won't be any Christmas."

Teréz shook her head.

"A soldier came from Germany to-day. He brought a letter from Mummy. You know, there isn't any post any more. . . ."

Eva's heart stood still. That there was no post was nothing new. Why didn't Auntie Teréz come to the point? Was she going to tell her that Mummy wasn't coming for Christmas?

"Mummy has had bad news from your father," said Teréz.

"From Daddy?"

"Well . . . his commanding-officer has written to her."

Eva broke angrily away from her aunt. Why didn't Auntie Teréz tell her the truth straight out? She knew what it meant when the commanding-officer wrote. Mothers of her friends in Berlin had received letters from the commanding-officer.

"You're Daddy has been killed," said Teréz. She said "Daddy"; usually she referred to him as "your father."

382

Eva tore herself away. She started to cry. Crying, she flung herself on the couch. In hot waves the feeling flowed over her that she loved her father more than anyone, more than Teréz, more than Mummy. She blamed herself for having seldom thought of him. He had always been away. It was a very long time since she last saw him, but now it seemed to her as if she had seen him yesterday, as if he hadn't been away at all. Yesterday he had brought her a doll. They had been to the Zoo and stood in front of the giraffes, her favourite animals and his. He had sat on her bed and read to her. Since she had been in Kisnémet she had almost forgotten him. She included him in her bed-time prayers, but occasionally she forgot to say her prayers at all. It was all her fault that he had been killed.

Teréz had sat down behind her and now tried to take Eva in her arms.

Eva shook her off angrily. It wasn't her fault that he had been killed. It was Auntie Teréz's fault, Mummy's fault. What rubbish was Auntie Teréz talking now? Saying that she had Mummy and her. . . . She didn't want either Mummy or Teréz. Her aunt's touch hurt her. She wanted to be alone; to think of her father; to make amends for what she had failed to do.

"Why didn't Mummy come?" she asked through tears.

"It's impossible at present, you know that," said Teréz. "But she will come . . . she really will."

Eva sat up. Teréz gave her a handkerchief. She held it in her hand but didn't use it.

Then snowballs banged against the window. Adél was down below with two boys. They had come to call for her.

She ran into her room and locked the door, as though to lock herself in so that she couldn't go out and play with the children.

She heard her aunt's voice.

"Go home, please," said Teréz. "Eva doesn't want to play today." The children seemed to be asking some question. "Her father has been killed," said Teréz.

There was silence outside. Eva went to the window and watched the children walk away.

2

Zita went from one office to another. She had nothing else to do. The 'building project,' because of which she had been sent to Munich, had come to nothing. The only possible 'building project' consisted in clearing away the rubble.

When she went to the window in the morning she saw nothing but ruins. It was the same almost everywhere: in one street destruction ran along the even house numbers, in another along the odd. On the opposite side of the street one single wall was standing. You could tell it had been a four-storey house by the four lavatories that seemed to be suspended in mid-air one above the other. Living-rooms, bedrooms, nurseries had been destroyed. Only the lavatories had been spared.

Then Zita started on her trek from office to office. They were hard to find. They had vanished or moved overnight. Zita clambered over bricks, piles of rubble, broken staircases; went through doors behind which no house stood; looked for houses that were no longer standing. Sometimes the direction signs were still hanging undamaged on the walls, but in the direction in which the arrows pointed there was nothing but bricks, piles of rubble, broken staircases. Everywhere there was a smell of dust and ashes.

She grew accustomed to being looked at as though she were insane. Since Christmas she had given up trying to get to Hungary. The Russians were in Hungary; since the beginning of January Budapest had been under siege. But there must be a way of getting news from her child. Half pityingly, half angrily, she was sent from one office to another. She went to the Red Cross. Next day the Red Cross was gone. She found it again. Yes, they would write to Geneva. When could she expect an answer? They shrugged their shoulders. Back to the German authorities. Her husband had been killed, she said. Major Konrad Severin, Knight of the Iron Cross. People exchanged looks. The Iron Cross? The woman must be mad. They got rid of her by telling her to go to a neutral organization, Swiss or Swedish. Where? Nobody knew. Then she found the Swedish relief organization. Your child's in Hungary? Be glad she is, Frau Severin. Just wait, Frau Severin. What for? No one dared to answer. They were all waiting for the end.

In the evening she went to a tavern near her home. She still had enough money for the next few months. The pearls her mother had given her were under the mattress on her bed. Zita didn't trust her landlady. She could still sell her pearls.

The tavern-keeper had taken a liking to her. He was a man of enormous girth. At the beginning of the war his right arm had been shot off, in France, where such occurrences were rare. It didn't suit Herr Pernstorffer to have lost an arm. He was too fat to be a cripple, and he didn't wear an artificial one. The right sleeve of his shirt dangled from his shoulder and flapped about the tavern. He supplied Zita with brandy, and after the third or fourth glass he refused payment. He used to sit down at her table. To begin with, he used to ask her every evening how she had got on during the day. She showed him photographs of Eva. "She's better off in Kisnémet," he said, remembering the name of the Hungarian village. Later he stopped asking how she had got on and just put the brandy-bottle down in front of her. When she had drunk a great deal she told him about her life. She had grown communicative. "You must have loved him very much," said Herr Pernstorffer when she talked about Konrad. She had tears in her eyes; therefore he imagined she had loved Konrad very much. There was no point in telling him how little Konrad's death had meant to her. She had felt nothing but surprise when she read the C.O.'s consoling letter, as though it had informed her that some one who was dead long ago had died all over again. Konrad wanted pity, but she had no pity for him since she needed all her pity for herself. The dead imagined they were making amends for everything when they died. They had no idea how little courage was required to sacrifice oneself. The dead don't weep. They expect one to weep over them, to remember the anniversary
384

of their death, to put flowers on their grave and remain true to them. It was a good thing she didn't know where Konrad was buried. But she didn't tell the tavern-keeper this. She talked about her family, her mother. She also mentioned her father. "He was a Baron Rattowitz," she said. "Ferdinand Maria Leopold Freiherr von Rattowitz. But I don't believe he was my father at all. My father was probably a Prince Kontowski. The last Austro-Hungarian ambassador to the court of the Tsar." Then she told him that her mother had been to the Tsar's court. "She was immensely beautiful. The Tsar once sent her flowers." She said her mother was in America. It suddenly struck her that she owed Pernstorffer for fifty or sixty glasses of brandy. "When my mother comes back," she said, "I'll pay for everything." The tavern-keeper sat with her less and less often. One day he took her hand. "Listen, Frau Severin," he said, "I wish you well. There's no need for you to tell me any fairy-tales. What you say about your child may be true, but the rest. . . . It makes no odds to me, Frau Severin, but people laugh at you. The story about the Tsar's court and the conductor, whatever his name was, and the house that's supposed to have belonged to you, and the Prince, whatever his name was. . . . You get it all muddled up yourself." He wiped the sweat from his forehead by taking hold of his empty sleeve with his left hand and using it as a handkerchief. "Besides, it's dangerous. The other day somebody wanted to denounce you, for espionage or spreading alarm and despondency or something. I calmed him down, I told him your imagination was running away with you. There's no need to tell me any fairy-tales," he repeated, "so long as I have any schnapps left you can always have a glass." Then he tapped her on the cheek.

She left. The icy rain ran down inside her collar; she didn't walk along by the wall of the houses, however, but out in the middle of the street. The walls of the houses seemed to be swaying in the wind.

She came to a stop outside her front door. She laughed so loud that she had to lean against the door. She was laughing with anger, or with despair, or because the whole thing was really laughable. When her mother came back she would go with her to Herr Pernstorffer. She would drive up in a big black limousine. How many glasses of brandy does my daughter owe you for? Fifty, a hundred, two hundred? She would throw the money down on the table without a word and drive away. Or was her imagination really running away with her now? Her mother would never come back. She would never be able to prove to Herr Pernstorffer that every word had been true. She stopped laughing. Herr Pernstorffer was right. It all sounded very unconvincing.

She didn't go back to Herr Pernstorffer. She found another tavern.

3

In February 1945 Eva wrote in her diary:

WEDNESDAY, FEBRUARY 14.

At last I have settled down to write my diary again. I haven't written anything for a week, although there has been plenty to

*write about. I am going to start at the beginning. Or rather, I think
I shall start with what happened to-day, because that's more important.*

*We still don't have any school. We were just sitting with Auntie
Teréz having breakfast when the bell rang. We were very frightened.
I looked out of the window and saw a green car. It was a Russian
car. Auntie Teréz didn't want to open the door because she was
afraid our house was going to be requisitioned. A lot of houses are
being requisitioned now. But in the end she did open it.*

*There were two Russian soldiers outside and a man who spoke
Hungarian.*

*Auntie Teréz was terribly excited after they had left. She could
scarcely speak, she was so excited. She said her brother was here.
Her brother is Mummy's uncle. So he's your great-uncle, said
Teréz. I asked her if my great-uncle was a Russian, but I couldn't
quite understand what she answered. His name is Lajos, she said,
and Mummy must have told me about him. But Mummy has really
never told me anything about him.*

*At lunch Auntie Teréz was so excited she couldn't eat anything.
Then I had to put on my best dress, the blue one. And Auntie
Teréz combed my hair till my head was sore. Of course it was
much too early and we sat around waiting for at least an hour.
Then the car came back, but this time with only one soldier. As
we got in, he got out and saluted. He was very polite, although he
couldn't talk to us.*

*We drove to the castle. Teréz said it used to belong to a count.
She told me his name, but I can't remember it. I was much too
excited.*

*The castle is very big, but it doesn't look like a castle at all. Un-
less it's like an enchanted one. There is almost no furniture in it.
It was full of soldiers.*

*They took us into a room. There, a very old man came to meet
us. He was wearing boots and a uniform, but it wasn't really a
uniform. He had a short white beard. He kissed Auntie Teréz.
Auntie Teréz immediately began to cry. Then he kissed me. He told
me to call him Uncle Lajos. He was surprised that I understood
Hungarian, but I think he was very pleased about it.*

*He sat down behind a big desk which was so loaded with papers
that I couldn't see him properly. But I think he looks very much
like Great-grandfather, only he's much older. I know that's impossible, because he's Mummy's uncle and Auntie Teréz's brother.
I sat down on a chair which was so dusty that my dress got quite
black. I sat down very carefully, because I saw straightaway that
one leg was wobbly.*

*They talked for at least an hour. Mostly I didn't understand what
they were saying. I kept looking at a picture that was hanging behind Uncle Lajos. It was a picture of a woman in a white wig. She
looked like a queen. The picture was hanging all crooked.*

*Uncle Lajos told Auntie Teréz there was nothing to be afraid of.
He kept stroking his white beard. I knew at once that he was*

tremendously powerful, because soldiers kept coming in and saluting. He only nodded his head. Afterwards Auntie Teréz told me that he is something like Hermann Goering is with us, but she said I mustn't repeat that. It must be a secret.

And now comes the most important thing. Uncle Lajos said he would arrange for Mummy to visit us or for me to go to Mummy. I wanted to jump up and throw my arms round his neck, but Auntie Teréz told me to keep calm. As we left she told me it might take a long time, because there was still a war going on in Munich. But I know it can't be very much longer. He said he had to leave again to-day. He gave Auntie Teréz a piece of paper with his address on it.

I have forgotten to write that he kept on talking about my grandmother, who is in America. I have a lot of photographs of her. She is very beautiful. Mummy told me I look like her.

And that is really all. Of course I'm very happy. Auntie Teréz is very happy too; that's why I'm allowed to stay up late and write my diary.

But now I've written so much that I can't write any more about everything that has happened. Since the Russians have been here there hasn't been any school, but it's supposed to start again next week. I'm looking forward to it. There are Russians living in almost all the houses. They are very kind to children, but we have been told not to talk to them.

The main thing is, I shall soon see Mummy again.

4

It was almost midnight when Stefan and Ilona came home from Broadway. They sat down in the two armchairs under the standard lamp.

"Do you know what keeps coming into my mind?" said Stefan. "Something that happened during the First World War, nineteen hundred and fifteen. I don't think I ever told you about it." He smiled, as if to say that there couldn't be very much left which he hadn't told her about. "I was going home on leave, in October, just before my birthday. Travelling was very difficult. I had to use all my ingenuity in order to get home in time—in time for my birthday, that is. I had made up my mind to celebrate it at home. I almost managed it, or to be more exact I did manage it, though I was a little late. I arrived in Berlin at midnight, took a cab, and drove home. The house was brilliantly lit up. No one heard when I rang the bell; I grew impatient. At last the manservant opened the door. Yvonne and Mama rushed out into the hall. They took me by the hand and led me into the lounge. It was full of people celebrating my birthday, having no idea that I was going to take part in the celebrations myself. I was quite moved by the whole thing till I gradually noticed that my presence was unwanted. I don't mean by Yvonne and Mama—they were probably also aware of this feeling that was depressing me. But Yvonne had to carry out her duties as a hostess, and Mama was afraid Yvonne would steal the limelight. So I sat in a corner and watched the celebration of the absentee's birthday—in the eyes of the guests I was still absent. They drank my health and sang; they even danced, if I remember rightly. Only they couldn't grasp the fact that I was there. I felt wretched and wished my train had been late. Do you understand?"

She understood.

An hour ago they had walked down Broadway, pushed to and fro by the jubilant crowds celebrating VE Day, victory in Europe. The neon signs of the *New York Times* ceaselessly flashed out over Times Square the announcement of Germany's unconditional surrender in the Rheims school. It was a cool May evening, but the asphalt of Broadway seemed to be radiating the heat of a midsummer day. Men and women who were total strangers kissed. Brass bands blared from the cafés. Ten or twelve sailors had linked arms and were blocking the sidewalk, staggering from side to side as if there were a heavy sea running under their feet. They were singing *It's a Long Way to Tipperary*, the song which the soldiers had sung as they went to the First World War. During the war no one had bothered very much about the soldiers; now anybody in uniform was lionized. Soldiers were dragged into bars, filled up with alcohol and put back in the street, like cars whose tanks have been filled up. The mounted policemen in their dark-blue uniforms sat high up in their saddles, their horses tightly reined in. The horses' heads soared above the crowd, growing out of a thicket of human heads. The buildings had been dressed in flags. The stars of the banners danced over Broadway as if the stars of the sky had become hugely enlarged.

"I'm unjust," said Stefan. "And the story I told you doesn't fit at all. I only remembered it because I envied these people."

"Envied them?"

"I should have liked to celebrate myself. Perhaps not so noisily, in any case alone. All the evening I kept thinking that they were celebrating our victory. I felt ashamed of this thought, because they won the victory. We only ran away. We only hoped and prayed. We only died, because we had no alternative. And yet now I had the feeling that I ought to say to them, 'This victory isn't like any other.' I wanted to take the alien victory out of their hands, our victory, even to give a little of it to the defeated. . . ." He raised his eyebrows. "Who would have understood me?"

She nodded. "I think it is something different. You arrived in time for your birthday. You felt as though they were celebrating somebody else's birthday, but you got there in time."

"I know," he said.

There was no need for her to say more. For those celebrating on Broadway victory had not come too late. They were young and the day of victory was like any other day, only rather happier. But what about the two of them? Next year she would be sixty. Stefan was already sixty-five. The last twelve years had stolen spring from some and summer from others. After spring came summer, after summer, autumn. Many had fled into winter, a season when everything lay in the past.

From these two the years had stolen autumn. Now winter was coming. It wasn't a season to sow, nor to reap.

"I clearly remember November nineteen hundred and eighteen," said Stefan. "There was the same jubilation. We had no inkling that we had placed our destiny in the hands of history. Since then it has been in miserable hands. History will never again let our destiny out of its cold, senile hands. It isn't doing so to-day."

"The great helplessness. . . ." said Ilona in a low voice.

She thought of Kontowski. He was dead. The stationmaster was dead. Probably Ginsburg and Sales were dead. Where was Zita? Where were Eva and Teréz? No sooner had these ideas crossed her mind than she regretted having followed Stefan's gloomy train of thought. During recent years it had often seemed to her as if he were standing on the coachman's box with a blazing whip, lashing on the horses to gallop faster into the abyss. She would do better not to watch his frenzy.

She sat up in her armchair and said, "We've talked enough nonsense now, Stefan. It's nothing but the reaction setting in as our nervous tension relaxes, the sobering-up after the intoxication. If you say now that we are too old to begin again from the beginning, I can only tell you to look at yourself in the mirror." She laughed. "Anyhow, I don't want to have anything to do with an old man. For twelve years you have been talking about going home. And I was silly enough to believe that it wasn't just talk, but that you really meant it. You ended by convincing me, and now you want to give up the struggle. It's all very well persuading women to join in your dream and then telling them it was only a dream. Perhaps it will take time, but that doesn't matter now. I've listened long enough to you telling me that you brought me disaster. I want to spend my last days as the wife of the famous publisher. It's high time you started thinking about the future of S. H."

He smiled, stood up, and kissed her hand. How young he looks all at once, she thought.

He took her by the waist, she put her arm round his shoulders.

"How do you manage to remain eternally young, Ilona?" he said.

He walked into the bedroom in front of her to put on the light; she lagged a little behind, closing her eyes. The lights she had been looking into the whole evening danced in front of her eyes. It mustn't be too late, she thought.

5

A hot summer had been followed by a rainy autumn. Late September resembled early November.

At the end of September Zita received the first news from her mother, transmitted by the Red Cross.

We are doing all we can to get back as quickly as possible [wrote Ilona]. Doubly good news: Stefan is intending to settle in Munich. His former reader, Anton See—he was very young then—I believe you know him—remained faithful to him through these difficult

*times and is already in Munich making the necessary preparations.
I am giving you the address of an American soldier, the son of a
friend of ours, through whom we can correspond. Tell me all about
Eva; send lots of photographs!*

Zita could tell her mother little about Eva and had no photographs
to send. She received the first letter from her child only two days after
Ilona's. It had travelled by a roundabout route. Lajos had sent Teréz's
and Eva's letters from Kisnémet, via Budapest, to the Soviet authorities
in Berlin; the latter had forwarded them to the Russian military
mission in Frankfurt, who had finally conveyed them to Zita. There
was no hope of her seeing Eva again soon. Zita, who was German by
marriage, could scarcely move from one town to another, let alone to
Hungary. There was no prospect whatever of the child returning to
Germany.

In spite of everything, the two letters had changed Zita's life. She
felt it every morning. In order to sleep, she still needed tablets, which
she had to make great sacrifices to obtain, and which only helped if she
repeatedly stepped up the dose. But whereas up to now she had
struggled every morning, sometimes for hours on end, against coming
back to life from a kindly state resembling death; whereas the anguish
of morning had exceeded the anguish of the day, great as this was,
because her consciousness, though awake, was still too weak to force
the black thoughts below the threshold of consciousness, she now woke
quickly and painlessly.

She began to worry about the untidiness of her appearance. When
she sat in front of the mirror she sometimes imagined that her mother
might come into the room, and the thought, which in her girlhood had
frightened her, filled her with happy excitement. She had been forty in
January; there was no need for her to look like an old woman. The
hairdressers reopened long before the grocers. Zita's dark hair hadn't
lost its lustre. She needed a little more powder, rouge, and lipstick;
after a while her skin became soft and white again, grateful for the
care and attention it had lacked for so long. Soap was always to be
had and the blouses she wore for preference became radiantly clean,
even in cold water.

She began to attract the attention of men again. In spring, in that
unforgettably terrible spring, when the world seemed to be foundering,
Zita had observed dully and yet alertly that fresh grass was growing
among the ruins, that the impudent yellow of a flower ventured to
emerge between shattered walls and charred furniture. It was just the
same with human eyes. The men who stood in queues; who forced their
way on to trams as though it were a matter of life and death; who
hurried past with tattered brief-cases—the brief-case had become the
German uniform—nevertheless turned their heads and looked round
when a pretty woman hastened by.

She still feared the evenings. Between the darkness that descended
upon the city and the darkness into which her sleeping-tablets finally
carried her off, lay countless hours. Out of the darkness rose her
familiar enemy—loneliness. The thought that other people were asleep

390

dismayed her, as though she were living in a threatened house and knew that the protecting night-watchman had fallen asleep. But the idea that other people might be awake, that the happiness for which she was now beginning to crave once more was waiting for her like a lover who would go to bed disappointed if she herself went to bed, disturbed her no less.

If she was alone she had to stupefy herself; to stupefy herself she needed alcohol; when she drank she needed cigarettes. She had very little money left, and anyhow alcohol and cigarettes were not to be bought.

At this period two letters towered up before the German-speaking world, wreathed with laurels, as all-important as the 'N' of the victorious Emperor Napoleon had once been. The victors' monogram was 'PX.' It stood for 'Post Exchange,' Zita was told, a word dating from America's pioneer days and meaning something like 'barter shop,' but now possessing a much less commonplace, more fateful significance. The PX stood in the Brienner Strasse, formely Munich's Nobelstrasse, and since the victors were open-hearted one could see through the glittering window-panes a magic world of cigarettes like ingots of gold, of gleaming bottles containing drinks of every kind and colour, of cameras, scent, penny dreadfuls, handbags, pipes, fashion magazines, sweets and blue mountains of a magical toilet tissue. The pioneers stood on one leg leaning against the wall of the 'barter shop,' or squatted on their heels, for hours on end, without speaking a word. The storks and frogs in uniform, many of them with black skins, smoked cigarettes, chewed gum, and waited—since PX meant 'barter shop'—for a chance to trade cigarettes, whisky, and toilet tissues for a little love. Women and girls gathered on the other side of the street, not daring to speak for fear of infringing the iron law of non-fraternization. There could be no fraternization, only barter.

Zita avoided the Brienner Strasse. She thought of her mother, of Eva. Occasionally Konrad occurred to her. Herr Pernstorffer hadn't believed her, but she was still, or rather was once more, Baroness Von Rattowitz; although the expression struck her as ludicrous, she was also a 'war widow'; she dreamed of her future life with her child. And her mother would soon come back from America, had perhaps become a victor herself. There was no longer any bitterness in the thought that her mother had been victorious.

When she finally decided, in spite of everything, to go to the Brienner Strasse, she did not remain standing by the wall like the other women. She walked in through the door to paradise.

6

Stefan's endeavours to obtain the papers necessary to return home proved fruitless. He had given up his badly paid job. Now they knew how long what they still possessed would last. He sat for days and nights bent over questionnaires; next day he handed them in or mailed them to Washington; received fresh ones. There were many questions that didn't appear in the questionnaires. Why was he, the refugee Stefan Herrdegen, in such a hurry to return to Germany? Hadn't America afforded him a safe asylum? Wasn't he happy in 'God's Own Country'? Why did he want to exchange the comfort of his American home for the ruins of Germany? Had he merely fled, had he not wanted to immigrate? Was his return in the interests of the Occupying Power? Or did he actually feel sympathy for the defeated? Stefan could have asked questions himself. Was there anything suspicious in a mother wanting to see her daughter, a grandmother her granddaughter? Must the last twelve years count for more than the forty before? Were there not vanquished who had waited eagerly for the victors? Was his homeland only the ruins and not the graves too? How many years could a man in his mid-sixties afford to lose? Stefan wrote and spoke and replied and asked no questions.

At the beginning of 1946 he received a letter from his collaborator Anton See, who, in order to avoid reading the books of trashy writers in the 'Third Reich,' had preferred to read account-books and had taken a job as a book-keeper. In his letter he wrote:

> *A stray bomb—the Grunewald is virtually untouched—destroyed your house. You know that the house was occupied by the man who was your servant and later my 'boss,' Reinhart Stuck. There was a drinking party going on at the time. Reinhart's 'harem' was a byword throughout the city. Two ladies of easy virtue met their death in the servant's arms. All three were undressed. Don't imagine, dear Herr Herrdegen, that this was an unusual occurrence. I shall be able to tell you of countless similar, absolutely incredible cases. Incredible, above all, is the subtle precision with which Destiny works. If one were religious one would assume that Christ had returned to hold the Last Judgment. But we know that this Last Judgment is human handiwork.*

He added a postscript:

> *After a long search I have succeeded in tracing your friend Dr Sales, whom you inquired about. He spent several years in a concentration camp, where he lost his left arm. Nevertheless he is alive and kicking, and has asked me to send his best wishes to you and your dear wife.*

Such letters, reaching America only one at a time and by illegal— that is to say, human—routes, raised for a few fleeting instants the curtain behind which lay the dark, destroyed, enchanted land, the land of longing. But the more often the curtain was raised, only to fall again, the greater became Ilona's impatience.

Unlike Stefan, she had not been unhappy in their new home, was still not unhappy. But just as in the years of exile her love had imposed upon her the duty to instil patience and yet more patience in Stefan, so now her task, the meaning of her love perhaps, was to lead him home. And her instinct told her, naggingly, robbing her of sleep and finally rendering her desperate, that she who, in her youth, had so often abandoned her child must now get back to her quickly and at any price.

At the end of 1946 she was still in New York. In December the State Department informed Mr and Mrs Herrdegen that "permission for civilian personnel whose presence is not in the interests of the Occupying Power to enter Germany cannot be granted before the end of next year, and possibly not till the beginning of 1948."

7

Between Christmas and the New Year the PX was closed to the public. Two days after Christmas a sergeant had brought Zita her mother's letter. "Perhaps at the end of the new year. Perhaps not till the beginning of 1948. . . ."

On the day before New Year's Eve she went to the PX to collect her wages.

When she left the building it was dark. Piles of black snow stood at the edges of the street. The snow had tried to cover up the dirt of the city, but the dirt had covered up the snow. Only every fourth or fifth street-lamp was alight; the electric bulbs looked like squeezed lemons. There was almost nobody in the street. The street was naked, as though it had been stripped of its clothes—its lit shop-windows, street-lamps, cars. A street that had been turned out naked into the street.

Zita began to walk, although she lived a long way from here. The farther she walked the shorter the evening became.

She stopped in front of the Theatiner church. The door was ajar. She could hear the prayers of the faithful, a rumbling murmur. The light from the candles fell upon the black snow, dying cinders in a pile of rubble.

It was years since Zita had been inside a church. The people in the church were to be envied. They were unaware that the cold seemed to be flowing out of the house of God into the street. The house of God was colder than the street. The faithful were to be envied and at the same time to be pitied, because they were speaking softly, in murmurs, to a deaf God. Zita pictured them looking up with a reverent mien to their image, to the crucified God whom God had not succoured. He had suffered His own houses to be reduced to rubble and ashes. He had not heard His own son's prayers, the deaf God. Had she not prayed that He should reunite her with her daughter, with her mother? Was that asking too much? He didn't answer. The deaf God was dumb.

As she hurried past the church she heard melted snow splashing against the pavement. She heard her name as a jeep pulled up.

It was Captain Howard. Captain Lee M. Howard. She had met him in the PX and had gone out with him two or three times.

"How about a drink?" he said.

"A drink would be fine," she said.

A drink was always fine, and Captain Howard was particularly fine. He was one of those Americans who were neither sentimental nor slipped their hands up under your skirt. He might have been thirty, or

393

at most thirty-two, slim, with a frank, youthful face. He looked like Lindbergh, the aviator, when the aviator was still young. Only he wore spectacles, reassuring rimless spectacles. She couldn't understand why he went out with her and was glad that he had no reason.

She climbed into the jeep as though into a lifeboat. The thought that she would have to spend the evening alone seemed to her all at once so terrible that she didn't dare to think it through to the end. Only now, when she had escaped from loneliness, did she become aware of the mortal danger.

They went to the Gnat, a black-market restaurant in Schwabing. Lee—she called him Lee, he called her Zita—had nothing to do with the black market. It was because of the non-fraternization order: an American officer couldn't take a German woman into a less secret restaurant. The Gnat stood in a hidden position, a wooden hut among ruins. It might have been taken for a builders' hut—if there had been any building going on.

When they had sat down she asked Lee how it was he had dared to take her in the open jeep. "I'm allowed to," he said, but he didn't explain what he meant. He ordered wine and paid with cigarettes.

The customers were almost all Germans. They wore new suits that had obviously been made for some one else; suits belonging to people who had bartered them for bread. Two Negro soldiers were standing at the bar with a girl between them. One had his hand inside the neck of her dress, the other had his hand on her buttocks. The soldiers pretended not to have seen the officer, or else they really hadn't seen him—every one knew that Americans couldn't take wine

Zita couldn't take it either. It was a sweet adulterated beverage, ostensibly from North Africa. Lee ordered something to eat, but by the time it was brought she had drunk too much to be able to eat.

Conversation was easy: Lee asked questions, she only had to answer them. They were impersonal questions, pleasantly impersonal. When had the Germans known that the war was lost? And why had nobody been prepared to murder Hitler? And when did they first hear about the concentration camps?

She answered and hoped he would ask more questions. As long as he asked questions she didn't have to go home. At home lay her mother's letter. Another year, perhaps at the beginning of 1948. She counted. If she became a year older every month she would be sixty by the time her mother came back. She laughed.

"Why are you laughing?" asked Lee. He watched her through his affable glasses. "You have a pretty laugh," he said. She thought of Eva's letter, the big, childish, neat writing. "And were you proud when he won the Iron Cross?" asked Lee. "My daughter was very proud," she said. Lee's eyes came closer. He was good-looking, but his eyes were too big, like cow's eyes. There were men who went to prostitutes, didn't undress, but simply asked questions. How had they become prostitutes; and was it bad sleeping with six men every night; and did they still feel anything after two hundred men? These were the inquisitive men, the Lee Howard's. The landlord brought a fresh carafe. She answered. Now both Negroes had put their hands on the girl's buttocks their fingers were touching; they were like one man's hands on the girl's buttocks. Lee asked no more questions. He was sorry for her, he said. She was a nice girl, the nicest girl he had met in Germany. She said she wasn't a 'nice girl,' but a woman over forty. Slightly taken aback, he said one could be a nice girl even at forty. He had only loved one woman in his life, she was thirty-five, but he too had been younger at that time. Then he talked about his mother; it was on her account that he hadn't married. The restaurant began to rock, pleasant-ly, as though they were sitting in a slightly rocking boat. Would her mother come over by plane or boat? How long did a boat take? It didn't matter, since he wasn't going away. The bar at which the Negroes were standing went away; the floor under her feet was moving like the dance-floors at the fairs. "I'd like to ask you a lot more questions," said Lee. "Ask away," she said encouragingly. Anything rather than go home! "I'm leaving to-morrow, for a few weeks," he said. The Negroes were singing in husky Negro voices. The black marketeers joined in the song; they too sang in English. "We can't go to my place, unfortunately," said Lee. "Have you a flat?" She said she had a flat. Perhaps he really only wanted to know why nobody had murdered Hitler. But it didn't matter what he wanted to know. All that mattered was not to be alone.

The entrance hall was a large, almost circular room. She didn't put the light on. Lee lit his 'Zippo,' a lighter of which the victors were almost as proud as of their victory.

As she walked ahead of him on tiptoe a memory came to her out of the darkness. She had walked through the dark hall with Georg, and through the bedroom with the pictures of the family and the pictures of the Holy Family. It seemed to her that the place smelt of apples. Wherever you were merely a tenant the place smelt of apples. Her room had a door of its own. Next to it was the dining-room. Nobody would hear them.

"This is where I live," she said.

He looked round appreciatively. It was cold. He offered her a cigarette, gave her a light. The 'Zippo' worked, as always. He hung his wet trench coat on a nail.

Her eyes fell on the unmade bed. It was a brass bedstead. The rods looked like golden prison bars. She wondered whether to pull the blanket up. Then she sat down.

"I'm not inquisitive," said Lee. "I only ask questions because I have to. It's my job in the army."

"Ask away," she said.

He looked at the photographs of Eva.

"You're a nice girl," he said. He paced to and fro.

She wanted to help him ask questions. If he couldn't think of any questions he would go away.

He polished his glasses.

"I don't really need glasses; I'm only a tiny bit short-sighted," he said, but he put them on again. "By the way, it isn't true that I'm only going away for a little while. I'm going back to America." He came to a stop in front of her. "Are you a bit sorry?"

"Yes," she said, "I'm sorry."

She was sorry. She knew he hadn't come to ask questions. She had known all the time, only now she knew it a bit more clearly.

"I'm no good at lying," he said. "I can't say that one day I shall send for you to join me."

She stood up and went to the washstand. She had concealed half a bottle of brandy underneath it. She filled two glasses and gave him one. She was glad he had stopped asking questions. He wouldn't go away.

"Everything else is true," he said.

"I know," she said. Her mother's letter was lying on the table. "From my mother. You can read it."

He took the letter hesitantly and skimmed through it.

"I'm sorry," he said.

She shrugged her shoulders, as though to shake off his pity.

He paced up and down again, passing the brass bedstead, the golden prison. She thought of the beds in which she had slept. The others had been made of wood, a forest of beds. She shivered.

As she was about to fill her glass he took the bottle away from her. He drew her to him, kissed her.

She twined her arms round his neck. He kissed her differently from what she had expected. She knew very well, because she had cold-bloodedly imagined how he would kiss her. His kisses were greedy, as if his mouth didn't belong to the cool, neat, well-pressed Captain Lee M. Howard, who asked questions. Then his hands didn't belong to him either. They were hands that became clumsy with passion. He tugged at the zip-fastener of her dress, which wouldn't run, he tore her skin with the fastener.

She freed herself from his arms and undressed.

He switched on the bedside lamp and switched off the ceiling light. She put out the bedside lamp as well.

She made love to him as she had never made love to a man before. When he tried to speak she put her hand over his mouth. She seized his hands and wouldn't let go of them. She stroked her body with his hands as if they were her own. Once, when he laughed, she pressed her lips to his mouth and smothered his laughter. He must be imagining she had been hungry for him. She didn't care what he imagined. She did everything any man had ever desired of her; she didn't ask whether he desired it. She did everything she had ever pictured in sensual dreams; she didn't ask whether she desired it. She merely thought, if I love him enough he won't go away.

"I must go now," he said in a low voice, apologetically.

She pushed him away. He stammered a troubled apology. She didn't understand what he was saying, turned to the wall, covered her ears.

He kissed her hair. She didn't move until she felt that he was about to switch on the lamp. Then she held his hand fast.

She heard him moving about. He put on his coat, stumbled over a chair, came back to the bed, kissed her again.

The 'Zippo' flared up once more in the doorway.

She listened for the front door, but he closed it behind him so quietly that she heard nothing. She switched on the light and sat up.

On the table lay two packets of Chesterfields and beside them his glasses.

8

It's three o'clock, she thought. If I take four instead of two sleeping tablets I shall sleep right through the day. She put her nightdress on and wrapped her dressing-gown round her shoulders. If I take six instead of four I shall sleep right through New Year's Eve.

As she fetched the jug she began to multiply the number by the days and nights. The numbers confused her. Then, like a revelation, the thought came to her: after a certain number of tablets each single one represents a hundred days, a hundred nights, a thousand days, a thousand nights.

She put down the jug and began to count the tablets. She had been collecting them for years for fear that one evening she might find she had none. Once she had asked a doctor how many tablets one would have to take in order never to wake up again. Thirty, he had said, looking at her in an odd way. If she still had thirty. . . . At forty she stopped counting. Forty lay counted on one side of the table, four in a row, ten times four; the rest lay in a little pile.

The hand of the clock seemed not to have moved. It was still three. She thought the matter over. Her landlady wouldn't notice that she hadn't left her room until ten at the earliest. Perhaps not until eleven or twelve. Or not till the afternoon.

She reached for the tablets, but drew back her hand. She still had things to do. She had to write a farewell letter. The expression 'farewell letter' seemed to her grotesque. "Letter giving notice" would have been better. She was sending her life a letter giving notice. It was a maliciously satisfying thought, as though she were sending in her notice to an employer who was sure that he was the only one entitled to give notice.

The intoxication had vanished. It was a long time since she had been so sober. She took her wages out of her handbag, put the rent due in an envelope and wrote the landlady's name on it. That was done. She enclosed the rest of her money in a second envelope. That's the legacy I'm leaving, she thought. This word too seemed to her ludicrous. She didn't know who to leave the money to. She wrote "Police" because she couldn't think of anything else. Then she went to the bed, lifted the mattress, and looked for the pearls. She would put those with the letter to her mother. After she had found the pearls she tidied the rumpled bed. It smelt warm, of man and love.

Finally she sat down at the table and picked up the pen. It occurred to her that this was the last letter she would ever write. She didn't want to get sentimental. She remembered Georg, who had told her that sentimentality was a sign of inferiority. To be sure, this was now a matter of indifference to her. You were only afraid of your own inferiority because of its possible consequences. Dying was easy, because after that nothing had any consequences.

She couldn't write yet. Up to the present she had only thought of the

397

fact that she would sleep for a long time. If you slept for a very long time you were dead. That was new. The saying "Man dies alone" occurred to her. She regretted that it wasn't accurate. If you died alone it would have been something special. But you didn't die alone. Thousands died at the same time. Millions had died before her, millions would die after her. It was commonplace; "plebeian" Paul would have said; 'plebeian' was one of his favourite words. What did being dead mean? Not much. Only that the others went on knowing something which you yourself no longer knew. So it really didn't mean anything more than sleep.

She normally wrote quick, unconsidered letters. No she brooded. The sentences formed within her, but she didn't get them down on paper. Why was she writing at all? Many reasons occurred to her, but they cancelled one another out, since she would know nothing of the consequences which she was considering. Who would weep? Who would remain unmoved? Who would be surprised? Who would say, "I foresaw it?" It wasn't difficult to imagine being dead. The difficulty was to imagine that it didn't matter what happened afterwards.

As she twisted the pen this way and that the suspicion arose in her that she didn't want to die. She despised herself, as we despise ourselves when we give alms and think at the same time that we shall be rewarded for doing so. It was high time she started to write. You wrote the letter giving notice so that you couldn't change your mind. Or because you wanted to accuse the person to whom you were writing. But this too was the thought of a living person who considered consequences. You ought to write the letter after you were dead.

All right then, "Dear Mummy." Or "Dearest Mummy." Or "My dearest Mummy." I am voluntarily taking leave of my life. A revolting banality, like the whole letter, like suicide.

She lit a cigarette, stood up, poured the rest of the bottle into a tumbler. She observed the effect of the alcohol like a doctor watching the reactions of an intoxicated rabbit. Would alcohol arouse her will to live or strengthen her will to die?

She had no will to live left, she observed with satisfaction. Why? She would have to give a reason in her letter of notice: otherwise her notice would be rejected. She could think only of two words. Too much. It was too much. That her mother hadn't come, wasn't coming. That Konrad had promised her peace and run away to war. That she hadn't locked the door and Zoltán had come in when she was in bed with the Italian. That she had tried to take her child to safety and had taken her into a prison. That Werner had gone back to his wife. That no one had moved a finger when a dozen men slept with Consuela one after the other. That she hadn't stayed in Kisnémet. That Pernstorffer didn't believe her; that the first lieutenant had slipped his hand under her skirt; that Lee had left two packets of Chesterfields behind. That her mother had left her in the lurch; that the patience wouldn't come out; that she had been alone on her fortieth birthday; that she had wrinkles; that Teréz had gone away; that Konrad had believed in victory; that the place smelt of apples; that her child had deserted her, like her mother and Hermann and Teréz and Georg and Lee M. Howard. That it was

398

too much and that it was senseless. Dear Mummy, Dearest Mummy, My dearest Mummy. That isn't all. That everything I caught sight of became opaque; everything I touched melted away; everything I found I lost again. That of two roads I always chose the wrong one. At every crossroads, the wrong one again. And that I could never act differently, because I am not you, but myself. That I should never imagine tomorrow that I was choosing the right road, but at the same time I should know that it was the wrong one because I was choosing it. I'm giving notice because I'm incompetent. Too much. Too much.

"Dearest Mummy—forgive me. . . ." the letter started. She smoked and drank. Her eyes fell on the packets of cigarettes, the forgotten glasses. Suppose Lee came back to fetch the glasses? Didn't she want to die? You only wrote in such detail when you felt sorry for yourself. She did feel sorry for herself and went on writing. Every time she wrote about Eva she stopped. The word 'responsibility' occurred to her and immediately afterwards appeared to her as ludicrous as farewell letter, legacy, and suicide. Eva didn't need her. It would be good for the child if she no longer existed. She wouldn't follow false paths which Zita might point out to her. Why were tears running down her cheeks? Because she felt sorry for herself. Because she thought that Teréz and her mother would weep. But perhaps they wouldn't weep. Why ask forgiveness? It was her own like; she could do what she liked with it, for the first time. "Eva must never find out," she wrote.

She put the pearl necklace in the envelope and sealed it.

As she swallowed the tablets she counted. One, two, three, twenty-nine, thirty-eight. She counted, although forty already lay there counted in advance. Then she swallowed the others, with a triumphant smile, as though she had at last succeeded in disarming her own mistrust. She thought of how she would be found next morning. She really ought to have beautified herself. Rouge. The long evening dress. To have sat in front of the mirror. She was glad she hadn't done so. At least she had escaped this hackneyed gesture.

She lay down on the bed and closed her eyes. To-morrow people would say she had slept quite peacefully. With a smile on her lips. She tried to smile.

Suddenly a single thought rose to the surface of her dull, pounding, dark brain shot through with will-o'-the-wisps. She had forgotten to write on the envelope the name of the soldier who would forward it. It didn't matter whether it was forwarded. Let the living bother about that! Seized with panic, she sat up. She felt as though her body were floating away, or as though her soul were standing up and her body lying down. She dragged herself up by the bed-post. The golden bars, the golden prison. The cold went through her body. Perhaps her body had already gone cold.

It was a long way to the table. What was the soldier's name? Exerting all her remaining strength, she drove out every other thought. What was his name? Then his name appeared before her as though written on the wall. Sergeant William E. Stoane, A.P.O. 765, Postmaster General. She knew it exactly. She wrote the name and address on the envelope.

She stood up. The bed moved away into the distance, became a golden sun. She looked for the prison bars, but they were rays of sunshine; she couldn't take hold of them.

She never reached the bed.

9

"Eva must never find out," said Ilona.

"There's no reason why she should," said Lajos.

They were sitting facing one another in the book-filled attic room of a Budapest apartment house. The crooked window looked out on to the Danube. The suspension bridge, broken in the middle, hung down into the water. Ilona thought of a prisoner who had escaped with his hands chained, and fallen into a river.

It was autumn, autumn 1948. She had arrived in Munich with Stefan a fortnight ago. Yesterday she had received a permit to go to Hungary for three days. She was allowed to fetch the child, but had to leave the country immediately afterwards.

Brother and sister looked at one another. Whenever they looked at one another silence came over them.

Ilona had been sixty-one the previous year. Lajos sixty-four. Ilona's hair was grey, but one could still see that it had been blond. Her brother's hair was an icy-grey and icy-grey his small beard. Both of them were sitting upright, rather too upright, like old people.

"You must stop blaming yourself," said Lajos.

"I've failed."

"She was forty."

Ilona shook her head. "You know it started long ago."

"You couldn't change the times you were living in."

"I was too busy being a woman. I wasn't a mother."

"That you had no time for both was also the fault of the times," he said.

The sound of a steamship's siren came from the Danube.

"I've lost my assurance since then," she said. "I wondered for a long time whether I ought to take Eva to live with me. Who can say that I shan't fail again?"

It was more than eighteen months since she had received Zita's letter, but she still couldn't utter her daughter's name without tears coming to her eyes. At first she had believed that she couldn't survive Zita's death. The letter hadn't contained a word of blame. Ilona had read nothing but blame between the lines. Stefan's love alone had led her out of the darkness which for months on end had lain over everything around her. Now there were hours, if only hours, during which she didn't think of Zita. There were times when she could smile again. Her smile was tired. When you grew old you felt grief not as though it pierced your heart, but as though it came down like a heavy burden on your shoulders. You suffered more violently in youth; more heavily in old age. Grief joined forces with the years, as if it had turned into time.

"You talk as though people became what one made of them," said Lajos. "If that were so humanity would have become perfect long ago."

He filled his pipe. "I've seen Eva a few times. You'll get a shock when you see how much like you she looks."

"A shock?" she smiled.

"She is probably the most unspoilt creature I have ever seen," he went on. "I mean . . . unspoilt in spite of everything that has happened around her. Not even Teréz's smothering love was able to spoil her."

"Teréz . . ." said Ilona. She felt a pang in her heart.

While they talked about Teréz, Ilona observed her brother. She had always loved him, but she felt that she loved him more now than in her youth. Stefan was kind, but there were things that only a brother understood. How greatly Lajos had changed! One could never have talked to him in the past for an hour on end about the little personal things that were so big. The ardour in his dark eyes seemed to have gone out; the cold ardour had turned into warmth.

"I shan't see much of you on my way back," she said.

He had risen to his feet and was standing with his back towards her, looking out of the window.

"We have never been so close to one another," he said. "People talk about youth as if it were a great community. Youth feels this, youth wants that. . . . Have you noticed that all old people look alike? What is that due to, I wonder? Perhaps it's because we set out to learn a thousand different things and end up by all having learnt the same thing. The closer you come to truth the narrower grow the paths. In my youth I was often surprised that the same mother had borne us. Now we are both old and alike." He spoke of their shared youth, even mentioning her visit to the Emperor. "It isn't hollow sentimentality when old people suddenly start thinking about their long dead parents. Nor is it fear of death. It is solidarity with the old, with those who are living and those who are dead."

What is he trying to say to me? she asked herself. He is trying to confide something in me. She couldn't see his face, she could only see the slim, erect figure in the green uniform. It made her think of the last pictures of the Tsar. He looked like a dethroned king in a uniform stripped of all insignia. From the back he also reminded her of the stationmaster during his last years, when he had looked like a retired general.

"There is hardly anyone left to whom I can talk," he said. His voice seemed to grow harder, sounding almost metallic. "Don't imagine that is wounded vanity. I'm an old man. I don't mind their having dismissed me after six months. I'm quite happy among my books. I enjoy teaching young people at the university. What hurts me is that the peasants are being deceived again. I thought the Communists wanted to help us redistribute the land. That's why I went to Moscow, that's why I came back. Now they're herding the peasants like cattle into collective farms. Our peasants aren't moujiks. What the Aporfalvys were to them in the past, the collective farms are to them now."

His neck grew straighter and straighter, stiffer and stiffer. His neck was young. She remembered the young soldier in Sopron, the deserter. She thought of the summer night on which the policeman had taken him away.

"Won't you at last leave it to others to save the world?" she said.
He turned to her.

"You've guessed it," he said. "When I was young I believed one couldn't leave it to the old. Now I know one can't leave it to the young. Well, don't you worry about it any more. You can't go to the Emperor in any case. I simply want you to know that no injustice has been done to me . . . if something is done to me."

She wanted to warn him, to entreat him. Had he not just spoken of age? Had he not said that he was an old man? But when she looked at him she knew that it was pointless. The familiar ardour was back in his eyes.

Dawn was already breaking when she left Lajos. She walked to her hotel, a small hotel whose name had not been known to her in the past. The hotels on the Danube embankment were burnt out; they stood there like black lackeys of their former glory. Here and there the fronts were undamaged and the old names still up over the entrances— Dunapalota and Hungaria and Carlton. Ilona remembered a clown she had seen in her childhood. He carried a small garden-gate along in front of him; put it down; opened it; stepped through the gate out of nothingness into nothingness. The rubble was piled high behind the empty fronts. On the other side of the Danube the walls of the royal castle rose up to an empty dome whose flying buttresses looked like gnawed bones. The last rays of the sun came in through the bare dome. A few Russian soldiers passed. A ragged old woman was rummaging in a dust-bin. The bandstand in the Hangli had collapsed. Before the monument to the freedom poet Petöfi lay wreaths of flowers and laurel. The river smelt mouldy; rotten timber and blackened bricks floated and rolled along with it; but it flowed calmly on from inexhaustible springs into the endless sea.

Ilona involuntarily turned to the left in the direction of the Váczi ucca. Not still she was standing in front of Aunt Rosa's house did she realize that she had picked the Galamb ucca. The house was undamaged and undamaged the little marble plaque saying "Salon Rosa."

Two men stared after the old woman. Ilona hurried on.

10

Eva stood by the railway-lines with a pounding heart. The round disk of the signal had already changed from red to green. The train would appear in a moment.

The fifteen-year-old had difficulty in calling her grandmother to mind. Too many pictures confused the picture. The photos showing her as a young girl didn't count, but there was the one from St Petersburg; a snapshot taken at a ball in Berlin; a portrait study from America. In Eva's imagination her grandmother had once been old and had then grown young again, but since she had known that her grandmother was coming she had thought of her as younger and younger. Anyone who was so beautiful, wore such fine clothes, was so rich and powerful, couldn't be old.

Teréz and Margit were standing behind Eva. She didn't look round, but stared fixedly at the railway-lines. She wanted to avoid Auntie Teréz's sad, reproachful eyes. How could she explain to her that she loved her? That since her mother's death she had loved her more than anyone in the world? She would long for her. But, after all, Kisnémet was only a large village and Debreczen a small town. Teréz herself had often called her a 'city child': she had been born in Berlin. "What is so wonderful about Berlin?" Auntie Teréz had sometimes asked her. She hadn't been able to explain. When she thought of Berlin she remembered her mother, and sometimes her father. The picture she had of him was blurred, of course, as though made up of many photographs. When she thought of Berlin she also recalled the nights in the air-raid shelter; she could still hear the dull explosion of bombs, the *rat-tat-tat* of anti-aircraft guns; she could still smell the odour of old and new fires—she had been able to distinguish clearly between old and new fires at that time. And yet it was something different from Kisnémet. Berlin was a jungle with many dangerous beasts lurking in the undergrowth. They threatened you, but you could escape them. In Kisnémet it was as though there was only one wild beast, but with this you were shut up in a cage. She thought of the men who had hung on the apple-tree. The wind had swung him to and fro; he had looked like a dangling scarecrow.

The smoke of the train became visible behind the cemetery. It passed the barrier.

Ilona was the only passenger to get out at Kisnémet. Teréz and Margit went to meet her: Margit with her long strides, as though she wanted to embrace the whole train; Teréz with the short, tripping steps of an old woman. Eva, suddenly shy, stayed behind.

Then she overcame all her shyness. It was her grandmother's reassuring appearance as she looked round for her. She was taller than Teréz and Margit, but she was trying to wave to Eva between the heads of the two women.

Ilona's heart too beat louder. It was as though she herself were standing by the railway-line countless years ago. She didn't know which moved her most deeply: Eva's resemblance to her own youthful appearance; the child's almost womanly beauty; the meeting with Zita's daughter; or the sudden realization that a being so close to her had been able to grow up for fifteen years far away from her. She took Eva in her arms.

Eva's first thought was that she had been right. It was incredible that this slim woman with the white skin, in the dark-grey autumn costume, the dark-grey travelling coat, and carrying a graceful umbrella should be her grandmother, anyone's grandmother. It was true that grey hair peeped out from under the little hat, whose colour matched the coat and costume, but after all even young people sometimes had grey hair.

Ilona took Eva's arm and hurried ahead of the two women.

"Shall we speak German or Hungarian?" asked Ilona.

"Whichever you like, Grandma."

It was the first time Ilona had ever heard the word.

"I speak English quite well too," Eva went on. "And a little French.

You can speak every language, can't you?"

"Not all, but quite a few."

"When are we leaving?"

"Are you in such a hurry?"

"No, no. . . ." Eva blushed.

"We're leaving the day after to-morrow," said Ilona in a low voice so that the two women couldn't hear.

A feeling of happiness such as she hadn't felt since Zita's death came over Ilona. Why had she been afraid? Naturally Eva was glad to go with her. Naturally she ran to her, already belonged to her. Naturally.

She walked faster, so that Teréz shouldn't hear the conversation. She walked faster, so that Eva shouldn't imagine she was old. She thought of the stationmaster.

11

The paradise that opened up to Eva was a dilapidated paradise, but none the less a paradise.

It was Munich after the currency reform. At first the ruins had frightened Eva, but she soon got used to them, hardly saw them any more. It didn't seem to her as though the houses had collapsed recently, but as though they were ancient ruins, like the ones in pictures of Greece and Rome. Everywhere men were sawing, nailing, plastering; a smell of cement and paint hung over the whole city; the hammering and banging kept one company all day and even during the night. It wasn't a disturbing sound; it was rather like the hammering of fairy-tale dwarfs and gnomes.

The Herrdegens' flat was in a two-family house in Schwabing, not in the entertainment district, but at the point where the city approaches the countryside. The ground floor was occupied by a poet whose name Eva had never heard before, but whose old books of poetry she read with enthusiasm. He was a small, tubby gentleman who seemed to be made of balloons and shared with the latter, in spite of his heavy body, the same weightlessness. He might have been taken for anything except a poet; and even less for a hero, although he had been that too. He had lived for several years hidden in a cellar, and was so tubby only because he had since eaten at a single sitting, so to speak, all the food which he had gone without during his 'cellar years,' as he put it. He often visited Herrdegen, read his poems aloud, and politely asked Eva for her opinion.

The Herrdegens' flat consisted of a lounge arranged in rustic style, whose ingle-nook delighted Eva, a study, and two bedrooms. The study, which became increasingly filled with books, was subject to a special ritual, the 'desk ritual.' In the morning, when Eva was at school, the desk belonged to Ilona, who saw to it that her papers and correspondence disappeared before Eva came home; in the afternoon Eva used the desk for her homework, but cleared away her exercise and text-books before supper; during the night the desk belonged to Stefan, who brought home books, manuscripts, and proofs from the publishing house, but removed them all again in order to clear the decks for

Ilona. On the other side of the passage, separated by the bathroom, lay the two bedrooms. The balcony opened out of Eva's charming room, arranged in Bavarian peasant style. In the summer, when they break-fasted out on the balcony, Stefan always jestingly apologized to Eva for having to pass through her room.

The fifteen-year-old hadn't been mistaken: she had entered Paradise. Not till she was seventeen did she discover that in Paradise there stood a dangerous tree, the "tree of the knowledge of good and evil."

12

Martin called for Eva to take her to a fancy-dress ball. He didn't come into the flat; he never did. He waited outside the front door while Eva's friends, Karin and Florentine, ran upstairs. Once again they had difficulty in persuading Ilona of the innocuousness of the Fasching carnival, the first Eva had been allowed to attend.

While Karin was dressed as a circus acrobat in tights and Floren-tine as an apache's sweetheart, Eva had chosen a Mary Stuart costume and had thought up an original, if gruesome detail: she was carrying her own head, made for her out of papier mâché by a young sculptor, under her arm. She looked charming in the lace cap and high-buttoned black-velvet dress with the white ruff and white ruche cuffs—Ilona's evening-dress from London had had to serve as the basis of her costume.

Eva sat in the back of Ulrich's tiny car between Martin and Karin. Her cheeks were glowing with excitement. Her conscience was not entirely at ease.

A few weeks ago she had met Christian Grooth, a reader in the S. Herrdegen publishing house, at a party given by the firm. He was just on forty and had lost his wife during the war. He had devoted himself to her throughout the whole party. Since then she had lunched with him several times without telling her grandmother, from whom she had never concealed anything. She had mentioned that she was going to the carnival and he had said, "Then I shall go too." That was all, but she felt this rendezvous to be a betrayal of Martin.

Martin was six years older than she and a student of journalism. They had been going out together for the last six months. Her friends regarded her as 'Martin's girl,' although neither she nor Martin had ever spoken of love. Martin seemed to regard love as like measles, a children's disease that was unpleasant, but didn't last long.

She took a look at him. He was dressed as a bandit. He wore a striped jersey under his overcoat, had a brightly coloured scarf round his head, and a black patch over his eye, for he was a one-eyed bandit. His brown hair peeped out from under the head-scarf and hung down over his forehead. He had let his hair grow long, although Eva didn't like it, because he had been forced to wear his hair short during the war and now did everything he had not been allowed to do in the army. It sometimes seemed to Eva that all his actions were dictated by a spirit of protest. As a protest he avoided the Herrdegens' flat, although Eva

405

didn't know what he was thereby protesting against. As a protest he never spoke of love. He probably thought love was soft, bourgeois, and old-fashioned—concepts which he detested. No doubt he thought that something you didn't put into words didn't exist.

Karin declared that they must separate as soon as they got inside the hall. She began to argue about this with Ulrich, whose 'girl' she was. Her eighteenth birthday had taken place a little while before. She had blond hair which she wore combed in a curious fashion: the parting was low down, only a little above her right ear; the long hair hung over her left eye. Martin claimed that she had had at least five love-affairs, and he said it so disparagingly that Eva couldn't help laughing, because Martin condemned in practice what he condoned in theory. To annoy him, Eva immediately agreed with her friend. Of course they must quickly separate; after all, they didn't go to a fancy-dress ball to see the 'same old faces.'

The carnival was being held in a theatre converted into a ballroom. "Mirror, mirror, on the wall" was the theme, and it enabled young artists to exploit all sorts of mirror-effects in the most skilful manner, allowing all the feminine visitors to believe that they were "the fairest of them all." The chandeliers, decorated with fragments of mirror, cast a sparkling light on the parquet floor; the mirrors on the walls of the boxes turned a thousand pretty legs into ten thousand; the columns seemed to be rotating in the glitter of the mirrors; every masquer had been given a hand mirror, so that as they danced the mirrors were reflected in the mirrors; the glasses and bottles became focal points of merry lenses. There were few tail-coats and evening-dresses to be seen. Apart from apaches, cowboys, sailors, and dominoes there were a number of more original fancy dresses—Henry VIII, late nineteenth-century street-walkers, Jacobins, babies with nursemaids, circus manageresses, and even figures out of *Faust,* Parts I and II.

Eva and her friends actually had split up soon after arriving. Although Mary Stuart, with her head under her arm, won universal applause, was approached by strangers and torn away from her un-known partners, she was overcome by a feeling of anxiety. She had never felt anything like it before, except during the nights of air raids or in Kisnémet under the Russians. She told herself that she was in Munich at her first Fasching, that the people were good and gay and she herself must be gay. She found it hard, to-day of all days. She looked round for Martin.

As she was squeezing past a box some one seized her arm. It was Christian Grooth. He was not in fancy dress but wearing tails.

"Would Mary Stuart like a drink?" he said, leading her to his box.

She considered that Christian looked magnificent in tails. He was tall, slim, and his face, which was made up of ugly parts, created an attractive effect as a whole. His nose was big and hard, an aquiline nose, his mouth a double dash; his dark eyes were set deep behind eyebrows that were far too bushy. He had scars in his face, so that his skin looked like tanned leather; but one didn't notice any of these defects, which somehow added up to a personality.

He explained to Eva why he wasn't in fancy dress. Masks, he said, were treacherous, they unmasked one's wish-dreams. The Napoleon over there was undoubtedly a hen-pecked husband; Charlie Chaplin a dispirited book-keeper; the whore a good little housewife. Why had she chosen to dress as Mary Stuart? Eva wanted to know. "Perhaps you failed your history exam," he laughed. "Don't misunderstand me," he added, "I like these colourful gatherings. If there were no mirrors I too should have dressed up."

"And what is your wish-dream?" she asked.

"Youth," he answered. "But I don't know whether any mask can fake that."

A seat in Christian's box became free. They sat down. Christian poured her champagne. "Wouldn't you rather dance?" he asked at the same time. "No," she said quickly. Did she know what a strange creature she was? he asked. She laughed. He began to talk about her, seriously, as if he were talking about a third party, as if they were not at a Fasching ball. What he said hit the nail on the head. He had obviously made inquiries about her life. He didn't speak like an inquisitive detective, however, but more like a radiologist dictating his findings in a darkened room. He was the first person who had troubled about her. She thought of Teréz, who had often taken her temperature and then said, reassured, "Your temperature is normal, there's nothing wrong." You could have a normal temperature and still be ill. Christian was the first person who seemed to know that.

The couple who had stood up earlier now came back to the table. The man was dressed as a clown in knickerbockers with a red nose and a chalk-white face; the woman wore black stockings, out of which her naked thighs bulged, and a corset, out of which her breasts bulged. Eva was about to stand up, but the clown said they could all move closer together. He was an acquaintance of Christian's. Christian introduced him to Eva.

"Severin?" said the clown when he heard Eva's name. He bent forward closer to her across the table. His pointed nose almost touched her face. "Severin . . ." he reiterated. "I had a friend . . . Konrad Severin."

"My father," said Eva, turning pale.

The clown stared at her with red-rimmed eyes. "I knew your mother too," he said. The two furrows that he had drawn with charcoal at the corners of his mouth deepened.

Eva leant back. Little beads of sweat broke out on her forehead. Why did the clown speak about her father, her mother? She hardly ever thought of her father now, and rarely of her mother. Her life had begun on the day she left Kisnémet. She was two years old. In the dancing, mirrored crowd she suddenly felt that she was not two years old. She had a past of her own, perhaps a past that was not her own. The gaiety appeared to her sinister, as though it might suddenly turn into panic and savagery; sinister the masquers, who were perhaps wearing masks with evil intent; sinister her own Mary Stuart's head, which she had put down on the table among the bottles and glasses. They were dancing a boogie-woogie. The space was too small for dancing. Every one was fighting for room. The girls flew into the arms of unknown partners. The toes of shoes stuck into the calves of unknown dancers. The faster the rhythm of the jazz band became, the more serious became the dancers' faces. The effort of trying to keep time left them nothing to laugh about. None of the dancers wanted anything to do with his partner; only the fact that they occasionally held hands revealed that they were together. Every one was dancing on his own. If anyone touched a body it was a stranger's body. A few were singing, but nobody spoke. The dance seemed to symbolize the attraction and repulsion of the sexes, both taking place in a terrible mood of depression. Eva caught sight of the mirrors on the pit-boxes and the room looked to her like a shoe-shop gone crazy.

The clown was whispering with his wife, the lady in the corset. Eva felt a pitying glance fall upon her. Her father had been killed in the war. So what? Millions had been killed. It was more than five years ago. Was she supposed to be in mourning? Hadn't she the right to go to a Fasching ball?

Then Martin appeared.

"So there you are," he said. "You went off," she said angrily. "That's obvious," he retorted. She wanted to introduce the two men. "We know one another," said Martin roughly. "May I invite you to a glass of champagne?" said Christian politely. Martin didn't reply. "You're coming with me," he declared, seizing her so firmly by the hand that she cried out. "Bring your head with you," he said. Christian had already risen to his feet. He seemed amused. "I shall stay here," he said.

Martin didn't utter a word as they went down the stairs. She had difficulty in keeping up with him in her long dress.

Not until they were in the Coca-Cola Bar did he say, "I know you had a date with that fellow."

She protested.

"I don't care if you make dates," he said, "but not with that fellow. I know his kind. For Führer and fatherland till the last minute. First lieutenant retired. And a Nazi swine."

He was silly, she said, silly and jealous.

"I, jealous? Not of that rat. He's finished, washed up, done for."

He didn't know who Christian was, she said.

"Oh, don't I just!" he said. "He's Herrdegen's reader. I'll tell you something. We expected an example from people like your grandfather—or stepgrandfather or whatever he is. But what do they do? They employ Nazi swine. They come home from the emigration and employ Nazi swine. Wet their pants with emotion because they hear the divine German forest rustling again. Questionnaire in order? Then everything's fine. Yesterday on the parade ground, to-day behind the publishing-house desk, but always the same First Lieutenant Grooth. I know that lot, you don't have to introduce them to me." He emptied his glass of Coca-Cola as though draining a cup of poison. "Anyhow, you can do as you please. The ape in tails is waiting." He leaned back. "I think he suits you pretty well. A knight in armour and a girl of good family. You really ought to marry him. You might have half a dozen nice little kids."

She interrupted him. "I wouldn't mind half a dozen nice little kids," she said. "But I do mind your conceit. I'll tell you something, though you won't like it. You're hopelessly old-fashioned. Only old people continually live on their memories. I've been out with Christian, and he didn't say a word about parade grounds. I've just spent an hour with him, and no one would ever guess what he did in the past. He looked at me instead of looking at himself in the mirror. You're constantly looking at yourself in the mirror. Anyway, he wasn't a Nazi. Not every officer was a Nazi. My father was a major, which shocked you terribly when I first told you. I'm sick and tired of your blather about justice." Tears were choking her. "Besides, I came here to enjoy myself." She stood up.

He had gone white in the face, but he remained seated and laughed heartily. "Go on, enjoy yourself!" he cried out after her with histrionic scorn. "And don't forget your head. It's lying on the table!"

13

She was sitting beside Christian in his Volkswagen. It was three o'clock, and the ball was in full swing. She had spent two hours with him. They had danced tangos and foxtrots and waltzes—dances in which the dancers didn't dance alone, smiled at one another, sometimes exchanged a word. She had several times caught sight of Martin, in the ballroom, leaning on bars, sitting on stairs, with witches and corsets and prostitutes, and girls in grandmothers' nightdresses. She had smiled; he had turned away. He had turned away from his partners too. Then she had sat at various bars with Christian, at the champagne bar and the whisky bar. When he had suggested fleeing from the din and dazzle, going to his place and continuing their conversation in peace, she had said "Yes."

Since they had been sitting in the car they had both kept silent; a man and a woman after a decision, before a decision.

She pressed her head against the window-pane. Her head was heavy with the drinks she had drunk. There was a thick layer of ice on the glass. The small car became smaller still, the interior of a cube of ice. The glaring lights sped past the window like out-of-the-way stations in the night. Through the windscreen they could see staggering figures, pierrots and cowboys and men in tails and Americans in uniform. The car skidded into the frozen tramlines and jumped out of them again. A few burnt-out walls were still standing; the carnival figures seemed to disappear into them. Eva saw the face of the clown in front of her, the face of the lady in the corset. "Her mother . . . you know. . . ." What was there to know about her mother? She wondered why her grandmother so seldom spoke of her mother; why she so often went alone to the grave in the Waldfriedhof; why Stefan and her grandmother sometimes exchanged furtive glances; why her grandmother seemed to lower her eyes when she passed photographs of her daughter. She was surprised that she hadn't asked Christian about the clown's strange remark while they were still at the ball, but now that she wanted to ask

409

him her voice failed her. She heard herself say, "I think you'd better take me straight home, Christian."

"Are you afraid?"

"No."

"It's still early."

She wasn't afraid. Most of her friends had lovers. It wasn't reprehensible to have a lover; nor virtuous not to have one. What happened between a man and a woman, if they desired each other, was always natural. Pleasure and love were one: there was no sense in denying yourself either. Nevertheless Eva felt some inexplicable connexion between the uneasiness that had come over her in the box at the ball and her willingness to go with Christian. Since then she had been looking for a refuge. Christian's voice had reassured her. Christian's arms were a sanctuary.

He still kept silent as he helped her out of the car. She found it touching that he was afraid, more afraid than she; he had not spoken for fear of spoiling something.

He occupied the ground-floor flat in a villa in Schwabing, not far from her own house. The villa had belonged to his mother. Two American families had been billeted in it, but two rooms had been given back to him; next month the whole house would be his again.

She put Mary Stuart's head down on the table in the hall. He helped her off with her coat.

The drawing-room with the dark furniture and bronze lamps reminded her of the dining-room in Kisnémet. It was a room that ought to have been warm, but it was cold. Christian switched on one of the bronze lamps and lit the gas fire. The blue flame darted up through the bars; they looked like piano keys catching fire. There was a warm smell but no warmth.

Christian sat down beside Eva on a wide couch. The couch was out of place in the room, a memory of the time when every room was a bedroom. The piano keys were humming softly. Eva thought of a waxwork exhibition she had seen, probably in Berlin, a very long time ago. Christian, sitting there stiffly in tails next to Mary Stuart, looked like the president of a state. In the waxwork exhibition presidents stood next to the queens of history.

"I suppose you would have preferred to go on dancing till morning," he said.

She shook her head. How was it that among the dancers they had talked continuously and that now they found nothing to talk about? When a man and a woman have made up their minds to make love to one another there is nothing left for them to talk about.

"May I lay my head in your lap?" he said.

She nodded. He stretched out on the sofa and laid his head in her lap. She looked down at him. Although it was almost dark, she saw every wrinkle in his face, every scar. The gaslight danced between his eyes; his eyebrows became blue and even bushier. She laid her hands on his head.

He sat up and took her in his arms. She turned her head a little to one side. He kissed her neck. His hands played round her ruff, excited hands. He couldn't find the fastener of her dress, took her round the waist, kissed the velvet of her dress. She felt his kisses on her breasts, muffled, velvet kisses. He took her head in his hands and pressed his mouth to her lips.

She pushed him away, so violently that she immediately regretted it. Her body had remained cold under his kisses, was growing colder and colder. Her only thought was, how can I get away from here without hurting his feelings? She wasn't afraid; she simply didn't want to hurt his feelings.

"Christian!" she said.

He let go of her at once.

"Christian, it was very stupid of me . . ."

He looked at her uncomprehendingly.

"I don't know," she went on, "perhaps I shall one day become your lover. Then you can be sure that I love you. To-day I don't know and you don't know."

He stood up and walked across the room. The gas flames went with him.

After a while he began to speak. What was it they had been talking about? Ah, yes, living in the country. City or village. Landscape and character. He developed theories, intelligent and superior, and yet it seemed that he was becoming entangled in his sentences, couldn't extricate himself from them.

He sat down beside her again. Youth. Modern youth. Young women and old men. Like her and him. He laid his head in her lap and looked up at her, but didn't touch her.

"You're right," he said. "Old men like me are crazy."

"You're not old."

"Too old. But you needn't comfort me. I don't cling to you because you're young, but because, since my wife died, I can't find any more women. The women of to-day make me think of very old butterflies. As long as they are in the state of the caterpillar and the chrysalis you imagine they are going to turn into butterflies. By no means! What crawls out of the chrysalis is some indescribable creature that is certainly not a butterfly. Only while it is still a chrysalis do you imagine it might turn into a butterfly."

"So I'm a chrysalis," she said with a smile.

"You understand me perfectly," he said rather irritably. "I may have been the first old man who tried to seduce you, but I shan't be the last. Just look around—nothing but young women and old men. Freud would explain that by the father complex: most girls have no father. . . ." He stopped and only continued when she laid her hand on his forehead. "The explanation is too logical to be true. It rests on a fallacy that has been widely current ever since Adam and Eve: namely, that in love the woman is bound to be the seductress. Eve led Adam to commit an act of extreme stupidity, but there was nothing erotic about it. Since the man's erotic urge is stronger than the woman's—even the modern woman's, indefinable creature that she is—the seducer is generally the man. Therefore the father complex doesn't explain anything." He put his hands round her waist again. "I love you," he said, "because you don't imagine you know everything. Because you are still capable of asking questions. Because you can keep silent with big, tender eyes. Because even if you loved me you wouldn't tell me how to love you. Because if you loved me I should have the illusory hope that you would stay with me for a lifetime." He sat up slightly. "I'll tell you a secret, little Eva. We old men have never hated the young so much, because we have never envied them so much. In my youth an old man could have seen you and Martin together without the blood rising to his head. The old man would have imagined that you were inviolable; and that would have consoled him. Now he knows that you sleep together, or have slept together, or will sleep together. He finds the thought unbearable. He asks himself, why he and not I? But he dare not give himself the answer, because the other man is young and I am old. We hate the young, Eva, because we hate your freedom and our obscenity."

He drew her down to him. His hands slid over her breasts again, as though he had excited himself with his own resignation. He only stopped when she went stiff in his arms. This was the second attempt, more humiliating than the first; the cold attempt that was solely a matter of pride. Poor Christian, she thought, poor old man.

He stood up again and once more walked across the room, once more accompanied by the flames. What had they been talking about? Whether she should come into the publishing firm. There was a great deal in favour, a great deal against. The new literature, the destruction of values. Houses could be rebuilt. Souls took longer. He tried to cover up his defeat with words. Eva shivered. She wondered how she could make him forget his defeat. He couldn't forget it, and was afraid of being left alone with it.

"I must go now, Christian," she said at last.

On the way he didn't utter a word. When they were close to her house she said, "Christian—your friend, the clown at the ball, said something about my mother. What do you know about my mother?"

She watched his face in the early morning light. His lips had narrowed, as though blocking the path of his words.

"Nothing," he said. "Nothing in particular. . . ."

At the garden gate she quickly kissed his cheek. He gazed after her in surprise.

She opened the front door and pretended to go in, but waited there until the car drove away. She drew deep breaths of the cold morning air. The thought that there was some secret connected with her mother merely passed over her mind like a transitory cloud. She was happy. She didn't love Christian!

14

Ilona didn't know which she was most worried about, Stefan or Eva.

Because Ilona identified herself with the man she loved even more than in her youth—like the chameleon that takes on the colour of its environment—she felt Stefan's joys, and also his disappointments, more and more acutely.

The atrocities committed by the lords of hell during the years of darkness grew more personal, as it were, but they were not new to Stefan; he had heard about them for twelve years, had probably known more about them than his countrymen. He also understood the callousness with which people spoke of them: the experience was still too close, the horror still too great, the suffering of every individual so inconceivable that it had turned entirely inward. What amazed, disappointed, almost shocked Stefan, was the closing of the ranks between the torturers and the tortured, the solidarity of persecutor and persecuted. They seemed to be keeping a common secret, like the occupants of a house who had been held captive all night by armed bandits, and after their liberation refused to say what had happened during the night; either because they still feared the bandits; or because they distrusted the police; or—and this was what Stefan believed—because they were ashamed of their cowardice, which the bandits might have revealed if arrested.

In his second disappointment Ilona was even less able to help him. As his friends often said, he was a knight of literature. He had sought to set the gagged literature free and found that it did not exist. From a distance he had imagined that it was still possible to think with a gag in one's mouth: now he saw that the inability to think had gone hand in hand with an inability to write. He had opened the locked drawers of desks only to find that they were empty. How great must the hopelessness have been; how deep the conviction that terror would reign for ever! He had heard of the horrors while in America; he had not learnt of the hopelessness until his return. Well, they would have to start from the beginning, and the septuagenarian was stout-hearted. But here again, what difficulties! The young had grown up without examples. But literature, as Stefan had long known, does not grow out of untilled soil, as the untalented primitive geniuses claim: it grows out of books. Geniuses build roads so that talents can travel: without geniuses talents perish. Moreover, Stefan, who spent a great part of the day in conversation with young authors, felt that by comparison with these refractory old men he had remained a youth. He had thought that they would now reach for the bricks with urgent idealism, but in reality they were like children who, because the top storey of a castle made from building-blocks has collapsed, despairingly destroy the foundations as well.

It was hard work digging for the hidden treasure that must exist somewhere. As in America, Ilona could help Stefan only by constantly assuring him that the old miner wasn't yet too old to dig.

Ilona observed her granddaughter with no less concern. Ever since Eva had been living with her, Ilona had enjoyed the happy feeling that her granddaughter kept no secrets from her. At times Eva's honesty appeared to her positively brazen, as though she concealed nothing because she didn't believe that anything whatever could be shameful. Nevertheless Ilona was more and more convinced that a woman's friendship had developed between her and her granddaughter, quite understandably, since the young girls who visited the Herrdegens' house all quarrelled exclusively with their mothers and blamed all their

troubles entirely upon the generation immediately preceding them
Stefan, whom Ilona had once proudly told that Eva's friends envied
her for her grandmother, had commented, "It's a perfectly natural
process. The 'ultra-modern' woman hates the woman of yesterday—
that is to say, the 'modern' woman; against the woman of the day
before yesterday, the old-fashioned woman, she has no complaint."

And now Eva suddenly appeared morose, irritable, quick-tempered,
sometimes actually rude. What was worrying her? It could only be
a man. Was it Martin Mainoni, who still wouldn't enter the house?
Was it Christian Grooth, who telephoned Eva far too frequently?

15

It was a spring evening and Eva and Ilona were both alone; Stefan
was entertaining visitors from abroad. Grandmother and granddaughter
were sitting in the living-room. They had both been reading
manuscripts.

Eva shut the notebook with a bang. "I'm going to bed," she said.

Ilona put down her spectacles. "I'd like to talk to you."

With a gesture of reluctance Eva remained seated.

"You have changed a great deal recently," said Ilona. "Something is
worrying you. Can't I help you?"

For weeks Eva had been wondering whether to reveal what was on
her mind to her grandmother. Several times—in a casual manner, she
imagined—she had brought the conversation round to her mother. She
had also asked Christian, whom she saw now and then, about her
mother. She had run up against an elastic wall.

"I want to know what happened to Mummy," she said.

Ilona couldn't face the girl's eyes and had to lower her own. "Eva
must never find out," Zita had written in her farewell letter. It had been
a last will and testament. Had she obeyed the testament? Or had she
merely kept silent because it was convenient? Convenient and cowardly.
For years she had feared this moment. Wasn't the truth a heavier
burden than ignorance? Could she tell Eva the truth without harming
her?

"You're grown up now," began Ilona, as though she had to apologize
for her silence hitherto. "Until to-day I couldn't. . . ."

"Mummy killed herself," said Eva.

"How do you know . . .?"

"I'm not as stupid as you think."

"I never thought you were stupid."

"Why did you keep it from me?"

"It would have been too heavy a burden for you."

Eva laughed. The truth—too heavy a burden! Martin was right. That
was why there was no bridge between the young and the 'grown-ups.'
They considered the truth a burden. They considered the truth all sorts
of things: superfluous or dangerous, thoughtless or rude. As though
you could haggle with truth! As though you could water it down, like
full-bodied wine! As though you could postpone it, like an unpleasant

414

rendezvous! And as though you had the right to decide for whom the truth was suitable and for whom it was unsuitable.

"I want to know everything," she said.

Slowly, hesitantly Ilona told her. If only she could find the right words now! The person who commits suicide accuses the living. That is why the living accuse those who have taken their own lives. To exculpate themselves the living have to blame the dead. The living and suicides are enemies. At all cost no accusations, thought Ilona. She went far back into Zita's life. She spoke of her early disappointments, of her loneliness. When she came to the war she found the story somewhat easier to tell. The 'great helplessness' was a good excuse. Then she broke off. By defending suicides we accuse them. Only the accused require defending. Natural death is kind, because it acts without reason. Murder and suicide have one thing in common—the motive. If the decision is taken out of death's hands there must be a motive. Now Ilona paused at Zita's decision to take Eva to Kisnémet. The separation, the lost war, the Russian occupation, the curtain that came down. But this wasn't easy either. Was she to present Zita's separation from Eva as the motive? That would mean laying the blame on the child, innocent as she was.

Eva listened with compressed lips. The dull pain was so great that she could scarcely think. It was as though she had only just received the news of her mother's death. Her grandmother wasn't telling her the truth, not the whole truth. She wanted to know what had happened in the years before her mother's suicide. She wanted to know every minute immediately before her death. What had her mother felt as she reached for the poison? Had she taken poison? And whose fault was her suicide? That was the most important thing. A suicide had to be avenged, like a murder. Was she, the daughter, to blame? An absurd idea; when she last saw her mother she was barely twelve. And yet she accused herself, not because she had done something, but because she might have omitted to do something. She looked at her mother; saw her in a different light from hitherto. What had her grandmother done? What had she left undone? Why had she remained silent until now about what happened on that December 30, 1946? Where had her grandmother been? Where had they all been, what had they all done, while her mother was dying?

"Did she leave a farewell letter?" she asked, threateningly, as though to forestall a lie from the outset.

"Yes."

"I want to see it."

"Must you, Eva?"

Eva stood up. She was as white as chalk. Her suspicion had grown stronger. She was still being lied to.

"Show it to me!" she said.

Ilona went into the bedroom and came back with a key. Eva watched her in silence, as though she were a criminal who had been caught and compelled to lay the proof of his own guilt on the table. She remembered that the right-hand drawer of the desk had always been locked. So that was where her grandmother kept the proof of her guilt.

Ilona opened the drawer of the desk and took out a folder containing personal papers. In it was the envelope bearing the name of the American soldier: Sergeant William E. Stoane, A.P.O. 765, Postmaster General.

Eva sat down with the envelope in her hand.

Ilona stood beside her granddaughter, not daring to touch her arm or her head. If only Stefan were here, she thought, but she was immediately ashamed of her weakness. It was a good thing Stefan wasn't here. He had a weak heart; at his last visit the doctor had shaken his head. Ilona was also ashamed of having thought of Stefan's illness. All her life she had only thought of the man. That was why she had failed as a mother. Now she was thinking of Stefan and failing as a grandmother. Poisonous vapours seemed to be rising from the letter her granddaughter held in her hand. Ilona was old: the vapours could no longer poison her. But Eva! She laid her hand on the girl's hair.

Eva shook it off and stood up.

Tears were constricting her thoat; not tears of pity, tears of rage. Her rage sought an object, as a ship lost in the mist seeks a harbour. The figure of her grandmother faded, became faint, incorporeal. Her anger was directed against her mother—not because she was dead, but because even in death she had not spoken the truth. Since the letter contained no accusation it couldn't contain the truth. Again she thought of Martin. "They only whine," he used to say. "They'll run a mile in order to get away from the truth. They find explanations for everything, so that they don't have to ask who is guilty."

"Why did you leave her alone?" she asked.

Ilona sat down. She was exhausted. She felt the burden of the years as never before.

"She didn't want to come with us," she said. "You know that we had to go."

"Did you try to persuade her?"

"That was impossible."

"Why?"

"She wanted to stay with your father."

"And afterwards, when he was dead?"

"The war was still going on."

Eva stood in front of her grandmother like a public prosecutor.

Ilona straightened up. It seemed to her that the whole tragedy would not have happened if she had not always given in to Zita. She wouldn't give in to Eva now. It was no longer the daughter who was at stake. She mustn't lose the granddaughter. Up to now she hadn't defended herself. It was time to do so.

"You don't understand," she said. "I did all I could to prevent your mother's marriage. Stefan and I knew that it would end in disaster...." Now bitterness rose in her too.

"Why?" Eva interrupted.

"Because . . ."

"Tell the truth at last!"

"Because your father was a Nazi. Because he wanted the war in which he was killed. I'm not blaming him. He was consistent. He died

416

for Führer and fatherland. But Führer and fatherland were more important to him than his wife and child. Your mother sought tranquillity and he took her into turmoil. Your mother was always lonely and he left her alone. Your mother was good, but she became his accomplice. That was why life became unbearable to her, for no other reason."

Eva's lips moved, but she could neither weep nor give any answer. Turmoil, loneliness—whose fault was it? Her grandmother acted as though she had nothing to do with it. A Nazi. Accomplice. That was all she had to say. She suddenly felt that she loved no one but her father. Not her grandmother, not her mother, not Stefan, not Teréz not Martin. She loved her father, the Nazi, who was held to blame for everything; the scapegoat who couldn't defend himself; who lay in a mass grave somewhere in Russia.

Before Ilona could hold her back she dashed out of the room; tore her overcoat from the peg; ran down the stairs and out into the street.

16

Not until she was racing up Martin's stairs did it occur to her that she should have gone to Christian. Christian understood her. Christian didn't condemn her father. Christian didn't content himself with bitter comments. She didn't know why she had hurried to Martin. She knocked at his door.

Martin opened it. He was wearing blue jeans and a brightly coloured checked shirt. Jazz echoed from the room. Martin looked at her in surprise.

His flat, or rather his room with a kitchen recess, looked out on the Viktualienmarkt. It was a large, untidy room. Books and newspapers lay everywhere, and a few unwashed dishes. There was a smell of beer and vegetables. The jazz was pounding.

"What's the matter?" asked Martin.

"Turn the radio off!"

When he had done so she sat down on the studio-couch.

"I'm not going home again," she said. "I've had enough."

She told him what had happened an hour ago, not omitting a single detail.

"Now it's all supposed to be my father's fault," she said. "I'm not going to have him abused." She narrowed her eyes threateningly. "Not by you either."

He had pushed away the table that stood between the couch and the armchair, the only chair in the room, a disabled soldier that had lost an arm. Martin shifted it towards the couch and seized Eva's hand.

"First, you must calm down," he said. "When your mother died you were only thirteen. You have no idea what sort of a time that was."

"People didn't all do away with themselves."

"Will you please listen to me? I don't know your grandmother, but she seems to me to be a decent woman. The fact that she stuck to Herrdegen when he had to leave Germany speaks in her favour."

"Are you attacking my mother?"

"I'm not even attacking your father, although I'm quite sure I shouldn't have liked him. I don't like him any the better for having been killed in the war. I've no use for heroes and least of all for heroes from conviction. You're furious because your grandmother didn't tell you the truth, but you'll be furious when I tell it to you. Either or. Please forget your grief for a moment: it's too late now for you to put things right. If we're to get along at all in this rotten world we must throw romanticism overboard. Your father was probably a romanticist, but that doesn't excuse him any more than his heroism. Romanticists are a menace. And not only to their contemporaries. You're the best proof of that." He stroked her hand with a gesture that belied his words. "Just think of me. My father was a Nazi. Probably a thousand times worse than yours. You know he became rector of his university under the Nazis. He was tremendously proud when I was sent to the front. He considered it his life's work to turn the students out of the university as fast as possible, so that they could perish as fast as possible on the field of honour. In the same year in which Ossietzky received the Nobel Peace Prize in a concentration camp, my father received the golden Party badge. Now, of course, he tries to deny it all, but the fact remains that he makes me sick. According to him I ought to say, 'My father, right or wrong.' In short, we should introduce a tax on inheritances so high that none of us ever again comes into possession of these wretched inheritances. Let the old people moan that we are cynical. Or without traditions. Or lacking in respect. The dung-heap our fathers have left behind doesn't smell any better because it was they who left it."

Eva didn't draw her hand away from him, but she scarcely heard what he was saying. She knew Martin's principles. She had heard them often and she had begun to believe in them. But to-day she hadn't come to him to hear a political diatribe. He didn't understand her.

He noticed that she was listening to him with only half an ear. He let go of her hand; sat down beside her; put his arm round her shoulders.

"Your grandmother has been through a lot," he said. "Perhaps she's a little unjust. Anyhow, she is not guilty of your mother's death. In her place, I should have told you the truth long ago, but at the time when your grandmother grew up the truth wasn't in demand. She wanted to spare you. I can understand that the news upset you, but you must stop striking out blindly around you. It's true that people didn't all do away with themselves at that time, but it's a miracle that they didn't." He straightened a cushion. "Now lie down quietly and close your eyes. When you've had a rest I shall take you home."

She obeyed. All at once, she didn't know why, her heart felt warm. It didn't matter whether Martin was right. He wanted to help her. She could put herself in his hands. Christian might have understood her better. But he wouldn't have helped her.

With her arms crossed behind her head, she stared up at the ceiling. He stood up, went over to the radio, switched it on. A dance band was playing. Then he sat down beside her again.

She twined her arms round his neck.

"Couldn't I stay with you to-night?" she said.

"The old woman would be worried to death."

He bent down over her and kissed her on the lips. She embraced him more passionately than ever before.

"I'm not at all sorry I came to see you," she said.

"And why ever should you be sorry?"

"I'm not quite sure whether you love me."

"Rubbish!"

"You never invited me to your room?"

"It's not very pretty here." He gently released himself from her arms and pushed the one-armed chair away.

"I think it's beautiful. And you don't come to me either."

"I don't like family connexions. Besides, I'll let you into a secret. I've submitted my novel to Herrdegen. Herrdegen might think I'm trying to influence him."

She laughed. "If he gets to know you he's bound to turn it down. By the way, he's never mentioned it."

"Perhaps he hasn't even seen it. Herr Grooth will sling it out for sure."

She sat up. "Do you know, I think you're wonderful."

"I am wonderful. The news just hasn't got around yet."

She lay back against the cushions again. "Do you know what happened after the ball?" she asked.

He wrinkled his forehead.

"I went to Grooth's flat."

He stood up, walked over to the radio and furiously twiddled the knob, as though to put some life into the soft music of the dance band.

"Nothing happened," she said. "He kissed me. And nothing happened."

"He kissed you—that's enough."

"I wanted to go to bed with him, but I couldn't. Do you think it's very bourgeois of me to refuse to go to bed with anyone I don't love?"

"What do you mean—bourgeois? You're not a whore."

"Then Florentine and Karin and Helga must be whores."

"I don't care a damn about them. I've no idea whether they do it for love." He sat down beside her again, but he didn't touch her. He held a cigarette between his fingers without lighting it. "Anyhow . . . if you and I . . . then it's got to be right. That's why I'm going to drive you home now. It may be that you only think me wonderful now, because for the moment you're all mixed up. Which isn't surprising."

She stood up, took his head between her hands and kissed him. She had always felt protected. In Berlin, when her mother had come to look for her in the school air-raid shelter. In Kisnémet with Auntie Teréz, even during the nights when the Russians roamed round the house. With her grandmother, to whom she had probably been unjust. Then one day she had gone to a fancy-dress ball; a clown had said something about her mother; Martin had abused her; she had gone to Christian's flat. The ground under her feet had begun to sway. Now it was standing still again, as after an earthquake. Perhaps it didn't matter all that much what happened to you; what happened around you; not

419

even what you did. The only thing that mattered was to love and be loved. Could it be that her mother hadn't loved enough, hadn't been loved enough . . . ?

17

Summer came suddenly, as though it had been waiting outside the school gates for the reports to be handed out. The trees in the Englischer Garten seemed to have dressed behind the screen of the spring mist: now they stood there in their green frocks. Half-naked people were to be seen on the slopes of the Isar; they looked like white skeletons, but the skeletons ran down into the water, and when they came out of it again the water had woken them into life. In the parks the old people nodded their heads, as if they had played a trick on death and lived to see the summer after all. The birds twittered all day long, as if to make up for lost time. The women wore light frocks and the men gazed after them, as though seeing them for the first time.

It was Sunday. Eva and Martin had walked through the woods along the Isar with four friends. They had picked flowers and lain in the grass, which was full of the stirrings of young life. It was a day that seemed to say, "More, more, more." And because they couldn't part from the day and from each other they had gone to the station in Rudolf's car and bought sausage and rolls and beer and hot liver pâté. Then they had gone up to Martin's room. Eva and Helga had covered the table with paper serviettes—Ursula, who was less domesticated, had taken no part in this—and they had agreed that three glasses were sufficient for six people. Now the plates were piled up in the cooking recess; only the beer-bottles still stood around. As always, there was a smell of beer and vegetables and a slight odour of bloody meat, for although the green stalls of the Viktualienmarkt were closed the smells were not taking Sunday off. The warm air that streamed in through the window carried the smells in its arms, as the market women carried the vegetables and the butchers the meat.

Conversation revolved around the founding of a student magazine. Rudolf, a gaunt, bespectacled law student in his third year, the son of a well-to-do family, asserted that he could raise the money, a statement that was greeted sceptically by both Martin and Heinrich. Although—as Eva had observed, not without pride—Rudolf and Heinrich were agreed that Martin should run the paper, Martin would have nothing to do with the project.

"I ask you, what's the sense of it?" he said, turning to Rudolf. "They'll kill us dead after the third number."

"Who?" demanded Rudolf.

"Who, who? Every one. Above all, our fellow-students. The gang are German nationalists to the marrow once more. When I see those faces, the neatest duelling scars appear before my mind's eye. The young gentlemen's great dream is to become old gentlemen."

"We shan't be running the paper for them but against them," said Rudolf.

"Martin is quite right," commented Heinrich. He wore his hair long and his forehead was as wrinkled as a dachshund's. "Against is also for. But for whom?"

"Start asking me for the positive cause—that's all I need," retorted Rudolf.

He went to the radio. Their conversation was now accompanied by soft jazz.

"Assuming they don't kill the paper," said Martin. "Assuming we find one or two idiots to put up the money. Assuming advertisers aren't afraid of advertising in an independent paper. Assuming the governing body of the university doesn't put its foot down. Assuming the printer doesn't yield to outside pressure. . . . What then? Then at best we shall have lit a miserable little candle. And in a vacuum it will go out." He jumped up and strode to and fro, bumping into things on all sides. "Just stop to think, for heaven's sake. They conduct a war in the name of humanity and end it gloriously by wiping out a hundred and fifty thousand people with their rotten atom bomb. Declare war on Fascism and let Franco go free. Bomb Dresden to bits and leave the I.G. buildings in Frankfurt untouched. Were outraged by the union of Austria with Germany, but join Silesia to Poland. Divide up Berlin like a birthday cake and now suddenly discover that uniforms suit us splendidly. And then Germany, is supposed to be de-Nazified, my foot! What they mean is whitewashing the Nazis. But don't worry, everything is going to be all right. Messrs Ostermann, Heger, and Mainoni are going to found a student magazine and teach every one common sense and good manners. Count me out!"

"And a fellow like you is studying journalism!" said Rudolf Heger. "May I ask why?"

"Of course," replied Martin. "In the first place, I find it comforting to learn that the Press has always been corrupt. In the second, I intend to take an active part in the corruption. You don't imagine I'm going to sit back all my life and watch the scum filling their bellies." He dropped into the one-armed chair, which almost lost its second arm in the process. "They're actually letting my father teach again. When he thinks back on the rows we used to have he must be convinced I'm crazy."

Eva stood leaning against the window-frame. Her feelings were in conflict. She was proud of Martin; many of his arguments had convinced her. But was he right in everything he said? And where would it lead, for him and her?

As she looked at him—the powerfully built young man of medium height with soft brown hair, impertinent, almost audacious eyes and the rather too wide but infinitely loveable mouth—as she watched him marching up and down the too-small room again in his Texas trousers and checked Texas shirt, she caught herself including herself in his plans, or rather in his lack of plans. He was always running his head against a wall, just as he was doing now—even where there wasn't any wall. Stefan, for example! He had read Martin's novel; had praised the author as exceptionally gifted; had instructed Eva to invite him to the house. What did Stefan want with him? Martin had asked. Stefan wanted to suggest one or two changes in the book. "Aha," Martin had said, "I suppose I'm to turn the sergeant-major into a Father Christmas and the captain into an English lord." She hadn't been able to persuade him that all Stefan had in mind were a few stylistic changes and possibly a modification of the dramatic structure. "I'm not going to walk into the trap," Martin had said. "Before I know where I am I shall have an advance in my pocket, and in the end the whole thing will stink of rotten compromise." All right, no compromise then, she had said, but what did he hope for from his book? Nothing. People were blind, deaf, and unfeeling; that was why the mighty could 'play ducks and drakes with them.'

In the meantime they had long ago stopped talking about the students' magazine. They were now talking about Helga's mother. The subject regularly cropped up when Helga had to go home early in the evening. She couldn't get used to her mother's 'double morality.' Helga's father was still a prisoner of war with the Russians; her mother was having an affair with an American colonel. The case was dissected; it lay on the table between sausage-wrappings and beer-bottles. The surgeons couldn't agree. "Devil take it," said Ursula, "your mother isn't forty yet, even if she did make the mistake of bringing you into the world. Your father went to the front nine years ago; you can't expect her to wait till she's covered in cobwebs." She had nothing against her mother's love affair, objected Helga; only her mother should kindly leave her in peace. "What has double morality to do with it?" lectured Heinrich. "Morality isn't the issue here at all, that's obvious. Neither single nor double. It's purely a question of coming to an understanding. I'll give you an example. You catch me stealing this handbag. Next day you come and demand half the contents, otherwise you will report me to the police. That's blackmail. If I report you to the police you will be imprisoned. But I shall also be imprisoned, for theft. I'd rather give you half. But who is to say that you won't report me to the police just the same? Because I have once yielded to blackmail, I shall live under a constant threat. So there's no way out. Wrong! If I go halves with you as soon as the crime is committed there will be no legal action. We shall be accomplices. Neither of us can report the other, neither of us can blackmail the other. It's a clear case. Morality is a mutual agreement to do everything immoral in concert. You, Helga, should go to your mother and say, 'I know perfectly well that the Colonel doesn't come to have German lessons, but to sleep with you. And I shall come home when it suits me, because I'm sleeping with Rudolf.' In that way morality will be saved and the case settled by a gentlemen's agreement."

What will Martin say? thought Eva. He said nothing, but simply drank his third bottle of beer, this time direct from the source. He was sitting with his arms folded and his feet on the couch. Eva knew that he was utterly disgusted. She also knew that in a moment he would vent his feelings and the evening would end with a tremendous row. Whom he would throw out wasn't quite certain, but some one would be thrown out, there was no doubt about that. "It's time we went home," she said.

Rudolf stood up and took Helga's hand. There were tears in her eyes. "Now I can race from one end of the city to the other with my car,"

422

said Rudolf. "Why doesn't the equality of the sexes go so far that women can travel home alone at night?"

Every one laughed except Martin, who turned off the radio as though wringing its neck.

"I'll take Eva home myself," he said.

18

When they were alone Eva began to tidy up. Martin turned the radio on again, just as impatiently as he had previously turned it off. He didn't help her with the washing up. She left the door to the kitchen recess open and hummed the tune of the radio. Martin stood by the window.

"It wouldn't injure my masculine pride to help you," he said. "I'm merely expressing my disapproval because you can't leave the stuff as it is. In the first place, they could have washed up themselves. In the second, there's no point anyway."

She calmly completed her work.

When she came back into the room he put out the light. The radio dial emitted a faint orange glow, and the rising moon cast its shy beams into the room.

They both stood by the window.

"A romantic moonlit night," he said.

"I find it romantic," she retorted stubbornly.

The smell of beer and vegetables and bloody meat had grown stronger. The air stood still. The moon put little silver roofs over the green stalls, a heavenly tiler. A drunken man staggered out of an inn. As he opened the door they could hear a zither playing.

"That green down there," said Martin, "is of course fir-trees. The moon is playing in their tops. What glistens over there is not tram-lines, but the silver tracks of the deer. That door over there which is just opening isn't the door of the *pissoir*, but the door of a hotel in the mountains. Who do I see approaching? Devil take me if it isn't Marlon Brando. What is that splashing over there? The mountain stream." He put his arm round her waist. "Moreover, my princess, we are not in a student's room above the Viktualienmarkt, but are looking down from the balcony of our hotel on to the mountain landscape. The orchestra is discreetly playing our favourite song. And the smell coming up from below is of course the ozone of the Swiss forests." He sniffed. "Can you smell it?"

"Yes," she said. "I can smell it."

They stood in silence, their arms round each other's waist, looking at the moon, which was as red as the setting sun.

"The forester's hound is giving tongue," she said.

"It scents game. Deer perhaps." After a while he said, "Heinrich makes me sick. I felt like punching his face."

She put her arm round his neck. Her heart was beating so loudly with happiness that she thought he must feel it through his shirt.

"Do you know that I love you?" she said.

"It would be too bad if I were the victim of unrequited love," he said.

They stepped back from the window, but the moonbeams followed them, and as they sat down on the couch the moon flowed past them, like a river on whose banks they were sitting.

They gave one another a long kiss filled with all the passion of their youth. Under her thin summer frock he kissed her firm little breasts. He looked up at her and said, "If you don't go now, I disclaim all responsibility."

She undid her dress.

The moon was high over the Swiss Alps when they left the room.

"We'll walk," she said.

"All the way to Schwabing?"

She laughed. "Farther than that."

She slipped her arm under his and they walked between the green stalls of the Viktualienmarkt as though between pines and firs.

19

A happy year began for Eva.

Martin was working on his thesis. His subject was "The Development of War Reporting since Cæsar." He hoped to prove that Cæsar's army newspaper during the Gallic Wars contained the first, but also the last, truthful war reports ever written, and that these were truthful only because the Gauls had no reporters, so that there was no need for the Romans to outbid the lies of the other side. Martin's professor wasn't exactly delighted, but he couldn't resist the vast mass of material, which included contrasting descriptions of battles given by the two opposing sides.

While Martin worked on his thesis with a diligence for which he felt obliged to apologize, he earned his daily bread in the archives of a Munich newspaper, where his badly paid and dreary task was to remove the dead from one filing-cabinet and arrange them in another, known as the 'charnel house.' On 'good days,' when few eminent citizens had passed away, his work in the archives left him leisure to attend to his studies and rewrite his war novel. He was doing the latter not under the influence of Herrdegen, whom he had still not met, but in response to his own urge and after long talks with Eva.

Eva worked in the publishing house. She enjoyed her duties in the reading department; they were nothing new to her, since Stefan had long ago taken to asking her opinion of manuscripts and often discussed his plans with her. She worked directly under Anton See, who, with Stefan's increasing age and failing health, was coming to bear more and more of the burden of running the firm. She saw Christian every day, but they avoided each other as far as possible, as though they both had a bad conscience.

Eva had not exactly admitted her relationship with Martin to her grandmother, but neither had she concealed it. Ilona and Stefan noted it in silence; Ilona initially with a certain resignation, Stefan in good spirits. But the longer the relationship lasted, the more favourably disposed towards it Ilona too seemed to become: she inquired after Martin, gradually seemed to get to know him from a distance, and, it appeared to Eva, to take him to her heart.

Eva and Martin mixed chiefly with people of their own age, young men and women between eighteen and twenty-five. They were often astonished themselves by their ability to manage with a few hours' sleep. They used to sit till two or three in the morning in the artists' cafés of Schwabing, danced all night long, went from café to café, and were up and about early next morning. In the winter they skied in the neighbourhood of Munich, frequently staying away over the weekend. They saw the new films people were talking about, went often to the theatre, collected gramophone records. When they quarrelled, which was not infrequently, it was generally because Eva accused Martin of being 'two-faced.' Whereas he was almost always cheerful and relaxed in her company, he was capable of joining in the chorus of other people's gloom as soon as he came into contact with them. It seemed to Eva that his actions were optimistic and his views pessimistic. His moods, like those of most of his friends, were mercurial: they seemed to be watching one another to make sure that none of them felt too happy. Between two dances Martin would suddenly declare that they were dancing on a sinking ship; the sight of a well-fed product of the 'economic miracle,' of whom there were many about now, could spoil his evening; it also happened more than once that he picked a quarrel with some one whom he suspected, perhaps without reason, of being a 'Nazi.' Martin was also quite capable of reproaching Eva with her high spirits and accusing her of being superficial and bourgeois. Although she never forgot that he had stood by her when she turned to him in trouble, she now felt that he blamed her for getting over it so quickly. Slight as was the difference of age between them, Martin's behaviour sometimes seemed meant to emphasize it. Once, in a Schwabing café, he imagined he had spotted one of his former sergeant-majors, and when the latter disappeared in the crowd he actually dragged Eva from café to café because he absolutely had to 'bash him in the kisser.' At four o'clock they found the man, but it turned out that he wasn't Martin's superior officer at all. Another time they quarrelled about a book published by Herrdegen, which Eva had recommended on the grounds that it was a harmless light novel, but which Martin condemned as serving the interests of dishonest hero-worship. It often seemed to Eva that Martin felt obliged to apologize for his enjoyments and therefore filled the pauses between dances with social criticism. Again and again, however, her own *joie de vivre*, which was now expressing itself in a positively eruptive manner, drew him back to her. She thought with a shudder that she might have become Christian's lover. Once when she was talking about it to one of her many girl friends she said, "Christian would have grown old beside me. Martin is getting younger and younger. . . ."

20

One August Sunday in 1953 Eva and Martin had gone out to the Starnberger See in the company of Karin and Philipp Lobmeyer, a well-to-do Munich businessman. In the evening Karin and Philipp had gone back to town. Just before they left, Karin had confided to her friend that she and Philipp were getting married in a few weeks.

Eva and Martin were sitting in a little open-air restaurant by the lake. They could see the scattered lights of the houses on the other bank. It was so quiet that they imagined they could hear the fish rising to the surface. The water was lapping against the walls of a boathouse. A slight breeze had risen and from the tree under which they were sitting an early leaf fell, the first sign of autumn.

Eva was telling Martin about Karin's wedding plans. She wasn't indiscreet, but she was incapable of keeping anything secret from Martin. Moreover, she was in the habit of always passing on news of marriages to him while it was still hot, with the conscious or unconscious intention of reproaching him for his own silence.

To begin with, Martin expressed himself disparagingly about the plan.

"If I'm not mistaken," he said, "Philipp is twenty-five years older than Karin. Did you watch him while we were swimming? He absolutely insisted on racing with me. . . ."

"I couldn't help laughing. You let him win."

"I didn't want him to have a stroke. Why do these old men insist on behaving like young men? The swimming race wasn't too bad. But that conversation about Picasso! I know perfectly well that the whole of modern painting goes against the good Philipp's grain. He simply wants to prove that his taste doesn't lag behind Karin's. I don't consider Philipp a shining light, but he has more sense in his little finger than Karin in her pretty head. I ask you, why doesn't she try to learn from him? Instead of that, he is doing his best to become as stupid as she is."

She nodded. "We couldn't think of anything so stupid that they wouldn't promptly copy us." She looked at Martin out of the corner of her eye. "So you don't think much of their marriage?"

"To be perfectly frank, I don't give a damn. I merely think that Philipp will get tired of Karin just as quickly as the other way round. She's a crazy sex-bomb, but you can't spend a lifetime with a piece of sexual high explosive like that. I sometimes think that women like Karin humble themselves more than our grandmothers, whom Karin describes as domestic animals."

"Karin certainly doesn't humble herself."

"Of course she does. She can't seriously believe that Philipp is attracted by anything but her bosom, her backside and the other parts of her body. All honour to bosom and backside, but it's not very flattering to be married simply for your anatomy. What's left of a woman like Karin once you've weighed out her charms like piece goods? Probably young women have never fetched such high prices, and women over, say, twenty-five such low ones."

Eva emptied her wine-glass and said nothing. She was slightly irritated. Karin was getting married. Ursula and Helga would probably be marrying soon. Not that she herself was in any hurry. She felt young and wanted to preserve her youth as long as possible. Only the fact that Martin had never dropped so much as a hint about marriage annoyed her, especially on evenings like this. Martin contradicted himself. Since he had, as they seemed to her, old-fashioned ideas—why wasn't he old-fashioned enough to marry her?

Martin laid his broad hand on Eva's hand.

"I suggest you stop envying Karin," he said. "I'm quite sure you won't be left on the shelf."

"No. I can get a Philipp Lobmeyer any time."

"You wouldn't be happy with him. Besides, you're far too old for him and you haven't enough bosom."

"There's nothing wrong with my bosom. And Karin is older than me."

"I didn't mean to offend you. Karin may be older, but she makes herself younger. Women start doing that when they're fifteen. Only you're an exception. That's why you'll have to put up with me."

She bit her lip, because she felt the tears welling up into her eyes.

"Of course we'll get married," he said. "I've thought it over carefully. We're an ideal couple. We'd be an ideal couple even if we didn't marry, but I don't want to make it too easy for you to ditch me. Of course, I've drawn up a whole list of conditions."

"Maybe I shall make conditions too."

"We'll come to yours later. Do you want to hear mine?"

"Without commitment."

"First we shall live on my income. But since my income will feed a man only meagrely and his wife not at all, we shall wait till I'm earning enough. Agreed?"

"But I'm earning too."

"In your father's firm. That's pocket-money, which bears no relation to the work you do."

She protested.

"I don't want to offend you, but you really are overpaid," he said. "Besides, I don't think much of women working. Heaven knows, I don't blame them: people do what they have to. But why do what you don't have to?"

"I enjoy working."

"Then there's something wrong. Only amateurs enjoy working. I don't mean that women work amateurishly. Only that it's amateurish to work when you don't have to."

"Church, kitchen, and children," she said.

"Church can be left out." He stopped her from speaking. "Point two, you won't try to change me."

"I like you quite well as you are," she said.

"I know. But women are like purchasers who buy a house because they like it and then promptly have it rebuilt as soon as they've bought it. I don't imagine that I'm perfect, but I've gradually got used to myself. I don't want to stop picking my bosses; going around in jeans; punching Nazis in the kisser; discussing Sartre and jitter-bugging;

scratching myself in public when injustice makes me itch; not wearing a tie; standing up for my own views without consideration for my income; not taking bribes; and so on and so forth. It's a bit of a muddle, as you can see, but that's me. Third. . . ."

"You're really not making things easy for me, Herr Mainoni," she interrupted him.

"Last point, you're not to change." He squeezed her hand. "I want you just as you are. Romantic, level-headed, feminine, wilful, sentimental, tender, pert—and all the other contradictions you're full of. I want three children, two boys and a girl, the girl between the boys. And I insist on your never ceasing to think me wonderful."

"Much as you may regret it," she said, "I accept your conditions." He kissed her cheek and they drank to each other.

Eva's heart seemed to overflow with love. Only now did she realize how much she had been waiting for a word from Martin. You could be above all prejudice, could unceasingly despise prejudice, but a man proved his love only when he asked a woman to share his life. You could stay young when you were married; you really became young when a new marriage put an end to an old relationship. The years that lay behind Eva suddenly appeared to her far more difficult than she had realized. She seemed to herself like a walker who is picked up by a car after a long march, and only then realizes that he has been marching exhaustedly on because hitherto nobody has picked him up. She couldn't help laughing when she thought of Martin's conditions. She would have made the same or similar. They wouldn't always agree, and she wouldn't always give in to him. In time she would convince him that she wasn't 'overpaid,' as he had put it, and that a woman could have her own interests. He wanted to change the world, although he regarded it as lost; he was an enthusiastic advocate of freedom, but he had queer ideas about his wife's freedom; despised money and wanted to start a family of three children. It would all work out. She remembered that he was six years older than she, and a man; that meant that he was perhaps the younger. That was why he thought she contradicted herself. Now she had time. Now she had tranquillity.

They had to catch the night train to Munich. It wasn't very late yet. They walked slowly along the avenue to the station. He was carrying their little case with the bathing things. He had his other arm round her waist. The August sky was filled with stars. Through her thin dress Eva felt Martin's hand on her skin; it was as though they were both walking naked through the warm night. The telegraph wires were singing above their heads, as though they had learnt the song of the birds which sat on them during the day. Every now and then Eva and Martin stood still and kissed. They had to run the last bit of the way, because they could already hear the whistle of the approaching train.

21

A few days later Stefan received a letter from Dr Sales which he immediately showed to Ilona. The letter said:

My Dear and Esteemed Friend,

Your suggestion that I should come to Munich and 'pick' a job in your firm touched me. I imagine the reason for your invitation is that you have heard that things are not going too well with me. Actually this is not altogether true. Although I am approaching seventy-five, my health is excellent: even as a professional hypochondriac—as doctors are—I can observe no particular signs of failing strength in myself. I have got used to the loss of my right arm: you can see that I have learnt to write with my left, and occasionally to hit out with it too. The compensation for my imprisonment, though not large, keeps me afloat, and various contributions to medical periodicals assure me a tranquil old age.

This brings me to the real reason why I cannot accept your kind invitation. At the same time, however, it means that we shall soon see one another again. I have decided to retire to a Bavarian monastery. Have no fear, my dear friend, I am not going to don the monk's cowl in my old age, nor am I returning repentant to the bosom of the only saving Church. I merely intend to spend the rest of my days in wholesome solitude, so as to appear before my Maker in the cleanest possible state. Anyhow, it's the same with the washed soul as with washed hands: we doctors know that there are still quite enough germs adhering to them.

The idea of a monastery is bound up with the idea of resignation. This idea, though extremely one-sided, is in my case not entirely without foundation.

It is not political events that have disappointed me, not the war which, as people say, was fought "in vain." It is simply that since the atom bomb was dropped on Hiroshima I doubt mankind's ability, or even will, to halt the Flood, and do not wish to waste my last ounce of strength in futile endeavours.

I do not mean by this that mankind is necessarily preparing for another war. I am not so much impressed by the warlike character of the atom-bomb tests—the earth cannot be blown up more than once—but, since, probably in our lifetime, every single State, including Liechtenstein and Andorra, will be able to blow it up, the athletic exercises of the Great Powers appear to me utterly infantile. Let me tell you why I tend towards resignation, and, as far as I am personally concerned, have no intention of taking any more part in the hurly-burly.

When we look back we can clearly see the course of development—though too late. Holy Scripture contains all the philosophy man 'needs.' But the more practical humanity becomes, the more unpractically it thinks, and having lost interest in any living philosophy, it has extended its thinking beyond Holy Scripture, and as a result evolved a 'Philosophy of Pure Unreason.' With the elimination of a personal God, little by little silently condoned by the Church, Christ has, of course, also to be 'eliminated,' since only God or man, but by no stretch of the imagination a philosophy, can have a son. From Spinoza the road leads to Freud, from the elimination of the God above us to the elimination of the

God within *us. Philosophy created the launching bases for the atomic rockets. But just tell men that they should stop thinking, that they are surfeited with useless knowledge—and that's what it amounts to; tell them they would do better to ponder the still unresolved concepts of good and evil, which alone govern life and death—the result would be as I have described above. So long as people only painted abstractly and surrealistically it was tolerable. Now they think abstractly too. We no longer depict the nightmare: we make it real. Abstract thinking, however, does not by any means imply deep thinking: it implies thinking not checked against the facts. Good and evil determine value: where good and evil become meaningless, values cease. Do you understand my resignation?*

I see I have once more been unable to resist my old disease of putting into words everything that is weighing upon me. Ilona knows this disease; she has had plenty of opportunity to observe it in me.

I really only wanted to thank you. People like you give one hope—hope for the individual at least. I shall call and see you on my way to the monastery. It might interest you, incidentally, to know that I was offered a professorship by the university here: so I have no grounds for personal bitterness. This opportunity, too, I turned down. If, in spite of my last efforts, I should end up in Hell, I don't want to fry in the company of scholars, who, it seemed to me, will arrive there in hordes—though I regard it as unjust that they will suffer no worse torments than thieves, adulterers, highway robbers, and other modest rascals.

Please embrace Ilona for me and accept the good wishes of your old friend,

SALES

22

It was summer again, a year later, when Martin entered the Herrdegens' house for the first time.

They had just moved to the new house in the residential district of Bogenhausen. Ilona had planned and supervised the construction of the small house and the large garden in every detail.

They were sitting in the garden. The night was warm and filled with the scent of acacias. The candles were burning in the lanterns. Eva was sitting between Stefan and Martin. She had shaken off her constraint. Up to Martin's arrival she had wondered whether he would submit to putting on a decent suit instead of jeans and a shirt, though she hadn't dared to suggest it to him. In fact he was wearing his grey lounge suit with a white shirt and a shiny tie, and he had brought flowers for Ilona. After only a few minutes she also lost her fear that he would offend Stefan and Ilona with one of his abstruse utterances. He seemed to be getting on excellently with Stefan. Neither of them was making an effort to please the other; conversation was lively and spontaneous. She had nothing to worry about.

430

Ilona sat in her armchair, erect, and as usual a little stiffly. She forgot her constant concern for Stefan's health. He was in a cheerful mood, ate with a good appetite, and visibly enjoyed talking to young Mainoni.

During the last year Stefan had grown increasingly sceptical—was it the result of his illness, or was his illness the result of his frame of mind? He had found it hard to make up his mind to build the house. His joy at the success of the publishing firm, which had regained its old standing, was mingled, as he admitted to Ilona, with a feeling of discomfort. German life was growing too fast; it was like a fantastic countryside that was not burnt up by a rain of fire, but fertilized by the fire. Stefan was not comforted by the fact that he profited from the unnatural blossoming himself; it brought him into conflict with his conscience. Hadn't he a right to a belated renaissance? Of course, of course, he said, but things couldn't be explained as easily as that. Maybe what had happened in his beloved country did not enter his consciousness till after the war, and then only gradually. How could it have happened? How was it possible for people so quickly to gloss over the horrors? He was inclined to forgive—but could one so lightly forget? Had the evil been torn out by the roots, or were the roots still proliferating underground? His longing for his homeland hadn't decreased since his return, perhaps it had even increased now that he was back. There were times when he longed for the homeland of his exile—even if it only now seemed to him that he had felt at home there. Ilona knew that he felt ashamed before those who had voluntarily remained in exile; she felt answerable to them; he envied their consistent attitude, although he called it unjust. Ilona and Stefan mixed with a small circle of friends, almost as small as before their flight from Berlin. Then no one knew who was capable of doing evil; now no one knew who had done evil. The villa in Bogenhausen was a luxurious but uncomfortable exile within the homeland.

Ilona couldn't help thinking of all this as she tried to follow the conversation between the two men. She was grateful to Martin for stimulating Stefan to contradict. The young man's pessimism was a challenge to Stefan's buried optimism. For the first time since his return he pleaded as passionately against the idea of collective guilt— 'a barbaric generalization'—as he had done in America, where his views had been unpopular. When conversation turned to literary topics the old man also took a more optimistic view than the young one. "Wait and see. . . . You'll be surprised. . . . It's a natural desire to lay the ghost of the past . . . just think of your own book."

When it grew cooler the men retired to Stefan's study. Martin, for the first time gruff, almost rude, had avoided discussing his novel; but Stefan had put his arm round Martin's shoulders and acted as though the latter were doing him a favour.

Eva went indoors to fetch her grandmother a shawl.

She told herself that she had built a bridge. It might be that the two men were still standing at the bridgeheads, hesitating whether to cross, each unsure how far the other would come to meet him. But the bridge was standing, spanning half a century. Eva was glad to be able to share her love between Martin and her grandmother without neglecting

431

the one or the other. Although she had been reconciled with her grandmother immediately after the clash, the residue of her uneasiness seemed only to-day to have vanished for good. She still didn't quite understand her grandmother, and imagined that she wasn't completely understood by her. Her grandmother was convinced that life moved on straight tracks, that it was clear and self-contained. When she discovered contradictions in Eva's nature she felt she had to resolve them, like a sum that didn't tally when checked. Eva resisted this simple mathematics, but she was now convinced that her grandmother meant well by her; felt that the old woman was trying to understand.

Ilona gazed after Eva as she ran along in her gauzy summer frock with the wide, swinging skirt, showing her slender legs, a creature of exceptional beauty, her granddaughter. She looked like her and yet was quite different. God forgive me, thought Ilona, I can't help comparing her with Zita. How hard Zita had not tried to walk like Ilona, although she bore no other resemblance to her but this walk. Eva had run across the lawn, light and girlish, more girlish perhaps than her years would have led one to expect; but it seemed to the old woman in the armchair that the light-footed girl never lost touch with the solid ground under her feet. She walked while she soared. Zita had wanted to grow up fast and had remained immature. Eva was growing mature without wishing to.

Ilona smiled. Since the morning on which Eva had come home from Martin, an intolerable burden had fallen from her shoulders. Eva had done what she would have done in a similar plight. She had gone to the man who could help her. Zita wouldn't have allowed herself to be helped. No one was spared illness, thought Ilona; the question is, who succumbs to the illness and who resists it. The burden that Zita had had to bear from the outset was lighter than the burden that had rested upon Eva. The daughter of a fanatic, the daughter of a suicide. And yet what a difference! Zita had picked up and carried every stone that lay in her path, until she collapsed under the load she had assumed. Eva seemed to throw off the inherited load, seemed to remove the stones or to avoid them. Perhaps Ilona had contributed to Eva's ability to ward off disease. Perhaps it was possible to put right in your grandchildren the mistakes you had made over your children.

Eva came back.

"They seem to be getting on splendidly," she whispered to Ilona.

She put the shawl round the old woman's shoulders.

23

The world found no peace. On May 26, 1952, Britain, France, and the United States had signed a pact with Germany declaring that the war was over. Thousands were dying in the hills of Korea. Germany undertook to pay compensation to Israel. Egypt elected an army colonel President. The first British atom bomb was exploded in northwest Australia. The secret was no longer a secret. Joseph Stalin died in the Kremlin. New show trials were held in Prague. Soviet tanks fired on workers demonstrating in East Berlin. Edmund Hillary scaled the highest peak in the Himalayas. The Soviet Union announced that it had a hydrogen bomb. People no longer talked of wars of position or of movement. They talked of wars of annihilation. German newspaper readers read about the 'injustice of the Nuremberg trials'; the word 'war criminal' appeared in quotation marks. The first atomic submarine, the *Nautilus*, left the port of Groton in the state of Connecticut. Paris raised skirts higher. New atom bombs were tested by the United States near the Bikini atoll. The woman-murderer John Christie was executed in London. The first atom spy was put behind bars in London. The fire was smouldering in Kenya, Indonesia, North Africa, and Indochina.

It was smouldering in Hungary. On a March day in 1954 Ilona read in the newspaper that thirty leaders of a planned uprising had been arrested. They were said to have incited the peasants to revolt against the collective farms. Among those arrested was the former minister of agriculture in the Károlyi government of 1918, the subsequent 'commissioner for the redistribution of land,' seventy-one-year-old Lajos Horváth. A month later Lajos Horváth was condemned to death by hanging. On account of his age the penalty was commuted to life imprisonment.

Ilona couldn't weep. When she left Lajos's garret in Budapest she had known that she would never see him again. Life imprisonment. For the septuagenarian the word meant exactly what it said. In the photograph of the trial Lajos was the third from the left in the front row; he was standing between young men and seemed as young as they. What had the septuagenarian wanted? Oh, she knew. Like a black magnet the black earth had drawn him. Life imprisonment. How long was his life? How long was her own?

24

That year Stefan Herrdegen died. Death came in a quiet and friendly way.

It was autumn. The rain beat against the window-panes, soft and friendly, as though announcing a welcome visit, blowing the last leaves up against the glass, the trees' letters of farewell.

Stefan hadn't felt well the previous evening. He had played a game of rummy with Ilona; had lost, as always; had gone to bed early. The following morning she persuaded him to stay at home. He gave way unwillingly. Soon after ten he dressed. He hated to 'let himself go," to lounge about in his dressing-gown. At eleven he sat down at his desk to deal with happy, private correspondence. When Ilona called him to lunch he didn't answer. He was sitting in his armchair. His head was bent forward, as though over a letter. There was no terror on his face, but something more like an amiable thoughtfulness. He had his pen in his hand. He had been dead for an hour.

Ilona did what she had to do without knowing what she was doing. She rang the doctor, talked on the 'phone with Eva. That he was dead, she could grasp; that she was alive, she could not grasp. They had sometimes asked each other what the one or the other would do if left alone. Neither had believed that the other might die first. When Ilona was young she had asked herself: how can people live knowing that they have only a few years left? How do the old live, condemned to death? Since she had been old herself she had found out about the kind of lies of time. They turned the coming days into weeks, the months into years. A decade lay in front of you when a year lay in front of you. Now the illusion was at an end.

Eva came; then came Martin, Anton See, Stefan's colleagues, friends. Ilona sat in the lounge; shook hands with the visitors; murmured thanks; let them file past her; didn't see them. She could have withdrawn, have abondoned herself to her grief. When Eva suggested she should go and lie down she merely shook her head. Her carriage became stiffer and stiffer, more and more erect. When she had to weep she turned away. Finally the visitors ventured to ask her questions. She answered clearly.

She didn't think of herself—it was as though she were dead and Stefan alive. Scenes from her life floated past her, apparently insignificant incidents. There was an occasion when he had pushed the little wheel-basket in front of him in an American grocery-store. An occasion when he had cursed loudly because the lace of one of his patent-leather shoes had snapped just before they went to the theatre; she had knelt down and tied it. When she was ill and he had read to her from *Atta Troll*. When she had bought him an overcoat for his birthday: he had had to try it on at the tailor's blindfold. Memories mysteriously shifted emphasis. The scenes floated past, but she saw only Stefan; her own image was swallowed up by the mist. Eva suggested she should sleep in her room. Ilona retired to her own room. All night long she lay awake with her hand on Stefan's pillow.

He was buried in the Waldfriedhof. It was still raining. Eva walked on Ilona's right, Martin on her left. Martin held an umbrella over her. She walked quickly ahead of him, as though fleeing into the rain past an endless lane of umbrellas. She saw no one. Many people had loved Stefan. The sympathy increased Ilona's grief. Behind her thick black veil the tears streamed down. The voices of the pastor and the funeral orators sounded to her like the splashing of the rain. They praised the dead man and knew nothing about him. When they came home she asked her granddaughter to leave her alone. She sat down on the couch in the study and stared unwaveringly at the desk.

25

Two years had passed. This year Ilona would be seventy.

It was the end of October. She hadn't gone to the publishing house. For days she had sat by the radio, only turning it off for a few minutes at a time.

Revolution had broken out in Hungary. Ilona had succeeded in finding the wavelength of the freedom radio-station. She listened to the news in her mother tongue. The call sign was the long-drawn, sweet and sad note of a *tárogató*, a Hungarian shepherd's flute.

The garden was bathed in mild October sunshine that played among the cactuses on the windowsill.

Ilona picked up a piece of embroidery, put on her glasses and moved the armchair closer to the window. In an hour Eva would be home. In the morning she had told Ilona she had something important to discuss with her.

Ilona thought back over the last two years.

Stefan's will had been a declaration of love to his wife. He had written it out by hand shortly after his first heart attack. It had been attested before a notary in accordance with the law; everything was in order, nothing forgotten; a love-letter and a portrait photograph were enclosed with it. He had left Ilona not merely his money and his publishing house, but also every possible power of attorney. No question as to the dead man's wishes remained; he had written everything down. He asked Ilona to promote his friend Anton See general manager of the firm. He had set aside a fund for a prize for young authors which was not to bear his name. He specified that she was to maintain the house "in a suitable condition." In the event of her death. . . . (He had thought of that too.)

Three times a week she went to the publishing house. In response to her wish, Anton See had moved into Stefan's office. She herself occupied See's former office, small and light and full of books. The windows looked out on new buildings, the reborn city. Ilona saw only the house in which she had lived with Stefan; the rooms in which he had worked. In her black dress, with the thick hair combed back from her forehead in soft waves and showing a slight glint of yellow, she was still beautiful. She rarely mentioned Stefan; never asked what he would have done; never invoked the dead man's name. It was as if Stefan had stayed at home on account of the snow or the heat; she had gone to the publishing house in his place; was carrying out his instructions. She listened to every piece of advice; learnt what she didn't know; reached a decision. She never had the feeling of being a working woman. If she was going out she would sit in front of the mirror and give herself a friendly nod, as though Stefan were doing it. If she remained alone she would dress as though he might come home at any minute. Every week she went out to the cemetery. Even when there was deep snow she refused to be accompanied.

There was no sound in the room but the plaintive notes of the *tárogató*. Ilona turned down the volume.

When she picked up the embroidery from the table again she looked down at her hands. Gout had hardened them. The fingers had grown a little broader, a little clumsy. She wrinkled her brow and went on working. Before Stefan's death she had occasionally fallen ill. While still in America she had suffered from rheumatic pains; in the harsh climate of Munich they had grown worse. Now she had no more pains. Men can't bear sick women; so one just wasn't sick. As long as Stefan was alive, whenever an acquaintance died, or she read of the death of a public figure, she inquired their age, as though counting the years left to her on the basis of the dead man's age. At that time she had been delighted to see old women hale and hearty; but secretly she had also been glad when they were not so. She no longer compared herself; neither with the hale and hearty nor with the ailing, neither with the living nor the dead.

She asked herself whether everything had ceased to matter to her since Stefan's death, whether she were waiting for death. For the first year it had seemed so. At that time she had invented an illusory game to enable her to go on living. Every morning she drew up a time-table and kept to it to the minute. She was like a mechanical doll who wound herself up. She moved mechanically, spoke mechanically; she even managed to think mechanically. When the key began to turn more slowly she wound the mechanism up again. She had lived solely from outside inwards. Almost in dismay, she asked herself why this had long ago ceased to be so. Did the automaton imagine it was living? Or had she been unfaithful to her grief? Had she conspired with the few years left to her? Had she really 'consoled' herself?—that self-pitying, renegade, apologetic word. She thought of Dr Ginsburg. What was it he had said about time? Could it be that time was like the frightened author of an atrocity, who binds up the very wounds he has inflicted?

There was the announcer of the freedom radio again. The Government buildings were in the hands of the insurgents. The singing and jubilation of the crowd could be heard from the street, the Budapest street. Some one declaimed in the midst of the announcement. *Talpra magyar, hí a haza. . . .* From the distance machine-gun fire was audible. Were they once again going to war singing? "The abolished national day, the day of the March revolution of 1848, has been restored." Ilona thought of the day on which she had come from Berény to the revolutionary city. Then, too, they had celebrated the memory of 1848. They had torn down the nameplates of the aristocrats from the walls. Now the monument to Stalin in the municipal park had fallen. The present reached far back into the past. It threw down memorials. Did it erect new ones? The present sang old hymns. Were there no new ones? "The prison in the Markó ucca has been thrown open," said the announcer. Ilona put aside her embroidery. Lajos, she thought. Was it possible that the doors of the prison were opening before the old man? That the crowd were carrying him shoulder-high? That he was striding through the streets of the celebrating city as though the walls were spreading out to the plain around Kisnémet? "Further news in an hour." The shepherd's flute rang out again.

What does Eva want to talk to me about? thought Ilona. It must be something to do with Martin. Her heart grew warm. After Stefan's death he had offered her his help only hesitantly, as though she might think him intrusive or suspect him of selfish motives. She had turned to him more and more frequently, not without intention. His judgment was astonishingly clear; his actions sensible and purposeful. Even his occasional self-mockery she found charming. His book had been published—not by S.H.—and had enjoyed a moderate success. He hadn't allowed himself to be discouraged, but had written a second novel, parts of which he had read to Ilona. Excellent passages, she thought,

436

excellent passages. Why didn't they get married? Because Martin wasn't earning enough, said Eva. What did they call enough? They weren't adventurous, these young people, but was their caution not deserving of respect? They were harsh and impatient towards weaknesses, but might this not be their strength? How correct and in the best sense bourgeois was their contempt for what was bourgeois! Wasn't Sales wrong? Weren't these young people already on the way back?

Ilona's thoughts returned to herself. Martin wasn't the only one who had stood by her. Anton See had become her friend. None of Stefan's old friends had abandoned her, nor had any of her own. Once a month Dr Franz Sales travelled from the Allgäu to Munich to see her. Zoltán hadn't merely sent a wreath for Stefan's funeral: the maestro, surrounded by more admirers than ever, wrote regularly from his travels. A few months ago he had sent her a collection of his most famous gramophone records. One evening she had listened to the *Alpine Symphony* with Eva and Martin. She had observed her granddaughter's shining eyes. Tears had come into her own. Eva and Martin had looked at one another. They had no idea that she was thinking of Zita. Zoltán and See and Sales and the others—pride mingled with Ilona's gratitude. It wasn't pity that people felt for her. Men were incapable of pity, but they felt all the more respect for the mastery of grief. When you grew old you stopped looking for motives. You began to be grateful for deeds.

Ilona was startled by her own contentment. She stood up and walked a few paces towards the study, as though she had to tell Stefan she had betrayed him. What could it be? Did people become as selfish as children in their old age? Were they so afraid of death that they didn't even dare to think of the beloved dead any more? Did they cast from them everything that might provoke, attract, conjure up death, might draw its attention to them? Did they imagine they could keep life hidden? Did they imagine death was infectious? Did they face life with such courage because they were so afraid of death?

The voice from the radio brought her to a stop. "More and more towns and villages are joining the revolution," announced a warm female voice trembling with emotion. "It has just been reported that the towns of Györ, Vázc, Veszprém, Kaposvár, Zalaegerszeg. Püspökladány, Kiskunhalas, and Esztergom are firmly in the hands of the insurgents."

Ilona heard only "Püspökladány."

The rays of the afternoon sun were dancing among the cactuses. When is Eva coming? thought Ilona.

26

Grandmother and granddaughter were sitting facing one another. The notes of the *tárogató* accompanied their conversation.

"Do you thing it possible that the Russians will invade Hungary?" asked Eva. "That's what Martin heard at the newspaper offices. The French are supposed to have bombed Egypt. That would mean war."

Ilona shook her head. She had only heard the freedom station, knew nothing of the latest news and was scarcely in a position to form an opinion. It was simply that she didn't believe in another war. When the first began Fate had taken the tiller of destiny out of her hand. In recent years she had felt as though her old hands were gripping the tiller again. There mustn't be a third war in her lifetime.

"I have a bad conscience," said Eva. "I really shouldn't discuss this with you to-day of all days. . . ."

Ilona made a gesture of dismissal with her hand, but was immediately ashamed of it. That was old age, which tried to ward off everything unpleasant. She wasn't old, she could listen to anything.

"It can't be postponed," Eva continued. A Frankfurt publisher had offered Martin the post of senior reader, 'a dream of a job,' and also well paid. "We want to get married at once. . . . Of course, we shall have to move to Frankfurt. As early as the first of December. Even before your birthday."

Ilona laughed. "And you have a bad conscience about that?"

"The thought of leaving you alone. . . ."

Ilona stood up, embraced her granddaughter, sat down again. The weariness in her legs, which she had felt before, had gone. I mustn't become a burden, she thought. I mustn't become a burden!

"You couldn't give me a lovelier birthday present," she said.

"Frankfurt isn't far. . . ."

"And what if it were far? There's a train, isn't there? By plane I could be in Frankfurt in an hour and a half."

Now Eva was laughing too. "You seem to be delighted at getting me married off."

"Heaven knows it's high time." She wiped her eyes. "First, I shan't be alone, and second, I'm not afraid of being alone." She spoke with conviction, believed it herself. "When I come to think of it," she added quickly, "I've never been afraid of loneliness. That was it—not being afraid of loneliness," She wrinkled her forehead, rather angrily, because nowadays she often caught herself repeating a sentence. "I'm relieved to know that you haven't hesitated——"

She broke off, for fear of becoming emotional. The whole afternoon she had been seeking an answer as to why she had been able to survive Stefan's death. The answer was beginning to form in her mind. She had led Eva on to the path which she had followed herself. Had it been the right path? It must have been. The right one? No path was right from beginning to end. You strayed from it, lost your way. You took wrong paths, roundabout paths. Stony paths, when pleasant avenues lay before you; pleasant paths when you should have taken stony ones; you went forward when it would have been better to turn back. The important thing was to find the right path again. She had always found it again. In her childhood, when she lost her way in the company of Teréz and Margit and other children, the others hadn't wanted or hadn't dared to ask the way, but she had always said, "Of course we must ask!" It was so simple if you asked. She had asked Feri and Kontowski and Sales and Stefan, and, again and again, the stationmaster. Most of them were now dead, but she still asked and they still answered.

"Never stop asking," she said, not noticing that she was putting into words the end of a chain of thought of which Eva hadn't heard the beginning.

Eva nodded. She knew the old woman's principles.

"The worst thing is that I shall have to leave the publishing house," she said. "Because of Frankfurt and . . ."

"And because Martin doesn't want you to work."

"That too. Although I intend to start again later. Martin has enough sense not to forbid me to do anything. Only he says at the moment . . ."

"Yes, yes, at the moment . . ." repeated Ilona. Don't start preaching, she told herself. But then she changed her mind and said, "When I was young, as old as you or a bit older, women marched through the streets demanding equal rights. I'm afraid that even in those days I was a traitress. You won't believe me, but I thought more about old age then than I do now. I thought, something that is only right for a young woman can't be right. That which is feminine doesn't age." She looked round. "I haven't regretted it. I have a house that I love. My old friends have remained true to me. I don't think you can say that I have forced myself on anyone. . . ." She waited for corroboration, then continued, "Yet I have gained plenty of young friends."

"Martin loves you," said Eva.

"And I have always let people help me. The world is full of men who want to help women, if the women will only act as if they needed help. Martin is no exception. Stay weak. We women have no other strength."

She knows what she's saying, thought Eva. I needn't worry about her. She has never worked, in our sense, yet when Stefan died she took over the reins of the publishing house with a firm hand. She is as true to herself as I am to myself; my life will be like hers. She is a great woman. Perhaps I shall never be a great woman. But I'm glad I have listened to her. I shall go on listening to her in the years that remain to her. With a smile, she said, "I shall try to stay as young as you."

Ilona nodded. She didn't feel what Eva had said to be an empty compliment.

The notes of the shepherd's flute fell silent. The woman announcer reported the battles for the Honvéd barracks in Ujpest and on the Muzeum-körút. Ilona listened with folded hands. The 'great helplessness,' she thought. If only the 'great helplessness' doesn't descend upon my children. . . .

"I hope nothing is going to interfere. . . ." said Eva.

"Nothing will interfere."

"Do you think they are fighting in Kisnémet too?"

"No one bothers about Kisnémet."

They spoke of Eva's move.

Ilona studied her granddaughter's face. It was young, full of magnificent impatience. She was no longer afraid, neither for herself nor for the child. The thought that she would be alone had frightened her for a moment, but it was already over.

She said, "Go to Martin and reassure him. I've still got a lot to do."

Then she gazed after her granddaughter as she ran across the garden.

Ilona remained standing at the window after Eva had disappeared behind the fence. The notes of the *tárogató* rang out again, melancholy and warning, plaintive and full of promise. It seemed to the old woman at the window as though she herself had just run across the garden to a man who was waiting for her.

What was the meaning of this strange contentment, this strange happiness? She smiled, a small secret smile, as though she had long known what she now knew. Eva had come to her, would always come to her. She would always be there for her granddaughter. Her granddaughter. Her child.

Naturally I shall always be there, she mused, repeating her thought. And naturally Eva won't need me. Naturally I asked old age the way; naturally it took me by the hand and led me home. Being old meant being superfluous. But a woman was never superfluous. Wasn't happiness entrusted to women? It was good like that, because that was how nature intended it. Naturally.

THE END